ALSO BY

WILLIAM GADDIS

THE RECOGNITIONS

J R

CARPENTER'S GOTHIC

A Frolic of His Own

A Novel

WILLIAM GADDIS

Poseidon Press

NEW YORK LONDON TORONTO

SYDNEY TOKYO SINGAPORE

POSEIDON PRESS

Rockefeller Center
1230 Avenue of the Americas
New York, New York 10020

This book is a work of fiction. Names, characters, places and incidents are either products of the author's imagination or are used fictitiously. Any resemblance to actual events or locales or persons, living or dead, is entirely coincidental.

DESIGNED BY BARBARA M. BACHMAN

Manufactured in the United States of America

1 3 5 7 9 10 8 6 4 2

Library of Congress Cataloging in Publication Data

Gaddis, William, date.
A frolic of his own : a novel / William Gaddis.
p. cm.
1. College teachers—United States—Fiction. 2. Copyright—United States—Cases—Fiction. 3. Dramatists, American—Fiction. I. Title.
PS3557.A28F76 1994 93-26098
813'.54—dc20 CIP

ISBN: 0-671-66984-2

A portion of this book originally appeared in *The New Yorker*'s October 12, 1987, issue as "Szyrk v. Village of Tatamount et al. in the United States District Court, Southern District of Virginia, No. 105-87."

Details of the battles at Ball's Bluff and Antietam which appear in this book are drawn from *The Army of the Potomac: Mr. Lincoln's Army* by Bruce Catton, Doubleday & Co., 1962. Copyright © 1962 by Bruce Catton. Lines on page 30 are from *Literary Democracy* by Larzer Ziff, Viking, 1982.

Permission to reprint from the following is gratefully acknowledged: From *The Poetry of Robert Frost,* edited by Edward Connery Lathem. Copyright 1951 by Robert Frost. Copyright 1923, © 1969 by Henry Holt and Company, Inc. Reprinted by permission of Henry Holt and Company, Inc. From *White Mischief* by James Fox. Copyright © 1982 by James Fox. Reprinted by permission of Random House, Inc.

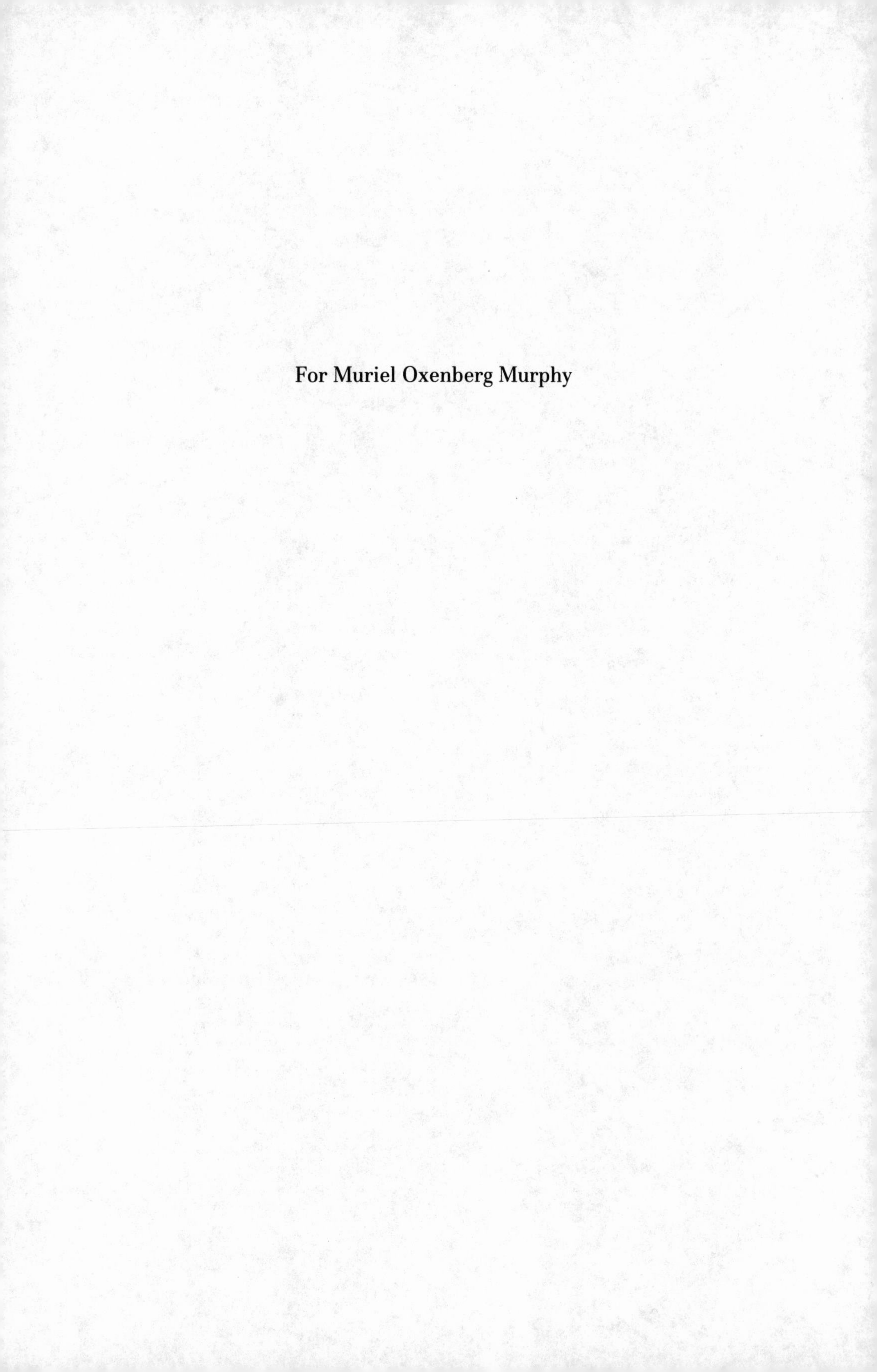

For Muriel Oxenberg Murphy

What you seek in vain for, half your life, one day you come full upon, all the family at dinner. You seek it like a dream, and as soon as you find it you become its prey.

—Thoreau, to Emerson

Justice? —You get justice in the next world, in this world you have the law.

—Well of course Oscar wants both. I mean the way he talks about order? She drew back her foot from the threat of an old man paddling by in a wheelchair, —that all he's looking for is some kind of order?

—Make the trains run on time, that was the...

—I'm not talking about trains, Harry.

—I'm talking about fascism, that's where this compulsion for order ends up. The rest of it's opera.

—No but do you know what he really wants?

—The ones showing up in court demanding justice, all they've got their eye on's that million dollar price tag.

—It's not simply the money no, what they really want...

—It's the money, Christina, it's always the money. The rest of it's nothing but opera, now look.

—What they really want, your fascists, Oscar, everybody I mean what it's really all about? She tapped a defiant foot against the tinkling marimba rhythms seeping into the waiting room somewhere over near the curtains, where the wheelchair had collided with a radiator and come to rest. Trains? fascism? Because this isn't about any of that, or even 'the opulence of plush velvet seats, brilliant spectacle and glorious singing' unless that's just their way of trying to be taken seriously too —because the money's just a yardstick isn't it. It's the only common reference people have for making other people take them as seriously as they take themselves, I mean that's all they're really asking for isn't it? Think about it, Harry.

—I've thought about it, now look. How long do we have to wait. I've got to be in court in an hour.

—He's been in therapy they said, it shouldn't be long. The nurse said he's in a highly agitated state.

—Ever see him when he wasn't?

—Well my God can you blame him? She was digging deep in the

shopping bag on the floor there between them —after all, being run over by a car?

—Looks like he's planning a long stay.

—Well of course he wanted his own robe and pajamas, the rest of it's mail, notes, papers, how he expects to get any work done here.

—Probably as much as he ever gets done anywhere.

—And do you have to start that? I mean that's why I asked you to stop up here and see him isn't it? to show a little family concern for him? Maybe you can even pretend it was your own idea, here... coming up with whatever brightly wrapped, —you can give him this.

—But what...

—It's just a jar of ginger preserves, the kind of thing he likes with his toast in the morning. I'm sure all he gets here is that loathsome Kraft it's grape because it's purple.

—You don't think he'll believe it do you? that I went out and bought him ginger preserves for his morning toast?

—I think he'll think you were very thoughtful.

—I was. I picked up a copy of this Opinion in the Szyrk case for him.

—That was very thoughtful Harry, it was just the wrong thought. You know he and Father hardly see eye to eye on anything as it is, do you think this asinine business about the dog all over the papers will help matters?

—And something else here about that big Civil War movie, he may want the...

—Well my God you're not going to show him that! I mean I just told you he's in a highly agitated state didn't I? Isn't it all bad enough? When I drove out there to pick up his things the lawns hadn't been cut, that south veranda still hasn't been repaired I don't know what holds it up, he was going to have the garage doors painted and they haven't been touched, the way he's talked about getting the ignition on that terrible car fixed for months, and then of course Lily drove in, that was all I needed. In a BMW. I wish you wouldn't drum your fingers that way, and can't you do something about that awful music? His hands came to grips on the attaché case flat on his lap, and she closed her knees as though in restraint against the tum, tum, tum tum tum, tum being accompanied without great success by stabs from the wheelchair. —A new BMW, she'll probably be here any minute. I didn't want to tell her what had happened but of course I knew Oscar would be furious if I didn't, it's like everything else. I thought it was that real estate woman driving in but it turned out he's never even called her, it's just as well though. You can't imagine anyone wanting to buy the place the way it looked this morning.

—Exactly.

—What do you mean, exactly. It's Father who's making noises about selling it after all.

—That Oscar doesn't want to see the place sold.

—Well I know that Harry my God, we've gone over it for a hundred years. I mean we used to talk about one of us buying the other one out when we grew up, but if something happened to him and the whole place would come to me he'd get violent because it had belonged to his mother when Father married her and he'd say he'd come back and haunt me, he'd jump out from behind doors to show me what he'd do, grabbing me and tickling me till I screamed, till I couldn't breathe till, till somebody came, until my mother came and pulled him off, or Father. That's all he was afraid of. Father.

—Sounds a little unhealthy, if you ask me.

—Well I didn't. I mean we were just children, after all.

—Exactly.

The music had taken up a Latin throb livened by haphazard thrusts, lurches, abrupt leaps of hands from the wheelchair where she turned her back, left an awkward leg behind in her impatience, and which opera, if it came to that, 'true love defying family hatred'? a 'tragic tale of family ties and superstition'? tapping the deviant foot behind her —but where he ever thought he'd get the money, unless he married it like Father did. I mean you can see why Lily's parents gave up on her, he told me her father's putting all his money into her brother's hands, getting around the estate taxes in case he dies, so of course she pictures herself marrying Oscar and moving right in if she can ever get her divorce straight, which of course she can't. Where are you going.

—Look he's probably going to be here for a while, why don't I come up later in the week when he...

—You can come up later in the week too Harry, I mean this

whole thing will give you both a chance to get to know each other a little better won't it, spend some time just chatting? Because I still think he paid off her first lawyer when she went on to this second one, half Oscar's age and she's already managed a mess of a marriage and this mess of a divorce and her mess of a family and now this mess she's got herself into getting her purse stolen? Of course they won't give her a penny no, no but Oscar will, lending her money as though she could ever pay it back while he's talked about getting the ignition on that car fixed for months, the way he's talked about his teeth, will the car last long enough to justify getting new tires. Two thousand dollars for new teeth no, no he'll give it to Lily but he won't go out and buy himself new oh my God! What happened!

—Woman getting off the elevator, she sailed into that nurse with a tray of blood samples and wait, wait Christina sit down, don't...

—But it's Trish! and she was up. —Trish!

—Oh God. Teen how sweet, how did you know I'd be here, look at it. Blood and broken glass all over the floor, it's just like home.

—But what wait, it's all over your coat wait, nurse?

—Nurse! Whose blood is this no, don't touch it Teen God knows what you'll catch, nurse? Can't you do something?

—Just step over here Ma'am so we can, Jim? Where's Jim. Tell him to bring a mop I've got to go wash my hands, tell him to put on gloves.

—Will this blood come out of my, where did she go. No I'd better just burn it, like that floor in the upstairs foyer it will never come out, it's as bad as red wine stains on a marble table people can be so damned careless, simply facing that smirking bitch at my cleaners after the last time she'll come up with cela va devenir une habitude Madame? and have it all over the upper east side, but how thoughtful of you to be here Teen. Always thinking of others.

—No it's Oscar, a car accident, he was run over by...

—But how clever! I mean he can sue for millions can't he, if you read about these marvelous awards they're handing out every day in the papers? Is he still at that dreary writing or teaching business or whatever it was? He'll be quite set for life won't he, I remember the time he took us all to the beach at Bailey's and lost his, oh God look at that! She thrust out the point of a 9AAA in mauve peau-de-soie, —look at them!

—But they're lovely, simply exqui...

—Don't you see it? right there on the toe, the blood?

—It's only a speck, no one would...

—Do you think Gianni would ever sell me another pair if they could see that? She seized the near shoulder, —just steady me...

—It's only a speck wait, don't...

—You can't think I'd wear them now, spreading God knows what disease all over town? kicking off one, then the other, —I mean they were designed to go with the coat in the first place, maybe they've given Oscar a pair of these little paper slippers like that mad man over there in the wheelchair waving his arms around conducting the music Teen don't look now, a rather slick looking fellow over by the door giving you the eye.

—Where, what oh, oh it's Harry. Harry? Harry this is Trish, we were at school.

And as he came in reach —Oh! seizing his hand, —and he's your doctor?

—He's my husband Trish, Harry Lutz. He's a lawyer, we...

—Teen I didn't dream you had a husband!

—Well I didn't a year ago, we...

—But how clever of you. Getting one right in the family I mean, where he won't send you these ridiculous bills and then sue you like mine always do, because I've got to call Bunker the minute I get home. Of course I'd hate to sue over this mess but after all he's on the hospital's board isn't he? and it's not as though I haven't given those damn white tie diamond benefits year after year till that night in the elevator when they ripped the diamonds right off my throat and took poor Bunker's billclip, his old daddy's gold billclip shaped like an outhouse it was just the sentiment, he advertised for weeks and now it's black tie and we just call it the Winter Party to keep it low key which is simply incongruous isn't it, I mean Harry Winston doesn't turn you out for a church supper in Kalamazoo and Gianni wouldn't make me a shroud if they could see this coat right now with God knows whose blood on it spreading God knows what, this new depravity they've come up with just to get back at the rest of us who thought the bad news for a good fucking went out with penicillin but it's not like that loathsome Mister Jheejheeboy anymore is it, making a career out of marrying us we were all such damn schoolgirls but so long after school was out, now you don't dare touch anybody under thirty Teen I've got to talk to you.

—Yes but just, Harry? Harry wait a minute...

—Because I mean marriage at our age Teen, suddenly it's half the fun at twice the price will you call me?

Maracas, bongos, chichicaboomchic, he'd got as far from the commotion in the wheelchair as the waiting room allowed, standing there drumming his fingers on the attaché case when a nurse tapped his arm, pointing down the corridor to —six twelve B.

—Christina?

—Yes I'm coming. And that shopping bag will you, oh you've got it. Trish? Call me?

—Love to Oscar, and Teen? I meant to say how devastating for your father, all over the papers with that horrid dog, and you'll call? Someone should simply shoot it, nurse? Are you going to simply leave me standing here like this?

—Here, this way... and down the corridor, —talk about Lily...

—Well what about Lily! Striding out ahead —no, there are two kinds of people in the world Harry, one of them gives and one of them takes, think about it. You don't think those benefits that Trish gives are breadlines do you? Her third husband owned half the timber in Maine, and here's Lily squeezing money out of poor Oscar when he won't even buy himself new teeth, like that car, buying new tires for the car or will it fly to pieces first.

—Like that... catching her aside as a nurse came bearing down on them with the wheelchair from behind.

—Like what.

—Parkinson's, as the wheelchair passed with silent leaps of a hand, jerks of the head, —palsy, Christina. Palsy.

612 B: in the first bed an inert figure lay absorbed in the chaos of a traffic report from a hand sized radio; and beyond the drawn curtain from a welter of newspapers, —Well. You're finally here.

—We've been waiting out there for hours Oscar, they said you were in therapy or something.

—Did you think I'd be out playing baseball? Hand me that glass of water will you? Hello Harry.

—Harry wanted to stop in and see you Oscar, he brought...

—Did you bring my mail? and the papers?

—I was going to but I thought they'd just upset you. Of course you've got them all anyway.

—I didn't say newspapers did I? Of course I'm upset. Did you see that item Harry?

—Item? How could he help it, it's the whole front page! She came rounding the end of the bed gathering them up, flourishing the bold headline, —someone should simply shoot it, will you just look at this?

OUT, DAMNED SPOT

—You think somebody won't? He'd taken the only chair, snapping the attaché case open on his lap, —police, firemen, torchlights, hot dogs, cotton candy, see them on the news last night Oscar? Stars and Bars and the good old boys with six packs in both hands, the hound in the pickup with the shotgun rack behind the seat, they're probably burning the old man in effigy down there right now, he...

—What else can you expect, being a Federal judge in that outlandish place Oscar move your leg.

—I can't, wait, those newspapers, what are you doing...

—Throwing them out, you've read them all haven't you? If you want to keep right on being upset, Harry's brought you a copy of Father's Opinion that's made all the trouble, that's the...

—That's not why I'm upset! There's something in one of the papers, can you just leave them there? Something about that big Civil War movie, somebody suing that man Kiester who made it, did you see that Harry? the one that made that Africa movie with those special effects that had people passing out in the aisles?

—Those lawsuits are a dime a dozen, Oscar. Nuisance suits, people who hope to get paid off just to go away, look I've got to get downtown, the...

—No but if he stole my idea, the same story all of it, it's even the same battle it's not a, just a nuisance it really happened, it was my own grandfather wasn't it?

—Oscar you can't just, you can't own the Civil War. You can't copyright history, you can't copyright an idea now here, here's your father's Opinion. It's great bedside reading, you can see if they could get their hands on this Szyrk character down there they wouldn't bother with burning an effigy.

—No but Harry?

He was up, closing the attaché case with a snap, —frankly I think he'll be overturned on appeal, a poisonous atmosphere like that down there the newspapers are already going after him just for being past ninety years old...

—Harry!

—Racist, leftist, they'll dig up anything they can to kill his chances for the circuit court and a reversal won't help.

—Will you just sit down for a minute? Oscar's asking you something.

—Well what Christina, what. I just told him copyright law isn't my field and...

—Maybe that's not what he's trying to ask you.

—Well what is he trying to ask me!

—He's expecting the insurance man about the accident and he told me he wanted your advice.

—Look I just said I'm in corporate law, I'm not one of these ambulance chasers I don't even know what happened, now let me...

—I told you what happened. He's been talking about getting the ignition on that car fixed for years, the way he's talked about getting new teeth but he...

—Oscar what the hell happened.

—Well this car, it's not new, I mean it wasn't new when I bought it and about a month ago the ignition switch broke and the garage didn't have one, they had to order a new one but it hasn't come in yet so they showed me how to start it by touching a wire from the coil to the battery and usually I stand beside it but this time...

—He was standing right in front of it Harry. When it started suddenly it slipped into Drive and I mean why were you standing in front of it Oscar, how could the...

—Because there was a puddle beside it and I didn't want my...

—Look nobody's asking him that, Christina. The insurance covers the owner of the car so he just sues the owner.

—But he owns it Harry, it's his car he owns it.

—The owner's insurance would probably go after the driver.

—But there wasn't any driver that's the point! The car ran over him and nobody was driving it.

—Let them worry about that, go after the car's maker for product liability, it couldn't have been in Drive or it wouldn't have started, probably the only proof they'd need, just the incident itself. Res ipsa loquitur Oscar, like the chandelier falling on your head. What kind of car is it.

—It's a Japanese car a red one, whatever got into him to buy a red one.

—When you buy a used car Christina you can't always choose the colour, I saw the ad in the paper and when I...

—Look Oscar I've got to get downtown, hope the next time I see you you're out playing baseball... with a clap on the supine shoulder and —I hope there's nothing under that bandage, you could have a nice lawsuit right there. Christina? I'll be late. Oh and Oscar? He was through the door, —don't sign anything.

—Why does he want to see me playing baseball? I've never, ow! What are you doing!

—Just cranking your bed up a little, laid out like that it's like talking to a corpse.

—Well stop it stop! It's fine it's, listen I've got five cracked ribs and this shoulder throbs like a, it's like a hot poker and my leg, I can't even...

—I know all that yes, you told me on the phone. Don't they give you anything for pain in this place? And these pillows...

—Please they're fine!

—I mean they don't seem to care what happens to you, lying around here in this slovenly mess. I've brought your robe and pajamas, at least you won't have to greet people wearing this shroud looking thing.

—Why do you say that.

—Say what.

—This shroud. And being laid out like a corpse.

—Well, you look like you're ready for the potato sack race, is that any better? And I mean does anyone? come to see you?

—That's what I'm telling you. Last night, a man in a black suit I thought he was a, that it was one of those pastoral visits but it wasn't, it was frightening, he ow!

—Well don't wriggle then, can't you just lie still? She'd snapped the sheet straight, tucked in the corner. —Who was it.

—Because this medication they give me, I think it's Demerol, it's as if there are holes in my memory and things that are happening to me are happening to somebody else, because all you really are is your memory and...

—Well who was it, a black suit Harry wears a black suit, black raincoat black shoes there's nothing frightening about Harry.

—I didn't say that Christina, that was just why I thought it was a pastoral call but he kept talking about taking messages to the other side and I, gradually all I could think of was that mysterious stranger calling on Mozart offering him money to compose a requiem when he asked me if I was a terminal case and offered me money to...

—Well my God of course it's these drugs they're giving you, just a hallucination nobody came offering you money to compose a requiem, now...

—He was here! He was here ask the nurse, call the nurse and...

—And he offered you money.

—To carry messages to the other side, yes.

—Well really.

—Yes well really! He puts ads in the papers, he reads the death notices and finds people who've lost a loved one and they pay fifty dollars to have a message delivered by somebody on his way to the other side when he gets there and we split it. I'd get twenty five for each message I took over and, I mean you would, once I'd departed, and then he asked me if I spoke Spanish and where the charity ward was where maybe he could find some Puerto Ricans, don't you see?

—I see nonsense, a lot of morbid nonsense.

—That mysterious stranger offering Mozart money to compose a requiem and he thought it was his own? for his own death? while he was trying desperately to finish The Magic Flute? Did you bring those papers? those notes I asked you for?

—Oscar you're not going to die, you're just banged up and how you expect to get anything done here flat on your back in the first place, it's as bad as that pain in your left arm when you were trying to finish that monograph on Rousseau and you were so worried about tenure? Because if you'd had a fatal heart attack it wouldn't have mattered whether you had tenure or not would it? She'd pulled forth the robe with its worn quilted facings and something beige all arms and legs from Hong Kong, reaching deep in the shopping bag for —these notes, it's all I could find the way you've piled things up in the library, those stacks of old newspapers why you can't simply clip something out instead of marking it with a red pencil and saving the whole paper, it's like everything else. The whole place looks disgraceful, not that anyone's coming to look at it. You hadn't even called that real estate woman.

—We have to talk about it Christina, the housing market is down and this whole inflationary...

—Talk about it, my God we've been talking about it for a hundred years since you used to jump out at me behind the door to the butler's pantry it's got nothing to do with the housing market, it's not a house, it's a place. Someone spending two million dollars isn't just looking for a...

—Two million four, we said two million four but...

—All right two million four! Do you expect two million four from somebody who's looking for a handyman's dreamhouse? Are you just going to lie here till somebody shows up and that veranda caves in on their heads then you'll have a lawsuit, since you seem to be getting so fond of them. Here's the mail. Where shall I put it.

—Anywhere just, where I can reach it, do you see my glasses?

—They're right here where I put them, with your precious newspapers. I thought we'd paid this plumber.

—I thought I'd wait till the end of the month when the...

—And these tree people? They should pay us, those broken limbs when you come up the drive, have you talked to them?

—Well I, not exactly, no.

—Not exactly? I mean either you've talked to them or you haven't.

—Well I called but the line was busy, it's all been, since you left trying to do everything there myself and get my own work done, it's been...

—How long does it take to write a check, you know you're going to pay sooner or later but you just can't part with it till you have to? I mean no one's asked you to do everything yourself Oscar really, since the day I got married you've behaved as though Harry had simply come in and stolen a good housekeeper from you. We are all kind of related now after all and you could make a little more of an effort with him, couldn't you? He's awfully busy in court today but he took the time to get this copy of Father's Opinion and come all the way up here to see you, like one of the family I mean wasn't that quite thoughtful?

—But he just doesn't look like anybody in the family, even on your mother's side, and I don't think Father...

—He met Father once, last year when he had to be in Washington, it wasn't awfully successful but that was hardly Harry's fault, was it? if you remember the shape Father was in? And I went out and got you a housekeeper after all, didn't I? Two of them, after you said the first one burned your socks, and what's happened to this new one? I didn't see a trace of her.

—If you'd like to see a trace of her look at that Sung vase in the sunroom. She put cold water in it for some blossom branches Lily brought over and of course it seeped through the terra cotta and completely destroyed the glaze. A thousand years go into that exquisite iridescent glaze and one coarse stupid woman can destroy it overnight.

—I'll look around for another one, now...

—Another one? Do you think you can just walk down the street and pick up a real Sung dynast...

—A housekeeper Oscar, another housekeeper, and what Lily's doing bringing over blossom branches in the first place, aren't things in enough of a mess there without blossom branches? You complain about disorder and then open the door for chaos herself, I mean she certainly doesn't look like anyone in the family if that's what you have in mind, driving in there this morning in a new BMW as if she owned the place. She'll probably show up here any minute. I told her what happened.

—A new BMW?

—You're lying here smashed to a pulp by that second hand wreck while she's driving around in a...

—No but whose BMW?

—Well I certainly didn't ask her, I mean I certainly don't want to know, do you? Think about it Oscar, because I should think you might after all, a breezy blouse half unbuttoned, blonde hair flying and enough lipstick to paint a barn I'm putting the mail right here. I'll bring checks, I'm sure you don't have any. Who is John Knize.

—Who is who?

—There's a letter here from someone named John Knize. Shall I open it?

—Oh, no that's probably just someone who...

—Dear Professor Crease, he's got one of those awful typewriters that writes in script. Perhaps my earlier letter did not reach you. I am researching material for a book on the Holmes Court, of which I understand your grandfather, Justice Thomas Crease, was a colourful member, well known for his conflicts with his associate Justice Holmes though it was said they were warm friends through their shared youthful experience in the Civil War, both having suffered wounds, I understand, at Ball's Bluff and Antietam. Since your grandfather lived to age ninety six it occurred to me that you might well have known him as a small child and, you're not planning to see this person are you?

—I just thought it might help to...

—Well whatever you thought, just remember people don't come out of nowhere to help you, people help themselves, I mean you don't picture sitting down with this utter stranger telling him how Grandfather dandled you on his knee when you were five and rattled on about the Civil War? These papers you had me drag in here because you're afraid somebody's stealing it from you and Harry's right isn't he, the rest of it's nothing but opera. I'm the Queen of the Night and here's your mysterious messenger haunting the wards for a terminal case, wheedling a requiem for the old Count to pretend he composed himself, trying to frighten me when we were children saying you'd come back and haunt the place the way I felt out there this morning, the mist just lifting from the pond and suddenly the swans, a whole fleet of them coming by as still, as still, and across the pond those reds and russets...

—Where the sedge is withered from the...

—Well exactly! the letter she'd been crumpling gone to the floor as she stood. —Alone and palely loitering, I mean if Keats could see you now. How long do they plan to keep you here.

—They don't know yet. Could you hand me my glasses? It depends on when I can walk again if I can, if I can Christina, they don't even know that yet.

—Well I hope they don't plan to turn you loose till you can, do they expect you to ride around that house in a wheelchair without breaking your neck? She reached down to where he'd just put on his glasses with some difficulty, and took them off. —Can you see through these things at all? dipping a tissue in the water glass —let alone read through them, doesn't it ever occur to you to do this yourself? and she set the sparkling lenses back astride his nose —though this bandage hardly helps. Will there be a scar?

—Probably, they said...

—Poor Oscar. She stooped to kiss his forehead. —It may give your face a little character, like Heidelberg. I'll start digging up another housekeeper.

—Yes but, Christina? If Harry doesn't mind I mean, or if he's away or anything? I just thought maybe you could come back out there and spend a little time with me? Just until, and wait, this creamed ham they gave us last night...

—We'd still need a housekeeper, oh and I meant to tell you, Trish sends love, Trish Hemsley? She's quite fond of you you know, it's a shame you never pursued it Oscar, she could be such a help. You don't mind if I take these? folding together the crinkled paper slippers she'd just found on the night table, —I mean it's not as though you're going anywhere? sweeping back the curtain, past the lively concert of traffic backed up for seven miles at the eastbound entrance to the George Washington bridge for an overturned tractor trailer, seizing the arm of a nurse passing the door with —the far bed in there, Mister Crease? He's rather anxious about the supper menu, and whatever this medication you're giving him I wish you'd check with the doctor, he's seeing little men in black suits coming in asking him to carry messages to the other side and he's not even packed... on up the corridor and —oh my God...too late to turn elsewhere, —hello Lily.

—Oh! Is he okay?

—If he were okay would he be here? Six twelve B, do try not to tire him.

—Oh yes I, but Christina?

—What is it.

—Just, I just wish you liked me.

—So do I Lily.

612 B: past the horn concerto on tiptoe with an apologetic gasp, bursting past the curtain with —oh Oscar! Are you okay? and a lipstick smear on the bandage. —Does it hurt?

—Yes.

—Where, the bandage on your face?

—Everywhere.

—Oh Oscar. Can I get you anything? I was going to bring you flowers but then I saw I only had four dollars.

—Look in my wallet. In that drawer in the night table, Lily?

—Yes, yes can I get you anything?

—Where did you get a new BMW.

—Where did you hear that. Is fifty all right?

—Christina says you drove up to the house in a new BMW.

—It's just this person I borrowed it from Oscar. To come over and see you, I only wish she didn't dislike me so much. She just always makes me feel like a, she's so superior and smart and her clothes, she's just always so attractive for somebody her age and...

Her hand fluttered by and he caught it. —It's just that you're a little young, I think she worries about you, this divorce and your problem with your family, and the...

—It's not my fault! She recovered her hand, —is it Oscar? Because that's what I have to talk to you about.

—What's happened now.

—Because it's this lawyer. She wants another twenty five hundred dollars Oscar I just don't know what to do.

—Twenty five hun, but we gave her a three thousand dollar retainer after we paid off the first one.

—Yes but now she says I still owe her this twenty five hundred more dollars or she won't release all these papers.

—All what papers, where.

—To this other lawyer. Because since she withdrew from the case and I need another lawyer she said this new one can't be the attorney of record unless I pay her and she gives back all these papers.

—No wait what do you mean, she withdrew from the case.

—Because she said you've kept interfering writing her all these letters and calling her up and telling her what to do about the separation agreement and everything so she's withdrawing from the case, it's not my fault is it?

—Well she can't. She can't Lily, she can't withdraw just like that. Fifty five hundred dollars for what has she done, that long garbled separation agreement she couldn't wait to give away everything in sight and even that isn't signed, it's ridiculous. She can't.

—But I asked this new lawyer and he says she can Oscar.

—What new lawyer.

—Well I thought I'd get a man one again, like before, so...

—It's ridiculous, no. No, we can take it to arbitration, take the whole thing before a grievance committee and...

—But he said those committees are just all these other lawyers so they have to protect each other because they may be next so...

—Who said! And what if she can quit, listen I don't even know what these hospital bills will be, an insurance man's coming up here later and I'm not even sure that they'll pay, can't you ask your brother? I'm afraid to write a check for a dollar, all this money he's getting from your father so the government can't get it, can't you ask Bobbie?

—Bobbie wants to buy a Porsche... Her head came down to rest on the edge of the bed, —I just get so tired, Oscar... and her hand followed, burrowing under the sheet. —It's just all Bobbie, it's everything for Bobbie, they won't even talk to me and they've joined some church down there, that's the only letter they've sent me about how glorious it is to be saved and how happy I'd be if I'd just accept the Lord while this woman that stole my purse is out there someplace pretending she's me with all my credit cards and everything where she used my bank credit card before I could stop it so these other real checks I wrote bounced, I can't even identify myself and she's buying these plane tickets she could be in Paris right now being me and I don't even know what I'm doing there till I get this bill for these lizard skin shoes I bought at some store in Beverly Hills where I always wanted to go, and it's spooky.

His hand had come down to smooth her hair, a finger limned her ear, traced her brow; hers came deeper, soothing a rise there under the sheet. —We'll get it straightened out as soon as...

—She'll find out it's not so easy being me though, that it's not as much fun being me as she thought, does this hurt?

—Just, be careful, I...

—Mommy kiss and make it well?

—Not, not here no, no not now...

—But won't it make you feel better? Where's a tissue, I'll get rid of this lipstick.

—Not, not now no, a nurse might come in and...

—We can just pretend I'm down straightening the sheet...

There was a great thump on the curtain. —Hey there!

—What's the, who...

—Send her over here!

—Who do you, what are you talking about!

—She knows! and another thump on the curtain, —if you don't know then send her over here. Hey, Mommy?

—Of all the damned, ow!

—Oscar don't try to, just be still I think somebody's coming. I better go anyway.

—Wait who is it.

—Just this man Oscar, I better go. I'll see you real soon.

—What man. In a black suit? Lily wait, how are you getting home.

—This car I borrowed.

—But wait, whose is it.

—This new lawyer... and she squeezed his hand, left a blot of lipstick on it and brushed past the curtain, past the next bed with a heated whisper, —You dirty man.

And from the doorway, —Mister Crease?

—Back here, wait. Wait who is it...

—Frank Gribble, Ace Worldwide Fidelity, may I come in? in a black suit, —how are we feeling. May I sit down? and he'd done so, flattening a plastic portfolio on his lap, —I hope you're not in pain? and he had out a yellow pad, —now. Let's not take too much of your valuable time, Mister Crease. If you can just tell me what happened.

—Of course I can, I...

—In your own words.

—Well of course. The car's ignition was not working. I had to start it by opening the hood and touching a wire from the coil to the positive post on the battery.

—I believe that's what they call hot wiring. We constantly have reports of cars stolen that way, please go on.

—This is my car Mister Gribble.

—Oh yes, yes I didn't mean...

—The car was in Park. I touched the wire, the engine started, it slipped into Drive and ran over me.

—I see. Then we assume you must have been standing in front of the car? Why were you standing in front of the car, Mister Crease.

—Because there was a mud puddle beside the car Mister Gribble, and I felt it wise not to risk the combination of water and electricity. But all this is irrelevant isn't it. The insurance covers the car's owner, doesn't it?

—But I understand you are the owner.

—I am also the victim Mister Gribble. Now I believe that the usual course would be for the owner's insurance to pursue the driver, but...

—But I understand no one was driving it.

—Which I suppose would leave you the alternative of suing the maker for product liability? It slipped from Park into Drive of its own accord didn't it? If it had been in Drive at the outset it wouldn't have started at all. Res ipsa loquitur Mister Gribble, as clear as the chandelier falling on your head.

—Yes well it might be a little difficult, if we could dig up some similar cases and we'd need to examine the car, wouldn't we.

—Examine the car of course, I only want justice after all.

—It's garaged at your, at the place of the accident I can't find the, what kind of car is it.

—Sosumi.

—I'm being quite serious Mister Crease.

—So am I! It's a Japanese car, a Sosumi.

—Oh. Oh dear, yes I'm sorry, it's so hard to keep track of them all nowdays. We had a whole family killed last week in an Isuyu and I made a similar error. I think we've covered all the preliminaries Mister Crease, I don't want to tire you. You'll hear from us promptly, I don't think there should be any problem about your hospital bills here and I may even be able to squeeze in your television rental without anybody noticing, no sir. Our only problem now is getting you the very best care, if you'll just sign this right here at the bottom and we'll have you up in no time ready to go out and, here's a pen...

—And play baseball?

—Right at the bottom there yes, just a formality.

—Quite a lengthy formality, Mister Gribble. I don't sign things I haven't read.

—Oh, if you, go right ahead. I just didn't want to take up your time, I saw the supper cart in the hall and I think you have quite a surprise coming. I'll just read the newspapers here while you...

—You'd better just leave it with me, some other things I've got to take care of first, those papers right there on the night table, if you'll hand them to me?

—This? It looks like something legal, I should have guessed. You're a lawyer, Mister Crease?

—Thank you. No, I dabble in it, Mister Gribble, I only dabble. Good night.

—You only dabble, do you? came from behind the curtain over eager revelations of a six car collision on Route 4. —Like a little dab of that myself, that was some hot number.

—Be quiet.

—A little dab'll do you, a little dab'll...

—Shut up! and he settled back into the pillows, squaring his glasses as best he could, managing some sagging measure of dignity commensurate with the pages before him. And so we may as well begin this sad story with the document that has set things off or, better, that merely paced the events that follow, spattered as it was all over the newspapers, since it had nothing directly to do with them, much less its remote participants, distant in every way but the historic embrace of the civil law in its majestic effort to impose order upon? or is it rather to rescue order from the demeaning chaos of everyday life in this abrupt opportunity, as Christina has it, to be taken seriously before the world, in an almost inverse proportion to their place in it, their very names in fact and the inconsequential nature of their original errands, like that woman intending no further than Far Rockaway suddenly lofted to landmark status by Justice Cardozo in Palsgraf v. Long Island Railroad, or the mere passerby rendered eternal by Baron Pollack in Byrne v. Boadle beaned by a barrel of flour whence the doctrine of res ipsa loquitur tendered by Harry in an image more suiting those unnatural persons mounting, in an almost inverse proportion to the millions, billions in settlements, the frivolous legal heights of corporate anonymity, in Harry's hands become the chandelier he's dropped here in Oscar's path, arching his good knee, squaring the pillow, his glasses again, licking a thumb to flick over the cover page of Szyrk v. Village of Tatamount et al., U.S. District Court,

Southern District of Virginia No. 105–87, haunted by the sense that 'reality may not exist at all except in the words in which it presents itself.'

OPINION

CREASE, J.

The facts are not in dispute. On the morning of September 30 while running at large in the Village a dog identified as Spot entered under and therewith became entrapped in the lower reaches of a towering steel sculpture known as Cyclone Seven which dominates the plaza overlooking and adjoining the depot of the Norfolk & Pee Dee Railroad. Searching for his charge, the dog's master James B who is seven years old was alerted by its whines and yelps to discover its plight, whereupon his own vain efforts to deliver it attracted those of a passerby soon joined by others whose combined attempts to wheedle, cajole, and intimidate the unfortunate animal forth served rather to compound its predicament, driving it deeper into the structure. These futile activities soon assembled a good cross section of the local population, from the usual idlers and senior citizens to members of the Village Board, the Sheriff's office, the Fire Department, and, not surprisingly, the victim's own kind, until by nightfall word having spread to neighboring hamlets attracted not only them in numbers sufficient to cause an extensive traffic jam but members of the local press and an enterprising television crew. Notwithstanding means successfully devised to assuage the dog's pangs of hunger, those of its confinement continued well into the following day when the decision was taken by the full Village Board to engage the Fire Department to enter the structure employing acetylene torches to effect its safe delivery, without considering the good likelihood of precipitating an action for damages by the creator of Cyclone Seven, Mr Szyrk, a sculptor of some wide reputation in artistic circles.

Alerted by the media to the threat posed to his creation, Mr Szyrk moved promptly from his SoHo studio in New York to file for a temporary restraining order 'on a summary showing of its necessity to prevent immediate and irreparable injury' to his sculptural work, which was issued ex parte even as the torches of deliverance were being kindled. All this occurred four days ago.

Given the widespread response provoked by this confrontation in the media at large and echoing as far distant as the deeper South and even Arkansas but more immediately at the site itself, where energies generated by opposing sympathies further aroused by the police presence and that of the Fire Department in full array, the floodlights, vans, and other paraphernalia incident to a fiercely competitive television environment bringing in its train the inevitable placards and displays of the American flag, the venders of food and novelty items, all enhanced by the barks and cries of the victim's own local acquaintance, have erupted in shoving matches, fistfights, and related hostilities with distinctly racial overtones (the dog's master James B and his family are black), and finally in rocks and beer cans hurled at the sculpture Cyclone Seven itself, the court finds sufficient urgency in the main action of this proceeding to reject defendants' assertions and cross motions for the reasons set forth below and grants summary judgment to plaintiff on the issue of his motion for a preliminary injunction to supersede the temporary restraining order now in place.

To grant summary judgment, as explicated by Judge Stanton in Steinberg v. Columbia Pictures et al., Fed. R. Civ. P. 56 requires a court to find that 'there is no genuine issue as to any material fact and that the moving party is entitled to a judgment as a matter of law.' In reaching its decision the court must 'assess whether there are any factual issues to be tried, while resolving ambiguities and drawing reasonable inferences against the moving party' (Knight v. U.S. Fire Ins. Co., 804 F.2d 9, 11, 2d Circ., 1986, citing Anderson v. Liberty Lobby, 106 S.Ct. 2505, 2509–11, 1986). In plaintiff's filing for a restraining order his complaint alleges, by counts, courses of action to which defendants have filed answers and cross claims opposing motion for a preliminary injunction. The voluminous submissions accompanying these cross motions leave no factual issues concerning which further evidence is likely to be presented at a trial. Moreover, the factual determinations necessary to this decision do not involve conflicts in testimony that would depend for their resolution on an assessment of witness credibility as cited infra. The interests of judicial economy being served by deciding the case at its present stage, summary judgment is therefore appropriate.

Naming as defendants the Village Board, the dog's master James B through his guardian ad litem, 'and such other parties and entities as may emerge in the course of this proceeding,' Mr Szyrk first alleges animal trespass, summoning in support of this charge a citation from early law holding that 'where my beasts of their own wrong without my will and knowledge break another's close I shall be punished, for I am the trespasser with my beasts' (12 Henry VII, Kielwey 3b), which exhibit the court, finding no clear parallel in the laws of this Commonwealth, dismisses as ornamental. Concerning plaintiff's further exhibit of Village Code 21 para. 6b (known as 'the leash law'), we take judicial notice of defendants' response alleging that, however specific in wording and intent, this ordinance appears more honored in the breach, in that on any pleasant day well known members of the local dog community are to be observed in all their disparity of size, breed, and other particulars ambling in the raffish camaraderie of sailors ashore down the Village main street and thence wherever habit and appetite may take them undeterred by any citizen or arm of the law. Spot, so named for the liver colored marking prominent on his loin, is described as of mixed breed wherein, from his reduced stature, silken coat, and 'soulful' eyes, that of spaniel appears to prevail. His age is found to be under one year. Whereas in distinguishing between animals as either mansuetae or ferae naturae Spot is clearly to be discovered among the former 'by custom devoted to the service of mankind at the time and in the place in which it is kept' and thus granted the indulgence customarily accorded such domestic pets, and further whereas as in the instant case scienter is not required (Weaver v. National Biscuit Co., 125 F.2d 463, 7th Circ., 1942; Parsons v. Manser, 119 Iowa 88, 93 N.W. 86, 1903), such indulgence is indicative of the courts' retreat over the past century from strict liability for trespass (Sanders v. Teape & Swan, 51 L.T. 263, 1884; Olson v. Pederson, 206 Minn. 415, 288 N.W. 856, 1939), we find plaintiff's allegation on this count without merit (citation omitted).

On the related charge of damages brought by plaintiff the standard for preliminary relief must first be addressed. Were it to be found for plaintiff that irreparable harm has indeed been inflicted upon his creation, and that adequate remedy at law should suffice in the form of money damages, in such event the court takes judicial notice in directing such claim to be made against the Village Board and the dog's master in tandem, since as in the question posed by the Merchant of Venice (I, iii, 122) 'Hath a dog money?' the answer must be that it does not. However, as regards the claim that the dog Spot, endowed with little more than milk teeth however sharp, and however extreme the throes of his despair, can have wreaked irreparable harm upon his steel confines this appears to be without foundation. Further to this charge, defendants respond, and the court concurs, citing plaintiff's original artistic intentions, that these steel surfaces have become pitted and acquired a heavy patina of rust following plaintiff's stated provision that his creation stand freely exposed to the mercy or lack thereof of natural forces, wherewith we may observe that a dog is not a boy, much less a fireman brandishing an acetylene torch, but nearer in its indifferent ignorance to those very forces embraced in the pathetic fallacy and so to be numbered among them. We have finally no more than a presumption of damage due to the inaccessibility of this inadvertent captive's immediate vicinity, and failing such evidentiary facts we find that the standards for preliminary relief have not been met and hold this point moot.

Here we take judicial notice of counterclaims filed on behalf of defendant James B seeking to have this court hold both plaintiff and the Village and other parties thereto liable for wilfully creating, installing and maintaining an attractive nuisance which by its very nature and freedom of access constitutes an allurement to trespass, thus enticing the dog into its present allegedly dangerous predicament. Here plaintiff demurs, the Village joining in his demurrer, offering in exhibit similar structures of which Cyclone Seven is one of a series occupying sites elsewhere in the land, wherein among the four and on only one occasion a similar event occurred at a Long Island, New York, site in the form of a boy similarly entrapped and provoking a similar outcry until a proffered ten dollar bill brought him forth little the worse. However, a boy is not a dog, and whereas in the instant case Cyclone Seven posed initially a kind of ornate 'jungle gym' to assorted younger members of the community, we may find on the part of Spot absent his testimony neither a perception of challenge to his prowess at climbing nor any aesthetic sensibility luring him into harm's way requiring a capacity to distinguish Cyclone Seven as a work of art from his usual environs in the junk yard presided over by defendant James B's father and guardian ad litem, where the progeny of man's inventiveness embraces three acres of rusting testimony thereto, and that hence his trespass was entirely inadvertent and in good likelihood dictated by a mere call of nature as abounding evidence of similar casual missions on the part of other members of the local dog community in the sculpture's immediate vicinity attest.

In taking judicial notice of defendant's counterclaim charging allurement we hold this charge to be one of ordinary negligence liability, already found to be without merit in this proceeding; however, we extend this judicial notice to embrace that section of plaintiff's response to the related charge of dangerous nuisance wherein plaintiff alleges damage from the strong hence derogatory implication that his sculptural creation, with a particular view to its internal components, was designed and executed not merely to suggest but to actually convey menace, whereto he exhibits extensive dated and annotated sketches, drawings, and notes made, revised, and witnessed in correspondence, demonstrating that at no time was the work, in any way or ways as a whole or in any component part or parts or combinations thereof including but not limited to sharp planes, spirals, and serrated steel limbs bearing distinct resemblances to teeth, ever in any manner conceived or carried out with intent of entrapment and consequent physical torment, but to the contrary that its creation was inspired and dictated in its entirety by wholly artistic considerations embracing its component parts in an aesthetic synergy wherein the sum of these sharp planes, jagged edges and toothlike projections aforementioned stand as mere depictions and symbols being in the aggregate greater than the sum of the parts taken individually to serve the work as, here quoting the catalogue distributed at its unveiling, 'A testimony to man's indiminable (*sic*) spirit.'

We have in other words plaintiff claiming to act as an instrument of higher authority, namely 'art,' wherewith we may first cite its dictionary definition as '(1) Human effort to imitate, supplement, alter or counteract the work of nature.' Notwithstanding that Cyclone Seven clearly answers this description especially in its last emphasis, there remain certain fine distinctions posing some little difficulty for the average lay observer persuaded from habit and even education to regard sculptural art as beauty synonymous with truth in expressing harmony as visibly incarnate in the lineaments of Donatello's David, or as the very essence of the sublime manifest in the Milos Aphrodite, leaving him in the present instance quite unprepared to discriminate between sharp steel teeth as sharp steel teeth, and sharp steel teeth as artistic expressions of sharp steel teeth, obliging us for the purpose of this proceeding to confront the theory that in having become self referential art is in itself theory without which it has no more substance than Sir Arthur Eddington's famous step 'on a swarm of flies,' here present in further exhibits by plaintiff drawn from prestigious art publications and highly esteemed critics in the lay press, where they make their livings, recommending his sculptural creation in terms of slope, tangent, acceleration, force, energy and similar abstract extravagancies serving only a corresponding self referential confrontation of language with language and thereby, in reducing language itself to theory, rendering it a mere plaything, which exhibits the court finds frivolous. Having here in effect thrown the bathwater out with the baby, in the clear absence of any evidentiary facts to support defendants' countercharge 'dangerous nuisance,' we find it without merit.

We next turn to a related complaint contained in defendant James B's cross claim filed in rem Cyclone Seven charging plaintiff, the Village, 'and other parties and entities as their interests may appear' with erecting and maintaining a public nuisance in the form of 'an obstruction making use of passage inconvenient and unreasonably burdensome upon the general public' (Fugate v. Carter, 151 Va. 108, 144 S.E. 483, 1928; Regester v. Lincoln Oil Ref. Co., 95 Ind.App. 425, 183 N.E. 693, 1933). As specified in this complaint, Cyclone Seven stands 24 feet 8 inches high with an irregular base circumference of approximately 74 feet and weighs 24 tons, and in support of his allegation of public nuisance defendant cites a basic tenet of early English law defining such nuisance as that 'which obstructs or causes inconvenience or damage to the public in the exercise of rights common to all Her Majesty's subjects,' further citing such nuisance as that which 'injuriously affects the safety, health or morals of the public, or works some substantial annoyance, inconvenience or injury to the public' (Commonwealth v. South Covington & Cincinnati Street Railway Co., 181 Ky. 459, 463, 205 SW 581, 583, 6 A.L.R. 118, 1918). Depositions taken from selected Village residents and submitted in rem Cyclone Seven include: 'We'd used to be this nice peaceable town before this foreigner come in here putting up this [expletive] piece of [obscenity] brings in every [expletive] kind of riffraff, even see some out of state plates'; 'Since that [expletive] thing went up there I have to park my pickup way down by Ott's and walk all hell and gone just for a hoagie'; 'Let's just see you try and catch a train where you can't hardly see nothing for the rain and sleet and you got to detour way round that heap of [obscenity] to the depot to get there'; 'I just always used the men's room up there to the depot but now there's times when I don't hardly make it'; 'They want to throw away that kind of money I mean they'd have just better went and put us up another [expletive] church.'

Clearly from this and similar eloquent testimony certain members of the community have been subjected to annoyance and serious inconvenience in the pursuit of private errands of some urgency; however recalling to mind that vain and desperate effort to prevent construction of a subway kiosk in Cambridge, Massachusetts, enshrined decades ago in the news headline PRESIDENT LOWELL FIGHTS ERECTION IN HARVARD

SQUARE, by definition the interests of the general public must not be confused with that of one or even several individuals (People v. Brooklyn & Queens Transit Corp., 258 App.Div. 753, 15 N.Y.S.2d 295, 1939, affirmed 283 N.Y. 484, 28 N.E.2d 925, 1940); furthermore the obstruction is not so substantial as to preclude access (Holland v. Grant County, 208 Or. 50, 298 P.2d 832, 1956; Ayers v. Stidham, 260 Ala. 390, 71 So.2d 95, 1954), and in finding the former freedom of access to have been provided by mere default where no delineated path or thoroughfare was ever ordained or even contemplated this claim is denied.

On a lesser count charging private nuisance, H R Suggs Jr, joins himself to this proceeding via intervention naming all parties thereto in his complaint on grounds of harboring a dog 'which makes the night hideous with its howls' which the court severs from this action nonetheless taking judicial notice of intervener's right inseparable from ownership of the property bordering directly thereupon, to its undisturbed enjoyment thereof (Restatement of the Law, Second, Torts 2d, 822c), and remands to trial. Similarly, whereas none of the parties to this action has sought relief on behalf of the well being and indeed survival of the sculpture's unwilling resident, and whereas a life support system of sorts has been devised pro tem thereto, this matter is not at issue before the court, which nonetheless, taking judicial notice thereof should it arise in subsequent litigation, leaves it for adjudication to the courts of this local jurisdiction.

We have now cleared away the brambles and may proceed to the main action as set forth in plaintiff's petition for a preliminary injunction seeking to hold inviolable the artistic and actual integrity of his sculptural creation Cyclone Seven in situ against assault, invasion, alteration, or destruction or removal or any act posing irreparable harm by any person or persons or agencies thereof under any authority or no authority assembled for such purpose or purposes for any reason or for none, under threat of recovery for damages consonant with but not limited to its original costs. While proof of ownership is not at issue in this proceeding, parties agree that these costs, including those incident to its installation, in the neighborhood of fourteen million dollars, were borne by contributions from various private patrons and underwritten by such corporate entities as Martin Oil, Incidental Oil, Bush AFG Corp., Anco Steel, Norfolk & Pee Dee Railroad, Frito-Cola Bottling Co., and the Tobacco Council, further supported with cooperation from the National Arts Endowment and both state and regional Arts Councils. The site, theretofore a weed infested rubble strewn area serving for casual parking of vehicles and as an occasional dumping ground by day and trysting place by night, was donated under arrangements worked out between its proprietor Miller Feed Co. and the Village in consideration of taxes unpaid and accrued thereon over the preceding thirty-eight years. In re the selection of this specific site plaintiff exhibits drawings, photographs, notes and other pertinent materials accompanying his original applications to and discussions with the interested parties aforementioned singling out the said site as 'epitomizing that unique American environment of moral torpor and spiritual vacuity' requisite to his artistic enterprise, together with correspondence validating his intentions and applauding their results. Here we refer to plaintiff's exhibits drawn from contemporary accounts in the press of ceremonies inaugurating the installation of Cyclone Seven wherein it was envisioned as a compelling tourist attraction though not, in the light of current events, for the reasons it enjoys today. Quoted therein, plaintiff cites, among numerous contemporary expressions of local exuberance, comments by then presiding Village Board member J Harret Ruth at the ribbon cutting and reception held at nearby Mel's Kandy Kitchen with glowing photographic coverage, quoting therefrom 'the time, the place, and the dedication of all you assembled here from far and wide, the common people and captains of industry and the arts rubbing elbows in tribute to the patriotic ideals rising right here before our eyes in this great work of sculptural art.'

Responding to plaintiff's exhibits on this count, those of defendant appear drawn well after the fact up to and including the present day and provoked (here the court infers) by the prevailing emotional climate expressed in, and elicited by, the print and television media, appending thereto recently published statements by former Village official J Harret Ruth in his current pursuit of a seat on the federal judiciary referring to the sculptural work at the center of this action as 'a rusting travesty of our great nation's vision of itself' and while we may pause to marvel at his adroitness in ascertaining the direction of the parade before leaping in front to lead it we dismiss this and supporting testimony supra as contradictory and frivolous, and find plaintiff's exhibits in evidence persuasive.

Another count in plaintiff's action naming defendants both within and beyond this jurisdiction seeks remedy for defamation and consequent incalculable damage to his career and earning power derived therefrom (Reiman v. Pacific Development Soc., 132 Or. 82, 284 P. 575, 1930; Brauer

v. Globe Newspaper Co., 351 Mass. 53, 217 N.E.2d 736, 1966). It is undisputed that plaintiff and his work, as here represented by the steel sculpture Cyclone Seven, have been held up to public ridicule both locally and, given the wide ranging magic of the media, throughout the land, as witnessed in a cartoon published in the South Georgia Pilot crudely depicting a small dog pinioned under a junk heap comprising old bedsprings, chamber pots, and other household debris, and from the Arkansas Family Visitor an editorial denouncing plaintiff's country of origin as prominent in the Soviet bloc, thereby distinctly implying his mission among us to be one of atheistic subversion of our moral values as a Christian nation, whereas materials readily available elsewhere show plaintiff to have departed his birthplace at age three with his family who were in fact fleeing the then newly installed Communist regime. We take judicial notice of this exhibit as defamatory communication and libellous per se, tending 'to lower him in the estimation of the community or to deter third persons from associating or dealing with him' (Restatement of the Law, Second, Torts 2d, 559), but it remains for plaintiff to seek relief in the courts of those jurisdictions.

Similarly, where plaintiff alleges defamation in this and far wider jurisdictions through radio and television broadcast we are plunged still deeper into the morass of legal distinctions embracing libel and slander that have plagued the common law since the turn of the seventeenth century. As slander was gradually wrested from the jurisdiction of the ecclesiastical courts through tort actions seeking redress for temporal damage rather than spiritual offense, slander became actionable only with proof or the reasonable assumption of special damage of a pecuniary character. Throughout, slander retained its identity as spoken defamation, while with the rise of the printing press it became libel in the written or printed word, a distinction afflicting our own time in radio and television broadcasting wherein defamation has been held as libel if read from a script by the broadcaster (Hartmann v. Winchell, 296 N.Y. 296, N.E.2d 30, 1947; Hryhorijiv v. Winchell, 1943, 180 Misc. 574, 45 N.Y.S.2d 31, affirmed, 267 App.Div. 817, 47 N.Y.S.2d 102, 1944) but as slander if it is not. But see Restatement of the Law, Second, Torts 2d, showing libel as 'broadcasting of defamatory matter by means of radio or television, whether or not it is read from a manuscript' (#568A). Along this tortuous route, our only landmark in this proceeding is the aforementioned proof or reasonable assumption of special damage of a pecuniary character and, plaintiff failing in these provisions, this remedy is denied.

In reaching these conclusions, the court acts from the conviction that risk of ridicule, of attracting defamatory attentions from his colleagues and even raucous demonstrations by an outraged public have ever been and remain the foreseeable lot of the serious artist, recalling among the most egregious examples Ruskin accusing Whistler of throwing a paint pot in the public's face, the initial scorn showered upon the Impressionists and, once they were digested, upon the Cubists, the derision greeting Bizet's musical innovations credited with bringing about his death of a broken heart, the public riots occasioned by the first performance of Stravinsky's Rite of Spring, and from the day Aristophanes labeled Euripides 'a maker of ragamuffin mannequins' the avalanche of disdain heaped upon writers: the press sending the author of Ode on a Grecian Urn 'back to plasters, pills, and ointment boxes,' finding Ibsen's Ghosts 'a loathsome sore unbandaged, a dirty act done publicly' and Tolstoy's Anna Karenina 'sentimental rubbish,' and in our own land the contempt accorded each succeeding work of Herman Melville, culminating in Moby Dick as 'a huge dose of hyperbolical slang, maudlin sentimentalism and tragic-comic bubble and squeak,' and since Melville's time upon writers too numerous to mention. All this must most arguably in deed and intent affect the sales of their books and the reputations whereon rest their hopes of advances and future royalties, yet to the court's knowledge none of this opprobrium however enviously and maliciously conceived and however stupid, careless, and ill informed in its publication has ever yet proved grounds for a successful action resulting in recovery from the marplot. In short, the artist is fair game and his cause is turmoil. To echo the words of Horace, Pictoribus atque poetis quidlibet audendi semper fuit aequa potestas, in this daring invention the artist comes among us not as the bearer of idées reçues embracing art as decoration or of the comfort of churchly beliefs enshrined in greeting card sentiments but rather in the aesthetic equivalent of one who comes on earth 'not to send peace, but a sword.'

The foregoing notwithstanding, before finding for plaintiff on the main action before the court set forth in his motion for a preliminary injunction barring interference of any sort by any means by any party or parties with the sculptural creation Cyclone Seven the court is compelled to address whether, following such a deliberate invasion for whatever purpose however merciful in intent, the work can be restored to its original look in keeping with the artist's unique talents and accomplishment or will suffer irreparable harm therefrom. Bowing to the familiar adage Cuilibet in arte sua perito est credendum, we hold the latter result to be an inevitable consequence of such invasion and such subsequent attempt at reconstitution at the hands of those assembled for such purposes in the form of members of the local Fire Department, whose training and talents such as they may be must be found to lie elsewhere, much in the manner of that obituary upon our finest poet of the century wherein one of his purest lines was reconstituted as 'I do not think they will sing to me' by a journalist trained to eliminate on sight the superfluous 'that.'

For the reasons set out above, summary judgment is granted to plaintiff as to preliminary injunction.

They heard the racket before she got out of the car, through the rain running up the wet steps of that veranda to tug at the door, down the hall past the library and into the sunroom with —Oscar! What's going on!

—Damn.

—Well stop thrashing around, you could tip that thing over and hurt yourself. I mean what are you trying to do.

—Hurt myself! What do you think I, where is she what does it look like. She sat me here in a draft and just left me here and the rain starts I've been trying to close this damned, damned...

—Yes all right just, if you'll just relax and let me wait, will you just let go of it! She twisted the cane's handle free of the blind's louvers where he'd thrust it through trying to snag the catch on the casement window, —there. And she got it closed. —Did it occur to you to simply move your chair out of the...

—Did it occur to you that the damned thing won't move? The wheels locked or something, maybe it's the battery. Can you make me some tea?

—My God, you do have trouble with vehicles don't you, where is she, what's her name.

—If I knew where she was do you think I'd been sitting here in the rain? She hates that little room you've put her in I'll tell you that Christina.

—I'll put her in your old room on the top floor when you were a little boy, she can go up there and play with your rock collection, just turn your head a little. No, this way.

—What's the...

—It's not bad at all is it, your scar. You'd hardly notice it.

—You'll notice it, I just have to ask Harry, I thought he was coming out with you.

—He's getting some things from the car Oscar listen, before he comes in, he doesn't want to make a Federal case of it but these phone calls you've been making to his office, he's been terribly busy and he just can't put up with them. He even said that you'd...

—Well if that's what he, if he hasn't even got time to...

—No but that's what he said Oscar, it isn't his time, it's their time, the law firm's time, they charge their clients for fifteen minutes if they talk for three he'll explain it to you, it's...

—Their clients? I thought he was my brother in law, I thought you wanted me to make him feel like a member of the family, isn't that what you do if you're a member of the family? help out when somebody in the family needs your advice?

—But that's the point Oscar, you're not a client, you're not paying them for his advice, that's why he's come out here today, a Sunday, he brings work home, he eats late, this case he's been working on it's in the millions of dollars it's been going on for years, he hasn't a minute to himself he said you'd even asked him to go to this movie for you we just haven't had the time. That's why we're late getting out here now, he had to make some calls before we left and I told the garage to bring the car around while I got your groceries together and I'd meet him in front of the building, and of course it was raining...

And of course they'd both been out there, waiting in the rain by the time the car appeared, the grocery bag already split down the side. He'd drive, he told her, get it over with and make an early start back, —and you? You've decided to stay out there?

—My God Harry I don't know, my coat's caught in the door here can you wait? She got it open, slammed it and —I won't know till we've seen him. He's been out of the hospital for three days and he's already got everything in a turmoil, that nine hundred dollar chair I got for him he'll probably break his neck in it and this woman I brought in, white columnar thighs to break a bull's back isn't that what you said once? Whether she can cook but she may get his mind off of Lily long enough to be careful! She'd seized the dashboard, clinging there with a tremor —my God...

—Did you see that?

—No but please just, be careful...

—Did you see that? his knuckles gone white on the wheel, —steps right in front of the car and holds up his hand, did you see that?

—God Harry just be careful. They're crazy. I mean you're the one who told me that aren't you? take for granted everybody in this city's crazy till they show you otherwise? You could have killed him.

—Better than just knocking him down, see a car like this one they know how much liability you're carrying and you're in court for the rest of your life.

—Just the rage. If you saw his eyes, that's what this city runs on, where it gets its energy. Rage.

—It's the money, Christina. The rest of it's...

—It's not The Marriage of Figaro I'll tell you that. She's got a new lawyer for her mess of a divorce who wants to handle Oscar's accident, shock, injury, loss of income, disfigurement, a million, five, God knows what nonsense, you said he's called you?

—Called me? sweeping up the avenue through the burst of a cab's horn so close she started, freed into traffic lifting both hands from the wheel for a gesture —called me! I told you, look Christina. I told you to speak to him, he gets me at the office and I can't get him off the phone. I don't want to hurt his feelings but you know the pressure we're under down there. A client calls and knows it's costing him seventy five dollars just to pick up the phone but Oscar, it never occurs to him that...

—Well it doesn't Harry, that's just the point, it just doesn't occur to him. Flat on his back, I mean what's more natural than to reach for the telephone and he's been simply frantic since this movie opened, he's just getting used to the idea that he has a brother in law he thinks he can turn to and when he can't reach you, when they tell him you're in court...

—Because I've finally told Doris that whenever he calls I'm in court, that I'm in conference, that I'm out of the office, I'm not trying to make a Federal case out of this Christina but you've got to do something. I thought he resented me intruding on the family by marrying you, try to show him some family concern, fine. That's what I'm doing today, now, Sunday, but even that woman we met at the hospital? the one with the blood bath, you actually gave her my number too?

—Trish?

—Well who else. Maybe you should just tell your friends I'm a public relations man, that I'm in ladies' underwear, an ad account executive, something completely useless that...

—Trish would love you in ladies' underwear Harry.

—Look I'm serious! She got on the phone with her whole life history, the time they took her to Payne Whitney when she cut her wrists? Patched her up, gave her some pills, when they sent her a bill for eleven thousand dollars she tried it again, now she wants to sue this hospital for something she calls foetal endangerment?

—Because that's what she was doing there. I mean she came in for that amniosomething, centesis, that test they give pregnant women our age to make sure the baby won't be born with one leg or eight thumbs and she'd have it aborted, she's already got a sweet little boy about ten named T J and when that blood got spilled on her obviously that's the first thing she thought of. She just wants to be sure before she marries Bunker.

—I see.

—I don't think you do, Harry. I mean if she married him first and then got these tests and had to have the abortion, she'd be stuck with Bunker on her hands for no earthly purpose until God knows when, he'd be awfully expensive to unload and of course he doesn't know a thing about the boy.

—If she's thinking of making him a stepfather, I don't...

—Of making who, Bunker? You see you don't listen, I mean this boy she's been seeing, where do you think the pregnancy came from. Of course she hasn't mentioned it to him, he's trying to be a writer and obviously hasn't got a penny you can't seriously picture her married to him, she's twice his age and I mean Bunker's twice hers but he's so pickled he'll last out the century and if Bunker got in there and anything happened to her T J would never see a penny.

—The rate she's going looks like old Bunker's onto a sure thing.

—Well you can't laugh at them Harry, making fun of people's troubles I mean that's the way it sounds sometimes, if you could just stop and try to see their good side?

—Married the wrong man, Christina. We don't get to see much of the good side, greed, stupidity, double dealing, a system like ours you expect it to bring out the best in people? One lawyer to every four or five hundred and most of them can't afford one anyway, the ones who can like your friend here are even worse, make a mess of things and expect to be rescued, they...

—You didn't need to be rude to her.

—I was not rude to her! When I finally got a word in...

—That all you could talk about was money.

—Exactly. Look. I told her I don't do matrimonials. I told her I don't do negligence. I told her I could set up a conference for her and there'd be a charge, if the firm took her case there'd be a retainer, it happens every time. The minute you mention money they think you're being rude when that's all they've got on their minds in the first place, look at Oscar. Perfectly happy if the insurance company would just pay his hospital bills till Lily drags in this ambulance chaser whetting his appetite for damages? Why I went into corporate law in the first place where it's greed plain and simple. It's money from start to finish, it's I want what you've got, nobody out there with these grievances they expect you to share, have you got a dollar? Another dollar, for the toll.

—I don't, wait... she dug deeper, —here. It's just what I...

—Look at Oscar with this damn movie, you've got to explain to him Christina, these phone calls and the rest of the...

—I don't see why you can't explain it to him yourself, I mean it's just what I said earlier isn't it? about being taken seriously? Simply explain to him that you look out! My God Harry, you shouldn't drive when you're upset, that little green car anybody who drives a car like that don't you know he's going to try to prove something?

—Cuts me off because he wants me to take him seriously, exactly. Look, I can't explain things to Oscar because I can't get a word in. Because you want this great show of brotherly concern I'm supposed to get as upset as he is over this monstrous injustice, the minute I mention money we'll end up just like your friend with her foetal endangerment. He probably doesn't have a case. If he does the chances are it can't be won. They get these nuisance suits all the time, people with grandiose ideas about suing Hollywood for millions even if he's got one, even if Oscar's really got a case with this play of his he's got to know it will cost him money. He's got to know you can always lose a lawsuit and your money with it, that's the point, has he got it? the money? Because you don't start something like this on what they pay a college history teacher.

—Well I know that, no. He just does that, the teaching I mean, it just goes in to the bank every month I don't think he makes any connection between it and these students he detests no, there's a trust his mother set up for him before she died because Father married money that first time, just the way his father had, so what does Oscar show up with? Somebody whose idea of share the wealth is getting her purse stolen, but I mean all that was before Father married again, married my mother I mean so I've never known what it amounts to and Oscar's always been awfully careful about what's his and what's mine. Why is that funny.

—Careful.

—Well why is that...

—First time I met him, first time I came out to the country to see you? That downstairs hall bathroom, I hadn't closed the door tight and I hear Oscar's footsteps come creaking down the hall, suddenly as he passes his hand slips in and switches the light off and leaves me there sitting in the dark.

—I don't think that's odd at all, he's just not used to having strangers in the house, I mean with half the place shut off to save heat there's nothing odd about being upset by sheer waste is there? It's the way we were brought up, you get letters from him with the address pasted over some political fund raiser or cripple benefit or God knows what because he can't bear to see the postage wasted, you don't waste you don't want and putting up with my mother my God, you couldn't blame him. I mean if you're brought up like that you're going to go one way or the other when the times comes, throw your money out the window or separate the clean bills from the dirty ones, right side up, the twenties and tens inside and then the fives, the ones think about it, I mean you couldn't blame him. That egg he wouldn't eat at breakfast when he was what, seven? and she puts it in front of him again at lunch? Roast chicken for dinner and he's still sitting there gritting his teeth against that egg it went on for two days, he just wouldn't give in till that second night he finally went to pieces, threw the whole thing on the floor and shouted which came first! the chicken or the egg! and he was sent to bed, he went up the stairs singing it and he stayed there, he even managed to run a fever. God knows what went on between Father and my mother, he never said a word but I'd see him looking at Oscar sometimes, watching him with that cunning little smile he gets when you don't know whether he's pleased or that you'd better watch out.

—Tell you one thing, I'd hate to argue a case before him when he's sober.

—Well you only met him that once Harry, he was hardly at his best.

—Kept calling me counselor, that courtly manner and the gravy spots on his tie I'm not even sure he knew who I was. He seemed to think I wanted to discuss Justice Holmes' dissent in the Black and White Taxicab case, he's got total recall for the year nineteen twenty eight when he was clerking for his father on the High Court and now the press down there trying to heat things up over this Szyrk decision, madness in the family and all the rest of it, have you seen that ad for this damn Civil War movie? Based on a true story, have you seen it? All they'd need is a look in his chambers there, sweltering, cigarette smoke you could cut with a knife, must have been a hundred degrees and that Christ awful life size plastic praying hands thing of Dürer's standing there on the window sill upside down like somebody taking a dive, think that's his idea of a joke?

—God only knows, he's...

—If it is it's a pretty good one.

—Well of course that's why Oscar's so frantic, I don't mean this mess about Father but this awful movie, you can't blame him. I mean that's why he tried to write his play in the first place, for his grandfather, you can imagine, I mean even after he'd retired from the Court he used to dress to go out to dinner and Oscar had this solemn little task, transferring his gold watch and chain and the gold pen knife and change from the pockets of the suit he'd had on to his evening clothes it went on right till the last, he didn't die till he was ninety six and then suddenly there's this little boy with his own mother gone and his father marching his new wife into the house dragging this little girl behind her, my God. Because he'd have died before he'd have taken a penny changing his grandfather's money from one suit to the other but now he'd watch his chance to go through the seat cushions in that big chair in the library where Father sat when he read the papers, I mean think about it. Because his grandfather was really the first friend he ever had.

—Fine... He ran a hand over her knee, drawn up that close to him on the seat there, —take a nap. Because I've tried to tell him, haven't I? that he can't copyright his grandfather?

—And the rain, Harry? her voice already falling away, —just don't drive so fast?

And the rain, steady as the highway stretching out ahead like the day itself, lightened at last now the car turned south off the highway into a road, a byroad, as the —Sorry!

—Well my God! seizing the dashboard again, —you knew that bump was there didn't you? through the gates, past **PRIVATE ROAD MEMBERS AND GUESTS ONLY,** passing **STRANGERS ARE REQUESTED NOT TO ENTER** down a ribbon of disrepair prompted at discreet intervals along its way by names on the order of Whitney, Armstrong, here a Kallikak freshly lettered, even a Hannahan posting driveways off to the right, to the left turning in at a weathered Crease to splash up the pitted drive —and these dangling limbs look at them, twelve hundred dollars to those tree people they should pay us for damages, drive up as close as you can will you? by the steps there?

They heard the racket before she got out of the car, through the rain running up the wet steps of that veranda to tug at the door as he came round the side of the car for the grocery bag, a suitcase, newspapers, round the side of the house to the tradesmen's entrance where a door led through to the kitchen and —Harry? in here, we're in the sunroom, maybe you can help?

It was the obstinate chair of course, —a little safety lock down here Oscar, you must have brushed a hand against it.

—I did not brush a thing against it. Hello Harry. Christina's making some tea.

—Well it's late enough Oscar, I brought out some sturgeon, maybe we'll just want lunch? But he'd already ordered up tortellini for lunch, told that woman to fix it in some broth and then something in an Alfredo sauce and salad if anyone could find her, bad enough just trying to find anything herself, scissors, any scissors, those ginger preserves, his copy of Fitzhugh's Cannibals All! because he certainly couldn't scale the shelves in the library the mess it was in since they'd moved things around to put a bed in there for him where he couldn't reach the phone that had already rung twice since he'd been left sitting here in the rain, abandoned was really the word for it, he'd had her look in his room upstairs for his play in a black pebbled binder and she finally came down with an old address book and the papers, had they brought out the newspapers? Not that he could read them if they had because that was the worst of it, his glasses, —what that woman could have done with my glasses I haven't been able to read anything but the headlines since the day before the, the mail even the mail, wherever she's hidden the mail like every illiterate in this whole illiterate country I have to watch the news trimmed to fit that damned little screen between the hemorrhoid and false teeth commercials, can you imagine what the rest of the audience looks like? America has taken Spot to its heart, did you see it last night? Every idiot in sight down there with something to sell, dog candy, hot dogs, Free Spot! buttons, Free Spot! T shirts, Spot dolls with huge wet eyes and that whole hideous Cyclone Seven? peddling this take apart puzzle model and a game where you try to get the dog out with magnets shaped like a dog bone? Marching around for animal rights, artists' rights, black rights, right to life, abortion, gun control, Jesus loves and the flags, Stars and Stripes, Stars and Bars and then somebody...

—Oscar, just...

—Yes and then somebody throws a beer bottle and they...

—And Father right in the midst of it, that's...

—And why shouldn't he be! Why shouldn't he Christina he started it all didn't he? with that, that decision he wrote for this awful little dog? Schoolchildren sending in donations so this cheap sentimental vision of our great republic shall not perish from the earth, you know that story by Stephen Crane? A Small Brown Dog? where a lonely little boy and a simpering brown dog make friends and the whole thing gets so syrupy the drunken father finally throws the dog out the window? I'd do the same thing, it's being reprinted everywhere how the same man who wrote it could have written The Red Badge of Courage, you think they're not making that into a television special too? Everybody grabbing part of the act, the Civil War nobody gives one damn for it till they see these headlines PATRIOTIC GORE IN NINETY MILLION DOLLAR SPECTACULAR, have you seen it?

—That review in the Times? It was...

—No the movie! the movie! Isn't that what I asked you? if you'd just go see the movie? They steal the whole, how many, two years? three years I worked on that play? They step in and steal the whole thing and you can't even take three hours to go see what they...

—Oscar it's not that simple. You know Harry's up to his eyes in work and you don't really know what they've done after all, I mean you haven't actually seen the movie yourself yet and...

—Yes I know I haven't actually seen the movie myself yet! I haven't actually been out playing baseball myself yet either! if that's what you, why I asked you to go see it I can't even read about it where is it, that review will you look over there? on the sideboard there? unless she's burned it, all I could read was that headline. And that ad. Did you see that Harry? that full page ad? Based on a true story with the picture of that idiot Christina wait, where are you going.

—I'm just going to look for...

—I just told you I can't read it didn't I? without my glasses? If neither one of you can bother to go to the movie can you at least take a whole minute and a half to read me the review?

—Oscar try to calm down. Here it is, Harry can read it I'm just going to look for that woman, I mean you know it's quite rude of you to call her that don't you, I'm sure she has a name and Harry? that bag of groceries?

—In the kitchen, on the floor by the sink, no look Oscar. The whole point of the...

—That ad yes. Based on a true story, did you see it?

—That's what I'm talking about, that's the...

—And the review there it is yes, there it is read it. Read it.

—Do you want the credits and all the...

—No no no later, no just read it.

—PATRIOTIC GORE IN NINETY MILLION DOLLAR SPECTACULAR. The full fury of what remains our nation's most searing rite of passage, the American Civil War, bursts from the screen in the epic proportions of this three hour, ninety million dollar saga of historical artifice and grisly reality, The Blood in the Red White and Blue, produced and directed by Hollywood's reigning wunderkind Constantine Kiester. Unlike the big budget pictures which followed Mister Kiester's initial gory box office triumph, the Africa extravaganza Urubu...

—Do you believe it? He made a big movie about Africa with these special effects that made you throw up so they give him ninety million dollars to make a Civil War movie with battle scenes that make you throw up, Constantine Kiester. Do you believe it? Nobody's named that. If you were named that you'd change it no but go on, read it. Go on.

—Unlike the big budget pictures which followed Mister Kiester's initial gory box office triumph, the Africa extravaganza Uruburu, both the Vietnam comedy Armageddon Blueplate Special and his 'twenties gangster satire The Rotten Club appeared to have been filmed unfettered by the restraints of a script, with a story patched together as an afterthought, whereas here he is fortunate in dealing from the start with a story line strong enough to accommodate even the severely limited talents of Robert Bredford in the leading role, that of a young man who resolves his divided loyalties in the country torn asunder by Civil War by sending up substitutes to fight in his place in both the Union and Confederate armies, where both are killed in the bloodiest...

—At Antietam isn't it! Isn't it?

—in the bloodiest single day of the war, September seventeenth eighteen sixty two, at the Antietam creek in...

—There, I told you! It's the same story it's exactly the same, they stole it. It's that simple, they stole it.

—You'd have to prove they stole it, Oscar.

—Well of course they did, it's my grandfather isn't it? the play I wrote about my own grandfather, it says it right there in their ad. Based on a true story, they...

—What I'm trying to tell you Oscar, don't you see? That can put it right out in the public domain where they can claim fair use, where anybody can use it, it's even been in some of the papers down there hasn't it? This trash they're printing about madness in your family? Trying to use these stories about your grandfather to get at your father over this Szyrk case they'll dig up anything they can, if you...

—Do you think they haven't called here? One of these, these

mushmouths from something called the South Georgia Pilot and how familiar was I with my grandfather's voting record on the Holmes Court back in the 'twenties pretty far over to the left he thought, maybe a little tainted with a breath of antiSemitism? anti-niggra? That my great grandfather was in the diplomatic corps over there in France when the communists were acting up back in the eighteen forties and maybe I could tell him a little about my grandfather's second marriage? Ask him what the hell business that is of his and he says not his, no, the public, that it's history, it's the public's right to know, that the...

—What I'm trying to tell you Oscar. If they dig up things like this in the public domain they've got their First Amendment rights to publish pretty much whatever they...

—But why! Just to, talk about Father smoking three packages a day he didn't even start smoking cigarettes till he was seventy five whose business is that, just a good thing they never caught him on a spree examining his false teeth in the glass to see whether he'd had dinner the night before.

—Look just be patient, the village has appealed his decision and all this trash is just to build up pressure on the circuit court appointment, frankly I think he's going to be reversed and then he's out of the picture and the whole thing...

—Fine he's out of the picture fine, what about me? What about this movie they stole that's what this is really all about isn't it? What else does it say, go on.

—While his boyish charm is wearing rather thin, under Mister Kiester's energetic direction Mister Bredford manages the part of young Randal with enough brio and costume changes to bolster a sagging career, plunging into the early battle scenes with commendable bloodthirsty zeal, and handling himself convincingly enough in those steamily explicit sexual encounters where all eyes are, in any event, on the voluptuous attributes of the tempestuous daughter of the neighboring plantation, played with an abandon obscuring any notions of her own acting ability by the stunning Nordic-Eurasian discovery Anga Frika in her first American starring role, had enough?

—Yes. Go on.

—The crisis precipitating Randal's abrupt...

—The most ridiculous rubbish I've ever heard, there's nothing voluptuous about Giulielma at all that's the whole point. She's a shy lonely girl, she's not even supposed to be particularly pretty just, go on no, go on.

—The crisis precipitating Randal's abrupt departure from the Confederacy, following his heroic showing in the blood drenched battle sequence at Ball's Bluff, attested upon his return by a raw scar on his cheek which will lend him the credential of a dueling scar through the rest of the picture, is the threat of confiscation by the Federal government to extensive coal mining properties he inherits from an uncle in Pennsylvania where his cry for...

—No wait, stop. Stop! Did you hear that? that, that scar? on his cheek? Harry that's mine, that's in my play right at the start the same thing, the same battle Ball's Bluff the same battle he comes back with that scar on his cheek it's mine, it's right there in my play, Christina? Where is she, she's got to find it where is she, yes and then what. And then what.

—Pennsylvania, where his cry for justice, demanding...

—Yes in Pennsylvania, the uncle who dies in Pennsylvania and the coal mines yes and then what.

—demanding only what is his, echoes beyond the bugle's battlefield summons to the fatal confrontation between the Southerner's fierce love of the warm and fruitful land, and the cold hard cash to be blindly torn from the black depths of the Northern mines.

—Yes that's exactly what I...

—In more responsive hands, the characters of the two substitutes might have reflected the deeper opposing dualism of man's nature, but Mister Kiester has no time for such subtleties. The Northern substitute is no more than a brutalized excrescence of blind industrial slavery, while the South is personified by Ziff Davis, acclaimed for his portrayal of the sadistic pederast in Sick City, who seems to have wandered into the wrong picture from some subdivision of God's Little Acre in his depiction of sly depravity with all the...

—Yes listen to that! you see? That's exactly what he's not, what William in the play is not, he's a sensitive intelligent wait, Christina? Where have you been, listen...

—Her name is Ilse, Oscar. She was down in the laundry, she...

—Have you heard any of this? Listen you've got to find it, my play you have to find it, it's...

—In a black pebbled binder, I'll look for it after lunch. She's putting it on the table, now...

—No but wait, that's not all, Harry? Go on, that's not all is it?

—In the part of the father of the bride, as grossly overplayed by aging exstar Clint Westwood in his first role since A Hatful of Sh*t, the Confederate Major is the archetypal cigar chewing duplicitous Southern planter with a taste for drink and an unsavoury eye for the fatal charms of his own daughter, all of which blossoms in what will undoubtedly be the most widely discussed mass rape scene in screen history.

—Well that's just, of all the revolting nonsense there's nothing like that anywhere, it's...

—Well my God Oscar what's the problem then. You're furious because they've stolen your play and then you're furious because there's nothing like it in the movie anywhere, how do you expect anybody to take you seriously if you...

—Well ask Harry! What he's just read to me that's in the movie right down to the same battles and this scar on his cheek if he takes me seriously ask him, did you hear that? about the scar?

—You'd hardly notice it, I told you that the minute I walked in didn't I?

—That's not what we're talking about! This is the movie, he comes home from the war with a raw scar on his cheek where he's been wounded it's right out of my play, and in the same battle, do you think that's an accident? A detail like that, do you think that's just a coincidence?

—I think a lot of people to hear you carrying on about this little scar on your cheek from a play you wrote a hundred years ago would wonder about a coincidence, let's go in to lunch.

—No wait, stop. He's not finished, are you Harry? Would anybody believe that's just a coincidence?

—As the bloodiest single day of the entire Civil War, the battle of the Antietam was the ideal vehicle for the real stars of The Blood in the Red White and Blue, the special effects technicians whose grisly spectacles under Mister Kiester's direction established his reputation at the box office with his original extravaganza Uruburu. Billed at the time as not for the squeamish, that epic of modern Africa broke all bounds not only for screen violence but, as in the notorious sledgehammer scene, good taste, obliging him to seek dubious refuge in the First Amendment, and perhaps as a result the more excruciating excesses of the earlier film are somewhat modified in his latest epic. This is not to say that those who thirst for blood and hunger for patriotic gore will go away unrewarded. From the massing of the Union troops of Hooker's I Corps in the early morning mists for his opening attack on Jackson's two divisions spanning the Hagerstown turnpike at five thirty in the morning of that fateful day dawning over the Antietam creek, the carnage of war fills the screen for an unprecedented twenty four minute sequence in which, as a measure of the degree to which Mister Kiester's audiences have become inured to the agonies of their fellow men, the real terror reaches us in the flaming uncomprehending eyes, the violent throes of death, the hoof thrust heavenward of the suddenly rigid corpse of the horse in the din of battle.

—Harry? I said lunch is...

—Wait, there's only this. In other hands...

—Just bring it with you then!

—In other hands, The Blood in the Red White and Blue might have offered a vivid, once in a lifetime opportunity to explore the more profound implications at the heart of its story in the dramatic portrayal of man the microcosm of his nation's history, of man against himself, of self delusion and self betrayal, of the very expediency at the expense of principle we see blindly laying waste to our hopes and our future today, of the urgings of destiny, and the unswerving punctuality of chance. What we have instead, is a ninety million dollar glorification of the horrors of war, an inspired, lavishly illustrated text for those of our reigning political patriots who will never cease to extol the spilling of blood so long as it is not their own or who, pray, would there be left to extol it?

—Yes wait, wait that whole last part read it again, that's what it's about, my play that's exactly what it's about justice, self betrayal, destiny that's what it's all really about read it again, you've got to find it for me Christina you've...

—Harry don't you dare read it again, we're going in to lunch Oscar if you think you can drive that thing without Harry wait, just get hold of it he can't see where he's going, steer him this way through the no, this way, so he can sit up at the end of the table and look out! My God, another case of vehicular homicide we'll all be in court, will you just sit up Oscar?

—I can't.

—Well you're not going to just loll there like some Roman emperor spilling tortellini down your front and drinking wine through a bent straw are you?

—I thought you might help me. What's this.

—It's your old tricycle horn, I found it in the cellar. Just hook it onto your pram there and Ilse will come running the next time you're left out in the rain, really you've got to get something done about the driveway. Anyone coming to look at the place after a day like this it's like fording the Amazon with those limbs dangling over your head, have you paid those tree people yet?

—You don't expect to show the house with me here in this condition do you?

—It's not a very appetizing prospect no, but I don't think they'll think you come with the house, when you're back on your feet...

—And nobody's asked about that course, have you, when I'm back on my feet? Because it's if, it's not when it's if I'll walk again that's what they're saying, this sciatic nerve if it's as badly damaged as these doctors think I might not, that maybe I'll never walk again.

—Well that's the most, did they actually say that?

—Maybe not exactly but that's what they think, the therapist's coming tomorrow and the driveway, I called about the driveway and the tree people no, I haven't paid them yet, I thought we might save some money if...

—Maybe if you'd just stop thinking about how to save money and start thinking about how to make some, your sleeve is in the broth there can't you use your spoon?

—It's cold anyway, she didn't...

—It got cold while you were entertaining Harry in there with your battle scar, unless she's planning a whole new career for you just going around and suing people?

—She who, what do you...

—Well who else Oscar! You said this ambulance chaser she's got for her divorce wants to sue your insurance company for a million dollars damages?

—I never said a million dollars Christina. She says that Kevin said if my basic economic loss is limited to fifty thousand dollars under No Fault including all these medical and hospital expenses and lost earnings up to a thousand dollars a month for up to three years, that we...

—Has the school stopped paying you?

—Well no but we don't know what's going to happen do we? because I don't have tenure? and the reason I still don't have tenure is because I don't hand out As and Bs to these kids who won't learn and don't want to learn the first thing about American history. Talk about the Civil War they think Longstreet is an address in New Jersey and you can imagine the ribald fun they have with Hooker, so she says Kevin thinks we should file a claim to assert my rights to the, my common law rights to a regular trial and...

—Why don't you ask Harry if that makes any sense, wheeling you into the courtroom in this getup...

—Not my field Oscar but it might be risky, your insurance company probably move to dismiss your claim based on their alleged immunity under the No Fault laws and then where are you, can't collect damages for noneconomic loss that's what your No Fault is for isn't it?

—No but pain and suffering Harry, if they...

—I think you've really got to establish serious injury, lose an arm or a leg or some real disfigurement to start an action for...

—Well look at me! I still can't move this leg if I try to turn this way or sit up straight it's like a hot pitchfork right through here, I was on the critical list in there wasn't I? in the hospital? Isn't that enough to convince somebody that I...

—If it's not Harry, he can tell them about his little visitor in the black suit coming to take him to the other side like Dante and...

—No stop it Christina, that wasn't it at all and you know it. If you think it wasn't serious do you know they even came in and asked if I wanted a summary of what was going to happen on If the World Turns and the rest of these idiotic soap operas, will kindly old Apple Annie die of a brain tumor? will Gary the star halfback test positive for AIDS? They have those, they provide them confidentially to terminal patients who don't want to leave without knowing whether friendly Frank really stole that money or if beautiful Jessica will have that abortion, if that's the...

—No look Oscar, I didn't mean to seem to shrug off your injuries. Point is once you get these lawsuits started they can drag out for years, they give you some docket number in the hereafter and the insurance company's in no hurry. They're getting fed up with these million dollar awards and settlements and they're starting to really fight them, get one postponement after another and by the time you come to trial you'll be...

—I'll be out playing baseball, will you tell her to bring in that Alfredo dish Christina? Because she says Kevin said I'm probably already well past the threshold limit on all these medical bills so what we're talking about is all this pain and suffering and lost income because of this permanent disfigurement.

—I think he means his battle scar, Harry. Just turn a little so he can see it Oscar, which cheek is it?

—It's right here! Can't you see it?

—If you know where to look. Get it in the right light it's quite distinguished, don't you think so Harry?

—You said the school's still paying you Oscar, I don't see where loss of income is...

—Maybe he could get a slouch hat and take his play on the road.

—Christina stop it! I'm trying to...

—I mean anyone who could take his girlfriend on a vacation trip to visit a Civil War battlefield, she probably asked which side was George Washington on, talking about all this lost income Oscar I can't imagine what you're talking about.

—Because that's exactly what I'm talking about, this same battlefield because that's the trip we made down to Maryland when I was going to lecture on the battle at Antietam at the Army War College in Carlyle, lecture fees like that and the whole lecture circuit even if I can finally walk again, that this facial disfigurement can cause my loss of earning capacity that's what it's about.

—Well I must say it's the first time I've ever heard you talk about the whole lecture circuit, Ilse get that bottle away from him before the whole thing goes, just pour a little in his glass and put some sauce right on his noodles there, where did that come from.

—It's a nice Pinot Grigio, just a table wine really but...

—I mean all this talk about the lecture circuit that's going to be deprived of your brilliant contributions.

—Yes well that was really Kevin's idea, those fees are at least three thousand dollars and even five because...

—And he thinks people would line up in droves to hear you talk about the Civil War?

—Well as he says Christina, I've got the credentials and with the interest that this movie has stirred up we can...

—You can sue them both.

—Not with Kevin no, she told me he's just writing the complaint for this accident and then we'll...

—She told you, what has he told you?

—Well I haven't met him yet but...

—Haven't met him? You mean he hasn't even seen your, your battle scar, this facial disfigurement you're so pleased with and he's writing the complaint anyhow? And you expect to pay him for this nonsense? have you thought of that?

—I told her to ask him about that and she said he just laughed and said to tell me not to worry about it.

—And you believe that? Harry tell him what you said about...

—Probably doing it on a contingency, if Oscar loses he doesn't pay him, if he wins this Kevin takes thirty, forty, maybe fifty percent of the settlement, you ought to clear that up Oscar.

—No but, half? he'd get half? But that's, that's robbery that's...

—No worse than your art dealer is it? or your concert booking agent? It's the middleman Oscar, it's always the middleman.

—And that's how he's handling her mess of a divorce?

—Well that's not my, I don't know Christina, she doesn't tell me every, all the details, she's been trying to get a separation agreement signed and there's some trouble with that woman lawyer she had about money...

—It's always about money, I know her. Served on a committee with her once, she's running for city judge.

—She was supposed to be known as this great negotiator but all she's done is to...

—Look, a lot of people out there who mainly enjoy giving away what isn't theirs some of them make it a profession, the bigger the numbers in their negotiations the bigger their reputation, you walk in and they're on the phone saying we said four million three and the New York town house Jim, my client can't do better than that, expect him to spend the rest of his life on a lousy sixty foot yacht?

—Well that's hardly the case here is it, I mean unless her lawyer is busy giving away what isn't even hers if you see what I mean, I mean you do don't you Oscar. See what I mean I mean. I mean of course what is hers to give away is something else again after all isn't it, if you see what I...

—Just put down the wine Christina you've had enough, nobody's giving anything away here. No lawyer's going to take a case on contingency unless he's sure he can win it look Oscar, all I'm saying is bringing lawsuits like this movie business can get really complicated. The worse they get the more they cost the little guy who just can't begin to put up the kind of money that...

—I'm not a little guy! I told you what I, that all I want is justice that's what it's all about, what the play's all about in the first place, it's my whole...

—Oscar look. If they've spent ninety million dollars on this picture, you're the little guy. They're ready for you, any chance they could lose these nuisance suits their insurance wouldn't get near them, the exhibitors wouldn't touch it, they're ready to spend anything to protect their investment it's that simple.

—What Harry's trying to tell you Oscar is whoever takes your case it's going to cost you money, that even if you're right you can lose it maybe you don't care, I mean obviously you can't pay Kevin in the same coin Lily can, you...

—The, what do you mean the same coin! That's not fair Christina, I already told you she said he said if I want to sue anybody in the movie business out there that I better get myself a Jewish lawyer and he's not the...

—What this Kevin person's trying to tell you Oscar is going to cost you money, whoever takes a case like this is going to cost...

—I know that! That's what Harry just told me didn't he? that they wouldn't take it on some contingency arrangement where they'd get half that's not what I asked him for is it? I just thought maybe if we worked things out that maybe we could get some kind of a discount or maybe he could just sort of do it on the side where his law firm wouldn't even have to know about it would they? because it's all right in the family isn't it? If he wants to use some of his spare time just to do something for somebody in the family who...

—Oscar look at him. He's exhausted, he doesn't have any spare time, can't you understand that? I mean just look at him, Harry you got some of this sauce on your, no there on your chin there yes, there, even his own time isn't his own even if he wanted to, even if he could Oscar just because he's your brother in law and wants to do you some special favour, he...

—All right! If you think I expect some special favour just because he's my brother in law? that I'd ask him to take a case he thinks is a nuisance that he's already said he could lose, didn't he? Because maybe...

—Yes all right, just calm down Oscar, calm down. Is there anything you want me to do while we're...

—No. If you can find my play that's all, if you can look for it before you go. It ought to be upstairs in my room.

—Well I hadn't really thought of leaving Oscar, I mean Harry has to go but I thought you wanted me to come out and...

—Just do what you want to, I have to take my nap now there's no reason you should both have to sit around for that. Thank you for coming out.

—Well really Oscar, if that's what you want. Blow your bicycle horn there will you? I want to show Ilse that upstairs room before she, oh Ilse? Will you come upstairs with me?

—Oscar? Look...

—I just get impatient with her sometimes Harry. She just won't listen.

—All right, look. I appreciate your confidence in me Oscar but it wouldn't be fair to you. I couldn't give it the kind of time a case like this one deserves trying to do it on the side and my firm would know anyway, file the suit with the courts and my name's right there on it as the attorney of record, and look... He had out the slimmest of gold pencils, a pocket calendar gilt edged writing Lepidus, Shea & —here, tearing the page out, —ask for Sam, it's a small firm I knew him in law school, I'll call him in the morning, tell him to go easy and you're not in shape to come into his office but you can get your picture across on the phone, and he was up. —Bathroom's down this way isn't it?

—Next to the library yes... a hand up that might have been waving departure to finally settle it unsteadily on the glass, tipping its bent straw for the slurp of depletion and then wavering there in midair till the glass was suddenly seized and replaced on the table.

—Where's Harry.

—The bathroom, he...

—Where do you have your nap, I don't see why you can't have it right here in this thing, you're practically laid out flat as it is. When do you see the doctor again.

—I don't know Christina, but the insurance company's doctor when we file this lawsuit they'll probably...

—It's the most ridiculous thing I've ever heard. This Kevin person, filing a complaint when you've never even met him? that you haven't even read?

—But she's bringing it over. I told you.

—You did not tell me. When.

—Well I, later.

—After your nap? You certainly did not tell me no, my God we drive a hundred miles just to, Harry? We can leave when you're ready, it's Oscar's nap time and here, here's what you've been looking for Oscar. It was in your old room on the shelf with your rock collection, I've put Ilse in there.

—But it's, you found it yes, it was right where I said it was wasn't it? where I told that woman to...

—You told that poor woman it was in a black pebbled binder Oscar. This is a manila folder.

—Yes that's what I, Harry? She found my play wait, that part about the scar in that review? It's right in the opening scene, let him read it Christina.

—Just steer him back into the sunroom Harry.

—Or wait no, listen this whole opening scene it's between Thomas and his mother, you can both read it. Harry you read the Thomas part and Christina the mother so that way when you see the movie you'll remem...

—Oscar we're leaving. I'll call you tomorrow, I brought out some groceries Ilse can see to them and I put out some cash on the kitchen table in case she needs it.

—But wait no, you can't leave now wait, now that we have the play but I don't have my glasses and...

—Let Lily read it to you, I assume she can read?

—No but wait, Harry...

—Good luck Oscar. Watch out for laches. If you're going to do it don't put it off.

—And he's got his little horn there? in case he needs something? My suitcase, I think it's still in the kitchen Harry my God, I mean we might as well have just stayed in town and gone to the movies. But she paused there, looking out, where the rain had stopped, down over the lawn where a mist settling over the pond dimmed the opposite bank, to say, before she turned for the hall, for the door and out to that veranda and those wet steps down to the car, —but my God, it is beautiful isn't it.

> The sparsely furnished room is represented by two walls, their angle meeting to the left of center of the stage. To the right

he rubbed his eyes, held the page off, held it close,

> THOMAS is a tall lightly bearded man in his thirties, whose studied manner of folding his long legs out before him, and abrupt bursts of exuberance, combine the casualness of the born aristocrat with the energy of one who insists that youth cannot be gone. He is dressed in boots and a rumpled grey fieldcoat buttoned to the throat. The scar on his cheek is evident, but not so prominent as to be disfiguring. HIS MOTHER is more a desolate presence than

but without his glasses all this floated before his eyes in a blur, the effort of separating it into words echoing in broken gasps till he gave it up and the whole thing, manila folder pages and all, went to the floor as the gasps leveled off in mere measures of sleep and even the rattle of dishes elsewhere gone, settled in silence like the steady accumulation of gloom of the late afternoon shattered, all of it, all at once by —Oscar? and the light streaming on overhead, —are you okay?

—What's the, will you turn that off?

—What are you doing sitting here in the dark? Lights snapped on, snapped off like the lighting on a stage set, —and these papers all over the floor? sweeping them together with a wayward foot, —are you okay?

—Yes and stop walking on them will you? Can you just pick them up?

—And I brought this thing over.

—What thing. I said carefully! Can you pick them up carefully and keep them in order?

She got the pages slithering, back to front, upside down, —this thing about your accident, Kevin says will you read it and change anything that you...

—I can't read it. I can't read a damned thing, that woman lost my glasses I can't even read the paper.

—But I put them right up here didn't I? She was reaching behind an antique tea canister on the mantel, —these?

—When did, damn it Lily what did you hide them up there for!

—So nothing would happen to them. You don't need to be so cross, I'm just trying to help aren't I? If you'd, ow! Ow, Oscar!

—What is it now.

—You're running over my foot where are you going, didn't you learn to drive it yet? The last time...

—Into the library, just bring those papers and the, don't push it!

—I wasn't but, but don't drive it so fast, did I tell you? Bobbie bought a Porsche?

—No you didn't. That chair there, move it away from the door, I want to back in there by the bed.

—Bobbie just bought this Porsche.

—You told me.

—You just said I didn't, didn't you? She got busy pounding the pillows out of shape, —he just bought a Porsche. Was I ever in here before Oscar?

—Just help me on the, get my leg up there will you? And those papers, this thing Kevin's got going?

—I told you didn't I? he hasn't got anything going? that he can't do anything till we pay off this sleazeball woman lawyer, I even called up Daddy this one last time to see if he'd help or if maybe Bobbie would but since they all joined this church down there he said he has to ask this Reverend and, is that what you mean?

—No it's not what I mean. Turn on the light, it's right behind you. I mean this complaint you brought over from Kevin about my accident, let me read it over.

—Here. And that he said he probably couldn't help me out either? She squeezed the chair closer to the discomfort he'd strung out on the bed there, —Bobbie I mean.

—Yes, just let me read the, to file this claim declining inclusion under No Fault protection in asserting his full common law rights to seek tort recovery for damages for personal injuries including pain and suffering, and the...

—Because he just bought this Porsche, I even went over to the phone company but they said they're not hiring anybody even on the long lines, you could always get work on the long lines before all this technology screwed it up for everybody. I can't even pay my rent, did I tell you what the bank did?

—plaintiff's loss of earning capacity attributable to the scar.

—Where these checks I wrote bounced so they won't let me write any more because this other person may be cashing them who's going around being me?

—Listen just let me find what he's asking for damages here, where's the, consisting of a facial scar extending...

—Where I can't even pay to go see this doctor for this pain I told you about once right up here?

—facial scar extending below the right eye approx...

—No up here, give me your hand. Feel it? this lump?

—Yes. Now just let me, a facial scar extending below the...

—Not there no! You know what that is, wait... and another button of her blouse came undone, —there. Can you feel it?

—No. Yes. Listen, this facial scar under the right eye about two inches in length, where did he get that.

—Who, this scar? Her own hand came up tracing the line of it, —I think it's cute.

—God. Listen. I mean where did he, where did Kevin get this description.

—I don't know, just some movie he saw how do I know. Wait... a buttonhole burst, the blouse came away, —there. Now you can...

—That's what I'm asking you, how do you know. What movie.

—Just some movie he said he saw, how do I...

—I called you last night, I called you two or three times is that where you were? at the movies?

—I thought you'd be mad Oscar, I just thought...

—Well I am, no. No I just want to know, was it this big Civil War movie that just opened everyplace?

—It was real long, yes.

—No but was it the Civil War was it, what was the name of it.

—It was just a movie Oscar I don't know, who cares what the...

—Well I do, that's what I'm telling you I do! Was it The Blood in the Red White and Blue?

—There was blood in it. That's all I remember, there was blood...

—No now listen, listen...

—See I knew you'd be mad, he just said do you want to go to the movies so we went to this Chinese restaurant after with this crispy duck like these rubber bands and he's talking about your accident and this scar where this man in this movie has this scar that wasn't my fault was it?

—I didn't say your fault. I'm talking about the movie.

—I just told you. He said do you want to go to the movies and...

—And then you went to a Chinese restaurant, fine. Now the movie.

—Like you said, there was all this blood. Right here, can you feel something?

—In the battle scenes, but what about...

—I just closed my eyes. Where you see this soldier get almost cut right in half and, and his, where this soldier waving a sword rides right over him I just closed my eyes.

—Listen, just start at the beginning.

—This first time they meet? where he's out hunting and she rides up on this horse? So she's acting very superior and says what is he doing on their land, only then she gets off the horse because it's real hot and then you know what? Her hand had come burrowing under the quilt he'd pulled up —where he's wearing these kind of overalls?

—I can guess. Listen...

—Where her hand down there is unbuttoning these buttons? The mound under the quilt stirred —and you can practically see what her hand is doing in there. Like, remember in the hospital? where you didn't want to do anything because the nurse might come in? The mound gently receded, gently rose, —Oscar? Who's that picture.

—The, who?

—Up there by those books, in this black bathrobe.

—It's not a bathrobe he's a judge, it's my grandfather when he, what are you doing...

—I just don't like the way he's watching what we're doing here...

and she had, in fact, drawn up her blouse clambering off the end of the bed to reach up and turn the picture's face to the wall —because it's none of his business is it? her blouse falling open again —look. Do they look lopsided?

—Do, what?

—I said don't they look lopsided? like this one's higher than...

—Listen! I've got to clear things up about this movie. We're going to read the play right from the start and you tell me if you saw the same thing in the movie, here. You read the part of the Mother.

—Me?

—Just read it! I'm Thomas, I'm standing silhouetted against the window, left, my back on the room and a letter clutched in my hands behind me and I say, Dead! Now go ahead.

—But I thought we...

—Just read it! Where it says His Mother. Is that the place?

THOMAS

(IN A HOARSE WHISPER)

Dead!

HIS MOTHER

Is that the place? On your cheek? Where you were wounded?

THOMAS

(INSTINCTIVELY RAISING HIS HAND TO HIS CHEEK)

It's healed.

HIS MOTHER

Like a kiss...

THOMAS

(TURNING SLOWLY TO FACE HER)

Is it so bad, then?

HIS MOTHER

No, not bad Thomas no, only... you look surprised. Is it true then, what we heard? That you were a hero?

THOMAS

Where?

HIS MOTHER

On the... battlefield?

THOMAS

I mean where did you hear it.

HIS MOTHER

Ambers heard, up at Quantness. What happened?

THOMAS

(DISMISSING IT IMPATIENTLY)

What happened? A shot, or a flying splinter. How's one to tell at a moment like that...? I didn't know myself when it happened.

Seating himself in the window, THOMAS raises a boot to the sill and smooths letter out against it, intently as though trying to read.

HIS MOTHER

(ANXIOUSLY)

Didn't know yourself, Thomas?

(SHE PAUSES, AS HE PAYS HER NO ATTENTION)

You don't look well, Thomas. I couldn't see when you came in, coming before it was light, but I knew your step. You look like you've scarcely eaten or slept the whole year you've been gone, since it started... You're thinner and tired, too, now I can see. You might have lost an eye.

THOMAS

Tired...?

HIS MOTHER

Or been blinded for life.

THOMAS

(EXCITEDLY PLANTING BOOTS, BRANDISHING LETTER)

I told you I hadn't slept! How could I, with this?

HIS MOTHER

Your uncle never gave things away before. Not a smile, not a penny, and his own brother lying dead and buried in a foreign land...

THOMAS

(WITH ELATION)

And he never died before either! Dying intestate, Lord! I admire that, I must confess it. I don't know why, but I admire that 'intestate.' For him, of all men, to die without leaving a will! And after the way he talked to me then, when we came back from France like beggars looking for a new exile, and you sent me up there to see him? 'Coming in here in your fine French clothes demanding your rights,' he said to me, when I asked him for the money that he owed to my father, when I'd spent the morning trimming frayed cuffs and pinning the hem on my father's coat to try to look fit to call. Five hundred dollars! What was that to him, 'the prominent coal magnate' this letter calls him, and here...

(LOOKING AT LETTER AGAIN, WAVING IT)

'The eminent Pennsylvania political leader,' shabbier than I was with his tarnished buttons, and a coat gone green at the seams. And not for want, mind. He was proud of it, of saving the cost of a coat. Do you know where he'd got it? Off his coachman's back, when even the coachman was ashamed to be seen in it. And even at that, would he part with the five hundred dollars? Three hundred, take it or leave it, he said, and a deed to oblivion, the deed to this place he'd been stuck with on a bad debt.

(CHUCKLING WITH RELISH)

What a fine pair of tramps we must have made, and this fortune between us, when he sent me off to see his man Bagby. This same one, his General Manager, the same Bagby that's written this letter. 'Bagby takes care of such things,' he said when he sent me off. Seven years ago, this same one, this same Bagby.

(PACING THE ROOM, MUTTERING WITH RELISH)

Sitting up stark naked in the middle of his bed gaping at a comic print, a bag of jawbreakers beside him and a hard hat on his head. 'Come in,' he says to me, into his dingy furnished room. 'There's your money on the chiffonier, I've no doubt you'll want to count it.' 'Here? The devil it is,' I told him, without even touching the envelope. 'My uncle said gold, and where's the deed that he talked about?' 'Suit yourself,' says Bagby, cracking a jawbreaker in his teeth, 'in the top drawer,' and back he went to his comic. There it was, three hundred dollars counted out in the drawer, and the deed to this place with it. And now...!

(TURNING HALF TOWARD HER)

'Bagby takes care of such things...' By God, and he does!

HIS MOTHER

Thomas!... Language fit for the battlefield, you're not in camp now among strangers and animals.

THOMAS

(APPROACHING HER)

A battlefield, that's what it's been all our lives! And now? Isn't it a time for... 'language,' as you say? To owe no one, after... all this. The years of all this, and of talking poormouth at Quantness...

HIS MOTHER

You've earned your keep up at Quantness.

THOMAS

And to never be forced into any man's debt again!

HIS MOTHER

Do they know?

THOMAS

Know? Up at Quantness? Of course. And the first thing the Major said, when I told him about it last night, was 'Get up there and claim it.' Do you think he wants the mines, the coal, all of it seized by the Federal government? Confiscated, if I don't claim it? Do you now how much we need coal?

HIS MOTHER

(LOOKING PAST HIM TO WINDOW)

I do know, Thomas.

THOMAS

When I rode in there last night, on furlough, and found this news waiting, why I... I was a hero, home from the war, as though I'd lived there all my life and not just these three years since I married.

HIS MOTHER

(RUEFULLY)

They've needed you more than you did them, Thomas. The work you put in on Quantness cotton while this place ran to ruin...

Standing over her, THOMAS gestures imploringly, then turns and crosses to the window, where he stands staring out.

THOMAS

By heaven, what a day!

HIS MOTHER

(AFTER PAUSE)

They've stopped the pension, Thomas.

THOMAS

(TURNING)

Pension?

(STARES AT HER FOR A MOMENT, THEN BREAKS INTO LAUGHTER)

My father's pension? That... how-much-was-it-a-month?

(ADVANCING TOWARD HER AGAIN)

Listen, don't you understand? This, what we have now, it's worth all the pensions they ever paid?

(HALF TURNING FROM HER DOWNSTAGE CENTER)

It was an insult, that pension, coming year after year to remind us what injustice was, in case we'd forgotten. In case I'd been able to forget all the plans that he had for me, for a great career in public life, bringing me up to read Rousseau, believing the 'natural goodness of man...'

Turning to her impulsively, THOMAS goes down to one knee beside her chair, and she throws up a hand to save the lamp from falling.

Listen, we can wait our lives out, Mother! Waiting for something like this... Waiting for something to happen, isn't that what people do? What keeps them alive, this waiting? What... even my father, wasn't he? Waiting for something to happen? to come out of nowhere and change things... and then?

As his enthusiasm fails to kindle her, THOMAS regains his feet slowly, turning away pensively toward the window.

Why, they die that way, waiting.

Letting himself down slowly half seated against the windowsill, THOMAS opens his coat and takes out a tobacco case and a cigar.

(HALF TO HIMSELF)

Free to be something, all the things... things we've talked about, to make choices. Yes, free to make choices, instead of being driven to them, will you get ready Mother, please? They're waiting for us, up at Quantness.

As though regretting this show of impatience, THOMAS seats himself back against the sill, and picks up a strip of rag he finds there.

They're expecting you...

HIS MOTHER

Is that the same uniform you went off in? Yes, it looks like it, now I can see.

Restraining himself, THOMAS crosses a boot over his knee and begins to rub it clean with the rag.

I remember when it was new, before you went off, you'd lay a handkerchief over your knee when you crossed your leg up that way, with your soiled boot...

THOMAS

(WITH EFFORT, NOT LOOKING UP, CONTINUES RUBBING)

They've done things, at Quantness, getting ready. A room...

HIS MOTHER

That cloth, Thomas.

THOMAS

(HOLDING UP THE RAG, PERPLEXED)

What?

HIS MOTHER

Please don't use it, for that. We've kept it for lampwick.

THOMAS

(STANDING, BARELY ABLE TO CONTROL EXASPERATION)

Listen, will you get ready? They expect you. They're waiting. They expect you up there to stay while I'm gone.

HIS MOTHER

(QUIETLY)

I've kept well here this whole year you've been away Thomas, and the chance that you mightn't come back at all. I can't leave here now.

THOMAS

(BURSTING OUT AT LAST)

Can't leave? Here? Look at it! The gate off, the fence fallen, corn dead on the stalk and tobacco rotted on the ground. The door latch was broken when I came in. I'm not blaming, I know it's been hard, I'm not blaming anyone. You or old Ambers, or John Israel, no, I know it's been hard. But now? You can leave it! Leave all this behind, things broken and worn out and saving precious rags, the cold and... all this.

THOMAS flings the rag to the floor between them and stands confronting her.

HIS MOTHER

(WITH A SORROWING CALM)

I was proud of you here, Thomas.

THOMAS

Proud!

HIS MOTHER

(AS THOUGH TRYING TO REACH HIM)

Of your work, your courage, that you'd found a place, your... you loved this land, Thomas. The life, things growing, even your new tobacco, your new bright leaf, you called it? It's still down in the barn where you hanged it to cure. I gave orders no one to disturb it. I've thought I've heard you down there at night sometimes, Thomas. The way you used to go down and grind corn? Do you remember?

THOMAS

(BROODINGLY)

Remember...!

HIS MOTHER

And the way you went off, when the war came...

THOMAS

(WITH BROODING INTENSITY)

Yes, and who do you think I've been fighting up there, but my uncle and all his damned Bagbys? Fighting, for this? For the right to lie down at night counting the minutes, the years, the days that can't be told one from another? And a red stripe in that flag of theirs for every year of... humiliation, straining side by side in the mud with old Ambers and John Israel, two black wretches who can't call their souls their own, planting and putting in fence. Yes, four years of that, and then three talking poormouth at Quantness, and you ask me to hesitate? With these seven stripes across my back, and now this on my face to remember?

(PAUSING, AS SHE JUST LOOKS AT HIM, HE ADDS WITH BITTER AFTERTHOUGHT, LOOKING ROUND)

'One of the finest private mansions in the Carolinas,' and look at it. Look at it now. That's what my uncle called it that day, just to get rid of us. Lord! the way he described it. Had he ever come down here and seen it? Why, he talked as though he'd seen Quantness.

HIS MOTHER

(COLDLY DIRECT)

The way you did.

THOMAS

(DRAWN UP SHORT)

I...

HIS MOTHER

The way you saw it that first day we came, and you drove that old rig right up to Quantness as though you'd lived there all your life. Standing up as you drove and pointing things out with the whip, the house and the tall white columns, and seeing it all for the first time yourself. I might have thought that you'd been born there, if I wasn't your mother and knew.

THOMAS

(ANNOYED BUT TAKEN ABACK)

And why not? It was just a mistake, following what directions we had and after he'd described this place as 'one of the finest private mansions...'

HIS MOTHER

(CUTS IN SHARPLY)

And this now? This great fortune? No Thomas, your father had a friend, what was his name from back in the old whaling days, they called him the Sage of Sag Harbor and what he used to say. There is never a treasure without a following shade of care...

(HOLDING UP A HAND TO FORESTALL HIM)

And you sound like you did seven years ago, like you did when we drove into Quantness, standing up in that old rig and crowing. Pointing out things that you thought were yours, horses, stables, I won't forget, even that sundial by the drive, there wasn't a tree or a blade of grass, a dog or a darkie that wasn't yours the moment you saw it, not a fear or a doubt in your mind, and now...

THOMAS

(CUTTING HER OFF FIRMLY)

Quantness is my home now.

HIS MOTHER

(SNIFFING, FUMBLING AS THOUGH SEEKING A HANDKERCHIEF)

It has changed you, Thomas. A year from home and people.

THOMAS

And people! By heaven, people? What do you think war is?

HIS MOTHER

No, mindful of others, I mean to say. I cannot see you, a year ago, using such language in the parlour, lighting up your tobacco without excusing yourself, putting your feet up on the woodwork... No, not only this, only this as a part of you now. Coming so sudden at dawn, you look so big to me, so different, so like and so different. Some dream of yourself, coming in so rumpled, your beard not trimmed and the way your face is drawn on that one side... you look outraged. I've dreamt of you Thomas but not my dream. Someone's dream, someone else, yours perhaps, coming in with this letter from your Mister Bagby and your talk of going north now, today, when you've scarcely laid eyes on your family at Quantness, when you haven't been home yet once round the clock...

THOMAS

(BLURTS OUT)

Listen...! If all this is to keep me here, Mother? Because I can't stay, isn't that clear? If you'd... tell me what it is that you want. When war came you didn't want that, you didn't want me to go, and now you don't want me to leave it? When I planted tobacco you didn't want that, we couldn't eat it or wear it, and now you were proud of it. You said I was vain when I put on this uniform, now when I cross a boot over my knee... what is it you want? And when this fortune was out of our reach, why you... and now, you won't have it? What is it!

HIS MOTHER

(WITH REPROACHFUL CALM)

What I have always sought, for myself and those in my keeping Thomas. To know the Lord's will, and submit. To lay up treasures in heaven, Thomas, treasures even for you, while you seek here below...

THOMAS

(HOARSELY CHALLENGING)

Only justice!

THOMAS draws both hands down his face and stands staring.

All of this came when my spirit was almost broken... or when I suddenly knew that it could be, and that's the same thing...

He turns away slowly as he speaks, nearing the door and there staring at an old shotgun racked on the wall.

When I've laid out there with their screams in my throat, the screams of men being torn to pieces in my own throat because I had to be next, but I couldn't be...

He takes down the shotgun as he speaks and with the suppressed horror of somnambulism goes through the scene which he describes.

All of it couldn't be happening. There? to me? It couldn't be, no... But what happened once, what happened there, what happened before still happens at night. It happens the way it happened then, when I went up hunting on their property, over the rise where the chapel looks across the fields and over the creek, staring through rail fence and that creek to Quantness house itself. It was when we first came here, we knew no one, and I'd never hunted a thing in my life. With this gun... there's a path that runs up the rise and broadens into a wagonroad straight through a clearing a half mile long and brown with cornstalks standing uncut where the woods farther on fall back. And there, coming over the foot of that rise, three cock pheasants burst up off the ground with the terrible slowness of things in a dream. They wheeled, I fired, and they were gone... but there on the ground with a broken wing one of them struggled across the stones, and I fired again, and it kept on, struggling until it reached a wall where it fought its head in amongst the stones. I wanted to leave it, and let it live, to remember as something I hadn't seen. Worse happens in nature that we never see. Worse happened. I killed it cutting its throat, too kind to do it the violence of wringing its neck or snapping its head against a stone. But around its throat, the brilliant feathers, I couldn't get the knife through... It wouldn't cut without... God! The absurdity of it. It wouldn't stop fighting, and not fighting me... It was fighting to fly from what was happening.

(MORE DISTANTLY, STANDING AS THOUGH DAZED)

She was a child, Giulielma then, come up behind me demanding to know what I was doing on their property. And it was as though I'd strayed into a kingdom, a fool from nowhere with blood on my hands and that bird dropping blood on the ground between us. I gave her father the bird when I met him, as though I'd been out and shot it for sport. 'I never knew anyone to hunt without dogs,' was what she said when she took me in...

(SHUDDERING, HE CLUTCHES A HAND OVER HIS EYES)

And I never climb that rise today without seeing them wheel up before me, without a tearing ache in my stomach. I was hunting because we were hungry.

HIS MOTHER half rises from her chair, her arms tendering an embrace which she drops slowly as he stares without seeing her.

HIS MOTHER

(SINKING BACK IN CHAIR, QUAVERINGLY DIRECT)

And you married her... for Quantness and, you're going there? now?

THOMAS

(SPEAKING WITH EFFORT, NOT LOOKING AT HER)

Out to wake John Israel and Ambers, to pack up your things.

HIS MOTHER

(COLDLY)

John Israel's gone.

THOMAS

(STOPPING SHARPLY IN THE DOOR)

Gone?

HIS MOTHER

John Israel's gone, Thomas. He ran off.

THOMAS

(AMAZED, STEPPING BACK INTO THE ROOM)

But... why didn't you tell me? Or write?

HIS MOTHER

(WITH RUEFUL SATISFACTION)

What could you have done, so far away?

THOMAS

When? When did he go?

HIS MOTHER

In dead of winter. We worried sick, if he was running away up north, where it's colder.

THOMAS

But... him run off, and you worried for him?

(HE COMES SLOWLY TO REST AGAINST THE DOORFRAME)

And after I left him safe behind, instead of taking him up to the war...

HIS MOTHER

(DISTANTLY RESENTFUL)

The way you used to take him to work up at Quantness, and you and her brother used to devil him up there.

THOMAS

(WITH EFFORT AT WEARY INDULGENT LAUGH, AS THOUGH THIS IS AN OLD ARGUMENT)

Mother... devil him? Why, John Israel, he was our 'noble savage,' and Will wasn't more than twelve years old. Did you know that the Major wanted to buy him? that he offered me six hundred dollars for John Israel once? And that it was Will that talked me out of it? giving me back all my own ideas, that I'd brought back here from France?

HIS MOTHER

You took him to build that fine staircase at Quantness when our barn roofs needed mending right here.

THOMAS

(IMITATIVE)

'A niggra like that that can turn wood and read,' the Major said...

HIS MOTHER

(IN A SUDDEN OUTBURST OF BITTER AND DESPERATE ACCUSATION)

I taught him to read in the Bible, Thomas! John Israel was given into my keeping, Providence gave him into my keeping and I taught him where to seek the Lord's grace, to find his duty in the Lord's will... to submit to the Lord's everlasting mercy... to fight the temptation to... harden his heart...!

THOMAS

(BURSTS OUT AS DESPERATELY)

The Lord's grace! And... is it my heart that's hardened? Mine? You ask me if I remember those nights, when I used to go down to the barn and grind corn? Remember? I went out and worked in the darkness because I was trapped, because I was baffled, because I was through but I couldn't end it, I... I died too, but I couldn't lie down. I still had strength that was left from the day, I still had anger that I hadn't spent pulling stumps, or putting in fence, and there was nothing to do with my anger and strength but to stand in the dark and grind corn. To stand, like a blind horse chained to a millstone, and accept it, as though it were mine... but knowing it... couldn't be! You... you talk of laying up treasures in heaven? I... I want order here. And the way, Mother the way you cling to this place, to that pension, and even the way John Israel ran off, it's as though you... cherish injustice. When I left John Israel to keep things up here, I gave up a commission, if I'd taken a servant I would have accepted an officer's commission, but I... left him here safe, for you... for you, that pension? When my father died in an embassy post where they gave him nothing, no promotions, they let him rot there until it was over and every idea he had was dead, and we had to come back and beg from his brother what was his? what was ours? And then to be put off with this?

(HE MOTIONS ROUND HIM INDICATING THE HOUSE)

As HIS MOTHER sits, deadly motionless, THOMAS stands away in a monumental effort to gain control, and snaps his watch open in his trembling hand.

Without John Is... with only Ambers to help you, I'll send a wagon down with a boy. I'll send Will's boy Henry down with a rig, from Quantness.

HIS MOTHER

(IN A VAGUE, DISTANT TONE AS THOUGH LOOKING FAR AWAY)

He will come back, when it is time. He will come back here, if he is able... hunted down to earth somewhere he has never been... Alone, deviled, and what will he know, what will he know then but what he learned at night to read here, when no angels' hands are offered... Yes, 'Thou shalt not tempt the Lord thy God' when no angels' hands are given, to bear him up.

THOMAS

(STUPIDLY, IMPULSIVE)

Mother... will you... come north with me, then?

HIS MOTHER

(TURNING, SLOWLY, VACANTLY, STARING AT HIM AFTER A PAUSE AS OVER A GREAT DISTANCE)

Is that a rent in your trousers, Thomas?

(PAUSE AS HE STARES AT HER HELPLESSLY)

There, by the pocket...?

THOMAS

(HOPELESSLY)

There's a... house there.

HIS MOTHER

You can't go north dressed like that, Thomas.

THOMAS

(BACKING SLOWLY AWAY FROM HER TOWARD THE DOOR)

Mother, will you...

HIS MOTHER

Will you... want to take that coat, Thomas? I've mended it up.

THOMAS

(NEARING THE DOOR, WATCHING HER AS THOUGH ESCAPING HER)

I... won't need mended coats, mended anything... Clothes pulled from the casket, no... I'll have coats, everything... as it should be...

The gauze curtain of the Prologue lowers as THOMAS exits backing through the door. HIS MOTHER remains rigidly still until a horse is heard outside, at which she rises and hurries to the window, staring out until silence falls, and then, turning and recrossing the room slowly, is stooping in a shaft of sunlight to pick up the rag as the scene fades out behind lights up on the gauze curtain scene. There is the morning sound of birds, and the trot of a horse rising and falling away.

—Did you write this all by yourself Oscar?
—Of course I wrote it.
—It's spooky.
—It's not spooky! It's a serious play that I, what are you doing.
—What does it look like? buttoning her blouse as she stood up out of reach, —I have to go Oscar, I only came over to bring you that thing about your accident and I haven't even got money for gas.
—There's some on the kitchen table but listen, that was only the beginning, the prologue we haven't even read act one and...
—You better read it to somebody else Oscar, she said from the door there turning for the kitchen, —I don't even know what it's supposed to be about.

ACT ONE

Scene One

From stage right to left, the parlour, front hall, veranda and lawn path of Quantness. White columns rise on the veranda, running from downstage left to upstage left center; and at the extreme right of the stage another column, obviously one of four, supports the corner of an unfinished pediment, all in the Greek Revival style. The parlour carries through the stark elegance of the house, with plain chairs flanking a sideboard upstage right center, a fireplace with long straight mantel at right, and the corner of a spinet showing at downstage right. From the parlour a door opens upon the hall at stage center, plain but lofty, with an exit at rear hidden by the gentle sweep of a curved staircase.

THE MAJOR, a man in his sixties, is turned out to a fault in military uniform which lends authority to his patronizing manner, his apparent satisfaction with all that is familiar and mistrust for what is not, his forthright lack of imagination or sympathy for all he does not understand, and his distress at anything that threatens to disturb established order.

MR KANE is shorter, somewhat stout and balding, his loose beard, prominent nose and carelessness of dress giving him an unwieldy appearance which he belies with his attitude of shrewd appraisal for everything he meets and a presence of lively, attentive dignity.

Because the play, wasn't that what this was all about? Waving Mister Basie to the chair where his father'd used to sit reading the paper there in the library, change spilling from his pocket down the cleft of the cushion, just take the opening scene here, after the prologue between Thomas and his mother, where the Major's showing his guest around Quantness (with a sweeping gesture to offstage left)

THE MAJOR

All that out there was cotton, growing up now in rabbit tobacco and Queen Anne's laces. That cotton that's down at Wilmington now piled on the dock there waiting to be shipped, that's all the Quantness cotton that's left after what we lost at Beaufort.

KANE

(POLITELY)

They tell me Quantness is the biggest plantation in the county.

THE MAJOR

In some ways, Mister Kane, you might say it is the county. You stand right here, sir, any way you look, Quantness runs as far as you can see.

(TURNING TO LEAD WAY INTO HOUSE)

It was a good piece of the next county, until my own father, he seceded it. He took and joined it onto this county here, the same way we seceded the county from the state three months before they got the state seceded from the Union. I figured he would have done that, my father. He wasn't one to wait on other people making up their mind.

As THE MAJOR and KANE enter hall crossing toward the parlour, right, WILLIAM, hearing their approach, retires to a corner upstage center with a hitch to his trousers and smoothing back his hair. He walks with a marked limp.

(IN THE HALL)

You're a history teacher you said, Mister Kane? Up in Virginia?

KANE

(ANXIOUSLY SELF-DEPRECATING)

No, no, I was a fellow. A resident fellow in philosophy.

THE MAJOR

(LEADING WAY TO THE PARLOUR)

Yes, there's some books in here that would probably interest you, the set of books my father left that he was building the house here from. The Antiquities of Athens is what they're called. I took up in these books myself right after we buried him, everything that he had marked, every line right down to the inch. The oak beams were hewed and morticed right here where they're laid, and the floor is the heart grain of pine.

(ENTERING THE PARLOUR)

It's still not all finished, all my father had planned.

Noticing WILLIAM immediately, KANE has stopped, and THE MAJOR, as though forced to do so by KANE's attention, turns to introduce WILLIAM with the almost apologetic manner he reserves for his son, as one whose presence seems to dismay him as does anything he does not understand, and for this reason almost fears.

Ah... Mister Kane, my son William...

(AS THOUGH FORCED TO EXPLAIN WILLIAM'S PRESENCE, AS KANE AND WILLIAM SHAKE HANDS)

William's kept things up here the whole time I've been gone. This whole year since the war started.

(THIS ACCOMPLISHED, HE TAKES UP HIS EARLIER TONE; TO KANE)

You might notice the tilt to this mantel shelf? It killed him, this mantel shelf did. It killed my own father. It's solid Maryland marble, the whole thing. There wasn't a floorboard laid when it arrived here, just the oak beams to climb on, but he couldn't wait. My father wanted that mantel shelf up, and he wanted it just so. They had it swung into place, and he stepped in there to set it right. He was like that, stepping right in like that to move it just that much of an inch, the hair breadth between it being perfect and not, and it crushed him. It slipped and crushed him right down on the beam.

(PATTING THE MANTEL WITH APPARENT SATISFACTION)

It's still not finished, all my father had planned here. Wrought iron running in a balcony up there inside the el of the house, that never got here from Pennsylvania. And the mirror for over the mantel shelf here...

—Excuse me there Mister Crease, maybe...

—And the mirror for over the mantel shelf here, it got broke on the way. Just to give you the feel of it Mister Basie, would you like some tea? Tea? No, no, just some coffee if it wasn't that much trouble, already had one hell of a morning just getting out here and finding the place, got lost two or three times looking for the gates with that **STRANGERS REQUESTED NOT TO ENTER** sign and finally must have come in the back door, the service entrance there with that woman barring the way in the kitchen, planting those splendid thighs that could have swallowed him whole and the toot of this horn, it was tooting right now, threatening the crippling rush of a four year old on a three wheeler down the long hall where no one's expecting you, make you feel like a thief in broad daylight, nobody expecting Harold Basie wasn't that about it? —No well you see Mister Basie they didn't ah, oh Ilse? with stabbing motions toward his guest, —you bring coffee? She doesn't speak much English.

—That great big not, requested NOT to enter, what you'd call xenophobia isn't that about it? Not too friendly, walk down Worth Avenue after sunset they pull right up beside you, who you work for boy? Not too friendly.

—No well that's just ah, they don't mean anything by it it's just ah, when I talked to Mister Lepidus on the phone, Sam Lepidus, I didn't mean...

—Don't mean anything by it yes, that's good to know Mister Crease. They don't ordinarily send people out like this but they said you came recommended by your cousin Harry Lutz?

—Not my cousin no, he's my brother in law. You don't, do you know him?

—Know of him. He's on this big Pop and Glow case.

—Pop and what?

—You get these Episcopals tangling assholes with Pepsico you're really in the big time.

—Yes I, I see. The big time I mean. That's why Harry thought your firm could handle this case of mine, a ninety million dollar movie it could be a landmark.

—Could be if you won it.

—Well of course that's why you're here isn't it, why I want to give you some feel for the thing before we get down to cases on this Kiester person. He should be drawn and quartered.

—Probably will be, you see him in the paper this morning?

—It's on that pile right there beside you no, no I don't read that kind of rubbish, these movies they're making are all of them rubbish, you saw that review? the most widely discussed mass rape scene in screen history? That Uburuwhatever it was, people throwing up in the aisles?

—You didn't see it?

—The notorious sledgehammer scene the papers talked about, whatever that may be. I certainly did not see it.

From a flurry of the newspaper, —what this is about, here. Charges of malfeasance and deceptive practices surfaced today involving the producer director of the recent motion picture Uruburu, an extravaganza set in Africa promoted as 'not for the squeamish' which made his overnight reputation as 'king of special effects' and led to the multimillion dollar backing for his current gory Civil War blockbuster, The Blood in the Red White and Blue. The producer, Constantine Kiester, is charged with using actual film footage of the gruesome sequences which made Uruburu an overnight sensation and broke box office records throughout the country. The charges involving Mister Kiester emerged from an analysis by a second year film student at UCLA, Barry Gench, isolating one widely discussed sequence purporting to show in extreme slow motion close up a man's face being smashed by a sledgehammer. Mister Gench contends that the notorious sledgehammer sequence, cited by reviewers and critics as a grisly triumph of the latest in special effects technology, actually took place and was filmed with an ultra high speed sixteen millimeter camera at up to two hundred forty frames per second, requiring from four to ten times the lighting employed in routine production shots. The sequence was later slowed and blown up to the thirty five millimeter format as evidenced, according to Mister Gench, by the rough edges and difference in grain structure of the continuous shot in which no cutaways occur and where microscopic examination reveals the contrast between the more intense colour values characteristic of sixteen millimeter Ektachrome and the Kodachrome reversal negative reduced to the common stock. If substantiated, the charges could provoke severe restrictions on a film industry which is already, in the words of one critic, saturated with blood and guts, and will at the least open the way for a variety of lawsuits. Efforts to reach Mister Kiester were unavailing, and his office disclaimed any knowledge of his whereabouts. How about that.

—Well? How about it.

—He's got a lot on his plate, Mister Kiester has.

—Just what I've been saying about him isn't it? Just another rotten, a scandal like this maybe it will put him out of business.

—Afraid you've got it exactly backwards Mister Crease, bigger the mess you make out there the more they want you. Forge a few checks, get caught with your hand in the till, the more you steal the more you're in demand, figure you've got just the kind of smarts they need out there. It's all just money.

—It's not all just money! Stealing money is...

—You want to sue them for damages, that's money isn't it?

—Because that's the only damn language they understand! Isn't that what you just said? But stealing a whole world somebody's created and turning it into a hogpen just because there's money in hogs? Steal poetry what do you sue them for, poetry? and the court sentences Kiester to two hundred hours of community service? Two hundred hours teaching Yeats to the fourth grade? Expect me to pay your legal bill with Maid Quiet?

—Match her up with Mister Clean.

—With what?

—Where has Maid Quiet gone to, Nodding her russet hood?

—The winds that awakened the stars Are blowing through my blood. Well! Well, we share something then don't we Mister Basie, no small thing either.

—That's good to know. Now getting back to the...

—To where we left off yes, I can see now you'll be sensitive to these nuances I tried to get in here, the Major's still talking when Thomas walks in.

THE MAJOR

(OVERBEARING, GESTURING TOWARD DOWNSTAGE RIGHT)

That and the porch there on the east front. It never was finished, just left like it is.

(ABRUPTLY VAGUE AND RESIGNED)

I never could find it there in the book. I never could figure what my father had planned there...

THE MAJOR stands abandoned with the remains of his empty gesture as THOMAS enters the parlour, directly embracing WILLIAM familiarly round shoulders. WILLIAM behaves throughout with a hurt but heightened almost self-conscious masculinity in his presence.

WILLIAM

(WITHDRAWING FROM THE EMBRACE, HIDING HIS SHOCK AT THOMAS' SCAR)

One of those Yankee women kissed you there, Thomas?

THE MAJOR

(APPROPRIATING THOMAS)

Mister Kane, my son in law...? Mister Kane is just down here from Richmond, Thomas. He thinks he may be able to help us with that cotton we have tied up down at Wilmington. To get it all shipped over to France before it's lost like we lost that at Beaufort.

KANE

(TO THOMAS)

I understand you're acquainted in Paris? That your father ranked in the embassy there.

THE MAJOR

(HASTILY, TO THOMAS)

Yes, Thomas, I... I told Mister Kane, about your father's... ah, ambassadorial work over there, and your contacts that might help in reaching the Emperor.

THOMAS

(STARTLED)

The Emperor?

THE MAJOR

(HURRYING ON)

Mister Kane is going over himself, to France. There's a shipyard there going to build a ram that will sink the Union blockade to the bottom of the Atlantic Ocean. The importance... you can see the importance, if we want them to see us as anything better than what they do now, a belligerent. The Emperor there can't seem to make up his mind, he wants cotton, he wants Mexico...

THOMAS

We left there seven years ago, when my father died in the year 'fifty four.

KANE

Still, you might have known some fine Bonapartists? Fleury, perhaps? Persigny...?

THOMAS

(AGITATED, LAUGHS UNCOMFORTABLY)

Fleury's wife...

KANE

(TO THE MAJOR)

You didn't tell me you had a diplomat here, and one in the very best French tradition? One who might know the boudoirs of Paris even better than the court itself?

THOMAS

I? I was brought up there in the Second Republic. Even when the Empire came back, my father had me reading Rousseau. 'The supreme guidance of the will of the people,' and the reign of universal reason.

KANE

All we heard over here from France in the 'forties was the voice of the people crying 'Get rich quick!'

THOMAS

(TURNING TO WILLIAM, AS THOUGH TO INCLUDE HIM)

Do you remember, Will? How we used to talk? 'Its power has no limits,' Its... its punishments are simply a means of 'compelling men to be free...'?

(PAUSING, AT A LOSS AT WILLIAM'S SILENCE, TURNS BACK TO KANE)

Yes, I... I came back here to America with my mind stuffed with ambitions and the Social Contract in my pocket, looking for Rousseau's noble savage and a great career in public life...

KANE

And you were disappointed?

THOMAS

Till now!

WILLIAM

(IMPULSIVELY, TO THOMAS)

It's true, then? You're going up north today, Thomas?

THOMAS

(TAKEN ABACK)

Didn't they tell you...?

THE MAJOR

(OVERBEARING, TO KANE)

Thomas got word here last night of the death of an uncle, a prominent coal magnate in Pennsylvania. The Federal government's ready to confiscate everything, what's rightfully his, if he's not there to claim it. You know how much we need coal.

WILLIAM

(IN A COMPULSIVE UNDERTONE)

If I had a chance to be up there myself...

THOMAS

(CONFUSED)

Up... north?

WILLIAM

At the war! Oh, I'm not saying a thing about you Thomas, it isn't you haven't done four men's part...

(HIS OUTBURST BECOMES A MOCKING RECRIMINATION)

To hear them tell it, you won that battle up at Ball's Bluff all by yourself, didn't he now Papa? And coming back here with a scar to show? No, just myself, if I could be up there, how I'd let anything to keep me away, missing it like I've missed it now a whole year.

THOMAS

(AFTER LOOKING FROM ONE TO THE OTHER DURING EMBARRASSED PAUSE, STUNG BY WILLIAM'S RECRIMINATION, TURNS TO HIM)

Well, you should! You should see it! Isn't that so, Major? Yes, the spectacle, isn't that so, Mister Kane? The spectacle of it? Of men before battle...? And now? Now that it's almost over, and probably never the chance again...

WILLIAM

(MORE SHARPLY)

Over? For us? The coast blockaded, our ports all closed, a hundred thousand Union troops right outside Richmond and Jackson off in the Shenandoah...?

THE MAJOR

(INTERPOSING OVERBEARINGLY, TO KANE)

Yes, you might know something of that battle, sir? The battle we fought them up at Ball's Bluff? Thomas distinguished himself up there, in a Company under my command. He's made us proud to have him in the family here.

(WITH AN AWKWARD ATTEMPT TO BE SPORTIVE)

He's from a fine family himself, of course, but it's not a Southern family, strictly speaking. This uncle that's dead up in Pennsylvania was an eminent figure in politics there, and I've told you about his father's post, that he held till the day he died.

(TO THOMAS, ARRESTING HIS DEPARTURE)

Mister Kane tells me that he was formerly an instructor in history up in Virginia, where General Jackson taught.

(WAITS FOR KANE'S RESPONSE)

I meant to point out, sir, that you had been a friend of General Jackson?

KANE

I knew him.

THE MAJOR

A totally remarkable man!

(PAUSES)

Yes... did you not find him so even then, sir! At the Virginia Military Academy?

KANE

I believe he has found his vocation.

THE MAJOR

(WARMLY)

He has indeed, sir! The God-fearing certainty with which he goes about his business? Is there anything you cannot help admiring about such a man?

KANE

(THOUGHTFULLY)

His nose. Yes, I cannot help admiring that, now you mention it.

THE MAJOR

(STARTLED)

Sir?

KANE

(TURNING TO THOMAS)

Yes, as I do yours, sir.

THE MAJOR

His... nose? We are speaking of General Jackson, sir!

KANE

Yes, yes, I can envy him, the God-driven man. I can envy the man who knows, who knows without question, and acts. But... admire him? Heroes like that can cost us all dear before we're done. What happens when they're needed?

(GESTURING, HE KNOCKS A GLASS TO FLOOR AND STARES AT BREAKAGE)

There, I'm sorry, but like that. I'm sorry, but there. Like that, it just happens, thrown from a horse, shot down when the light's bad or something else that we can call... accident.

THE MAJOR

(BETWEEN BAFFLEMENT AND INDIGNATION)

But... indeed sir!

—Mister Crease? Let me ask you, where are we going here.

—Going? I told you, give you some feel for the play before we...

—Talking about the movie. You haven't seen the movie, I haven't seen the movie, you know anybody who's seen the movie?

—If you'll just be patient yes, yes I do, and there are similarities that simply can't be explained by coincid...

—He spell them out?

—It's a she no, no except for these sexually explicit scenes she was quite clear about those but they're not in the play anyway, matter of fact she wasn't sure whether she'd actually seen certain scenes or if the words just made her think she had but the man she was with, she...

—Maybe doing a little groping there in the dark?

—That's occurred to me Mister Basie! It's a, she's not too reliable about movies, they showed that old Laughton picture once and she got quite confused, thought it would be about football, the halfback of Notre Dame but this scar now, she was clear enough about this scar on his cheek it's even mentioned in that review, coming home from the battle at Ball's Bluff and his uncle's just died up north with these coal mines? It's right there in this scene isn't it? You call that a coincidence like mine? this one of mine?

—This what, I don't...

—My scar, this scar right here on my cheek can't you see it?

—Now you point it out, it's...

—Of course it is, that's why I'm suing and it's not just the money, loss of earning capacity, career in jeopardy no, it's the principle of the thing. It's the pain and suffering, mental anguish, simple justice after all, I'm just claiming my constitutional rights aren't I?

—Might put it that way, but you get up and try to prove it in court they...

—No question of that once I can assert my full common law rights, you're a lawyer aren't you? Break out from under all these petty restrictions, provisions, limitations under the, just hand me that folder on that pile of books there it's all spelled out, you think they won't take it seriously? Just look at me, tell them the hospital wanted me to sign something in case of death donating any left over usable parts for some perfect stranger? Like that fellow who left his skull to the Royal Shakespeare Company for the graveyard scene in Hamlet you could specify which organs or parts and what use they could, here, here it is yes, whether the Federal and State Constitutions' equal protection and due process clauses are violated by here, quoting Montgomery v. Daniels where the court held that New York's Article 18 was not unconstitutional nevertheless supporting the 'concept that the individual is the basic and ultimate unit in society must be supported by recognition of the value of one's physical, mental and emotional integrity, including freedom from pain and suffering and the ability to live an uncrippled life.' You see?

—Can't say I see exactly where the...

—Well it's right here, it's perfectly clear, quoting Falcone v. Branker. 'A disfigurement is that which impairs or injures the beauty, symmetry, or appearance of a person or thing; that which renders unsightly, misshapen, or imperfect, or deforms in some manner.' You see what we're getting at.

—Can't say I do, exactly. You write this up yourself did you?

—Certainly not no, my attorney drew it up, he...

—You say you already got an attorney?

—Well of course, this is the complaint he drew up, he goes on from Montgomery. 'The automobile, a modern bane and boon, daily threatens that integrity for millions of people. And Article 18, while not in any way alleviating that threat, strips a class which includes most automobile accident victims of the right to be fairly compensated for injuries and pain and suffering,' you see? Just because it provides these full first party benefits accruing to the injured person regardless of fault or negligence on the part of the covered person, that's where they're claiming immunity from lawsuits like this one without, where is it, without here, without permitting nonduplicative recovery by suit against tortfeasors at common law. That's what the whole, where are you going. It's down the hall on the right.

—Thought I'd see how she's coming with that coffee.

—Just be patient... A hand broke free to squeeze the horn, —now. Can we go ahead?

—You say you already have an attorney Mister Crease, now why you had me to come all the way out here frankly I'm just not clear what we're talking about.

—Talking about this scar aren't we? We're talking about coincidence, my scar and the scar on the face of this character in my play that's a coincidence, his scar and the scar on the face of the character in this movie is not a coincidence, it can't be, the same battle, the Major there home from the war and the whole...

—Problem you run into with these similarities though you've got to prove it, prove they stole it, be surprised how many times somebody will make something up like a song maybe, he writes this song maybe just honestly forgets somewhere a long time ago he heard practically the same thing, even if he didn't there's just so many combinations of notes isn't there. Talk about a play now, you take O'Neill, Eugene O'Neill, see I did some, took some acting classes you might call them once, sort of little theatre, you know, even thought of being a serious actor for a while there and...

—If you want to play O'Neill fine, play your heart out. Go right ahead Mister Basie, the Emperor Jones is a powerful role, almost operatic isn't it but that's not what I'm talking about.

—Neither was I.

—What? Oh. Oh I meant, I didn't mean just because you're...

—Didn't mean anything by it no, that's good to know. See what put me in mind of O'Neill was some old Civil War play he wrote where there's this old Southern mansion with all these Greek columns and...

—Well it ends right there, believe me! Because his play's about the Civil War too? Which of course it's not is it, it's a clumsy warmed over schoolboy parody of Euripides with a few vulgar Freudian touches thrown in for good measure.

—No but see that's what I'm saying here, just the appearance, why just this appearance of even some real close similarities won't hold up in court, have to match them up line by line, prove they knew about your play, that they saw your play performed or had the easy chance to? or that they...

—Well of course they never saw it performed.

—Then how come you...

—Because it's never been performed that's how come! Nobody's ever seen it performed, a serious play of ideas like this one you expect to see it in lights on Broadway? All Broadway wants is tits and ass, a chorus line of stupid self indulgent idiots cavorting around the stage singing about tits and ass and the whole loud vulgar, tickets bought on company expense accounts to entertain your out of town buyer you think he wants to sit through something that requires one grain of intelligence?

—You been to the theatre lately Mister Crease?

—Me? God no. Wad up your coat and jam it under the seat you've paid sixty dollars for where you can see exactly half the stage, hot as blazes and you can't cross your knees, the curtain goes up on a torrent of obscenity or some burntout star who's decided a revival of an old chestnut like your O'Neill there's his vehicle for immortality the minute he staggers onstage the audience explodes in applause and goes to sleep till intermission for the cigarette in the alley and that watery five dollar orange drink. End of the limited engagement the investors grab their tax breaks and status as patrons of the arts one thing you can be sure of, they're having a better time up there on the stage than you are. Whether it's spouting tits and ass or your O'Neill chestnut they're all just having a good time at your expense.

—Let me ask you then, clear up one thing for me while we...

—'A gross, coarse form of art,' Pound made it pretty clear didn't he? writing to Joyce when Joyce ground out that dreary play Exiles, 'speaking to a thousand fools huddled together...'

—Feeling like that then, how come you'd want to write for the theatre in the first place?

—Did I say that? write for the theatre? Get back to our friend Yeats here when he and Pound were going to write plays together that Pound said wouldn't need 'a thousand people for a hundred fifty nights to pay the expenses of production.' They can read it can't they? produce it in their own minds if they've got any probably do a better job of it than these money grubbing producers, stagehand unions, actors unions and the rest of the...

—No that's good to know, you had it published? Access, see that's what we're talking about that constitutes access, chance for somebody to read it and lift whatever they...

—I didn't say it was published! No, I submitted it with some excerpts written as a novel, the way I'd treat the whole thing as a novel and they turned it down because of my age, they liked it they liked it a lot but they said I was too old to market, not the book but me, to market me! Talk shows, book tours all the rubbish that publishing's turned into, not marketing the work but selling the author in this whole revolting media circus turning the creative artist into a performer in this frenzy of publicity because I wasn't a baseball player with AIDS or a dog that lived in the White House I was just too old, try to deal with these publishers all they want is your coffee, put it down there Ilse not on the books! on those newspapers there, I sent a copy to myself registered mail in a sealed envelope against just such a piece of dirty work as this one, I did that when I...

—Takes care of your copyright then, already protected if it was never published or performed in public anyplace, send it to yourself in a sealed envelope you don't even have an audience of one if it never circulated out in the...

—I'm coming to that, just be patient. I sent it to some television director I can't remember his name, that was back when I wrote it when television was still occasionally doing things with some kind of artistic and intellectual content not this rubbish where a man's rushing around in a simian crouch jamming an enormous pistol at you, mindless action for the sake of action just like everything else out there, no. No, when Hector's body is dragged around the walls of Troy there's action, action with some meaning in it because Hector has meaning as a hero, put him up against Achilles and...

—Don't remember his name?

—Hector?

—This television director you sent your play to.

—No. It was a nice name like Armstrong, Montgomery but, no, I can't remember.

—He like it?

—No. He rejected it, he...

—You have his rejection letter? Did you sign a release? Usually they won't even read something without a release, won't even send it back without a postpaid envelope.

—It's around here somewhere no, I didn't sign a release. He probably never read it himself anyhow, probably some twit of a secretary right out of business school who'd ask which side George Washington fought on.

—Name couldn't have been this Kiester could it?

—God no! I said it was a nice name didn't I? You think I'd have submitted it to somebody named Kiester? That whole gang out there that's why I was told to call a firm like yours, dealing with a Montgomery or an Armstrong I would have called in Davis Polk or Cravath, but Kiester? you follow me?

—Can't say I do, Mister Crease.

—Go after that gang out there you'd better get a Jewish lawyer, that's what they told me.

—Why you were real surprised to see me walk in here.

—Well I, matter of fact, yes, I...

—Don't mean anything by it, no. You can send me right back you know, pay the consultation fee and that's it.

—Well that's not, no, no that's not what I meant at all we, after all Mister Basie we, you're obviously a civilized man with your theatre experience and the, and Yeats of course yes I think we're off to a good start here aren't we?

—That's good to know.

—Getting into slavery here and that whole sentimental myth about the old antebellum South, Thomas is leaving and trying to get his mother up to stay at Quantness while he's gone and the Major...

—You come to think about it though, it's those Jews in Hollywood you're talking about that pretty much gave us that myth, spread it around.

—That may well be yes, but...

—Butterfly McQueen twittering around and old Hattie McDaniel grousing all loving and faithful, horses and beautiful women and Leslie Howard off to fight the good fight?

—Just a shame they didn't win it, two separate countries like we've got right now but I mean really separate, borders, passports, import duties, rural economy down there growing God knows what for the mills in the North and religion, God, talk about another country, there's your nice Baptist lady on election day right behind the local bootlegger both of them voting dry, ever been in the South? Beautiful horses and bad teeth, sit down in a restaurant first thing you're offered is coffee, then the salad course and you finally get to the meal, getting it backwards like everything else. Ever been there?

—Been in Texas but that was...

—Well Texas of course. Texas is unspeakable. Here, you'll see what I mean.

THE MAJOR

Your, ah, mother, Thomas? Is she all settled in?

THOMAS

(SNAPPING HIS WATCH OPEN NERVOUSLY, LOOKS UP)

I had to send Henry down in a rig to get her. No one had told me about John Israel.

THE MAJOR

Told you what.

THOMAS

Why, that he ran off.

THE MAJOR

(TRANSFERRING HIS INDIGNATION)

John Israel, run off? We'll have them out to hunt him, and fit punishment...

THOMAS

No, it happened in winter, months ago.

THE MAJOR

Well why didn't... they didn't anyone tell us. William?

WILLIAM

(TURNING TO THOMAS SLOWLY, WITH A SMILE OF INNOCENT BUT ALMOST CUNNING INTIMACY)

'The punishment it inflicts on those who refuse to obey it is nothing more than a means of compelling them to be free...'?

THE MAJOR

(TO KANE)

Yes, you might have noticed the staircase out here? This same niggra John Israel built it. I offered Thomas six hundred dollars for John Israel. They'd taught him to read down there at The Bells. Isn't that the gratitude you bound to expect? Teaching a niggra like that to read, that he's bound to run off with his head full of nonsense? The newel post out there, it's carved like a pineapple, and then to go teaching him to read? A niggra that can turn wood like that, filling his head up full of ideas? How do they expect he's going to turn out?

KANE

A black Epictetus?

THE MAJOR

Yes, a black... what?

KANE

The philosopher Epictetus, a Greek slave...

THE MAJOR

Yes, they had the proper idea of these things now, didn't they. Aristotle, he was the Greek philosopher, I can show you somewhere what he had to say about natural slaves. That there's some just naturally meant to be slaves.

KANE

Ah... but to let a man's colour decide it, sir? Why, every Greek knew the threat of enslavement. Think, on the day he set off to war, how he must have pondered what the poet meant with 'The day a man's enslaved, Zeus robs him of half his virtue.'

THE MAJOR

(HEATEDLY)

Exactly, sir! And who ended up taken prisoner and enslaved? Those with neither the skill to win nor the courage to die, like these niggras out here. What do we get over here from Africa? Not the ones with the courage to fight off the slavers, or smart enough to escape them, no. What we get here is the natural slaves, they're the ones that are already slaves where they come from, that can't do a thing but what they're told, that have to have everything laid out for them right down to the line, that can't do a thing but follow orders. We don't get the warrior class, the aristocrats...

(PAUSES, BUT IS PROVOKED BY KANE'S SILENT APPRAISAL OF HIM)

Yes, I can show you in these same books, sir. The Acropolis there in Athens, Greece, it was built the same way this house was built.

KANE

(PROMPTS, AS THOUGH PRIVATELY AMUSED)

For the same 'arms-bearing aristocracy... '

THE MAJOR

Indeed it is, sir. I can show you in any Southern camp right today, the courtesies between officers and men, if you care to see these... arms-bearing aristocrats.

(TURNING TOWARD THE DOOR)

If you care to see the stables, Mister Kane?

(CROSSES TO THE DOOR, STOPS AND TURNS IN THE DOORWAY)

My own men, sir, have never wanted for my respect.

THE MAJOR pauses in the hall, looking round as KANE follows him, exiting left.

WILLIAM

(EAGERLY)

Thomas, you're leaving?

THOMAS

(ABRUPT, VEXATIOUS)

Why, should I wait? Wait and see everything up there taken? What's mine, the way all this is yours?

WILLIAM

(DISCONCERTED, WITHDRAWING A STEP)

No, you... you go. You go, Thomas.

THOMAS

Yes, and think what you like. Think what you like of my leaving.

WILLIAM

(DISTRESSED)
Anything I said Thomas, back in the parlour, anything I said there with Papa, Thomas...

THOMAS

(PAUSES, STUDYING HIM)
You knew, Will, didn't you. About John Israel.

WILLIAM

(MOCKING, AS THOUGH OF THEIR PAST FRIENDSHIP)
The 'noble savage...'

THOMAS

(ABRUPTLY TAKING HIS SHOULDER)
You helped him!

WILLIAM

(FALTERING BACK)
The way we'd talked Thomas...

THOMAS

You... helped him run off, Will?

WILLIAM

(DEFENSIVELY DESPERATE)
Wasn't he the 'noble savage' when we used to talk? That was naturally good, yes, like it was myself, to be free, the 'natural goodness of man' and then... with the war, and both of us left here and me no better off than him, except I could do what he couldn't do for me...

THOMAS

Yes, free him, for what! To be hunted down somewhere and killed?

Seeing someone offstage left, where he is facing, THOMAS waves, calls out as he descends from the veranda and WILLIAM follows to downstage left.

(CALLING)

Here, Henry? You bring me that bay mare round here, saddled.

WILLIAM

(APPEALING, HORRIFIED AT THIS INTERPRETATION)

Thomas... no! No, it was if life could be good, the day I saw that if life could be good at all then it had to be good for all men...

THOMAS

(AS DERISIVE AFTERTHOUGHT)

Yes, there, why didn't you set Henry off, your own boy instead of mine?

WILLIAM

But... Henry, he wouldn't have understood...

THOMAS

And my mother, do you think she understood? Left alone down there at The Bells with only old Ambers and Emma to help? And after your father offered to buy him when I brought him up here to work on that staircase, when our barns needed mending at home...

(TAKES OUT HIS WATCH, SNAPS IT OPEN AND LOOKS AT IT IMPATIENTLY)

WILLIAM

(WITHDRAWING A STEP, QUIETLY ASSERTIVE)

You were too proud to sell him Thomas. You only brought him up here to show. A niggra that could read and turn wood, to show what you'd made of him down there. Proud, like you were of me...

—This John Israel now, when does he come in.
—Into the play? you mean come onstage? He doesn't.
—Well then how come they...
—Because that's the idea, Mister Basie. Thomas' mother has

taught him to read, that was against the law in some of the slave states so here he is suspended, between what he is and what he never can be. I had an experience last year that will give you the idea. I was robbed. On the Fifth Avenue bus. The Second or Third Avenue you could expect it, but the Fifth Avenue bus? I carry my cash in my left trouser pocket and getting off, changing buses, a tall black fellow right in front of me fell, dark suit, nicely dressed, well built like you are, he fell on the step there with his trouser cuff caught on the open door and I came down holding his shoulders so he wouldn't fall all the way, land on the street. He was twisting and turning, having a hard time freeing his trouser cuff or that's what I thought, what I was supposed to think, somebody pressing behind me but I was so busy holding him up I hardly noticed till finally he got loose, shook himself off and walked away he didn't even turn to thank me, have to say I was annoyed but I thought, there you are, that's New York. Not even that's a black for you but just that's New York. The driver wants to speak to you somebody said, they took your wallet the driver told me, you should call the police. No it's right here I showed him, I carry it in the inside breast pocket like everyone, then a woman standing there said no they did, they robbed you. I was afraid to say anything she said, she was a coloured woman too, they robbed you. They? There were three of them, but here's my wallet I showed her, thanked her, got on the next bus and rode six blocks reading the paper suddenly thought, suddenly put my hand in my pocket and it was gone. I couldn't believe it. Why I'd always carried cash in that trouser pocket, nobody's going to get a hand in there without your knowing it but it was gone. I couldn't believe it.

—You mind if I smoke?

—What? Oh, if you, well no go ahead and smoke if you, you see they all knew what was happening, this coloured woman, the bus driver sitting up there like a tub of pale lard watching it in his rear view mirror now that's New York. A friend of mine did jury duty on a mugging case, the judge picking the jury asked if any of them had ever been mugged and every hand went up, you come out relieved that you weren't stabbed. They all knew I was being robbed except me, I was even cooperating.

—You get the police?

—No, I just said I got on the next bus. I couldn't have identified them if I had, probably why he turned away without thanking me so I wouldn't get a good look at him.

—All look the same though, don't we.

—That's not, no! That's not what I meant at all. Of course I was annoyed, not the money but nobody likes to be made a fool of, but I thought about it later and realized I was just giving something back, paying my dues you might call it. All I've been given in this world you can just look around but you take these three fellows, they'd probably been given damned little but look what they'd done with it. Probably'd never made it through sixth grade but the skill they pulled this act off with, the sheer artistry, smooth, unhurried, talk about theatre and the willing suspension of disbelief there I am helping the one down on the step while the other one's going through my pockets with the third one covering him? Didn't even bother with the wallet, nothing that obvious, no threats, nothing ugly, an elegant piece of theatre and they were gone, didn't even wait for the applause. They were just doing their best with what they'd been given, la carrière ouverte aux talents as Napoleon had it, you had to admire it. You see what I'm getting at.

A smoke ring billowed from the chair, growing larger, heavy with purpose. —Afraid I do, Oscar... and another pursuing it, careening off at a tangent. —Afraid I do.

—Yes well, because the whole idea there, what I meant was simply making the best with what we...

—I know what you meant. Take this idea about natural slaves now, you believe all that?

—I don't have to be a murderer to write a murder mystery do I? The Major believes it that's the point, to make the Major believable as a character defending his beliefs and principles here, it's right here a few pages later he's talking with Mister Kane again.

THE MAJOR

(SENTENTIOUSLY RETURNING TO TOPICS OF CONSEQUENCE)

That interested me what you had to say earlier, the Greek philosopher that said 'The man without fear cannot be a slave.' The exact thing I was saying myself, I believe. Yes, they had an idea of these things, the Greeks did, looking after the natural order of things.

KANE

(MASKING HIS AGITATION WITH EFFORT)

And the slaves who worked in the mines, what of them? Who worked in the mines until they died, because they had no immortal souls, and could die in the darkness, was that it? Was that the natural order?

THE MAJOR

Yes, we've improved there, as a purely practical question. They are too valuable for such treatment here. When they are sick or injured, who takes care of them? No sir! We cannot afford to throw them aside here, the way men who can't work any longer are thrown aside by the Yankees. Of course it's the natural order. Why, hasn't Lincoln himself let the Southern leaders know that he has no intention or power to interfere with slavery down here?

—You mean he's acting on his principles, the Major is? Or he's digging them up afterwards to justify his whole...

—That's the whole idea isn't it? It's all up there in a book by George Fitzhugh from before the Civil War, Cannibals All! it's right up there somewhere, take it and read it, why the Major brings up this whole question of wage slaves in the North we get into all that later, when Thomas takes over these coal mines in the second act and...

—Doesn't sound much like the movie.

—I'm not talking about movies! I'm talking about ideas.

—I thought we're talking about this movie, why you had me to come all the way out here, talking about infringement aren't we? this movie you say they stole from you? You talk about ideas this, ideas that, you can't copyright them. Talk about these natural slaves, you just finished saying it's all right up there in Fitzhugh didn't you? I know it is. I've read it. They can read it, anybody out there can read it, lift whatever they want to. You tell me this play here is a play of ideas, I have to tell you I don't think you've got much of a case.

—Well that's not, wait a minute, you're not leaving? We haven't even got to the main...

—No, just stretch my legs, pace up and down helps me talk while

I'm thinking, like the courtroom, makes the juices flow. I see you laid out there what I'm really seeing is this jury, all...

—If you want to pace up and down you'll have to do it in the hall, here you can't even wait, the phone there, can you hand me the phone? I can't quite, yes. Hello? Yes hello, what...

—Down the hall on the left?

—On the right. Hello? Yes well what is it now I'm busy, I'm... No I'm in conference, in a conference with a new... No but can you just tell me quickly what's the matter? I'm... What do you mean it's too terrible, if it's so terrible you can't even talk about it why did you call, can't you just tell me quickly what it's about? What...? Well not this minute no, no I told you I'm in conference with a new lawyer who... It's not about the accident no, it's my... Well it is really important! It's about my... All right then! Maybe it's not as important as what you're calling for but if you won't even tell me what it's about how can I... about Bobbie? What, go where...? All right do all that first then, pick out the dress and go to the shoe store and stop at the hairdresser and then come over if you... yes, goodbye. Mister Basie...?

—Right here.

—Your cigarette there, just worried it could roll off on the floor and set the whole place...

—Sorry. Here, let me hang that up for you. This is a beautiful place you've got here isn't it. Probably go for a million these days.

—Add another million for the pond out there.

—And that sign at the gate.

—Well the privacy yes, that's worth more than ever now isn't it with these miserable little tract houses going up everywhere, not to speak of the people who infest them, it's really the only thing left worth having that money can buy.

—You own all of it?

—Let's not get into that right now. Where were we.

—Point with this movie, you come down to the difference between protection for an idea and the expression of the idea, the artistic...

—You've seen that ad for the movie they're running haven't you? Based on a true story? They're admitting it right there aren't they? that they took this story of my grandfather I wrote my play about?

—Not just admitting it no, see what they're doing is...

—I can't copyright my own grandfather all right, I know it. I can't copyright the Civil War I can't copyright history I know all that, but they...

—What they're doing there Oscar, they're heading you off at the pass.

—What pass, what do you mean.

—Means it's right out there in the public record doesn't it? Based on a true story means it's right out there in the public domain where anybody can pick it up for a play, write a novel, make a movie?

—All right then listen! Did they know that? They'd already made their revolting movie hadn't they? All this didn't come out before they made it, it came out afterward and they put their ad together at the last minute when the picture opened, when they'd seen these awful, these scurrilous stories about my father in the Szyrk case in the mushmouthed press down there digging up anything they can, anything to try to make the whole family sound mad I've got some of it right here. PAST COMES TO LIFE IN SZYRK DECISION, ECCENTRIC JURIST SPARKED HOLMES COURT. They've dug around in their musty old newspaper morgues down there, they keep everything, that's what the South is all about, come up with these yellowed clippings here's one, from nineteen thirty, listen. The soldiers who served as substitutes for Justice Crease in the Union and Confederate armies were both killed in the same battle, and it is said that his feeling of responsibility for their deaths now threatens to become an obsession, firmly convinced after discovering that their regiments faced each other in the bloody day long battle that, among the thousands of troops engaged, the two substitutes died at each other's hands. As an associate justice on the U.S. Supreme Court, it appears that his passionate opinions and outspoken clashes with Justice Holmes, who himself still bears wounds from Ball's Bluff, Antietam and Fredericksburg, arise from umbrage taken by Holmes over what he regards as his colleague's expedient use of substitutes in order to avoid the, that's ridiculous right there, it's plain libel. Holmes knew he'd fought at Ball's Bluff, he knew the whole story, William James said that Holmes would vote for anybody who'd fought in that awful war, no. What it was between them, for Holmes everything was the law and when somebody held forth about justice like my grandfather did Holmes argued that he was refusing to think in terms of the evidence, to think in legal terms that's what it was all about between them right to the end, these clashes and passionate opinions he was as obsessed with justice as Holmes was with the law you can see it in his face up there, that picture up, wait, before you sit down will you turn it around? Up there facing the wall where she, where that woman must have been dusting in here yes, because that's what it's all about, this character in my play who's based on him there's a whole passage here where he's just gone down to see his mother for the last time before he goes north and he'd had an accident, he comes in all torn up and interrupts a conversation Kane is having with William.

THOMAS

Coming over that rise, down, there by the chapel, we flushed a bird square up in front of us and the mare shied and lost her footing. She went down, the cinch broke, and I fell on the stones, crawling, when she reared up over me, crawling across the stones on the battlefield...

(SITTING MORE UPRIGHT, HE DRINKS DOWN WHISKY)

There, I'd gone down to accept what she'd offered, to meet her terms, and then... no! What I want, after what I've seen now...

KANE

(SOLICITOUSLY, AFTER PAUSE)

What is that?

THOMAS

(ALMOST SNARLS)

Only justice!

KANE

(WITH RENEWED EFFORT AT LIGHTNESS)

Well! William and I here have just been looking for the same thing. I hope you have better luck than we did.

THOMAS

(TONELESSLY BELLIGERENT, STARING AHEAD)
And what did you find, then?

KANE

(AS THOUGH HUMOURING HIM)
I'm afraid we found that it was nothing much at all, didn't we William.

(AS THOMAS MUTTERS WITH CONTEMPT; TO WILLIAM)
Or had we gone further? Were we quite finished, William?

THOMAS

(WITH ANNOYANCE, HOLDING UP HIS GLASS TO KANE)
Finish, then. No, damn it, let me hear. I insist.

KANE

(TO WILLIAM, WITH MOCK RESIGNATION, AS HE FILLS THOMAS' GLASS)
Do I remember correctly then, William? You said it was right for the just man to injure bad men and enemies?

(WILLIAM NODS)
Well, let us take horses. We've had an injured horse, haven't we. And when horses are injured, do they become better or worse?

WILLIAM

Worse.

KANE

Worse in the qualities, the virtues of horses? Not, say, of dogs?

WILLIAM

Horses, of course.

KANE

But injured dogs are worse, then, are worse in their qualities as dogs, are they? And what about men? Aren't they worse in terms of human virtue when they're injured? And isn't justice a human virtue? Then, my young friend, if men are injured, aren't they made unjust?

(WILLIAM NODS, HALF SMILING)

All right, we'll take horses again, the art of horsemanship. Can the horseman use his art to make others bad horsemen?

WILLIAM

No...

KANE

And can the just use justice to make men unjust? Can the good use virtue to make men bad? Any more than heat can produce cold? or drought moisture?

(WILLIAM SHAKES HIS HEAD)

Then if the good cannot injure, and the just is good, it isn't the work of the just man to injure anyone, is it, friend or not. No, that's the work of the unjust man.

—See now right there where all that almost sounds familiar, that's what happens. Like I said, you take a song now, take that song about, full moon and empty arms...

—Stop singing! Of course, it's that Rachmaninoff piano concerto obviously they lifted it, the way they plundered Chopin for I'm, always chasing...

—Don't need to sing it for me Oscar, see what I'm saying is where maybe you can't protect an idea, what you can protect is the expression, your original artistic expression of this idea in these characters, what they do, how they talk, but you try to prove they stole all that from your play it doesn't exactly sound like what you hear these days in the movies.

—It's not teeming with obscenities if that's what you mean.

—I just mean for instance right there where they were talking about justice, they...

—Right there where they were talking about justice, Mister Basie, happens to be some of the greatest dialogue in the history of western civilization. That passage, the whole scene is from the first book of Plato's Republic that's why it sounds familiar. You're supposed to recognize it because it's, what's the matter.

—That's good to know.

—What do you mean now it's good to know, what are you shaking your head for.

A match flared and died in an aimless cloud of smoke. —I mean maybe that's something not to get into if you try to go ahead with this, go pointing around at Fitzhugh and your Plato there they go ahead and claim fair use once they establish this whole story idea was in the public domain, show that clipping you read where the...

—We just settled that didn't we? You're telling me that two or three years ago this Kiester happened to see it in the Gastonia Sentinel for December third, nineteen hundred and thirty thought it would make a good movie?

—Need to prove it.

—Fine yes, I'd like to see them try to prove it.

—You. You do, need to prove he didn't.

—Well that's absurd. It's obvious isn't it?

—Not to the law Oscar. What the law's all about.

—All right then listen. Get hold of their records, subpoena their records or whatever you do, prove right there that they came up with this based on a true story ad at the last minute just to cut me off at the pass? that they got it from these cheap stories about my father in the yellow dog press down there trying to poison the atmosphere over the appeal in this Szyrk case? Any court could see that.

—Never tell what any court will see. They granted the appeal didn't they? overturned his decision?

—What? When. I didn't...

—Got him for error before some new judge on the Third Circuit down there, I thought you'd know about it from your father.

—Well not, we're not in very close touch but, but that's just what I've been saying isn't it? All of it down there, it's nothing but mean dirty politics, twist anything around to damage him because he's a damn yankee they're still living in the Reconstruction, you show one spark of civilized intelligence and...

—What I saw it all looks pretty legal, struck down his summary judgment where there's still triable issues of fact. Some mixup over a clouded title to the land where Szyrk put up his Cyclone Seven, threw in the court's failure to cite the Virginia statutes in his citations even got some of the locals there recanting on their interrogatories, claim they were tricked by the fancy language where Szyrk claims his sculpture is site specific for the moral torpor and spiritual vacuity of the place the only words they got hold of were moral and spiritual, thought it was all some big tribute.

—Just what I've been saying? Exemplars of our moral and spiritual values they've never heard the word torpor and the only time they've heard vacuum is a vacuum cleaner, so stupidity triumphs and the law celebrates it?

—Wouldn't be the first time would it. Take Szyrk naming this James B kid as a defendant now you've got the two of them joining up to sue these toymakers over this Free Spot game, James B suing over these Spot dolls and Szyrk suing over these T shirts and tinny souvenirs of his sculpture claims it's a protected statement, dog lovers suing all of them over animal rights while they're trying to find somebody in California who keeps sending Spot dog candy with ground glass in it, got a lot on their plate down there.

—It's got nothing to do with this crazy Szyrk anyhow, you've seen that monstrosity he calls a sculpture? Just their way of staining my father's judicial record, a good thing he's out of it.

—May not be if they send it back to him for a jury trial. Why this Szyrk didn't plead his First Amendment rights as a protected statement right from the start's how I would have handled it.

—Well why don't you then. Handle it. Call them up and tell them you'll handle it, or maybe you don't want to. Maybe you wouldn't want to walk into a courtroom down there.

—If I thought that way Oscar I'd still be out behind a plough, more likely up front pulling one. Nothing please me better but I've got a lot on my plate too and I'll tell you one thing. He's got a way better case than you do here. He could shit on a shingle and call it a protected statement under the First Amendment, you can't find that letter rejecting your play you don't even know who you sent it to. You go and serve a complaint on this Kiester they'll respond with an answer and motion to dismiss and they'll probably get it. If they don't and you have to subpoena their records they come after yours too and that means that letter and all that doesn't even come till the discovery process, depositions, documents, interrogatories all the rest of it, motions for summary judgment if that's denied you get ready for your pretrial conference maybe get a settlement. If you don't you go to trial, you lose there and you go to appeal spending your money every step, every step you take, disbursements, stenographers, transcripts, all that plus your legal fees I'd just hate to see it, case like this where it looks like you've hardly got one I'd just hate to see you laying out money like that even if you've got it, like it looks like you do.

—Yes well I thought though, these legal fees I thought maybe we can work something out. I mean Harry said he'd talk to Mister Lepidus he knew him in law school and he thought, I thought maybe we could, that we might work something out.

—You better talk to him, find it's all pretty cut and dried though. See they have what they call these billable hours where an associate like me, I have to turn in two thousand of them a year, that goes to the firm, comes out of your pocket and out of my hide. That's the way it works.

—Oh. Well do you think, I mean how much an hour would you think...

—Better talk to him, say he's a friend of your cousin's there but see that's if we take the case and like I say, so far I can't frankly see recommending it.

—Yes well, yes maybe postponing it would be a good idea wouldn't it, let the movie run in the theatres while their profits pile up and then sue them and the theatres and distributors and advertisers all of them sue all of them, that way we'd get...

—Try that and they'll get you on laches first cat out of the bag.

—Oh. Well what, Harry warned me about laches but what...

—That's where you do exactly what you're saying here, what they call sleeping on your rights even if it's plain negligence, leges vigilantibus and the rest of it. The laws aid the vigilant, you hold back like that and give them grounds for laches you're out of the ball game before it hardly starts.

—Oh. I see what you mean yes but I thought, these legal fees I was thinking once we break through this No Fault nonsense and get down to the damages for the pain and suffering in this accident case and my scar, my academic career and the whole lecture circuit where I, what are you doing...

—Just show you something.

—But you, why are you taking off your shirt what...

—Not taking it off, just show you something here.

—God!

—Collar bone right down to the groin, how's that. See if I was this male model or some ballet dancer there goes my living, see what I mean? I mean maybe you haven't got the greatest case there either.

—I, yes I see what you mean but I, but this case it's all on a contingency basis so even if I...

—Tell you what I'll do. I'll go see the movie and you give me a copy of the play, read it on my own time I just got kind of interested in it and if...

—But this is my only copy, this and the one in the sealed envelope I can't...

—No, you keep that like it is then. I'll go see the movie for the hell of it and that letter, you call me up if you find that rejection letter maybe we can still get someplace.

—Yes wait, wait your shirt's not tucked in... squeezing the horn, —she can let you out through the front.

—I'll find it. Sounded like a car pulling up out there. Hope you're feeling better.

—Yes and thanks Mister Basie, thanks for coming out here.

—You'll get the bill.

A cry pierced the hall —Eeeeeeee! a glass door slammed, the clatter of heels and then —Who was that!

—I told you on the phone, he's the...

—When I saw him I thought you were being robbed. Then I heard your little horn, are you okay Oscar?

—Yes but what are you doing here? You said you had all this shopping and something so awful you can't even tell me running around buying shoes and dresses what...

—Well look at me! Can you just look at me? My hair's a mess I know it, you don't have a comb do you you never have a comb and I broke a nail trying to open the window this morning, the way you sounded on the phone you probably think I just came to see you to get some money you always look so uncomfortable whenever it's mentioned the way your lips get real tight the way you're looking at me now because you hardly ever look at me when I've got any clothes on and look at them, I can't go to the funeral like this can I? All I've got are these tight skirts and blouses in these bright colours I don't even have shoes to go with this black dress that I just...

—To what funeral!

—It's Bobbie! Didn't I tell you it's always Bobbie?

—God. What, look there are tissues right there by the lamp here, sit down and tell me about it but, ow! my leg...

—It's like a matte jersey only they have to let the skirt down with this real low cut V neck but I can pin it with that bunny rabbit pin you gave me that time when we went to that battlefield place where the motel had that bed with the magic fingers and you wanted me to, are you even listening to me?

—Will you just tell me what happened?

—Don't you even remember? where the bed kept jiggling and...

—To Bobbie! What happened!

—I told you didn't I? that he got this Porsche? I don't know what to do. Did you eat yet? All I had was some coffee I'm starved, maybe it's something else feel right here, that lump? No inside, you can't feel through my clothes, did it get any bigger since last time? No, harder...

—If you'd go see a doctor...

—How can I go see a doctor if I can't pay him, I haven't even got that insurance they gave me at the phone company that's why I didn't ask you. I thought you were mad at me.

—About what, why should I be angry.

—When I went to that movie with Kevin, why shouldn't I. You never take me anyplace.

—How can I take you anyplace! I can't even, you didn't even really see the movie anyhow did you except for the parts about, where did you sit.

—Where did I sit?

—In the back? in the dark? where he could...

—Where he could what, what do you mean after this favour he's doing for you with this accident case where you haven't even paid him anything?

—It was his idea wasn't it? that he gets paid if we win? that he might take almost half? And what about your divorce? how are you paying him for that unless he, unless you're paying him with some different kind of coin...

—I don't even know what you're talking about.

—You know exactly what I'm talking about I, have you? been to bed with him?

—What?

—I said have you slept with him.

—No!

—All right then, if that's...

—No stop it! Get your hand away, you hurt my feelings you don't even think I have any, everything I say you insult my intelligence right to my face while you're trying to put your hand in my...

—All right then. If you, oh Ilse? Wait, listen do you want some of that Alfredo sauce with the...

—I'm not hungry! I have to go anyway, I don't know why I even came over here to see you. I thought I could talk to you but you don't even listen, do you think I came over here to beg? The way you're looking at me right now that's all you ever...

—Listen. Sit down. Do you need...

—I can't sit down. I told you I have to go didn't I? to get my hair done, do you think I can go to Bobbie's funeral down there like this where everybody's looking at me? They won't even do the alterations on that dress till I pay them a hundred seventy nine dollars and they can still get it done by tonight if I can even go in the first place because the airplane fare is over four hundred dollars and...

—Listen. Right over there, my checkbook's right there where you left it the last time, there's a pen...

—That's round trip. You want me to come back don't you? Here. And two dollars for that stuff you spray underneath so the dress doesn't cling to my, with this minister they've got down there that's why I need the skirt lengthened or they'll think I'm some kind of a...

—Wait. Wait, before you go there's just one thing, there's a letter I have to find it may be in one of those boxes over there behind the...

—I can't! I can't Oscar I have to hurry before the stores close and this hairdresser... folding the check, leaving a streak of lipstick on —your little scar, I'm glad it's all better you'd hardly notice it... and after the clatter of heels, the slam of the glass doors, the parting roar of the car left a stillness broken finally, hesitantly, by a toot, toot, echoing into the hall, and then abruptly more insistent, as though fusing despair with a note of defiance, of hazard, even merriment, envisaging the rakish tilt of that careening tricycle rounding the blind corner, toot! toot! toot!

—You can see the shape the lawns are in, and the painting, of course the whole place needs painting, all the trim I mean, it's too late to do anything about the shingles the dampness comes up from the ground and simply rots them but you can't really be surprised, standing out here for almost a hundred years in the weather that comes in from the ocean, the way the veranda sags you came in that way, didn't you? You wonder what holds it up. I've asked Ilse to bring in some tea, the therapist has him out there in the sunroom, they shouldn't be much longer. Would you like some toast or anything?

—Just take some coffee if it's not that much trouble.

—And the driveway of course, you saw that. He usually takes care of these things but the shape he's in now, I thought I'd better come out and get the work started before the weather turns and the, yes here she is. Ilse? Will you bring Mister Basie come coffee? And an ashtray, it seemed like a good opportunity while Harry's away. I will thank God when this case of his is over with.

—Episcopals been around for maybe five hundred years, probably good for five hundred more.

—Well Harry's not God knows, neither am I at this rate I hardly see him at all. Something always comes up like this conference where you just met him, the first time in ages I'd thought we might have a few days to ourselves.

—Should have come along Mrs Lutz, plenty of wives down there, golf courses and all the amenities you could have had a nice...

—The state things are in here? No, no we did it once but that was Japan, it was when we'd first met and of course that's why I went, because it was Japan, Sapporo, up in the north. Harry had these endless meetings and I simply wandered around their museum, I learned more about the Ainu than I know what to do with.

—About you knew, what?

—No, the Ainu, the earliest inhabitants, they were a Neolithic people, short, dark, thick and hairy, heavy beards and hair all over their bodies I suppose for the terrible cold. It's on Hokkaido, one of those brand new utterly primitive cities, there were little pictographs posted over the toilet showing how to use it, little stick figures sitting and standing they'd thrown up these hotels overnight for a winter Olympics, God knows what they expected in the way of contestants. Women tattooed around the mouth and bear baiting, apparently that was the big event, slaughtering a bear.

—That's some Olympics.

—My God no, no I mean the Ainu, a ritual sacrifice of bears I suppose they believed they were some kind of totem ancestors with all that hair, more than any other human race if you call that a race of course, even their language something utterly outlandish they're known as the hairy Ainu. We still joke about it, we, I mean Harry has to shave twice a day when we're going out I'm awfully glad you met him. He's talked to you about all this hasn't he.

—Tell you the truth I don't recall he ever talked about your hairy Ainu there but...

—No of, of course not no... clearing her throat sharply —I meant the, this lawsuit Mister Basie you see frankly what I'm concerned about is the money. I mean if I'm not who will be, the state Oscar's in with these medications he's on it's all bursting out in some sort of folie de grandeur, I'm sure you had a taste of it when you were out here last week and I'm really quite surprised to see you back. Harry thought you both agreed it's all little more than a nuisance.

—Before that story in the paper, see that gives us kind of a handle on this Kiester if Oscar's dug up that rejection letter, that rejection letter for his play maybe's something to go on, he tell you about that?

—Tell me, my God he called in the middle of the night I'd just come in from taking Harry to the airport I thought he was having a seizure, I mean he's never been someone who drinks but I think he's been getting overfond of this Pinot Grigio he's discovered here waving the newspaper at me yesterday morning the minute I walked in the door shouting read it! Read it! Of course the first thing I asked him was whether he'd called you. I assumed you'd convince him it was all hopeless nonsense but I had to read it just to calm him down.

Hollywood, September 30. In response to allegations made by a second year film student regarding the notorious sledge hammer scene in the recent African film sensation Uruburu, the office of producer director Constantine Kiester brushed off inquiries with a brief statement conceding the possibility that the sequence might have depicted an actual occurrence but stating that they had been approached by an itinerant documentary maker, who was not named, offering the sequence at three hundred dollars a foot. The offer, according to the statement, came as the rough cut of the film was being assembled, and under production schedule pressures no effort was made regarding its source or veracity. 'It brought out the spirit of the picture and there was a perfect slot for it so we bought it and cut it in,' the statement said. The eight minute scene largely accounted for Uruburu's billing as 'not for the squeamish' and its overnight success as a box office favourite, heralding Mr Kiester's meteoric rise in the film industry. Before coming to Hollywood, he had earned a reputation in the east for quality television productions of American theatre classics ranging from Elmer Rice to Eugene O'Neill and Tennessee Williams under his own name, Jonathan Livingston, adding the surname Siegal when he turned to motion pictures and adopting a unique new identity as Constantine Kiester when he came to the West Coast, where he is known as the 'king of special effects' on the strength of the sensational Uruburu and his current Civil War extravaganza, The Blood in the Red White and Blue, which has already garnered $59 million in its first week at the box office and a further $74 million in cassette and foreign distribution rights. He lives in Bel Air in the rental property of a former radio evangelist which he 'picked up for a song' following the sordid and far reaching scandal which...

—All right Oscar, now I've read it. What's the point, have you called that lawyer? the one you saw last week who...

—Basie, Mister Basie of course I've called him!

—Well you needn't be so snappish, he convinced you it was all hopeless nonsense didn't he? I told you Harry met him at that outing down at the Greenbrier didn't I? and they agreed you don't have a case with the remotest chance of winning? Harry thinks he's brilliant.

—Brilliant! I had to do all the work myself Christina, lead him along step by step pointing things out trying to get a straight answer from him, trying to get him to take the whole thing seriously while he rambled on about his acting career in some thimble theatre sitting there blowing smoke rings as though we were having a chat about baseball with the evidence right there in front of us that they'd taken this whole based on a true story idea from these sleazy attacks on Father down there in the Szyrk case they reversed it, did you know that? that Father's decision in the Szyrk case was overturned? Telling me how he would have handled it he sounded about as professional as a delivery boy, got a lot on their plates I won't repeat the rest of his language but you can imagine what a legal brief he'd write would sound like he thinks Harry's my cousin. He calls me Oscar.

—Well that's your name isn't it? If you want to throw your money away on...

—Yes and that's another thing, trying to pin him down on their fees and how much it can cost these same vague evasive...

—Well my God Oscar if you feel this way, why on earth did you call him?

—Who else can I call! Harry wouldn't help me would he? Telling Basie that I don't have a case that was before this piece in the paper here about Kiester that his real name's Livingston, that's who signed that rejection letter before he changed it to Jonathan Livingston Siegal covering his tracks and then to Constantine Kiester, Basie told me to call him when I found it and he said then we can get someplace. I said once if anybody had a name like that they'd change it didn't I?

—And you've found it? this letter? That's what all these boxes are doing stacked in the hall?

—Well not exactly but...

—What do you mean not exactly. Have you found it or not.

—This letter? One letter, one piece of paper do you expect me to find one piece of paper overnight in all this material that I've had to save for the, that I've saved? I told Ilse to bring down all those boxes from my closet and the upstairs storeroom I can't go up there to go through them myself can I?

And so she turned now to her guest over the tea and coffee cups that had clattered to rest on the low table between them with —this letter no, I don't think Oscar's found it yet but, oh and Ilse? some sugar? and will you bring some cream if there is any, I asked you to bring Mister Basie an ashtray didn't I, honestly. Training them is almost as tiresome as doing it one's self.

—My mother now, she would have gone with you on that.

—Oh? I didn't, what I meant was the, was those boxes you can see them piled up all down the hall it's what Oscar's pleased to call his archives, every piece of paper he's ever had his hands on, letters, old Playbills, scraps of newspaper, invitations, papers written by his illiterate students, recipes he's never tried, he read that letter a thousand times storming around the house here. We had an old dog then and he read it to the dog. The first act is entirely superfluous, anything useful it contains can easily be incorporated in the second act. As for the last act, how did they put it, something like the last act resolves problems which have never been raised except for any reason for the play to have been written in the first place. The author makes it clear throughout that he does not trust the director, he does not trust the actors and he does not trust any audience he would be fortunate to have.

—Pretty rough all right, maybe a little taste of revenge in this lawsuit he's after.

—A little! I tried to tell him he was lucky, if he'd had his wish and seen it produced that could have been the review in the Times I mean that's what makes it all so painful, this rather desperate need of his to be taken seriously but I suppose that's why people go around writing things in the first place isn't it, and of course this miserable teaching business hasn't helped matters. These useless students probably all know exactly how little he gets paid which is the way everything's measured and it's not as though he needs the money after all, that's really the fine irony because since money's never been the problem going into teaching was his way of trying to be taken seriously in the first place.

—Now you bring it up though, seems he takes this money about as serious...

—No it's not as though he hasn't always been terribly careful about money, I mean I suppose he got rather peevish with you over fees and things like that didn't he. He's so used to being terribly meticulous, I mean he carries it loose in his trouser pocket the clean large bills folded face in down through the smaller bills all of them right side up with the soiled dollar bills on the outside, he means to spend the crumpled bills first, insofar as he means to spend any of them of course, it's all quite surreptitious but I've seen him in agonies folding a crisp new five over a soiled ten you can see what I mean. I mean I think he feels your approach to all this is a bit, a little bit casual as though you don't really take any of it terribly seriously. You see what I mean.

—See what you mean Mrs Lutz but cases like these, they can go anywhere. Try to tell him the clock's running every minute, running right now while we sit here talking but he's just not the easiest man to get things straight with, pin things down now is he.

—Oscar? My God no he can be a perfect pill but I've got to ask you, I mean honestly Mister Basie does this whole thing make any sense to you at all? I mean you've had experience in the theatre or so he tells me and these grandiose notions he's got of this play of his, you must have read it?

—Only had the one copy no, no but he took me through some of it, said he wanted to give me the feel of it but...

—Well I pried it away from him first thing this morning and went out and had ten copies made, God knows why he needs ten copies.

—But see what I think of it, maybe I think it's a little old fashioned these characters getting up there and making speeches at each other you might say, awful lot of talk but if I think it's a good play, if I even think it's maybe a great play or this Livingston Kiester thinks it's a real bad play that's all just what you call irrelevant, see what we're talking about here is infringement. You take the movie. I went out and saw this movie he says they stole it for whether it's a good movie, whether it's a great movie or just trashing up history with all this blood and gore and some naked woman see we're not talking naked women here. We're talking naked theft. Fish in these waters here a little today and see if we come up with enough to file this complaint he's hell bent on, see if they'll settle. If they don't offer to settle like for damn sure they won't, they respond with their answer and motion for dismissal of all charges like for damn sure they will, they don't get a dismissal and we figure our chances, drop the whole thing or get in deeper.

—Yes well of course it's that getting in deeper that's all rather frightening, your alarm clock running my God, what can be keeping them.

—Thought I just heard a car pulling out, maybe...

—Because someone's got to stop and think about the money before everything goes overboard, I mean I didn't mean it to sound like Oscar has all the money in the world just now talking about his teaching, I think he's got some wild vision of a lavish settlement in this accident case you'd think he'd already won it, crowing about this petition they've just granted getting him out from under some

No Fault protection whatever that means, I'm sure you've noticed that scar he's so proud of?

—Means his insurance will claim immunity under the No Fault statute and try to get it dismissed, he files a claim for what you call tort recovery probably take him a year or two just to get on the docket and by the time he walks into court with a scar like that he'll need the best negligence lawyer around.

—Well of course he's got one, a lawyer I mean not the scar but considering how he got him God knows Mister Basie, I've simply got to count on you to discourage him when you think things are going too far, I don't mean this absurd ambulance case obviously that's gone too far already but this...

—Just let's make sure we have one thing real clear Mrs Lutz, see we're not out looking for business, not ambulance chasers. Sam put me on this like kind of a favour to look into it, if I go and get us into some drawn out tangled up case just because the client's got money where I know we'll probably never win it I'm out on the street tomorrow. Maybe we've got something here, maybe worth a try, have to admit it all kind of intrigues me. And now Oscar here, see I've come to like Oscar.

—You actually, you like Oscar?

—Always have to like a man that's at the end of his rope, came over the table to her in a cloud of smoke and then, piercing her through it, toot! toot!

—My God why did I ever dig that thing up, you expect him to come wheeling around that blind corner from the hall on that awful tricycle he was still riding when his legs were so long that he could hardly, Oscar? I'm in here with, look out!

—Well. You finally got here.

—And he's been sitting here with the clock running since wait, will you just park over here by the windows before you knock these cups over?

—But my students, aren't they here yet?

—What on earth would your students be doing here.

—Because, Christina. Because we're going to go over these points for the complaint, Mister Basie's seen the movie now and while we go through the rest of the play he can note down the things they've stolen and...

—And these dense students of yours will sit here and applaud?

—They can have the chance to get a real sense of the complicated issues that were at stake in the Civil War I should have thought of it before, having them read the parts aloud and feeling they're taking part in the whole atmosphere of the...

—No wait. You can't mean you're going to have them read your play to us out loud? Here? Now?

—They're bright talented kids Christina, they just need to be stimulated maybe some of them have even seen the movie and can point out...

—You mean you're going to put on this circus while Mister Basie just sits here with the clock running? Is that why I just spent something like two hundred dollars getting all these copies made? Is there any earthly reason to have ten copies?

—Probably need more than that if we get in deeper Mrs Lutz, see but now you have copies Oscar maybe I could just take one along and then talk on the phone later?

—Oscar will you listen to him? Mister Basie's trying to tell you that you can save time and money if he takes a copy with him and reads it himself, couldn't you have simply mailed one to him? without dragging him all the way out here? and then discussed it on the phone? Isn't that why they invented the ungodly thing in the first place? to save people from tramping around the countryside on some stupid errand that no one in his right mind would, how many of these socalled students do you expect.

—Maybe only a dozen or so, I left the message that it would help their grades and...

—My God. Listen, I want that two hundred dollars I spent on those copies.

—Did you get a receipt? I'll need it for tax...

—I did not get a receipt! Simply give me the two hundred dollars.

—All right but, later yes listen, before they get here where are my glasses, listen. This might be useful in my complaint Mister Basie listen, it's a letter of Bernard Shaw talking about making movies from plays he says here 'set your analytical faculty, if you have any, to tabulate all the techniques involved in these extraordinary exhibitions...'

—Oscar, please...

—'Up to a certain point it pays. Most of the studios seem to live by it. But in such studios the dramatist can find no place. They know that they can do without him.'

—Oscar for God's sake what has this got to do with...

—'They don't even know, poor devils, that there is such a thing as a dramatic technique. Get drama and picture making separate in your mind, or you will make ruinous mistakes' and then he says...

—Might come in handy later on Oscar, see all we want right now is a few clearcut causes of action, opening guns you might say like this rejection, show they had their hands on it. You found that letter?

—I...

—Can't you simply say no Oscar? that you had that poor woman hauling a hundred heavy boxes down all those stairs and you don't really know whether it's in any of them? One letter, you expect to find one piece of paper in this whole mess, you've saved every letter anyone ever wrote you God only knows why they bothered, there are letters all over the place. What about that bundle you had me cart in to the hospital for no earthly reason but to cart them back out here, if you can't bear to simply throw them away you've a marvelous chance to get rid of them haven't you? this socalled historical society down there begging to add them to their distinguished collection?

—Why! For some doddering old women to paw through them wheezing over their sacred past, I've got my own archive haven't I? And this family correspondence they already claim to have should be in it too, it's mine isn't it? Ours?

—Why don't you ask your lawyer, he's sitting right here with the clock running.

—I don't have to ask anyone! It's our family correspondence, it's ours Mister Basie isn't it?

—Might have some trouble contesting who owns the actual letters but what they say, that still belongs to whoever said it, whoever wrote the letter, father, grandfather, grandmother, the rights pass right on down to the survivors. Might not be that bad an idea just to go ahead and register the copyright in your name, that way if some problem comes along you...

—Yes well do it then, you've got your yellow pad there write it down, can we do it?

—Just need some particulars, where they're deposited, who they...

—He didn't even know they existed till he heard from this preposterous historical society, he's probably lost that letter too.

—What do you mean too!

—I mean this rejection letter you're so pleased with that Mister Basie's sitting here with his clock running waiting for you to produce.

—Don't have to produce it right this second Oscar, state in the complaint they had this access and face the problem of proof when we have to, taking a little chance on these reasons they gave for rejecting it when we try to claim breach of implied contract as a cause for action but...

—They weren't reasons at all, nobody could have written that letter who'd really read the play it was probably just some twit of a secretary who typed up a form letter for Livingston to sign and...

—What Mister Basie is trying to tell you, Oscar, is that your Livingston Kiester person had to have read it if he was going to steal it, isn't that what this whole asinine business is all about?

—Well he, that's what I mean, would you believe anything he said? You can see how shifty he is just the way he's kept changing his name yes and I want that in, fraud and deceit changing his name twice to cover his tracks to put in the complaint?

—Put it in Oscar, but this intent can be real hard to prove, why somebody goes and changes his name? Smoke took shape in a ring billowing gently upward in the thin sunlight, —now you take your name, suppose you just decided that you...

—I've certainly got no intention of changing it yes and that's another thing, the way they're advertising this based on a true story with this cheap vulgar movie defaming my grandfather what about that.

—Can't defame the dead, Oscar.

—Well I'm not dead am I! Neither is Father, they got his decision reversed down there isn't that what they wanted? Dragging our name through the mud what about me, what about my professional reputation if anybody thought I had anything to do with it, if...

—Oscar, look out the...

—Christina, please! Because I don't care if you can't defame the dead I want that in there, I don't care if I can't copyright my own grandfather I want that in this complaint for the very first cause of action because it is, because it will let them know immediately that they're not just dealing with some, some nuisance.

—Oscar calm down, a dirty van just pulled in out there I think it's your cast of thousands.

—Oh! Oh yes let them in, have Ilse let them in, are they coming in?

—My God.

They could all sit on the floor he thought, mainly concerned lest they waste any time, passing round copies, assigning parts, sizing up the first act's tribulations with a haste such that it might indeed have been he who had first labeled it superfluous pressing on, now, with all the urgency he'd endowed in his protagonist, to get out, to leave the South behind with all its sacred past and simpering postulates and seize reality by the throat in an office in a western Pennsylvania mining city, midsummer eighteen sixty two, Act II, Scene i.

> Smoke and evidence of the colliery are visible at the large window, upstage left. At downstage left center a rather ponderous desk littered with mail and newspapers, two chairs, and the effect of being partitioned off in a large glassed enclosure from the rest of the office beyond, reached by a glass-paneled door upstage right. Outside the door, at upstage right center, is another desk, far less pretentious but more littered. Cabinets of some sort, acceptable in but hardly designed for an office, stand within the inner office downstage right.

> Neatly but unostentatiously dressed, THOMAS is standing at a window left staring out, as MR BAGBY advances from upstage right toward downstage center desk. Despite a concerted effort at florid respectability, there is a seediness about BAGBY that goes beyond his overtight clothes: shrewd, pompous, ingratiating by turns, he is constantly eyeing his man and the main chance without missing any of the minor ones by the way.

BAGBY

Why, we've one shaft sunk four hundred and thirty eight feet, and you cannot expect men to have kindly thoughts down there, whoever they are. And now, the kind that's come in, with the need for coal what it is? There's foreigners and all manner of undesirables, with their striking and looking for trouble. They get down there in the dark together and think up some new deviltry the minute you've settled an old, you meet one demand for them and they'll think up another. There's no end to their ingratitude. No, they want a tap on the head now and again, as your uncle would say, to knock some gratitude back into them.

Edging up to the desk at downstage center as he talks, BAGBY twists his head to get a look at the letters opened there as THOMAS turns thoughtfully from the window and crosses to downstage center slowly, treating BAGBY in an almost humouring but patronizing way, and with an assumed reassurance he had not had in Act I.

THOMAS

My uncle has said all he had to say. I don't know how I shall convince you, Bagby, if the sight of him didn't, hunched lifeless here over his accounts, as you told me, one morning when you came in?

(PICKING UP PAPER, HOLDS IT OUT)

And his house up in Norwegian Street? Here's a bill from the Pinkertons, for a guard on it. Who are you guarding, his ghost? I told you to sell that house, not to guard it.

BAGBY

But to sell it off now? Ah, for you to stay in it yourself, that's another matter. I wouldn't care to stay in it if I was you, of course, and the men in the temper they are. It wouldn't be the first that they'd burned it to the ground, and you in it, watchman and all.

THOMAS

(IMPATIENTLY, SITTING DOWN AT THE DESK)

And why should they harm it? Haven't I been fair to them? Don't they know me by now? Yes, you've said so yourself, they know me for a just man. And has there been one accident? Even one, since I took up here?

(HOLDS BILL OUT TO BAGBY, RETURNING TO MAIL ON THE DESK)

No, here. I've told you, I want order. I want order here... but

(MUTTERING)

I won't hire murderers...

BAGBY

(STANDING BEFORE THE DESK, WITH MOCK AFFRONT)

Murder? Now how many's been murdered then? Surely a head knocked in now and again an't murder? And when two days later you'll see the same head bobbing up and asking for it again?

(PICKING UP A NEWSPAPER, POINTING OUT HEADLINE)

Here, 'Coal operators may be forced to suspend operations until the militia draft is ended.' You're an owner, whatever else you may be, fair or not. And that's reason enough for them to burn you and your house to the ground right there. Do you see...? where it speaks of the 'lawless foreign element' that's come in, with the demand for labour what it is now?

(PAUSING TO TAKE A JAWBREAKER FROM HIS WAISTCOAT POCKET AND POP IT INTO HIS MOUTH)

When men behave like savages, after all, with no respect for law and order, how must they be treated? Why, like savages! Take them one by one they may be fine fellows, as you say, but get them together they'll rise up and go wild with their brawling and drink and howling for justice, with no respect for decent people like ourselves.

(CRUNCHING DOWN ON THE JAWBREAKER)

You must knock a bit of justice into them now and again...

(SITTING A HAM FAMILIARLY UP AGAINST THE DESK, LEANING ACROSS)

And I might add, sir, you've made no friends here since you came, and it's not as though you mightn't need them, before you're done.

THOMAS

(SITTING BACK, HALF DERISIVELY)

We've made friends, haven't we Bagby?

BAGBY

(IMPULSIVELY CANDID, AS THOUGH TAKEN OFF GUARD)

I hope so sir...

(RECOVERING HIS CONFIDENTIAL DETACHMENT)

Ah, but I meant... them with influence. The other mine operators, the foundry owners, the bankers... they wonder about you, now and again, you know. I've stood up to them for you of course, but it's some of the changes you've made for the men here, giving in to them where your uncle stood fast. It's not... playing the game, you might say, doing such things on your own without consulting together... though I've told them, of course...

THOMAS

(AMUSED BUT ANNOYED)

Told them what.

BAGBY

(REASSURINGLY)

There, I haven't repeated some of the things you've said, no. Of your being the master here with the men's consent... no, have no fear of my repeating such things. I've stood up to them for you. But if you was to get out a bit more yourself...

THOMAS

(DISDAINFULLY, WAVING HAND TOWARD THE WINDOW)

Out? In that?

BAGBY

Out in society I mean to say, not tramping the streets alone at night, as you've done and unarmed at that. No, there's some that pass through here, United States senators and the like, cultured people like yourself, and speaking the French language and such things, and your father that served in that embassy there... and then that you've seen a bit of the South, it don't hurt in these times, you know, with many of them's never been down there. And a bit of influence, now and again, it don't hurt when you want things done...

(LEANING CLOSER OVER DESK, IN SPICY CONFIDENCE)

And then, if you cared to do yourself up a bit, that and move from the place you've been living up into a decent establishment, up in Mahantongo Street perhaps, dressed up a bit more in the fashion, you might say, instead of such worn clothes as mine here that's all I can afford, why... I know of a lady or two who'd find it an honour...

THOMAS

(SARCASTICALLY)

And how would you have me dressed, Bagby? In a uniform...?

(LOOKING AT A LETTER FROM TOP OF THE PILE)

From Brooks Brothers?

BAGBY

(DISCONCERTED, LOOKING ANXIOUSLY AT THE LETTER)

Ah, you... know the firm, sir? In New York?

(CRANING NECK TO LOOK AT THE LETTER)

Gentlemen's clothiers... a fine old firm...

THOMAS

(HOLDING THE LETTER BACK, READS AND COMMENTS ACIDLY)

It sounds like just the place. Here's a mention of a contract for 'twelve thousand uniforms which were delivered at a net price of nine dollars fifty...' You've dealt with them?

BAGBY

(GUARDEDLY, BACKING OFF)

Not directly myself, I've had friends, influential friends...

THOMAS

(READS AND COMMENTS ACIDLY)

Yes, I'd like to see myself in one of these uniforms! Here, 'of inferior material, strange and outlandish cut, and ingenious construction...' I like that. 'Pocketless, buttonless, and otherwise devoid of necessary entity...'

BAGBY

(RECOVERING EXPANSIVELY, STANDING BACK)

There, that was all straightened out you know. The newspapers tried to make it a scandal but some very prominent people stepped in and straightened it out. There was some that let on that the state officers had conspired with the manufacturers there, but it was all straightened out. The soldiers was left with some rags, the Brooks Brothers with some money, and the people reading the papers with a new scandal. Why, some of them prominent people that straightened it out, I know them myself, you know, people with influence...

THOMAS

(COLDLY, HANDING OVER THE LETTER)

I gathered you did. This letter is addressed to you. And let me tell you, Bagby, when I want company, when I want influence I'll find it myself. If there's one thing money can buy that's worth the having, it's privacy, do you hear? Privacy...! there. Where are the walls I've asked for here, instead of this glass cage I'm in?

BAGBY

But you wouldn't be able to see what's going on, with walls all about you and nowhere to look but the window? and out at the pits? Your uncle liked to see what went on. Here, he'd tap on the glass with the ring he wore, and I'd be in in an instant. A look from him through the glass, and I'd know what he wanted.

THOMAS

(CURTLY, RETURNING TO THE MAIL)

Now you know what I want, and you see to it.

BAGBY

(SOMEWHAT APPREHENSIVELY, LOOKING AT THE MAIL)

As you say sir, and I shall explain to the staff...

THOMAS

(WITH ANNOYANCE)

You need explain nothing to anyone. Do you think I come into this office every morning just to watch that parade of sharpers that lines up there at your desk?

BAGBY

(REPROVINGLY, BUT PREOCCUPIED TRYING TO SEE THE MAIL)

There's problems come up with the mines you know, details... unless you might be referring to the man in here yesterday? Him with the hair down his back? Now there's a man, sir, you wouldn't speak so slighting if you knew what he's up to. He's an inventor, a rare fellow you might say, and I may let you into a confidence. He's built a rapid-fire gun that will end the war in a day. Yes, once it's brought into the line, once it's seen by the right people... them with influence... was there... any more of my mail? that might be... mixed in?

THOMAS

(WITH FEIGNED LACK OF INTEREST, HOLDING UP A LETTER)

Two hundred barrels of mess pork, shipped to Washington?

BAGBY

(TAKING IT WITH A SHOW OF INTERESTED IGNORANCE)

Possibly...

THOMAS

Sabres at four dollars and twelve cents 'for ornamental purposes'? Are they for the mines?

BAGBY

(TAKING THE LETTER)

No sir, a small commission...

THOMAS

Small? And priced to the government at eight dollars? And here, pants at two dollars fifty cents on government contract for five?

BAGBY

(TAKING THE LETTER, DISTRACTED)

Yes, five... dollars a pair, it may mean? At two fifty each? And... was there nothing else, then?

THOMAS

No. Not if we've worms in the mines, that is.

BAGBY

...Worms?

THOMAS

(HOLDING OUT A PAPER)

A shipment of vermifuges, from something called Pfizers in Brooklyn. You signed this order?

BAGBY

I... I didn't know what they was sir. 'Vermifuges.'

THOMAS

Will you tell me the meaning of all this, then? You knew the cost and the mark-up, and that was enough...

BAGBY

(INTERRUPTING DEFERENTIALLY)

There, sir, you mustn't be... outraged... An occasional small commission that passes my way. There, and an't it a man's place to come forward and offer a hand? Yes, with times what they are, and the government fighting to preserve the Union, and equality for people like ourselves? A bit of business on the side now and again, when I find I can help things along, a chance to be of assistance...

(TAKING A PAPER FROM HIS INSIDE COAT POCKET)

To help out a friend... as you called me...

(HANDING THE PAPER TO THOMAS)

To lend a hand against fate, you might say, I might let you into this... Not that you're off on a boat trip. It's a marine insurance policy indeed, but you needn't go anywhere to collect on it.

It's a new thing, an accident clause. You don't even need to drown, an accident in the parlour will suffice. Surely you've paid fifteen cents for twenty four hours protection on a train journey from loss of life and limb? This don't end overnight, it goes on, on until you collect. Yes, I have it myself, you know, and it's them plays the game, this company here, making up odds against death and accident, and nobody loses. It's a fine new dodge for all concerned. Why, you may manage things anywhere, and collect what they call the principal for no more than the loss of both hands, feet, eyes, or a winning combination...

THOMAS

(THRUSTING THE PAPER BACK AT HIM EXASPERATED)

A fine new dodge! Is this how you spend all your time here? And that parade past your desk, your Pfizers and Brooks Brothers peddling worm medicine and one-legged trousers...

BAGBY

(BURSTING OUT DEFIANTLY)

And what would you have! No, it's all honest goods. I've broken no law. Do you think it's like the army buying sand for sugar, and being sold rye for coffee? paying for leather no better than brown paper? The governor of the state himself, and I've met him, before the war was a week old he'd contracted for ten thousand suits of clothes and a half million dollars was gone in a month. And a single firm here last November got a state contract for eight hundred and fifty thousand yards of army cloth. A million three hundred thousand dollars to a single firm! And I should hang back? When a beef contract runs from three dollars ninety cents to eight dollars thirty a hundred pounds, on the hoof at that? And you ask me to hesitate?

(COMING IN MORE CLOSELY, IN CONFIDENCE)

I've a friend now, he's a major for the moment, his company got a contract for ten thousand head of cattle at eight cents a pound and he let it out very next day at six and a half. Thirty two thousand dollars overnight, without the risk of a penny! Do you think he ever saw the cattle? He knows as much of cows as I do of these vermifuges, and here was thirty two thousand two hundred and sixty eight dollars and seventeen cents overnight, without risking a penny. Why, before the new war secretary came in there was feed contracts let for mixed oats and corn, and who knew the difference when the ratio was switched about? Must you know oats from corn? or only the difference in price. And who knew what had happened, the mules? blown to pieces with grape shot when they'd fairly finished eating?

(HALF TO HIMSELF)

And how long can it last now, what's left...

THOMAS

(IMPATIENTLY)

Last?

(RISING ABRUPTLY, WALKS TO WINDOW LEFT, MUTTERING)

It can't!

BAGBY

(HALF FOLLOWING)

Now they've called up three hundred thousand volunteers, right here in the state alone? Even if some of them's already saying it's only a war to free the naygers...

THOMAS

(IMPATIENTLY)

It can't last. Don't you read the papers?

BAGBY

Three million naygers...!

THOMAS

Since the battle of Seven Days? McClellan's great campaign of invasion that was to destroy the Southern armies and capture Richmond... what happened? It went to pieces in front of Lee and Jackson. And with Lee in command now? The Southern armies have been sweeping north ever since. They'll be here before summer's out.

BAGBY

(ALMOST WISTFULLY)

Yes, and then... that's all there is... All at once, one fine day, things is only what they might have been again, and there you are. It's all over before you know it, it ends up and leaves you behind.

(INTENTLY)

No. A man must put himself forward. You get my meaning, sir? There's no harm in trying to better myself a bit, now? While it lasts? To better myself while I can, more like you if I may say? A gentleman...?

THOMAS

(LAUGHS DISTASTEFULLY, RETURNING TO THE DESK)

If you like, Bagby.

BAGBY

(AN EDGE CREEPING INTO HIS VOICE, PARADE SOUNDS OFFSTAGE)

And is it so different, then? You may laugh at influence, like them Brooks Brothers have that I told you about. But isn't influence the next thing to power itself? And power no more than the advantage of the man who can make things go forward, staying inside the law? That's justice enough, isn't it? What works? Yes, you may afford to mock at influence, with your resources spread out there wherever the eye can see...

THOMAS

(ABRUPTLY, CURBING ONE HAND IN THE OTHER)

This... blackness, wherever the eye can see...?

Distant parade sounds have now given way entirely to tumult.

Dirt? and strife, do you hear it? Yes, are these my resources? Even without it, without the strike, that clanking machinery tearing the earth, and the darkness, digging deeper, darker, men whose voices are the clang of metal, whose lives are death and whose white faces...

(TURNING TO BAGBY, ABRUPTLY MOCKING)

Do you know what coal is, Bagby? that it's death by the billion in every handful?

BAGBY

Ah, but its uses...

THOMAS

Uses? No, is that like owning a... a thing for itself? A place? Where there's order and life? The order of everything growing, alive... and the sun itself is a part of things, not the blazing stranger that it is here, lighting up ugliness better hidden, the lives of men who bring darkness up with them from under the earth to spill it out... listen...

Sounds of tumult erupt closer.

(REMOTELY, LOOKING OUT)

Yes, 'Lay not up for yourselves treasures upon earth,' do you know that one, Bagby? 'Where moth and rust corrupt, and thieves break through and steal...'

BAGBY

There, it's using things that keeps rust off of them, and the moth and the thief have no chance...

THOMAS

(ALMOST RECOVERING HIS PATRONIZING IMPATIENCE)

Uses! Your uses be damned! For what then, more uses?

BAGBY

(QUIETLY SHREWD)

And what would you do with your place that you speak of, to own 'for itself'? A farm, to grow fat like a vegetable?

THOMAS

(FEELINGLY)

No, in all that a man can... take hold and grow, and be something real to other men, to do something, something real in public life...

(BREAKING OFF, AS THOUGH HE'S GONE TOO FAR BEFORE BAGBY, ADDS SOMEWHAT LOFTILY AS HE RETURNS TO DESK)

Never mind, no, you wouldn't understand me...

BAGBY

(FOLLOWING HIM, OBLIGINGLY)

But I would indeed sir, for it's politics, an't it? And an't that just uses, and a means to an end then? Your farm? And does it stay the same, the end then, whatever the uses, them that gets it and them that it's used for?

(COMING ROUND FRONT OF DESK, MORE CANNILY OBLIGING)

You may find your free white savages here all strife and darkness if you like, and your black slavery part of life and order, things growing, you say? Like the... plantation you speak of? No, it all has its uses, that's all, and what's better using than politics? for this plantation, as you say? This place... with the shares, that you're after? With the curious name... 'Quaintness,' is it...?

THOMAS

(SITTING SLOWLY BACK, STARING AT HIM)

What... what do you know of it? What business of yours...!

BAGBY

Ah, not mine, not mine at all sir. I know nothing more than I heard, just in passing, from a banking acquaintance...

THOMAS

(CRUMPLING PAPERS ON DESK IN DISMAYED EXASPERATION)

By... heaven! Your bankers here... call themselves bankers, do they? Talking over my business in public?

BAGBY

(HASTILY REASSURING)

In privacy you may be assured sir, and only with them that they trust... If you'd spoke to me first, now, we might have bought these shares up cheap. Then there'd be nobody about, pressing you for the profits as they're ready to do to you now... Them that owns them, now they know what you're after, there's no telling the price, with your resources spread about here wherever the eye can see... The streets an't safe for you wandering out alone, and... you value yourself very high, I know. It's not to be a safe night out, not for anyone but most not for you. There, that insurance I spoke of earlier...? You're a very good bet to collect!

THOMAS

(RISING TO HIM BEHIND THE DESK, TENSELY)

I've fought that, do you hear? I've fought it, and I've won!

BAGBY

(BACKING OFF A STEP, AS THOMAS STARTS ROUND DESK TO HIM)

Yes, you didn't find that scar in a parlour, I suppose? No... a bit nearer the battlefield I should imagine.

(AS THOMAS DRAWS CLOSE TO HIM)

I... I've seen a bit of that too, you know.

THOMAS

(STOPS, LOOKING AT HIM)

You? the battlefield?

BAGBY

Why yes, at Bull Run you know, I...

> Offstage sounds of violence increase, with breaking of glass as THOMAS slowly takes BAGBY's arms and speaks with the impulsive appeal of having found here a comrade in arms, an opponent only in battle's appearances since both fought the same thing, death.

THOMAS

You...? At Manassas?

BAGBY

(UNCERTAIN, DRAWING BACK)

Why yes, yes but I...

THOMAS

(ALMOST HUNGRILY)

You... my opposite in every way...

BAGBY

(CONCERNED, STEPPING FROM REACH, HASTENING TO EXPLAIN)

No, no, I was just there in the gallery, a spectator as you might say. Yes, this senator I spoke of? with a lady friend, all as a lark. But there, we'd no sooner got our picnic laid out on a spot that gave us a view than a soldier on horseback rides through it, smashing bottles every which way. Here, a bit of flying glass... I'm marked from it still, do you see?

(OFFERS HIS WRIST TO THOMAS, WHOSE LOOK TURNS TO ONE OF THOROUGH CONTEMPT AS HE TURNS ON HIS HEEL ROUND BEHIND THE DESK)

The whole army of the Potomac rode over that picnic cloth, every man jack. I lost a boot myself before we was safe back in Washington...

(AT A LOSS, UNABLE TO UNDERSTAND THOMAS' REACTION)

The lady was very put out...

They stare at one another as offstage sounds die into silence.

THOMAS

(WITH A STERN EFFORT, SEATED BEHIND THE DESK)

Listen to that! What's the meaning of it? I tell you, I will have order here! Obedience, yes, to authority, things as they should be, and that brought to an end.

BAGBY

(HELPLESSLY)

What, sir?

THOMAS

(VEHEMENTLY)

All that... outrage, that... chaos, do you hear?

BAGBY

(RETIRING UPSTAGE RIGHT, ALMOST PLAINTIVELY)

If we can't crack a skull here and there...

THOMAS

And Bagby!

(BAGBY STOPS)

This scar? For your information, this scar that you wondered about? It was an accident, it happened... a fall from a horse...

As BAGBY stands upstage right, facing THOMAS with a look of shrewd understanding taking place of bafflement in his face, sound of crashing glass offstage and a quick fade-out.

Toot! toot toot!

—Thank God.

—No sit down Christina, wait. That's only the first scene, I'm just calling Ilse for...

—Mister Crease? Where's the...

—Down that hall, past those boxes it's the second door on the right. Now. Was any of that familiar? Who's seen the movie.

—It was gross.

—I'm sure it was, Frank, that's not what I mean. Did any...

—I'm not Frank, I'm Jed. This is Frank.

—All right then, Jed. Or Frank, any of you, did anyone recognize, oh Ilse? Will you bring me a glass of that Pinot Grig...

—Ilse? I think he'd prefer a nice cup of tea.

And yes, there were certainly movie scenes in the offices looking out over the mines, the noise, the smoke, but this character Bagby, they remembered a minor character in the movie, kind of a straight man, a foil, short, fat, foul mouthed, —a kind of a Punchinello, Oscar, real opera buffa, Bagby in one or two crude dimensions maybe, a stock character, a comic device. But where had he come from? They just took Bagby and made him an Italian to cover their tracks, like changing Livingston to Siegal? —Look at it that way Oscar, they just claim parody, the worse this cartoon character of theirs is, the more they hold Bagby with all his posturings around up for ridicule the stronger their parody defense.

—All right but listen, what comes next. Listen to what comes next it's a specific scene, there are five or six characters they couldn't take it, they couldn't just take it and call it a parody...

> That evening, or one soon thereafter. A scrim curtain scene of a street corner, dark toward stage left. Some tattered evidence of a parade earlier that day, such as patriotic bunting, litters street, and torn recruiting posters deck the walls. The main illumination shed on the characters in this short scene comes from offstage right in flashes with the illusion of a fire with increasing steadiness and brilliance.
>
> As the scene opens all is still but for a sound from abovestage left, of a child crying, not loud or desperate but mounting from a whimper. THOMAS appears walking slowly from downstage right, head bowed, unaware of the figure awaiting him near stage center, a SOLDIER dressed in the worn blue uniform of the Union army and displaying a decided limp, played by the same person who plays WILLIAM in Act I but made up a good twenty years older so there may be no confusion that it is WILLIAM. He is barefoot, his shoes knotted by their laces over his slumped shoulder.

SOLDIER

(STANDING OUT IN THOMAS' PATH, HIS HAND ON THOMAS' ARM)

Sir...?

(AS THOMAS STARTS, STEPPING BACK IN ALARM, CONFRONTS HIM)

If you've a moment? You'll understand. You... you look like you've seen it yourself...

THOMAS

(RECOVERING, BRUSQUELY)

What's the meaning of this?

SOLDIER

(HANDING OVER PAPERS)

I'm not begging. Here, I'm an honourable man. I want nothing for nothing.

THOMAS

(BEWILDERED)

What's this?

SOLDIER

Four months' soldier's pay's what it is. It's yours for the price of three. With clothing benefits there at three fifty a month that's sixty six dollars all told for fifty, yours for fifty dollars gold.

(AS THOMAS STEPS BACK LOOKING AT HIM ALARMED, CONFUSED)

Or paper, then. Gold or paper then, damn it!

THOMAS

No, but... why mine? What do you mean?

SOLDIER

(BECOMING BELLIGERENT)

I mean you may cash it and I may never, that's what I mean! There's been no pay master, that's what I mean, and they told us it was over, that the whole damn bloody thing would be finished, and now I'm called back to my company. Can my children eat them papers? Can I leave them here without a penny and the chance I'll never come back at all? They're used to food and clothing, that's my mistake, and I'll leave them money before I go... if you'll... buy it?

THOMAS

(HORRIFIED, THRUSTING PAPERS AT HIM)

But... by heaven! You ask me to... would that be just? Do you think I could... buy your pay? What do I look like?

SOLDIER

(ANGRILY, GRABBING PAPERS FROM HIM)

Don't get high and mighty with me, by God! and... to tell me what's just! When I've seen your damned justice swallowed up in more suffering pain and fire... With a pound of grape shot in my leg, and does that make you the better man? What do you look like in your damn fine boots? Yes, I'd like to see you taking my place in the line now, going back in...!

(WITH HEAVY LIMP, STARTING TO THRUST THOMAS ASIDE)

Make way then, Christ! Make way!

THOMAS

(SEIZING HIS SHOULDER, FORCING COINS ON HIM)

Hear me out...

SOLDIER

(STANDS BACK, STARES AT COINS IN HIS HAND)

Twelve dollars?

(WITH SCATHING CONTEMPT)

You... funny fellow!

(FLINGS COINS DOWN)

Four months of a man's life, and war... you'd buy that for twelve dollars!

THOMAS

(KNEELING, SEARCHING FOR THE COINS, IN DESPERATE TONE OF APPEAL)

Wait! No, I don't want your pay... This, it's all I have with me, take it...

SOLDIER

(STOPS, EMBARRASSED, TAKES COINS SLOWLY AND REACHES FOR THOMAS' ARM TO HELP HIM UP)

I... your pardon, sir...

THOMAS

(REMAINING RIGIDLY ON ONE KNEE, COVERING EYES)

Take it and go!

(AS THE SOLDIER PERSISTS IN APOLOGETIC ATTENTIONS, THOMAS SHOUTS)

And go!

Withdrawing his hand, the SOLDIER stares a moment longer in consternation, then hurries offstage right. THOMAS remains rigidly kneeling, then draws a hand over his face and starts to rise as a cry and shout offstage left bring him slowly to his feet, still unaware that a YOUNG MAN has emerged from darkness left, running as though pursued, and now seeing him circles behind him and leaps upon him like an animal. Almost to his feet, THOMAS casts him off, and confronts him: the YOUNG MAN, in torn and soiled working clothes, is simply brute force incarnate.

YOUNG MAN

(BACKED UP AGAINST THE WALL)

You!

THOMAS

You know me?

(ADVANCING UPON HIM)

You know who I am?

(SEIZES THE YOUNG MAN BY SHOULDER MUSCLES, SHAKES HIM)

What's the meaning of this then? I demand it!

(FLINGS HIM BACK)

YOUNG MAN

(COWERING, DEFIANT)

There's none!

THOMAS

None!

(ADVANCING UPON HIM AGAIN)

I'll have it, do you hear? I'll have... order here!

As they confront one another sounds of laughter and broken song come from offstage right.

(SLOWLY SEIZING HIM AGAIN BY SHOULDERS)

If... you... think...

YOUNG MAN

(AS THOMAS' HOLD TIGHTENS)

I... was made...

THOMAS

(HOARSELY, HIS HOLD APPROACHING THE YOUNG MAN'S THROAT)

Made!

YOUNG MAN

(STRUGGLING TO HOLD THOMAS' HANDS AWAY)

...for something... better!

Laughter and sounds of revelry come closer offstage right as the YOUNG MAN, held down by THOMAS standing over him with his hands on his throat, stares up with fascinated horror but speaks with simple wonder, as a brilliant burst of flame offstage right illuminates them.

You would... kill me!

They stare, in flaring illumination, transfixed with one another, THOMAS' hold loosening until the YOUNG MAN, with sudden twist away, escapes him, takes wild step toward stage right, sees figures approaching and turns and flees across stage to exit left as BAGBY enters from right with two others: a flamboyantly dressed and mannered elderly man, white-maned, pompously absurd, THE SENATOR, and a stridently caricatured TART, both somewhat drunk, and played respectively by the persons who play THE MAJOR and GIULIELMA in Act I.

BAGBY

(HURRYING ONSTAGE OFFICIOUSLY)

Ah, it's you sir! I saw it, I saw it myself! and they'll get him, have no fear... yes...

(AS THOMAS STARES AT THEM WILDLY, DRAWING A HAND DOWN HIS FACE LIKE A MAN TRYING TO SHAKE OFF NIGHTMARE)

Yes, out having a time for yourself...! Here, you must meet my friend, my close associate the Senator, yes... and this lady...

(TURNING TO THE SENATOR, WITH HIGH-HANDED CORDIALITY)

I've spoke in the past of our new owner, yes... a gentleman...

(TURNING BACK TO THOMAS)
You're all right, sir? and... there, that tear in your pants? There by the pocket?

TART

(TAKING THOMAS' ARM, PUTTING A HAND UP TO HIS CHEEK)
Here, you're hurt dear... Here? on your cheek...?
(AS HE PULLS AWAY ABRUPTLY, COVERING THE SCAR WITH HIS HAND)
I'm sorry dear, there! I didn't do it!
(TURNING TO OTHERS)
It looked like it had just happened!

BAGBY

(EXPLAINING IN AN EMBARRASSED PAUSE)
The militia draft's what's turned their heads...

As THE SENATOR speaks, the SOLDIER reappears from stage right, to engage BAGBY in transaction.

THE SENATOR

An odious necessity, the militia draft. As odious to those who have volunteered their very lives in the noble, the enduring, the steadfast and the noble service of their country... as to those souls too craven...! too craven to give, to offer, the last full measure of devotion upon the field of battle! Who? who among us? would want such a man for his comrade in arms? To share the strife, the heartaches and the glorious pains of battle!

BAGBY

(ASIDE TO THOMAS)
The Senator is a very influential man, you know.
(RETURNS HIS ATTENTION TO THE SOLDIER).

THE SENATOR

Where union and strife face one another, across the terrible abyss of war! Where only union! the Union! can unite, and only strife put asunder...

TART

(PULLING THOMAS ASIDE)

Will you come with me, dear?

(AS HE PULLS FROM HER)

You're not going to run off...?

(MOCKINGLY, REACHING FOR HIM AGAIN)

You, the only man here?

BAGBY

(JOVIALLY UPSTAGING ALL, TO THE SOLDIER)

Yes, that's a fine way to wear shoes, or did no one ever tell you what they was for? Here, you wear them on your feet, so...

(EXTENDING A FOOT BEFORE THE SOLDIER)

SOLDIER

(SULLENLY)

You do when they're made of calf leather and don't rub you raw to the bone, don't be clever with me. What do you say now, six for five.

BAGBY

You have my offer.

THOMAS

(LOOKING ABOUT HIM)

Where are we?

TART

Norwegian Street, dear. Yes, the fire? That's Mister Bagby's home, where he's always entertained us so nice...

SOLDIER

(TO BAGBY, HOLDING OUT MONEY AND LOOKING AT IT)

Wait a minute, you said...

BAGBY

(TO SOLDIER)

Take it or leave it!

(POCKETING PAPERS AS THE SOLDIER WITHDRAWS, LIMPING PAST THEM TOWARD STAGE LEFT)

And be glad to have it while you're still alive...!

TART

(TO THOMAS)

They set it on fire as we finished dinner... but we can find another place, dear...

BAGBY

(FOLLOWING AS THOMAS STARTS OFFSTAGE RIGHT TOWARD THE FIRE)

I've just kept an eye on it now and again, sir...

THOMAS exits offstage right, BAGBY, the TART and THE SENATOR following in that order.

I suspected some trouble brewing tonight, and come down to defend it...

TART

(CALLING, TO THOMAS, FOLLOWING OFFSTAGE)

You're not running off, dear...? You coming back here to us at all...?

Alone on stage, the SOLDIER crosses limping slowly left, counting the money and stowing it inside coat as he reaches shadows. The sound of a child, crying as at opening of scene, brings his head up; he stops, and from darkness the YOUNG MAN leaps upon him and bears him to the ground where they struggle an instant, are still, and blackout, with the sound of the child's crying declining to a whimper.

—Now! Was that in it? that scene? Was there a scene like that in the movie? Jed? Any of you?

—Only I didn't quite get it Mister Crease, right at the end there where the...

—Didn't get what. It was a mugging wasn't it? Do you think muggings are a modern phenomenon?

—A what?

—A mod, a new invention, listen. All this crime, greed, corruption in the newspapers, you think they're just part of the times we're living in today? that our great Christian civilization is breaking down here right before our eyes? It's just the other way around. These petty swindles of Mister Bagby's outfitting the Union army, the only difference is all that was in the tens and hundreds of thousands and today it's in the millions and billions, false invoices, double billing, staggering cost overruns and these six hundred dollar toilet seats all wrapped up in the American flag? Pick up the papers and it looks like our defense industry's one gigantic fraud, that nothing gets built without bribes and payoffs, that Wall Street's nothing but a network of fraud?

—Oscar...

—It's not the breakdown of our civilization that we're watching but its blossoming, greed and political corruption it's what America was built on in those years after the Civil War where it all got a start, so it's not whether corruption's a sign of decay but whether it's built into things right from the beginning. All these cases Bagby's talking about were in the newspapers then just like ours today, that's where I got them. This soldier selling his pay slip for food for his family those things really happened and this brutalized young man who mugs him, they're both victims of this world of vast overpowering greed and corruption and industrial slavery that built this great country almost overnight that's the irony, that they're each other's prey isn't that clear? whoever said you didn't get it?

—No I just meant the child, at the end there where there's this child crying, so you mean it's supposed to be this soldier's child crying because it's hungry and...

—It's no one's! It's no one's child it's the whole world's, it's the cry of desolation and innocence and, and of sadness and loss for all humanity in these two men, that they're each other's victims that's the tragic irony, that's what makes drama if there's a scene like this in the movie they stole it didn't they? in this complaint?

—Right there in the charge of unjust enrichment Oscar, see but the problem is...

—How can there be a problem! If you can't call a mugging unjust enrichment right on the face of it I don't know what the language is for!

—See but you have to prove it, now where you're talking about something really happened, based on a true story, things you saw in these old newspapers you're putting it all right out there in the public domain again where anybody's got a right to...

—I just said that's what makes great drama didn't I? the dramatic expression of the idea that...

—Oscar what your lawyer's trying to tell you is it's not a question of great drama. There's no question of tragic irony, no question of greed and corruption that built this great country overnight or whether it's a great play or the movie's a ghastly movie. It's all simply whether somebody profited taking something from you even if it wasn't great drama, even if it was something stupid and fatuous that was yours in the first place, isn't that what this circus is all about?

—All right then! Just, if you'll just stop interrupting Christina that's what I'm talking about, you're just wasting time and you don't have to call it stupid and fatuous either. Just because something really happened doesn't mean I can't use it in a play does it? Didn't drafting men for the Union army and people hiring substitutes really happen? That's where Mister Kane from the first act shows up here in this scene where Bagby's looking for something in the morning mail.

THOMAS

(COMING DOWNSTAGE TO HIM, HANDING HIM A PAPER)
Possibly this? A wholesale order for trusses?

BAGBY

(TAKING IT)
Yes... a small commission. There's many wearing them now, with the draft boards springing up all about. A rupture has become quite the thing, you might say. And... was there... nothing else?

THOMAS

What you have in your hand behind you.

BAGBY

This? Yes, I picked it up from the floor where it had fallen.

THOMAS

It didn't fall. I threw it there.

BAGBY

(READING FROM IT)

Yes, to 'report to the county seat within five days...' Well, that journey won't take you long, for this here is the seat of Schuylkill County, you know.

THOMAS

(TAKING THE PAPER, CRUMPLING IT AGAIN)

And you expect to see me marching off to the draft office in one of your trusses? Do you think I take this seriously?

BAGBY

A bit of influence, and you might have...

THOMAS

Have you looked at the paper? It will be over in a matter of weeks, of days...

BAGBY

That's still time enough to find yourself court-martialed, and when you can buy your commutation for three hundred dollars...

THOMAS

And you want me to pay three hundred dollars for a week's peace of mind?

BAGBY

That's what Section 13 of the enrollment act is for, you know, to provide for the better class of people like ourselves. Of course this commutation is only good until the next draft, and the rate things are going that might be tomorrow. You'd do better to pay a bit more, wouldn't you, to buy a substitute to go up in your place. I can dig one up for five hundred dollars, and then let the war last as long as it likes. You can put it out of your mind.

(AS THOMAS SITS DOWN, LOOKING AT NEWSPAPERS, WAVES HIM AWAY)

Of course if it was me, you know, if I was financially situated like you are, there's the owner of the iron works here, you may know of him? He raised a regiment of cavalry for twenty thousand dollars and for that they made him a colonel. And where is he? Why, in Washington, showing his uniform, rubbing his elbows at the White House with high officials and senators, and nuzzling their wives when they turn their backs. And what will become of him? They'll nominate him a brigadier general and set him off somewhere to guard an empty barracks until things settle down, and you'll see him back here with 'General' printed on his visiting cards...

(RETIRING A STEP UPSTAGE)

Shall I dig a man up for you, then?

THOMAS

Dig up nobody. It's all nonsense.

BAGBY

Nonsense? And when you're court-martialed and shot for a deserter, will that be nonsense?

THOMAS

(ABRUPTLY, LOSING PATIENCE)

I've seen that, do you hear? That's... enough!

BAGBY

Seen... what, sir?

THOMAS

(GLANCING UP TOWARD UPSTAGE RIGHT)

Just tend your business, Bagby. A particularly unattractive bundle of it just arrived at your desk.

As THOMAS speaks, KANE has appeared at desk upstage right carrying a small case, and is heedlessly entering door as BAGBY hastens to intercept him.

BAGBY

(TO KANE)

Here, where are you going? You don't just march in and see him like he was a public monument. I'm the man you see here.

KANE

(STOPPING, AS THOMAS TURNS SLOWLY TO LOOK, CONFUSED)

You might be... Mister Bagby?

BAGBY

You got my name at the barber shop in Coal Street, did you? Let's see your teeth.

(KANE OBLIGES)

Not that you'll need them for eating. And you've got all your fingers and toes, have you? You'll do, if your breath don't knock them flat first. Go back to that barber shop, do you hear? Tell them I sent you. Mister Bagby, do you hear? They'll know what to do with you. Trim you up and get this thing off your face, why, they may find a boy of twenty hiding behind it! And then you come back here to me, do you hear? And I'll take you down and enroll you. Now get on!

THOMAS

(STANDING, SLOWLY)

Wait a minute!

BAGBY

(TURNING TO HIM, HOLDING KANE'S ARM)

You want him, sir?

(STANDING OFF, LOOKING KANE OVER AGAIN)

I'll be frank now, on second look, he don't look like he'll get far. They can't shave that belly off him in a hurry, and his breath would stop a train. I'll dig up better by sundown.

KANE

(ALMOST APOLOGETIC)

I'm sorry if I've misled you, sir. All I have to volunteer is my wares here. I'm a commercial traveler in tobaccos,

(COMING DOWNSTAGE TO DESK)

and I've a fine bright leaf that may interest you...

THOMAS

(COMING ROUND, PROFFERING A CHAIR BESIDE THE DESK)

Yes, sit down. You'll forgive Mister Bagby here. His enthusiasm to recruit, feed, worm, and outfit the entire Union army from head to toe sometimes gets the better of him.

(TO BAGBY, DRILY)

Though I hadn't realized you were recruiting.

BAGBY

I, sir? Yes, volunteering my services, you might say. Why, since Lee crossed the Potomac there hasn't been a moment's peace, and a man must come forward and lend a hand...

THOMAS

And you've been lending hands from the mines? Is that why the payroll is smaller every time I look at it?

BAGBY

And why not, with the mines closed down? If we've been ordered to suspend operations until the draft is ended, should we let the poor men go unemployed?

KANE

Yes, I understand Harpers Ferry has fallen, and General McClellan is marching out of Washington with every division he can pull together to meet them before they reach the Pennsylvania line here. I passed a fine set of lads drilling down near the river...

BAGBY

Them? Buckeyes, you mean? And do you think they're getting ready to fight Lee and Jackson? They're getting themselves ready to fight off the draft officers, that's what they're doing.

KANE

(HIS FACETIOUSNESS LOST UPON BAGBY)

Such an attitude must make your noble efforts quite difficult.

BAGBY

Ah, but it's not that I don't see their point, you know, now the word is out that it's no more than a war to free the naygers. Why, they've had high wages here in the mines. Do they want to go off and get killed fighting to free a lot of naygers that will come in and work for a penny a day? Why, the President himself said when it started that he had no power or intention of freeing the naygers, and now? Well, I've learned from a friend, he's a highly placed man down in Washington, that he's already written a proclamation freeing the naygers! Yes, he wrote it this summer, the President did, and he's read it off to his Cabinet there. Yes, preserve the Union! with four million naygers running around free? Why, the woods is full of them right now, and do you expect a nayger to go back into slavery once he's been as free to come and go as yourself?

KANE

(WITH SUDDEN ILL-CONCEALED INTEREST)

Reading such a thing to his Cabinet hasn't freed anyone.

BAGBY

And who should he read it to, you? He'd be a laughing stock if he read it out in public now, the way things are going. No, he must wait for a victory. Then people will listen and it will make sense. With a real victory behind it, he can give the slave states a choice of coming back into the Union or having their slaves freed right under their noses.

THOMAS

A victory? Winning a battle, what difference will that make. No, you'd better say winning the war!

KANE

(THOUGHTFULLY)

But even a battle... and a battleline advancing as a crusade... While the South is waiting for France and England to intervene, if only to free the cotton. And they might still in a rebellion, yes, in a civil war, but... a crusade against slavery?

BAGBY

Yes, and the victory is all the President lacks to make it so! There's nobody seen what war can be, that hasn't seen the next battle!

BAGBY exits importantly upstage right.

THOMAS

(LEVELLY)

You dislike me, don't you Kane. You showed it at Quantness when we met. What is it you want, then.

KANE

(TURNING, AGREEABLY)

Or perhaps it's just my unfortunate manner? Yes, my manner may be like your scar there, the expression it gives you? When I walked in, you looked outraged to see me, but... surely you were not?

THOMAS

And that cotton, what's happened to it? Was it ever shipped from Wilmington?

KANE

It was shipped. That's what I've come to tell you about...

THOMAS

And what's happened to it? There are obligations attached to it, and I've heard nothing. I had a special interest in that cotton, you know, an arrangement I made with the Major, and I've heard nothing. No remittance, nothing...

KANE

The shipment was impounded by the French government.

THOMAS

Im-pounded? but... I owe nothing, I left no debts...

KANE

A firm of French shipbuilders got out a lien against it. The ones who are building the battle ram Stonewall. The cotton was shipped from a Southern port, and they hadn't been paid...

THOMAS

A ram! But... by heaven! I'm being pressed for those profits now, the shareowners here... a ram! What the devil are they building a ram for!

KANE

To break the blockade...

THOMAS

The blockade! Why, damn the blockade, what does it matter now? With the army that's sweeping up here? Lee has probably invaded Pennsylvania itself while we sit here, he's right on our doorstep, and they're worried about a blockade? The whole thing will be over in a matter of days.

KANE

I seem to recall your saying that the last time we met.

THOMAS

(WITH DEFIANT ANNOYANCE)

Well, and... isn't it?

KANE

But not as it would have ended then, with a hundred thousand Union troops massed on Richmond.

THOMAS

Yes but... damn it, that's not the point now! Don't you see the shape things are in here? These militia drafts and the rest of this nonsense? They're terrified. The Southern armies will sweep through like hail in a cornfield.

KANE

(QUIETLY, EYEING THOMAS' BOOTS)

In boots like that, they might.

(AS THOMAS CLAPS HIS BOOT AND STANDS IN EXASPERATION)

You talk as if Lee's army were... a machine. You've seen it. Have you forgotten? Men and boys without shoes? Ragged, forced marches on one dry biscuit? Why... is there ever a... body left on the battlefield, to be buried in a whole pair of pants?

THOMAS

Do you think I don't still live it at night! ...When the battle is over, it's not the men. Do men look dead that you stumble over? No, they've seen nothing, the death that happened had nothing to do with them, or life. But the horses...!

(HE SHUDDERS)

The horses had seen it, it was still in their eyes, their heads flung up and their nostrils wide and their eyes... wide opened on it still... It's still there, on a field that just that morning was nothing more. Why, you might have lived there half your life or you might never have seen it before. Fields, fences, trees, a creek... has it ever made any difference before if the fence were here? or there were a ditch? if the corn was cut, or the trees had leaves? Until the morning the sun comes up and finds it a battlefield? Why? Here? Not a mile, or twenty miles away but here! And now everything takes on meaning, now none of it could have been any different. Not a tree or a stone to crouch behind, none of it could have been any different, if men are dying? hidden in the corn? lying in the ditch? If these were trees? and that were barren? Then who would have lived and who would have died? Who would have suffered and who... gone free... Because if each tree, because if each stone and rail of fence had no reason to be right where it was that day, that instant, then our pain and death had no more meaning than the stones...

KANE

But when you said that you'd... you'd fought death, and won...

THOMAS

And I did! When that whole sky wheeled and burst, the woods swept clean up the wagon road and the cornstalks glittering stalks unsheathed behind the rail fence, where the stupid face of that chapel stared down across that creek at the house with its windows blazing with the sun as though it were afire. That bay mare had dragged me over the stones with one rein twisted around my wrist, and I pulled myself up on the strength of her terror. And when I brought down her head and fired, her legs came up like a folding toy. She didn't stagger or fall, she went down square... doubled up running from what was happening... But if all of it... had no more meaning than this?

(PACING AWAY, AND BACK)

I don't even... know myself anymore. On that battlefield, when I suddenly knew that the man I saw coming up against me, my opposite in every way... that he was not my enemy, but death, that we were fighting together... And since then, now... it's like meeting myself down some dark street, waylaid round a corner and thrown to the pavement, and left to fight myself off! Is that why you mistrust me then! Just for being a hero, was it? Yes as my mother said, 'being a hero in war...'

KANE

I? But I mistrust it no more than you do yourself, as a boy's idea, seeing the threat come head-on, and you run or you meet it, that's cowardice or... 'soldierly fortitude.' But courage itself, it takes the courage of wisdom to stand trial when we never suspect it.

—Oscar, is...

—I said please, Christina! Please don't interrupt, what is it.

—Never mind then. It's just someone down on the lawn with a camera.

—With a, who! Who is it what are they doing!

—Oscar be careful, you'll tip over the whole...

—Well find out who it is! Taking pictures of, somebody spying out there they...

—Just calm down, my God. Who on earth would want to spy on us.

—That's exactly what I'd like to know. The way Kiester and these people sneak around there's such a thing as invasion of privacy isn't there? Can't that go in the complaint?

—If you haven't filed your complaint yet Oscar they don't even know who you are, so why should Kiester's people want to spy on you.

—I'm not talking to you Christina, will you just go and find out who that is out there? I'm talking to Mister Basie about this complaint.

—Thing is Oscar this is an action for infringement. You get privacy and things like that in there you just confuse things, run a good chance they throw the whole thing out, just stay right with your play there.

—All right then, what about the horses.

—What about the horses.

—The way he just described the horses on the battlefield, how death was still in their eyes, the horror, that was all in the movie wasn't it? the way that review described them in the movie?

—Describing them's one thing, show them right up there on the screen you can't prove they...

—You don't expect me to have horses crashing around dying on the stage do you? Because we have the battle, you'll see, it's at the end of the act but it's all effects, light and sound and the...

—You ever see Errol Flynn in The Charge of the Light Brigade Oscar? Don't know how many horses got killed making that movie, actually injured and killed so bad they got the laws changed, these Kiester people didn't need to steal from you. Just claim they went to see Errol Flynn in The Charge of the Light Brigade.

—Listen. I did not see Errol Flynn in The Charge of the Light Brigade, no. That's the point, that's exactly what I'm afraid of, people connecting my name with this mindless nonsense if they think I took my play from Errol Flynn in The Charge of the Light Brigade there goes my whole reputation and loss of income as a scholar and a, a playwright, now what about that. What about that.

—Why you'll ask compensatory and triple damages for mental and professional distress.

—Oh. Good. That's what I meant yes, good that's what I, what's she doing out there look, they're coming right up on the veranda who's that woman, Christina? One of you open the window there so I can, Christina! Will you stop him taking pictures? Who are they!

—Maybe we better just clear out Mister Crease.

—Sit down! All of you, just sit down we're not finished, these constant interruptions you lose the whole thread of...

—Just go ahead Oscar, it's only this real estate woman getting pictures of the place for their brochure.

—Well stop them! It's just an invitation, people who rob houses that's where they get their ideas get them out of here!

—They're not going to rob the house, they...

—Just get rid of them will you? They've already broken the dramatic tension this whole scene depends on the, where are we now...

As KANE stares up at THOMAS, whose expression turns to one of perplexity, BAGBY appears upstage right disheveled and hurries down to them.

BAGBY

Here, the guard took me out for a look at them, getting their heads punched up at shaft seven, and what do you think we found? They'd come to set it afire, if you can believe it, shouting about having their rights, yes, and who do you think we found! Sprung out of the ground, out of the pit itself, blind on destroying, fighting anything just to fight... And who do you think we caught up with? The boy that assaulted you that night, in Norwegian Street where your house was burned. The same night that soldier got himself murdered there, and they know this boy done it. They're bringing him here, as I instructed, the guards are bringing him here for you to identify.

THOMAS

For me? I saw no murder.

BAGBY

No, not for that, for the murder they cannot prove though we know that he done it. To identify him for assault, and you'll see! If he will go trying to make a fool of justice, not owning up to the murder, he may wish that he had!

The YOUNG MAN, haggard, unshorn and dirty, is flung onstage with a final effort by the GUARD and BAGBY.

(CIRCLING THE YOUNG MAN WARILY)
Here's your savage, sir. A fine specimen, an't he? One of nature's noblemen, you might say. Do you know him? There, you might not recognize him at a glance. He an't got any prettier, hiding away until he was hunted down to earth... here, guard! Stand by here!

BAGBY gets the GUARD between himself and the YOUNG MAN, who stands looking askance at THOMAS; and THOMAS in turn appears to avoid looking too closely at him.

(TO THOMAS)
An't he the one that done it, sir? That laid for you that night?
(TO KANE)
He was lucky I happened along, you know, or the boy here might have killed him, for that's what he meant to do...
(TO THE YOUNG MAN)
Wasn't it! Like you went on to kill that soldier boy? Speak up, you young ninny! Like you tried to kill your master here?

KANE

(UPSET)
What do you want him to say! That he tried to change what he was himself by trying to destroy his master?

BAGBY

(DISDAINING KANE, TO THOMAS)
Why don't you have a word with him, sir. You might know from his voice...

KANE

(IN EXASPERATION)

And what do you want them to say! You expect them to sit down and have a chat, do you? when all they share is the... terrible silence of slavery?

BAGBY

(TURNING LOFTILY ON KANE)

There, that's going too far now. Why, who brought the boy to the mines here but the boy himself? Yes...

(TO THOMAS)

Isn't that true enough, sir?

(TO KANE, MOTIONING TO THOMAS)

Yes, he's said it himself more than once, that they're here by their own consent...

THOMAS

(IMPATIENTLY)

Let's get all this straightened out quickly, do you hear? I'm leaving, I'm going abroad, to the Continent...

BAGBY

(TAKEN ABACK)

But when, sir?

THOMAS

I don't know, as soon as I can.

KANE

(STILL APPEARING RELUCTANT)

There's a ship from Philadelphia tomorrow night.

BAGBY

And you in the militia draft, with U.S. marshals watching every port...?

BAGBY, KANE and then even the GUARD fall back as THOMAS slowly approaches and confronts the YOUNG MAN, staring him full in the face.

THOMAS

(TO THE YOUNG MAN, AFTER PAUSE, AS THE YOUNG MAN STARES HIM BACK)

You... know me? Yes... your face that night in a flash of flame, in the street, that night of the fire. I know you... too well!

YOUNG MAN

(HALTINGLY, AS THOMAS SLOWLY PUTS A HAND TO HIS SHOULDER, LOOKING AT SCAR)

And I gave you that, did I? Well... good enough!

BAGBY

(HURRYING UP TO THEM)

Here now, be careful...

THOMAS

(GRIPPING THE YOUNG MAN'S SHOULDER, PUTTING FACE IN HIS)

Yes... you know me!

(AFTER AN INSTANT'S BINDING PAUSE, STEPS BACK ABRUPTLY ALMOST UPSETTING BAGBY, ON WHOM HE TURNS, CALMLY)

He's going up in my place.

BAGBY

(BEWILDERED, AS KANE STANDS APPALLED)

But... him? In your place in the draft, sir? Why... why...

THOMAS

If he's willing.

BAGBY

If he's willing! Why, why what has he got to be willing about?

(TURNING ON THE YOUNG MAN WITH THOROUGH CONTEMPT)

There! Are you willing?

YOUNG MAN

(STEADILY, TO THOMAS, WITH HINT OF SMILE, DRAWS HIMSELF UP)

I am willing.

BAGBY

(HURRYING TO TRY TO GET COMMAND OF THE SITUATION)

Yes, and why should you not be? If it's that or prison...

THOMAS

I said no such thing!

KANE

(APPROACHING THOMAS UNSTEADILY, LAYS A HAND ON HIS ARM)

What... you're doing...

BAGBY

(HAVING CALCULATED SHREWDLY AND SWIFTLY, TO THOMAS)

Yes of course sir, you'll want to do the right thing by him...

(HASTILY TAKING OUT A THICK WALLET, EXTRACTING A PACKET OF MONEY WHICH HE COUNTS QUICKLY AS HE SPEAKS AND HANDS IT TO THE YOUNG MAN)

And I happen to have the fee right on me, is six hundred dollars...

THOMAS

In gold! Get it from the safe now, do you hear?

BAGBY

(AGAIN SWIFTLY, SHREWDLY CALCULATING, WITHDRAWING UPSTAGE RIGHT)

As you say sir... in gold.

KANE

(STILL APPALLED)

Do you know... what you're doing?

THOMAS

(IMPATIENTLY, SHAKING HIM OFF)

I've told you! And... by heaven, what do you want! Now? for me to retreat? With the war, all of it, almost over? And still the chance to straighten things out...?

KANE

(IN DISTRACTED HORROR AND CONSTERNATION)

And you still think a battle will end it! Battles, battles, can't you see? They can be fought until not a soldier's left standing, and still no one will win? No, that's what soldiers are for, fighting battles and winning or losing them but... no, they are no longer war. War is attrition... not of armies, but of people, people, people...! Not wiping out soldiers in battle but... wiping out hope in the heart!

BAGBY

There!

(TURNING ON THE YOUNG MAN)

He an't much to look at, but you're not doing badly, you know, and times what they are... No family, no home, no history to him at all you might say, but he's good with mechanical things...

(OFFICIOUSLY APPROACHES THE YOUNG MAN)

Straighten up! You're not in the pits now!

THOMAS

(TO NEITHER OF THEM)

Nothing to fight for at all...?

BAGBY

And what would he want with something to fight for? with all he's got to fight against? Here now...

(TO THE YOUNG MAN)

Let's see your teeth... Not that you'll need them for chewing salt horse, but tearing your cartridges. You've got all your fingers and toes have you? and no rupture?

(STABBING THE YOUNG MAN WITH A STRAIGHT HAND IN THE GROIN, AND THE YOUNG MAN STARTS TO SURGE AT HIM, THEN RECOVERS WITH THE SAME HALF SMILE AS BAGBY STEPS BACK)

THOMAS

But... his eyes there...

BAGBY

It's nothing, it's something they all get down in the mines. You'll see some of them with their eyes rolling from side to side like a minstrel show. It's from lying on their sides and using the pick, in a narrow seam in the dark. Why, sometimes you'll see them come up from the pits and they'll bang around out here in the sunlight like we might in the dark, or blind...

(TO THE YOUNG MAN)

You watch your eyes when you're examined, or there won't be a penny.

(TAKING UP A SACK FROM THE DESK, TURNING TO THOMAS)

And you'll want to give him something for expenses now and again, tobacco and the like... two dollars a week say. If you sign the order, I'll see to it myself...

(HANDS THE SACK TO THE YOUNG MAN)

Here, and you don't get nothing free, you know. Transportation, clothes, you can pay me and I'll see you're outfitted.

(TAKING A PAPER FROM HIS INSIDE POCKET, DROPS A CARD WHICH THOMAS PICKS UP AND LOOKS AT)

Coat, six dollars seventy one cents. Over coat, seven twenty. Hat, two eighteen. Pants, three oh three. Shoes, one ninety six. Drawers, fifty cents. Leather collar, eighteen...

THOMAS

(HOLDING UP A CARD, TO BAGBY)

Where did you get this?

BAGBY

(STARTLED, RECOVERS QUICKLY)

Ah... that night. You dropped it. I'd meant to give it back, for it's pretty enough. It looks enough like a hotel. Hand painted? Or is it that farm, with the quaint name, what is it? that plantation...?

THOMAS and BAGBY stare at each other a moment longer as THOMAS pockets the picture and BAGBY turns upstage right to the GUARD.

That's all now, is it? Unless you'd like to give the boy here your blessing?

As BAGBY speaks THOMAS has approached the YOUNG MAN and they two seize one another in a kind of equal stand-off.

THOMAS

(MUTTERING)

Yes by heaven...! You will!

BAGBY

(AS THEY BREAK APART)

Here!

(TO THE GUARD)

Take him for his examination and then lock him in the courthouse overnight.

(TO THOMAS)

There's a train for Harrisburg in the morning loaded with bacon and cordwood and two hundred fine recruits, twenty Chippy-wa Indians that's never seen a suit of clothes and fifty more that can't speak English, every one of them a substitute. There, for the Union forever...!

The YOUNG MAN shakes off the GUARD's hand and marches off upstage right before him.

A fine thing at the last here, wasn't it, for him to attack you...

THOMAS

No he didn't...

BAGBY

No? And what did he say then, to your blessing?

THOMAS

He said... he was made, for something... better...

BAGBY

Did he now...! And perhaps he shall have it...

THOMAS

(STANDING OVER THE DESK, AFTER PAUSE)

He... stole my tobacco case.

BAGBY

But what can you expect...

THOMAS

(WITH SUDDENLY VICIOUS DEFIANCE)

Are you any better?

BAGBY

(AFTER PAUSE OF SIZING THOMAS UP)

Let me tell you, sir... I and this boy here, and you? It's been you, you the master? And you say war is history, but no. No, the difference between us, you see, is that I, I and that boy there, we can improve ourselves... we can while you cannot and that... that, I call history.

Scene fades slowly as BAGBY faces THOMAS, upstaging him, to darkness and silence which, after a moment, is broken by the distant sound of cannon.

—It's charming Oscar, what it's got to do with the movie I can't imagine but...

—Charming! Is that all you, charming? I'm not asking you to shout bravo Christina but the least you can...

—Well of course you are, I mean isn't that all any writer really wants? everyone jumping up shouting bravo? I thought we'd have chops for dinner, I want to get down before the stores close. Will that suit you Mister Basie? lamb chops?

—Can't stay, sounds real great but I'm on my way, get on the highway before the rush.

—No but wait! Listen there's another scene, there's the whole last act you can't all go. There's the whole last act, we haven't even talked about the...

—I heard a phone ring.

—Got enough going to run up your complaint Oscar, any problems I'll call you.

—Shall I answer it Mister Crease?

—Oh and before you go Mister Basie, one more thing? if we can come back to the real world for a moment? A friend of mine who's going in for an abortion, the father's got a court order to stop her and...

—That's not his field Christina! We're not talking about some indecent...

—Oscar don't be ridiculous, I'm just asking the...

—Well he's, he hasn't got time to get into all that, you seem to forget who's paying his bill, he's...

—Mister Crease? You got a collect call from Disney World.

—My God.

—Plenty of copies here now Oscar I'll just take one along, get things off the ground. Better get that phone.

—That reminds me yes, that two hundred dollars Oscar?

—No but wait, hello? Yes I will. Hello?

—Two twenty one sixty to be exact.

—But what about the funeral, why are you still down there...

—Mister Basie? We can go out this way.

—No wait! Wait what do you mean, Disney World was right on the way...

—You can get a court order for most anything Mrs Lutz, she goes ahead with this abortion she'll get a citation for contempt but it's a real grey area, get these foetal rights going it could turn into anything, turn into a landmark like Roe v. Wade.

—How much? What do you mean you drove all the way down there!

—Thanks Mister Crease we better go, that was fun.

Fun? And they were gone. Clattering up the hall, the glass doors banging, car engines, the blurt of a horn, fun? He got the phone back in its cradle, paused laid back there as though listening to the silence, as though observing that word, literally observing its semblance dissipate and vanish, and then abruptly he got both feet off to the floor and stood, his teeth gritted, holding to the back of the chair before he took a step, and another, and enough of them to get him across the room to the table there and back clutching a sheaf of pages rolled like a stave, like a staff, like a weapon, falling open in his hand as he let himself down, squaring his glasses, muttering it again as though spitting it out, —fun!

Pyrotechnic lights rise over stage with reeling effect and fade gradually as smoke clears to reveal the body of one SOLDIER draped over an inclined cannon barrel and three or four figures flung still at downstage left. Battle sounds drop, lights die, pause of stillness as stars appear and the stage is suffused in violet darkness.

BAGBY appears from stage right, looking vaguely about, shaking his head and pausing, popping a jawbreaker into his mouth philosophically.

BAGBY

There now... you wouldn't think...

(AMBLING TOWARD STAGE CENTER, LOOKING ABOUT)

Them that would make such fine sense of things...

(KICKING A STONE OVER)

To find meanings in stones...

(DIGGING AT THE DIRT WITH HIS TOE)

And this earth here soaked with the blood of twenty thousand men that will fight no more? In a battle that was no more than that, a battle, where one side lost because it did not win, and the other won only because it did not lose...

As he speaks BAGBY is drawn with a sort of dread curiosity toward figures lying still at stage left.

There, it's ended and left you behind here? with the kisses of death upon you all, why, the way you cling... one to another...

(GINGERLY ADVANCING A FOOT TO PRY TWO FIGURES APART)

you might have been comrades in arms here, fighting together against... haaah!

(DRAWING BACK WITH SHOCK AS THE FIGURE TURNS OVER FACE UP)

Smashed, like a bird with a broken wing, running...

(VISIBLY SHAKEN, STARTS TO KNEEL)

Yes... your dancing days are done...

(PUTS A HAND TO THE BODY BEFORE HIM)

You wasn't taken a prisoner, there's that... And you've still your fine teeth but set in a look... of such outrage! what is it!

Would you try to hold all this suffering world in the beauty of your own agony? Let me tell you then! It don't end!

(WITH A BRIEF SHUDDER HE STRAIGHTENS AWAY, HOLDING A CASE LIFTED FROM THE FIGURE)

Yess... So he freed you then, did he? Once he'd gave you his blessing? and brought you right up to himself? You was made for something better, was that it? And he freed you to be what you are now? Ahhh! must a man be scourged then, and racked, have his eyes burnt out and then be set up on a pole, to know that he should wish, not to be just... but to seem it? Yes, and the unjust man, an't he above that? Above living for opinion? Him, he don't wish to seem unjust, no... but to be it! Yes, and then he may hold public office because he is thought to be just, he may marry wherever he likes, and be partners with whoever he chooses, and still make a profit...! now and again, for he don't mind being unjust, only seeming it! There, and won't he grow rich, then? and be able to help a friend and hurt enemies, and serve gods and men better than any...!

(STANDING OFF, EMBRACING IT ALL)

Yes now, this much... and no more! Up to this point yes but... beyond it...? No! By... by heaven...! there are limits!

(WITHDRAWING TOWARD RIGHT, LOOKING OFFSTAGE LEFT)

Because... this is how it must be!

A shot is fired, with shout of warning, from offstage left.

A burial detail, is it? And they'd take me for... a looter?

(POCKETING THE CASE, PAUSES AT STAGE RIGHT)

Let them look up in the sky then...! if they must be so blind, that cannot see the truth in broad daylight, but must have the whole world in darkness to see the conceit of the stars...

Stillness as BAGBY exits hastily, right, a star glitters beyond silhouetted scene, then another, as the curtain falls.

COMPLAINT Filed with US District Court, S.D. New York, September 30, 1990, naming the Parties,

1) Oscar L CREASE, Plaintiff, v.
2) EREBUS ENTERTAINMENT, Inc., Ben B F Leva, Constantine Kiester a/k/a Jonathan Livingston (Siegal) and others, Defendants

Allegations Applicable to All Causes of Action:

3) That on or about July 1, 1977, plaintiff submitted a copy of a script of an original play dealing with certain fictitious characters and events in the American Civil War titled 'Once at Antietam' suited to stage production or television adaptation to the defendant Constantine Kiester, who was at that time employed as a television producer in New York under the name Jonathan Livingston, and
4) that shortly thereafter plaintiff's play was returned to him with a note from the said defendant citing reasons said defendant found the play unsuitable for television production wherewith plaintiff withdrew it from further circulation, and
5) that some thirteen years later the motion picture 'The Blood in the Red White and Blue' made and exhibited by and at the behest of the defendants individually and severally and in concert with others and bearing resemblances of such substantial similarity to plaintiff's play as to have been appropriated directly therefrom in utter disregard of his rights therein

As and For a FIRST CAUSE OF ACTION:

6) Plaintiff repeats, reiterates and realleges all of the allegations of this complaint contained in paragraphs (1-5) inclusive as if fully set forth herein at length,
7) that on or about July 1, 1977, plaintiff submitted a script for an original play titled 'Once at Antietam' dealing with certain fictitious characters and events in the American Civil War suited to stage production or television adaptation to the defendant Constantine Kiester at that time employed as a television producer in New York under the name Jonathan Livingston
8) and that shortly thereafter plaintiff's play was returned to him with a note from the said defendant citing reasons said defendant found the play unsuited to television production wherewith plaintiff withdrew it from further circulation
9) and that some thirteen years later the motion picture 'The Blood in the Red White and Blue' made and exhibited by and at the behest of defendants individually and severally and in concert with others

bearing resemblances of such substantial similarity to plaintiff's play as to have been appropriated directly therefrom in utter disregard for his rights therein as a result of which infringement plaintiff has sustained general damages in an amount to be determined.

As and For a SECOND CAUSE OF ACTION:

10) Plaintiff repeats, reiterates and realleges all of the allegations of this complaint contained in paragraphs (1-5) inclusive as if fully set forth herein at length, as a result of which fraudulent conduct on the part of defendants conspiring together and with persons unnamed plaintiff is entitled to special damages in an amount to be determined.

As and For a THIRD CAUSE OF ACTION:

Plaintiff repeats, reiterates and realleges all of the allegations of this complaint contained in paragraphs (1-5) inclusive as if fully set forth herein at length, wherein the fraudulent conduct on the part of defendants individually and severally conspiring together and with persons unnamed was willful, wanton, malicious and in utter disregard of the rights of the plaintiff causing him mental and professional distress entitling him to compensatory and treble or punitive damages in an amount to be determined.

As and for a FOURTH CAUSE OF ACTION:

Plaintiff repeats, reiterates and realleges all of the allegations of this complaint contained in paragraphs (1-5) inclusive as if fully set forth herein at length whereto, being of unassailable good character and heretofore good health he has been subjected to extreme mental and physical distress as a result of which he is entitled to a constructive trust benefit on all profits and gross revenues from 'The Blood in the Red White and Blue' up to and including the effective date of an injunction halting its exhibition unless and until he is credited on a separate card in letters no smaller than those accorded the film's producer and director and of no shorter duration on the screen with his originative role in its creation, an accounting, interest, costs, and reasonable attorney's fees.

—Is this all? Where's the rest of it. Where's my grandfather.

—Get to those details later Oscar, all we want now's a complaint they can't claim is defective on its face when they cite grounds for dismissal and you lose before you begin.

—Well it all just sounds muddy and repetitious. If you can explain it as we go along maybe I can help you cut down some of these tedious lines where you keep repeating yourself and save some money.

—Look, what you've got here is this judge sitting there reviewing this complaint and their answer under Rule 12 of the Federal Rules of Civil Procedure looking for grounds for dismissal where they try to claim it's legally insufficient, like it doesn't state a cause of action for a claim where relief can be granted, or they say it fails to allege an essential element of the claim or it alleges some element defectively here where there's these different kinds of damages you're asking for, see you're alleging general damages, compensatory damages, special damages, punitive damages, you comply with these procedural necessities for each one or you're out on your ass.

—Oh. All right but listen, that last part there I certainly don't want to be credited with creating this revolting spectacle, isn't that one of the things we're suing them for in the first place? Byron did it didn't he? Lord Byron, did you know that? A bad poem going around with his name on it and he sued them, took them to court and cut them right down, connecting my name with this mindless trash like Errol Flynn in The Charge of the...

—Would have made a great movie now wouldn't it, Errol Flynn playing Lord Byron don't worry about it, they're not just about to put your name up there in lights, see we're just putting them on notice here under Section 502 where once we start this action we get an injunction pulling it out of the theatres all over the country, impound their prints, masters, negatives any time while the action is pending, you see where they sold thirty one million dollars in tickets over the weekend? over a hundred million now in just the first ten days?

—A hundred million dollars!

ANSWER TO COMPLAINT

Defendant named herein as KIESTER for his answer to Complaint herein alleges as follows:

1) Denies the allegations contained in paragraphs (1-5) according to knowledge and information sufficient to form a belief.
2) Denies the allegations contained in...

—Herein, herein, the same repetitious hereins what comes next.

FIRST AFFIRMATIVE DEFENSE
Plaintiff has been guilty of such laches as to bar any recovery herein...

—We settled that right at the start didn't we? that we wouldn't let them get us on this laches business Harry warned me about when you talked about holding back and letting their profits pile up so we could...

—Not quite how I remember it Oscar, but...

—Yes well it doesn't really matter, I'm just trying to keep the record straight but when do we stop wasting time with this name calling and go to court, stop wasting time and money passing papers back and forth and do something.

—Going through the motions, that's where you get that phrase just going through the motions, next thing they'll want a bill of particulars to get the facts established and make a motion for summary judgment under Rule 56, trying to keep you out of court Oscar not get you in it.

PLEASE TAKE NOTICE that the undersigned hereby demand that you serve upon them within twenty days particulars of the Complaint herein as follows:

1) With respect to the allegations contained in paragraph (3-5) of the Complaint, state separately with regard to each alleged negotiation:
   a. the date and place;
   b. the name and address of each person, other than plaintiff and defendant, who was present or participated in the negotiations;
   c. the substance of statements made by each participant in the negotiations;
   d. whether the negotiations were evidenced in whole or in part by written documents, and, if so, annex a true and complete copy of each such document...

—They're steaming right along here Oscar, you find that rejection letter yet?

—Not, no I...

—What I'm trying to tell you, see that can be crucial, the judge sees that letter and it proves they had access, makes it a fact they can't argue with. See what they're doing here is they moved to dismiss our complaint under Rule 12 but they stuck some other documents in there where if this judge has to go look beyond the pleadings at these other affidavits their motion to dismiss gets converted automatically into a motion for summary judgment under Rule 56 where the court reaches a decision without going to trial once there's no more questions of facts for some jury to dick around with, get these cleared up in an Amended Bill of Particulars and your depositions and...

—And it's all just more words and more words until everything gets buried under words, you said...

—Said you wanted me to explain every step as we went along didn't you? hoped you could find a few short cuts where you could maybe save some money?

—Yes but now it's probably beginning to cost more to explain it than anything I could save when these words all begin to sound the same and cancel each other out, that's what I...

—Get to these depositions Oscar, you haven't seen anything yet. What I tried to tell you right from the start. Words, words, words, that's what it's all about.

PLEASE TAKE NOTICE, that pursuant to Article 31 of the Civil Practice Law and Rules, defendant KIESTER named herein will examine plaintiff Oscar L CREASE as the adverse party, by taking his deposition upon oral questions at 8295 Sunset Boulevard, Los Angeles, California 90046, before a notary public of the State of California or before some other person authorized to administer oaths, in compliance with Rule 3113(a) of the Civil Practice Law and Rules.

The aforesaid party is to be examined regarding all evidence material and necessary in the prosecution or defense of the above captioned action and is required to produce the following items or copies thereof:

All books, papers, writings, letters, written communications and records of oral or written communications, including, but not limited to, bank records, contracts, diaries, recordings, log books, call slips, memoranda, drafts, and worksheets, and other documents or things which pertain to all such evidence...

—California? When you can't even walk across the room? Have you tried?

—Tried what.

—Walking across the room she said, doing so herself just then to lower a blind where pale sun streaked the chair she'd been sitting in shuffling papers, —worksheets, drafts and other documents, old concert programs? Just ship those boxes in the hall out to California the way they are, old Playbills? menus? invitations? they don't know what they're in for, what about those family letters that doddering historical society is wheezing over down there? and that rejection letter, had he found that? —I mean it's Exhibit A isn't it?

In the first place he wasn't going to California he told her, in the second place no, he hadn't found the letter but Basie said they could try putting in a sworn affidavit, see if they could get it admitted in evidence, as for that damned historical society no action for infringement can be started until the copyright claim is registered and if the Copyright Office turns it down Basie can start an action by serving a notice on the Register of Copyrights with a copy of the complaint, it was our family's correspondence wasn't it? letters between that uncle with the coal mines in Pennsylvania and Grandfather's mother and father, when they went to France in that diplomatic post where he died —and that's all I know except the rights, there's no question about the rights descending directly to me through Father on this per stirpes basis where the...

—Oscar please. Don't explain it. Obviously you can't go to California so the whole thing...

—I thought Harry must have told you. They've just retained his firm, they've retained Swyne & Dour where Basie said they've put some snooty Hindu on it and I thought maybe I'd ask Harry to sort of get him aside and...

—Don't you dare ask Harry to get anyone aside, my God. He got you a lawyer, isn't that what you wanted?

—Look Christina, here's Harry with this blue ribbon law firm and I ask him to help me and end up with Mister Basie, meanwhile who ends up with the blue ribbon law firm?

—You asked him for a Jewish law firm Oscar, I was standing right here I heard you.

—And what's Mister Basie then, one of the lost tribes? That's why I'm not going to go to California, because they're coming out here to take this deposition, do you think I'd ever collect a penny for all this pain and suffering if anybody saw me up running around the room? Five hundred dollars, that's what they offered me Christina, the insurance company said they'd settle for five hundred dollars and pay these terrible hospital bills now they're trying to get my claims dismissed completely by pleading immunity under these No Fault statutes and if they saw me up running around the room they'd...

—They'd think you were exercising your common law rights, wasn't that what you wanted? It's not your constitutional rights this socalled lawyer is asserting, can't you see? He's asserting his own right to exploit your misery for every dollar he can, it's not his pain and suffering is it? his brilliant lecturing career that's in jeopardy? Is he going to pay your hospital bills when you lose? doctor bills? lab bills? this therapist? By the time you get into a courtroom that scar will look like you fell off your tricycle when you were five, think about it, when you start getting bills from Mister Basie sitting here with his clock running and these people taking your deposition, who's paying for all that?

—It's right there in the complaint, it's even stated right there in the copyright law, we're not just suing for damages you put in reasonable attorney fees too, that's part of the...

—If attorneys' fees were reasonable do you think Harry would be driving around in a car like ours? If they offer to settle for enough to get you out of the hole you're digging yourself into he thinks you should take it, just forget this fifty million dollars damages you're dreaming about.

—I don't know where you got fifty million dollars, we haven't even...

—The story in the paper.

—I haven't seen the paper. It's in the kitchen drying out, Ilse has to walk all the way out to the end of the driveway to get it and after a rain like last night, who told them fifty million dollars?

—I assume it's your friend Mister Basie, he couldn't let you sound like a piker could he? with this other ghoul suing them for twenty?

—What do you mean this other ghoul, who.

—Whatever his name is, he's suing over that revolting sledgehammer scene in Uburubu or whatever it is. He claims your friend Kiester commissioned him to go over there and set the whole thing up, paid all his expenses and promised him some earth shaking fee. It's obviously a better story than someone suing over an old play, your suit was just tacked on.

—Well what did it say Christina. About me, what did it say about me?

—Simply that, Oscar. That you're suing them, that your father's the judge in the Cyclone Seven mess and a little headline, CYCLONE SEVEN SEEKS NEW HOME. I'll get the phone.

—Well wait, wait if it's...

—If it's collect from Disney World she's probably seen your name in the paper with that fifty million dollar pricetag. Shall I just tell her the check is in the mail? And then, —hello? Oh, it's you... Yes... Yes I can take care of it tomorrow, it's not... Well it's really not that important Harry, don't worry about it... No, everything's fine, he's right here working himself into a state over this deposition they're coming for... Coming here yes, they've retained your firm, did you know? He says Basie tells him they've put some snotty Hindu on it and he hoped you might get him aside and... Well of course, he knows that... I'll tell him... Yes I'll tell him that... I hope so yes, as soon as you can... God, I do too... and she hung it up. —That was Harry.

—What did he...

—He said to tell you to relax about your deposition, just remember to tell the truth and don't volunteer. This Hindu is probably just their third world payback for being handed a token black. Just tell Oscar to tell the truth and don't volunteer.

—What, answers? I don't know what he thinks I...

—It's that fifty million dollars, Oscar. They're beginning to take you seriously.

APPEARANCES:
Messrs. LEPIDUS, HOLTZ, BLOMEFELD, MACY & SHEA
Attorneys for plaintiff
12 West 43d Street
New York, N.Y. 10036
BY: HAROLD BASIE, ESQ.,
Of Counsel

Messrs. SWYNE & DOUR
Attorneys for defendants
450 Park Avenue
New York, N.Y. 10022
BY: JAWAHARLAL MADHAR PAI, ESQ.
J. VENNER SMITH, ESQ.
Of Counsel

O S C A R L. C R E A S E, plaintiff, called as a witness by defendants, being duly sworn testified as follows:

MR. BASIE: Before we start, but on the record, I should like notice to be taken of Mr. Crease's physical condition confining him to a wheelchair in an almost prone position thus preventing the free expression of his feelings under the stress occasioned by this procedure in the hope of seeing it conducted as expeditiously as possible.

MR. MADHAR PAI: May I remind counsel for the record that it is plaintiff himself who in bringing this action has already seriously inconvenienced others to the degree of journeying some distance to his residence to examine him in taking this deposition at his convenience, and if he now feels suddenly reluctant to confront the possible rigours of a legal procedure which he himself has...

MR. BASIE: I only ask that his condition be taken into account in hopes that the procedure will not be unduly prolonged.

MR.MADHAR PAI: I assure you that we have no such intention consistent, of course, with a thorough airing of the situation for which he alone is responsible in bringing suit on the...

MR.BASIE: Excuse me. To call him solely responsible for creating the situation in which we find ourselves is a gross misstatement of the circumstances and I cannot let it pass unchallenged.

MR.MADHAR PAI: Are you quite finished Mr. Basie?

MR.BASIE: For the moment.

MR.MADHAR PAI: May I make clear at the outset that I do not like to be interrupted, and this is the second time it has happened in as many minutes. If you have an objection please make it for the record.

MR.BASIE: I am making it for the record.

MR.MADHAR PAI: What is your objection?

MR.BASIE: What makes you say I wasn't making it for the record?

MR.MADHAR PAI: I thought you were making a statement. What is the basis for your objection?

MR.BASIE: I am starting to state my objection.

MR.MADHAR PAI: And what is your objection? If you have an objection, object. You want to make statements and testify.

MR.BASIE: I have only made comments on your statement.

MR.MADHAR PAI: I am trying to go smoothly ahead so that this session will not be unduly prolonged.

MR.BASIE: Are you asking me to give up the plaintiff's rights?

MR.MADHAR PAI: We're not here to fight over the Fifth Amendment old sport, we are trying to conduct a nice quiet deposition. As soon as you feel there's something that might get us a little nearer the truth of the matter, we seem to...

MR.BASIE: I don't agree with that.

MR.MADHAR PAI: I withdraw it.

MR.BASIE: Thank you.

MR.MADHAR PAI: Now may I proceed to examine the witness?

MR.BASIE: He is clearly at your disposal.

EXAMINATION BY MR.MADHAR PAI:

Q Will you please first state your name and the occupation from which you derive the bulk of your income.

A Oscar...

MR.BASIE: I must direct him not to answer the question as it has been put.

MR.MADHAR PAI: If you have an objection will you please...

MR.BASIE: It's an objection as to form. There are two questions.

MR.MADHAR PAI: To which question are you referring.

MR.BASIE: The question that has just been asked.

MR.MADHAR PAI: But you say there are two questions, and I'm asking which one you are referring to.

MR.BASIE: And I am directing your attention to the question that has just been asked.

MR.MADHAR PAI: Let me understand you. You are objecting as to form.

MR.BASIE: I am objecting as to form regarding the overall question which comprises two questions, and I am objecting to the second of these two as being improper.

MR. MADHAR PAI: I'm afraid you are confusing the record by entering a second objection before your first one has been resolved. Please read back the question.

(Record read.)

MR. MADHAR PAI: Now perhaps your first objection will be met by restricting the question to a simple statement of the witness's name, Mr. Basie? Will that please you?

MR. BASIE: Delighted.

Q Will you please state your name.

A Oscar L. Crease.

MR. MADHAR PAI: Now I believe your second objection had to do with impropriety?

MR. BASIE: It carried the misleading implication that the witness might have a job on which he is dependent for his livelihood.

MR. MADHAR PAI: You would not want it thought that he must work for a living, is that what you object to?

MR. BASIE: That is not the question.

MR. MADHAR PAI: Then what is the question. Do you think we can move this along?

MR. BASIE: Are you asking me to deprive my client of the protection of the facts?

MR. MADHAR PAI: If you have an objection, please make it for the record.

MR. BASIE: I want the record to show that I have every clear intention of making it for the record. It is to a simple question of fact, and I want the questions to be proper. The question as stated is loaded.

MR. MADHAR PAI: In implying that, like most of mankind, he must work for a living?

MR. BASIE: Now come on Jerry, I'm

not going to be drawn into a discussion of Adam's curse here. The question as it stands makes the statement that his occupation provides the bulk of his income.

MR.MADHAR PAI: And you object to that as to form?

MR.BASIE: I object to it as improper and irrelevant at this time.

MR.MADHAR PAI: All right, we can pursue its relevance later if it appears to be material. Let's restate the question.

Q If you are presently employed will you please state your position, and how long you have held it.

A I have been a lecturer in American history at the community college at Lotusville for twelve years.

Q And before that?

A Before that?

Q The position you held before that.

A I pursued my own interests.

Q In your present position have you what might be called a specialty? If so will you please name it?

A The period of the American Civil War.

Q And was that among the interests you pursued before becoming a lecturer at the college here?

A It was.

Q Do you have tenure in your present position?

A I do not.

Q And this is your sole profession?

A I'd simply call it a job, you could say it's really nearer a hobby.

Q But you have no other profession. You're not a playwright for example, a professional playwright?

A I'm not clear what you mean by professional.

Q I think it is generally understood to mean someone who is paid for his services.

A A baseball player.

Q Professional sports yes, that's a good example.

MR. BASIE: You mean as opposed to amateur sports?

MR. MADHAR PAI: I am asking the questions Mr. Basie. If you have an objection please make it for the record.

MR. BASIE: I am making it for the record.

MR. MADHAR PAI: Well? What is your objection, is it as to form?

MR. BASIE: It is as to form, it was not a question but a leading observation and I want a proper question where the meaning is clear, whether you mean professional sports as opposed to amateur sports.

MR. MADHAR PAI: I think that is an assumption the witness is capable of making, that he can make that distinction.

MR. BASIE: Then it's incorrect, the witness is being led. If we mean distinction we should say distinction, if you mean professional sports as distinguished from amateur sports, that's one thing. If you mean as opposed to that's something else.

MR. MADHAR PAI: If you want to turn this whole thing into a tautological exercise, be my guest.

MR. BASIE: I want the questions to be proper and I will continue to object when I find them otherwise. Opposing professional to amateur invites an invidious comparison to the ordinary observer.

MR. MADHAR PAI: Are you implying that there is something pejorative in the use of the word amateur?

MR. BASIE: In this context that's exactly what I'm saying.

MR. MADHAR PAI: And that forms the basis for your objection?

MR. BASIE: Exactly. May I ask you...

MR. MADHAR PAI: I'm not here to be questioned.

MR. BASIE: I would just like your question cleared up.

MR. MADHAR PAI: It's a new question, Mr. Basie.

MR. BASIE: That was the other question. I said I object to this one too.

MR. MADHAR PAI: You are still having trouble with the word amateur.

MR. BASIE: I want to have it clearly defined. Without all the baggage.

MR. MADHAR PAI: In the sense of a dilettante, is that what you object to? Superficial, elitist...

MR. BASIE: Where it's not done just for payment.

MR. MADHAR PAI: Fine. We can proceed.

Q Since you do not derive your income from playwriting, would it be fair to describe you as an amateur playwright?

A If that is your characterization, I...

Q I want to clarify something with respect to...

MR. BASIE: I have to object. To question the witness and not allow him to respond, to finish his answer, that's entirely unprofessional.

MR. MADHAR PAI: I withdraw it. Since his answer was not responsive I'm just trying to move things along here and...

MR. BASIE: I want the record to show my objection to this flagrant abuse of the witness.

MR. MADHAR PAI: I withdrew it, Mr. Basie. Now in the interests of moving this along without unduly...

MR. BASIE: You withdrew it by calling his answer unresponsive when you hadn't allowed him to finish it, how do you know whether it would have been responsive or not.

MR. MADHAR PAI: Maybe we should adjourn this and do it elsewhere.

MR. BASIE: Why.

MR. MADHAR PAI: Because that way we could proceed without these constant interruptions, or at least under the supervision of a Federal magistrate. There's a contentious element creeping in here that I don't want to interrupt the sworn testimony of the plaintiff.

MR. BASIE: I think the record will be perfectly clear where the plaintiff's sworn testimony is being interrupted in an entirely unprofessional manner that I'm entitled to object to and I do object.

MR. MADHAR PAI: All right.

MR. BASIE: I don't mind if you ask questions on this subject matter. I am merely...

MR. MADHAR PAI: I am gratified.

MR. BASIE: I am merely asking that you make these questions in the proper form.

MR. MADHAR PAI: Fine. We can proceed.

(Document marked Defendants' Exhibit 1 for identification as of this date.)

Q The play on which plaintiff brings this action for infringement is titled Once at Antietam. Is this your own title, or is it meant to somehow conjure up something?

MR. BASIE: The witness does not need to answer that or even comment since the title's not protected by copyright in any case.

MR.MADHAR PAI: Are you objecting?

MR.BASIE: I want the record to show I am objecting on a matter of substantive law here.

MR.MADHAR PAI: I am not questioning the copyright one way or the other. I think the question will stand. Read it back.

(Record read.)

A In a way possibly, yes. It echoes a line in Othello.

Q For the record, you are referring to the play Othello by William Shakespeare?

A The Tragedy of Othello, the Moor of Venice, by William Shakespeare, yes.

Q Will you identify the line?

A In his death scene at the end, yes. 'And say besides, that in Aleppo once, where a malignant and a turban'd Turk Beat a Venetian and traduc'd the state, I took by the throat the circumcised dog, and smote him thus.' And he stabs himself.

Q And the title Once at Antietam is intended to evoke reverberations of that dramatic moment at Aleppo seized upon by Shakespeare in his memorable poetic rendition?

A Well it, yes.

Q To evoke these reverberations in a wide audience, would you say? Or a potentially wide audience?

A To anyone who's read Shakespeare.

Q Would you characterize that as a general audience? Or a rather narrow one?

A As the theatre going audience.

Q As a relatively narrow audience then, a traditionally elite audience? In other words you wouldn't have expected a mass audience to make this Shakespeare connection?

A Well, you made it didn't you?

Q I ask the questions. I am asking the questions and I want to move this along. As an amateur playwright, is that a fair assumption?

MR.BASIE: Excuse me, but I can't let the witness answer that. We're not making assumptions here.

MR.MADHAR PAI: Are you making an objection?

MR.BASIE: I am entitled to object to the form of questions, as you know, and I object as to form, yes. To any question based on an assumption, whatever it is that's being assumed.

MR.MADHAR PAI: I am assuming that one would not expect a mass audience to make an esoteric connection with a phrase from Shakespeare.

MR.BASIE: That's not the question that was asked.

MR.MADHAR PAI: My patience is wearing quite thin, Mr. Basie. I did not state that that was the question, I was repeating the assumption that formed the basis for your objection.

MR.BASIE: My objection is based on your assumption characterizing the witness as an amateur. It's disparaging and I direct him not to answer.

MR.MADHAR PAI: I thought we had cleared that up. Read it back, please.

(Record read.)

Q If we've defined services that are done for pay as those of a professional, can we distinguish those done without pay as the efforts of the amateur?

A Broadly speaking, but...

MR.MADHAR PAI: You have an objection, Mr. Basie?

MR.BASIE: The form is improper,

the form of the question employing the phrase 'the efforts of the amateur,' the word 'efforts.' It's disparaging.

MR. MADHAR PAI: It's a perfectly good English word.

MR. BASIE: In this context, the way it's used here it implies failure, just reeks of it. You've got your professional there being paid for these services where the amateur's efforts aren't making him a dime. It's pejorative on two counts.

MR. MADHAR PAI: You seem bent on turning this procedure into some sort of Chinese water torture. Can we move on?

MR. BASIE: I thought we'd cleared all this up. This word amateur starts out to mean doing something for the love of it, that's the root, doing it for its own sake without a price on it. Now these days where there's a price on everything, what's not worth getting paid for's not worth doing. You say something's amateurish means it's a real halfassed job. You want the best you hire a professional. A real pro, as they say.

MR. MADHAR PAI: So that accusing someone of unprofessional conduct is pretty damning.

MR. BASIE: Where you have money setting the standard for performance it's the worst.

MR. MADHAR PAI: Thank you.

MR. BASIE: See here's where you run into trouble with the arts. You want an example?

MR. MADHAR PAI: No.

MR. BASIE: You take van Gogh, the painter Vincent van Gogh? A painting of his brought over fifty million dollars a few years ago but in his whole lifetime he only sold one picture, that make him an amateur? Some hobby he had, turning out these halfassed pictures on Sunday afternoons? You get into this you're getting into apples and oranges.

MR.MADHAR PAI: Mr. Basie please! Are you objecting? Is it as to form? If you are will you state your objection for the record, if you can remember it? I'm sure none of us else can. You expressed the wish when we commenced of conducting this examination as expeditiously as possible and I am doing my best to accommodate you for all our sakes but you are wearing my patience extremely thin confusing the issue with your remarks about apples and oranges which I think you'll find, incidentally, to have been featured in the still lifes painted by Cézanne, not van Gogh, who favored sunflowers. Now if we may be allowed to move along, I wish to direct the witness's attention to plaintiff's Exhibit Number 11.

(Document marked Defendants' Exhibit 11 for identification as of this date.)

Q Your attention is directed to Defendants' Exhibit 11. Will you read it, please.

A Yes. I, Oscar L...

Q To yourself.

A I've read it.

Q And you can identify it for the record of your own knowledge and belief as your sworn affidavit describing a letter of rejection addressed to you and purportedly written and signed by the defendant named therein as Jonathan Livingston, whose professional interest you had solicited on behalf of and as sole author and proprietor of a play titled Once at Antietam, these events taking place on or around the dates indicated therein?

A Yes.

Q Dates which occurred quite a long time ago?

A Depending on how, on what you call a long time ago.

Q I would call a decade, well over a decade in fact, long enough for routine incidents of no particular interest when they took place to have fallen through the cracks of memory, as it were? Now would it be fair to say, sir, that a man beginning such a career working as both producer and director of a highly successful dramatic television series might, in the routine course of a busy day, be expected to receive numerous unsolicited proposals in the form of concepts, treatments, or scripts from aspiring playwrights in the high hopes that under his artistic and professional supervision their ambitions for their works will be realized and suitably rewarded?

A Yes.

Q Rewarded financially?

A Yes.

Q That in fact this hunger for financial reward might in many cases be the driving force behind the creation of the work in the first place?

A In too many cases, yes.

Q But not your own?

A As the driving force behind its creation no, no that's not why I wrote it.

Q But as the driving force behind its submission.

MR. BASIE: Again, you've made a statement. That was not a question.

MR. MADHAR PAI: Please don't interrupt the answer.

MR. BASIE: I object to the form of the question.

MR. MADHAR PAI: Mr. Basie, that is grotesquely improper. I am not a man of temper but that is just plain unprofessional. I wish you wouldn't do it.

MR. BASIE: I am entitled to object to the form of the question.

MR. MADHAR PAI: You may object if you will, but don't interrupt the answer. I am trying to go ahead smoothly here so that we may get to the heart of the matter before we break.

MR. BASIE: Break?

THE WITNESS: Break, on thy cold grey stones, O...

MR. MADHAR PAI: May I ask you to restrain the witness, Harold?

MR. BASIE: I don't understand your request.

MR. MADHAR PAI: I think it is obvious that he is not responding to the question. Would you read the question back.

Q Mr. Crease, if you understand it when it is read back, I would like your answer. If you feel that you cannot answer will you simply say, I cannot answer. I'd like to move this along before we break for lunch.

A I cannot answer.

Q Thank you. We were speaking of the public taste. Now in the case of television, of the television audience, this would embrace a very wide public would it not?

A Yes it would, yes.

Q One whose level of refinement, sensitivity, intelligence, attention span has often been described in terms of the lowest common denominator?

A The great unwashed, yes. Sweep on, you fat and greasy citizens!

MR. MADHAR PAI: Mr. Basie, you have no objection to that response remaining in the record?

MR. BASIE: No objection.

MR. MADHAR PAI: And the witness of course is aware that he is under oath.

Q And it was, in effect, according to your sworn complaint, to this forum that you submitted your work titled Once at Antietam?

A Yes.

Q Had you or have you since made numerous other such submissions of your work, other plays for example?

A No.

Q Have you sold any such work or works in this market?

A None, no.

Q And because of the money involved, may we infer that it is a highly competitive environment?

A I would think so, yes.

Q Still you had what we might call the audacity to try to enter this unsavoury environment with one lone, pristine product of your own unique vision, like the painting which brought fifty million dollars by the artist who was unable to sell his work during his lifetime.

A For the irises, yes.

Q For what?

A Fifty three point nine million, it was a painting of irises.

Q May I direct you to answer the question.

MR.BASIE: I have to direct him not to answer.

MR.MADHAR PAI: Are you objecting, Mr. Basie?

MR.BASIE: It was not a question. It was a statement. He was simply trying to set the record straight.

MR.MADHAR PAI: He is not here to set the record straight. He is here to be examined.

MR.BASIE: He is under oath.

MR.MADHAR PAI: That is the nature of this proceeding, and it does not oblige him to talk about irises. Will you read it back, please.

(Record is read.)

Q Will you tell me if you agree.

A It seems a little far fetched, but...

Q Will you answer my question?

A Yes.

Q Fine. Now let's go ahead if there's no objection.

MR. BASIE: I want something clarified here.

MR. MADHAR PAI: What is it now, Harold. Are you objecting?

MR. BASIE: The witness was asked whether he would answer the question. His answer was yes. I want it to be clear whether he meant yes, he would answer the question but had not yet done so, or whether counsel is abusing his privilege in assuming that the witness's response expressed his agreement with counsel's statement.

MR. MADHAR PAI: Read it back.

(Record read.)

Q Would you agree to that? You may answer simply yes or no.

A Well I, for the sake of the argument, yes.

Q Good. I believe we're making some headway. Now since you appear to like to associate yourself with Shakespeare, might not this dramatic work of yours in its lonely search for an audience have perhaps been better suited to the mercies of the rather more narrow, elitist theatre going public which we agreed his plays call forth?

A No.

Q Do you understand the question?

A We did not agree on this narrow, elitist notion. He was a very popular playwright.

Q I take it you mean in his own time?

A That's when he wrote his plays, isn't it? For

the whole general public, he played to the stalls and to the pits.

Q He made his living at it then, didn't he?

A Well he owned shares in his acting company too so he got a percentage of the profits and he was in real estate too, I think he even lent out money at exorbitant rates if you just read the Merchant of...

Q But we could certainly call him a professional playwright, couldn't we?

A Of course. He acted in some of them too.

Q Yes. And when you say the pits, you are characterizing this television fare that's addressed to the lowest common denominator, what's envisioned when we say, it's the pits? The great unwashed, in your own pungent phrase?

A The pit was the cheap section of the theatre behind the stalls at the front of the orchestra, yes. Yes it probably got pretty rank on a warm evening with the orange peels thrown in.

Q I'm sure. Now this broad audience, they were all fairly familiar with the material of the plays, the plots and stories, were they not?

A Yes, generally speaking.

Q How so? Can you be more specific?

A Well, Shakespeare took his material from familiar sources, contemporary fictions like the romance Rosalynde where he got As You Like It, All's Well That Ends Well from Boccaccio's Decameron, things like that.

Q All right. And the later historical plays, he raided Holinshed's Chronicles of England, Scotland and Ireland pretty freely didn't he, for Richard III and the Scottish history in Macbeth, even for King Lear? And Plutarch, he lifted Antony and Cleopatra and Julius Caesar right out of Plutarch didn't he?

A I wouldn't say lifted, he...

Q Took? That he simply took them? And no one

took exception to this practice that you know of, did they?

A Not that I, no.

Q In other words, these ideas, characters, twice told tales, odd quirks of history, it was all just there for the taking, wasn't it?

A All right.

Q Whether you were Shakespeare or Joe Blow, you could turn any of it into a play if you wanted to, couldn't you?

A Well not the, if Joe Blow could write a play?

Q Do you mean it would depend on the execution of the idea?

A Well, yes. Yes of course.

Q Not the idea, but the way it was expressed by the playwright? Isn't that what makes Shakespeare's King Lear tower above Joe Blow's King Lear?

A Obviously.

Q They are separate things, then?

A What, Joe Blow's King...

Q I mean the idea and the expression of the idea, they are separate things aren't they?

A Well, in the sense that...

Q I think we've been over the ground. Will you please simply answer the question? Read it back please.

(Question is read.)

A Yes.

Q Now may I ask you, as a lecturer in American history with particular expertise in the Civil War, would you say that during that conflict the hiring of a substitute to go up and fight in one's place constituted anything extraordinary?

A Well of course, in the South of course a planter who owned more than forty slaves was automatically exemp...

Q Mr. Crease, we are not here today to discuss that peculiar institution. My question was a simple one and I would like you to answer it. Read it back please.

(Record read.)

A No.

Q It was, in fact, a not uncommon practice on both sides of the conflict for those who could afford it, was it not?

A It, yes.

Q There was no real opprobrium attached, was there?

A Not, no but...

Q And the idea, the idea that a man of split allegiances might find himself in a situation obliging him to send up a substitute in his place in each of the opposing armies, while it was hardly an everyday occurrence, was certainly within the realm of possibility wasn't it?

A Yes, it...

Q And that the two might even meet in battle?

A Yes, yes that's...

Q In fact there was at least one such documented instance, was there not?

A That's what my...

Q Where both were, in fact, slain? In other words, a sort of quirk of history, the kind Shakespeare drew on freely when he needed a plot or a character? He could have pointed to Holinshed and advertised King Lear as based on a true story couldn't he?

A If he, I suppose so, yes.

Q So that in this action you're not claiming protection for an idea. What you claim has been infringed here then is not the idea which occurred to you over a period of time.

MR.BASIE: You have not been asked a question. That was a statement.

MR.MADHAR PAI: Please do not interrupt the answer.

MR.BASIE: It was not a question.

MR. MADHAR PAI: I believe it was a question. You object as to form?

MR. BASIE: I'm objecting to the form of the question, yes. It was not a question.

MR. MADHAR PAI: You may object if you want to, but please do not interrupt the answer.

MR. BASIE: Would you read it back, please?

MR. MADHAR PAI: I'd like to clear up this point before we break for lunch.

Read it back.

(Question read.)

Q Again, you don't claim protection for that idea do you?

A I claim protection for the idea too yes, if the...

Q You do?

A ...if the idea is copied in a vulgar, demeaning way.

Q The way it is expressed, is that what you mean? Can we separate the idea from its expression, sir? Do we understand each other?

A Yes, yes we understand each other. When the idea is used in the context of the expression, combined with the expression, then the idea becomes part of the abuse I'm referring to.

Q You don't claim any proprietary interest in the Civil War, do you?

A No, no, no.

Q In the battle at Antietam, any more than Shakespeare could lay a claim to the siege of Aleppo?

A No.

MR. MADHAR PAI: Let me take a moment to speak to Mr. Smith? Please note for the record that counsel are conferring.

(Counsel confer.)

MR.BASIE: Is it on the record that you took time out?

MR.MADHAR PAI: The difference is that I am not under oath.

MR.BASIE: I didn't say there was a difference. I said is it on the record that you took time out.

MR.MADHAR PAI: Yes.

MR.BASIE: I would like the record to show that there was no pending question.

MR.MADHAR PAI: We will continue the examination when we reconvene at one o'clock.

AFTERNOON SESSION

1:50 p.m.

O S C A R L. C R E A S E, resumed the stand and testified further as follows:

MR.BASIE: Before we start, but on the record, I want to say on behalf of Mr. Crease that he expects that this session will be more courteous and more civilized than the last one.

MR.MADHAR PAI: That's entirely up to you, Harold.

MR.BASIE: That's not Mr. Crease's feeling.

MR.MADHAR PAI: I understand that, old sport.

MR.BASIE: Quite often, when I was out of it, I recall that he was not being treated with courtesy.

MR.MADHAR PAI: He felt that he was not treated with courtesy?

MR.BASIE: Yes.

EXAMINATION (cont'd) BY MR.MADHAR PAI

Q Is that right, sir?

A Yes.

Q I'm sorry you felt that way.

We are dealing with the subjective here, and I imagine it is possible that people form different views of things, but I view you with consummate respect, and in doing my job, if you found me abrasive or discourteous, I would appreciate it if you would chalk that up to a misconception of the way I feel, both about you and about my work, which I take altogether seriously. I might note, in evidence of my good faith here, my acquiescence in delaying this afternoon session to accommodate the nap which your condition dictates and which commands my complete sympathy.

Let's proceed. You are still under oath. Fair enough?

A All right.

Q I am concerned about something. If I understood you, Mr. Crease, I want to clarify something with respect to the idea which led to Defendants' Exhibit 1 and its expression, which is Defendants' Exhibit 1, and I ask you again, are you claiming protection for an idea, an idea as separate from that work?

A I thought I'd explained that.

Q I understood a conflict in your answers, that you gave two. That at first you said it was not an original idea...

A I gave a clear answer. The idea executed is the idea expressed, transformed into a play, in other words it's definitely bound to the execution. So there are two things there to talk about. One is the idea and the other is the execution of the idea which is the work, the work we're talking about, the play. When the idea is tied with the execution, then they are both unique and separable as such and defendable.

Q The idea apart from the work is not protectable and is not claimed as protectable by your...

A Anybody can say, 'Here's a man who hired two substitutes in the Civil War on both sides and

they were both killed in the same battle.'
Anybody can say that's an idea.

Q I respectfully submit that is not what is expressed in Defendants' Exhibit 1, that what is expressed in Defendants' Exhibit 1 as testified by you is a far more egocentric notion than a mere battlefield, that it is heavily laden with symbolic overtones of death and suicide of a moral nature.

MR. BASIE: I must direct you not to respond. You have not been asked a question.

MR. MADHAR PAI: You object as to form?

MR. BASIE: Would you read it, please.

MR. MADHAR PAI: We are going to be a lot more businesslike this afternoon because I am not going to have this again.

Read it back.

(Question read.)

Q Do you agree or not agree?

MR. BASIE: Off the record.

MR. MADHAR PAI: Nothing off the record.

Q Do you agree or disagree with that?

A I have to, I'm sorry, I wasn't listening. You will have to read it again.

MR. MADHAR: Read it back.

THE WITNESS: I thought you wanted it read for your own benefit.

(Question read.)

Q Do you agree or disagree with that?

MR. BASIE: I'm sorry, but...

MR. MADHAR PAI: Do you have an objection?

MR. BASIE: Yes.

MR. MADHAR PAI: What is your objection?

MR.BASIE: It was a statement. There are a number of statements.

MR.MADHAR PAI: Do you have an objection?

MR.BASIE: Yes.

MR.MADHAR PAI: What is the objection?

MR.BASIE: The objection is that you have made a number of statements...

MR.MADHAR PAI: Is it as to form?

MR.BASIE: Yes.

MR.MADHAR PAI: Then let the witness answer.

THE WITNESS: I repeat. There are two things here. One is the idea and the other one is the execution of the idea.

Q Yes.

A Before I wrote the play, when I thought about the idea I had in mind, I could say here's the story of a man who sends up substitutes to fight in his place on both sides in the Civil War, both of them are killed at Antietam and he survives haunted by a sort of sense of self betrayal, that he's been slain by his own hand on the field of battle. That's an idea, anyone can repeat it.

Q Not an original idea, in the sense that someone made it up, created it so to speak, would you agree?

A All right.

Q So that anyone putting it to use would be taking only what the law allows wouldn't they, wherever they'd found it? In terms of general themes, motives or ideas, they'd be free to go ahead and express it artistically?

A I suppose they could do it their own way if that's all there was to it, but when I do it my own way that idea is substantial and connected with the execution.

Q So that the execution can be protected?

A And the idea related to the execution. They cannot be divorced because they...

Q Then tell me what the idea is that you expressed in Defendants' Exhibit 1 or Defendants' Exhibit 6?

A The idea that, what's Defendants' Exhibit 6?

(Document marked Defendants' Exhibit 6 for identification as of this date.)

Q Let me direct your attention now to Act I, scene i, page 3. Will you read it, please?

A Yes I, here. 'His Mother. Is that the place, on your cheek, where you were wounded?'

Q To yourself, please.

A I've read it.

Q And on the next page, she goes on to say, 'You're thinner and tired, too, now I can see. You might have lost an eye.' It's in the prologue to your play, the play titled Once at Antietam that's the subject of this action, is it not?

A Yes.

Q Now let me read this, and ask you whether it sounds familiar. '(Touching the bandage on his head, tenderly) Your head! Does it pain dreadfully? You poor darling, how you must have suffered! (She kisses him).' Do you recognize that?

A No.

Q Well let me try this. '(He wears a bandage on his head high up on his forehead) God, how I've dreamed of coming home! I thought it would never end, that we'd go on murdering and being murdered until no one was left alive! Home at last!' Is that familiar?

A I think it might be the...

Q I want you to be certain. Let me ask you to turn to the same scene page 8, at the bottom.

A Where his mother asks, 'Is that the same uniform you went off in?'

Q And she goes on, yes. 'I remember when it was

new, before you went off, you'd lay a handkerchief over your knee when you crossed your leg up that way, with your soiled boot...

A Yes, that's...

Q I haven't finished. I want to read you this now and ask if you recognize it. 'Oh, I know what you're thinking! I used to be such a nice gentlemanly cuss, didn't I? And now, well, you wanted me to be a hero in blue, so you better be resigned! Murdering doesn't improve one's manners.' Are those lines familiar to you?

A It probably has to be that dreary thing of O'Neill's.

Q For the record, can you identify it a little more closely?

A A play by Eugene O'Neill called Mourning Becomes Electra, I hope you don't think I...

Q Thank you. It's a trilogy really, isn't it. The Civil War is just ended and the character Orin returns home, wounded. His father, General Mannon, comments 'I've made a man of him. He did one of the bravest things I've seen in the war. He was wounded in the head... a close shave, but it turned out only a scratch.' Now here in the second scene we have the Major, in Once at Antietam, speaking of his son in law. 'The battle we fought them up at Ball's Bluff? Thomas distinguished himself up there, in a company under my command. He's made us proud to have him in the family here.' Do you see any similarity between these passages?

MR.BASIE: Excuse me.

MR.MADHAR PAI: Are you objecting?

MR.BASIE: I have a question.

MR.MADHAR PAI: I am asking the questions. Are you objecting?

MR.BASIE: I think you've made your point, but what is it?

MR. MADHAR PAI: We spoke of unprofessional conduct, sir, and I must say you exceed all bounds. I am conducting this examination and will make my points when I am ready, without your interference.

MR. BASIE: I'm just trying to help you move things along.

MR. MADHAR PAI: You can help best by refraining from these rude interruptions. They are counterproductive and I wish you wouldn't do it. Read it back, please.

(Record is read.)

A In a superficial way possibly, yes.

Q All right. The General, Orin's father in the O'Neill work, describes Orin's exploit crossing enemy lines, meeting and killing a Reb, and the same thing happening as he returns. Orin then describes it. 'It was like murdering the same man twice. I had a queer feeling that war meant murdering the same man over and over, and that in the end I would discover the man was myself!'

A But that's...

Q I have not finished. Will you direct your attention to the second act, scene iii of the play Once at Antietam on page 17, the line beginning 'On that battlefield...'?

A On that battlefield, yes?

Q And tell me if you see a similarity between the O'Neill passage and what follows? Let me read it. '...when I suddenly knew that the man I saw coming up against me, my opposite in every way... that he was not my enemy, but death, that we were fighting together... it's like meeting myself down some dark street... and left to fight myself off!' I repeat, do you find a resemblance?

A As I said, on a superficial level.

Q And in both cases we're talking about the execution aren't we? about the expression of the idea?

A About the play, yes.

Q But not the idea?

A Both. About both.

Q And what about the characters, are they an expression of the idea?

A In a manner of speaking I suppose, insofar as there's a...

Q It's a very simple question. I would like a direct answer.

Read it back, please.

(Question is read.)

A Well they, yes.

Q Take the Major, how do you describe him in your play.'The Major, a man in his sixties, is turned out to a fault in military uniform which lends authority to his patronizing manner... his forthright lack of imagination or sympathy for all he does not understand, and his distress at anything that threatens to disturb established order.' All right? Now here's O'Neill's General Mannon, who's also a judge if you remember. 'His movements are exact and wooden and he has a mannerism of standing and sitting in stiff posed attitudes that suggest the statues of military heroes.' Do they sound similar, seeing them up there on the stage?

A Yes.

Q Or on the screen?

A I suppose.

Q And as expressions of the idea, they cannot be divorced from it?

A I don't understand.

Q What is it that you claim not to understand?

A That this isn't an infringement action between my play and O'Neill's, is it? I mean are you saying that I took my material, that I took my characters from that sham thing of his?

Q Are you saying that you did not?

A Certainly not!

Q But you have agreed that there are certain similarities?

A I can't help that.

Q In other words, you agree that similarities can occur without copying?

A Up to a point.

Q Up to what point?

A Well. Appearances, certain appearances, coincidences, facts, historical facts but depending how they're arranged, how they're expressed.

Q And that expression is what is protected by law?

A Yes.

Q In a play, would you say that this expression you speak of resides largely in the dialogue?

A Yes. Yes that and the arrangement of it, of the characters.

Q That the dialogue does not just advance the action of the play, but in large measure actually defines the characters?

A Yes, yes you can see that in the passages you just compared, can't you? I mean you wouldn't see me writing 'Does it pain dreadfully? You poor darling, how you must have suffered!'

Q They don't correspond at all, do they?

A With my play? No.

Q Let me then direct your attention to the second scene in your first act, if I may. Page 30, the dialogue between the Major and a character named Kane. Will you read it, please?

A Starting with the Major? 'I'll grant you, even a reasonable man, he won't bear old age easily in poverty, but the unreasonable man he wouldn't be at peace even if he was rich.'

Q And then they talk about money, don't they, that the ones who care little about it are the ones who haven't earned it, but those who have take it seriously, and Kane asks what's the greatest good his wealth has brought him, do you follow that? And then?

A Yes, he goes on, 'When a man faces the thought he has to die, he begins to see fears and anxieties that haven't troubled him before. You think of the tales we hear of the next world, how justice is going to be done to those that have done wrong here. We've laughed at them before but now they begin to rack your soul. What if they're true!'

Q Now will you listen to this and tell me if you find some similarity? 'And to those who are not rich and are impatient of old age... to the good poor man old age cannot be a light burden, nor can a bad rich man ever have peace with himself.

'May I ask, Cephalus, whether your fortune was for the most part inherited or acquired by you?·

'Acquired! In the art of making money I have been midway between my father and grandfather' he goes on, they talk about money, and then the greatest blessing he has reaped from his wealth, and he responds as follows. 'For let me tell you, Socrates, that when a man thinks himself to be near death, fears and cares enter into his mind which he never had before; the tales of a world below and the punishment which is exacted there of deeds done here were once a laughing matter, but now he is tormented with the thought that they may be true...' Now. Do you find a similarity between those passages?

A Well of course, I...

Q I haven't finished. Here is another passage. They are discussing justice, and suddenly this character Thrasymachus breaks in. 'What folly, Socrates, has taken possession of you all? And why, sillybillies, do you knock under to one another? I say that if you really want to know what justice is, you should not only ask but answer... for there is many a one who can ask and cannot answer.' And so forth, to the response '...don't be hard upon us. Polemarchus and I may have been guilty of a little mistake in the argument, but I can assure you... If we were seeking for a piece of gold, you would not imagine that we were ''knocking under to one another...'' And why, when we are seeking for justice, a thing more precious than many pieces of gold...' they go on discussing the problem, giving evasive answers, till Thrasymachus loses patience. 'Listen, then, he said; I proclaim that justice is nothing more than the interest of the stronger. And now why do you not praise me? But of course you won't.' Do you recognize that passage?

A Of course I do.

Q Now here is your protagonist Thomas, page 39 of the second scene, arguing with the character Kane. 'This is rubbish! The two of you bowing and scraping to each other like a pair of fools. If you really want to know what justice is, Kane, don't just ask questions and trip him up every time he answers. You know it's easier to ask than to answer. You answer now, and tell me what you think justice is...' Kane responds. 'Don't be angry with us. If we've made mistakes we couldn't help it. Why, if we were looking for gold we wouldn't waste time bowing and scraping to each other, and we're looking for something worth much more...' until Thomas loses patience. 'All right then, listen. I say that justice is nothing but the advantage of the stronger. There. Why don't you clap for that?' You recall writing this passage, don't you?

A Of course.

Q And do you see a striking similarity between it and the one just before it?

A Of course.

Q Let me briefly review one more so that no doubts remain. Your character Kane again. 'The Bible certainly can't mean to give everything back on demand to someone who's out of his senses, a man whose shotgun you've borrowed, to give it back to him when he's out of his head. Still, it's owed to him, isn't it. So, the repayment of a debt is justice, but this case is not included?' Now if I may ask you to compare this, 'Concerning justice, what is it...? Suppose that a friend when in his right mind has deposited arms with me and he asks for them when he is not in his right mind, ought I to give them back to him?' And so forth, now again. Do you find a striking similarity here?

A Of course.

Q Can you identify the source of the passages I have cited in comparing your work?

A Of course.

Q Will you please do so for the record?

A The first book of the Republic, obviously.

Q Can you be more specific?

A Book One of Plato's Republic.

Q You say from, from the work by Plato. Do you mean lifted from? taken from?

A Paraphrased.

Q Do you mean the idea, or its expression?

A Both.

Q Now the principal idea set forth in the first book of Plato's Republic is the attempt to define justice, is it not?

A Yes, it...

Q It's simply there isn't it, the way you might find Richard III in Holinshed, or Caesar in Plutarch, all just there for the taking?

Q No but those are historical figures, this is an idea.

A Fine. And when Thrasymachus says, 'I proclaim that justice is nothing more than the interest of the stronger' he is simply expressing an idea, is he not?

A His own interpretation, yes.

Q Exactly. He's quite a cynic, isn't he.

A No. No he's a Sophist, quite a different school. The Cynics were...

Q Sophist of course, I stand corrected. A school as you say, they charged fees for their teaching and Thrasymachus now wants to be paid for discussing justice doesn't he? And when Socrates pleads he has no money and his friends, Glaucon and the rest of them, offer to pay his part he's posing as a poor student isn't he? But he's really turning the tables, compelling the teacher to explain what he means with his clever questions it's what's loosely referred to as the Socratic method isn't it, he is really the teacher who is just posing as the amateur, the dilettante as though all this is just a hobby of his? He's using the ruse that he doesn't charge fees like Thrasymachus does, the professional, the Sophist, the proud hack like the book reviewer instructing the great unwashed in the works of other professional hacks who...

MR.BASIE: I have to object to this line of questioning.

MR.MADHAR PAI: Is this as to form Harold? Is it for the record?

MR.BASIE: It's for the record and as to form yes, deliberately confusing the witness getting way off the tracks on book critics and...

MR.MADHAR PAI: Excuse me old sport, I did not say book critics I said reviewers, there's a world of difference although the reviewers are delighted to be referred to as critics unless they're on the run, then they take refuge in calling themselves journalists. Now if you'll let me proceed with my...

MR.BASIE: I can't let you proceed with this leading the witness and confusing him right along these lines you're talking about, that's not what we're here for.

MR.MADHAR PAI: One of the things we're here for Harold is to make the distinction between amateur and professional. The witness himself has practically characterized his teaching career as a hobby even though he's paid, while he's now seeking substantial monetary damages for work he says was not motivated by mere hopes of financial gain, and since he has placed it in this Socratic context that is the line I am pursuing. Now Thrasymachus is telling us what sort of fellow he is, isn't he, in the way he expresses himself here?

A Yes.

Q In the way that we agreed characters are largely defined by dialogue, the way they express ideas, and it's this expression that's protected isn't it? Even if the ideas themselves are not?

A I said the idea expressed is the idea executed, when it's transformed into a play it's bound to the execution.

Q I see. And so, in short, you felt quite free to simply incorporate whole passages from Plato without attribution into the play you are representing as your own in this action?

A That I what?

Q It's a very simple question and I think you can answer it. Read it back please.

(Question is read.)

A I just wouldn't say incorporate.

Q It's a perfectly good word isn't it? Shall we read it again?

A No, but I...

Q Would you prefer took? lifted? purloined?

MR.BASIE: No, I have to break in here.

MR. MADHAR PAI: Please do not interrupt the witness.

MR. BASIE: I have an objection.

MR. MADHAR PAI: Do you have an objection?

MR. BASIE: The witness is being led.

MR. MADHAR PAI: No one is leading anyone. We're simply searching for some suitable wording.

MR. BASIE: Didn't he use the word paraphrase earlier?

Q In short, you have used and paraphrased whole passages from Plato in your play Once at Antietam?

A Yes, that's...

Q In other words we are talking about very substantial similarities are we not?

A Yes. You see I...

Q In other words, these are not the sort of similarities that you agreed earlier can occur without copying, that may be plain coincidence so to speak, when the idea being expressed is common property as it were?

A Well not when the, I mean what I think I said was up to a point when what's being said is, when the idea and the expression are bound up together and the...

Q Let me get back to this essentially simple question. You see no harm in deliberately borrowing, to put a charitable face on it, in deliberately borrowing entire passages from the work of Plato and inserting them, with slight alterations, in work which you represent as your own. Is that correct?

A Yes and if you'll just let me explain, I...

Q Please take your time. We're in no hurry here.

A Because in the first place I obviously

expected people to recognize these passages, these pieces of Socratic dialogue, any civilized person would recognize them from the Republic. It's all simply, it was all simply meant as a kind of homage, that's obvious isn't it?

Q Please let me ask the questions. When you say any civilized person, are we back to that somewhat narrow, rather exclusive audience envisioned in connection with your play's title's slightly remote echo of Shakespeare?

A I answered that didn't I? That he played to both the stalls and the pits?

Q We are speaking now of Plato. Are you saying, then, that this very broad audience, which you have characterized as the pits, would be expected to recognize these random passages from his Republic?

A It doesn't matter, no. No not the specific passages but it doesn't matter, that's the...

Q Not the specific passages then, but the approach, the Socratic method as it's known. What Dale Carnegie called the 'Yes yes' response?

A Who?

Q Dale Carnegie, the author of How to Win Friends and Influence People.

A God! Yes, speaking of the pits but that's the point, it doesn't matter. They don't have to know it's the Republic, they may never have heard of Plato but they're carried along by it, by the dialogue, by the wit and the timeliness of it, and the timelessness of it. That's the greatness of Plato, finding a wider audience, that's the point. That's what I mean by homage.

Q You speak of the wit and timeliness of these dialogues, and you agreed earlier that the characters in a play are in fact largely defined by their dialogue, is that correct?

A Yes.

Q And in light of what might be called

popularizing the work of Plato, would it be fair to infer that the character named Kane in your play is to a large degree based on Socrates?

A It's obvious, yes.

Q As portrayed by Plato? Or the historical figure, which?

A Well, well both, I mean Plato's version is about all that we really have, isn't it.

Q Which was simply there for the taking, like Caesar in Plutarch?

A Well not really no, because...

Q Because we agreed that the idea and its expression are different things, did we not?

A Yes but...

Q The difference between Shakespeare's King Lear and one by Joe Blow, is that correct?

A All right, yes, but...

Q And Joe Blow's version would differ substantially from yours? In the sense that we wouldn't see you writing 'Does it pain dreadfully? You poor darling...' Is that correct?

A Yes, but I...

Q And in the passage from Plato we just looked at, you wouldn't be found using a word like sillybillies, would you?

A No but neither would Plato, that...

MR. BASIE: I object.

MR. MADHAR PAI: You are interrupting the witness.

MR. BASIE: That's the basis of my objection.

MR. MADHAR PAI: Are you objecting for form?

MR. BASIE: Yes.

MR. MADHAR PAI: For the record?

MR. BASIE: For the record.

MR. MADHAR PAI: All right. Let's move on. Read it back, please.

MR. BASIE: Now wait a minute.

MR. MADHAR PAI: Why should we wait a minute? Read it back.

MR. BASIE: I haven't finished. Why do you want it read back? He answered your question.

MR. MADHAR PAI: Then why are you interrupting?

MR. BASIE: Because I have an objection.

MR. MADHAR PAI: Would you like to state your objection?

MR. BASIE: You are badgering the witness by interrupting him before he can complete his answers.

MR. MADHAR PAI: I believe it was you who interrupted the witness.

MR. BASIE: I have a right to object when the witness is being baited by this pattern of repeated interruptions.

MR. MADHAR PAI: And I repeat, sir, the record will show it was you who interrupted the witness. Please read it back.

(Record is read.)

Q We stated earlier, did we not, that anyone is free to take an idea and express it in whatever...

MR. BASIE: I haven't finished.

MR. MADHAR PAI: I simply cannot put up with this, Harold. I've tried to conduct this procedure as expeditiously as possible in deference to your wishes regarding the condition of the witness. I've been trying to speed things up by shutting off these irrelevancies and digressions but you seem bound on prolonging things with your ceaseless interruptions and it's most unprofessional.

MR. BASIE: I think the record will

show that the entire course of the questioning has turned into a digression.

MR. MADHAR PAI: I don't know what you're talking about.

MR. BASIE: What I'm talking about is how we got off here into Plato, whether any passage in the play might have been borrowed from Plato is relevant to this infringement action where even just suppose Plato had a copyright, it would have expired before the birth of Jesus in any case.

MR. MADHAR PAI: I cannot resist the temptation to digress here for a moment myself, Mr. Basie, because it may be instructive and even of some later use to you in what you are pleased to call your career. I have never looked into the status of copyright agreements in fifth century Athens, which I agree would be quite remote from our present purposes. We are citing passages from the English translation of Plato's Republic by Benjamin Jowett copyrighted just a century ago by the Macmillan Company, renewed by Oxford University Press in nineteen twenty, and you may pursue it down to the present day as you see fit.

MR. BASIE: Well shit.

MR. MADHAR PAI: Shall we move on?

Q We stated earlier, did we not, that anyone is free to take an idea and express it in his own fashion, hence sillybillies might be called Jowett's expression of a detail of Plato's expression of a detail of the idea under discussion, would you agree?

A Yes, all right.

Q In this vein do you recall making the distinction between protection for the expression and for the idea unless the idea is copied in a vulgar and demeaning way, when it becomes an abuse?

A Yes.
Q I am directing the witness's attention to Defendants' Exhibit 29. Will you read it please?
(Document marked Defendants' Exhibit 29 for identification as of this date.)
A Starting where, 'as he was sitting among them...'
Q To yourself please.
A I've read it.
Q Will you identify it for the record?
A Of course, yes. Yes, it's the story Glaucon tells of the shepherd Gyges in the second book of the Republic.
Q And?
A Well he's obviously, Gyges is obviously a rather low ignorant type who stumbles on a dead body in some pretty bizarre circumstances, he takes a gold ring off the dead man's finger and by accident discovers it can make him invisible, and it goes on from there to describe his adventures, his rise to power using this new, this stratagem.
Q And is Plato just telling us a story here? A sort of Arabian Nights Entertainment?
A Of course not, no. He's placing the perfectly unjust man beside the just man in his nobleness and simplicity as Aeschylus says wishing to be and not to seem good. That's Plato quoting Aeschylus and I'm quoting Plato, what's the difference?
Q The difference is exactly why we're here. Plato attributes the idea and the words to Aeschylus whom he names, whereas you have simply lifted them from Plato without ascribing them to anyone the way you've done elsewhere I might add, Camus and Rousseau and I don't know who else, now may we get on with this? Glaucon's story is employed as an expression of this idea, is that correct?
A In expressing it, yes.

Q But you are not claiming property rights in an idea then, are you?

A In certain ideas yes, when I'm talking about ideas I'm talking about art.

Q Let's take that out. We're talking about an actual thing.

A I'm talking about work, you can't divide a work of art, the idea from the technique that expresses it.

Q Well that's exactly what you're going to have to do in a court of law. The idea is an abstract form and that's not what we're here to talk about. We're here to talk about your play and I direct your attention to Defendants' Exhibit 30. Will you identify it please?

(Document marked Defendants' Exhibit 30 for identification as of this date.)

A It's, yes it's from the second act of my play, the third scene. It's a dialogue between Mr. Kane and a character named Bagby. Mr. Bagby.

Q I would like it read into the record please.

BAGBY

And why not? An't they close enough to doing it now? And do you think they keep from injustice by preference, then?

KANE

(VEHEMENTLY)

I do!

BAGBY

Ah...! And that they practice justice willingly? No, only let both of them do what they like, and you will catch your just man in the act. It's only the law that keeps him to fair dealing.

KANE

The law...

BAGBY

Yes and what is the law but a thing got up by them that fear suffering injustice, and not them that fear doing it. No, I heard a story told once of a man that found a gold ring upon a dead body, and as he wore it one evening with friends he happened to turn it upon his finger, as nervous people may do. And no sooner had he done this, than he was invisible, and his friends spoke of him as if he was gone. He found that when he turned it outward he was visible again, and turned inward no one could see him. So he got a job as the king's messenger, and with this new dodge of his he soon humped the king's wife, and before you know it he'd killed the king and seized the empire... There, with a ring such as that, now, who could keep from taking what he liked wherever he found it, walking into anyone's house and humping whoever he found there, and setting free from prison any man he might choose... Why, with two such rings, for your just man and the unjust, you could not tell them apart...

Q There is no question here of a passage from Plato being copied into your own work in slightly altered form, is that correct?

A Yes, the...

Q And as a result of these alterations, the idea has been copied in a vulgar and demeaning way, do you agree?

MR. BASIE: Wait, I'm sorry, but...

MR. MADHAR PAI: Do you have an objection?

MR. BASIE: Yes.

MR. MADHAR PAI: I won't have any more of this, Harold. You have made your objection and I am going to proceed with this examination.

Q Do you, or do you not, find the term humping a crude and vulgar term to denote sexual activity?

A I, yes that's what I...

Q I'd like you to simply answer my questions without these rambling digressions. In the passage from Plato which we have just reviewed, the translator has employed such phrases as he seduced the queen, and lie with anyone at his pleasure, to convey these activities, am I correct?

A Yes.

Q Activities which in your own rendering of the passage take the form of humping, am I correct?

A I, yes.

Q Now you stated earlier, did you not, your belief that an idea is protected in its expression against being copied in a vulgar and demeaning way?

A What I meant was...

Q Please answer the question. Was that your statement or not?

A Yes.

Q And that you find the word 'humping' a crude and vulgar term?

A Yes but...

Q So on the one hand you would enjoin Joe Blow from presenting what you consider a crude, vulgar, demeaning expression of an idea which you feel you have made your own, exalting it to a protected status through your own unique artistic expression, while on the other hand you have no hesitation at all in offering us a parable from one of the greatest minds in western history dressed in this manifestly crude, vulgar and hence debased version, with the temerity to label it homage into the bargain. Am I correct?

A ...

Q I didn't hear your answer. Will you repeat it please?
A That's not what I meant.
Q I want an answer to the question.
A It's nearer to parody, this passage.
Q Did you understand the question? I said parable, not parody.
MR. BASIE: He's free to characterize it however he wants to.
MR. MADHAR PAI: Are you objecting? I want an answer to my question.
MR. BASIE: You asking him to characterize it as homage?
MR. MADHAR PAI: I am not asking him to characterize it as anything.
Q If you don't understand the question, say you don't. If you don't know the answer, say I don't know.
A I don't know.
Q Will you explain why it is that you don't know?
A It has to do with the subject matter, with the character. Will you let me explain?
Q I wish you would.
A Well, you see the character Gyges in Plato's story, this story told by Glaucon that is, Gyges is a crude unlettered shepherd, earthy, greedy, sly, fundamentally dishonest like the character Bagby, Mr. Bagby in the play, so he uses vulgar language. It's as if Gyges were telling his story himself instead of Glaucon, he'd use vulgar language, so it's not me using vulgar language, it's Bagby. The character Bagby.
Q Did you understand the question?
A We're talking about characters defined through their dialogue, aren't we? The three levels, from good men to bad, it's all right there in the Poetics. They're either above our level of goodness like the characters of Homer, like my

character Mr. Kane, or about our own level, that's the hero the audience identifies with here, or beneath it like Bagby, Mr. Bagby, who's beneath our level of goodness like the characters of Nicochares, who wrote the Iliad...

Q We are stopping short of response here. I believe you have strayed into Aristotle, and this is not the lecture hall. We are here to talk about your play, whether it's Defendants' 1 or 6, and the way you have seen it purloined or made substantially similar or even debased in the work of another, and on the point of what you like and don't like, what you find actionable or not actionable, I ask you again, do you understand the question?

A Well it's not the same thing, you talk about debasing someone's work with that one short passage from the Republic, if you look at the play, at the whole last act of the play? The scene with Kane in prison condemned to death when Thomas is trying to talk him into saving himself, it's the Crito isn't it? Right out of the Crito? And there's nothing debased about...

Q Did you ever have a discussion with anyone with respect to the subject matter of the lawsuit?

MR.BASIE: What does the subject matter mean?

Q Do you understand my question?

A Well I ask the same question, what does subject matter mean?

Q I am not inclined to answer your questions, Mr. Crease. Do you understand my question?

A I wanted a clarification from you.

MR.BASIE: I think we all know that Mr. Crease has not seen the movie.

MR.MADHAR PAI: I don't think that precludes his answering, but if you do, Mr. Basie, then he doesn't know. I'm sure he has been advised what the movie is about. If he hasn't, and you brought a lawsuit...

Q So that before you started the lawsuit, you personally made no investigation of what was actually portrayed in the film itself?

A I read some reviews.

Q Reviews customarily refrain from telling the ending, giving away the story so to speak. Was that the case here?

A I don't know.

Q So accordingly you really have had no way to know whether or not the scene, this last act scene you've just cited, whether it or even some character in your play actually occurs in the film?

MR. BASIE: I don't think you can defend an infringement on the grounds of what was not stolen.

MR. MADHAR PAI: Please don't interrupt. Will you read it back?

(Question is read.)

A No.

Q So that all you claim are certain similarities you have come upon at second hand, is that correct?

A That's what I'm talking about. I haven't finished.

Q I want you to finish.

MR. BASIE: I am sorry, he can't possibly finish. Not in these time limits.

MR. MADHAR PAI: He will have as much time as he likes.

MR. BASIE: He can answer that question only subject to later supplementation.

MR. MADHAR PAI: Is that because you want to talk to him before he goes on or because there isn't enough time, Mr. Basie?

MR. BASIE: Because there are some similarities here that he is...

MR.MADHAR PAI: Are you testifying, Mr. Basie?

MR.BASIE: You asked me a question. I am giving you the reason.

MR.MADHAR PAI: No, I didn't.

MR.BASIE: You asked me, is that because, and you were looking straight at me.

MR.MADHAR PAI: I meant the question which preceded it. Settle down.

MR.BASIE: Why should I settle down? You look at me and ask a question, when I start to answer you...

MR.MADHAR PAI: Why get excited?

MR.BASIE: It's the truth, though, isn't that exactly what happened?

MR.MADHAR PAI: I did speak to you, the preceding question was to your client.

MR.BASIE: I was objecting to it.

MR.MADHAR PAI: He didn't tell me he didn't have enough time. I thought he was the one under oath here. He said he wasn't finished.

Q I said I would like you to finish. Go ahead.

MR.BASIE: I am saying that he cannot be bound by what he says at this deposition as to the question of similarities between the play and the movie.

MR.MADHAR PAI: What is the reason for that?

MR.BASIE: Because there are so many that it's very easy for him to miss a few. If you are asking him to tell you every similarity that exists...

MR.MADHAR PAI: I am.

MR.BASIE: I will instruct him not to answer. My objection was simply that I believe you used the word 'claim.'

MR.MADHAR PAI: Your problem was that I stated it in terms of something that had not yet been proven in the case?

MR.BASIE: No, in terms of something that would be his contention, claim.

MR.MADHAR PAI: As opposed to that which is deposited?

MR.BASIE: As opposed to that which merely asks him about what he recalls at present.

Q Would you tell us, then, what...

MR.BASIE: In other words, when you use the word 'claim,' it sounds like an attempt to, or maybe I misinterpreted it as an attempt to limit his further testimony, something which comes later in the litigation.

MR.MADHAR PAI: The record comprehensively reflects our respective positions, in my view. You felt that Mr. Crease should be at liberty until the moment the trial closes to add to his list of similarities, I thought.

MR.BASIE: No, sir.

MR.MADHAR PAI: Then I did misunderstand you.

MR.BASIE: No. There is a later stage. Very often it is pretrial conference.

MR.MADHAR PAI: Up to that point then?

MR.BASIE: Yes.

MR.MADHAR PAI: I respectfully ask that he turn his attention to the task now and do it now, and you said to that, you directed him not to answer.

MR.BASIE: Yes. But only so as not to limit his testimony at the trial to what he...

A This may be a reason to postpone because I am getting tired.

Q We will stop right now. I would just like to know if there are any other forms of damage that you wish to have redressed in this lawsuit that we haven't heard from you about?

A Well it's both things, I tried to explain, on

the one hand it's taking the, it's the theft of my play without giving me credit and on the other what offends me is when my work is, when vulgarity and grossness and stupidity debase my work.

Q What sum of money do you seek for that?

A I'm not, I have to talk to my lawyer about it. I don't think it's something you want me to answer right now.

MR.BASIE: It is stated in the complaint.

MR.MADHAR PAI: There is not a dollar figure stated in the complaint.

MR.BASIE: That's right, because we don't know.

Q Do you have a figure in mind of what you want?

A I haven't really thought about it.

Q But you have thought...

A But I could very easily, yes.

Q Would you do it then?

A When the moment comes, yes.

Q This is the moment.

MR.BASIE: No, I don't think so.

MR.MADHAR PAI: You don't?

MR.BASIE: No.

MR.MADHAR PAI: What are we supposed to do, kind of tiptoe over this thing and maybe come to a special spot where we commune under a tree and you tell me about it?

MR.BASIE: For one thing, let me say to you that under the Copyright Act, you can make a choice of remedies after the trial.

MR.MADHAR PAI: Thank you. I would like to know what the witness's number is right now, if he has got one.

Q Would you please do that?

MR.BASIE: He said he didn't.

Q I'm asking you if you could do it now, if it's that easy.

A I can't.
Q You choose not to do it now?
A I choose not to do it now.
Q What are the reasons you choose not to do it now?
A Well it's not, it's very difficult for me to translate offense into money.
Q One last question occurs to me, Mr. Crease. Has it ever occurred to you to change your name?
MR.BASIE: Let me remind him he is still under oath, isn't he?
MR.MADHAR PAI: Of course.
MR.BASIE: I direct him not to answer the question.
MR.MADHAR PAI: I think we can call it a day. The witness is released. Thank you, gentlemen.

—Read the Cratylus.

—What's that, old fellow?

—I said read Plato's dialogue Cratylus, arguing whether someone's name is just a convenience or whether it expresses his true nature, if it doesn't it's not a name at all, change it any way you like.

—I'll look it up, by the way old sport I think you've got hold of the wrong end of the stick there with the Sophists. It was Plato who turned the word into a term of opprobrium wasn't it, slandered them the way he does there with Thrasymachus for his own purposes giving Socrates the high moral ground and all the rest of it? Always thought he was a bit of a fascist myself I'd like to chat with you about it some time, might even come out changing your name.

—I'd as soon change the shape of my nose.

—Had a client who did that once, wanted a nose bob and couldn't afford one so she got herself the wrong way in a revolving door and sued. What do you say, Harold?

—I'll take the Fifth.

—'Every dog is entitled to one bite.' Is that true?

—Is it the law, you mean? No.

—Well then why would he say it. What?

What he'd actually just said was —I like your outfit, where she'd come striding naked across the bedroom.

—Do you Harry? rippling her arms outstretched, —I'll get it in four colours. Meanwhile doesn't it ever occur to you to water these plants when I'm not here? He drew in his feet where she came down on the end of the bed with the newspaper. Plants? Never occurred to him, no, they were just there, pleasant furnishings like those fluted candlesticks, like the lamps, that Piranesi, she wouldn't expect him to go around watering lamps and pictures would she, one leg off to the floor and her knee drawn up parting the thatch to his gaze if he'd looked there before the newspaper interfered again with —Écrasez l'infame, of course the French are besotted by dogs, you remember those two giant hounds under the next table at Lipp's you'd know they couldn't resist it. Art vs negritude, the petit maître little James B they're turning it into an intellectual cause célèbre and the Brits, of course, a stern letter to the Times from the Pit Ponies Protective Association, my God. Do you want la Repubblica? They call the miserable creature Frugaletta, its soulful eyes brimming with the wounded innocence of the oppressed the world over. I mean you know how they treat dogs.

—They're an operatic people, Christina. In Vietnam you'd have Frugaletta on the lunch menu.

—No stop it, it's just not funny anymore, those stupid local papers down there trying to make Father sound like a monster and these foreign papers pick up the headline and suddenly it's an international incident, this stale cartoon of brutal Uncle Sam trampling the underdog. To turn a phrase, I mean my God, écrasez l'infame, why don't they simply tear the hideous thing down. CYCLONE SEVEN SEEKS NEW HOME, that was a headline wasn't it? why the Village went to court in the first place? They won their appeal didn't they?

—No demolition permit.

—Well that's ridiculous. You mean the Village can't tear it down because they haven't issued themselves a permit?

—Szyrk got a restraining order while he tries to take it to the high court so now everybody who was suing him is suing the Village, James B charging them with detaining and endangering Spot and now these animal rights people joining in with a writ for unlawful restraint, sort of a canine habeas corpus with some psychological expert testifying Spot's having a nervous breakdown.

—Well isn't it? simply ridiculous?

—But it takes a jury to say so. Little James B up there in his bandages telling them how he coaxed his beloved pet near enough to reach in and rescue him and snap, they corner Judge Crease and they've got their headline. EVERY DOG ENTITLED TO ONE BITE, SAYS JUDGE.

—Well my God, Father just lost his temper, he didn't say it in court did he?

—Wasn't even in his court, it's hardly a Federal case but they got their headline, you think their readers are going to make those fine distinctions? The ones down there who can read in the first place I mean, taking a hell of a chance with his circuit court appointment but it almost sounds like he's trying to get himself disqualified in the rest of these cases, these toymakers, the Free Spot game, the Spot dolls, figurines, keyrings and the rest of the junk with the insurance companies' batteries of lawyers in there in no hurry to settle anything, business as usual that's what they're paid for. Now he's got James B's father going after these same animal rights people, posters, T shirts with their new logo, Spot framed by those steel teeth claiming free speech, fund raising in a public cause against Spot's right to own, protect and commercially exploit his own name, likeness and persona following that Federal Appeals Court 1983 ruling for Carson in Carson v. Here's Johnny Portable Toilets and their lawyers contending this right of publicity attaches only to real people, homo...

—Harry he's a Federal judge! You mean with all the carnage going on in this country wherever you look that all the government can find to worry about is portable toilets?

—Not talking about portable toilets Christina we're talking about millions of dollars, that's what this country's finally all about isn't it? We're talking about free speech, about the right of publicity, names, symbols, trademarks what this whole case that I'm on is all about. I just hope your father's confirmed for the circuit court before he gets a chance to make any more headlines like this last one.

—Well my God, he simply lost his temper again do you blame him? Those obnoxious home town reporters down there bait him until they get another headline, you just said that yourself didn't you? Vilify him any way they can since this whole idiotic business started, this vicious gossip about his drinking and his three packs of cigarettes a day and when one of them got in there and saw that ghastly praying hands thing upside down they accuse him of sacrilege on top of these snide innuendos about madness running in the family, digging up any lie they can about his father in this whole Civil War mess Oscar's got himself into, printing whatever they like while you lie here stark naked and talk about free speech and Johnny's portable toilets?

—You're saying you want me to get dressed?

—I didn't say that did I? running her hand along his ankle where it came down against her, and from there her eyes without pause back up the rest of him —no, no I like your outfit.

—Only colour it comes in Madam, you'd like it with the tassel? or without.

—Oh with! running her hand up his calf, over his rising knee as he reached out an arm —no don't, don't answer it let the tape run, you can break in if it's important can't you? and the grating echo of her own voice reciting the litany, the beep, and then a voice, a filtered imitation of a voice —Oh Teen? It's Trish. It's Trish Teen you've got to call me. I've tried and tried to reach Larry, your husband Larry? They pretended they didn't know him and then they blamed me because they said I had his name wrong Teen I may have to go to prison. Even when I got his secretary he was always in conference or in court Teen it's that wretched boy, these loathsome right to life people got hold of him and had a guardian appointed for the foetus and won a court order to stop the abortion and my lawyers don't know what they're doing, they won't talk to me they just talk to each other and send me the bills and then one of them even had the impudence to call me at the hospital where Mummy died last night and I was snatched away from that marvelous new Basque restaurant everyone's thronging to, a month in advance for a table unless you're a rock star and of course it's très cher with hordes of Japanese so it's clear at a glance there's not a soul you know all simply glaring at my diamonds, I should never have worn them, the ones that were literally torn off my throat that night in the elevator after that jubilee with Bunker? These clever insurance people had actually bought them back from the thieves if you can imagine, like these shady deals for these tiresome hostages you keep reading about in the papers, it was like seeing old friends and now they have the gall to ask for the money they gave me when they settled my perfectly legal claim, isn't that why we pay these frightful premiums year after year in the first place? It just shows the lengths they'll go to, it's all sheer greed you almost want to lose your faith in human nature, I don't know what this poor boy thinks he's up to but oh, I have to tell you. I went back and bought that sweet little Lhasa, the one we saw in the pet store window coming back from the clinic? I've got to run, Bunker's persuaded me to press charges against that pitiful creature who threw the catsup on my sables when we came out of the clinic thank God it wasn't the chinchilla Mummy would kill me so I'll miss the vernissage for what's his name I can't pronounce it, are you going? I hate to miss it but Bunker insists it's our duty to stand up to these hordes who are out to destroy civilization Teen call me, I may need you. I hate to bother Larry but he may be all that stands between me and that island, Rikers is it? remember their sign NO FOOD AT ANY PRICE and those vile hamburgers at four in the morning the night Bim stole the hearse and we all went out to Jones Beach God, those were the good times weren't they Teen, how could we know it would all turn into such a...

—Harry, could you...

—No.

—But you haven't even...

—I said no Christina. Don't get me into it. Better watch out yourself too when she says she may need you.

—She just means my moral sup...

—If she's going to court she needs a witness. You were with her?

—At the clinic? I had to go with her Harry, I mean you never know what's going to happen at a place like that and of course it did, this nicely dressed young man in rimless glasses suddenly stepping up and throwing catsup on her fur coat, something about spilling innocent blood God knows what he was, animal rights or rights to life it was quite unnerving.

—Probably both, and the gun lobby thrown in. You mean she had the abortion.

—That's why she's terrified of going to prison, you heard her. This frightful boy demanding his paternal rights as though she were some sort of brood sow, she'd literally found him on the street picking up cigarette butts and pulling newspapers out of trashcans so she invited him to dinner and the police called just as they were sitting down. He'd stolen a book in a bookstore to bring her as a gift, some science fiction nonsense about people living under water, he kept telling them it was his book, he meant he'd written it there was his name on the cover but the price of books is so appalling these days he obviously couldn't afford it but of course they couldn't see it that way till she went down there herself and ordered fifty copies to calm them down. Now he's ready to send her to prison for murdering his child. His child!

—Nobody's going to send her to prison, certainly make the world safer for democracy if they did but she'll probably just be cited for contempt and fined, a good healthy one if she shows up in those diamonds. What was she doing at a public clinic?

—She could hardly go to her own hospital, I mean not while she's suing them could she?

—You mean she's got one set of lawyers bringing this suit for foetal endangerment and another set to defend her abortion. No wonder they talk to each other.

—I suppose that's exactly why she has two sets, I mean this way she probably counts on winning one or the other after the lesson she learned losing that dreadful custody battle over T J, she's still livid about it.

—But she won didn't she? Doesn't the boy live with her?

—That was the problem Harry. Neither of them wanted him. Of course the father paid through the nose for support and a trust fund, one of these quart a day louts in ostrich skin boots who owned most of downtown Lubbock till somebody shot him and she had to take his estate to court against six other paternity suits for a settlement, I mean that's hardly the case this time. God knows what this miserable boy thought he was up to, he's really not quite bright if you take a look at his book.

—Maybe just bright enough to figure if he got her pregnant she'd marry him, the inevitable divorce comes along and he ends up with the child and collects a bundle for its support. Like T J in reverse.

—Well you see you could help if you wanted to Harry, think about it. I mean of course he was planning something like that, he...

—Probably the only way he could get it up, if you marry money you're going to earn every penny and some kid fishing newspapers out of trashcans who...

—She said he explained that. He told her he was doing market research for some ad agency on what page people reached in the paper when they threw it away and how far down they smoked these different brands of cigarettes it all sounded rather bogus, she's been buying him the most lavish gifts like a twelve hundred dollar robe from Sulka's he tried to return for cash but they told him they'd be glad to credit it to her account so of course he kept it while apparently he's been going around complaining that whenever there's a ten dollar cab fare or she needs a lipstick she says all she's got are hundreds and he has to take care of it, if you call that gratitude, she no, don't answer it... motionless for the grating echo of her own voice, the beep and then, harsh and peremptory —Christina. I'd like you to call me.

—That was quick.

—I think he's terrified I'll pick it up and it will all go on his long distance bill instead of ours, he managed to steer that thing into the kitchen out there and saw that Ilse was throwing these five cent deposit soda bottles he has with his Pinot Grigio into the trash and made a dreadful scene, will you hand me those nail scissors? God knows what he expects to do about those hospital bills and how much he owes Mister Basie by this time, you'd think he'd already won the case from that grandiose interview in the paper and his, there's some cotton right there could you, no by your elbow, could you hand it to me? I mean with that headline JUSTICE'S GRANDSON SEEKS JUSTICE obviously that's what set Father off, pulling skeletons out of closets when they found they could manufacture a good story setting the father against the son my God, as though things hadn't been bad enough between them long before this revolting movie came along and all this nonsense about madness in the family, you can't blame him.

—Ever occur to you that he might be?

—Oscar? Mad?

—The Judge.

—Because he loses his temper? My God Harry they're just a lot of, it's just nastiness they'll say anything just to...

—No look, look. How much of it is just plain sloppiness, you see it every day. Read something in the Times if you were there yourself you saw something entirely different, look at me quoted on Royal Crown, Roman Catholic, R C Cola and Classic Coke, New Coke, Coke II and Vatican II, these Episcopals and the Pepsi Generation they take a case like mine in the hundreds of millions and label it Pop and Glow, pop for the drink and glow for the church, turn it into a circus because that's what newspapers are now, entertainment. No malice just freedom of the press, take the Spot logo or your cleancut young man with the catsup bottle it's all freedom of speech, prying into your father's private life? But you don't feed the fire, you don't lose your temper and hand them a headline like this last one. DAMN THE PUBLIC'S RIGHT TO KNOW, SAYS JUDGE. Not the way to get seated on the higher court and if he's been telling Oscar what the...

—Well my God Harry he hasn't been telling Oscar anything, I mean they don't even speak. Oscar tries to dig things out of that doddering old law clerk of his down there who's numb with drink most of the time because Father insists on doing everything himself and now of course that picture of the house they had in the paper, a rundown country mansion in an exclusive Long Island enclave they captioned it sagging veranda and all, one look at that and Oscar's panicked that Father will get on us again to sell it.

—Why he did it in the first place, nobody ever won an interview Christina the minute you let them in the door they...

—He didn't let them in, he asked them in Harry that's the point. It was his own ridiculous idea, he saw his name mentioned in the paper and thought he'd better set the record straight as he put it, make sure the whole world knows he's only seeking justice and then of course he got carried away and probably wrecked the whole thing.

—A little late even if he wanted to, nothing to do now but sit tight waiting for the ruling on summary judgment and pray you get the right judge. I got a look at our man on the case, real red brick university product all English tailoring really full of himself, Swyne & Dour's token ethnic they came up with when they got a look at Mister Basie.

—Well I mean it's Mister Basie who's got Oscar so carried away, I hope to God he's as smart as you say.

—No he's smart Christina, the way I hear he handled that deposition he's smart, even imagine them bringing him into the firm to dress up its image with a few more minorities before some loose cannon comes up with an antidiscrimin...

—Well for God's sake don't tell that to Oscar or he'll, Harry please. I mean do you have to stare? abruptly drawing her knee up hugged against her breast, biting her lip with concentration on a cuticle —like that story I never understood about John Ruskin taking years to tell that poor girl why he'd never laid a hand on her because he was so disgusted by what he saw the first night they were married? bent closer without a look up, and an emphatic snap of the scissors —going for ten year old girls who were more like those pristine Greek statues he was besotted with, I mean my God didn't he have pubic hair too?

—Read Freud.

—I've read Freud Harry. I don't want to read Freud.

—His little essay about Medusa's head sprouting snakes instead of hairs?

—That's why I don't want to read Freud.

—Talking about your friend Ruskin, Christina. He was horrified when he saw her naked because she didn't have a penis.

—Well that's the most absurd, I mean you've got it backwards anyhow. It's the girl who collapses with penis envy when she sees that he has one.

—That's what his daughter Anna came up with because she didn't have one. What panicked Ruskin was castration anxiety, so his fertile imagination transformed her pubic hairs into a den of what he didn't see there in Freud's version of the terrifying aspects of female sex, left poor Ruskin getting old obsessed with visions of snakes right to the end.

—It sounds more like the DTs but I mean Oscar's terrified of them too, he saw one sunning itself on a flat rock out there by the shed when he was a little boy and he's still petrified every time he passes it.

—Why doesn't he just get rid of the rock.

—Well obviously he's terrified of what might be under it, I mean he says what frightened him was how fast the thing moved. He'd heard about them crawling around without legs and thought they'd go about as fast as an earthworm, it's that without legs that frightens him.

—Like a penis, better still the ornaments in those brothels in Pompeii where they had wings but I wouldn't worry about Oscar, I'm sure Lily's got a really flourishing...

—I'm sure she has Harry, and I'm sure you'd like, my God, you know I made the most awful gaffe out there talking about Japan? as she came down on the bed beside him —when we were in Hokkaido? her voice falling with the reminiscent search of her hand through the hair thick on his chest, —those two days we barely left our hotel room to eat and I told him you spent them in those endless conferences while I wandered around that museum with the...

—Where's the gaffe, he knew we had a trial run on that Japan trip before we...

—Not Oscar no! No I'm talking about Mister Basie, telling him about that museum and I suddenly found myself talking about the hairy Ainu and the more I tried to get away from it the worse it got. Stocky, dark, thick and hairy I mean can you imagine? as her hand descended, exploring deeper till it came to rest as on a failed promise —God knows what he was thinking, he said he'd heard about that conference in Japan but he didn't remember you ever talking about your hairy Ainu I don't know what I said, I'm sure I was blushing I almost burst out laughing but he was cool and so serious I couldn't even, I mean can you imagine? And where her voice broke off abruptly muffled against him her hand took up down there moving in silent reciprocation, gone unrewarded for its defeat to rise and surface again in her voice. —Did you sleep at all last night? coming up on an elbow and examining him that close, —your eyes are bloodshot and these terrible circles, the hours you put in they're just wringing you dry. Your tooth aches it's probably an abscess and you just put it off with these painkillers they're destroying you, can't you see? These absurd Coke II and Vatican II Pepsi Generation Episcopals this idiotic case is destroying you?

—It's almost over Christina, I'm...

—It's not almost over. Somebody will win, somebody will lose, somebody will appeal and it starts all over again doesn't it? isn't that what happens?

—And if it didn't? reared up on his own elbow sweeping the space around them with an arm, space magnified, reflected in the mirrored walls, expanded without bounds through sheets of glass to the floor all light and space where no shadow found refuge, all crystal geometry, —if it didn't, Christina? Could we live like this?

—Like this? when you don't sleep, you don't eat, you left the key in the front door when you came in last night you've never done that, all your obsessions with order and security you've never done that, and the night you forgot our address here? You actually forgot our address? Do they know what they're doing to you? even care? I mean I just hope they'll pay your bills at Payne Whitney when the time comes.

—Look, nobody's going to Payne Whitney. I went to the doctor didn't I? Heart fine, EKG fine, liver, cholesterol everything fine? Just tired, just a little overtired that's all, he...

—Well then find another doctor! Do you think the doctor they send you to is going to tell you they're destroying you? My God, will you look at you? her own eyes spilling down the length of him, resuming the gentle motion of her hand —I don't know what I'd do if you, if anything happened? her frown suddenly melting —to the hairy Ainu? throttling the surge that was filling her hand there, —wait. I'll be back. The mirrored door swung open on the bathroom, and from there —Don't you dare answer it!

Her voice echoed in grating counterfeit and then, in brisk rejoinder, —Christina? I called you some time ago and I would appreciate it if you could take a moment from your thrilling domestic pursuits to do me the courtesy of calling me back. It might be important. I might be having a seizure. The house might be burning down. I'd like to speak to Harry too. Please call me back.

—Oscar?

—What is it. Will you hang this up?

Had he got that card she'd sent him, she wanted to know, abruptly straining upright to dislodge his hand, —with a picture of Mickey Mouse in a cowboy suit? But he wasn't talking about Mickey Mouse, he loathed him in fact, said he was everything that was wrong with this country, a cheap smug little racist no, no he was talking about the last time he'd seen her, he'd asked her then hadn't he? whether she'd ever slept with this, this lawyer of hers, and she'd told him she hadn't? —It was true, she sulked. Was, was true, what about now? She'd said she'd never been to bed with him hadn't she? —It was true, Oscar.

—I don't believe it.

—I don't care if you believe it! You haven't even said you're glad to see me. It's too late to say so now anyway so don't bother. Are you? But he just wanted, demanded to know what happened down there, she'd said she had to fly down for that funeral and instead she'd driven down there to Disney World with him and —I just told you didn't I? You don't believe me anyway you just said so, that I even went to the funeral? where this Reverend Bobby Joe gets his hand on my knee because the dressmaker didn't have time to let down that hem right up under my skirt while Daddy and Mama are sitting right there listening to him tell how my brother's sitting up there on the right hand of Jesus where he's already set this dinner table with these presents from his enemies while we can all see Bobbie laying right there in the casket ten feet away? It was spooky.

—I believe it, that you went to the funeral I believe it, that's why I gave you money for the plane ticket when you...

—I knew you'd say that, about the money. That you'd remind me about the money because it humiliates me, that's why you do it isn't it. Isn't it? That's even why you think I came over to see you now isn't it, the first thing when I'm back, you haven't even asked how I am. I'm exhausted, can't you see that? how my hand quivers, look. Why do you keep it so cold in here, what do you care about the money anyway, with this seventy five million dollars you're getting at least couldn't you turn up the heat? But this was getting ridiculous he broke in again, what seventy five million dollars, that was just a number, it could have been a million, a hundred million and what made her think he was getting it anyhow? —It said it right in the newspaper didn't it? in that story he showed me about that war movie we saw and your father down there with that dog he's got trapped in that junkpile that bit somebody didn't you see it? with that same picture of him you've got in there in the room with all the books?

—That's my grandfather no, they got everything wrong and that seventy five million dollars look, look at that pile of papers on the chair it's all motions affidavits and depositions I don't know how much it's going to cost, it's all...

—Well he said you'll win, he's always on the side of the creative individual he said standing up for your rights like he's helping you with your accident and you haven't even thanked him?

—Thanked him for what! Where is he anyhow, he's never helped anybody but himself has he? He's not standing up for my rights he's standing up for his own right to exploit my misery here for every penny he can, it's not his pain and suffering is it? it's not his scar he's going to wear to the grave, he's not going to pay all these doctor and hospital bills is he? I haven't heard anything from him since both of you were, what happened down there? Do you know how long you've been gone?

—I've been trying to tell you haven't I? When I thought by now you'd be all well and we can sit and talk without you getting mad like these two regular human beings now that you're almost able to sit up while I can hardly even, I think I'm catching cold here, put your hand back where it was, can't you twist around a little? Just unbutton my, feel it? how my heart's racing? her hand hard on his pressing it close there, lingering long enough only to make its absence felt as it emerged to trace a sharp nail down his cheek —where that old scar was that you're so mad about? You can hardly see it...

—Because it's on the other side! wrenching his face around, —there. Now can you see it?

—You're not even listening to me are you, no keep your hand there, you can be so cold Oscar. You don't think other people notice it but I do, you're thinking about something else I can tell when you do that with your eyes like the last time I saw you when tragedy struck? But all she got back for that was her own words scorned with a muttered edge to them —and that's all you can say? When my own brother gets killed in a car crash and you don't even call that when tragedy struck? just because this new lawyer was right there to help me I don't know what I would have done down there, Daddy sitting there just kind of numb with Mama staring at him and him staring at me like he didn't know who I am? Where I hardly got to ever talk to them alone because Reverend Bobby Joe was always there comforting them with how happy Bobbie is in the next world so Daddy wouldn't feel so bad about the car Reverend Bobby Joe kept calling the death instrument, that Daddy gave Bobbie the money to buy the death instrument and maybe this is all some grand design of the Lord where all this money's coming back because it was insured so Daddy can cleanse it by putting it in the Lord's service, look at these shoes. I just got them when I went down there where the heel's practically coming apart if I have to go to the Philippines but you don't want to know about that either do you where I can't even go to the doctor and...

—Well go to the doctor! I told you I'd help you with that didn't I?

—It's not my fault if they can't give me an appointment till he gets back from Acapulco is it? Can you feel it? that lump? if it got any bigger?

—It just feels harder, it's...

—That's not it, you know what that is. It's the other one anyway, the other side, no. Lower. Did it? I'm not getting any younger, look at my, now what are you looking at. You're thinking about something else aren't you.

—What do you think I'm thinking about! I'm thinking about you and that, that, about what went on down there with you and...

—See? You're not even listening. That's what I'm trying to tell you isn't it? How he was so kind and understanding with Daddy trying to help straighten up this old misunderstanding so maybe we can make up and have this reconciliation now that Bobbie's gone and they'll maybe give me some help where Daddy's going to get back all this money he put into Bobbie's name so the government wouldn't get it before tragedy struck?

—What about before tragedy struck. You said you hadn't gone to bed with him didn't you?

—I said I didn't go to bed with him because it was in his car, so there.

—But you, in his car? that BMW?

—Because I was mad at you that's why, because you hurt my feelings.

—What are you talking about.

—That you don't take me seriously as if I didn't have any feelings except my, don't squeeze it so hard, that's why.

—So you thought I wouldn't care if you climbed in the...

—If I didn't care for you it would never have happened in the first place! Because I care more for you than you do for me because if I didn't care for you then you couldn't hurt my feelings could you. Could you!

—So you climb in the back seat of his BMW and...

—Anyway it was the front seat, so there. When he was teaching me to drive.

—Front seat back seat and every motel in, you know how to drive! between here and Disney World that's the way you show how much you care for me? that you've thought of me once?

—I sent you that postcard didn't I?

—While you're, a picture of a rat in a cowboy suit while you're down there rolling around on a waterbed with...

—While you're laying around up here with those big ones she's got bending over you with this nice plate of spaghetti and a glass of wine look, look how flabby you're getting down here, I can feel it, feel it?

—I can feel it!

—That's not what I meant.

—Well what do you mean? How can you expect me to know what you're talking about, going to the Philippines because you're mad at me?

—I didn't say I'm going to the Philippines because I was mad at you, I said your, take your hand away I'm getting all upset, don't...

—Don't why not.

—Because I'm, because I can't, because he wouldn't like it.

—He wouldn't like it! Get rid of him, I don't care if he, just get rid of him!

—How can I? getting her knee free, delivering his hand, —he's my lawyer isn't he? catching her blouse together —how am I supposed to get this divorce where he's already getting this private detective to find my husband for abandonment on this boat someplace as a cook, that they said he got this job as a cook he couldn't even make an egg till I showed him and these Philippines where they think I'm some kind of a criminal and this whoever stole my purse now they're looking for somebody that had this prostitution ring there kidnapping these beautiful oriental girls with all my cards and ID from my purse that's how real.

—Wait, sit down. Nobody's going to come and arrest you.

—I can't. I just came over to tell you I'm all right didn't I? steadying herself against the sideboard tugging her skirt around, tugging its zipper. —I have to go anyway, I just need to get gas for the car that's all. Do I have to ask you?

—Listen. Sit down for a minute.

—No there's some right here, look.

—I don't have to look! It's out there for some wine they're supposed to deliver just, just take ten if you have to, now wait.

—It's just this bunch of twenties.

—Well take one!

—Because I need some cosmetics too I thought maybe you could help tide me over till I get things straightened up with Daddy and, why are you muttering at me like that, can't you even say it was very nice to see you? thank you for coming over to see how I am? Because you think I just came over for this don't you, you've just been waiting for me to ask, you thought maybe I'd refuse didn't you, well why shouldn't I accept it. I did before didn't I? Why shouldn't I now. You know I can't turn it down I only just wish I didn't have to.

—Sit down! Listen...

—No let go. Is my lipstick on straight? I have to go anyway Oscar, there's this man out there on the porch. I only wish you wanted me to be happy, that's all.

Toot! toot toot toot! The door clattered. —Wait! Who are you! How'd you get in here?

—The, your daughter? She was in such a hurry I couldn't...

—Well who are you!

—Mister Crease? I'm, here's my card I'm from your, from Ace Fidelity investigating your claim, your accident claim? May I sit down? and he'd done so, flattening a plastic portfolio on his lap, —I hope you're not in pain? and he had out a yellow pad, —now. Let's not take too much of your valuable time, Mister Crease. I've just examined your car out there and apparently your attorney has filed court papers containing what I'm afraid we feel to be a rather inflated claim considering the nature of the damage I've just observed. I don't mean to sound unsympathetic but am I to understand that the condition which confines you to this, this motorized chair is the ongoing result of injuries sustained in the accident we are discussing?

—Well of course! What do you think this is all about, you've seen my hospital records haven't you? my whole medical...

—Please, I don't mean to upset you, I'm only doing my job you understand. I'm simply pointing out that I will be obliged to note in my report to the company that your purported injuries appear to be rather excessive in light of the nature of the accident itself, Mister Crease. I hope that I'm clear? He had out a small blue book, rustling its pages —now. I believe I can speak for the company regarding actual damages that we could reach a settlement of, just a minute, the six thirty five i yes, here it is. Four fifty three and then the, I should say in the neighborhood of fifteen hundred dollars, if you find that in order?

—Fifteen hun, of course I don't find it in order what are you talking about!

—The new fender Mister Crease, there's no possibility of hammering out the one that is presently on the vehicle it's totally smashed in, I'd hate to see the other fellow as they say. I mean to say I trust there was no other fellow, some stationary object I assume. The fender itself for this particular model BMW runs four fifty three and then of course there's the fender moulding, lining up the hood, painting bringing the labour up around a thousand so altogether we...

—Now just stop. What are you, what in the hell are you talking about what BMW.

—The one right out here in the drive, I thought...

—You thought! You thought I'd be caught dead driving a BMW? Most vulgar car on the road? that mean little German snout with its two open nostrils cutting in front of you and roars away they're for showoffs, they're for ill-bred pushy people who have to prove they...

—Excuse me I, excuse me Mister Crease there's someone at the door there, shall I...

—Find out what he wants. Ilse? Toot! Toot! —Where is she. Ilse! Well who is it.

—He's delivering cases of wine, he...

—He doesn't plan to bring them in the front door does he? Tell him to go round by the tradesmen's, oh Ilse. Tell that fellow to go round by the back, he's delivering some wine and bring me a glass. Quickly! Now.

—Now. I'm sorry to have upset you, I didn't mean...

—Most loathsome car on the road today like the people who drive them. The car you're here to examine is a red car, it's out by the shed on the other side of the house. A Sosumi.

—I, I'm afraid I'm a little confused. I understood you were the one who was suing, your attorney filed papers regarding your status under the No Fault statutes prevailing in this state which my company has had dismissed since you appear to prefer to be relieved of this statutory protection but in the interests of simplifying matters without further drawn out proceedings which would tax us all unnecessarily the idea of a settlement agreeable to both parties would seem the most sensible approach as I'm sure you agree.

—Agree? Look at me! And you march in here, you have the gall to march in here with a settlement in the neighborhood of fifteen hundred dollars? That's not a neighborhood it's a slum, it's a gutter!

—I apologize, my error in identifying the vehic...

—Fifteen hundred dollars, look at me! The protection of the No Fault statutes do you think I can't see through that? They're not protecting me they're protecting you, they're protecting you insurance people with this No Fault idea it's not even an idea, it's a jerrybuilt evasion of reality of course someone's at fault. Someone's always at fault. It's all a cheap dodge chewing away at the basic fabric of civilization to replace it with a criminal mind's utopia where no one's responsible for the consequences of his actions, isn't that what the social contract is all about?

—I'm sure it is Mister Crease but you see...

—I'll tell you what I see Mister, Mister...

—Prislikh...

—Anarchy. Mere anarchy.

—hoviscel...

—This is what I see, sir.

—It's right there on my card, if you...

—I see the entire crumbling of civilization before our very eyes.

—I see...

—I see all around us the criminal mind at large appropriating, literally stealing the fruits of the creative mind and the dedicated labours of others without even blinking, isn't that what's at the heart of this cancerous No Fault epidemic? this license for delinquency? Society created the criminal, society's responsible and so no one's responsible, isn't that the size of it? demolishing the pillar civilization rests upon, each individual's responsibility for the consequences of his own actions? and the natural law which frames the concept of negligence, let alone deliberate transgression goes out the window and the Constitution with it, are you aware of that? Are you aware that you're toying with one of the first laws of physical nature itself?

—I, I hadn't meant to no, no I...

—The simple, obvious, natural law of cause and effect? That there are actually people out there trying to banish it from the civilized world of human intercourse? And they'd ask me to join in this conspiracy against every lesson in sanity since the Age of Enlightenment brought us the, will you hand me that glass please?

—I, oh, here it's, I'm afraid it's empty Mister Crease I think, I think if you can have your attorney get in touch with us, we...

—I have no attorney.

—But I understood that you, that, but how long have you been without counsel?

—In this matter? For about twenty minutes.

—I, oh. I think, I think I, your delivery here I think he wants to be paid.

—It's right there, on that sideboard by the door now wait, where are you going.

—Yes I think I'd better, here? There's nothing here, you meant a check? or...

—Bills! Twenties, there's at least a dozen twenties there, right there by your elbow.

—But, there's nothing here no, no I'm afraid not Mister Crease.

—But, damn her! Ilse? Find my checkbook will you? in the library there, where's that glass of wine. Now wait, where are you going?

—Yes I'd better get back to the office for new instructions I, thank you I hope I haven't tired you, I'm sorry to have interrupted your holiday but we have such a backlog of yes, yes that reminds me Mister Crease, your front porch out here? I hope your homeowner's liability is paid up someone could have a nasty there, there's your phone...

—Here, wait a minute! Toot! toot! —Ilse? Just bring the bottle. Hello? Well! You finally tore yourself away from whatever unspeakable... what? Down on your knees scrubbing the kitchen floor I'm sure, listen Christina I want to speak to Harry... What do you mean asleep it's the middle of the day, of course I know that, it's Sunday here too isn't it? I've just had a hopeless confrontation with some idiot from the insurance company offering a ridiculously insulting settlement and I want Harry to dig up a really good negligence lawyer who can... Because I changed my mind! I simply decided to get a new one, that's... Because Basie's out of town, he's down there registering those letters in that historical society it's a requirement under the copyright law, when you bring suit for infringe... I don't know... I said I don't know Christina! Of course I haven't talked to him, it's this broken down old law clerk who's stirring up the trouble, he's got Father convinced that this whole mess he's in with the papers down there is my fault, that I... That he showed him that damned interview of course that's not what I said, they turned everything upside down and of course when he saw that seventy five million number they pulled out of a hat he thinks I did it just to publicize my lawsuit, that I... Well of course I didn't! I haven't even... Because he's seen the movie Christina! This law clerk took him to see it and of course he was horrified, if I'm suing them for stealing my play of course he thinks that's what I wrote, he never read my play did he? never showed any interest in it at all, now he's even convinced I wrote it in the first place just to exploit Grandfather and this whole madness angle they're playing up down there so it's my fault his appeals court seat is in jeopardy because it's his father who's being maligned, that it's my fault the... Well of course I know it's his father! He can't copyright his father can he? You remember when I wrote it Christina? the play? when I thought I'd finally done something to please him? that he'd be proud of I, that I, when I actually pictured taking him to opening night and all the wonderful reviews and it was ours, it was our family, that it set us apart from the rest of the dumb insignificant meaningless swarms of people who, the unexamined lives because there's nothing in them to examine, something we'd have together finally after all the, after the... what? I know it Christina! but he wasn't that old when I wrote it was he? and now he thinks that I've sold him out that I've sold out everything we, that I've betrayed everything that I tried to, to glorify in a man who, what? but... From this law clerk where else, where else would I hear it? And another thing. Another thing Christina I've just heard from a director, a theatre director he's one of the most famous in Britain he's interested in my play and he, wait a minute. Just put it down there Ilse. And a glass? And get the bill from him over there will you? You've brought my checkbook, did it occur to you to bring me something to write with? Christina? are you there? What? Certainly not, why would I be having a seizure, I... It's not ridiculous, Christina! Out here all alone pinned down in this chair at the mercy of every stupid Tom Dick and, Ilse? A pen, I can't write a check in pencil, the pressures I'm under with nobody around who seems to care whether I live or I... Because that's what happens! Pressures keep building up suddenly a clot in some tiny blood vessel in the brain when you least expect it that's when tragedy strikes, and... That's what I said, yes! when tragedy strikes! These desolate grey skies out over the pond and the wind I just thought maybe you could come out for a few days and... well can you call me sometimes just to make sure I'm... all right! But call me! Ilse? Here's the check, get him out of here, and when I say bring me a glass I don't mean a water glass, a tumbler, how many times I've told you you don't drink wine in a tumbler. There are plenty of goblets out there, the ones with the heavy stems, those tall thin ones would all be smashed the way you pack the dishwasher. We've got to get things organized here, I can't do everything myself. These boxes of papers, they're just in the way, you can stack them back in the hall where they were I haven't got time to go through them right now. And these books. I want them piled right here where I can reach them, not over by the card table. And the card table? hadn't he asked her to move it so he wouldn't have to drive across the room whenever he needed a pad or a folder, taking the whole day to get things in order so he could get something done that he couldn't get anything done. The blue folder for accounts, there should be two of them, one for household accounts and one for bills to be filed until they were opened. Correspondence, mail, clippings, a separate folder for clippings and the morning paper, where was it? Where was she for that matter, not that he'd finished with yesterday's paper clipping that story on Chevitz settling his suit against Kiester for, or was it the day's before? Couldn't she simply leave the scissors in one place? borrowing them to cut open a package of bacon, was there any reason a household like this one couldn't provide two pairs of scissors? Using a paring knife to open the mail, where was it, hadn't she finally learned to stack it right there? There was always mail, even the trash it was still mail wasn't it? something important that might have slipped into a big sale on camping equipment, washers and dryers, choice pork roast center cut like that invitation to lecture on Shiloh almost thrown out with porch and patio furniture, outdoor barbecues, snow tires and God knows what, the oil bill, trash removal $26.75 he punched out on the pocket calculator x 2 with a month's arrears and the window lit up with 8s end to end. —Ilse? Here you are. The batteries, put two AA size batteries on your list and the corn soup with those scallops, you've got to poach them very gently just two minutes or so, now around the neck and shoulders the way you did it yesterday? These strong thumbs digging deep down the base of the skull, the warmth spreading through muscles and tendons kneaded harder setting in a kind of somnolent rocking motion as the darkness accumulated out there over the pond, a blue heron stiff as a branch and two gulls tossed aimless overhead, white seagulls adrift on the currents of another glass before the darkness and the silence took it all until finally —you'll have to help me here he told her —just, there, get my leg over the side of the tub and ow! Boil me like a lobster, eight or nine minutes is long enough, boiled too long they get tough, nothing fancy just the plain melted butter and was there asparagus in the stores? All really just different ways to eat butter, asparagus, artichokes, a baked potato and he'd want another blanket tonight, more rain, two days of it, the newspaper strung on a clothesline in the kitchen to dry and the mail, Ace Fidelity, Lepidus, Shea & Blue Cross into the blue folder and couldn't she remember to bring back the wastebasket when she'd emptied it? A smudged postcard picture of Mickey Mouse in a cowboy suit **(HERE'S GUNNIN' FOR YOU!)** flung in its general direction when it arrived and that matchbook he'd been looking for, this wasn't it **(NEED CASH? INSTANT CREDIT 24HR. CASH LINE)**, it was red, **(NEGLIGENCE? ACCIDENTS? INJURIES? MALPRACTICE? FREE PHONE CONSULTATION)** and another half glass, the sun finally streaming across the room blinding the television screen with reflections of furniture so it had to be moved for his afternoon nature program, those strong thumbs pressing deep along the muscles of his neck and shoulders hunched intent on the world of carnivorous plants in the warm marshy bog where dwelt Dionaea muscipula, the notorious Venus flytrap closing its barbed lips on a hapless victim and sticky doings in the milkweed occupied the screen, still aglow with catastrophe on the grander scale of the evening news embracing a wide variety of vehicles flung broadcast down a highway in a freak blizzard in the midwest and with it, searching the shadows in this room and the darkness beyond a sense almost of panic, of the room standing empty, sold, when he'd gone, but where? or as suddenly shaken with the clatter of strangers moving in with their hideous furniture, —Ilse? and the smell of cabbage, —the plain boiled chicken, yes, just let it simmer and peppercorns, put in some peppercorns and do the rice in the same broth when the time came, couldn't she tell the difference between a salad fork and a dinner fork? and not to use a carving knife to pry open a jar or spread butter just because it was there within reach? And when the time came —you'll have to help me here he told her, easing a leg over the side if she'd just hold his shoulders so he wouldn't slip, arched over him in the steam easing him down, the full size of her hands flushed red in the water cradling the dead white shimmer of his thighs going under, wisps of tow brushing her throat in the trickle of perspiration arched over him easing him down where the merest token tumescence broke the surface, the transparent falsity he'd choked on in that cramped overheated sixty dollar seat where the curtain went up on a chorus line cavorting down the stage hymning the mockery of tits and ass no, here over him laboured the sweated splendour of buttocks and breasts intruding the abrupt image of milking her into the morning tea, where might he have read that? The wind out there wrapped the house like shipwreck, the whole place seemed to heave in the dark, —Ilse? he'd call out, —there's a door banging somewhere, hear it? if only to muster the sound of her footsteps, but worse, when they came they might have been anyone's, off groping in some unfamiliar reach colliding with a chair, a table, in that case he might tell her to simply leave all the lights on till the day came round again, the day that brought a man to the door selling aluminum siding, the day a large potted azalea delivered by mistake with a note You saved my life! signed Gwen was left to wither on the veranda and the gas for the kitchen stove ran out just at suppertime, prompting a feverish search for the source of that hoary inquiry What is worse than treason to one's king: A cold boiled potato on a white china plate, but soon enough replenished to offer, when the day itself finally came round, poached salmon served with carrots and olives sautéed in the Spanish style, despite the chance that —Mister Basie may not care for sautéed carrots. In the Spanish style. It sounds greasy.

—Well if he doesn't he'll be more polite about it than you are Christina, is that why you finally came all the way out here? just to criticize whatever I...

—You've been begging me to come out for days, for weeks haven't you? telling me you were having a seizure and the house was on fire? While you're simply sitting here with your Pinot Grigio putting on weight like a, sitting here behind this barricade of books and folders and papers it looks like you're running a little store here like you wanted to when you were seven and made me buy those horrid shreds of coloured ribbon on safety pins you said were badges because I couldn't tell a penny from a dime, at least you're almost sitting up like a human being and not rolled in like a fish on a platter, at least you're getting your money's worth from this therapist aren't you?

—I got rid of the therapist.

—You get rid of the one person who's doing you any good, I should have guessed shouldn't I.

—Well you guessed wrong. Ilse's been doing my, those things, handling those things she...

—Handling what things. Does it ever occur to you to simply try to get up and walk, Oscar? Where is she.

—She's gone to do the shopping.

—You still have her riding around in a taxi to order your groceries? There must be a less extravagant way of buying a bunch of carrots. There is such a thing as the telephone.

—Well you don't have to eat them Christina! I just thought Mister Basie might like something a little diff...

—He's not coming all the way out here to eat carrots is he? I thought all these court papers were filed and you were just waiting for a decision.

—We are, but we, but he has some things he wants to talk to me about and, and he said he thought the two of us should sit down together.

—Well there is such a thing as the telephone, Oscar. For the two of you I mean, maybe you'd rather I didn't join you?

—I didn't say that did I? I just meant that I, that sometimes when I'm trying to...

—Well you do seem to get things rather muddled sometimes and need someone to step in and move them along, I'm sure he keeps the clock running even when he's eating carrots. I'm going for a walk, I'll be back for lunch. I wouldn't think of missing it.

Swans, a whole fleet of them, rumpled the still surface of the pond where she came down to follow the sandy edge of it, giving way finally to reeds and mud sending her up to the road past one silent hulk of a house well beyond a stone's throw from another closed, most of them, for winter, leading her on to the dunes, the shock of a wind borne in from the restless waves out there urging her down the empty beach all the way to the cut where the sea turned the pond brackish, harassing her every retraced step to the road till by the time the driveway led her in under those mangled pines she brought the chill right into the house and stood there shaking it off. —Oscar? Voices reached her rising on a tide of garlic and olive oil.

—Only problem there Oscar, see your only problem is you've got right there in your original complaint where you're alleging professional distress for your second cause of action.

—I'm sure that's not his only problem Mister Basie, how are you? She waved off a handshake across the room, —please don't get up. What has he done now.

—Just talking about this letter he's writing to the...

—It's nothing Christina, it's just, give it back to me!

But she'd lifted it lightly from his hand, coming round behind him, —this? scanning it, —is it a joke?

—I said give it back to me!

—Who in God's name is Sir John Nipples.

—He's none of your, he's a director, he's the prominent British theatre director who...

—Surprised you never heard of him Mrs Lutz, he's put on some of these great productions from the Elizabethans. Beaumont and

Fletcher, Ford, Webster, did a Marlowe's Tamburlaine there two years ago knocked them out of their seats.

—There! you see? You see Christina? How he could bring out the pure poetry in my battlefield scene at the end of act two? and Thomas? my character Thomas torn between his demands for justice and his destiny being stolen from him by, the whole last act, and the curtain, when John Israel comes back and...

—He hasn't even read it has he?

—That's what this is all about, this letter, he wants to read it. How many people do you think get a letter from Sir John Nipples asking to look at their play, to see the whole thing up there on the stage just the way you imagined it and the whole...

—That's a good question isn't it, how he happens to write to you of all people at a moment like this?

—What do you mean of all people! He probably, he may have read my interview in the paper when I set the record straight on the vulgar desecration of the great passions and paradoxes of man's existence that have been the very heart of theatre since the Greeks to bring them down to the...

—Oscar?

—to the cheap appetites of the movie, what.

—See when she says at a moment like this, only way he'd even hear about your play is from this lawsuit in the papers.

—That's what I just...

—Where you're asking these triple damages there for your second cause of action?

—And it ought to be quadruple, quintuple, profaning the ideas and passions in a thing like this it ought to be ten times the...

—Asking money damages Oscar see that's what you have to prove, you've suffered money damages. Say old Sir John here'd come along a year or two ago wanting to do your play, took an option on it, you've got grounds there to project your Broadway profits maybe a movie sale coming out of that, miniseries, merchandising, money, just plain money. Court doesn't give a good God damn about desecrating these great poetic passions you've got. What you're alleging in your complaint is this movie they made whether it's a great movie or just a piece of, whether it's any good or not that they stole it from you and shut you out of any chance of ever seeing a dollar on your own creation like it has it right there in Section 8 of Article 2, same thing if your play is junk and a movie turns it into Coriolanus there's your constitutional right to protect a piece of junk, see that's what these cases are mostly all of them about, protecting one piece of junk against another piece of junk and there's your precedents. Sir John gets your play up there in lights and you blow your whole case because without this movie he'd never have heard of it. You don't even want anybody to know you heard from him, they hear about it and they'll come back suing you for a finder's fee. That brings me to the next thing here. They just made us an offer to settle.

—To, you mean my lawsuit? to settle my lawsuit?

—Settle it out of court, clean up the whole thing. Two hundred thousand dollars.

—That they'd, you mean they'd give me two hundred thousand dollars?

—Thank God.

—No now wait Christina I, two hundred thousand dollars!

—Well my God Oscar what are you hesitating for! Take the money, forget about the movie and call up the great Mister Nipples, that's what you've wanted all the time isn't it?

—Two hundred thousand dollars! Cash? in cash?

—To clear up this whole mess of course he'll take it Mister Basie, won't you Oscar.

—No but wait, wait...

—Up to him Mrs Lutz. Help him out on these legal expenses here wouldn't it.

—No but, help me out?

—See I don't know right where you stand on our last statement there but they maybe haven't got my trip to the coast in there yet, that whole deal going out to the coast, you got your last statement?

—Well I, it's here someplace but I, but the coast you mean California?

—Well where is it Oscar.

—Where is what. You mean you went out to California?

—Had to go out there to take their depositions, the writers, Kiester, the whole gang, sat around the Beverly Wilshire for two days waiting for Bredford to sober up to where he could spell his own name, couldn't even remember making the picture.

—Their statement Oscar. Where is it.

—It's right there, Christina! It's, it's probably over in that blue folder with some bills I haven't had time to open yet but, now wait! Put it back!

—Even bumped into an old buddy out there from when I knew him back in the, back in my little theatre days, plays the main house slave in the movie and...

—Christina I said put it back! You have no business opening my...

—My God.

—Maybe didn't get my trip south in there either, down there trying to register those old Historical Society letters. Turned out the old Judge was one step ahead of us, got in there and registered them in his own name.

—My God Oscar.

—Doesn't hurt anything Mrs Lutz long as they're protected, this law clerk of his told me the old Judge says as long as he's alive this per stirpes stops right here at his door.

—I mean this statement, my God. Well here Oscar, look at it!

—See what I mean about this settlement they want to palm off on you, talking before taxes too probably just about eat it up.

—Eat it up! and what about, look at them! paper tearing all the way —doctors, hospitals, x-rays, therapy here's the one for mutilating our trees out there you haven't even paid them yet? Trash removal, eighty dollars and a quarter? How long have you...

—I just told you I, the battery in my calculator burned out and I haven't had...

—Haven't had time to open them my God Oscar what do you do here all day, sit there with your Pinot Grigio and plan your little luncheon menus in the Spanish style? Now who's this one, law offices of Kevin who's he, that ambulance chaser she dug up for you?

—Well that's not, I haven't seen it no that can't be a bill, it was all a contingency arrangement that he said would be...

—Hours, disbursements, filing your case with New York Supreme Court seventy five hundred dollars.

—No!

—You make a written agreement with him Oscar?

—Well no, it was a, it was clearly understood that we...

—Clearly understood! Oscar never even met him.

—No, I simply won't pay it that's all. I won't pay it.

—Might have a problem getting your file back from him if you get yourself a new lawyer on it.

—I've got a new lawyer.

—Where did you get a new lawyer, Oscar.

—Well I, never mind where I got him Christina I've already had a telephone consultation with them and they're taking it, they're specialists that's what they specialize in, they specialize in personal injury cases like this one, in negligence, they...

—They probably sent a request for your file to this Kevin so he sits on the file and signs off with a bill.

—No well wait now listen, listen. I've been through this before, listen. He stepped in and took a divorce case for my, for a friend of mine from another lawyer who did the same thing, she wouldn't release the file till we paid her off for the mess she'd made of it and I won't do it again. I won't pay him. It's blackmail, I won't pay him, isn't it? blackmail?

—Pure and simple Oscar, legal blackmail.

—Well what are you going to do. You have a check here, did you know it? from your college health care Blue Cross program?

—Where, no, no I thought it was a bill.

—It's a check from Blue Cross for thirty seven dollars and eighty cents. Subject of course to any other insurance settlement you may have received.

—Do you know what they offered me? this, this other insurance settlement they offered me fifteen hundred dollars for everything, for the whole thing, fifteen hundred dollars!

—That makes a grand total of two hundred one thousand five hundred thirty seven dollars and eighty cents if you accept all these generous offers, doesn't it. What do you plan to...

—Yes and that's, he just said that's before taxes too so it probably wouldn't even cover the, all this, I don't understand all this, these disbursements and these, all these depositions in California?

—Disbursements Oscar, see that's money we lay out. Travel, filing fees, duplication, stenographers, that stenographer who came out here taking down your deposition that's ten dollars a page right there.

—Well I'm not paying her am I? They're the ones who wanted the deposition, that revolting little Mister Mudpye?

—Just to give you an idea how these depositions can run into money, see the ones I took out on the coast there were all...

—That's what I mean, who are they these, Railswort? Afhadi? Probidetz?

—They're the writers on the picture, they...

—And this Button somebody, who in the...

—That's the old buddy I just told you about, played the head house slave from right there in their opening scene through the whole...

—No but wait, wait, I mean just because he's your old buddy sitting around drinking in the Beverly Wilshire for two days while this Bredford's sobering up? What's the...

—Try to calm down Oscar, just calm down.

—It's all right Mrs Lutz, ought to ask me anything he wants to. See we had a little setback there. About the scar.

—What scar. On his face in the movie? That's one of the best proofs we have that they stole it, that they stole my play it's right there in the first scene when the curtain goes up.

—What I thought too Oscar, I surely thought so. Turns out they've got affidavits from old Button there and the doctor who sewed him up for their claim that right before they started shooting those scenes where he comes in with his scar Bredford got in an altercation with a cab driver in New York right beside General Sherman there outside the Plaza Hotel and the cab driver bit him on the cheek, would have held up their production schedule losing half a million a day so they just wrote it in.

—But that's, I don't believe it.

—They've got their original script there without it and this affidavit from my old buddy who happened to be on the spot trying to babysit Bredford even have the cabbie they're holding for deportation when they can figure out what country he comes from, couldn't take his affidavit because nobody can figure out what the hell language he's speaking.

—I don't believe any of it!

—But see the court will Oscar, got the sworn affidavits right there to prove it.

—Maybe this solves everything Oscar. Turn down their settlement, lose your case, and you're perfectly free to go off on your Broadway honeymoon with Sir John Nipples and be in debt for the rest of your life my God, you know what Harry told you, that you can always lose a case? He said it would cost you money didn't he? Well here's the money Oscar, take their settlement pay the taxes and start to clean up this whole mess, it's the chance you always wanted isn't it? This great director you're so besotted with if he really wants to do your play isn't that everything you've dreamed of? seeing it done the way you imagined it when you saw it in your head while you were writing it, to let Father see what you really wrote and be proud of you? Isn't that, doesn't that make sense Mister Basie? Doesn't it?

—Hate to see it drop now we've come this far Mrs Lutz.

—But with your, with this story about the scar and the, and if you lose? if he loses?

—We appeal Mrs Lutz.

—Yes and if you win they appeal and the clock keeps right on running?

—We knew that right off from the start didn't we, like Harry said you bring a big lawsuit it's going to cost money? See we got a strong case here, real strong. Why do you think they want to settle? This about the scar here it's a bad break, there's always bad breaks you got to expect them but that's all it is, just one little bad break in a real strong case why do you think they'll pay up to a quarter of a million to settle? See most cases, like maybe ninety percent of cases they're settled out of court at the last minute like this one, like they're trying to bait the hook here on this one. Why do you think they just settled with that documentary maker, they knew he had them by the short hair on that sledgehammer scene he did in Uruburu, same thing here. You think they're offering to settle if they're sure they can win?

—Yes and if they lose, if they lose they appeal and...

—If we lose, what we're talking about here if we lose. See they've assigned this case to this brand new district court judge, no track record you can't tell which way she'll go, the ABA sits real hard on these appointments and she's got a real high priced reputation as a negotiator, can't tell which way she'll go then what. Say she finds for the defendant and throws it out, then what. Maybe that's good Mrs Lutz. You take how many cases lose in the district court and win on appeal because that's where this Second Circuit Appeals Court's got a real appetite for cutting down the court below so maybe you play to that. Maybe that's how we play it.

—I honestly don't know what you mean, to lose? You plan to lose?

—Plan to win, win or lose. See I'm telling you we've got a real strong case here, win in the lower court and fight their appeal or lose and fight it out on our appeal I'm telling you, won't go into all the legal niceties of it they call them but the long view, taking the long view they win all pleased with themselves and we'll take them in the higher court win or lose, we'll take them on appeal.

—I see. I mean of course I don't see, it all sounds rather risky. Oscar?

—What? Oh. Yes it's probably ready, lunch is probably ready.

—I'm not talking about lunch! Have you been listening to what he's said?

—Of course I've been listening!

—Well? What are you going to do, accept their, where are you going.

—To see about lunch!

—Can't you simply blow your little horn? Let her call us when she, my God. I'm not sure what you're in for Mister Basie, what you smell may be a warning.

—Didn't count on lunch Mrs Lutz, afraid I got to pass it up, get back to the...

—He'll be terribly disappointed, he's sounded like it's the only reason you came all the way out here.

—Didn't count on it, see we could have done all this on the telephone but he insisted, thought the two of us should sit down together coming down to the wire here, go over the whole case, why he had me to bring out the whole file, see all this? riffling through papers in the attaché case opened on his lap, —brought the whole file I would have needed a trunk I just brought out the latest hey, look. Look, see this? flourishing a streamer of newspaper, —brought this out to you, thought maybe you missed it, piece in the paper on your hairy Ainu you were talking about?

—Well I, no I didn't see it, I...

—Where they think now how the samurai, this fancy top elite

warrior class way up there in the nobility that's like it says here the epitome of everything Japanese in their Kabuki and all the rest, how these samurai are really descended right down from your primitive old hairy Ainu they've been treating like dirt over there for a thousand years like a field nigger down here in Fayette County, have to say I got a kick out of it.

—Yes I, I can see you might I, thank you.

—Never would even have noticed it there in the paper but I remembered you talking about your hairy...

—Yes I, I'm sure you do yes thank you for thinking of my, of me, Oscar? Mister Basie's afraid he can't stay for lunch.

—But we, I thought we could talk some more about the...

—Got it all talked out Oscar, talk any more we'll just get confused.

—But I, maybe I can call you later or, tomorrow if I call you tomorrow we can...

—May not be a tomorrow, we're right down to the wire here, the judge sitting on those papers right now. It's real simple Oscar. You take their settlement and I'll pick up the phone. You want to go on with it, we'll hold our breath for the decision.

—Then I, I'll hold my breath.

—Hey!

—Oscar you're, do you know what you're...

—I know what I'm doing Christina. I'm going on with it.

—Hey, Oscar! and a clap on the sagging shoulder there, —that's it!

—My God. Wait, I'll see you to the door Mister Basie. I just hope you're right, I know you've worked awfully hard on it and, and I know you're not foolish. Harry's told me you're very much in demand.

—How's he doing?

—Harry? If he comes through this case alive I suppose he can come through anything.

—You want to see legal bills take a look at those. Thanks Mrs Lutz, you give him my best?

—Yes and, thank you... She stood there until the slur of tires on the gravel turned her back into the house and that lunch —and Ilse? That Pinot Grigio, bring it in to the table, did you hear me? And over the cold corn soup, —what's this floating in it. You don't plan to hoard that whole bottle of wine over there do you? I only hope your Mister Basie is as brilliant as Harry thinks he is oh, they're scallops aren't they, I mean if you have anything left once you've paid his bar bills buying drinks for his old buddies at the Beverly Wilshire? and over the carrots —you can start thinking about that seventy five hundred dollars for that ambulance chaser that blonde plaything of yours dug up I'm sure you still give her money? over the poached salmon —her divorce is probably as far off as ever thank God let me have the salt, I mean I hope she didn't find these new lawyers you've got that you're so secretive about, and the wine please? Of course it was quite senseless of that law clerk of Father's taking him to the movies in the first place but it may all blow over when you lose your lawsuit which Mister Basie seems to be planning on but I mean that should convince them that your play wasn't worth anyone bothering to steal so it's all just as well isn't it? her chair scraping the floor as she pushed the emptied wine bottle aside —here, let me help you. You're aware that you're putting on weight aren't you, whatever these rubdowns this woman is giving you if that's the word for it, handling things I won't ask exactly what it is she's handling but your body really never has been your friend has it, because you never learned to play. I mean you never really learned to play did you.

—To play what! he muttered, making their way back to the empty room already falling into shadows.

—No I mean, I just meant like other boys with...

—What other boys! You mean out playing baseball? There were no other boys, I used to play all the time I didn't need other boys, right down there by the pond I used to play all the time didn't I? By the shores of Gitche Gumee?

—Stood the wigwam of Nokomis, my God no I didn't mean that, where she stood now looking out over the pond, looking out where dark beyond it rose the black and gloomy pine trees and the firs with cones upon them —it was all just too heartbreaking, by the shining Big-Sea-Water where a tall and stately birch tree once had rustled in the breezes, where he'd cleft its bark asunder just beneath the lowest branches, just above the roots he'd cut it down the trunk from top to bottom, stripped away the bark unbroken for the birch canoe he'd made there puffed with pride at his achievement turning turtle when he'd launched it, filled with terror when his father saw the great birch torn and naked till its sap came oozing outward and the swift Cheemaun for sailing floating upside down and sideways through the reeds and tangled beach grass come to rest there in the mud —and it should have been a warning that you could never please Father.

Out there now the rising west wind rushed the surface of the pond toward the sea like a spring freshet, a flash flood, —look! he whispered, —how it's tossing up the branches of the pine trees like some wild saturnalia, flinging up their skirts all lust and rapine ravished like the Sabine women, like the...

—Like the beautiful Wenonah. I think it's a time for Hiawatha's nap, I'm going up for a bath. I mean if there's any hot water of course.

Dark had taken the trees and the torn surface of the pond out there by the time she came down where bursts of colours dancing across his face from the illumination of the screen belittled its repose till the sound of his name restored all its accumulated anxiety in an instant, in the blink of an eye caught up in a wince.
—What?

—I said are you awake? what on earth are you watching? and a voice from the screen obliged her with 'a sea anemone which looks like a harmless flower but is in reality a carnivorous animal.'

—It's my nature program he told her, slouching almost upright.

—You do have curious tastes don't you, she came turning on lights. —Has Harry called? And when it finally rang —We're fine, did you get to that new doctor? Well whatever you call him, you... I know that Harry but you've simply got to make time, if you don't you're going to end up like... that's exactly what I mean, he's sitting right here waiting for the evening news to whet his appetite for supper, I mean I can't take care of both of you can I? Scenes of mayhem from Londonderry to Chandigarh, an overweight family rowing down main street in a freak flood in Ohio, a molasses truck overturned on the Jersey Turnpike, gunfire, stabbings, flaming police cars and blazing ambulances celebrating a league basketball championship in Detroit interspersed with a decrepit grinning couple on a bed that warped and heaved at the touch of a button —because they offered him a settlement Harry, almost a quarter million dollars but of course he insists on going ahead with the case or rather Mister Basie does, he was out here for... what? The

Stars and Bars unfurled in a hail of rocks and beer cans showering the guttering remnants of a candlelight vigil —but if you can just try to be patient with her Harry, you know her mother just died and she's been in an awful state trying to... to what? Oscar will you turn that down! that now she wants you to help her break her mother's will? I don't see what... well they never really got on after her mother was converted by that wildeyed Bishop Sheed was it? a million years ago convincing her that it was more exclusive with Clare Luce and all that after the wads of money she'd been giving St Bartholomew's with these millions of Catholics jamming every slum you can think of if you call that exclusive, she...

—Look! Christina look! Placards brandishing **KEEP GOD IN AMERICA, MURDERER** —come quickly! and caught in the emergency vehicles' floodlights towering over it all the jagged thrust of —that, that Szyrk thing that, look!

—I'll talk to you later Harry, something's going on. What in God's name...

—It was struck by lightning and the dog, they said it killed the dog that's what all those candles...

—Well thank God for that.

—No but look at them look at the, that sign that little girl was carrying that said murderer that's Father, they said that was Father they, look! Did you see that? The effigy swung back into view and away to reveal a collision between a hot dog cart and a sandwich board purveyor of novelty flags, Spot dolls, keychains, T shirts bearing the Spot logo blazoned beyond on chests and unrestrained breastworks engulfing a frail girl whose meager bosom cautioned **You may play with my dog but leave my pussy alone** abruptly swept away by **PROCHOICE, IT'S MY BODY, ART IS FILTH,** a siren's wail and a bullhorn exhorting Go home now, youall uns just go home, hear? **BLACK PRIDE, THE LAVENDER COALITION, SMOKE WHITE OWLS, HE MARKS THE SPAROWS FALL** as the camera nosed its way through the streaming candles for a jarring glimpse of fur wadded there in a spotlit glare broken off in the shadow of the effigy swinging closer, close enough to read **MURDERER JUDGE THYSELF** pinned to its robes —because he called it an act of God, the lightning, that's what they said, that's the candlelight vigil.

—My God.

—No don't turn it off! Wait... The screen brightened. A leggy blonde cycled down a country lane and they were told she'd found relief from hemorrhoids as she passed them beaming, a woman gnashed gleaming dentures and they were told how she kept them in place, a sometime movie star pursued the active life with a tennis racket no longer hampered by incontinence —well try another station! and once again the sirens wailed, flags, placards, beer cans and fists flew, a moment's inattention and an armoured personnel carrier spewing tear gas down an emptied street —my God look! but the black body necklaced with a blazing tire turned out to lie at a crossroad in Soweto and now, poised at a casement window, a lady in impeccable negligee stirred by a gentle breeze over phantom breasts smiled serenely on the unruffled landscape of a country morning after a satisfactory bout with an overnight laxative in the day's early light, mist rising on the pond out there and the smell of —some more coffee? Ilse? over the morning paper's rehearsal of flying fists and beer cans, rocks and occasional items of intimate apparel culminating in twenty seven cases of injury, one of alleged rape and two arrests heralding a national outpouring of grief signaled on highways and byways throughout the land in lighted headlamps blinded by the sun as screens everywhere came to life with each delicate step in extracting the limp twelve pound remains from their fatal entrapment following emergency measures taken by the Village under the watchful eyes of dark suited local officials in unaccustomed neckties knotted once for all and hung over bedposts during the week, assorted insurance adjusters and senior citizens, white minister, black pastor, and the media cornering a stoic James B shouldered aside by his expansive father confronting their microphones in a mix of cordiality and vengeance, survivors of the night's melee and the entire resident dog population of every hue and cry, their numbers to be swelled in these days to come by gifts from many points of the compass and as various a herd of givers, a mastiff from a black coalition in Chicago and a pit bull from an anonymous donor in Mississippi, two salukis and an Afghan signed ChubbyChasers International and a registered cocker spaniel from a former First Lady and a springer from a more recent one but none, elegized the press, could take the place of little Spot in the heart of little James B, or in the heart of America, or, as it soon proved, in the astute vision of the boy's guardian ad litem filing suit against the Village charging negligence, distraint, conversion, conspiracy, loss of companionship and restraint of trade where it all might have ended down the road in Judge Elbert Haynes' Wink County Supreme Court with no more than the usual racial abrasions and related high jinks attendant on jury selection thereabouts but for the shrewd eye of presiding Village Board member J Harret Ruth surveying the wider prospect of Federal jurisdiction and so proceeding by impleader to provide the requisite out-of-state litigant in the odd bedfellow of the original creator of the vehicle of entrapment and 'rusting travesty of our great nation's vision of itself' thus satisfying the simmering local appetite for a proven common enemy —landing the whole enchilada, as Harry phrased it standing there in front of the smoking fireplace rattling the law newsletter he'd been reading from —right back in the old man's lap.

—Whatever all that means.

—Means they've dragged this sculptor Szyrk into it makes it a Federal case, diversity of citizenship.

—A name like that what could he expect.

—Nothing to do with his name Christina, just meant to protect somebody from another state against getting chewed up by your local rednecks.

—Which is exactly what will happen. Can't you fix that fire?

—Exactly. Get a jury trial going they'll chew him up and spit him out, something wrong with the damper I just opened it. The old man they're really out to get, this J Harret Ruth with his own cheap political agenda's nose up so far between the cheeks with that Neanderthal senator of theirs up for reelection, if they can kill the Judge on this appeals court seat that's what he's after, you'll see. Perfect forum, you get the...

—You've got to do something about it Harry, my...

—Not a damn thing I can do about it, just told you it's the law. Demand a jury trial within ten days after the pleadings and they've got one, a perfect forum. You get the...

—The fire, I'm talking about the fire. My eyes are burning I can hardly...

—Wood's probably wet. Or green, you get a leading old time states' rights advocate like Bilk up there in front of these hambones talking about the Federal government spending their tax money where it's got no business, he's already stood out there on the Senate floor and said art today is spelled with an f hasn't he? right in the public's face? Product of warped sick minds, sexual deviants, degenerates and foreigners Szyrk's made to order. Where are you going?

—To open some windows, why on earth you had to build a fire.

—Just seemed, Sunday afternoon in the country a fall day like this it seemed like what you do.

—You ought to turn on the football game then, you always like seeing somebody lose. You're simply not a country person Harry, you shouldn't go around building fires, any minute Oscar will be out from his nap and he'll have a fit.

—Nothing unusual about that.

—Well you can't blame him can you? Day after day waiting for this decision he calls Mister Basie and he's told he's out of the office, out of town, we're both nervous wrecks and these lawyers he got God knows where on his accident case now what are you doing.

—This, damn, damper keeps slipping closed trying to, damn. There. All be clear by suppertime.

—I can't wait till suppertime Harry, another day of this, another hour I'll lose my mind, if I have to watch one more nature program. No deer or bears or anything healthy no, no the ones he watches are all animals pretending to be flowers, deadly insects that look like twigs, harmless looking creatures simply seething with poison just lying in wait it's all rather unwholesome, and Ilse. If you could hear the splashing and carrying on in there when he has his bath God knows what they're up to, at least he hasn't mentioned that mess of a blonde I think I hear him coming, Harry for God's sake. A cup of tea and we'll leave. I'm all packed and I cannot endure another discussion deciding whether we'll have salmon with the dill anchovy butter or poached in an aspic glaze, simply tell him your office called and, oh Oscar? We've got to be off.

—But I thought, but Harry just got here Christina I thought he'd come out for a rest look, look he's built a lovely fire and I've told her to make tea I thought, about supper I thought...

—So did I, but they called and want him in there first thing in the morning. We want to miss the Sunday night traffic.

—But when did, I didn't hear the phone ring, I...

—It's ringing right now.

—No, I can reach it but, hello?

—Harry, can you bring down my bags?

—Who? But, oh, later, call later I, goodbye.

—Oh Ilse, you needn't bother with the tea. Well who was it.

—Who was, oh. A wrong number. They got the wrong number.

—Then why did you tell them to call back later.

—I just meant, you said Harry was exhausted that he needed a rest and I wanted to talk to him about the...

—My God Oscar we're all exhausted, we all need a rest Harry? can you hear me? She passed to fight a casement window closed, —there's a small makeup case in the bathroom, will you bring it? And she stood arrested, looking down the lawn where only the day before he'd stared out, even called her to see the only thing that moved out there, a bluebird hopping across the discoloured grass? or was it only a jay, but she'd been too busy to look, picking up streamers of newspaper, scraps of notepaper —if there's one thing I can't stand it's litter, will you ever learn to keep your things in one place? And now, —you've got to get that damper fixed Oscar, before somebody burns down the house. Are we ready? The squeeze of a hand, of a shoulder, —let me know if you hear from Father, perhaps you should call him, Ilse? Will you help us with these bags? And out on the veranda, —I wish you'd look down on the front lawn Ilse, there's a blue plastic bag blowing around out there where someone's been eating potato chips or something, don't things around here look shabby enough? Bracing herself against the bound of the car up the pits in the driveway, —that veranda is one thing, but if there's one thing I cannot stand it's, look out! throwing her arm up.

—Did you see? He skidded back into the rut he'd swerved from avoiding the old car cutting a swathe through bull vine and bittersweet down the driveway behind them.

—No, what. Who.

—Lily.

And see what she'd brought him, —Oscar? banging the outside doors, clattering down the hall —are you okay? It was a chocolate icecream cake and look, he already had a fire going in the fireplace, it was like old times, everything was so cozy, it was like he expected her, when she'd called and he hung up in her face she just came right over, to tell the truth she wasn't too sure what kind of welcome she'd get, coming down beside him, didn't he even have a kiss for her? sitting here all alone like old Mister Grouch with the silent television already aglow where a mouse flattened a cat with a sledgehammer, —you're not watching that are you? Look at me. Aren't you even going to ask how I am? But all he wanted to know was what she'd done to her hair. —I had it cut and shaped, do you like it? Me neither. Is that why you're so standoffish? You're not mad are you? But he seemed suddenly absorbed in the predicament of the cat, who was being stamped into smaller editions with a cookiecutter. —Oscar? Is everything okay?

—Is everything okay! Of all the stupid, you show up here like this out of nowhere just to ask me if everything's okay?

—I only meant, I thought maybe by now you're up walking around again and that, that everything...

—That everything was okay. That I'd forgotten all about the way you walked out of here with that, that, that all these medical bills were paid and I'd won my suit against the movie sitting here with seventy five million dollars in my pocket? Will you just tell me why you came? without making a big scene about it, just a plain honest answer?

—Oscar you can't! seizing both his hands —no, I've thought about you every day, how kind and gentle you are I forgot, I forgot how cold you can be, how you can look at me like you're looking right through me like I'm not even there. Do you know how that cuts right through somebody that cares about you like I do like this big knife cutting right through them? I never said anything about your seventy five million dollars, is that why you think I came? That's why you think I came isn't it, I don't see how you can be so cruel to me, how you can be so suspicious the minute I walk in the door that you won't even look at me because you're afraid I might ask you for money, even just a little because all this time you thought well I won't have to go through that again didn't you. You thought I'll never have to go through that with her again because I told you with Bobbie gone maybe I'll have this reconciliation with Daddy over this old misunderstanding where now I'm all they've got so maybe he'll help me out where there's all this money he put in Bobbie's name in this joint account where the government wouldn't get it when he died in these death taxes only now it's

Bobbie that died instead so he has to pay all these death taxes on Bobbie's estate for his own money coming back to him which was really his all along, are you even listening to me?

—Now you listen to me. This miserable ambulance chaser you got to help everybody out, do you know how he helped me out? Sending me a bill for seventy five hundred dollars for filing some court papers someplace in my accident case and he won't hand anything over to the new lawyers I've got looking into it till I pay him, you remember right back at the start? When I asked you about paying him and you told me he said don't worry about it? The same trick that miserable woman lawyer played on us when he took your divorce case away from her after she made some feeble excuse and pulled out? Now he does the same thing.

—You know why Oscar? Because now she's this judge. Because he told me how they made her this judge and he got scared if he crossed her that some time he might have to appear before her in court where she'd wipe up the floor with him for revenge like she ought to do anyway just because he's such a real sleazeball.

—Then why did you let him get your, get you in the back seat of his BMW and every motel bed from Disney World to...

—I told you!

—You did not tell me!

—Because I was mad at you, because...

—Why! You didn't tell me why, you just...

—Because you hurt my feelings, I told you.

—You've told me that a hundred times, how. How did I...

—Because you just did again, you said I was stupid right when I came in, just because you're smarter than I am with all these books that doesn't mean you're better than me does it?

—Listen, just tell me what I did that made you get into bed with that, that real...

—The way you treated me laying there on your back with this big erection sticking up right in front of somebody as if you never saw me before you didn't even...

—No wait, wait. In front of who...

—I don't know who! Because he didn't have any clothes on either like you were just laying there showing off and there were these cans of shoe polish on the bed, there were these three kinds of shoe polish and you...

—No wait stop it, stop! You mean this was some dream you had? some stupid dream that made you so mad when you woke up that you...

—It was real! It was as real as anything, it was just as real as that little man in the black suit you dreamed came to see you in the hospital to take these messages to the other side and...

—No that happened! That really happened, it was as real as we're sitting here now with your...

—That's what I just said! It was just as real as right now with your hand on my, I still get mad when I remember you laying there with it sticking up like I never saw you have one like that before and you looked at me like you never saw me before when I reached over and...

—Of all the, the shoe polish? three kinds of shoe polish? Of all the, dreams like that all of them, they're the junkyard of the mind all of them of all the crazy, and you want me to believe that? that that's why you did it?

—Oscar why are you doing this to me! When you're all I've thought about day after day crying myself to sleep sometimes at night remembering all the nice things I did for you when it was just you and me? Like that time that we, I can't even talk about it, that sweet sad kind of smile you'd always have when I came in the room I thought about it all the way coming over here but you just look at me like you wish I'd go away, I can feel it, you don't even want to look at me but I can feel it, don't you even think I have feelings? And finally letting go his moist hands to look up where his gaze lay fixed —at her? a full bosomed blonde crossing a knobbed knee on the screen, —you'd like to be feeling hers wouldn't you, did you think that's what I meant? This lump I've got, I think it got worse since I saw you, can you feel it? No don't then, you didn't even ask, it's too late please don't try, can't I say anything to make you listen to me?

—No wait, look! he startled upright, —where's the, here! The room shook with the sound of cannon fire, the screen with a tumult of plunging horses, flaring rockets and the Stars and Bars and men, men —look!

—How can you do this! I can't believe you're actually doing this just to drive me away when I came here to...

—Please! as the smoke cleared, and now the room echoed with

the clop clop of a horse and carriage seen approaching up a drive adroop with Spanish moss from the pillared veranda of an antebellum mansion by an imposing liveried black, the sun gleaming on the strong lineaments of his brow arching disdainfully as a decrepit horse and buggy bearing an aging woman and a handsome intense young man standing to snap his whip imperiously came close for an exchange of unheard words to be pointed scornfully on their way, glimpsed from behind a curtain by a ravishingly beautiful young woman in negligee in their retreat back down the drive. —Good God! he barely whispered.

—If that's all you can...

—That was the first scene of my, did you see it! And here was the blonde again, seated knob knee to knee with a black man of imposing dimensions and sartorial splendour introduced as 'our guest today' by a name she was sure their wonderful audience out there would want to know if it was his real one? —Yes it's that friend of look it's, listen!

—No I'm going! I'm going right now Oscar, if you think I came over just to sit and watch television I can't believe how much you've changed, maybe I can't still expect you to feel like I do about you but I hoped at least you could be kind, are you listening to me? She'd lurched up only to come down closer as they were being told it was a long story, how he'd taken this name, because his old name was way behind him, far enough behind him that now he could talk about it, because he'd done time under his old name, —can't you see what I'm going through? she came on, —that you're looking at somebody that's practically coming to pieces? You're not even looking at me, can't you even hold my hand if you can't bear to look at me? It was back in Illinois, he'd been sent up for three years for something a dumb kid would do stealing a car and he didn't even realize he'd driven across the state line that made it a Federal crime and a Federal prison and he felt like his life was over before it hardly began but maybe you wouldn't believe it, that was the best thing that ever happened to him. —Don't you believe me? and she had his hand again, tight —if I told you it really didn't mean anything? that I was all upset about your accident seeing you in pain and then Bobbie when tragedy struck down there and I hardly knew what I was doing when I let him do it? The best thing that ever happened because they had a program there, kind of play acting therapy for the prisoners to help them understand their anger by venting their hostility in these plays they chose, The Emperor Jones, he'd done The Emperor Jones —when I was really crying out for help Oscar and you weren't there on account of your accident, nobody was, can't you understand? He'd always been pretty vain about his looks, had to admit it now with the studio lights gleaming on the strong lineaments of his brow arching in a deprecating sort of way but they'd never brought him anything but trouble and now suddenly here was a place for them, a place for all his anger and strength and talent if you'd call it that and he'd never have made it without the others, the other prisoners when he heard their applause he knew he had something, one buddy in the program in particular kind of a jailhouse lawyer in there for something that would curl your hair tried to help him out on his appeal, told him if you're black in America you're always playing a part, no way around it just got to find the right part to play where you aren't going to take your bows in a cell block and that did it, —Oscar?

—Just listen will you!

—Can't you just listen to me for a second? please? her voice broke in what might have been a sob, and that was when he swore he knew what he'd be, who he'd be when he got out of there, when he took that name from one of the signers of the Declaration of Independence because this was his own declaration of independence from who he'd been, who they'd told him he was when they took one look at him, who they'd tried to make him, besides he'd had a little brother once they called Button, died from meningitis they'd thought was just a bad cold, didn't have any doctor, couldn't afford one —because I need you to help me Oscar, won't you just listen?

—How! I've got my own doctors' bills to pay haven't I? He'd snapped off the sound as the screen abruptly confronted them with a lively fellow fleeing the torments of diarrhea at what appeared to be an international airport, —after the mess you and that lawyer you brought me made of things? He ought to be shot.

—That's why I came, Oscar.

—You've done enough haven't you? Will you just come right out with it? without all this, all these maudlin theatrics, just come right out and tell me what you want?

—Revenge.

—For what, against who, what...

—Him.

—A little late for that isn't it? He's already got me into this mess, and then he sends a bill for seven...

—Not for you, for me, what he's done to me.

—We know what he's done to you don't we? in the front seat, the back seat and every bed from here to Disney World, that's all he's good for isn't it?

—With my girlfriend.

—What girlfriend, what...

—He's been screwing my girlfriend! That's what. My girlfriend from the phone company where we worked together on long lines, she needed this divorce so I sent her to him and they did it the second time she went there, right on his desk, she said he just pushed all these papers away and fucked her right up there on his desk and they're doing it now someplace, I bet they're doing it someplace right now.

—She told you this?

—After I got my hair cut and shaped like this because he wanted me to that makes me look like some scarecrow?

—Take him before a grievance committee, that's what I...

—Are you crazy? because it's just all these other lawyers, didn't he tell us that himself? when we wanted to do that with that sleazeball woman lawyer he took my divorce away from that we had to pay off and now she's this judge? Because they're all these other lawyers that are screwing their clients so they're scared if they give him a hard time they're going to be next, no. I mean revenge. I mean like in the movies, you're always writing these plays where you have to think up these characters and plots and everything and here's this real sleazeball character you have to start right off with, it would make some movie. You ought to see my girlfriend, she's really built and she's got all this red hair you ought to see her. Are you hungry? We could watch television while we eat and maybe you'll think of something.

And so over Pinot Grigio and cold salmon with mayonnaise and a boiled potato they watched Errol Flynn in The Charge of the Light Brigade. —Do you have to go? over that sodden icecream cake.

—I have to get this car back where I borrowed it.
—Where, from who.
—My girlfriend at long lines.

When the telephone rang later that night he let it ring, drawn up tight with one knee clenched against him as though cringing from some featureless dread there under the cover where he had a terrible dream which he could not remember, transfixed over coffee and the morning's headlines, or even on the mornings after that, vaguely following the course of jury selection and the trial in U.S. District Court, Southern District of Virginia, kept alive in the press pandering to Senator Bilk's electioneering appetite for attacks by the liberal northern media on his perennial states' rights stance against Federal interference in general and his vow to his constituents to employ every measure at his command to prevent the elevation of Judge Crease to the U.S. Circuit Court of Appeals in particular; by the homespun support of his veteran colleague from Iowa's Twenty Fourth Congressional District sponsoring a bill to restore the arts to their pristine decorative function; and finally by fleeting interviews with the artist himself, just now busied elsewhere defending a suit alleging wrongful death in the collapse of another of his creations in securing the delicate balance of its three ton steel appendages, denying any intention of meaning to be construed in his sculptural works beyond the raw arrangement of their actual materials in which any meaning, if there were such, resided in this very meaninglessness hence the vacuous site specificity of Cyclone Seven being embraced, even then, in testimony before the jury by expert witnesses called at appropriate expense on his behalf and in the farflung vapourings of art critics in the press confronting 'the challenge to decipher its iconography in its forceful maneuverings of space by steel beams bending, leaning, reclining and thrusting themselves forward, light as plumes of a gigantic bird curving around us with gentle solicitude in the sculptor's wish to appeal to all people in sympathy with their lives and needs in the energizing myth of participatory democracy characteristic of American postwar art to fit in everywhere yet stand defiantly alone in its solitary monumentality, restless and dominating, even menacing in its threat of instability finding few echoes in the surrounding architecture, dwarfing the people with an intimidating authority but also a sense of informality and fun, toying with our anxieties of inclusion and exclusion in experiencing the full immensity and vertigo of space, tapping the explosive feelings trapped within its sense of emotional and physical accessibility, its suggestions of Christian sacrifices and suffering...'

—That's enough! Giant bird plumes, my God.

—The confusion of tongues was the way Harry put it, simply another language, art theory referring only to itself 'stripping the forms of art to the bone, shaking off the emotional excesses of abstract expressionism' reducing art itself to theory with no more substance than that swarm of flies the Judge stepped on in his Szyrk opinion while Szyrk himself is out there somewhere right now hearing it exalted in terms of death and transfiguration, of the sacred seizing the profane in an embrace seething with sexual ferment saying it all 'makes him puke' with these 'hints of Christian sacrifice and suffering, its suggestions of journeys without end as the sculptor seems to turn away, smitten to the point where its beams buckle in shyness yet remain as firm and vigilant as a dog who has cornered his prey' —to coin a phrase, as Christina broke off with the front page picture of the thing itself, towering over the new dining area at Mel's Kandy Kitchen like the one at Babel rising toward heaven till the Old Testament Sculptor up there was smitten to the point of sending down a confusion of tongues so that nobody knew what anyone else was talking about where the judge below explicated the Village defense resting on an act of God in his charge to the jury while assorted Baptists sang Amazing Grace and the high school band played America the Beautiful and Tubby the Tuba on the courthouse steps as policemen ticketed cars with out of state plates and one of them smashed the camera of a newsman from the liberal northern press out to make trouble playing up the race angle on the piebald jury's black and a few poor white faces from the Possum Hollow end of town where long smouldering resentment over lacking streetlights, neglected garbage collection, road repair and ruptured sewer lines threatened to surface in a verdict against the Village already crippled by its foreign foulmouthed red atheist cross-claimant under the local headline STRANGE BEDFELLOWS IN CYCLONE SEVEN CASE and a vexatious God strangling in the bedclothes, the pied jury as finders of fact decided parti pris for plaintiff little James B with a judgment for damages, —talk about stepping on a swarm of flies said Harry, here was Judge Crease himself reported as saying some of these jurors had lied during jury selection when they declared they could hear the case objectively, reading what they told the newspapers after the trial their minds were made up before they walked into the courtroom, —all God fearing men and look, that reminds me. Your friend Trish.

—What in God's name has Trish got to do with it.

—That nice looking young man who threw catsup on her chinchilla coat, he...

—It wasn't the chinchilla Harry, it was an old sable, I was with her wasn't I?

—At any rate, the...

—She only took the chinchilla because she thought her mother was going to give it to Mary, this old housekeeper companion Mary who's causing such a problem with the will. It's worth thousands.

—At any rate...

—She never wears it.

—So she poured catsup on it to bring into court suing this poor guy for assault and the price of a chinchilla coat?

—What if she did! This poor guy, the insurance company pays for it what do you mean, this poor guy.

—He's in there claiming the court lacks jurisdiction, says he was acting under the guidance of a higher authority that's what reminded me of it, God in the courtroom like that Cyclone Seven jury down there, look. Just tell her to pay her retainer will you? You retain a firm like Swyne & Dour you pay their retainer. It's putting me in a hell of a spot.

—I thought they were delighted. You bring in a client with deep pockets, isn't that what you told me? that that's how you get made a senior partner?

—I didn't know a damn thing about it Christina! She gets in there and corners a senior partner about breaking her mother's will, waltzes right into Bill Peyton's office using my name when I was away I didn't know anything about it till he stopped me in the hall to congratulate me. She's already got them handling her pre-trial hearing on this assault case, even had the firm representing her in small claims court over a hundred seventy two dollars she owes some shoe repair place. Swyne & Dour in small claims court? Our billing will run her three or four times that, they sent Mudpye down there to keep her happy and she still hasn't put up a dime, that snappy dresser who handled Oscar's deposition with Basie, will you...

—Yes and where is he Harry. Mister Basie, where is he. Oscar's been in a frenzy trying to reach him.

—Basie? He's, I don't know he's, how would I know, nothing he can do now anyhow but wait for...

—No it's something Oscar saw on television, I couldn't make out what it was all about on the phone he was in such a state, he just kept saying he thinks something's terribly wrong. That black actor who played the house slave in the movie, Button somebody? He says he's got to talk to Basie, he can't even reach Sam, your friend Sam, they don't return his calls and he's in a state anyway over his accident case with Lily back in the picture, God knows where she's been. That seventy five hundred dollar bill from that ambulance chaser she found for him filed court papers that have him suing himself, he can't even...

—Look he can't sue himself, can't be plaintiff and defendant in the same suit. He said he had some new lawyers on it didn't he?

—And do you know where he got them? He got them off a matchbook cover, he finally blurted it out, specialists in negligence and personal injury because they offered a free telephone consultation now he's up to his neck with them pressing him for a retainer like Trish, like you're pressing Trish for some miserable payment for...

—Look Christina you don't get Swyne & Dour off a matchbook cover! We don't even bother to litigate anything under a million, three quarters of a million, you retain Swyne & Dour you pay them a retainer nothing miserable about it either, probably asking her twenty five, fifty thousand it's putting me in a hell of a spot.

—If you're just trying to protect yourself Harry, I...

—Not protecting myself I'm protecting the firm! What do you want me to do, walk into Bill Peyton's office and tell him she's a...

—Well my God I mean can't they look out for themselves? They've been around haven't they? They've heard of her, haven't they? All over the papers with her diamond jubilees and that front page robbery?

—Of course they've heard of her, that she's litigious and difficult that's why they're giving me these gentle hints about this retainer because they think I brought her in and she wants the firm to handle that too, that insurance settlement she got on those diamonds they bought back for her? What do you want me to do, tell Bill Peyton she's a friend of my wife's who thinks everybody from the shoe repair man to her mother's old housekeeper and the Catholic Church are out to get her? and this cousin, some cousin who's suing her over some diamond bracelets?

—And you don't think these Catholics are out to get her? This Father God knows what his name is, some unpronounceable Pole they put on her mother's case he'd come over and ring around the rosary with the old crone in that dark cavernous drawing room every afternoon till she put them in this will of hers for enough money to cover sixty years of masses for the repose of what she called her soul?

—It will take sixty years from what I've heard of her, but...

—And these diamond bracelets Harry, that was just a question of language. There were two pairs of bracelets, one was described in the will as a matching pair of diamond bracelets and the other a pair of bracelets of matched diamonds and the cousin, she's fifteen she's only a child and so...

—And so your friend Trish walked off with the matched diamonds worth a hundred times the two matched bracelets the poor girl ended up with?

—She's only got two arms hasn't she? She, I mean she was perfectly happy with them, wanted to wear them out playing field hockey till her father made a scene over the wording, he's a basketball coach so you can imagine, it was only the wording, it was only a question of language.

—But, but damn it Christina that's what we're talking about! What do you think the law is, that's all it is, language.

—Legal language, I mean who can understand legal language but another lawyer, it's like a, I mean it's all a conspiracy, think about it Harry. It's a conspiracy.

—Of course it is, I don't have to think about it. Every profession is a conspiracy against the public, every profession protects itself with a language of its own, look at that psychiatrist they're sending me to, ever try to read a balance sheet? Those plumes of the giant bird like the dog cornering his prey till it all evaporates into language confronted by language turning language itself into theory till it's not about what it's about it's only about itself turned into a mere plaything the Judge says it right there in this new opinion, same swarm of flies he's stepping on down there right now with their motion to throw out the jury's verdict if they've got any sense.

—He can't do that can he?

—Wait and see.

—But how can he. I thought that this was in the Constitution, a jury of your peers?

—A story you hear in first year law school, same argument Oscar's grandfather got into with Holmes and here's his son, here's old Judge Crease down there following Holmes down the line. Justice Learned Hand exhorting Holmes 'Do justice, sir, do justice!' and Holmes stops their carriage. 'That is not my job,' he says. 'It is my job to apply the law.' Wait and see.

—And see what! My God Harry what's he trying to do down there, the whole world flying to pieces war, drugs, people killed in the streets while this brilliant Federal judge up for the high court spends his precious time on this piece of junk sculpture and some dead dog, what's he trying to do!

—Trying to rescue the language, Christina. Wait and see.

OPINION

James B., Infant v. Village of Tatamount et al., U.S. District Court, S. D. Va. 453-87

CREASE, J.

This is a motion under Rule 50(b) of the Federal Rules of Civil Procedure for a renewal of a motion for judgment as a matter of law after trial.

Towering over this case both figuratively and literally stands the massive outdoor steel sculpture known as Cyclone Seven which occupies a freely accessible open space in the Village of Tatamount. In an earlier action before this court the creator of this unique work, R Szyrk, sought and was awarded a permanent injunction barring the Village from removing, altering or damaging this artistic structure in any manner for any reason or for none, in a suit occasioned by its clear intention to deliver forth an animal which had by misadventure strayed into and become entrapped therein (Szyrk v. Village of Tatamount, S.D. Va. 105-87). Upon appeal this judgment was struck down thus granting the Village the right of removal in the course of which it might be presumed the animal would gain its freedom; in the event, however, before these measures were carried out, Cyclone Seven was struck by a bolt of lightning, and its reluctant tenant found to have been released forever from the travails of earthly existence.

James B, Infant, acting through his curator bonis and guardian ad litem, filed an action as owner and bailor of the chattel, a dog of tender years named Spot, alleging negligence on the part of the Village. In a cross claim for indemnity under Fed. R. Civ. P. 14 the suit was joined by impleader in the person of the sculpture's creator R Szyrk whose diversity of citizenship has brought the matter before this jurisdiction under 28 U.S.C. 1332; 72 Stat. 415 (1958). The case was submitted to the jury with instructions to which plaintiff objected. The jury nonetheless found for plaintiff and defendants appeal seeking a judgment N.O.V. for the setting aside of the verdict.

The issue involved is whether the Village in its capacity as bailee, however inadvertently and unhappily arrived at, failed in its duty to bailor under the requisite standard of care and through such alleged negligence is liable for damages so incurred.

The relationship of parties in cases of bailment constitute the large body of law pursued with a vengeance over the centuries in Justice Holmes' The Common Law Lecture V 'dealing with persons who have a thing within their power, but who do not own it, or assert the position of an owner for themselves with regard to it, bailees, in a word.' In the instant case the defendant has urged dismissal of this designation arguing not only that no agreement was entered into with the plaintiff to so commit his chattel in trust for a specific purpose to be returned unharmed once such purpose was accomplished, but further that its efforts to rid itself of this unwelcome guest were a matter of court and public record. Here plaintiff rebuts, answering that whatever the originating circumstances as scrutinized in Szyrk, supra, any encumbrance was lifted by the decision of the appeals court restoring the Village as master of its own house and the duties assumed therewith. 'For the bailee being responsible to the bailor, if the goods be lost or damaged by negligence, or if he do not deliver them up on lawful demand, it is therefore reasonable that he should have a right of action' 2 Steph. Comm. (6th ed.), 83, cited Dicey, Parties, 353; 2 Bl. Comm. 453; 2 Kent, 585 as quoted by

Holmes op. cit. In alleging negligence so construed, plaintiff asserts therewith the further charge of conversion linked to irrecoverable loss of the chattel wherein his claim for damages resides.

Central to actions in bailment are the concepts of possession, by the bailee, and of ownership by the bailor. We have skirted the former to return to it below in considering the charge of conversion, and proceed now to re-examine the latter as giving upon the nature of the chattel at the heart of this action.

Due to their known peculiarities and wide variety, dogs are regarded by the law as in a class by themselves, and while under ancient common law deemed to rank low as property compared to cattle, sheep and barnyard fowl, the law has since evolved to recognize them as things of value in which the rights of property generally prevail within the statutory meaning and use of the word 'chattel.' While it has been granted that dogs have no intrinsic value as dogs unlike, in our own and other civilized cultures, animals domesticated for the purpose of being eaten where a fair market value may be rendered without undue difficulty, actions for damages arising from a dog's injury or death are not confined to its owner's showing of its market value as a dog, but most frequently on evidence warranting its value attaching to such individual qualities as pedigree and rarity of breed, intelligence, talent in the field or at herding, prize winning credentials at dog shows and the like (Wilcox v. Butt's Drug Stores, 38 N.M. 502, 35 P.2d 978, 94 A.L.R. 726. See also McCallister v. Sappingfield, 72 Or. 422, 144 P. 432, quoted with approval in Green v. Leckington, 192 Or. 601, 236 P.2d 335). None of these qualities distinguished the dog Spot. Of indeterminate breed, undetermined lineage and unprepossessing appearance, a follower not a leader, neither hunter nor gatherer, his only talent lay in his uncritical and colourblind offer of companionship the loss of which plaintiff alleged among his causes of action dismissed by the jury under instructions from this court holding that sentimental value may not be allowed as an element of damages (Wilcox v. Butt's Drug Stores, supra).

However it is well established that where an animal has little or no value for sale or consumption, that assigned to the uses to which it is put provides grounds for recovery where loss of profits in a business enterprise relying on these uses is due to its detention and wrongful taking (U.S. v. Hatahley Ca. 10 Utah) and its unjustified injury or destruction (Moses v. Southern P.R. Co. 18 Or. 385, 23 P. 498) whether by wilful act (Helsel v. Fletcher, 98 Okla. 285, 225 P. 514, 33 A.L.R. 792) or by negligence or omission (Brown v. Sioux City 424 Iowa 1196, 49 N.W.2d 853; Bombard v. Newton, 94 Vt. 354, 111 A. 510, 11 A.L.R. 1402). In the case at bar, the value of the decedent as the wellspring of a burgeoning trust in plaintiff's name composed of royalty and licensing fees pertaining to its various profitable configurations as dolls, ceramic items, mugs, keychains, puzzles, T shirts, logos, comic strip rights and a projected animated series for television is plainly evident and even, in point of fact, inadvertently attested to by defendant in an earlier and wondrously ill considered action filed and dismissed in a lower jurisdiction claiming a generous share of such profits as having provided the circumstance for its notorious predicament in the first place.

Here by peradventure we re-encounter the defendant in his alleged capacity among bailees 'who have no interest in the chattels, no right of detention as against the owner, and neither give nor receive a reward' (Holmes op. cit., Lecture VI, Possession), and thence to the subsequent charge of conversion wherein plaintiff's claim embraces what might be termed the last act by defendant in this drama, referring not to Spot in vivo but, as on the corpse littered stage with which Shakespeare brings down the curtain on Timon of Athens and elsewhere, to Spot's remains, summarily removed by agents of the defendant under the eyes of the press and a wide national television audience exercising its obligation under a century old municipal ordinance mandating the speedy and orderly removal of the carcasses of dead animals as ranking in value no higher than garbage with which they share a pungent attraction to flies threatening the spread of disease germs among the local population. However an owner's property rights in an animal are not foreclosed upon its death (Knauer v. Louisville, 20 Ky. L. Rep. 193, 45 SW 510, 46 SW 701), and while granting that the body of a dead animal may not pose a nuisance per se, it may be or become one in fact (Schoen Bros. v. Atlanta, 97 Ga. 697, 25 SE 380; Richmond v. Caruthers, 103 Va. 774, 50 SE 265), plaintiff has claimed that in depriving him of the opportunity to remove and dispose of the remains within a decent interval after death (Richmond v. Caruthers, supra) his constitutional property right to due process under the Fifth and Fourteenth Amendments has thereby been violated irreversibly since the whereabouts of said remains are not now known. Notwithstanding the dark commerce of the Resurrectionists Burke and Hare, corpus humanum non recipit aestimationem, but property value in the animal remains in question is attested by purchase offers in evidence from taxidermists in Chicago, Dallas and Kamakura Japan, by an enterprising glover in San Francisco seeking the pelt as a prototype for a line to be marketed as 'Hiawatha's Magic Mittens' labeled 'Genuine Simulated Spotskin® Wear 'Em With The Furside Outside,' and an urgent bid from Bao Dai's Tasti-Snax in Queens Village, New York, for purposes undisclosed. Pending a search at the Village dump defendant demurred and the charge was dismissed ex mora at the discretion of the court.

The issues of animal trespass and the conflicting portrayal of Cyclone Seven as an attractive nuisance which were disposed of in an earlier action before this court (see Szyrk, supra) surfaced again in the jury trial here under review. As held in Baker v. Howard County Hunt, 171 Md. 159, 188 A. 223; Pegg v. Gray, 240 N.C. 548, 82 S.E.2d 757, and elsewhere, no liability attaches to the owner of a 'reputable dog' for its straying without his consent and unaccompanied by him onto the land of another, and defendant's claim excluding the dog Spot from this category on grounds of his disreputable companions on neighborhood outings was dismissed. Where there is some authority for liability attaching to unfenced lands whereon are to be encountered erections or machinery negligently maintained so as to constitute a trap (Malernee Oil Co. v. Kerns, 187 Okla. 276, 102 P.2d 836), defendant denied such liability claiming as ordinary use free and open access to the subject premises and the erection thereon as public art where, by permitting the trespassing animal to roam at large, its owner assumed the risk for any harm or injury befalling it and thus yielded any right of action. Here the court concurred, since where plaintiff is found exempt from liability for the beast's trespass this does not make such trespass lawful rendering defendant liable for injuries not wilfully or wantonly inflicted (Pure Oil Co. v. Gear, 183 Okla. 489, 83 P.2d 389; Tennessee Chemical Co. v. Henry, 114 Tenn. 152, 85 S.W. 401). On the related charge of distraint, where the distress is lawful it is well established that the distrainer is obliged to feed and care for the animal which stands uncontested in this action and only in the event of his negligence will he be held liable (Kelly v. Easton, 35 Ida. 340, 207 P. 129, 26 A.L.R. 1042), but where such distraint is for any reason illegal the distrainer regardless of negligence remains liable for any injury to the beast while under his care (Dickson v. Parker, 4 Miss. (3 How.) 219), and here such failure resulting in unjustifiable pain and suffering on the beast's part through any and each act of neglect or omission may appear in the garb of passive cruelty where intention is not essential, as in such wilful acts as tying a flaming oil can to a dog's tail in State v. Kemp, 234 Mo. App. 827, 137 S.W.2d 638, or setting the dog itself afire (Commonwealth v. Gentile, 255 Mass. 116, 150 N.E. 830). Thus where an action may be maintained on a case for unintended injury or destruction, it is obligatory upon the animal's owner not only to allege facts showing defendant's negligence, but that such injury or destruction came about through this negligence as the proximate cause.

Nowhere in all of law are we confronted by a concept that has sired more confusion and disagreement and so presumably swelled the coffers of the legal profession than that of 'proximate cause,' a phrase derived from a formulation by then Lord Chancellor Sir Francis Bacon some four centuries ago, In jure non remota causa, sed proxima, spectatur, summoning shades of Ockham's razor from a past yet more remote. 'Cause and effect find their beginning and end in the limitless and unknowable,' wrote Judge Powell in Atlantic Coast Line R. Co. v. Daniels (8 Ga. App. 775, 70 S.E. 203). 'Therefore courts, in their finitude, do not attempt to deal with cause and effect in any absolute degree, but only in such a limited way as is practical and as is within the scope of ordinary human understanding. Hence arbitrary limits have been set, and such qualifying words as "proximate" and "natural" have come into use as setting the limits beyond which the courts will not look in the attempt to trace the connection between a given cause and a given effect.'

In alleging a bolt of lightning as the proximate cause of the victim's destruction in the instant case, defendant contends that the court erred in submitting the question of negligence to the jury and should have declared as a matter of law that an act of God was responsible for the dog Spot's death. Further, it has been held that this need not be the immediate cause, if it followed in a logical and unbroken sequence originating with the act of God (Blythe v. Denver & R.G.R. Co., 15 Colo. 333, 25 P. 702), and thus even absent the corpus delicti where singed fur might have evidenced that direct encounter with the Deity the fright so engendered would without physical impact be sufficient in its internal operation in that ghastly interval to cause death (Louisville & N.R. Co. v. Melton, 158 Ala. 509, 47 So. 1024).

It is quite universally held that a casualty cannot be ascribed exclusively to an act of God thus excluding liability where any human agency has intervened in or contributed to the result (Cachick v. U.S. (D. Ill.) 161 F. Supp. 15), and hence where by act or negligence such intervention is alleged it becomes a matter for a jury as triers of fact. 'Negligence, it must be repeated, is conduct which falls below the standard established by law for the protection of others against unreasonable risk. It necessarily involves a foreseeable risk, a threatened danger of injury, and conduct unreasonable in proportion to the danger' (Prosser, Law of Torts, 4th ed.). While lightning is notorious as an act of God within the comprehension of the law, 'when the negligence of a defendant "concurs" with an act of God, which is to say an unforeseeable force of nature, he is to be held liable' (Prosser op. cit., and see Manila School Dist. No. 15 v. Sanders, 1956, 226 Ark. 270, 289 S.W.2d 529). Honouring the familiar maxim causa causea est causa causati plaintiff avers, albeit in more homespun language, such concurrence on the part of party to the action by impleader the creator of Cyclone Seven in situ and there stipulated 'to stand freely exposed to natural forces' (Szyrk, supra). Where plaintiff further alleges that these impediments to its removal were swept away by the appeals court decision reversing this major provision in Szyrk, supra, defendant's disclaimer on grounds of the lack of a demolition permit required by municipal ordinance for such a procedure which, in the usual course of events would be issued by and to itself, has provoked the further charge of conspiracy wherein plaintiff cites the prominent presence on the Village Board of one Mel Kandinopoulis as chief obstacle to such issuance, submitting in evidence the expanding premises of Mel's Kandy Kitchen in the form of a sunny new dining area overlooking Cyclone Seven and a printer's dummy of a projected new menu offering quiche Lorraine, caesar salad with arugula, sangria and similar enticements to the sophisticated palates of prosperous out of town visitors where hoagies and a Bud by local custom had hitherto prevailed. These charges were dismissed by the court under common law immunity for public officers, based less on the 'desire to protect an erring officer... (than on) a recognition of the need of preserving independence of action, without deterrence or intimidation by the fear of personal liability and vexatious suits' Restatement, Second, Torts 895D, see also Learned Hand, J., in Gregoire v. Biddle (2d Circ. 1944) 177 F.2d 579.

In dismissing these allegations in toto the court found plaintiff's claims to be lodged in pure conjecture with no facts alleged to support recovery of the chattel safe and unharmed upon or during removal of the vehicle of its detention. Were we now ourselves to stray beyond these posted limits in further pursuit of the matter our path would soon be joined with that taken at excessive speed through the State of New Jersey by the defendant who arrived therewith for an on time appointment in Philadelphia with a bolt of lightning (compare Berry v. Sugar Notch Borough, 1899,

191 Pa. 345; Doss v. Town of Big Stone Gap, 1926, 145 Va. 520, 134 S.E. 563), an appointment better kept in Samara by that special breed of novelist driven by despair to embrace 'the unswerving punctuality of chance' (cit. omitted), sinking us deeper in the twilight of confusion from whence we shall now emerge inter canem et lupum, as it were.

In examining defendant's claim that plaintiff should have been non-suited by the court and the case dismissed as a matter of law as an 'act of God,' we have taken judicial notice of plaintiff's objection to the jury charge as it centered upon that phrase time honoured since its introduction by that contemporary and rival of the aforementioned Francis Bacon at the court of Elizabeth I, England's first Lord Chief Justice Lord Edward Coke. While far from questioning his piety, it behooves us to recall Lord Coke's diligent concern for the common over the ecclesiastical law then so prevalent in addressing ourselves to its vulgar version confronting the bench today in modern dress.

By 'an act of God' the law denotes a natural and inevitable phenomenon occurring beyond human origin and intervention. It is that simple, and the high tension natural discharge of electricity in the atmosphere known as lightning must clearly qualify to head such a list. 'But just as the clavicle in the cat only tells of the existence of some earlier creature to which a collarbone was useful, precedents survive in the law long after the use they once served is at an end and the reason for them has been forgotten. The result of following them must often be failure and confusion from the merely logical point of view.' (Holmes op. cit. Lecture I). Like the cat's clavicle, this 'act of God' has survived elsewhere as Deo juvante, Deo volente, ex visitatione Dei from depictions of the supreme god Jove in Roman mythology clutching bolts of lightning, hearkening back to prehistoric man cowering in terror from these flashes splitting the heavens with the voice of thunder to be placated, at any cost to reason, by fabricating privileged relations with the Deity as magic despaired and became religion. Thus even in our own time if not careful we may find ourselves sharing a ride with the defendant in Breunig v. American Family Ins. Co. whose special relationship to God as 'the chosen one to survive at the end of the world' led her to 'believe that God would take over the direction of her life to the extent of driving her car' so that just before striking the oncoming truck she was confident 'that God was taking ahold of the steering wheel' (45 Wis.2d 536, 173 N.W.2d 619).

On the other hand the proceedings in the case here under appeal were only further inflamed by the brief submitted by an ironically labeled amicus curiae on behalf of cross-claimant Mr Szyrk quoting from the writings of E M Cioran '[c]ontemplating this botched Creation, how can we help incriminating its Author, how—above all—suppose him able and adroit? Any other God would have given evidence of more competence or more equilibrium than this one: errors and confusion wherever you look!'

'When an issue of proximate cause arises in a borderline case...' wrote Chief Judge Magruder in Marshall v. Nugent (U.S. Court of Appeals, 1st Circ., 1955. 222 F.2d 604), 'we leave it to the jury with appropriate instructions. We do this because it is deemed wise to obtain the judgment of the jury, reflecting as it does the earthy viewpoint of the common man—the prevalent sense of the community' which found broad expression in the testimony of witnesses called to assist this jury in its deliberations. There, 'God struck that (expletive) pile of (expletive) with his good old lightning because it's a (expletive) abomination on this beautiful land the Lord give us here, some old pup got in the way that's just a accident,' contended with 'God He don't have accidents, wouldn't never have struck a poor dumb little creature like that, Bible says right there He marks the sparrow's fall don't it?' provoking the rude rejoinder 'Don't say He does nothing about it though does it?' However these earthy viewpoints may reflect disagreement, God presides over both in common with plaintiff's objection to the court's instructions to the jury as implying divine culpability in the matter before us through its use of the phrase 'an act of God.' With all respect due the parties, the jury, the God fearing community, and the common man of which it seems to have more than its share of over half this country's population planning an afterlife in the felicitous company of Jesus and even God himself, belief in God has neither bearing upon nor any relevance to these earthbound proceedings. In short, He may enjoy as much room in your hearts as you can afford Him, but God has no place in this court of law.

In our instructions to the jury the court may have erred in its effort to shed this confusion and should better have issued a directed verdict for the defendant and his cross-claimant. The jury verdict is set aside N.O.V. and judgment for damages to plaintiff dismissed.

The black robed effigy swung closer, close enough for the cameras to read IMPEACH pinned to its skirts before the flames con-

sumed it, SPOT LIVES, GOD IS JUDGE, Stars and Bars, rocks and beer cans, US GOVT KEEP OUT and hands crowding forward unfurling the headline CALLS GOD CAT'S CHINBONE through smoke swirling from the pork barbeque pit where a suited man in string tie hailed the thronged white faces buttoned to the throat many even clean shaven as their friend and neighbor stood to welcome our distinguished guest the honourable United States Senator here from championing your sacred rights in the black crime and drug capital of the nation wiping grease from his chin with a paper party napkin blazoning his name as he struggled to rise to the occasion from a folding chair flourishing a rib in response to their yelps of the name on the napkin with a scattering of more neighborly familiar salutes to Old Lardass since he'd 'growed up right down the road here apiece' well, he'd come back here looking for friends and by Golly he'd found them, they hadn't changed a bit in all that time and their moans confirmed that they heard this as a compliment —but you all mean so much to me it means so much just to be with you here like this. He wasn't much good at making pretty speeches but he didn't think they wanted to hear a lot of pretty words at a time like this while the Federal government had its Federal courts trampling their sacred rights to religious freedom, carry guns, trial by jury enshrined for all to see right up there in the U.S. Constitution —like we just witnessed here right before our eyes how this Federal U.S. judge just steps in there to suit his fancy and throws out a verdict reached after calm deliberation by a jury of you honest citizens black folk and white, right there in the Fourteenth Amendment in black and white, the jury that's the bulwark and cornerstone of American justice like you don't see in these dictator atheist countries slaps them right in the face and hands it over to this foreigner who came in here and put up this monstrosity he's from one of these atheist countries himself, says right here someplace in black and white this Christian sacrifice and suffering make him puke. You don't hear that kind of language before women and children at my house and I'm sure at yours neither but when I read that I was most like to puke myself, your hard earned Federal tax dollars going on things like that while they want to kill subsidies to our good hard working tobacco planters and growers of other nutritious crops supporting art and pornography to where nowadays you can't hardly tell them apart and paying these welfare women to go get their abortions. You put them together with all these homos parading around in the arts and pretty soon there won't be any taxpayers left, we keep going down this Godless path till one day they'll go and abort the Second Coming and nobody know the difference. And that's where this government interference with our sacred state's rights so many died for is leading us, sending in these Federal judges that take our great American language and twist the words around to mean whatever they want, calls God no better than a cat's shinbone, calls this beautiful land of ours a botched Creation and throws God right out of the courtroom, you heard him, do whatever they please because they're appointed for life. Well we have an answer for that, call it impeachment right there in the Constitution and that's the message I'm taking back up to Washington. They pay him with your good U.S. tax dollars and I'm going to tell them to take a look at one, take a good look at a U.S. dollar bill where it says In God We Trust and that U.S. dollar's gospel enough for me. That's the country I served back in the dark days of war right down here at Fort Bragg and the U.S. Constitution I swore to protect and defend from enemies foreign and domestic and we're seeing more than our share of both right down here in our own backyard. Now let's have us a little sip of that good bourbon.

And sure enough, there on the split page of the morning's paper flamed the black robed effigy of the craggy Federal judge who, like the sharp edges and jagged peaks of the controversial steel sculpture Cyclone Seven, had become a lightning rod for the passions of this once sleepy community, erupting last night in a virtual replay of an earlier melee which left seventy-two injured and extensive property damage in its wake. Among the dozen arrests that evening, that of Billy Pinks, thirty-two, an unemployed auto body worker charged with assault was later reduced to statutory rape on his plea that the 'provocative message on her T shirt got his juices going' and the admission by the twelve-year-old victim that she had deceitfully led him to believe she was fourteen. Mr Pinks was sentenced to thirty days probation and an apology to the victim identified only as Millie K, minor. The latest disturbance centered about an outdoor pork barbeque rally for U.S. Senator Orney Bilk, who is visiting the area on a campaign swing for the first time since he left his boyhood home in nearby Stinking Creek to enlist in the army following the end of hostilities in Southeast Asia. After graduating from army cooking school he was placed in charge of a field oven unit at Fort Bragg, N.C. Senator Bilk's interest in politics was kindled by the conviction on bribery charges involving unorthodox liquor procurement of an uncle whose place he later filled in the state legislature.

Known for his strong stand on states' rights in Congress, Senator Bilk took vehement exception to a decision by Judge Crease reversing a verdict by a local jury as undue interference by the Federal judiciary and called for his impeachment. Talking with the press later in the evening when the bourbon had been flowing freely, the Senator cited as an article of impeachment the possibility of a strain of madness running in the Judge's family, an allegation which has gained credence with the Civil War spectacle The Blood in the Red White and Blue, which is said to be based on the life of his father who later served as associate justice on the U.S. Supreme Court with Justice Oliver Wendell Holmes until his death at the age of ninety-seven. Through his law clerk Judge Crease dismissed the charges as 'foolish fabulation.' His son Oswald, a wealthy recluse living alone on a family estate on Long Island who wrote the original script for the spectacularly successful motion picture and, in an announcement made by the studio late yesterday has lost his multimillion dollar lawsuit against its producers, could not be reached for comment. Speaking on condition that he not be identified, Village official J Harret Ruth, who introduced Senator Bilk at the rally and who makes no secret of his own political ambitions, said my God. Harry?

—In the shower.

—In the paper, this perfectly asinine story about that circus going on down there in Father's courtroom, carrying him around in a flaming effigy, talk about madness in the family and all kinds of nonsense. Can they get away with that?

—What? He'd emerged in the folds of a towel. —With what.

—This story in the paper, they've got everything possible wrong. There are laws aren't there?

—Have to prove malice. Can't make laws against plain sloppiness can you? He'd commenced the towel in a vigorous rubdown, —against stupidity?

—Well my God, impeaching a Federal judge by saying his whole family's crazy? Isn't that malice?

—Have to prove it Christina, get into a case like that you end up like the tar baby, open up all kinds of cans of...

—And his son Oswald, a wealthy recluse who wrote the original script for The Blood in the Red White and I just hope to heaven Oscar doesn't see this he'll explode, that he's lost his million dollar lawsuit against them?

—It says that? The towel stopped, draped from a shoulder. —What does it say.

—That's what it says, in an announcement by the studio late yesterday that he's lost his multimillion dollar lawsuit against the producers right here, look.

—Well they, no, no it's true.

—What do you mean it's true! His son Oswald, they got everything else wrong didn't they? that he wrote the original script for the...

—No it's, it's true Christina, only thing they got right. Decision came down late yesterday, he lost.

—Well he, I mean you knew this? I mean my God Harry you knew this and haven't told me?

—I came in late last night and...

—Why didn't you tell me!

—I'm telling you! What should I have done, waked you up when I came in so we both could have had a sleepless night? Look...

—A sleepless night! and poor, we'll have plenty of those I'd better call him, poor Oscar God knows what he'll, does he know yet? Give me the phone, I...

—Now just wait, Christina. Wait! Look, there's no hurry. If he'd seen it, if he'd seen this thing in the paper he would have called. He'll call the instant he sees it won't he?

—I'd better go out there. And the money, he'll be frantic.

—I told him he could lose didn't I? right at the start? In a lawsuit somebody loses, I told him it would cost money didn't I? that he should have taken their settlement? We both told him he should have taken their...

—Well he didn't! If you knew he'd lose why did you, how did you know it, that he'd lost.

—I didn't say I knew he'd lose Christina, I said he could, that he could lose, you never know which way a judge will go, and this one, this woman? No track record at all, a real wild card one of the first cases she's tried no telling which way she'd go. I had to stop in at the office to get some notes transcribed when I got back last night and there's your friend Trish waltzing down the hall with Mudpye steering her toward the door, I think she'd had a few and out comes Bill Peyton. She was all over him, she...

—I'm not talking about her I'm talking about Oscar! And, and will you stop standing there dangling like that, will you...

—You don't usually mind do you? If you'll just...

—Well I do now! Will you...

—Will you listen? He got the towel around him, a foot up on the bed rubbing down his calf, —Peyton with his hand on Mudpye's shoulder congratulating him, he'd just heard the decision on Oscar's case patting Mudpye on the back and the insufferable little bastard preening like a damn bantam rooster and when I, who are you calling.

—And it's not just these thousands of dollars he owes your friend Sam and the mess he's in with these medical bills and that idiot lawyer Lily got for him suing himself for his, hello? Oscar? Yes how are you, I didn't wake you did I, are you... No I just thought I'd call, are you... Well take some aspirin then, it looks like a lovely day I thought I might come out if you... Nothing no, no of course if you don't want company I... No I just wondered, you haven't seen this morning's paper have you? It's... no nothing, a garbled story about... what? Oh... No, no but call me if anything... no, goodbye. Well. He hasn't seen the paper yet, he's got it drying out in the oven.

—Kind of puts me in a spot doesn't it, he'll probably blame me for the whole...

—Well my God Harry you are in a spot, you sent him to Lepidus, Shea & God knows who didn't you? up against your own fancy blue ribbon white shoe outfit? What did you expect.

—Where should I have sent him, some other white shoe Cravath? Davis Polk? string it out for another ten years like the case I'm on where the money really gets going? More depositions, more transcripts, pretrial conferences, coaching your expert witnesses at three or four hundred an hour and sorting out your trial strategy, accountants, overhead, talking about years and hundreds of thousands look, Christina. In the first place I didn't know that Kiester'd come to Swyne & Dour. Whole question of venue, a case like this you have to sue in the district where the defendant resides, for Kiester that's the Central District of California, if Oscar couldn't travel and it was just going to amount to taking a couple of depositions and an oral argument on one motion his lawyers could have flown in from California and taken care of it but Kiester got in under the studio's umbrella because they were named in Oscar's suit too and Swyne & Dour's their outside counsel in New York so that's where Basie served his summons and complaint and fell right into the trap Mudpye laid for him, what the little bastard was preening himself about there with Bill Peyton. I didn't know anything about it, I didn't even...

—Well why didn't you! What trap, what do you...

—You know damn well Christina, because I've been up to my eyes there, I haven't seen the judge's opinion it just came down, that's all I know.

—Can't you call your friend Sam and find out what in God's name is going on? if they plan to appeal? Oscar can't reach him, he can't reach Mister Basie they don't return his calls, will you? call him now so we can tell Oscar what they...

—In the first place Christina, you don't just walk in and file an appeal because you don't like the verdict, have to sit down and study the opinion to see if there's grounds to appeal on. It takes time, and money. Time and more money, what if they do dig up grounds for an appeal, there were grounds for the suit in the first place weren't there? and he lost? See him lose on appeal and you'll have to pick up the pieces. Just put it behind him, swallow hard and cut his losses, drop the whole thing. Now wait, wait, before you call him again...

—I'm not calling him Harry I'm, hello? Yes, this is Mrs Lutz, will you bring our car around? The, no the dark green Jaguar, can you have it at the door in about ten minutes? I think I'd better go out there Harry, the sooner the better, any minute now he'll see that story in the paper and call in a frenzy, you can just tell him I'm on my way and if you want to be useful will you call them? Sam or Mister Basie or anybody, tell them to call him out there. They told him he could win on an appeal and that's the first thing he'll ask.

—They, who. Who told him, Christina. Wait...

—Basie, Mister Basie did, I've got to hurry. The last time we saw him, is there gas in the car?

—But wait, that's not what you, Oscar must have misunderstood him that's not the way you...

—I was there Harry! Lose the decision we'll take them on appeal Basie said. Now will you call them while I dress?

—But that's not, you go in to win you don't plan to lose so you can win on appeal look, there's something I've got to talk to you about before you...

—We went all over that with him Harry, that's what I, my God there he is now, he's seen the paper will you answer it? just tell him I've left?

—But wait, there's something I, hello? Who? No you've got a wrong number, it's... I said the wrong number! He banged it down, —it'll ring again, one of those insistent idiots who gets a wrong number and sits right down and dials it again look, I, before you go something I have to talk to you about before you...

—Well come with me then! You don't have to go in today do you?

—Have to be in court first thing in the morning but...

—Well get on some clothes, you can tell me in the car, now...

—There, didn't I tell you? He grabbed up the phone, —I told you you had the wrong, what? Oh, Oscar? Yes... yes I know it, we... yes we've seen it, we... but... yes but... Oscar? Look, we're coming out, we... out there yes, we're leaving right now, we... when we get there, go over the whole thing when we... Yes I know it said Oswald, but don't... Right now no, she can't come to the phone she's dressing, she... I said she's getting dressed Oscar...

—Oscar?

—Tell her to hurry!

—Oscar?

—And don't talk to me when I'm on the phone! Here, hang it up.

—I just wanted to say do you want to eat?

—To eat what!

—Eggs? you want me to make eggs?

—You can't make eggs.

—I can so. I can make them boiled, or scrambled, or...

—Listen Lily you can't make eggs. Chickens make eggs, ducks

make eggs, those swans on the pond out there make eggs but you don't make eggs. You cook eggs, you prepare eggs. You don't make eggs.

—Oh Oscar. You always make everything so complicated, all I meant was...

—Isn't that what language is for? to say what you mean? That's why man invented language, isn't it? so we can say what we mean?

—What man. Anyway I'm not talking about language I'm talking about eggs, you knew what I meant. Do you want me to prepare you some eggs?

—No.

—I thought that's why you wanted me to come over because you were alone, to help you out. Who was that old man.

—Who was what old man.

—This old man walking around the room when I drove in before.

—There was no old man walking around the...

—I saw him through the windows Oscar, just for a second when I looked up, he was sort of stooped and slow right here walking across the room, by the time I got out of the car and came in he was gone.

—Oh. Oh. That, oh yes I forgot I, must have been old Mister, Mister Boatwright yes he's the, he's our plumber he's quite old yes, been with the house as long as I can remember.

—You better get a new one pretty soon, he didn't look like he could hardly make it across the room.

—Well he's, an old house like this he knows every pipe in the house he's replaced most of them, get some new young plumber in here it would take him a year to figure things out and have to start all over again.

—I think you better start all over again pretty soon before the whole place falls down like that porch out there.

—They'll be after it next, a wealthy recluse living on a family estate on Long Island when they see that! He had the torn page of newsprint he'd held crushed in his hand up trying to smooth it against a quivering knee, —Oswald! His son Oswald who wrote the original script for the spectacularly successful no wonder he's furious, that fool law clerk of his takes him to see this vulgar misleading twisted deformed perverted distortion of my, exploiting my grandfather, exploiting his father exploiting the family exploiting the whole Civil War and he thinks I wrote what he's seeing up there on the screen where is it, this madness in the, here, as an article of impeachment the possibility of a strain of madness running in the Judge's family which has gained credence with the, credence! No wonder he's furious, just the word, impeachment just the word. Impeachment! Madness, all right but a man whose whole life is the law, who's lived and breathed the law for his whole, for almost a century a century! It would kill him they, look at them look at it! He spread up the flaming effigy IMPEACH frozen there in print before the flames caught it —as an article of impeachment the strain of...

—You just read me that, you've read me all of it ten times Oscar it's all just...

—What! all just what!

—Just, Oswald? You want me to call you Oswald?

—If I, Lily if I could reach you to hit you I'd...

—It's the same thing! but she stepped away nonetheless, —this wealthy excuse living on this big fancy estate they got everything wrong didn't they? this Oswald that wrote this big movie is that you? where he just lost this big lawsuit that's not you is it? so they pretend they know everything because nobody knows anything?

—Basie knows, this lawyer Mister Basie he must know but there's something wrong somewhere. I can't get him on the phone they don't call me back I know it, I know there's something terribly wrong I've known it since the, you remember that black actor? the one we saw on television who was in the movie when he talked about being in prison? that he learned to act when he was in prison and...

—The telephone, you...

—Well answer it! If it's this collection agency tell them...

—Hello? It's who?

—Say I went to California.

—It's The People Magazine.

—No. Tell them...

—Hello? He went to California... No he didn't leave a num...

—Just hang up! Listen, if it rings again if it's Basie let me have it, or these other lawyers the ones with my accident case I...

—They called already Oscar.

—When! Why didn't you...

—Just now, when you were in the bathroom. I forgot.

—They're supposed to stop this collection agency from calling me in the middle of the night, that bill for seventy five hundred dollars for suing myself he ought to be shot.

—That's what Daddy said too but Reverend Bobby Joe said that could get him in real trouble, because Daddy already gave him this money to sue the insurance company and make them pay up on Bobbie's car where Reverend Bobby Joe said it was all this grand design of the Lord where Daddy could take this big insurance settlement and cleanse it by putting it in the Lord's service? Only now they won't pay it because they said Daddy's responsible because he gave Bobbie the money for the car where they found this empty sixpack in the wreck when tragedy struck so Daddy has to sue this dealer who sold Bobbie the car because he already failed his learner's permit three times so he didn't even have a driving license and they never should have sold him the car in the first place. So now Daddy and Reverend Bobby Joe they're both of them mad at me because it's my fault I brought down this lawyer that took money from Daddy to help him out when the only reason he did it with me in the first place in his car and at Disney World and these water beds all over the place he thought he was going to get in on all this money I'd have from Daddy now that Bobbie was gone when we reconciliated and he's up there right now spreading my girlfriend from long lines on his desk unzipping his big...

—Wait, no wait he was, that was before, you did it with him in his car before Bobbie's accident because of that stupid dream you...

—I don't care! I said I want to get revenge and don't call me stupid either, you said you'd help me didn't you? If we could do something to his car that would be funny, so he could have an accident like Bobbie wouldn't that be funny? Did you see that old movie where she thinks Cary Grant did something to the brakes so she'll go over the cliff? Only this time...

—Funny? getting run over by a car do you think I...

—Or I read someplace where they put this rattlesnake in this man's mailbox so that when he reached in...

—No! No this is all...

—Then you think of something! You just sit around here all day reading and watching the television where all everybody does is kill each other and you still didn't think of something?

—Wait what time is it. My nature program, what time is it.

—I don't know! I didn't come over here to watch some smelly animals and funny looking fish Oscar, can't you even talk to me?

—I, I can't no, I can't talk to anyone I can't think I can't even, everything's just spinning around I just want to get my mind off the whole, off all of it for a minute.

—Do you want me to...

—No, no don't. Later.

—I'm hungry she said, straightening up as the screen came dispiritedly to life on a visit to a lackluster member of the Cistaceae or rockrose family, Helianthemum dumosum, more familiarly known in its long suffering neighborhood as bushy frostweed for its talent at surviving the trampling by various hoofed eventoed closecropping stock of the suborder Ruminantia, to silently spread and widen its habitat at its neighbors' expense like some herbal version of Gresham's law in Darwinian dress demonstrating no more, as his head nodded and his breath fell and the crush of newsprint dropped to the floor, the tug at his lips in the troubled wince of a smile might have signaled no more than or, better perhaps the very heart of some drowned ceremony of innocence now the worst were filled with passionate intensity where —we share something then don't we, no small thing either —That's good to know, demonstrating simply the survival of the fittest embracing here in bushy frostweed no more than those fittest to survive not necessarily, not by any means, by any manner of speaking, the best, so that when at last the outer doors clattered open, clattered closed and down the hall with —My God, he's sound asleep! it was upon some lowlife in the bogs from the sundew family, Droseraceae to their betters, busy here supplementing their nitrogen spare diets in this gloomy habitat with insects captured on their leaves so purposefully endowed with sticky glands or hairs.

—I'm not asleep!

—Or had one of those seizures you talk about, how are you Oscar. Blow your little horn will you? I really need a cup of tea.

—It's broken, the rubber bulb's worn out and...

—Well then call her. Ilse? Where is she. Ilse!

—She's in the Bronx Christina, her sister has a cataract and...

—And whose old car is that out there, don't things look shabby enough around here? She picked up the torn streamer of the paper with a glance at the flaming effigy there before she crushed it again, —disgraceful. It's all simply disgraceful.

—Listen I've got to talk to you I, where's Harry I thought he was coming out with you.

—He's getting my sweater from the car, the house is cold as a tomb. And will you turn that thing off!

—Turn it up then, turn up the heat listen, there's something terribly wrong Christina. In the paper there, did you see it? where it says I lost this lawsuit against the...

—Why do you think we broke our necks getting out here, of course we saw it. He's got some rather upsetting news.

—Well so have I! Something that was on television, I haven't been able to get it out of my mind. I tried to tell you about it on the phone and you wouldn't listen, I've been trying to reach Basie day after day and I can't get him they ask me to leave my number they have my number don't they? Nobody calls me back they don't even, Harry? Harry listen. There's something wrong.

—Rotten luck Oscar. The chance you take though isn't it, we said at the start you can always lose a lawsuit didn't we, even when you're right you can't always...

—Yes well maybe, it barely mentioned that in passing they got everything else wrong didn't they? No there's something terribly wrong I know it, I...

—Afraid not no, the one damn thing they got right, we said you probably should have...

—That's not what I mean, I...

—Harry will you simply tell him what's happened?

—Said you probably should have taken their settlement didn't we...

—Well he didn't Harry! Now will you...

—Will you listen to me both of you! Listen. This actor named Button something, this black actor who plays the head house slave in the movie he was on television, I just happened to see him being interviewed on television he'd been in prison, that's where he discovered acting, where he learned to act in some acting therapy workshop they had acting out their hostilities and the more he talked. The more he talked about how he discovered himself there, best thing that ever happened to him he said how he'd found his true vocation, acting, The Emperor Jones they did The Emperor Jones and when he heard the applause and then he talked about another prisoner who was kind of a jailhouse lawyer told him if you're black in America you're always playing a part, just find the right one so you don't end up taking your bows in a cell block in there for something that would curl your hair and I've kept thinking of Basie, he showed me a scar once from his collarbone right down to the groin when they had these drinks in the Beverly Wilshire? this old buddy from back in his little theatre days? And that just sounds like him, being black in America you're always playing a part that just sounds like Basie, like something he'd say and, yes she saw it too. Lily? You remember the...

—No go ahead Oscar, I didn't mean to bother you, I was just in the kitchen making something Mrs Lutz. Can I get you anything?

—I'd be eternally grateful for a cup of tea Lily, now...

—Hard as hell to second guess a judge Oscar, a wild card like this one no track record it's practically impossible to...

—It's not that no, no it's just this feeling something's terribly wrong about the whole...

—Well there is Oscar! There is something terribly wrong my God Harry if you won't tell him I will! Our friend Mister Basie's a fraud Oscar, he never went to law school he lied on his bar exam and every place else and he's going right back to prison where he came from!

—But, but he, but...

—That's why you haven't heard from him, going on about his little theatre days his little theatre was the Federal prison where his buddy found his true vocation as the Emperor Jones while he sat in the prison library looking for ways to get them all out, finding his own true vocation buying drinks for his cellmates with your money in the...

—No but how could, how do you know!

—Harry just told me in the car driving out here, he...

—But he, Harry? is it true? What she just said is it true?

—Not, no, no not what she...

—Well what is then!

—He didn't lie on his bar exam Oscar, took the New York bars and passed on his second try but he'd falsified his application, falsified the document affirming he had a degree from an approved law school, he may have altered some inadmissible correspondence school diploma in the same state where the prison was and falsified the affidavits they require attesting to his good moral character all adds up to a Class A misdemeanor, a fine or a year in prison and they revoke his license to...

—To what! What about me why didn't you tell me! If you knew all this Harry why didn't you tell me!

—Haven't known it that long Oscar, look. If you'd won there'd be no problem over whether you'd been represented by a properly accredited attorney or not so why give you a few sleepless nights making the wrong move by dismissing him and throwing away your chances before we heard the decision, just seemed for your own good to wait and...

—But, for my own good! what do you...

—Look, once you'd turned down their settlement offer there was no place to go, a judge like this one with no track record so your remedies the way it stands now, if you've got any remedies they'll just spring from the fact that you lost.

—Well my God Harry he did lose, that's why we're sitting here! Sleepless nights, what do you mean if he's got any remedies of course he's got remedies, a new trial he can certainly get a new trial.

—Have to check it out Christina, a civil case like this one. If it was a criminal case and his lawyer hadn't been admitted to practice there'd be grounds to have a conviction vacated but of course there you've got a lot more protection under the Constitution than you do in a...

—Well he's not a criminal! If there's a criminal it's, where is he. Mister Basie, where is he.

—He'll turn up sooner or later, back in county jail or someplace else, a man like that can't stay out of trouble. He'll turn up.

—Why should he turn up if nobody turns him up, what about your friend Sam. Aren't they after him?

—Don't know what he'll decide to do Christina. If Basie was a partner at Lepidus, Shea they could sue to make him sell his partnership share if they could lay their hands on him, in fact under the disciplinary rules they'd have to but just an associate they put on the case that's not their, not up to them it's the State, up to the State to chase him down if they want to bother. Take the volume of cases we handle or Lepidus, Shea for that matter, the size of our staffs there's always the chance of a slip somewhere, try to help out these minorities give them a leg up you get some smooth laid back ex-con like Basie slips through the cracks just a stroke of luck that we...

—Of whose luck! Oscar's? My God Harry I've never heard such, help out these minorities I've never heard such a ridiculous, what is it now Lily?

—I'm sorry but, I can't find any tea bags I looked all over and...

—Of course you can't find any tea bags, you're not making one cup are you? for three of us? There's loose tea in a square yellow tin that says tea on it you make a pot of tea not a cup, you want tea don't you Harry?

—I think I want a drink.

—I should think you might! Pour yourself one and sit down, just stop walking back and forth you're not in a courtroom Harry I've never heard such nonsense from you in my life. From you Harry! Swyne & Dour and your friend Sam trying to give these minorities a leg up like your little bastard Mister Mudpye? Out of two, three hundred lawyers you've got there every one of them white? male? and you need a black face or two in the window before some antidiscrimination law wakes up and hands out a good stiff fine in the only language they speak up there, money? Put a pair of white shoes on Mister Basie make him a partner your friend Bill Peyton would think the place looked like a minstrel show and you can stand there with a straight face and, will you sit down! I feel like I'm talking to a...

—Look Christina, a place like Swyne & Dour you're not even proposed as a lateral partner unless you're bringing along a million and a half or two in billings with you, I've told you that. You think Basie or any of them's got that kind of a client base? Never been a black partner the whole time I've been there, never even more than two black associates at once and they didn't last long either, did I ever say it wasn't about money? You want to live in a place like Massapequa and drive around in a broken down Japanese, look at Oscar. Why do you think I referred him to Lepidus, Shea, smaller firm no white shoe trying to keep his costs down because Sam would try to give him a break on rates and...

—Keep his, my God have you seen the bills they where is it, that blue folder Oscar where is it. Keep his costs down, they've charged him for everything here but paperclips. Long distance calls, telecopier, deposition transcripts, photocopying thirty cents a page? They must have done the whole Britannica, car rentals, travel that's our friend Mister Basie off to California, Mister Basie buying drinks for the house at the Beverly Wilshire they all could have flown to the moon, you call this giving him a break?

—I said on the rates Christina, those are costs, I said the hourly rates.

—Mister Basie sitting here with his clock running showing me pictures of the hairy Ainu?

—Not exactly what I, what I'm talking about rates Christina, we'd price somebody at Mudpye's level out at one eighty six an hour, Basie's probably priced around a hundred, maybe less, two or three hours of conferences for his client to explain the situation, a couple of hours of reading whatever's relevant and a couple more preliminary legal research, another conference you're up to a thousand before he's even taken the case, then he drafts the Complaint. Twenty hours research, four hours to write it and we're up to thirty five hundred and you've barely started. Kiester's brief comes in filing for dismissal and the heavy research time comes in, maybe forty more hours preparing Oscar's cross motion for summary judgment. Depositions, discovery documents if Kiester handed them all over, if he didn't more conferences, more briefs, deposing your witnesses probably count on at least ten hours of preparation for every hour of actual deposition time and an important deponent like Kiester himself figure his deposition lasts ten hours so there's a hundred and ten billable hours right there and you're still pretty early into the pretrial stage when things begin to get really expensive...

—Harry?

—Trial strategy and preparing your witnesses, the whole...

—Why in the name of God are you telling us all this.

—Just trying to explain how these things can mount up, even a fairly simple case like this one you take the case I'm on multiply every figure by a hundred, a thousand, I told you it would run into money didn't I? right at the start? If he'd won...

—He lost! He didn't win Harry he lost! my God how many times do we have to...

—Win or lose Christina, I told you at the start you begin running up bills the minute you...

—You don't think he's going to pay them do you?

—What?

—I said, by any remote stretch of the imagination you can't think that Oscar or anyone in his right mind would even faintly consider paying these idiotic bills for one instant, can you?

—Just telling you they put in a lot of time and work on the case Christina, take a look back there at Oscar's deposition I think Basie did a pretty damn good job for the...

—For a fraud, so the State can put him away for a year, what about your friend Sam. How long can they put him away for, he knew about it before the decision didn't he? You knew didn't you? didn't you call him?

—Look I've been out of town, it still might have been just a rumour and I've been so damn busy with the...

—Is that what you're worried about Harry? what the State can do to you? You sent Oscar to Lepidus, Shea and the whole...

—No wait Christina, look. The State's got nothing to do with it, no law that we have a duty to look into the credentials of lawyers we make referrals to. The whole thing's a self regulating profession, deal with things like that under the ABA's Code of Professional Responsibility doesn't mean a client has a cause of action against a lawyer who's violated the Code just because he loses a...

—The Code! My God you sound like a, a self regulating profession! Your friend Sam got us into this mess didn't he? Is anybody going to regulate your friend Sam or do we just put it down over here Lily, do try not to spill it.

—Do you want the...

—Just put it down!

—Have to research that Oscar, end up putting you to a lot of trouble entering a claim citing the elements of damages you've incurred here needed to make you whole, as they...

—To make him what?

—Legal phrase Christina, just means what it says, to make him whole, restore someone who can prove he's suffered damages to his...

—Well look at him, he's sitting right here in a thousand pieces if you want proof of damages to make himself whole, he can't get a new trial he can't find anyone else around to sue so he's suing himself is that what you mean?

—Of course it's not. Whole heart of the Fifth Amendment, you can't be made to testify against yourself, you've got a new law firm on that haven't you Oscar? Isn't that what they've told you?

—Well he, there's a letter here from him somewhere, from Mister Mohlenhoff, he thinks maybe they could get around that by granting one of us immunity to testify against the other one under threat of perjury or contempt he's looking into it. They want a five hundred dollar retainer to look into it.

—Most ridiculous thing I ever, don't send them a nickel, these the ones you got off a matchbook cover?

—Which one of him are you talking to Harry, the one who got Mister Mohlenhoff off a matchcover or the one Lily found for him who wants Oscar to pay him for suing himself in the first place.

—I didn't know what he'd, I know it was my fault Mrs Lutz but I just thought he was this lawyer that would help Oscar out now he's doing the same thing to Daddy, he took this money from Daddy where Daddy gave my brother Bobbie all this money to buy this Porsche that Reverend Bobby Joe calls the death instrument so now Daddy's in trouble where they want to sue him for something they call I forgot what they call it but, but maybe I better go Mrs Lutz I didn't mean to start...

—Probably a suit for what they call negative entrustment Lily, like handing a shotgun to somebody who isn't resp...

—Harry leave her alone, just sit down and be quiet Lily, and bring in some sugar will you? Didn't you get a cup for yourself? Five hundred for Mister Mohlenhoff off a matchcover or seventy five hundred for Lily's ambulance chaser my God Harry we're talking about thousands, these tens of thousands for your friend Sam who hands us a convicted felon and loses the case into the bargain?

—Just what I mean, you get a look at our billings to Kiester's people probably a hundred times what we saved Oscar with a small firm like Lepidus and...

—And who pays those, Oscar? because he sued them and lost?

—Well he, it's not a requirement in civil cases that the losing defend, the losing plaintiff I mean pays defendant's costs but I told you, I haven't seen the decision I told you, unless this judge holds him liable for reasonable attorney's fees but a judge like this one, no track record to go by you can't tell what the...

—You don't need that, Harry.

—What. Need what.

—Another drink. You don't need another drink. You haven't eaten a thing and those pills you're on to keep you from jumping out of your skin they told you not to drink didn't they?

—Just cuts down their effectiveness, one or two won't make any diff...

—Well you've had one or two, now will you sit down until we straighten this out? I don't care what this decision says about your thieving defendant's reasonable attorney's fees, you just said they were a hundred times what they ought to be didn't you? Oscar wouldn't even dream of paying them, I want to know who's going to pay Oscar. To make him whole.

—Well it won't, it's not that simple Christina, the...

—My God I know it's not that simple! Would we all be sitting here tearing our hair if it were? Your friend Sam got him into this mess, what are these elements of damages he's incurred you were talking about.

—Just the, just these elements things like fees, costs, the profits and accounting he went after originally but the, I think when I've had a chance to talk to Sam we can...

—Well pick up the phone. There's your chance right over there, call him up.

—Once we've read the decision Christina, no sense in...

—Well there's no sense in Oscar trying to do anything if he doesn't know what he can do is there?

—Well he'd just, he'd probably make either a tort or a contract claim, file a notice pleading to put the defendant on notice of the claim against him but if he's going to plead fraud, it isn't that simple if he's going to plead fraud he's got to state every element of the common law tort of fraud, prove he was injured by intentional misrepresentation of a known fact, leave out one of the elements and his complaint's dismissed but if they can show it wasn't intentional, that nobody knew Basie was fraudulent he'd passed his bar exams hadn't he? showed them his certificate to practice?

—On Oscar yes, to practice on Oscar with Sam at the piano playing Nearer My God Harry either he knew or he didn't. If he knew, it was fraud wasn't it? and if he didn't know he should have.

—Well that would, you'd have to prove negligence. Take a hypothetical case, if the...

—I'm not taking a hypothetical case, we've got a real one wriggling around right here in our laps. Was it fraud or negligence.

—Well the, that would be for a jury, if the law allows claims of fraud and of negligence rising out of the same operative facts and it had to go to trial...

—That's what trials are for isn't it? My God Harry this is like pulling teeth! Either they injured him deliberately or they didn't. If they did he can charge them with fraud, if they didn't he can charge them with negligence is that what you're trying to say? or trying not to say? Either they're lying or they were plain careless and irresponsible, it's that simple, isn't it?

—Matter of fact it's, I'd have to research it but he might not be able to bring a malpractice claim till all his appeals were exhausted because up till then he hasn't suffered any injury.

—That's the most ridic, will somebody answer that?

—I will yes, Oscar told me hello? It's who? Oh... no. No, he's... No he went to California no he didn't leave a number.

—Who went to California.

—Nobody, that was just what Oscar told me to tell them.

—To tell who! Who was it, Lily.

—They said it was the South Georgia Pilot.

—There! You see Christina? as though they have the right to call whenever they, aren't there laws Harry? laws of privacy? The rights of, it's what Father used to say, the right to be let alone?

—A hundred years ago, that was a judge named Cooley coined the phrase opened up the whole can of worms, it came down from the invasion of property rights but in the courts these days if you're a public figure you haven't got any.

—Well I'm not. I'm not a public figure, I've done everything to avoid it, it says right there in the paper doesn't it? calls me a recluse?

—Call you Oswald too don't they? First Amendment freedom of the press to get things wrong Oscar, they...

—It's not just that it's the whole, when Father reads it he'll...

—He'll probably just chuckle like he did when that old woman with the withered hand? the one who frightened us on your mother's side, she asked him why on earth they'd named you Oscar? Nobody's family name she said, and he just chuckled and said well, we had to call him something, heat up some more water will you Lily? This tea's quite cold, of course it might come in handy for telling you apart if you insist on suing yourself Oscar but...

—I'm not suing myself Christina! And I'm, it's not funny, the whole thing, don't you think Father will read it? that his law clerk will show it to him? He already thinks I wrote that vulgar grotesque perversion he saw up there on the screen now when he reads this, if he had any doubts and he reads this where they say I wrote the original script for this spectacularly successful motion picture exploiting madness in the family did you see that? as an article of impeachment did you see that Harry? Impeachment! Just the word, a man who's lived and breathed the law for his whole, for almost a hundred years a century, a century!

—Look Oscar, one thing old Judge Crease is not, he's not stupid. Not thinskinned either. People paying press agents through the roof to get their names in the paper you sit here trying to protect your privacy the more vulnerable you become, call that the people's right to know. You think he doesn't see right through it? that they're just using you to get at him? Aiming for a seat on the appeals court and damn the people's right to know gets him the front page, you think he blames you for this rubbish about impeachment? How the hell do you think you sell papers, stir up a little controversy, create ill feeling wherever you can, bait the hook, stir the pot, stay away from them. Just stay away from them.

—No but listen Harry, just to set the record...

—Want to write them an indignant letter for calling you Oswald? They'll print letters from every Oswald in the country from Lee Harvey's widow on down a few libel suits thrown in, no malice intended? Whole damn thing's malice out there waiting for you. Stay away.

—No but listen! I, when they say I wrote the original script for this, this distorted travesty of a movie that bears no resemblance to what I really wrote to this blood and sex ninety million dollar spectacular they...

—Going to write them an indignant letter and tell them that?

—I have to! To set the record straight so that when Father sees it he'll see I had nothing to do with this warped twisted...

—Fine. And when Kiester's lawyers see it, when Mudpye reads it he'll mark it Exhibit A if you show up throwing away more money on an appeal, see what I mean Oscar? Just digging up grounds for an appeal if there are any you're one step deeper in the whole...

—My God Harry what do you want him to do, just forget the whole thing?

—Might not be a bad idea Christina, he fought the good fight didn't he? That's the important thing, fought the good fight and lost no disgrace in that is there? Might even be able to take a good tax loss on the...

—Harry look at him! Does he look like he needs a good tax loss? My God of course he'll appeal, you just finished saying he couldn't do this malpractice business till all his appeals are exhausted didn't you? I told you Mister Basie said we'd win on appeal, he...

—And who's going to handle it, Basie? He's probably busy right now making brooms at a dollar twenty three an hour in a Federal prison, gives them something to do to keep them from killing each other, you expect Sam to handle these appeals with a malpractice suit waiting for him at the end of the road? Look. I'll talk to Sam minute I get a chance, considering the whole situation he might take it on at a cut rate once these other obligations are settled and...

—A cut rate! What do you mean these obligations, this stack of bills Oscar's sitting here drying his tears on? and you think for an instant I'd let him pay for one single...

—All right look, Christina. Look. Give me a chance to talk to Sam once he's studied the decision, can't promise anything but considering the whole situation might even get him to let these billings slide for a while.

—Harry. You don't seem to understand me. I'm not talking about letting anything slide for a while, I'm...

—All right! Suppose we, not promising anything but suppose he'd consider letting them slide till, keep sending them through to satisfy the IRS he'd made every effort to collect and eventually write them off, just let Oscar pay the disbursements and...

—Harry?

—Don't have to make a big thing of it Oscar, getting it all over the newspapers just make trouble for the...

—Harry!

—Settle up what they've already laid out and drop the whole...

—Harry what in God's name do you think you're talking about! Those car rentals? photocopies? transcripts, telecopiers that whole trash heap you just spelled out for us? For what. Plane rides, depositions, drinks for God knows who at your Beverly Wilshire for what! You imagine he's going to pay one penny for this, this rollercoaster ride he's been taken on? Make a big thing of it my God it is a big thing, get it all over the newspapers he should shout it from the housetops, can they make it any worse? Can they?

—It's all, look Christina, get it all over the papers the way they twist things around make us all look bad that's all, this little mixup about Basie shows up there in your South Georgia Pilot gets picked up by some stringer for the Atlanta Constitution the Charlotte Observer grabs it by the time it gets to the Times here, the Wall Street Journal you've got those five blind men describing an elephant look. I'll talk to Sam, no reason we can't work something out before the whole thing gets out of, out of look, look Christina...

—I've looked! All I've been doing I've been looking it's taken me this long to finally see what I'm looking at hush things up, keep out of the papers, fight the good fight and lose there's no disgrace in that is there? Your great Code of what was it you just told us? of professional responsibility and every profession's a conspiracy against the public who told me that. Who told me that! Your self regulating profession no reason you and Sam can't work something out what about us?

—It's, look Christina.

—You look! I said what about us Harry, a conspiracy against the public my God we're your family! Protecting yourself, protecting your friend Sam, protecting Swyne & Dour and your whole ridiculous self regulating white shoe conspiracy against your own family?

—Look, I've got a lot of, we can discuss it in the car Christina I've got to get back, Oscar? Got to be in court first thing in the morning, a lot of paperwork to get through tonight try to, just try to get some rest I'll call Sam first chance I get and straighten things out, try to get some rest. Coming Christina?

—No.

—But, look I can't wait around I...

—I said no Harry!

—Well what do you, Oscar's fine he's got Lily here to look out for him you can't just, I've got to take the car I can't just...

—Well take it! Just don't break your neck like we did getting out here.

—Oscar look, will you tell her you're...

—And get me a cloth from the kitchen, will you Lily? I've spilled some tea here. Is there any food in the house?

—There's some eggs.

—Never mind, here's a napkin, now...

—Can I help you Mrs Lutz? I could prepare some...

—And for God's sake stop calling me Mrs Lutz.

—But I thought, I have to go in a minute anyway, I have to get this car back to my girlfriend but if there's anything I...

—We're all right Lily, we're fine. I'll just make some scrambled eggs, we'll be fine.

Down the bare hall the outside doors clattered again, the obstinate whine of a car's starter, the cough of the engine, the wrath of crows down there on the lower lawn where she looked out over the brown grasses stirring along the edge of the pond's surface teeming with cold which seemed to rise right up here into the room to wrap them each in a chill mantle of silence pillaged by the clatter of all that had gone before the more intense in this helpless retrospect of isolation where their words collided, rebounded, caromed off those lost boundaries of confusion echoing the honking tumult of Canada geese in skeins blown ragged against the uncharted grey of the sky out over the pond, each thread in the struggle strung to its own blind logic from some proximate cause blinded to consequence and the whole skein itself torn by the winds of negligence urging their hapless course, she'd told him to take their settlement offer hadn't she? and Harry, hadn't Harry told him the same thing? Then who'd got him into this mess in the first place? Get yourself a Jewish lawyer if you're going after these movie people, who'd handed him over to Sam Lepidus? passed him along to Harold Basie stranded here tugged between a Jew and a black drawn tight as the sullen line of his lips in this mute exchange raging between them, the way Basie'd not so much deceived him as let him down: Where had Maid Quiet gone to, nodding her russet hood? That's good to know, as though some breath of fondness lingered, tinging her lips with a smile the way he'd sat here with something he'd torn from the paper about the hairy Ainu gone on the instant, breaking out with —my God I hope he drives carefully, two or three drinks and those pills he's been taking. Isn't there some more of your Pinot Grigio? as the day drained away at last, and over the scrambled eggs in the kitchen —you've got to call him, Oscar.

—Call him where! Making brooms in some, why hasn't he called me? He's the one who...

—I'm talking about Father. You've got to call Father she said, and again more astringently next morning going through that blue folder adding columns of figures, going through the mounting heap of mail —my God, haven't you opened any of this? Overdue account Third Notice, a sale of boating equipment, of tulip bulbs, Final Notice Overdue, Hobbytime, The Bursar's office wishes to inform you that a $7500 lien has been placed against your salary effective immediately, in the event that Schriek Mohlenhoff & Shransky At your request we have applied for a hearing date for your appearance in connection with the above captioned product liability action brought by your insurance Ace Fidelity Worldwide against Sosumi Motors relevant to inconveniences allegedly suffered by you resulting from vehicular malfunction due to Delinquent Account Unless we are in receipt of your certified check in the above amount within five business days we shall Be the first on your block to sport a pair of Hiawatha's Magic Mittens Wear 'Em With The Ladies Historical Preservation Society eagerly awaits your response to our earlier request for letters documents and other memorabilia relating to the late Thomas Crease (later Justice Crease) Seventeenth Regiment Army of Northern Virginia in your possession which properly belong in our archives before we are obliged to take legal steps —for the love of heaven. You've got to call him.

—He already knows about these stupid archives doesn't he?

—I'm talking about these stupid bills and stupid overdue accounts and stupid liens against your stupid salary Oscar, this whole stupid mess you've got yourself into, what do you plan to do.

—What do you expect me to do! Burrow in the cushions for change that fell out of his pocket when he went to sleep reading the paper? That's what it would be like, asking him for money it would be like burrowing in the...

—Well you've simply got to make peace with him somehow, there's your mother's trust account in that Maryland bank you'd need his permission to go into that wouldn't you? There's something in this mess about an escrow payment on the mortgage, do you want to wait for them to step in and sell the place out from under us and try to explain that to him? Will you call him?

—Well I, maybe after lunch Christina, maybe...

—And what do you plan for lunch, poached salmon with carrots in the Spanish style? We've got to get some food in the house, if I look at another egg I'll turn into one.

—Yes well, you can call the cab in the morning and...

—I am not going to call the cab! Spend money on cabs after what we've just, you can call Lily. You can call Lily can't you? She's got a car hasn't she?

—But, to ask her to go shopping for us I don't...

—I didn't say I'd even think of doing that did I? She'd come back with God knows what, a frozen pizza and some Hostess Twinkies no, of course I'll go with her.

Bread, celery, tea, soups, oil, chicken breasts, onions, vermicelli, lamb chops, capers, sour cream, butter —You can put all that right in the refrigerator Lily, and tea, didn't we get tea? Put some water on will you? And I got this ginger preserve he likes with his toast, you might want to make tea for us right now I'm chilled to the bone and those dishes, maybe you can clear them up while we're waiting, that is of course if there's any hot water God knows what's wrong with it, there's scarcely enough to wash your face.

—Oscar had Mister Boatwright here, I thought maybe he fixed it.

—He had what?

—This old plumber, Mister Boatwright?

—I can't imagine what you're talking about, let me see if there've been any calls. Oscar? She burst down the hall, had Harry called while they were out? or had anyone? Well, had he finally got up the nerve to call Father? or would she have to do it herself, like everything else here. She'd asked Lily to stay to supper, a decent meal probably wouldn't hurt her it might be that appalling haircut makes her look like something the cat dragged in, if she could simply stop that incessant chatter, her daddy and mother say they're going to come up here and they're going to get everything reconciled when she's able to see them without that Reverend Bobby Joe always hanging around because she's all they've got left now with her brother Bobbie gone God knows where but they're still mad at her for where she went and made that dumb marriage outside the faith to this Jewish guy which Reverend Bobby Joe says like it's some kind of a disease that all of a sudden just turned up again like this bad penny who's suing your ridiculous accident lawyer for adultery so she's real scared he'll make her be this witness if he can find her —so you may have the chance to work another courtroom appearance into your own busy schedule Oscar, if you see what I mean. What are you reading there? He held up Hobbytime, —my God, like that ant farm you sent off for when you were seven and we had them all over the house oh, just put it down there Lily I think we can manage, before you wait, can you get that? If it's Harry tell him I'm not, no I'll talk to him give it to me, here. Harry? Oh... oh! followed by oh my Gods and but how awfuls, Nembutals? and finally —yes but do! It will do you good, you must be exhausted, when do you... Well whenever you can, if they need you in court then come out when it's over, it can't go on forever can it? resting the phone back in its cradle, cradling her head in her hand, —now. Where has she gone. Do you ever expect to see Ilse again? And will you do me a favour and call that therapist? unless you plan to spend the rest of your life lying around here like a beached whale. Do you think you can ask her to get rid of some of this trash?

—Wait, wait I want to keep that, I...

—This? She held up Hobbytime, —you're going to start another ant farm?

—No, there's a fish tank...

—My God Oscar. I'm going to have a bath. Unless she's used all the hot water in the kitchen of course, and remind me to tell her.

When she does those chops for dinner tonight for God's sake not to overcook them.

But a fish tank? when they could better be watched in living colour and much wilder variety spawning and feeding, fin ripping and vacant staring glassy eyed from far grander submarine vistas and exotic plant and coral strewn habitats right here on his nature program, spared those custodial concerns for wind and wave, temperature and salinity, aeration, pH balance, light and filtration and the daily toll of all those mouths to feed confined, best of all, where they could be summoned and banished in an instant like those hordes of his own species crowding the channels elsewhere rather than actually having them all over the house here firing guns, spouting news events, telling jokes, doing pushups, deep knee bends, shuddering with diarrhea, howling half dressed and full of passionate intensity humping guitars like the monkey with the greased football loosing mere anarchy upon the world where three's a crowd even in a house as large as this one, how long did he think she expected to stay? Just let her cool down, leave it to Harry, it couldn't all go on forever could it? and she wasn't still on the warpath like she'd been when he'd driven off without her, muttering —I could kill him! or, in the car when they'd gone shopping for groceries, snapping —Murder? yes. Divorce? never! interrupting a barrage of questions prying into everything from adultery to revenge and this lecherous accident lawyer, dry skin, depilatories, mammograms, reconciling with Daddy since tragedy'd struck coming down, all of it, to money, to the question of money right down to that faltering moment over seven dollars at the gas station but mostly, it was mostly just this feeling that —we never get to be alone anymore like it used to be Oscar, like remember that time we were doing it outdoors in the woods with those pine tree needles sticking into me with that squirrel watching us doing it and that rabbit where we were scared any minute she might see us? where any minute now she might come through the door with some new perplexity embracing household management, errands, the laundry or cornering him alone with —where in God's name she got hold of that car, it's really putting your life in her hands, she says it needs a new alternator whatever that might be, but I'm sure she imagines you'll pay for it, of course the reason she's never got a penny is that everything she's got goes on cosmetics, she's panic stricken at the thought of a wrinkle let alone this lump she rattles on about in her breast but I'm sure you've managed to find that all by yourself haven't you, is that the same shirt you've had on for a week? I'm almost afraid to trust her with the laundry after what happened to my beige cotton blouse and that little white alarm clock, have you seen it recently? I suppose she's managed to break it too like she did the last of those hideous Spode teacups, we simply can't go on like this Oscar do you ever expect to hear from Ilse again?

—Yes she called, while you were both out shopping she...

—Well thank God. When do you expect her.

—Well she, I don't. I told her I didn't think we could...

—That we can't afford her? My God, it's costing us more in sheer carnage than whatever her miserable wages came to isn't it? and you'd like to see everything around here taken care of by me and this poor girl out there right now mopping the kitchen floor just to save a few dollars?

—It's, no Christina it's her sister, she...

—It's no more her sister than the man in the moon, I think your mind's beginning to go Oscar. I trip over her every time I walk through the door don't I?

—I mean Ilse, Ilse's sister the one with the cataracts. She wants to get back out here to work but she's afraid her sister will have an accident because she can hardly see and gets confused about the gas stove, so she offered to...

—She offered to bring a blind woman out here for the rest of us to wait on while she's busy blowing up the house?

—No, no she just thought she could put her sister in the cubby in the top floor where she wouldn't be in the way, that she could peel vegetables and things like that to help out just until spring when the weather gets...

—Till spring! My God Oscar, has it occurred to you to worry about getting through the winter first? sitting here with the television running while you stare out at the, look. Look, can you see him out there? Reared up on the top step of the upper lawn beneath the window clutching an acorn, head darting, tail twitching, the squirrel scampered off at the wave of her hand, —did you see him? You think maybe he was trying to tell you something? One of Hiawatha's mangy little refugees setting up his layaway plan for the hard times ahead while Hiawatha sits here on the shore of Gitche Gumee, the minute old Nokomis walks into the wigwam he opens a book, his eyes seeking sanctuary on the page where *It seemed to me that the surface of the lake had changed, often dramatically, each time I looked back at the water* —you're not even watching this grisly thing then? are you? with a wave at the silent screen where, as though abruptly dismissed by the toss of her hand, the stretcher borne writhings of survivors of a tenement fire blazing away in the background gave way to the decorous designer sheeted writhings of a middleaging arthritic enduring languorous massage with a heat penetrating unguent and a Florida backdrop Kissing Pain Goodbye, had he called that therapist? Well not exactly, no, he'd told Ilse he didn't think things would work out so he'd just send her the money and —Send her what money! Well, that last week she was here and had to leave when her sister called on such short notice that —She left us in the lurch with nothing in the house but half a dozen eggs while we're paying her through the roof to handle your God knows what in there in the bathtub? Get that down to a quid pro quo now for every gallon of gas that goes into that death trap when we go shopping and maybe she can take right up where Ilse left off, of course I'm sure she already oh, Lily? you've finished out there? Yes sit down for a minute, something I meant to ask you talking to him till I'm blue in the face while he sits there staring at a book, will you look at him? *A minute later a sudden wind had transformed it into a blustering Scottish loch with a surface current and whitecaps. The light can change with an equal suddenness* —and can we turn that thing off if no one's watching it? Yummy! a waffle crowned with peanut butter being drenched with maple syrup abruptly displaced by a barefoot procession of bulging eyes and distended bellies fleeing a famine in Ethiopia —and bread? do we need bread? and flour, there's a pencil right there under that napkin we'd better make a list, go shopping without one when you're hungry and you come home with everything in sight, flour. I said flour didn't I, if we need it or not just to be safe there's no earthly reason you can't make a perfectly smooth béchamel sauce with this new processed flour Lily, you can try it again tonight with, write down cauliflower yes, we haven't had cauliflower it should be quite cheap now it's that time of year after all, isn't it. Oscar? do you think of anything? That time of year? watching those fragile fingers stumble paused over the spelling of cauliflower when yellow leaves, or none, or few he could have told them, and here came the squirrel again emptyhanded back down the steps to scamper off across the lower lawn toward a white oak for another acorn till at last when hard times came he'd have not the faintest notion where he'd buried any of them in this frenzy of survival serving neither himself nor even his kind but another vast kingdom, a different order entirely, planting white oaks broadcast —and while we're at it, tea, we always need tea, and yes sugar, just to be safe. Wasn't that what all this was about, after all? from the squirrel down there in the throes of its own monstrous miscalculations to that rabbit lunching nearby, panic quivering through every fibre of its being and beauty nothing but beginning of terror it was still just able to bear for what might that very instant be circling overhead or slithering toward it in the discoloured grass? All this, as she'd charged a minute before, trying to tell him something, there was simply no getting through a thought, let alone putting two of them together to make an idea, before she came up with something else out of nowhere, something in yesterday's paper about the parties in that ridiculous Cyclone Seven case exchanging places? renewing the fray now that horrid dog was out of the way with its genuine simulated Spotskin® and all the rest of it, Minjekahwun, Wear 'Em With The Skinside Inside, of simply getting through a page of the book here by the shining Big-Sea-Water, dark behind it rose the forest where the pigeon, the Omeme, building nests among the pine trees? *At times there is a clarity of detail at great distances when, for example, each branch of a thorn tree on the far bank is minutely sharp to the eye. Instantly it will become a dull strip of grey, and without a cloud in the sky to account for the change. This can produce mild hallucinations as the middle distance advances and recedes* where a moment before gusts had flung up the branches of the pines like the skirts of the beautiful Wenonah being ravished by the West Wind, by the heartless Mudjekeewis bending low the flowers and grasses *and you can soon begin to feel oppressed by the strange gloom of this lake, with its isolated houses and its wide lawns that slip into the water as if the lake were slowly flooding* and in flocks the wild goose, Wawa, flying to the fenlands northward and the squirrel, Adjidaumo, rattling in his hoard of acorns and the serpent, the Kenabeek —all coming right around full circle and probably getting it wrong at that, she came on, —have you heard a single word I've said Oscar? What is that you're reading. The jumble rattling around in your head, how can you expect us to know what you think when you simply sit here without a word, it's really quite rude. Pretending to read while I'm talking to you, can you answer my question? What was it I asked you. Have you thought any more about calling Father? Changing sides in that idiotic lawsuit they're just trying to drive him around the bend, as though things weren't already bad enough with all this nonsense about impeachment, about inherited madness running in the family, to simply sit down and write him a letter? Well? Well, he could have told them about all that, how John Brown's mother and grandmother both died mad —but on second thought he'd probably pass for Exhibit A himself will you take a look at him right now?

—Me? Oh, but they always told me that these things you inherit go from father to daughter, from mother to son like Bobbie had this nice head of hair, only Daddy was bald ever since I remember and Mama...

—Before you carry this too far Lily, Oscar is simply my step brother, I'm not his sister or his half sister either.

—Oh. I thought they're the same, he...

—Well thank God they're not, you talk about a nice head of hair if his gets any longer he can wear it in braids and stick in a couple of eagle feathers, the wealthy recluse on the family estate sitting here gaping out at the Big-Sea-Water while his father sits down there and lays down the law, of course he doesn't dare call him up, or put on his magic mittens and write him a letter.

—But maybe he'll just forgive and forget? Like Daddy, when Daddy knows how sorry I am that I did these things I shouldn't have done? and these things he thought I should do and I didn't? That it was all my fault, these mistakes I made and how sorry I am that I got him upset and I don't deserve him to pity me, and I can ask Mama to talk to him and help me out because I know deep down how he loves me and always wanted me to have the best so he won't stay mad at me, he'll forgive and forget and...

—You've made your point, but I think you should know that your mealymouthed Daddy and Oscar's father are about as alike as night and day, and the day Judge Crease forgives and forgets you'll know the moon is made of green cheese. Yes and write down cheese, let's get this over with before it rains. I thought we might try veal.

—Oscar liked the chicken the way we had it.

—Well he's always been fond of veal, we haven't had it in an age, Oscar? We'll have to have some wampum if you, my God now where has he gone. Sitting here pretending to read a book while we're in the midst of talking to him, the minute he hears me mention money he disappears while we're waiting on him hand and foot, you won't be warm enough in that. There's a jacket of mine you'd better slip on, it's a sort of grey tweed right there in the hall and bring my raincoat while you're at it. And you have the list? when they got outside, and then once in the car —drop me at the drugstore while you're getting gas, as they swerved up the ruts in the driveway —and for God's sake, will you please tell them to wash the windshield? If we're going to be killed I'd like to see what hits us, will you meet me right there in the grocery? Back by the fruits and vegetables, —mushrooms, while I'm finding those you can look for some heavy cream, just a small one, it goes bad so quickly with only the three of us.

—But what about Harry?

—What about Harry.

—But I thought, so we wouldn't have to go right out shopping again, I thought he might show up any minute.

—What in God's name made you think that.

—But you, back when he called? about how he was exhausted and taking that Nembutal? How he had to be in court and I thought you said well it can't go on forever, that he'll come out here for a rest when it's done?

—Well why on earth did you think that was Harry.

—Just if you weren't on the warpath with him anymore and...

—I'll tell you when I'm not on the warpath! I haven't heard a thing since the day he drove out of here after that disgraceful performance, I wouldn't think of calling his office with that ninny of a secretary he's got she'll say anything he tells her to, leaving calls on our answering machine I don't even know if he ever gets home. God knows he's exhausted but he'd never take Nembutal, he'd pour a drink instead no, that was for a dog.

—I didn't know you had one. You want me to carry that?

—A dog? My God no, here, you can carry both these bags out to the car. That was an old girlfriend I went to school with, she bought a snaggletoothed little Lhasa apso and has to hide the Nembutal in the pâté she gives it because it's simply driving her crazy. She forgets it's there and keeps stepping on it when she doesn't look where she's going and she hadn't slept for days since her daughter's breakdown, people calling her night and day to be of help and she thought she could get some rest out here but she may have forgotten it the minute she hung up, she's been in court constantly over her mother's will and that kind of thing can go on forever. You're sure you don't want me to drive?

—No, it's tricky sometimes just once it gets started. They said it needs a new alternator.

—Well I'm sure Oscar can help you with that.

—All he said was how much would it cost.

—He's always been quite careful with money, he hasn't changed since he was ten, digging under the furniture cushions for change that had slipped out of Father's pockets. We thought he'd be a lawyer when he grew up, that he was constantly reading those law books in the library but sometimes Father would use a dollar bill for a bookmark, or even a five, and that's what Oscar was looking for.

—From what I saw of lawyers that's all any of them's looking for, that and a little tail if you pardon the expression when you never suspect it, as they finally drew off the highway down a road, down a byroad and through the gate past STRANGERS REQUESTED NOT TO ENTER —you never know what somebody will do.

—My God Lily, as the car slid down the ruts of the driveway, —people will do anything.

—Look! as they turned in toward the veranda —there he is, this Mister Boatwright, I told you, see him in there? where he's barely walking all bent over? Didn't I tell you? he's...

—My God! Stop the car! it's...

—It's this old plumber, it's this Mister Boatwright I told you before when I saw him in there walking across the...

—It's, it's not Mister anybody it's, look at him! It's Oscar! Well what are you stopping for! hurry! and she was out of the car, through the rain running up the wet steps of the veranda to tug at the doors —Oscar! What's going on!

—Damn.

—Here take my arm before you, look out!

—Let me go I said!

—Can you, simply tell me? she'd sunk to the edge of the nearest chair —what, in God's name, is going on?

—What does it look like's going on!

—Well it's, look at it! Where are you going? Will you, my God Lily don't squeal like that! Made my blood run cold just, just put down the groceries and help me pick up this mess will you? Oscar? will you tell me what these papers are doing all over the floor? and where you think you're going with your be careful! Is it empty? on her feet again, —is this what you...

—Give me that!

—It's empty! it's, my God Oscar. My God. Leave you alone for ten minutes you open a bottle of your Pinot Grigio up running around the room like a, will you sit down! You're making me dizzy, is this what you've been doing? let us wait on you hand and foot and the minute we're out of sight you're up staggering around the room like a, will you tell me what this is all about?

—I called him.

—Who.

—Well who do you think?

—Oscar I'm not going to play games with you as though you were ten jumping out from behind the door, just answer me. You called who.

—Father.

—And that's why you're running around waving a bottle flinging books and papers all over the floor? Is this what you've, I asked you to sit down! I can't talk to you while you're, Lily why are you just sitting there. Can't you make yourself useful?

—But I thought...

—That's the one thing you didn't do. Mister Boatwright, my God, reeling around waving a bottle like a two year old learning to walk when nobody's watching, is that what this ridiculous performance is all about Oscar? What did he say.

—Well you do, you do have to learn to walk again, first time you stand up it's like a bed of nails, like walking on broken glass.

—That's not what I asked you! If you'd simply listen to me...

—That's all I've been doing isn't it! listening to you? Expect me to call him up and plead with him for, to sit here and tell Father the whole thing's my fault? that madness runs in the family did I ever say that? John Brown's body lies amouldering in the grave where his mother and grandmother both died mad? where one of his brothers, his sister and her daughter and some aunts and uncles were all of them in and out of asylums, if you want madness running in a family, his first wife and one of his sons died insane and his soul goes marching on while I'm sitting up here being yanked back and forth in this tug of war between a Jew and a black man over Grandfather's dead body and where is he? Father, my father too busy with this ramshackle piece of junk sculpture down there to listen to my, what am I supposed to do! Go down on my knees and beg for mercy as if I'd, as if I'm to blame for this talk about impeachment? and I'm supposed to have that on my conscience? Because that's what they're fighting over, isn't it? Like the parties changing places fighting over that rusty piece of junk, tugging both ways does it matter which one's at which end if I'm in the middle? Does it?

—Will you sit down! before you fall down, if you, where are you going!

—Right where I was going when you walked in the door there, into the kitchen to get another bottle of the, on the counter there Lily and bring the corkscrew will you?

—Sit down! Sit down both of you! My God, Lily didn't I just ask you to start cleaning up this mess? get a broom and sweep up these papers before we...

—These papers! sweep them up and I'll, it's my play where it spilled when I was trying to find the place in the last act where the, pick them up will you? help me pick them up Lily? It's all right there, he never read it did he, he wouldn't bother to read it but he went to the movie didn't he, listen. That's what we'll do we'll go to the movie. Call them up, get my shoes we'll...

—Oscar stop it, it's not even playing out here sit down I said!

—We'll go into town then, see it in town is there gas in the car?

—We're not going anywhere! Lily will you, here, get his other arm here will you? help him over to the...

—By the phone, over here, by the phone I'll show him, handle this appeal myself I'll show him.

—That's it. Just rest his head back, that's it.

—Feel awful.

—You want me to stay and help make supper?

—Just go along Lily, take those grocery bags out to the kitchen and go along. I'll just fix him some milk toast and get him to bed. Or, or Lily? and she raised her face from the flats of her hands where she'd covered her eyes rising suddenly overcast, dulled as her voice, —if you must go I mean, I mean must you? Because of course there's Oscar's old room up there now that Ilse's out from underfoot though he may go crashing up there himself, on second thought we'd better leave all the lights on tonight, God knows what he'll do next, you haven't left your keys in the car have you? if we hope to get a moment's sleep tonight, there. Do you hear it? a door banging somewhere? waiting for him to call that he's having a seizure? or the house is on fire? every sense tensed for the arousal of another blurring which one touched off the rest, the stab of the morning's light? the shrill cry? or the smell of smoke.

—Good morning he said, from the chair he sat in, —some coffee? oblivious to the night's dishevelment tumbled in from both directions —or, or tea? dispelling the cloud bluish in the sunlight at his elbow shattering its mantle of tranquility with the wave of a hand.

—You're, you're smoking!

—Sit down Christina, please, both of you, we can...

—Frightened us half to death, I smelled the smoke and, Oscar what in God's name are you doing! You haven't smoked for twenty years, where did you get that!

—Found them in the pocket of this jacket, now let's...

—I said where did you, are you all right? Sitting here in a suit and necktie what do you, you've been out and brought in the paper?

—I want a cup of coffee and I want to know what happened to...

—A cup! My God you'll need a pot of coffee after last night, you must have a really splendid headache, do you remember anything?

Getting up at midnight and marching up and down here reciting God knows what with your...

—Why, if 'tis dancing you would be, There's brisker pipes than poetry. Say...

—Please, don't start it again, if you...

—Oh I have been to Ludlow fair And left my necktie God knows where, And carried...

—Please! And will you put that vile thing out, it's smelling up the whole house, Lily for God's sake make some coffee, will you?

—Listen Christina, I want to know what happened to my play, to those pages that were on the floor here when you...

—What do you want it for. And that suit, where in God's name did you find that suit.

—I found it in the closet off the library. Now my play, where is it.

—You mean it's an old suit of Father's, isn't it?

—I just told you I found these in the pocket didn't I? when he first started smoking Home Runs? Now...

—My God no wonder. I mean no wonder I woke up with this sickening feeling when I smelled it as if he was still in the house, as if he was sitting down here waiting, just waiting for one of us to, will you put it out! Here, here use this for an ashtray you're already coughing like he was the last time we, put it out Oscar. Put it out!

—All right! Now where is it, you threw it out? My play, is that it? you threw out those pages on the floor?

—Just sit down, I put it somewhere God knows what you want to...

—I want it because it's mine Christina. I want it because I wrote it. I want it because it's the one thing I've got left out of this whole nightmare the one thing that's, that maybe I can rescue that's mine. Maybe that's why all this happened. Maybe it happened for a reason, to bring it back to life instead of just getting lost gathering dust on a shelf somewhere and when it's up there on the stage the way I wrote it, everything just the way I wrote it instead of this sleazy ripoff on the screen they...

—And who's going to put it up there on the stage, your friend Sir Nipples? My God Oscar, you...

—Yes. Sir John, yes you, you don't need to be insulting Christina. I want to read through it for the most effective passages when I arrange the reading for him, I don't think I should take up his time going through the whole thing the first time we...

—What on earth are you talking about, a reading! What about this appeal we've been tearing our hair over, you're just going to do what Harry told you to? forget the whole thing? Get your name in lights and leave your million dollar damage claim in the same shambles you've got my marriage standing up for you in this mess? Fought the good fight and lost, nothing wrong with that and I haven't heard from him since he drove out of here have you? Too obstinate just to pick up the phone and call me to say he's sorry for the way he behaved, to say anything and it's not even mine, this mess you've made of things, I told you to take that settlement didn't I? He did too didn't he? So now it's too late you're going to take his advice and forget the whole thing, am I supposed to forget it? when he can't even bother to pick up the phone and...

—Listen Christina. You're the one who's too proud to pick up the phone, you've been nervous and worried about the stress he's been under and the days going by like this the worse it gets. No I haven't heard from him since he drove out of here, I haven't fought the good fight and lost, I haven't given up this appeal at all. I've tried to reach Harry but they say he's in court, in a meeting, I've called Sam and told them to quit dragging their feet, to get this appeal filed and quit holding back while they haggle over bills and disbursements and the rest of this nonsense, they'll get paid when they get results. That's what I was doing up on my feet when you drove in here, the battery in that chair's gone dead and I got up on my feet to get to the phone and I'm going to stay on my feet, this play is still mine and I'm not going to miss this opportunity.

—Well let them then! Let them file your appeal and see what happens before you go off on some wild goose chase with, setting up readings, what readings? where? Call it an opportunity when you don't even...

—Because he's here Christina. He's in town, Sir John Nipples, he's here to direct a revival of Sheridan's School for Scandal it's right there in the paper, if that's not an opportunity?

—So you plan to have those brilliant students of yours over here sitting on the floor giving a spirited reading while you serve Sir John carrots in the Spanish style it's insane Oscar, you can't be serious. It's all perfectly insane.

—I did not say out here did I? Did I? I can arrange a reading in town, get some professional actors together and arrange a reading for him in town once I've chosen the most effective...

—And how do you plan to pay these professional actors of yours.

—Pay them? They'll jump at the chance Christina, the chance to be seen by one of the most prestigious directors in the theatre anywhere today? Of course they'll do it for nothing, they're so vain they'd probably even pay for a chance like this, we won't have to go searching for them we'll have to fight them off, we...

—I wish you wouldn't say we, I don't plan to have anything to oh, put it down here Lily, and those papers we picked up off the floor will you get them? I think I put them on top of the refrigerator, sitting up there in one of Father's old suits why don't you invite him up for your professional actors spieling these effective passages, I'm sure he'd have some suggestions.

—Father has a lot on his plate.

—You certainly read that line with relish. Is that why you're doing all this? just to prove to him that you...

—Why should I have to prove anything to him! He's...

—Well my God, I mean that's what set you off on this merrygoround in the first place isn't it? Up here staggering around when we drove in I asked you what was going on and you said you'd just called Father?

—I didn't say I talked to him did I? I said I'd called him no, no his clerk said he was too busy to come to the phone, another nice helping on this plate right here in the paper this morning, he's so busy down there now with some crackpot minister who drowned a boy he was trying to baptize he can't spare me a minute to come to the phone, where's the sugar. Put that on his plate with these Senate Judiciary Committee hearings any day now and that junk sculpture case turned upside down while this Neanderthal institutes his impeachment proceedings and he'll, didn't you bring the sugar?

—I hardly ever saw you drink coffee before Oscar, I didn't know if you wanted...

—Well what does it say, in the paper where does it...

—Well read it! Back in the entertainment section where it belongs, headline's LORD CALLED DROWNED BOY REVEREND UDE TELLS COURT, something like that.

—Who?

—Not your Bobby Joe no, this is some old quack up in the Carolinas, suit for wrongful death by the boy's father runs a junkyard in Mississippi so it's the same old diversity of citizenship lands it in Federal court and...

—No but it is! You know who that is? That's Reverend Bobby Joe's daddy, does it say Elton? Reverend Elton Ude? That's his old daddy, Reverend Bobby Joe moved down to Florida because Disney World's down there where the old people go and that's his daddy, I just know it is Oscar because Reverend Bobby Joe told Daddy once how his daddy was...

—Daddy daddy daddy, will you just give her the paper? The two of you, my God, sitting here in your old daddy's suit with your, now where do you think you're going.

—To get those pages you put on top of the refrig...

—Don't be ridiculous, Lily can get them and don't you dare light another of those things, up here parading around the room when some insurance adjuster drives in to check out your crippling disabilities, you think he's going to think you're Mister Boatwright our old family plumber in an outfit like that? And there go your damages for your idiotic accident pain and suffering, permanent disfigurement and all the rest of it down the drain along with your million dollar appeal when Sir John gets these professional actors up there prancing around the stage while your friend Kiester and the rest of them sit in the audience clapping their hands off and here you are gaping out at the shining Big-Sea-Water with nothing but a lapfull of bills from...

—Listen. This suit I'm wearing? a tremble in his hand clutching the package of Home Runs there as though armed however vainly, his own clothes were all up in his room and he hadn't wanted to try the stairs yet so he'd put this on from the library closet simply to dress like a civilized man again —because I am a civilized man! yes, and taking a look around maybe one of the last ones left. Hospital bills? medical bills? pain and suffering, he'd had enough of it, let his new lawyers worry about it, they'd get paid like the other ones when they got results and if anyone wanted a look at his permanent disfigurement he'd wear his scar right out where they could enjoy it, he'd accepted this invitation to speak on the battle of Shiloh hadn't he? had to get out his notes to prepare for that right now in fact, and if any brokendown insurance adjuster wanted to come peeking in the windows, let him. Just let him!

—I think you've got your wish, Oscar.

—Somebody just came up on the porch, shall I...

—That's what I mean. He looks sufficiently brokendown to play the part, will you see what he wants Lily?

—No, I'll go.

—I better not, if they find me here they could...

—I said I'll go! lurching upright, steadying against the sideboard and down the hall to clatter the glass doors open, —Well?

—Mister Crease?

—I am Mister Crease. What do you want.

—Hard time finding you back here. This is for you.

—Well what is it. Who are you.

—Process server, Mister Crease. It's a subpoena.

—It's, I don't want it! The envelope fell to the floor, —I don't...

—You've been served, Mister Crease. Nice place you've got, never know it was tucked away back here in the...

—Get out of here! Didn't you see the sign? This is private property, can't you read?

—One more word, get this porch fixed before it falls on somebody's head and you'll see me right back here again now I know the way, let's part better strangers as the Bard says? Have a nice...

—Go away! He stooped for the envelope, dropped it, caught it again and came up slowly, muttering back down the hall —God, what some people will do for a living. Here, he held it out unsteadily, —throw it away.

—People will do anything, what is it.

—I said throw it away!

—It's a, you're summoned as a witness for the trial in an action between Sosumi Motor Co. and the following defendants. Fan Tan Ltd., Productos Porqueria S.A., Wydawniczy I can't pronounce it, there's quite a list.

—Ridiculous, will you throw it away!

—Failure to appear may subject you to a fine or imprisonment, or both. Bring this summons to court with you, it sounds...

—Will you, here. Just give it to me, send it to the lawyers that's what they're paid for isn't it? I can't bother with it now, take all morning to get these pages back in order and try to read through the first act before lunch, just something light. An omelette? Consommé and a plain omelette, there must be thyme out there, tarragon, she'd have to show her, parsley? chives? a simple omelette fines herbes then, a little water beaten in with the eggs but cold water, it must be cold but she supposed she'd have to stand over her after that last milksop like something you'd get at a truckstop, and, when the time came —a little wine? It helped bring on the nap before he got back down to work, the pages sorted, squared, murmuring through them line by line broken by faint moans of pleasure, word by word shaping his lips and even escaping aloud —when we came back from France like beggars looking for a new exile and you sent me up there to see him? dropping to a whisper hoarse with indignation —Coming in here in your fine French clothes demanding your rights he said to me, when I asked him for the money that he owed my father, when I'd spent the morning trimming frayed cuffs and pinning the hem on my father's coat to, pinning up the hem, with a pause for the pencil, —pinning up the hem on my father's coat, on my father's threadbare coat to try to look fit to call. Five hundred dollars! in a gasp of outrage subsiding to a murmur, to muttering —for myself and those in my keeping Thomas, to know the Lord's will, and submit. To lay up treasures in heaven Thomas, treasures even for you, while you seek here below, on a sharp intake of breath —Only justice! falling away aggrieved —when my spirit was almost broken...

—Oscar? You want some tea or something before I do this laundry?

—What?

—I said do you want...

—I heard you. Don't you see I'm working? Do you have to interrupt me to talk about the laundry?

—I didn't mean...

—What time is it. I've got to make some calls, the thread's broken anyway. There's a shirt on the floor in the library, you can put that in, and will you make me some tea? The card table shuddered with his weight getting to his feet, getting to the phone with a torn envelope dialing the number scribbled there, —This is Mister Crease, may I speak with Mister Mohlenhoff? listening intent, clicking his teeth, slamming it down, and again —This is Mister Crease, may I speak to Sam? No, Sam Lepidus, don't you know your own... clicking his teeth, listening, slamming it down, thumbing the pages of the directory for —the Royal Court theatre? clearing his throat —yes, this is Mister Crease, Oscar Crease. I'm trying to reach Sir John... what? Oh. Thank you, may I try later? setting it down gently and lingering there over it as though fearful of leaving it untended till his vacant gaze settled on the vacant screen both of them, a minute later, asparkle with the flashy hues and fleshy petals of the promiscuous farflung family Orchidaceae, its wiles arrayed in every deceitful variation of shape and odour, colour and design to target randy insects with spurious promises of sex and nectar provoking frenzies of pseudocopulation and the consequent deposit of their pollen elsewhere it would do the most good, rearing up with —was that the phone?

—What? No I just brought your tea Oscar, I...

—Here, put it right here, sit down.

—I can't, I have to do the...

—Will you simply sit down? heaving aside to allow her room enough there for his arm to fall over her shoulders as a male wasp harassed an orchid artfully fashioned after his female counterpart, inadvertently picking up its pollen sacs for delivery to the ovarylike repository of the petaled temptress down the way, a hand slipping under the yoke of her blouse as the heady aroma of rotting meat exuding from another floral dissembler brought eager carrion flies on a similar skewed mission, bees stung with desire by the meretricious scent of female bees and bees elsewhere drunk with the fragrant promise of nectar staggering aloft so laden with pollen stuck to their backs they could barely complete their appointed rounds, his fingers parting a button, and another, delving deeper to pluck at the blossoming pink cresting to their touch, eliciting a moan mingling pleasure and distress as the screen swelled with the veined purple pouch of the lady's slipper —though it looks more like the Greeks' word for it, orkhis, for testicle, doesn't it? eliciting a giggle, —here, put your hand...

—No don't Oscar, please.

—It's all right, the laundry can wait.

—No but somebody might come peeking in the window.

—Christina's having a nap and nobody's peeking in the window.

—Like that man that came before? and he was peeking in before we even saw him out there? and if they're looking for me and saw me in here doing this with you that's all they'd...

—Doing what! Listen, nobody's looking for you, don't...

—They are too! That's why I'm staying here isn't it? and if Al's trying to find me he'll look everyplace. You don't know Al.

—Thank God. Who's Al.

—I told you, he's this husband I had that wants to get me in court with a summons like you just got to be a witness for screwing that sleazeball lawyer and if he saw me in here with your hand down my...

—Oscar?

—See? She squirmed free.

—I thought you were working. I've been doing the crossword upstairs trying not to disturb you. Are you watching this thing?

—It was my nature program, listen Christina. I'm not doing crossword puzzles down here, you can work for just so long with this creative tension I need and once the thread is broken you don't just sit there trying to think of a five letter word for...

—I think I just heard it. Now where are you going.

—I told you. I have to get together my notes for this talk on Shiloh, the battle at Shiloh, it was the second great battle of the war he went on, covering his wavering retreat from this hostile incursion with the haphazard deployment of Grant's forces in the face of the surprise Confederate advance on Pittsburg Landing in an April dawn near Shiloh church till he gained the redoubt of cardboard cartons still stacked there in the hall where he pawed through folders, loose notes, exam books, raw troops on both sides fueled by the exuberance of battle as disorder mounted among the Confederates under the howl of indiscriminate shells from Union gunboats on the Tennessee in two days of carnage leaving each side with ten thousand casualties and neither the winner, straightening up at last arms laden with folders spilling notes over the cartons like Grant brooding over the abandoned camps of the enemy, a carnival of bloodshed resumed elsewhere later and on a more modest scale on the evening news where religion seized the headline with an assault on the Babri Masjid mosque in far off Uttar Pradesh, exhausting its allotted news slot to make way for a moribund procession of sheer naked misery in the bulging eyes and distended bellies of a famine in the far away Sudan hastened to its destinationless close by good news nearer home for sufferers from athlete's foot, overweight, gas, and the spectacle of a two foot deep river of molten cheese, butter and lard issuing from a warehouse fire in the Midwest destroying thousands of tons of government surplus food, prompting no more than a reminder to put butter on the shopping list when suppertime came round, another night of winds vexing slates and shutters and the day bringing a show cause order from the Historical Society demanding an explanation for his failure to surrender those certain documents pertaining to Captain (later Justice) Thomas Crease which properly belonged to the ages —just daring to use those words it's, it's plain impudence.

—Well? Call your lawyers.

—I've called them, Christina. I called Mohlenhoff, they said he was in court. I called Sam and he was in court and I just called them again. They said Mohlenhoff would get back to me, they said Mister Lepidus said to tell me these things take time and I've been calling the theatre trying to reach...

—Calling the zoo and asking for Mister Fox, are you ten years old all over again? calling the drugstore to ask if they have Prince Albert in the can so you can tell them to let him out? Can't you think of better ways to waste your time?

—I can't send this script to an important director like this can I? It just needs a final polish, a fresh copy before he sees it, now will you...

—I thought you were polishing your great speech on Shiloh.

—I'm trying to do both! Now will you let me get back to work? his voice a minute later feigning the honeyed pomposity of the Old South with —the proper idea of these things, now didn't they? Aristotle, he was the Greek philosopher, I can show you somewhere what he had to say about, and the pencil again, —what he said about natural slaves. That there's some just naturally meant to be slaves? Ah... dropping to a rich baritone, —but to let a man's colour decide it, sir?

—And if you're going to light another of those things for God's sake do it outside, you smoked one in here last night after I went to bed and my eyes are still watering. Lunch? A sandwich, anything, right here at the card table so he could keep working, one day fading to the next on the repetitious drone of his voice dulled as the sky out there lowering over the pond where it might have been any daylight hour, to burst without warning like a break in the weather radiant in the surge of a brogue with —When men behave like savages, after all, with no respect for law and order, how must they be treated? Why, like savages! paused crossing through a line —but get them together they'll rise up and go wild with their brawling and drink and howling for justice, with no respect for decent people like ourselves. You must knock a bit of justice into them now and again, is the mail here yet?

—It's right there on the sideboard, something from your friends at Mohlenhoff Shransky and look out! You'll break your...

—Why didn't you tell me!

—Well don't smash the furniture, you didn't want to be interrupted did you?

Dear Sir.

In examining the situation surrounding your recent automobile accident we find Ace Worldwide Fidelity as the vehicle's insurers to have claimed immunity from any further participation in the matter pursuant to renunciation of the prevailing No Fault coverage by the former attorney for the vehicle's owner who remains, nonetheless, the attorney of record in that capacity having sequestered the file pertinent thereto pending settlement of allegedly unpaid billings to his client. We have, therefore, in the interest of expediting this matter to your satisfaction and to ensure that the controversy to be adjudicated will take place in an adversary context, moved to sever your claim for extensive personal injuries suffered as the accident victim, and are proceeding on these grounds with an action on your behalf for recovery of substantial damages against the parties referred to above. Please be confident that our long experience in these matters assures you of full protection of your rights. We advise you to refrain from discussing this matter with anyone and should you be approached regarding any aspect of it that you promptly refer such inquiries directly to us. We urge you to feel free to call us at any time with any questions that may occur to you in the course of these proceedings.

Sincerely yours,

—Jack Preswig. Look at that. Sincerely yours, Jack Preswig. They've put the whole case in the hands of some flunky who's probably not even...

—You find your lawyers on matchbook covers what do you expect.

—That's got nothing to do with it Christina. They all do it, these white shoe firms and all of them, look at Harry, a senior partner will bill you three or four hundred dollars an hour, look at Swyne & Dour, they put an associate on it and only bill you maybe one fifty. Look at Mister Mudpye.

—And look at Mister Basie. You're simply not making any sense Oscar, I don't know what in God's name you're complaining about. You want them to save you money don't you? Now where are you going.

—To get back to work! couldn't she see? spending all day here trying to capture these voices of men a hundred years ago swept by the tide of events toward the end of innocence? to bring them to life caught up in the toils of history, struggling vainly with the great riddles of human existence, justice and slavery, war, destiny, things are in the saddle and ride mankind in Emerson's voice cut short by the tin trivial interruption of Jack Preswig? It mightn't sound so trivial when he got their bill she prompted him, and it had sounded to her like he'd spent most of the morning that way on the phone himself, calling the zoo and asking for —But that's exactly what I mean! he broke out, calling hotels, he'd been calling hotels in the theatre district, he'd been calling the theatre he'd tried calling the Directors Guild he'd even called the newspaper, he couldn't make an appointment and just send this script off if he didn't know where to send it could he? If he had somebody to help him, if he had a secretary like everybody else to handle these miserable chores but he was the one who ended up talking to their secretaries who were paid to be devoured by trivia, his indignation swerving back to the lilt of a brogue from the pages he'd picked up again struggling to recapture a voice from a hundred and more years ago, to bring it to life —now the word is out that it's no more than a war to free the naygers?

—Is Lily in the kitchen? I forgot to ask her to peel those carrots for supper, and one of these days might it occur to you to shave.

—Yes, preserve the Union! he came on in a burst that brought him back to his feet —with four million naygers running around free? Why, the woods is full of them right now, and do you expect a nayger to go back into slavery once he's been as free to come and go as yourself? The phone's ring caught him off balance. By the time he got there it had stopped ringing; by the time he was back out of reach it rang again, stumbling over a wastebasket —hello? Well who is it... Well who are you calling! what... hello? hello? He slammed it down, —Idiot! his hand straying down to the bulge in his trousers, was she out there in the kitchen? her nimble fingers stripping the hard length of a carrot? but all he found was the wilted package of Home Runs down there distending his pocket and he had one out down the hall before he reached the door.

—Oscar? Who was that on the phone. Well where is he.

—I heard something fall down before. I thought maybe it was him.

—You'd hear more than that if it had been, my God it was simpler when he was in his little cart at least you knew where he was, like a baby. You can't wait for them to learn to walk, the minute they learn there's not a minute's peace you wish they'd never, what was that.

—Christina! The doors crashed closed down the hall —the car's gone!

—It's right out by the porch Oscar, I can...

—Not yours, mine! The one that was in the accident, it's gone!

—Well it can't be, it's practically dark you can hardly...

—It's gone Christina, it was right out there beside the shed it's gone.

—Why in God's name would anyone, well call the police.

—That's what I'm doing! Where the...

—The number's right there stuck to the, will you put that thing out! What were you doing out there anyhow.

—That's what I was doing! You don't want me to smoke in here so I, hello? Yes, yes I want to report a stolen car, it's... what? It's a red... No, my name? Yes it's...

—Take that thing away from him will you Lily? Throw it in the, not in the fireplace no and open a window before he gives us all cancer. They probably drove it away when we'd gone shopping and he was sitting right here gaping at his odious nature program, God knows who would want it. Oscar? when he'd hung up, —who was that on the phone.

—Well who do you think it was! I just called the police didn't I?

—I know you just called the police. When the phone rang earlier, who was it.

—I don't know. It was some hysterical woman who could hardly...

—My God. Was it Trish? But you wouldn't know her voice anyhow you haven't seen her for years, not that it's changed since her operation for, what did she say?

—Nothing, I told you, just a lot of garbled...

—I'd better call her. Do you have to turn that thing on right now? and she had the phone, —even hear myself think while somebody's trying to sell me toothpaste, will you see if that water's boiling yet Lily? I put the, hello? Hello? Yes it's Christina, are you... No, Christina, it's Teen, yes are you all right? You sound... yes, did you call earlier? who? No, a rude man who hung up in your face? No he, you must have had a wrong number, you don't sound... oh my God! She turned her back to the diverting spectacle on the silent screen where the evening news led off with the inevitable skeletal parade scantily tailored in garments of pounded bark against an arid landscape, distant Mozambique this time, a woman with milkless dugs lofting a child deprived of food had there been any by a mouth fungus in the swelling vanguard of Africa's twenty eight million famine orchestrated candidates for oblivion —but my God how awful, how did it happen? Far to the north, a gold mitred Pope in ankle length skirts rebuking a benumbed audience fresh from the potato fields with the revelation that all children born and unborn were gifts of God gave way, nearer home, to a fetid congregation of homeless being ousted from their digs under a railway trestle —still in court? But which was it, this nonsense about foetal personhood or for wearing the skins of these dead chinchillas my God that's all they're good for isn't it? a fur coat? A new denture cleaner and brightener, a new itch fighting shampoo, the radiant testimonial of a halitosis survivor nonchalantly sweeping up dead leaves with a bamboo lawn rake whipped up in a Chinese prison and back to news on the economic front, the trade deficit, a burgeoning bank fraud, a lugubrious President announcing China's most favoured nation status —chewing your bandages? Well stop him. Will you turn that thing down!

—Look! Christina look!

—Or an ambulance if you have to, you can find one in the phone book it will do you so much good. Can't you stop him? what? In court again tomorrow? No, pry his jaws open and push it to the back of his throat and then hold them closed till he... oh! did it break the skin? I'd better hang up yes, whenever you can, I'll get things ready, now. Did you have to turn that thing up while I was...

—But look! And surely enough, there looming over this dark tale with a happy ending the jagged planes of Cyclone Seven shed its scarred benisons down upon the wedding of Billy Pinks and Millie Kalikow, her fifth grade classmates clutching bouquets of bluebonnets side by side with the groom's ushers buoyed by the bonhomie of his colleagues on the loading docks at Miller Feed Co. drawn up at the patio entrance to the newly inaugurated Mel's Motel to be followed by the numerous guests into the generous dining area where the bride cut a cake topped by a spun sugar approximation of the towering artifact beyond the glass where their romance had first been kindled amid the passions that had blazed forth here on a darker occasion as the screen revisited the floodlit melee of flying rocks and beer cans, Stars, Bars and Stripes asunder, signs and placards brandished and trampled GOD IS JUDGE aloft and IMPEACH smouldering on the judicial robes of controversy lately put to rest by the conciliatory visit of Senator —wait stop it, what are you doing!

—I'm turning it off, what does it look like I'm doing.

—No but didn't you hear what he...

—I don't care what he's saying, my God do we have to go through that scene again? What time is it.

—Didn't you hear what he started to say about the...

—Please! before we, it's too late to go shopping isn't it, will you write down chicken? Lily? have you got a pencil, juices, soup, something bland, sole, plain flounder if they don't have it, rice, beef broth and, oh and do we have a heating pad Oscar? one that works?

—Yes but I've been using it for my...

—I'm sure you can manage without it for a few days, there's no sense filling the house with them, there's that old hot water bottle Father had for his gout you can find that and, yes and some gauze bandage she may forget to bring any she's been so distracted, this commotion over her daughter's breakdown when she cut her wrists last night and little T J called the doctor going to court like that all day or they might have thrown out this fight over her mother's will if she hadn't shown up and this sanctimonious idiot who threw catsup on her fur coat in a courtroom right down the hall where she has to show up tomorrow for that revolting boy with his absurd paternity suit when the whole thing literally went down the drain weeks ago my God she's so brave, if you could have heard her just now. Bright, cheerful, she even thought of you Oscar, the midst of all she's going through asking if it would upset you if she comes out?

—But, well no but how long do you think she would...

—For as long as she wants to! I've never heard anything so selfish even from you, we've taken your friend here in haven't we? She can sleep right there in the library, I think you're able to start staggering up the stairs to your own room again aren't you? You can help me air it out after supper Lily and get rid of those stacks of newspapers, they can go right down to the laundry room Oscar if you can't bear to part with them, it's not as though you're being asked to actually do anything my God, I'm the one who'll be waiting on both of you aren't I? And that little phone stand right there Lily, it can go in the library where you can take her tea in the morning, or coffee, write down some sort of muffins will you? or those frozen croissants though God knows she may just want to sleep, is that asking too much?

—No but listen, Christina...

—Is it? in a cry taken up next morning before a drop of coffee —or just tea Lily, and you can sleep on that couch in the sunroom can't you, I've napped there and it's quite comfortable, do you have that list? I'd like to get down there when the stores open, we'll have plenty to do here, will you try to pick up your things in the library while we're gone Oscar? that's not too much to ask is it?

—No but Christina, listen... but the doors down the hall clattered closed behind them, the car's engine thumped, thundered, and they were gone leaving him to falter his way back from the kitchen splashing tea in the saucer where he set it down, gathering up pages, clearing his throat, the words coming hit or miss, coming in chirps, descending for —Ahhh! must a man be scourged then, and racked, have his eyes burnt out and then be set up on a pole, to know that he should wish, not to be just, but to seem it? plaintive now, almost a bleat, was it the words? his choice of them? or the very words themselves, the strongest words in the finest language in man's history, God what they could accomplish with the simplest of lumber, the mansions they had built: Now he belongs to the ages! Maintenant il appartient à l'histoire, sheer tissue paper. Jetzt der gehört er der Welt? Geschichte? like a cow backing into a stall. Let them look up at the sky then! if they must be so blind... He stood gazing out over the pond where each branch on the leafless trees standing out sharply on the opposite bank blurred into a dull strip of grey without a cloud in the sky, putting down the pages to steady himself as the whole middle distance seemed to come closer and fall away, abruptly seizing up some pages he'd left on the sill there and bracing himself as though facing an audience intent for the facts not the words, not the sound of the language but its straightforward artless function, —Grant's army ascending the Tennessee River to disembark at Pittsburg Landing where Buell's divisions were to join it, the Confederate army deployed in battle lines near the Shiloh church barely two miles away in the gloom that had descended out there over the pond where the few isolated houses and the wide lawn below seemed to slip into the water as though the pond were flooding, and he took out the last Home Run to smoke on the veranda before he brought in the newspaper, settling back in the familiar embrace of his immobilized chair to fold back its pages in wide sweeps and mutterings, guttural sounds of impatience, aversion, an occasional mmmph of satisfaction, a gasp, ha! just as the sharp clack of heels down the hall brought him to his feet.

—Oscar? can you help us here?

—Listen to this! Listen. A new court case surfaced today in the boiling controversy that has engulfed the notorious outdoor steel sculpture known as Cyclone Seven since the initial uproar that greeted its first appearance in this sleepy rural hamlet, far from...

—Put some water on to boil will you Lily? in the big pot with a cover, will you help her with those bags Oscar?

—In a minute listen, made headlines recently when a small dog named Spot, trapped in its interstices, was killed when the towering structure was struck by lightning, provoking a nationwide outpouring of grief. The dog's body was accidentally disposed of, and its owner, a boy named James B acting through his guardian, has now brought suit against an enterprising glover for appropriating the dog's name in connection with a new line marketed as Hiawatha's Magic Mittens, which...

—Lily? The chickens are all cut up, just put them in to simmer and chop up a few onions, will you? and those carrots left from last night, have you picked up in the library Oscar? If that bag is too heavy for you let her come back for it, maybe you can help her in the kitchen?

—Yes in a minute, listen. Charging misappropriation of the dog's name for commercial exploitation in captioning the mittens Genuine Simulated Spotskin, Wear 'Em With The Skinside Inside, the boy's lawyer, J Harret Ruth, cites the provision governing false description and false designation of origin in the Lanham Trade-Mark Act, claiming unspecified damages for trade-mark infringement and of the rights of publicity and privacy. The community has been in turmoil since...

—Will you stop chattering about that damn dog! Lily? can you hear me?

—No but this is the part, listen to this part, the decision by a Federal judge questioning the good faith of a jury and reversing its verdict in a trial to determine the cause of the dog's death, for which he has been vilified as an unAmerican ungodly racist and even burned in effigy. These charges have been taken up by Senator Orney Bilk, appearing before the Senate Judiciary Committee which is considering the fitness of the judge, Thomas Crease, for a seat on the U.S. Court of Appeals. I mean he really has a lot on his plate, here's another helping listen, have spilled over into another lawsuit in his court, in which the attorneys for the defendant in a case of wrongful death occurring during a baptism have demanded that Judge Crease be removed in light of his amply demonstrated antiChristian bias which, Christina? Where'd you go. There's just this...

—Oscar? I'm in the library, will you please come in here?

—Just this last, yes. The controversy that has swirled around the sculpture Cyclone Seven itself has also taken a new turn, as...

—Now!

—Yes, as its creator the sculptor R Szyrk seeks its removal over the vigorous protests of the community where it has become a substantial source of tourist income reflected in the new fully booked motel and expanded Kandy Kitchen and the Cyclone Seven pin replicas worn by the townsfolk in their petition for according it Landmark status, to be joined by a theme park featuring strolls among artifacts of modern American history recently opened by James B's father, who...

—Will you put down that paper and tell me what you plan to do about that mess in there?

—A lot on his plate, he muttered getting up unsteadily from the crippled chair where he'd settled again.

—Well so have we! Will you, wait a minute. Your little cart there, you're sure it won't go?

—No I told you, the battery's dead.

—Well we'll get one, we can get one can't we?

—Yes but, but I don't really need...

—My God, you don't think I'm thinking of you do you?

—But I, but how long is she going to stay? Because I, I'm not quite steady on my feet yet, I might need...

—Marching around the room, I'm on my feet and I'm going to stay on my feet? isn't that what you told us? God knows what shape she's in, you heard her on the phone didn't you? what she's been through and you're too selfish to lend her your little cart? Like a three year old, my God, and when are you going to shave, are you planning to grow a beard too?

—Well why not! Why shouldn't I!

—And that suit, one of the last civilized men left with this whole ridiculous, oh Lily. When you've made up the bed in the library I want you to drive down and get a new battery for that chair will you? There was something else I, yes a deck of cards, get two decks of cards we may want to play cards, you can play bridge can't you or you can just be the dummy to have a little life in this house again after nothing but complaints day after day, as cheerful as could be on the phone with what she's going through maybe she can set you an example Oscar, all this mumbling and brooding if you see any other games Lily, there was a Scrabble set around here somewhere, look in the library, Oscar? have you seen it?

—No. No and listen, I'm trying to get this work done I can't spend the day playing cards and...

—Work? You were sitting here reading the paper when we came in weren't you? tiptoeing around as though you're ready for the last rites with this play of yours it's like running an intensive care unit, it's like living with a disease that permeates the whole house, it's a disease this play of yours thank God it's not infectious or we'd all be dead, where are you going now? Wait, just put those things down Lily and go help him clean up that mess in the library, and those boxes, let's get those boxes out of the hall there before somebody breaks their neck, I'll be in the kitchen, and pudding. I should have thought of pudding, vanilla pudding or something easy to digest. I'll think of something. And she did, after a day of almost speechless dolour relieved only by fetching and carrying, clean sheets, boiled onions, that little electric heater it must be somewhere, sitting down to supper but not the chicken, no, for tomorrow or whenever she gets here, there must be something in a can we can have, —it occurred to me, Oscar? over noodles with a tomato coloured sauce spiced with the taste of tin, —if it's not already too late of course, I mean she may have been dragged over the coals in court today over it but still it would make a nice gesture.

—I don't...

—It wouldn't cost you a penny if that's what you're thinking.

—But I still don't...

—If you'll stop interrupting, this absurd paternal rights case by this miserable boy who got a court order to stop her abortion.

—But she had it, I thought that was all...

—I know she had it, my God I was with her wasn't I? that right to life idiot throwing catsup on her and all the rest of it? Of course now he says it was animal rights because her insurance people are suing him for the cost of that lovely chinchilla while this revolting boy is after her for God knows how much in damages for killing his unborn child while they haggle about foetal personhood and the rest of this nonsense where you might make yourself useful, I know she'd be eternally grateful.

—But what could I, I don't know anything about...

—Well think about it Oscar. She's up before a judge who's already called legal abortions legal executions even if it was legal, even some church idiots trying to get in the act saying she might have been carrying the Messiah. Now do you see what I mean?

—No.

—Well I'm sure Lily does. There's no proof at all that this wretched boy was the socalled father is there? While they sit there splitting hairs over these absurd legal arguments is there any proof that he's the one who got her pregnant in the first place? I mean they can't do these fancy DNA tests and God knows what else on this dreadful little foetal person because it's off where it belongs with that dreadful little dog in its simulated Spotskin, it's exactly the same thing. Lily sees what I mean.

—You mean Oscar? that he was doing it with her too?

—That's a way of putting it, my God they've known each other for a thousand years he's certainly had the chance, he can say he did can't he?

—You mean if he just said it?

—Well my God I'm not trying to get him into bed with her, it's a little late for that, I've always thought it was a shame you never took the opportunity Oscar. She's always been quite fond of you.

—Is she cute looking?

—Cute isn't quite the word Lily, she's rather tall and, rangy you might say. She's lots of fun.

—And she's rich?

—She's very rich. She'd so appreciate it Oscar, think about it. It would really be the gentlemanly thing to do. You might even find you enjoy playing the gay Lothario.

—He did it with her too? And later, as they took their separate ways, —it was probably her money, that's probably how he got it up for her even if he was gay, Oscar? getting an arm around him, —did you? ever do it with her? He simply looked at her for a minute, sharing this weary half embrace there at the foot of the stairs where she'd cling to him as briefly late the next morning, descending carefully one step at a time with a raised finger hushing his lips. —No, she's already up, she's out in the kitchen making something. You want some tea? And by the time she brought it in he'd already begun his siege with the telephone, slamming it down when she said —I think I heard a car, and was gone up the hall.

—Well who was it.

—It's this real estate lady. She says would we mind if she goes through the house.

—If she, I certainly would mind! Barging in like a, what's she doing here. Who sent her.

—Oscar? I think I heard a car out there.

—Well you did, it's some real estate woman Christina. She wants to go through the house, of all the, just barging in like that?

—They always do. Did you make up your bed? And the sunroom, oh Lily have you put your things away in the...

—She's not coming in Christina! She's not putting one foot in this house, tell her she, where is she. Where is she.

—She said she'll just take a look around outside while we...

—Can't she read? This is private property, can't she read?

—Oscar wait, just try to calm down. That letter from the bank, did you ever do anything about it? About the mortgage, where is it.

—That they sent her here? That's got nothing to do with it Christina. The bank makes those payments right out of my account.

—Well there's a lien against your stupid salary isn't there? Maybe there's one at the bank too, where is it.

—It's over here someplace he muttered, dislodging a heap on the sideboard, and then —what's this. When did this come.

—It came yesterday, I forgot...

—Can't you tell me when these letters come? It's from these people on my Shiloh talk, it might be important, it might be a check...

—My God Oscar, you are a child. How much have they promised you.

—That's not your business Christina. Two hundred dollars, that's not the...

—Well a grand sum like that of course, they...

—I don't understand.

—That they don't pay you when they've never set eyes on you?

—No I, I don't understand...

—Well what is it, they've canceled it? She reached for the letter quivering in his hand but he drew it back, coming down unsteadily on the chair. —Well what is it.

—Dear, it says dear Doctor Crease. We are looking forward to your discussion on the events at Shiloh, and are sure it will contain an inspiring message for us all. While we certainly would not wish to appear to influence your approach, in view of the bitter feelings and prejudices engulfing the Holy Land today we suggest that you may not care to dwell at too much length on the bloodsoaked details of battle, and the slaughter of some thirty thousand by a barbarous enemy before victory and unity were bestowed by the forces of the Lord but at the cost of the glory of Shiloh departing forever. Unfortunately, this emphasis might only serve to add further fuel to the destructive atmosphere echoing down the ages in the voice of the Lord in Jeremiah, Go to Shiloh and see what I did to it for the wickedness of my people, and in the interests of healing the wounds of past generations you might find a more inspiring text in the words of the little child answering the vision that came to him there, Speak, for thy servant heareth...

—Oscar? Try to calm down. Think about it, what...

—But, what are they talking about!

—Well think about it. Who are these people waiting to hear what they think you know about Shiloh, who arranged this thing anyhow.

—I know everything about Shiloh! I know there were twenty thousand casualties not thirty thousand killed, ten thousand on each side they were all raw recruits no, no barbarous enemy, a lecture agency arranged it they take twenty five percent, for writers to give talks and readings...

—The whole thing is ridiculous. If you're a writer you write, why do you think people learned to read in the first place. All this tramping around giving talks and readings, are they all illiterates? You read stories to three year olds, if you're a writer you stay home and write.

—Well I, damn it Christina that's what I'm trying to do! These bills look at them, these lawsuits and these lawyers and these phone calls nobody answers and nobody returns, my car gets stolen and this salary lien and now this idiotic this, this glory of Shiloh departed forever healing the wounds of past generations? If it's madness they want, Go to Shiloh and see what I did to it for the, look! Look, she's out there peeking in the window, that's who sent her, selling the house out from under us when I'm barely back on my feet and I'll stay on my feet I'll, I'll go down there and see what he, what the hell is going on, I'll...

—Oscar for God's sake try to calm down, you're not going anywhere. Put on your magic mittens, genuine simulated Spotskin wear 'em with the furside outside and go down there and confront Father he'll eat you alive. Some poor real estate woman knocks on the door and you...

—Poor! I just saw her car, look out there, look at her car it's a block long it takes up half the driveway, tinted windows and the whole, listen! the door, she's trying to get in!

—She came in a little black car Oscar, it's...

—What in the, look! What in, how did it get in here!

—Teen? echoed down the hall.

—Oh my God... The door clattered, the dog barked —she's here, it's Trish, will you come and help her?

—Teen! in a flurry of mink —how marvelous! The dog barked —no down Pookie, stop it. Stop it! And Oscar, I said stop it! How simply marvelous! on a billow of scent —it's been a thousand years, I didn't dream we'd actually get here, the driver seemed quite lost I don't think he can read signs and then Jerry knew exactly where we were and the minute we saw your frightfully unfriendly sign at the gate of course he'd been here before, isn't it fun?

—Well old sport, emerged from behind the cloud of mink at about her shoulder's height, a hand extended —a small world, eh?

—It's, I, hello...

—Teen? This is Jerry, of course Harry knows him but you've never met have you, he hadn't the faintest notion we were coming here, we were in court on the stroke of ten, Jerry's made me frightfully punctual can you imagine? Waiting simply an eternity in this ghastly room filled with plastic coffee cups and teeming ashtrays and the Daily News all over the floor when they told us the lawyer for Mummy's estate got up and claimed this loathsome little priest who's a witness or something was unavoidably detained on official diocesian business doing God knows how many widows and orphans out of their last crust, I mean of course those weren't his exact words but they got a postponement and it suddenly seemed the perfect chance for this visit I've promised and here we are! I mean I did think of calling ahead, of course there's a phone in the car but Jerry was talking to a client and I thought it would be more fun to surprise you.

—Well you, you certainly did Trish, I thought...

—Will you get me out of this damn thing Jerry? as he reached up behind her to lift the fur away —just throw it anywhere, it's like wearing an animal farm, it was absolutely raw when I came out this morning, could you dream it would be such a beautiful day? shaking herself loose in a flash of diamonds —of course I shouldn't have worn them, they're for evening after all but I thought I should make it quite clear to the court and these estate lawyers and this whole den of thieves that I'm hardly a beggar but simply after my rights, I mean they're the ones who are howling about the money if you could see this unctuous little Father Stepan bleating over Mummy's eternal rest and this pitiful young man Mary's got from legal aid with his homemade sandwich in a paper bag, I'm sure he washes his shirts himself and of course Jerry simply took him to pieces stop it Pookie! Get down, all this glorious fresh air I'm simply ravenous.

—It won't take a minute Trish sit down, how does a little boiled chicken sound with a few...

—Frankly Teen it sounds rather revolting, you needn't bother we've brought something along Jerry? did you tell that savage to bring in the basket? It's why we're a little late, we stopped to pick up Pookie and I had them put together a sort of a picnic it's such a beautiful day I thought we might even have it out of doors, I don't mean that déjeuner sur l'herbe scene it's a little chilly for the girls to tear off our clothes while Oscar stands about looking every inch the gentleman poet and Jerry of course, can you picture anyone more fastidious? nodding after the midnight blue bumchafer receding up the hall, —I'd thought something in suede but he said something about cows so we settled on silk and thank God for Sulka's, I suggested some sort of yachting insignia for the breast pocket but he doesn't really own one yet and we settled for the plain gold monogram, can you help me with the catch on this bracelet Oscar? You remember that ridiculous child who wanted to wear them out playing field hockey Teen, her father's been arrested in some sort of betting scandal wouldn't you know? squeezing one wrist free, then the other —they're just in the way, I put them on to sort of hide these little bandages but you'd hardly notice them anyway would you.

—To tell you the truth you had me quite frightened, when you told me about T J calling the doctor I half expected bandages right to your elbows, what in God's name made you do a thing like...

—You simply wouldn't believe it Teen, that cut glass vase it was somebody's wedding present, I knew it had a crack in it just like that ghastly marriage I should have thrown them both out together but it was Baccarat and I hadn't the heart, I was putting some snapdragons in it Jerry had sent me when the whole damn thing came to pieces in my hands and while I was trying to mop up the blood there was T J on the phone to the doctor saying Mummy's cut her wrists again it was all too embarrassing, the way he looks after me he's such a dear, I don't know what he'd do without me, he's been bringing home some very odd friends one of them twice his age I could swear wearing lipstick and I've thought of getting a tutor to live in but after that poor Schofield boy, I heard they used a broom handle, that's really asking for it, he's so oh, here we are!

—Oscar? will you help him? and Lily, where is she, Lily? Will you tell her to bring in some plates?

—And silver, they've put in these horrid little plastic forks you'd think we were Kurds or something, Pookie get down. I asked them to give us some gravlax and it looks like they've simply put in a side of smoked salmon, you must have some dill? and some of that honey mustard and, never mind, it has to be pressed it would take all night but where is the pâté? We were in such a rush, I barely had time to tell Jerry we were off to the country to visit an old friend from school I'd been dying to see and of course he hadn't the faintest notion who and I'd never in my wildest dreams have imagined he might actually have been here himself when I was really the one who suggested it in the first place wasn't I Teen, that awful day in the hospital when that terrifying nurse drenched me with blood you know I've had to change cleaners four times, it's simply too mortifying to face that supercilious encore du sangre Madame? the moment I walk in, I've thought of finding one up in Spanish Harlem where it's no more than a little eggy mess on ve tunic in that charming story of Kipling's wasn't it with Oscar dying down the hall from his car crash and I said he could sue for millions, don't you remember? Of course I dropped that suit against the hospital to spare Bunker's feelings on the board but it's really the only language they understand isn't it, and when we turned in at your driveway just now and Jerry told me he'd been out here taking some kind of deposition from a poor man in a wheelchair of course I was thrilled, keeping things in the family and all the rest of it he's, where did he go. Oscar?

—He's, I think he went to the kitchen. He's been rather testy lately and it's better just to pretend not to notice when he...

—But my God Teen who can blame him, I mean what he's been through I didn't dream we'd see him up running around, I half expected to find you running some sort of intensive care ward here and of course I understand about the boiled chicken if he's still on hospital food but it's rather like killing the healthy chicken to make soup for the sick one and he might like to try this boned squab for a change if you don't think the truffles would disagree with his Pookie stop it, get down I said. I know I asked them for pâté, we might like it to start since the gravlax is oh, here he is, Jerry? will you help him with those dishes? You mustn't try to wait on us Oscar, I mean my God you're the patient after all and we've just been sitting here like wet rags marveling at your courage through this whole frightful ordeal.

—High marks, old sport. You've put on a little weight?

—Well don't stand there growling Oscar, let him help you.

—Straighten things out with your insurance people? They're all swine of course.

—And what are these little, oh. These delicious little cheese beignets but, is it Lily? Lily could you pop these into the oven for a few minutes, they really can't be served cold yes and just put the silver down here in a heap, we can fend for ourselves. And napkins? oh you've brought them.

—Clever move old sport, hauling us out here for that deposition, have your impairment wheelchair and all right there in the sworn record if these swine try to accuse you of malingering.

—But that's, they couldn't, I couldn't walk I couldn't even...

—Clever move... and, was it a wink? briskly cleaning his butter knife with a napkin —might want to keep your eye out for secret warranties if they get sticky about settling, a car with undisclosed defects that are covered by undisclosed warranties and the maker will pay up if you do the digging your insurance should do for you but of course they're all swine.

—Pookie you ate it! Nothing left but the waxed paper get down! Little bastard I'll break your, if all he wants is his Nembutal choking down all our pâté to get at it before we can even stop it I said! A lovely pâté maison, the foie gras was costing a fortune simply to shut him up and this is how he says thank you, Oscar while you're up can you bring in some glasses?

—Yes, some of your Pinot Grigio Oscar, ask her to see if there's any that's chilled.

—You don't want to drink that stuff old sport, here. We brought along a little Yquem, tried for the sixty seven but all they could come up with was the seventy five, of course the twenty one's all but impossible to find even at two thousand a bottle, got a corkscrew handy?

—Lily? can you hear me? will you bring in a corkscrew?

—Aren't you clever Teen, did you find her out here? But you're taking a terrible chance though aren't you, I mean when they're that pretty the first thing they'll do is go off and get pregnant in the back seat of a car somewhere, with bazooms like that I'm sure Oscar sees what I mean.

—I'm sure he does Trish, but...

—Now wait Christina, explain to her that Lily's not...

—My God Oscar, don't ask her to explain the facts of life to me of all people, the male animal's something that no woman in her right mind should even, Jerry? Where are you going.

—Taking the salmon in the kitchen to slice it.

—She can bring in a knife and we can slice it right here, you see what I mean? The poor thing ends up in court like me and God only knows who the father is.

—Well there Oscar. Isn't that exactly what I said? Oscar had an idea, Trish. I mean you've known each other for a thousand years, and he thought if he offered to appear in court and told them that he...

—You can't tell this Judge Weisnicht anything Teen, that tells you something right there doesn't it? This loathsome boy up there with his sleazy rights to life lawyer swearing he's in love with me and wanted to spare me the stigma of unwed motherhood but I didn't want to share the baby with him and then, I didn't tell you this did I? This little roach Father Stepan, that he's being served up in two helpings? when the judge ordered my doctor to give my medical records to this loathsome boy's lawyer and there's this little roach up there posing as an expert witness to get that ghastly little blob declared a person from the moment of conception so they can move it to juvenile court as a paternity suit while the one who threw the catsup gets off claiming his legal right to protect another person from harm, can you imagine anything more utterly insane? Well I couldn't either until we walked into the courtroom down the hall for the hearing on Mummy's will and there's this same little roach Father Stepan appearing as Mummy's confessor or whatever they call them presenting his bill for sixty years of prayers to keep what he has the gall to refer to as her soul out of purgatory or keep her in it God only knows which, I mean when you look at the hoard of money they squeezed out of her while she was still what you might call alive it's just the greed Teen, the greed written all over their faces it almost makes you ashamed for the whole human race if you, yes, our glasses at last. Just put them down here dear and, oh? you're joining us?

—I think we'd prefer the stemware Lily, these glasses aren't...

—God let's not stand on ceremony Teen I'm dying of thirst, Oscar don't sit there growling, look for the, Jerry? Where...

—He's in the kitchen slicing that salmon, shall I go and...

—Just sit still dear, I'm sure he can manage, hasn't she got the most beautiful skin Teen? I'd give simply anything for skin like that, I've seen this cream they sell for hemorrhoids on television I thought it might tighten things up here under the eyes before I have to go back to Doctor Kissinger for another tuck but I'd be frightfully embarrassed buying it I thought Oscar must have some I could borrow, I mean he's just been sitting around here for ages and Pookie stop it! Stop it! stop it! stop it! Dreadful little, did he tear your stocking dear? When you cross your knees with your leg out like that he simply cannot resist, God knows what goes on in his dirty little mind I suppose sooner or later he's got to be spayed but these horrid right to life idiots would come down in a pack, will you see if they put any lemons and capers in there for the salmon? Sheer poetry, look, put it down here Jerry, pale pink salmon served on a chilled white china plate it's perfectly exquisite isn't it. Turn your head dear, turn your face this way, do you see what I mean now, Teen? the same delicate glow on her clear white skin when they talk about being just a little bit pregnant like those French women in the eighteenth century for that glow that comes on the first month or so and then the curettage, it was all Bunker's idea. He thought it would be fun for me to get up in court and say I was just using this awful boy to try out this old French beauty secret but Jerry thought it wouldn't go over with this stupid fossil of a judge and Mary in the courtroom right down the hall with her pasty pudding face the perfect picture of a thousand years of Irish Catholic ignorance and that roach Father Stepan not letting her out of his sight while they read the bequest in Mummy's will to my loyal and faithful servant, nurse and friend I give and bequeath the entire contents securities bonds cash and God knows what else in my account with Loeb, Rhoades for her years of unselfish and devoted companionship in my service, his hands were simply trembling to get hold of every penny and if you could have seen their faces, he'd brought along three rapacious lawyers from the Cardinal himself to make sure none of these Peter's pence got spilled on the way to their pockets and you should have seen their faces when Jerry got up and straightened them out tell them, tell them Jerry. The most brilliant stroke you can imagine, Mummy'd had a fight with Loeb, Rhoades and, you tell them.

—Oh no, brilliant? with a smile dazzling in its modesty, —all quite simple, he held the glass he'd been burnishing with a napkin up to the light, —the old woman had had a fight with her broker when she'd told them to sell the minute that October crash came along and they'd taken a week to do it, lost her a few thousand so she moved her account over to a new broker and there was nothing left in the account named in the will but a few hundred in delayed interest payments, so as residual legatee everything in the new account goes right to...

—To me! To me, my God I mean if you could have seen their faces, the blood drained right out of them they stood there like living corpses which of course is exactly what they are and that little roach actually crossed himself, can you imagine? with Mary sitting there all in black fumbling her beads and her eyes red from weeping of course it was gin, I mean even a saint couldn't get through a day with Mummy without putting away a quart washing her and the bedpans and all the rest of it, haven't you got that wine open yet?

—Still it does seem a little harsh Trish, I mean the poor thing...

—We gave her something didn't we Jerry? a thousand or something? I mean my God Teen it's not as though she were a blood relative or anything, I only wanted justice didn't I? Do you think the poor thing would ever have seen a penny in the hands of that little black roach telling her she's a sinner every time she turns around when she's never been offered a stiff proposition in her miserable life till they'd squeezed every cent out of her they hadn't already squeezed out of Mummy? They're monsters Teen, all of them, simply monsters, did you find those capers? and the lemon? It's quite inedible without them. Do I smell something burning?

—You're not smoking one of those things are you Oscar?

—In the kitchen, it's those things I put in the oven to...

—My poor beignets!

—Let them go, old sport. Let them go, gives us a chance to talk. A drop of wine?

—It's too sweet. I don't like it.

—Not a bad year. Of course if you insist on the forty five it can run you twelve hundred a bottle. Never occurred to either of us we'd have a chance to just sit down and have a chat, did it. That's a nice suit.

—What's so nice about it.

—A nice cut, you don't see worsted like that anymore do you.

—Oh. This suit yes, it was made in, had it made in England. Thresher and Glenny.

—Down in Bond Street, they finally went under didn't they? You thought I meant this lawsuit? Can't blame you for being put out old boy, always annoying to lose a lawsuit, isn't it. Good to see you up and about though, that scar of yours healed up nicely didn't it. Hardly notice it.

—Well it's, what about it. That's what you want to chat about?

—No, no your play. Your play, a chance to...

—We've talked about it haven't we? You sat right here and talked about it for one solid day didn't you? You think I want to stand here and listen to all that again?

—All water under the bridge old sport, sit down, do sit down.

—Why. I don't want to sit down, sit down and talk to you about my play? my scar? that ridiculous story you got in there about that oaf in the movie being bitten by a cab driver? Her hand down there unbuttoning his trousers and the whole revolting spectacle, dragging these great themes through the mud just as an excuse to get her up there spreading her legs and pour blood and gore all over the screen? You won the case for your, for those swine, to use your word, you won didn't you? What else do you want.

—Of course I won it. Look, I think you're getting hold of the wrong...

—You got paid didn't you? What else are you asking for.

—Of course I'm being paid, and let's not start that squabble over the professional and the amateur. Afraid I'm getting a little bit impatient myself, old sport, I...

—You're, you? getting impatient with me? Barging in here and, getting impatient I'm the one who's getting impatient with this old sport business and the rest of your, I'm not old and I'm not, I'm certainly not a sport, expect to see me out playing baseball?

—Afraid you've got hold of the wrong end of the stick here. I just wanted to talk about your play. I don't want to talk about your lawsuit. You want to talk about your lawsuit. Find some back street lawyers out looking for business who drum up grounds for a nuisance suit happens every day, get you steamed up over a few similarities and her hands down there unbuttoning his trousers what's all that got to do with your work. You have your play, you've still got your play don't you? I get paid to win a case because it's my job to win, I lose it and I lose my bonus, lose a shot at a partnership, lose a few more and I'm out selling pencils. My clients never claimed to be artists did they? We can't all be artists can we? We don't all have the talents to be poets, writers, most of us just have to be content to do the world's work. Boring, repetitive, work anybody can do if they put their minds to it so you've just got to do a better job of it than they do. Nobody can write a better poem than Endymion. There's no such thing. It's unique. That passage in your prologue, when he's met her for the first time out hunting and the pheasant he's shot trying to escape into a stone wall, fighting to flee from what was happening, who else could have written that? The cadence, the poetic anguish of your imagery, we don't all have your gifts do we?

—Well I, that's not the...

—Go a step further. Suppose there were anything to your lawyers' claims that my clients stole your work, suppose they had actually seen your play, actually read it and suppose they'd come to you with a straight up front deal, two hundred thousand for the film rights. Have they ever claimed to be artists? Do you think you'd recognize one particle of your own work up there on the screen ten writers and twenty rewrites later? one scrap of your lofty Socratic dialogue on justice? one shred of the bleak lyric soliloquy on the battlefield that brings down the curtain on your second act? the poetry in that wrenching description of chance and panic in battle? No, they'd show you the battle. That's what movies are. They'd pour blood and gore all over the screen. They'd have her hands down there unbuttoning his trousers. In other words they'd make exactly the movie they did make. Only difference would be you'd be standing here with two hundred thousand in your pocket that wouldn't be wiped out in legal fees.

—But that's not my, I didn't sell it they stole it, I mean I think you've got the wrong end of the stick there. They stole it and desecrated it that's what this lawsuit is about, I only want...

—Talking about the real world out there old fellow, red in tooth and claw with ravin, tried to give you a second chance didn't we? You see nine in ten of these cases settled out of court, I even talked my clients into offering that substantial settlement, about what you would have got if you'd simply sold the rights, tried to clean things up considering your sister and Trishy, all in the family so to speak but your people turned it down. Just running up your costs, go to trial and run up your costs that's their business, win or lose. Our business too, keep running up your costs until you cry uncle and my clients have deep pockets, filing this appeal of yours you're just running up your costs a little further.

—But, it's filed? the appeal's been filed?

—All routine, just going through the motions. I ran through their brief and they're trying to get a reversal on some minor technicality, oral arguments the next day or two but it's just a formality the Second Circuit requires. Just running up your costs.

—But what is it, what technicality, they didn't show me the...

—I won't waste your time with it old boy, sit you down with a law book like looking for your symptoms in Merck's Manual and telling your doctor the diagnosis, leave it to the professionals. It's what we get paid for, what I just finished saying isn't it?

—But that's what I...

—Just stop here for a minute and let me put in a disclaimer, want to be clear that I'm not giving or even purporting to give you legal advice, just another formality. That's what you pay for. You think I want something else out of it? I got something else. I got a chance I'd have never had otherwise. I got the chance to read your play. You remember Conrad describing his task, to make you feel, above all to make you see? and then he adds perhaps also that glimpse of truth for which you have forgotten to ask? That's what I'm talking about, that's what you're giving us in your play old fellow, what you can do that none of the rest of us can. Maybe you're not even aware of how many of us envy these gifts you've got, look around at all the bad poems and bad art by people who can't spell and can't draw, bad books by somebody not because he wants to write, he wants to be a writer, millionaire stock peddler, car maker, general but he wants to be an author while the brilliant work of some real writer lies there gathering dust, a play like yours courts oblivion because there's no one around with the wit to grasp its possibilities, to see what you saw there and put it up on the stage where it belongs.

—Well there's a, matter of fact there's a director, there's a very prominent director who is interested.

—He's read it?

—Well he, not exactly but he's expressed his interest and it's just a matter of getting together with him, he...

—Splendid! Why didn't you tell me? and he swept the bottle up from the table between them, —here. Let's drink to it, shame you don't care for this it's really first class. Get someone like that behind it you shouldn't have much trouble lining up backers, people all over the place with nothing to do and money they don't know what to do with, no act of their own so they buy their way into somebody else's like the ones who litigate because they don't know who they are and it makes them feel real, gives them an identity when they see their name on a docket. Incidentally old boy, just between us, some time you or your sister get the chance to speak to Trishy about this retainer the firm's been billing her for, running up a lot of hours and the partners are on my back about it. I heard you're having a little billing problem with your people too.

—Well it's, I think it just comes down to the, to what you might call careless accounting procedures, they...

—Hardly surprised, I spotted that black they palmed off on you for a fraud the minute we got into your deposition, glad to see you've got new representation on your appeal. It's all a question of genes isn't it. The blacks lack a counting gene, you knew that didn't you? what keeps them right down there at the bottom of the heap? Lebanese, Palestinians, Pakistanis, weren't the Arabs the backbone of the African slave trade? Jews right through the subcontinent to the Pacific, Chinese, Japanese, Koreans that's where you find the counting gene. The Russians haven't got it, they can't count either, the only one who could was Chichikov and he was probably a Russian Jew at that, if you, what's the matter...

—Damn dog look what it's, Christina? Christina!

—Ghaa! and the flurry of white was caught square in the ribs with the polished thrust of a Ferragamo loafer and a splash of wine, —damn!

—Where are they, brought the plates in here and took the basket to the kitchen, Christina!

—Pookie? I heard Pookie yelp...

—Look at that!

—Be careful Trish, I think he had a little accident.

—Little! It was not an accident Christina, I saw him, he did it deliberately what have you been...

—Just put all that down here Lily and get some paper towels, will you take this Oscar? We put the food out on platters so we can see what we're doing, be careful Trish.

—No, they left out the squab, I'd hoped we could have it flambé if you had any Calvados but oh look! These zucchini flowers stuffed with chicken mousse and black truffles aren't they exquisite, poor little Pookie, here...

—For God's sake Trish don't feed him any more!

—Got hold of a great theme in your play there haven't you. Can't be too subtle about it with your theatre audience though, come right out with it.

—You're going to start in again with your narrow elitist notion of the theatre going public? I don't...

—Nothing like that no, problem with a real play of ideas like yours you try to keep things moving up there on the stage and they're liable to miss the whole point. Where's the real civil war going on, it's really raging inside your main character isn't it? what's tearing him to pieces from the minute he walks on? You've set up half your equation right there in the prologue with the old woman babbling about this runaway black slave, this John Israel she's loaded down with all her baggage about the Lord's everlasting mercy and laying up treasures in heaven, he's a living reproach by the time we get to what's the brother's name in the second act there who helped him escape.

—They do something divine with oysters in an oyster aspic with caviar and a sliver of smoked salmon, did we leave it in the kitchen? could you look while you're out there dear?

—That's Will yes, but it's in the first act, he...

—Noble savage and all the rest of it yes, rather heavy going with all the Rousseau you laid on there, and then you get the Major quoting Aristotle on natural slaves, bit of a stick isn't he.

—Well he's supposed to be, he...

—No no, high marks old boy, high marks, smug, dense, the inert status of property got him down to a T, his whole world flying to pieces around him in that passage you lifted from the Republic where the ones who haven't earned their money don't care much about it, but the ones who have take it seriously?

—It's what I've said before isn't it Teen, you don't leave the money to the children you leave the children to the money, I mean my God look at my Deedee.

—You'd just think they could see a breakdown like that coming and do something about it before it happened.

—It was really her own fault Teen, she's never had to learn to take care of things. I mean Jerry says money means entirely different things to different people but it doesn't mean anything to her at all. Isn't that what Jerry told us, Pookie? Run over there and tell him I need a little more wine. Of course if you look around you today it's all in the hands of exactly the wrong people. What is that awful smell.

—I think Harry would tell you it's the smell of money, Trish. Harry's read Freud. You've got the paper towels, Lily? Over there, under the sideboard, can you help her Oscar?

—Listen Christina, we're not...

—Here, give me the towels old fellow, no reason you should both dirty your hands is there? he came on, arm's length under the sideboard —for some people it's credit, for some people it's a way to make more, buy stock in pharmaceuticals, the big drug companies have got a license to steal, say they need the profits for their R and D, government puts a ceiling on one product so they reconstitute it and bring out a new one that's what their R and D is for. Some of them just use it to create envy, some of them pile it up as a bastion against death itself, read Tolstoy's Master and Man but she's right, listen to Freud these days and it's like diarrhea. Rock stars, ball players, developers, stock traders and arbitragers and your celebrity general who gets five million to write a book written by somebody else yes and who else? He straightened up holding away the wadded toweling, —the lawyers they bring in to clean up the mess. Money's become the barometer of disorder. Wealth and privilege, that's what it was with your Major there at Quantness wasn't it, money was the barometer of order, better go wash my hands. Down this way isn't it? second on the right?

—It's just the greed everywhere, that bandit in the shoe repair shop taking me to small claims until Jerry got a couple of postponements and he was losing business closing up shop to come into court till we finally won by default the day he didn't show up. I thought that was frightfully clever, don't you?

—It might turn out to be frightfully expensive, had you thought of that?

—It just costs a lot more to be rich today than it used to, I mean my God Teen I'm the living proof aren't I? Just getting Deedee out of this latest mess, can you imagine what that's cost already?

—Well a breakdown's a breakdown, they always cost money who knows better than you but after all it's the girl Trish, isn't it? the poor girl after all, whatever it costs?

—It's the car Teen, the car. It was one of those Lamborghettis or whatever they are she paid two whole months' allowance for, one of these high performance things you're supposed to change the oil every ten miles they told me and I said she'd never learned to take care of things didn't I? So the bearings or something burned out and it broke down on her way back from Diddy's wedding in Newport at four in the morning and she left it standing on the Merritt Parkway for a carload of I won't say what to run into on their way to work so they told the police but I'm sure you could smell whisky a mile away and the whole thing was simply demolished, the poor dear thought she was saving money not buying collision insurance so that's eighty thousand dollars right there Jerry thinks she hasn't a hope of recovering from the dip who hit her and even if she could on his salary it would take five generations, and then of course you've got the whole carload of them claiming broken legs and concussions and God only knows what, they'll say anything. I mean the rich are always lied to, it's one of our perks.

—Well at least be glad it's not your money, is it? I mean isn't that what her trust is for?

—It's the wear and tear Teen, the wear and tear. Jerry's tried to talk to this trust officer her fool of a father named in his will because they played baseball together at Princeton who wants her to invade the trust and set up a scholarship there in her father's name to get black people on the baseball team and he's frightfully sticky about anything like this that faintly resembles real life, I mean that's what I mean about leaving the children to the money, will you pour me a little more wine while you're standing there Oscar? You can open the other bottle can't you, I just thank God for Jerry, he's so quick isn't he, I mean life is so filled with coincidences. It's such fun that you two boys had already met over this marvelous lawsuit of yours and you have so much to talk about don't you.

—I'm not sure Oscar would call it fun Trish, he'd probably rather talk about something else because...

—No but listen Christina, he just told me the appeal's been filed, Harry's come through after all putting pressure on Sam or somebody, there are oral arguments the next day or two and they've put on a new man to handle it I've got to thank him, to thank Harry for...

—Poor Harry. It's the wear and tear isn't it, the terrible pressure he's been under it's really no wonder, have you talked to him Teen?

—No he's, whenever I've called they say he's in court but this case of Oscar's, I don't think you quite understand the...

—For God's sake don't burden me with the grim details, I know Jerry will win and then we can all have a marvelous party, where is he, he's not out in the kitchen with her is he? I asked her to whip up some heavy cream earlier for these delicious chestnut tart meringues, I mean for forty dollars you'd think they could add a dab of whipped cream but oh Jerry, here you are what on earth are you carrying?

—Oysters.

—I'm sure she could have brought them in herself. Is that what you've been up to all this time?

—Been thinking. I've been thinking about our Major there old boy, bit of a stick as you said and that's as he should be, all the pompous platitudes of wealth and privilege based on land and chattels where the body of English law came from in the first place, same things that are tearing your main character to pieces out there howling for justice but now what about Kane, this character Mister Kane. A little bit stuffy himself isn't he?

—Well he's, no he's not supposed to be, he's...

—Not talking about his ideas or his dialogue, hardly need to change a word of it no, no I mean his persona, this fellow in philosophy and all the rest of it? Just thinking maybe you want a little more contrast there, make him something else, something entirely contradictory, how about one of those itinerant peddlers who covered the countryside in those days. Pots and pans, scissors, handsaws, nostrums, a roll of calico for the ladies, plantations like your Quantness there were miles from anything, little worlds to themselves and he was the outside world, he was a real institution because his real stock in trade was news and gossip, welcomed with opened arms wherever he showed up with what they really hungered for.

—But that's not what I...

—You follow me? Who's just been shot over a card game or killed in a duel over some drunken insult, who shot his overseer caught sleeping with his wife, the price of cotton on the docks at Beaufort, prices at a horse auction, a slave auction and whose slaves have run off like you've set up John Israel right there in your prologue? He had his finger right on the pulse of the land in those dark days, wars and rumours of war he could show up anywhere with an ear to the ground, at a place like Quantness and nobody suspecting a thing, whetting their appetites for scandal where no household's secrets were safe, even theirs. Make him a bit more believable wouldn't it? a little bit more entertaining too up against your pompous Major, even works nicely when he walks in unannounced up north there in the second act peddling cigars and runs into Bixby.

—Bagby! If you want entertainment, if that's all you want Bagby's supposed to be a...

—Bagby of course yes, sorry old sport, a marvelous character, sort of your Greek chorus isn't he. The spoiler, the new man, the spirit of unbridled capitalism with his use versus own in the old Major's lexicon, the triumphant absence of integrity up against Kane who's the lonely heart and soul of it jangling across that desolate landscape with his pots and pans, the rootless wandering Jew who...

—Now wait, wait what makes you think he's Jewish!

—Because they were, most of them, weren't they? The Jewish peddler, a regular institution, make him a Jew and you've got half your Broadway audience right in the palm of your hand, you might even pick up a Pulitzer Prize.

—The Pu, good God talk about being famous for five minutes the Pulitzer Prize is a gimcrack out of journalism school you wrap the fish in tomorrow, talk about the great unwashed it's got nothing to do with literature or great drama it's the hallmark of mediocrity and you'll never live it down, what makes you think I want to get some wheezing Broadway matinee audience in the palm of my hand with a comic Irishman and a Jewish peddler telling dirty stories who...

—I wish they wouldn't fight, can you reach that wine Teen since they're too busy to notice? And for God's sake let me do something with this revolting mess they've made of this oyster aspic, put it on the floor where we won't even have to look at it, if she's still whipping that cream out there she'll turn it to butter, shouldn't you call her?

—Not it at all old boy, try to be patient with me for a minute, not suggesting a character who parades around up there muttering oy gewalt and picking his nose am I? No reason he can't be just as intelligent, just as shrewd and cultivated as your character is right now, just as well read without this stiff sort of academic veneer, a free spirit rattling along down those country roads all day behind his mule in his cart pots and pans jangling while he reads the Aeneid and oh, incidentally, running through your deposition again you ascribe the Iliad to some Greek nobody ever heard of, can't imagine why I didn't trip you up on it.

—Some Greek? I never mentioned the Iliad, you think I'd make a mistake like...

—Talking about characters beneath contempt like Bagby?

—Nicochares, the Diliad not the Iliad, the Diliad, characters beneath our level of goodness in the Diliad.

—Your point old sport, tripped me up that time, stenographers you get these days you've got to be grateful they've even heard of the Iliad. Comes a bit closer to your Socrates parallel too doesn't he? Informal, deceptively humble, a little unkempt, touch up his dialogue a bit here and there and there's your wry argumentative Jew with his own fierce hunger for intelligent talk, for this relentless doomed pursuit of ideas out there peddling his pots and pans in this intellectual wasteland, five cents, ten cents, the counting gene again, the second half of your equation, you follow me?

—No.

—Of course you do. The whole thing's your creation isn't it? the forces struggling against each other in this terrible equation that's still there at the heart of the matter today, obviously you've read your Tocqueville? You lay out the left side of it at the start with the apparition of this black runaway slave, he doesn't even appear, we don't see him we don't have to, the invisible man somebody called him haunting the whole play, haunting your main character with that flimsy pretext from the Social Contract of compelling men to be free to be hunted down somewhere and killed with no bands of angels waiting out there wails the dried old husk of a woman who's taught him to read in the Bible, about what it amounts to isn't it?

—But you can't say a flimsy pretext no, that whole noble idea of Rousseau's that for life to be good at all it had to be good for all men, and...

—Noble idea! About all it was, that pragmatic notion of ideas as instruments for guides to action never mind, I withdraw it, he's instrumental isn't he? Get on to the right side of your deadly equation where Kane's hounding him with his merciless logic about justice, manipulating all his hollow high sounding claims to moral rectitude leading him deeper into his dilemma, your cunning old Jewish peddler blackmailing him with four thousand years of Christian guilt, he isn't simply embattled, your main character. He is the battlefield, and there's your deadly equation, the black on one side and the Jew on the other fighting it out today wherever we look, you follow me?

Backed into a corner now silhouetted against the glass giving down on the pale light glistening on the pond, hands digging distracted in the pockets at his side for whatever they might come up with, a packet of obsolete design in one of them, coming out with —no... tearing it open with the other, —no it's going too far, a play about the Civil War I don't see how we got into all this, it's not about these quarrels between black people and Jews that burst out on the front page is it? It's...

—Not about these crude street fights that bring out the worst in both of them no, it's not about Hollywood Jews backing movies to show blacks as beasts in a jungle, Jewish doctors dispensing disease to black babies, it's not even about Jewish storekeepers in Harlem using the counting gene to exploit blacks who don't have it no, that's how they'd like it isn't it, your clean white Christian middle class watching it explode on the evening news worried to death about property values when the Jews move in, then the blacks and the whole harlequin spawn of the Caribbean and there goes the neighborhood as you say. Drugs, gunfire, let them fight it out, turn off the news and go in to dinner, not our fight is it? like your wounded pheasant burrowing for refuge in the stone wall, trying to flee from what was happening? the hollow essence of this Christian hypocrisy? And the burnished silk of Sulka's tailoring leapt up against that fine old worsted gripping a wrist there, —sorry...

—No I'll get it he blurted, excused for breaking away to recover the torn cigarette packet from what little of the floor remained between them, digging one out as he straightened up if for no more than to occupy his unsteady hand only to find himself abruptly caught by a lapel backed up against the window itself.

—John Israel and Kane out there, both sides of your equation manipulating your hero's profoundly hypocritical capacity for guilt, the black and the Jew parading their very real grievances they're not appealing to his conscience, they're not even fighting each other to seize hold of his conscience Oscar they're fighting for which one will fill this yawning sentimental churchgoing flagwaving vacant remnant of the founding fathers, which one will finally *be* the conscience of this exhausted morally bankrupt corpse of the white Protestant establishment and that! with an emphatic stab straight to the heaving chest —that's the heart of it, the heart of the American dilemma. Sorry, didn't mean to, didn't hurt you old sport did I? Here, need a light? What's that you're smoking, never seen them.

—Stop it Pookie, get down, he's not going to hurt you they're just playing, Jerry's simply so brilliant that sometimes he gets carried away Teen and people don't quite know how to deal with it, this mousse is too salty I don't think I can eat it can you? If you could have seen him in court with those three living corpses of lawyers sent down there by the Cardinal himself with that kind of money involved when they didn't really understand their own case until he had to get up and explain it to them before he destroyed it, do you think we...

—Just a minute Trish. Oscar what are you doing, you're not smoking one of those things are you? as the gold lighter flared up in his face.

—They're Picayunes he said, dropping the free hand pressed against his chest to steady himself against the sill, —an old brand probably don't make them anymore... breaking off with a cough. They both coughed.

—Can't smoke those old boy, here, try one of these? digging behind the gold monogram, —made for me by an old Cuban in Tampa for getting him a green card once.

—Well not in here! If you're both going to smoke go outside.

—Get a breath of air, shall we? like the old county host leading off up the hall, —rather painful confession to make old boy, do you mind? stepping ahead to rattle the doors opening on the veranda, —really embarrassing at this point you know, but your play there? Never read the last act. Nothing germane to the issue in your amended complaint when we called for the bill of particulars and all your people would surrender were the first two acts and the prologue, could have pursued it of course for another delay to keep running up your costs but I managed to convince my people to take mercy, always wondered how it came out. Here, don't stumble, get this fixed up out here or you'll have a fat liability suit on your...

—You mean you never finished reading it?

—Probably changed the denouement around for the movie anyway, not surprised are you? proffering the cigar, —got through the epitasis, that what they call it? proffering a light, —that's what matters isn't it?

—But the way you've been talking I thought, you never finished it? Then how could you stand there just now and dissect the whole, take the whole thing apart like that when you hadn't even, we talked about the Crito in that deposition didn't we? in the last act and you didn't even ask how it...

—No, no, can't blame you for being impatient but we got to the heart of it in there didn't we? The last act's always just tying things up and...

—How do you think it came out then! How do you think it ended!

—But we've always known the answer to that one haven't we, in death and madness old sport. Madness and death.

Blue smoke trailing behind them on the still air followed their steps down the veranda overlooking the lawn stretched below down to the unruffled surface of the pond and the leafless detail of the oaks on the opposite bank against the dark of the tall pines betraying their presence, recalling, Blake was it? Where man is not, nature is barren, —referring to King Lear?

—If you like. Based on a true story from Holinshed? like your grandfather there you tried to take out a patent on?

—That's ridiculous. It's just like the rest of this twisting things around to ruin my father's chances for the appeals court with talk about madness in the family and burning him in effigy he doesn't give a damn for all that but impeachment, this talk about impeachment if that happened it would kill him.

—Not a chance old sport, don't worry about it. The process is so complicated they've only managed to throw one Federal judge off the bench in the last fifty years for cheating on his taxes, finally tried an end run around Article I to impeach two more, one being tried for bribery and the other already in Federal prison for perjury but these pygmies in your congress haven't got the appetite for it, can't even stand up to this sleazy gun lobby can they?

—But that's not the...

—Can't expect to have a national policy on anything can you? Every national goal you set up there's some particular region or lobby or private interest out there to thwart it, that's what American politics are all about. It's not a country it's a continent, eight or ten million Italians, Swedes, Poles, fifteen or twenty million Irish, thirty million English descent, twenty five million Germans and the same for blacks, six million Jews, Mexicans, Hungarians,

Norwegians and this horde of Hispanics pouring in it's a melting pot where nothing's melted, what can you expect.

—I'm not talking about six million Norwegians! I'm talking about forty or fifty million Bible thumping illiterates and this Neanderthal in the Senate calling for my father's impeachment down there burning him in effigy talking about madness that's where it comes from, the Lord is a man of war says Exodus, two thousand years of slaughter since he came bringing not peace but a sword from the Crusades right down to your courtroom with the little black roach and his foetal personhood to the boy with the catsup bottle, the Dome of the Rock and the Temple Mount soaked with the blood of Muslims and Jews and your mosque up there in Uttar Pradesh with Muslims and Hindus drenched with blood wherever you find them, the true believers, revealed religion that's where it all comes from, those riots in Bombay with the Hindu mobs dragging Muslims out the front door and killing them? making men drop their pants in the street to see if they were circumcised and burning them alive, dancing and singing around their blazing bodies if that's not madness? if that's not madness!

—Of course it is old fellow, of course it is, the whole pantheon of...

—And those stories I heard about the Juggernaut when I was a child, that tremendous wagon they pulled in religious processions where people threw themselves under the wheels to be crushed?

—All nonsense old man, typical British bloody bedtime story. Juggernaut's a good fellow, ninth avatar of Vishnu, he lives in a temple on the east coast a town called Puri where he gets sick every summer, recovers, goes on vacation and these pilgrims show up in the hundreds of thousands to celebrate, build a huge chariot with him perched on top of it playing a flute and drag it to his aunt's temple a mile down the road to make a few Brownie points with the trinity all yelling and shouting, all the caste barriers broken down some of them trampled and run down in the melee, no worse than the carnage after a soccer game is it? Along comes the British raj and sees their little brown brothers having a good time, a few of them crushed under the chariot's wheels and they take it for a frenzy of human sacrifice to this bloodthirsty deity, give a dog a bad name and all the rest of it? one man's religion another man's madness?

—And you don't call that madness?

—Of course I do, let me finish. Of course it's madness, but the madness comes first. It's an essential of the human condition, the worse the human condition the greater the madness and your revealed religion simply comes along to channel the madness, give some shape to it. For these unlettered hordes mired in poverty the only things that are free are sex and religion, and the poorer and more illiterate they are the more they procreate and the more ornate these religious pantheons and rituals become. Some Filipino crucifies himself at Easter because Jesus drove him to it? No, no he's mad from the start and religion gives it an outlet, gets it organized, penitents flagellating themselves with scourges till the blood pours out in those streams of madness throbbing away skin-deep all over Mexico, Sikhs, Iraqis, Afghanis they're all raving maniacs to begin with looking for some grand design that they can fit into, some system of absolutes where they can find refuge, that's what the true believer is isn't he? And the more chaotic the times, the greater the demand for these absolutes, it's what drove Dostoevski's heroes over the brink wasn't it? this panic at living in a meaningless universe? Take the deep bedrock madness of the Germans from Peter the Hermit and Thomas Münster right down to the death camps they try to masquerade as nationalism, like that exquisite distillation of total madness that's peculiarly Japanese. The Italians channel theirs through the Vatican in a wholesale mayhem of crime and opera, the Russians drown theirs in a sea of vodka and the English cross dressing theirs under the skirts of the Anglican Church or they'd be as frankly mad as their neighbors across the Irish sea.

—Nothing to do with madness no, or even religion, the Church of England's just a framework for the comedy of manners holding together the ruling class with a social caste system that...

—What any organized religion is isn't it, old boy? But go to the Old Catholics for top drawer snobbism and your real streak of madness, the Anglicans are just the bastard child, perfidious Albion and all the rest of it, you want a taste of the social caste system in all its cruelty and duplicity? Such, such were the joys, try boarding at an English public school, you've got its pale offspring right here haven't you? your bankrupt Protestant Episcopal refuge for old families and old money?

—That's just what I'm saying! Good God look at Harry's Pop and Glow case, nothing to do with madness or religion, the only true Christian faces you'll see in this country are black and I don't mean your mad to begin with theory either, how anyone can grow up black in America and stay halfway sane is beyond me.

—Not arguing that with you, am I? The demands for being a true Christian what can you expect, give up all and follow me? They had nothing to give up in the first place, for everybody else this love thy neighbor as thyself's a plain oxymoron, turned the whole country into a cradle of hypocrisy.

—Fine yes, and when the bough breaks the whole thing comes crashing down baby and all, that's what I...

—What you're talking about's organized religion, the established churches, Episcopals, Presbyterians, Congregational losing members right and left out there fighting for market share in what's left of their elite spiritual supplyside economy but the blood of the martyrs, Tertullian wasn't it? the seed of the church? And there's your forty million to the rescue mad from the start and ready to spill it killing in defense of the right to life, no bleeding heart accommodation like your Roman Catholic confessional's end run around the seventh commandment, say a few Paternosters and Hail Marys and go and sin no more till the next time, try that in Islam and they'll stone her to death so there won't be a next time, steal a loaf and they'll lop off your hand. Remember T E Lawrence calling his Arabs a people of primary colours seeing everything in black and white? either truth or untruth? despising this doubt he called our modern crown of thorns, our hesitating retinue of finer shades, true believers go forth to war says the Koran. Turn your faces toward Mecca's what your young blacks are doing, throwing off the Christian names they were baptised with and calling themselves Ali and Muhammad reminds me, I looked into your Cratylus.

—My what?

—Plato's dialogue Cratylus, haven't forgotten the last time we talked have you? when you said you'd no more change your name than the shape of your nose? Cratylus claiming your name signifies your essential nature, if it doesn't it's not really a name at all and even if it is it's probably somebody else's with a real claim to the qualities it expresses like our friend Basie there, he's your perfect

Hermogenes isn't he? His cheery I'll take the Fifth on that, seeing names as nothing more than conveniences? change them any way you like?

—Can you blame him? His own real name lost back in some African savannah when the slave traders came through and what about yours then, would you change it?

—Tell you the truth when I was a boy I, Pai is an old name in the south of India but in England, I told you the cruelty of schoolboys and I hated it, needn't tell you what they called me and I swore I'd change it when I grew up, some of the finest old names going back to the battle of Hastings in sixth form there and even the future Duke of Wellington was called Washrag but all due respect old sport, I don't really trust your Plato, said that before haven't I? Look at his record on slavery, subjugation of women and the welcome mat out on Queer Street you get the feeling in this Cratylus that it's all really just a game he's playing, cardboard characters and their arguments so full of holes the whole thing ends in confusion and the flaws in his method show right through, your plea in your deposition back there as homage? as timely and timeless? In the end he's pretty much a dictator isn't he, a censor, can't trust him any more than your Major who's a sort of cardboard Cratylus himself isn't he? No more change his name than he would Quantness and the more chaotic things get the more he clings to them till they destroy him.

—That's the whole point isn't it? And there's Bagby, is he a cardboard Hermogenes? He's all expediency, change his name in a minute like your client Livingston changing his name to Siegal it was probably Siegal in the first place, and then Kiester? Constantine Kiester it's just a convenience, for Cratylus Socrates in the dialogue is really Socrates and the name Cratylus is the essence of Cratylus himself like the character Kane in the play, he's the Cratylus in the play and whatever gave you the idea he's some broken down peddler who...

—He's a free spirit Oscar, probably changed it from Kaminsky the point is he's a free spirit. Only thing he owns is a mule and his pots and pans till the day he sells them, up against the Major there with his slaves and real estate and illusions of permanence he...

—He did not change his name from Kaminsky! He's the...

—He's a free spirit! That's our friend Basie isn't it? freed himself of these illusions of absolutes? takes the name Basie because he likes the swing of it even if it was someone else's with more claim as its essence, the courage to live in a contingent universe, to accept a relative world, he's thrown out those Christian fictions that got his forebears through slavery, helped retain their humanity and turn it into the strength to survive the ones who'd used it to subjugate them, to accept misery in this world for peace and equality in some imaginary next one like the job you did on the old woman in your play, you know all this better than anyone, sitting there with poor John Israel at her knee, given into my keeping and all the rest of it you really did quite a job on her.

—What do you mean quite a job, she's a devout old Christian woman who's been embittered by...

—That's funny now, isn't it. You know I read her as whining grasping old hypocrite?

—That's not what I...

—A mean, lying old hypocrite, may have builded better than you knew, old man.

—No that's not what I, listen...

—Listen!

—Oscar! The glass doors crashed open —where are you!

—We, here, what is it? hurrying toward her, both of them, down the veranda —what...

—Hurry!

—But what's happened!

—Just hurry will you! back inside now, —I've got to leave as soon as we, we have to leave.

—But Christina wait, what...

—Where's my purse, he's had an accident why didn't they tell me, Lily? My coat, have you seen it? and my purse, whenever I've called they've just said he's in court, he's in court, that idiot secretary of his why didn't you tell me!

—But who Christina, what...

—My God Oscar will you stop asking stupid questions and, Lily, help Lily find my purse will you? instead of standing there like a, will you get rid of that cigar! A sweater, that tan cashmere, it's down here somewhere sitting here all this time talking about God knows what till Trish finally just happens to mention he's honestly Trish, honestly!

—But Teen, we thought you knew Teen, we thought you knew.

—Didn't want to pry you know, talked about it driving out here Trishy thought we could cheer you up, take your mind off it, really marveled at how you were handling it, stiff upper lip and all the rest between you and Harry after all, didn't want to seem to pry into your...

—But my God he's, where is he? Is he, how badly was he...

—He's all right Teen, I mean I didn't mean he was all smashed up in that marvelous car of yours, that lovely deep green and...

—Not a scratch, don't worry it's all...

—I'm not worried about a scratch on the car my God, if you...

—No, no Harry, she means Harry he wasn't hurt, a little confusion here. He wasn't in an accident, just some woman saying he caused one, cut her off and ran her into a storm drain and she's had him in court ever since. One of these little Mercedes SLs Harry said pulled right out in front of him going ten miles an hour and he tried to avoid it but her boyfriend got his number, leaving the scene of an accident and all the rest of it, broken wrist, whip lash, the lot. They brought Harry in for DWI, drug testing, tranquilizers he's been on but he said he hadn't taken any the firm's psychiatric counselor put him on for this stress he's been under, nothing but some codeine for a toothache but...

—Well my God it's their fault isn't it! Working twenty hours a day at this asinine case they've had him on since God knows when he's hardly eaten or slept, what do they...

—No no, they're behind him, trying to keep it from going to trial Bill Peyton's talking to the judge himself, an old classmate at Yale Law you don't have to worry, if it goes to trial we've got the expert witnesses already looking into this woman's background up to her ears in debt, bad credit rating and her boyfriend's just out of some rehab so don't...

—Not that jacket Lily I said my beige coat, have you found my purse?

—Teen I feel so badly, we didn't mean to upset you we thought you knew and Harry's all right, I mean now it's just going to be another of these dreary runarounds with courts and lawyers like Mummy's will and this revolting boy with his foetal personhood there's nothing you can do, you can stay out here and rest and Jerry can look after the...

—I've got to see him! My God Trish can't you, what do you want me to do take a train? I'll drive in with you right now can't I? Oscar have you found my, what are you looking over there for.

—That copy of my play, and my coat it must be in the...

—What in, your play what in God's name are you talking about!

—I'll come in with you, a big roomy car we can all...

—What are you talking about!

—Oscar watch where you step, I think the dog just got sick there.

—What? oh, no if I'm right there in town Christina it will be much easier to arrange things on short notice with this director for lunch or something and the hearing on this appeal, if I'm right there in court they might want me to testify tomorrow or...

—Don't bother with it old sport no, just complicate things it's all a pretty cut and dried procedure, a lot of legal technicalities nothing you can....

—Stop it! Oscar stop it I can't even, you're staying right here just my raincoat Lily take the jacket, keep it it suits you, can you help her with that fur coat? And the, there it is staring you right in the face my purse Oscar, just hand it to me please hurry Trish, I'll carry your coat you won't need it on in the car, Jerry?

—Coming yes, don't want to take along any of the food? Watch that plate on the floor there.

—I think that's where he ate that oyster stuff, do you...

—Are you coming! as the doors down the hall clattered open.

—But...

—Sorry to run like this, here... a hand burrowed behind the gold monogram —take these? Two cigars thrust forth with a sharp clap to the shoulder leaving him reeling as the car doors slammed outside, —coming! and moments later that veranda, the still house and the torn limbs fell away behind as the car seethed almost silently up the cratered driveway —sorry, that your foot there Trishy?

—This awful coat I can't see where I'm, here, pull it over your knees Teen sort of a laprobe, you wouldn't notice the spots on it would you after that awful boy but you should see the chinchilla. Bunker gave it to me, I think he got it on some kind of a bet he's having the most awful time, those odious neighbors of his in the country claim his butler raped one of their Filipino maids of course they're here illegally so she can't report it but they want him fired and Bunker won't budge, Victor's the best cook he's ever had and he won't lose him over some silly indiscretion and I mean he can't sit out there playing backgammon all alone can he? He had the whole place built an exact copy of the big old family mansion where he was born down in Georgia so they could put all the furniture right where it belonged when he moved in but he gets lonely there sometimes and...

—Have you talked to him Trish?

—He's in London no, he left yesterday on the...

—I didn't mean...

—He'll be back in a day or two, he just went over to have some suits fitted, why.

—I meant Harry.

—Who? Oh Harry, no just what Jerry's told me don't worry about him Teen, I mean Jerry's right there with an eye on things aren't you Jerry, I just hated to leave Oscar like that I didn't even get to say goodbye he looked so, but he's always looked rather lost hasn't he with that blonde there, you don't think they're up to anything do you?

—I'm sure they are, now...

—Well my God I hope so, don't you? I mean he really needs a little of that sort of thing, she reminded me terribly of that girl at school with that marvelous bosom I think she was Polish until her guardian took her out after that messy business with our Mister Jheejheeboy in botany, will you ever forget him Teen? He had fingers like velvet what was her name, that beautiful redhead from Grosse Pointe I went out to her funeral, Liz something she married him didn't she, Liz ow! That's my foot Jerry what are you doing down there.

—Just getting the phone, move over a little? as the car swayed from the road to the open highway ahead —there, that better?

—It was that Grimes girl Trish, they were best friends and he married that Grimes girl because he thought she had more money and her father had to pay him off to get it annulled.

—Edie yes, Edie Grimes, when they were caught smoking together in the laundry room, that pale white skin and red hair and the most marvelous cheekbones God how I envied her, I mean if I'm going in for these tucks I might as well have the whole thing done again, of course you come out looking like a mummy with two black eyes and have to hide out for a week someplace nobody goes anymore like Jackson Hole but simply everyone's using him, Bunker says that's why you see him at all these big benefits of course he's always somebody's guest, he's a frightful freeloader and when he started showing up at my Winter Parties for Bunker's hospital in his little tuxedo with his pants drooping over his shoes simply salivating over his little black book Bunker says he comes to all of them drumming up business I mean he adores titles and money, not one without the other not one of your ordinary restaurant Greeks because Bunker can't stand him and I mean Bunker's the only man you've ever known who asked for a copy of Debrett's for Christmas but you've got to wait ages for an appointment unless you're an old customer like Lettie Blanfors who used him when he was still a proctologist and they called him the shuttle surgeon racking up those charter members for his rosebud club till a sheikh and some African president sued him from their deathbeds for malpractice and that nasty business after the Pope's funeral in all the papers calling him some kind of double agent back when I first met him at one of those awful galas Edie was always giving, she was at the funeral too looking simply gorgeous but she was with that brutish man Liz was married to when she died, he did it of course, killed her I mean, you knew that didn't you.

—That was all simply talk Trish, he...

—They found him right there in the house that one morning with her body on the kitchen floor didn't they? It was all over the papers I can still see the headline HEIRESS SLAIN IN SWANK SUBURB, he tried to make it look like a burglar broke in while he was away and killed her with a...

—That was nonsense Trish, a lot of people thought that but it was nonsense, the kind they make up to sell papers, she simply had a heart attack, that's what came out later but you don't sell papers with a story about high blood pressure and a heart attack when the blunt instrument that hit her was really the corner of the table she hit her head on when she fell, anyhow he didn't find her there first the maid did. There were napkins and silver all over the floor from the kitchen drawer where they said she kept her household money and a check showed up cashed in Haiti when the maid disappeared that's what happened, that's what really happened Harry told me but it's not the way you sell papers.

—Well if you could have seen him out there at her funeral Teen, hard as nails I mean he looked like death was something he'd seen every day but she always went for the wrong men didn't she, like her Buddhist brother who was killed in a plane crash and her father who was an absolute monster hardly gave her the time of day because she told me once when she tried to stand up to him how he simply froze up and made a big show of pouring out his affection on these awful little Jack Daniel's terriers...

—My God can't we go a little faster? Dawdling along like this will you tell the driver to...

—Pookie. Pookie? Will you tell Jerry to put down the phone for a minute and tell the driver to, my God where is he! Pookie? No! Pookie where, we forgot him! Tell him, Jerry tell him tell the driver to go back!

—No! No we're not going back no!

—Teen it will only take a few minutes, we can't just abandon him with nobody to...

—Trish we're not going back! Oscar's there, they can feed him.

—But the poor little, Jerry call him. Hang up and call Oscar.

—Wait, hello? Hold on. Talking to my secretary Trish, she's reading me a brief and I can't...

—If you think that's more important than poor little, I'll just have to send the car back out for him, tell the driver to hurry then will you? I've really got to get home myself if I'm going to Aspen tomorrow for Lettie's party I forgot to tell you Jerry, you can get a postponement can't you, I'll have to let my maid do my nails now because everything in the morning will be such a mad rush and God knows what shape T J is in, I didn't mention this earlier Teen but I think that he drinks, are you having a nap? settling back with a knee outthrust for the hand slipping over it to disappear under her skirt and come to rest there lulled by the drone of the car and the drone of the voice on the phone as the fields gave way to a village and then houses and then villages and houses closer together and finally to towns and houses openly coupling in unrelieved ugliness now mounting in unrelieved layers of windows, and windows, all gone with the dive into the tunnel wakening on the sudden —Where are we?

—Thank God, yes. We're here.

—To your place first Teen, Jerry? will you tell the driver? and as they drew up, —call me Teen, won't you?

—Thanks Trish, thanks... breaking through the collision of doorman and chauffeur, biting her lip at her polished steel reflection in the elevator, hunting her keys and giving it up at the door, pressing the bell, again, —Harry? as it came open, —well thank God.

—Well. You're here he said, stooping for the towel that had gone to the floor fending off her embrace in the quick disguise of returning it, or was it the other way about? but she was already past him there like some naked statuary as she filled her gaze with the light and wonder of the place, unbounded light fading in the late pale sky pierced by lights coming on in the fenestrated heights of nearby buildings like some snug welkin all its own. —I didn't expect you.

—Well obviously. I mean you could have let me know couldn't you? She turned and dropped her raincoat on a chair and seemed to narrow her vision to take notice of him standing there knotting the towel at his waist. —Have you any idea what it's been like out there?

—Yes but, how did you...

—Your friend Mister Mudpye came out with Trish on a lark and I finally dug it out of them. We thought you knew they kept babbling, we thought you knew, it was like pulling teeth, I mean how do you think it made me look? I've called I've left messages here I've called your office and all your idiotic secretary would tell me was he's in court while I'm out there running an absolute madhouse losing my own mind waiting to hear from you after the way you tore out of there with a few drinks and these pills you've been taking I knew it would happen, I knew something like this would happen didn't I?

—That's not when it happened Christina, I...

—The way you tore out of there and left me to deal with Oscar and this mess you got him into it was bound to happen sooner or later wasn't it? and you couldn't even bother to call me? simply pick up the phone and call me?

—Look Christina, there's really nothing you could have done. Stupid predicament I got myself into no reason I should bother you with it, didn't want to upset you I knew you had your hands full out there nothing you could have done anyhow.

—Didn't want to upset me! My God Harry I'm your wife aren't I? Those two silly people babbling we thought you knew while I stood there like a fool telling me there's not a scratch on the car I mean you could have been lying in the hospital with a broken neck, how was it supposed to make me look? She was taking up cushions from the sofa, from the chairs, pounding them into shape and setting them right —I mean didn't it ever occur to you that I might be worried sick about the shape you were in not hearing a word from you day after day? And now she was turning on lights, one by one bringing the room into crystal concert as the glass expanses inviting the outside world abruptly shut it out with reflections of white walls and black onyx, fluted glass and the furniture and the lamps themselves and —the plants? have you bothered to water them? off to the wet bar in the corner for a pitcher before he could answer for the sudden peal of the phone, —will you get that?

—Probably for me yes, hello? Oh hello, how... she's right here Oscar, just walked in. How are you?

—Here... and she had it, —Oscar...? Well of course I am, what did you... I know it! We were half way in when we realized it, she... Well we couldn't turn back! She's sending the car back out for it, you can... I don't know when my God, you can just feed it something there's all that boiled chicken isn't there? and just shut it in the kitchen till the... well then just clean it up, you can clean it up can't you? your what? Well take an aspirin, take two aspirins Lily can help you if she's still there can't she? that she saw a mouse in the kitchen? My God Oscar listen I'm exhausted! I've been cooking running errands trying to hold things together for you out there since... Well there's nothing I can do, I mean you know I've got my hands full right here there's nothing I can do, I can't even think about it, I'm... who, Harry? He's fine. He's standing right here looking like the noblest Roman of them all while I... well my God see a doctor then, there's nothing I can do is there? I have to go.

—Christina look, before you...

—Is there anything in the house to eat? She was back at the bar filling the pitcher, —I mean I can't describe what I've already faced today in the way of food, an entire side of inedible smoked salmon and zucchini flowers stuffed with God knows what, he wanted to drive in with us can you imagine that?

—Better wait till he's back on his feet before he...

—Back on his feet my God he's on them all the time, marching around in one of Father's old suits growing a beard smoking cigars he calls himself the last civilized man, he's ready to come in and stage a reading of his play for some British director he's dug up and some outlandish notion of showing up in court tomorrow to testify on his appeal, I mean I said I'd been running a madhouse out there didn't I?

—But what, wait what appeal.

—His appeal Harry, this appeal he's got you to thank for getting your friend Sam to quit dragging his feet and run up his costs a little further, I mean has this little car adventure of yours completely destroyed your memory? All I find over there's an empty whisky bottle when I asked you if there's any food in the house didn't I?

—There's yes, I've sent out for Chinese there's some of that lemon chicken and some cold noodles but Oscar's appeal, you mean it's been filed?

—I just said it has didn't I? I mean you talk about language how everything's language it seems all that language does is drive us apart, I mean what did you think I meant.

—I don't know, I mean, what I mean is a matter of fact I haven't had a chance to talk to him, to Sam I mean, you mean the circuit court's already hearing oral arguments on Oscar's appeal?

—Well call him. Call Sam and ask him if you can't remember what you did ten minutes ago, is that all there is? this lemon chicken?

—There may still be some shrimp, that shrimp in black bean sauce but has Sam talked to him? to Oscar? he wants Oscar to come in and testify at the...

—Sam hasn't talked to anybody, Harry. Apparently somebody's talked to Sam and given him a good hard push, that's all I know and all I care to know. If you want the grim details I'm sure you can get them from your colleague in this self regulating conspiracy of yours. Are you going to go get some clothes on?

—Look Christina, just tell me what the hell's going on will you? What brought him out there anyhow.

—An immense grey limousine with a telephone and tinted windows, the kind Trish uses to épater the lower classes. They'd just been in court destroying some poor shoemaker and the miserable creature who's been emptying her mother's bedpans for forty years and thought it would be fun to come out and surprise us, I mean after all Harry you're the one who's getting the bonus for bringing in this wealthy client to get yourself made a senior partner aren't you?

—Look that's not the way it happened, you know it's not but the whole thing's highly irregular, him going out there to talk to Oscar while this appeal's pending it's just highly irregular.

—He didn't even know where he was going Harry, just some old school friend of hers he didn't know where he was till they turned in the drive but it didn't take him a moment, well old sport! Good to see you up and about, putting on a little weight? Never thought we'd have the chance to sit down and have a nice chat, that's a great play you've written, have a cigar while Oscar stands there in a complete muddle. His car's just been stolen, the lawyers he got off a matchbook cover have him suing himself as the accident victim and he's just written a speech about a Civil War battle for some bloodthirsty Hadassah audience lusting for slaughter in the Old Testament while your Mister Mudpye explains that his play is really about the war between blacks and Jews, never mind the lawsuit, all water under the bridge old boy, always annoying to lose one here, don't drink that stuff, we brought out a little Chateau something sweet enough to turn your stomach treating Lily like help while he stares down her blouse it was all perfectly revolting.

—Wouldn't worry about Lily, Christina. Lily can take care of herself. You'll see.

—Well we've taken her in because she thinks her husband's out to get her in this idiotic divorce while she moons around about reconciling with Daddy so he'll leave her all his money to spend on cosmetics and I do the cooking for both of them while the gentleman poet reads aloud from his play my God, it all seems like a thousand years ago. Trish completely besotted by him and Oscar lapping up his flattery like that loathsome dog of hers while he bustled around in a monogramed blazer she bought him at Sulka's calling her Trishy with his hand up her dress while he talked on the phone all the way into town he's so close to her money he can taste it, ingratiating himself with all of us so we'll give this revolting spectacle our blessing. He's already in there giving her daughter's trust officer a workout and you, you're not to worry, he and the firm are behind you while he shrugs off this appeal of Oscar's just a few legal technicalities, all in the family says Trish, when it's over we'll have a marvelous party the poor thing she thinks he hung the moon. He's so quick she says, telling us how he had to explain her mother's estate lawyers' own case to them before he destroyed it. He's so quick.

—Oh, he's quick. He's quick all right.

—What's that supposed to mean? She'd sunk back on the sofa, shoulders fallen and her knees fallen wide kicking off one shoe, then the other, the full pitcher on the floor between them, —the only one who seems to get anything done in this mess while the rest of you sit around and...

—Might mean sometimes he's a little too quick Christina, one of these men who has to show that he's smarter than you are even when nothing's at stake, what makes him a good lawyer but you get a feeling that he's got the answer ready before he hears the question, takes short cuts, doesn't look back, sets up the game himself as if he's the only player. He'd rather win than be right.

—That's what he's paid for isn't it? what all of you get paid for? what this whole insane business you're in is all about? If you stopped looking back and started taking a few shortcuts yourself you might manage to clean up this absurd case you're on and start living like a human being, I mean think about it Harry.

—You think I think about anything else?

—That's what I mean. If you stopped thinking so much about being right maybe you could get off this Episcopal merrygoround they've got you on, living on pills and drink while they drag expert witnesses on stress management into court for running old ladies off the road and we could both start living like human beings again, I mean I am your wife after all aren't I? Where are you going.

—Get some clothes on, I...

—Are you going to call Sam?

—Too late now to reach him, I'll try in the morning. Do you...

—Just a few legal technicalities, my God. Got a real strong case here, that's our friend Mister Basie, win or lose we'll take them in the higher court, we'll take them on appeal, it seems like a hundred years ago... sinking back into the cushions there, her legs slowly stretching out before her in a kind of languor rising to claim her voice with —the sun coming out over the pond while we sat there by the windows, play to the appeals court because that's where it's at he was so sure of himself, this marvelous energy just seething to break loose, this real appetite he had, his skin glistening in the sun and his hands, he had such masterful hands didn't he, as one of her own came up to scratch at her shoulder and slowly sink to ruminate at her breast, —do blacks have much hair do you think? on their bodies I mean?

—Frankly never thought about it, now...

—Waving that newspaper at me, piece in here on your hairy Ainu you were talking about, thought maybe you missed it? her hand fallen to stir the length of her thigh, —wouldn't have noticed it he said, he didn't remember you ever talking about your hairy...

—Look, do you want some of this lemon chicken now or...

—Don't be ridiculous.

Reflection limning reflection in the mirrored walls of the bedroom blew its dimensions, flashed with the mirrored door to the bathroom, caught the soles of her feet flung wide on the bed and her arm's impatient haste crushing his lips at her throat, at her breast, knees risen sharply akimbo forthrightly lewd intolerant of delay seizing the thick surge filling her hand toward the crest there heaving as his weight came over for the plunge withdrawn to plunge deeper in the pounding rise and fall of ravage, her nails dug in the voracious pillage of his loins, of the devouring dark and hairy paradox of intimacy mounting in a widening gulf with each silent thrust of this lubricious intercourse to distance them further one from the other in the helpless greed of separate revelation, eyes closed, tongue lax and indolent as hers diffused her saturated depths and his all panting earnest concentration on the burst that left his head buried on her shoulder, eyes closed, hers wide, as they slipped back in desultory concert to what remained of the day, of the lemon chicken and the shrimp in black bean sauce, the pointless flicker of dinner jackets and backless gowns on actors and actresses long dead and the papers, letters, briefs and memorandums —I mean do they have to be scattered all over the house, Harry? until at last the lights went out.

Sun filling the sky waked her to find a note on a yellow legal pad that he was off to an appointment with the firm's psychiatric counselor, God only knew the purpose of that, to prepare his court appearance? and which one, his or the firm's? to actually tend to the splintered inner shell of the man himself or merely blur it further, codeine, Darvon, Valium crowding her cosmetics off the shelf over the bathroom basin where the mirror snared her startled glance as someone passing in the street might have caught her eye to pause, as she did now, for closer scrutiny bent in a frown, dissembled in a smile provoking some remembered warmth of trust revoked too late in that blasted instant of recognition by the abrupt awareness of memory itself as the dissembler of some past betrayal that had turned it sour as she seized the familiar green capped clarifying lotion from among the alien crowd of pacifiers on the shelf there and a cotton ball to wipe it on, rescued the gold capped masque adoucissant applied en couche mince sur le visage et le cou avoiding the tour des yeux and too impatient to laissez agir fifteen minutes, retirer à l'eau tiède and dropping the face cloth for a silver capped clinging, creamy makeup base to conceal shadows, flaws and fine lines, a superb shield against the elements touched up with a whitener on the lids and stroke of the eyebrow pencil God knows who you might run into in the street in this smart part of town simply walking out to do the marketing and stop at the cleaners if just then the phone hadn't rung and of course it was —Oscar? Well who else would it be at this ungodly hour, you... all right noon, it's noon! I told you I was exhausted didn't I? that I can't help it about the dog, didn't I? She said she'd send a car out for it and... well if you've given it some boiled chicken and locked it down in the laundry what are you calling me for, if you just want to complain about these pains there's nothing I... Well what about Harry, my God he's got other things on his mind besides your appeal Oscar, he's... No, this morning's paper? Why would they put his picture in the entertainment section, if they think being in court over a car accident's a joke they... all right goodbye, I'll look for it now... and she found it, pictured here with senior partner William C G Peyton III neatly folded beside an empty coffee cup.

Final arguments have been scheduled in Federal appeals court in the longstanding $700 million damage suit brought by the Episcopal Church against Pepsico Inc., the multibillion dollar international purveyor of soft drinks and recreation snack foods. The charges allege trademark infringement and other related matters falling within the purview of the

Lanham Act, as well as libelous intent to disparage and make a mockery of plaintiff's good name. Following dismissal of the charges in Federal district court six years ago, the plaintiffs appealed and after a succession of law firms have retained Goldfarb Goldfarb & Mintz doubling the amount of damages sought in the original complaint.
'We regard the charges as frivolous in whole and in part,' said Harry Lutz of the blue ribbon firm Swyne & Dour retained as leading counsel by the defendants among the seventeen law firms involved in the dispute. 'Given a fair and thorough airing in court we are confident of the outcome,' Mr Lutz said. According to sources close to both parties, legal costs have already soared beyond the $33 million mark.

—It's the wear and tear, she'd repeat later, —not just on you Harry. I mean the wear and tear on all of us. Think about it.

—Think about it! See it right there in the paper don't you? how much is at stake here? Finally getting it cleared up and...

—My God I know what's at stake here, your bonus a senior partnership another million dollars for good old Bill Peyton and a nervous breakdown for all the rest of us? This fine psychiatric counselor they're sending you to, did it ever occur to him that this car accident might have been trying to tell you something?

—Well of course, stress, the whole damn thing he sees it all the time, he...

—Harry?

—That's his whole practice, lawyers under stress billing twenty five hundred hours a year it comes with the territory, as many quit practicing a year as kids entering lawschool and cases like this, a car accident like...

—Harry! I'm not talking about your car accident I'm talking about the rest of us! Does the firm plan to send us all for psychiatric counseling? or up to that rest farm where they get you off the bottle? Look at Oscar, isn't his case as important to him as your billion dollar client's is to them? Have you found out what in God's name is going on there?

—Look, Christina. Look, four hundred and twenty lawyers in the firm, a hundred partners, you think this is the only case we're handling? The court heard Oscar's appeal that's all I know, Bill Peyton's so damn busy on this case in the papers I don't even know who made the arguments, tried to reach Sam must have been somebody on his staff who handled Oscar's end but they said Sam's just gone trout fishing in Norway nobody there seemed to know a damn thing about it can't rush it Christina, can't rush the system, if he'd taken that settlement we'd all be...

—My God don't you dare start that again! Where are you going now?

—Getting a drink.

—Trout fishing in Norway. You can get me one too.

—Everything so damn complicated wherever you look, point's not that anything that can go wrong will go wrong he said, tipping the bottle generously over two glasses, —wonder that even the smallest damn thing goes right at all.

And surely enough, from one remote pinpoint on the globe to this one, among millions of doors to this very door in fact, in a negligible matter of days an array of trucks and airplanes stretching from Ultima Thule, of conveyor belts and sorters, diligent hands and trudging feet brought a picture postcard aptly captioned Ørret fiske i Surnadal, Norge, at a cost of a mere four kroner, little more than the price of the newspaper that same morning at that same door bringing

Tatamount, Va. An unusual development has surfaced in the troubled saga of the notorious outdoor sculpture known as Cyclone Seven towering over this sleepy rural hamlet where it has been engulfed in controversy since its unveiling. It first caught the public eye with the accidental entrapment of a small dog in its serrated steel cavities, leading to a confrontation by the Village in an effort to free the puppy and the sculptor's fierce defense of its artistic integrity. Following tumultuous demonstrations by partisans of both sides climaxed by the dog's death when the structure was struck by lightning, the Village won a court order demanding its removal, against the sculptor's claims citing its site specific status. The matter is again before the courts where each side has reversed its position.

The sculptor, Mr R Szyrk of New York, now demands the Village pursue its mandated course permitting the structure's removal, claiming his constitutional right to its eventual disposition as embodying a protected statement under the First Amendment. Pending the outcome of its petition for Landmark status the Village has refused removal or altering

of the unique creation which has 'put Tatamount on the map' bringing substantial tourist revenues and jobs to this chronically depressed area where unemployment runs thirty nine percent among whites and double that for blacks, with a twenty six percent overall literacy rate.
Since the plaintiff resides out of state the case will be heard in Federal district court by Judge Thomas Crease, who has already been subjected to vilification and abuse relating to lawsuits spawned by Cyclone Seven and is currently embroiled in his nomination to the U.S. Court of Appeals being vigorously opposed by Senator Orney Bilk, a native of nearby Stinking Creek, who is reported to have called for his impeachment.

—Oscar I said no! spilling her coffee with a tug at the phone's cord, and —I said don't even dream of such a thing! recounting it later over a half eaten supper —my God, I mean can you imagine it?

—Sounds like he wants us to adopt him.

—Harry don't even joke about it. He got hold of some old medical manual in Father's library and he's utterly convinced he's got a broken sternum when Mudpye poked him in the chest for emphasis in their insane conversation about blacks and Jews and cracked his scapular with a slap on the shoulder when we left, he...

—Any witnesses?

—Well of course, we were all...

—Sounds like he's putting together a brand new lawsuit.

—Do you think he hasn't thought of that? I mean it's perfectly ridiculous.

—Most of them are.

—Well you should know. I mean as revolting as he is he certainly wasn't attacking Oscar, the last thing in the world he simply got carried away.

—Nothing to do with it, Christina. Grabs his lapel it's a threatening gesture, don't have to exchange a word, it's assault. Poking him, hitting him, laying a hand on him without his consent it's battery.

—Well my God, I mean you don't break people's bones tapping them on the chest do you? slapping him on the shoulder? And you think he'd believe a doctor who told him that? No. He called one out there who asked him if he was an older person, any history of osteoporosis and of course that simply made him more hell bent on coming in here to see a specialist to drag into court, can you picture it? Sleeping in there on the couch he wouldn't be in our way at all, wouldn't be any trouble he'd bring his work with him he said, might get a chance to see Sir John, have him up here for a drink to go over his play and give him a look at this place to show him we weren't pikers, wouldn't bother us at all because Lily would take care of anything he needed and...

—No look Christina no, it's absolutely not, where would she sleep it's...

—Lily will sleep where she's sleeping right now! Do you think I've lost my mind too? I just said I'd told him not to even dream of such an idiotic idea didn't I? They wouldn't be in our way at all he said, drive in together when the car comes out to pick up that odious dog of course she's forgotten all about it, I mean I don't even want to think about it. The two of them sitting out there day after day eating boiled chicken, playing cards, watching the nature program looking out at that cold grey pond getting dark earlier every day while he turns into a nervous wreck waiting to hear about his appeal? I mean he even said he'd tried to call his new friend Jerry if you can picture that, ready to sue him for his broken sternum thank God they said he was out of town but by now Oscar knows when he's being lied to because that's all anybody...

—No, no it's true Christina, Mudpye's setting up a new client base out in Aspen, a lot of money out there and the firm thinks...

—My God.

—What.

—Nothing! Trout fishing in Norway, feeling up a new client in Aspen who in God's name is minding the store?

—Don't quite follow you Christina, talking about Oscar's appeal all I've heard is some young lawyer showed up at Foley Square and filed for admission to the Second Circuit bar pro hac vice must be out of state, went up to the seventeenth floor and filed the appeal, all strictly pro forma I didn't even get his name. An accredited member of some out of state bar, it's not our business where Oscar got him. Ask Oscar.

—Harry he hasn't a clue, you know what he's...

—Look Christina, some lawyer he got off a matchbook cover he can end up like that shark Lily got him for his car accident, lawyer has to know his client that's one of the most basic regulations in the whole...

—Your whole self regulating conspiracy my God, don't start that again. He knew Mister Basie didn't he? and look at the...

—No, no look don't start on that again, just ask him...

—Harry please! I just told you he's ready to have a seizure out there didn't I? Every time he looks up he thinks that real estate woman's peeking in the windows selling the place out from under us while the paint peels and the veranda caves in and he doesn't know who sent her, the bank or Father and he's afraid to ask either one of them. The high point of his day is reading something in the paper that means more trouble for Father, some boy who was drowned when he was being baptized and now this ridiculous Cyclone Seven mess starting all over again he's got a lot on his plate, you can almost hear the appetite in Oscar's voice when he says it, Harry? What is it.

—Just not hungry.

—I mean isn't the, is the meat too rare? raising her eyes from the plate in front of him —are you, do you want a drink?

—I'll get it.

—No I'll do it, sit still.

—Get the feeling they're not behind me, Christina.

—Who, the firm? your pal William Peyton third and his four hundred thieves? putting the bottle down sharply, —there's his picture in the paper with you for all the world to see, I mean doesn't that look like they're backing you up? speaking for the firm on this monstrous case that you...

—Not that case no, no it's this, this disagreeable little business about that car accident, all pretty routine let the insurance people haggle over it but I just get the feeling, if things get sticky leaving the scene of an accident just get the feeling that they're backing off, feeling Bill Peyton would just rather not hear about it, mention it to him and he comes up with a joke or some movie he's seen he, had lunch with him yesterday and he...

—Do you want ice in this? setting the glass in front of him, a mere interruption —because honestly Harry I think you're exaggerating, the smallest thing flies all out of proportion and you start to imagine things I mean you've known Bill Peyton for a thousand years, you know he's not...

—Not imagining that glitter in his eye when he'd had two martinis at lunch yesterday Christina, a few Scotches and he's fine, loosens him up even acts a little silly but that second gin martini you see that real streak of meanness, sounds like he's kidding but he's giving you just enough rope to throw you the other end when the moment comes that you...

—Well my God I mean you knew that didn't you? that he'd never have been made managing partner in a fine old white shoe blue ribbon outfit like Swyne & Dour without a good dose of that old school tie duplicity? that he thinks you think like he would, so he'll think it first, that you might sue them for the pressure they've put on you that got you into this accident? Sending you to their psychiatrist to save your sanity? to protect you? or protect the firm against you with an expert witness using everything he's wrung out of you to show that you're unstable? picking up her own glass already half emptied —because I can't stand seeing this happen to you that's why I, what's made me sound harsh and impatient and perfectly awful and I look at myself and see somebody I don't like because I can't stand what it's doing to me either, I'm your wife aren't I? with a hand on his arm that sent a tremor the length of it —I mean I love you Harry, I love your hands and your stubborn fighting yourself that drives me crazy when you won't take the shortcut like the rest of them and I love your hands on me and what they do and the stiff stubborn hairy Ainu that's like all the rest of you when I look around us at the pieces of my absurd pointless life before we met all strung out in front of us worried about Father, about the house and poor Oscar out there with his whole life in the lap of the gods and your smile, shaking your head it's such a patient, sad smile looking for what's right, what you said once, not what is just but what is right?

He'd reached out to hold her wrist, putting down his glass to say —lap of Judge Bone is more like it Christina, sitting on the Second Circuit bench as long as anyone can remember, cut from the same cloth as old Judge Crease, he doesn't suffer fools gladly I've seen him take a young woman prosecutor right off at the knees, got himself a name over the years for being a sort of misogynist so this wild card Oscar drew on the bench better have had her act together, do you want another? and he was up emptying his glass, taking them both back to the source and pouring it freely, —can't tell he said, handing hers back to her, —you can't tell. Little bit of the old puritan xenophobe too, get Mudpye up there with his secondhand red brick arrogance trying to deliver his oral argument and you can't tell.

—Well if you could have heard him out there Harry, I mean he's certainly got his act together if that's what you...

—May think so, he may think so but I don't think he's ever handled a case before the Second Circuit Appeals Court. Probably march in there with a twenty page brief ready to read every word of his brilliant legal analysis to these three old black robes sitting up there looking down at him and I mean looking down, he's standing at a lectern down in the well and they're up in their highbacked thrones behind this polished mahogany sort of horseshoe courteous, relaxed, really forbidding, almost informal that's what's formidable about it. He starts off with something like in order to fully understand this case one of them cuts him right off. We're familiar with the case, Counsel, is there anything you wish to add to what is contained in your brief? Your honour, if I may be allowed to outline the facts... I believe we understand the facts, Counsel. If it please the court, the public interest in the far reaching cultural implications of this case and Bone comes right in, I remind Counsel that we are here to serve the public interest. Your case is thus and so, goes right to the heart of it, sums up the argument in a couple of sentences and asks counsel to sit down, poor bastard's got himself up for a real performance and the place, the whole atmosphere's like a theatre but they're not there for a matinee and his whole star turn goes out the window, a few more questions and down comes the curtain.

—Well my God Harry don't tell, don't get Oscar's hopes up, I mean this whole brittle shell he's put together for who he thinks he is now but suddenly I look through that mangy beard and cigar smoke and see the face of the little boy down there by the pond that day with the little canoe he'd made, he'd spent days at it stripping the bark off a beautiful white birch that stood there and Father, Father looking at it without a word like some terrible open wound, looking at the canoe sunk in the mud and he had the poor tree cut down the next day without a word, gone without a trace he never mentioned it again but he never let Oscar forget it, just with a look, it was all too heartbreaking and now he's done it again.

Oscar's done it again setting himself up with these fantasies of producing his play when he wins this appeal and if he loses, this whole desperate pose as the gentleman poet, the last civilized man I mean he's just really so different from who he thinks he is and God only knows, when he loses...

—Not when he loses, Christina. It's when this who he thinks he is loses, what the whole thing's all about isn't it? He goes off on a frolic of his own writes a play and expects the world to roll out the carpet for...

—A frolic! Where in God's name did you get that, I mean have you ever seen anyone more deadly serious than...

—Just a phrase, comes up sometimes in cases of imputed negligence, the servant gets injured or injures somebody else on the job when he's not doing what he's hired for, not performing any duty owing to the master, voluntarily undertakes some activity outside the scope of his employment like...

—Harry?

—Like an office worker puts out an eye shooting paperclips with a rubberband they say he's on a frolic of his own, no intention of advancing his employer's business his employer's not liable, there may be a case if the employer knew about this horseplay and hadn't tried to...

—Harry! My God I'm not talking about shooting paperclips, I mean can't you say anything without writing a whole legal brief to go with it? and a swallow from her glass broke her off coughing —he, he spent a year, two years writing it and...

—All right, look. Look all I meant was Oscar takes off and writes a longwinded play about his grandfather he wasn't hired to do it, about somebody seeking justice nobody paid him to did they? And it gets him nowhere, does he keep at it? write another play? and another? No, no he splurges this one time and then lets it devour him year after year like this little birch canoe he made because it's safer to blame the world out there for rejecting who he thought he was, for all the work he's put in on a play that's not really about justice in the first place, not about injustice it's about resentment, it's resentment right from the start like his little canoe sunk in the mud and it poisons everything, blaming those faceless ogres out there instead of looking inside at the ogres we don't want to see, don't dare see our own hand in it, who we really are, and if he wins? pausing again to reach for the bottle, —if who he thinks he is wins on this appeal? What you see in the headlines out of Washington every day isn't it? caught redhanded destroying evidence, obstructing justice, committing perjury off on frolics of their own and when they get off on some technicality, everybody knows they're guilty but there's not enough there to prove it so they can proclaim they've been proved innocent, wrap themselves in the flag and they're heroes because now they believe it themselves, because the law has vindicated who they think they are like saying where would Christianity be today if Jesus had been given ten to twenty with time off for good behaviour, and if he wins? If Oscar wins and this whole cockeyed version of who he thinks he is is vindicated because that's what the law allows?

—I mean, but I mean isn't that really what the law is all about? and she straightened up as though to disown the slur in her voice setting her glass down emptied —where it's all laws, and laws, and everything's laws and he's done something nobody's told him to, nobody hired him to and gone off on a frolic of his own I mean think about it Harry. Isn't that really what the artist is finally all about?

—I've thought about it he muttered almost to himself, standing there staring at the drink swirling slowly in his hand like the words lost under his breath —I've thought a lot about it, melting away like the fixed resolve that had always seemed to map the hard features of his face, looking up at her. —Come to bed.

OPINION

Before Wakefield, Schlotz and Bone, Circuit Judges

BONE, C. J.

Oscar L Crease ('Crease') filed his complaint against Erebus Entertainment, Inc. ('Erebus'), its Chief Executive Officer Ben B F Leva ('B F') and Jonathan Livingston Siegal a/k/a Constantine Kiester ('Kiester') et al. in the United States District Court for the Southern District of New York for damages, injunctive and other relief. The action arises out of alleged infringements upon the dramatic presentation Once at Antietam written by plaintiff, a historian and fledgling playwright, for the stage or for television adaptation. The defendants deny infringement but admit production and distribution of the alleged infringing motion picture entitled The Blood in the Red White and Blue.

As provided in 28 U.S.C. 1400 (a), civil actions 'arising under any Act of Congress relating to copyrights... may be instituted in the district in which the defendant or his agent resides or may be found' plaintiff's summons and complaint were served on defendant's general counsel designated as agent for service in New York City in this judicial district where they do business and 'where the claim arose' (U.S.C. 1391 (a)), no claim of lack of venue having been asserted the objection to improper venue was waived. Before the pretrial conference stage in these proceedings was reached, defendant filed a motion to dismiss under Rule 12(b)(6) of the Federal Rules of Civil Procedure or in the alternative for summary judgment under Rule 56, submitting therewith certain affidavits and collateral supporting documents outside the pleadings affirming that no material issues of fact were in dispute and that given these undisputed facts one party was entitled to judgment on the law wherewith the district judge construed defendant's motion as one for summary judgment and so held. The plaintiff appeals.

An understanding of the issue requires some description of what was in the public domain, as well as of the play and the motion picture. As attested in exhibits submitted by the parties consisting in the main of journalistic and similar accounts published subsequent to the actual events, one Thomas Crease, a Carolina resident at the time the Civil War began, enlisted as a private in the Confederate army and fought in the battle at Ball's Bluff, where he was slightly wounded. He was intestate heir to valuable coal properties in Pennsylvania, and upon learning that these were in danger of confiscation by the Federal government, he received permission from the Confederate authorities to go north to protect his interests which he did, hiring a substitute to take his place in the army, a not uncommon practice. Complications arising in the North obliged him to provide a substitute to serve in the Union army as well, and both were killed at 'bloody Antietam.' In later years Crease looked up the details of that battle and, discovering that the regiments in which both were serving had confronted each other in 'the Bloody Lane,' became increasingly haunted by the conviction that the two had killed each other and that he was thus in some fanciful way a walking suicide, to which some ascribed his occasionally erratic behaviour in his late years as a prominent jurist. For his play the author used only this merest skeleton; the incidents, the characters, the mise en scène, the sequence of events and the events themselves all have been changed, embellished, lifted naked from classical sources or cut from whole cloth.

The play opens with a scene between the protagonist, who is named Thomas, and his mother, a long suffering, Bible ridden husk of a woman. He has just returned home from heroic action on the Confederate side in the battle at Ball's Bluff, to the news that his estranged uncle, a Northern coal baron, has died intestate, leaving him as sole living relative the heir to substantial mine holdings in Pennsylvania. It appears that some years before, with the death of his father in a minor embassy post in France, Thomas had returned to America to confront this same uncle, his father's brother, with the bitter charge, conveyed by his mother, of having cheated his father of his due a generation before, and in a humiliating scene has settled the matter for cash barely sufficient to launch a hardscrabble existence on a rundown Carolina farm his uncle had taken on a bad debt. The farm adjoins a large working plantation called Quantness where, mistaking it for his property settlement on his initial horse and buggy arrival 'driving up as if he owned the place,' further humiliation lay in store upon being directed on by a black house slave to the wretched dwelling where this present scene with his mother takes place. Here they have hammered out an existence, labouring side by side with the young slave John Israel, his mother's Biblical protégé, till the day of his chance meeting with Giulielma, the lonely daughter of the Quantness plantation, a further humiliation given his humble circumstances which nonetheless has blossomed into romance and marriage gaining him a foothold in the Quantness household itself. This whole scene has been presented through dialogue, and concludes with Thomas' consternation upon learning that John Israel has 'run off' during his absence, and his defiant resolution to go north and claim what he believes to be justly and rightfully his.

In the next scene we follow Thomas to the halls of Quantness where his father in law, a pompous Confederate major, is showing about a mysterious visitor, Mr Kane, amidst disquisitions on the war, the cotton market abroad, the French position and the Union blockade, slavery, Aristotle and other exalted topics. It is clear that Thomas' abrupt inheritance, plus his recent battlefield exploits, have greatly enhanced his value as a son in law, particularly when we learn in an aside that shares in Quantness, dependent on the cotton crop, have fallen into the hands of Northern bankers, and he may be the means to redeem them. This contrasts sharply with the Major's condescending treatment of his own son William, kept home from the war by his youth and a marked limp, whose hero worship of his brother in law anticipates a subterfuge by which he will, unbeknownst to Thomas, go up to the war in his place. Following a tender scene between Thomas and Giulielma in which he pleads with her to accompany him north, a fall from a horse leads somewhat inexplicably into a heated discussion of justice between Thomas, William and Mr Kane employing patches of Platonic dialogue lifted directly from Book I of the Republic, interspersed with unattributed views of Albert Camus on total justice and of Rousseau on absolute freedom, and Thomas departs.

The second act is set in the North where Thomas has arrived to take over the mining properties and the problems they present. His foil is a coarse, jovially venal man named Bagby, his uncle's mine manager and confidante, for whom no stratagem for self advancement is too petty or too grand, and who ridicules Thomas' efforts to deal fairly with the striking miners. A dramatic night scene in which Thomas is 'mugged' is followed by humorous scenes depicting Bagby's recruiting and profiteering activities, when Mr Kane appears unexpectedly with news of Confederate reverses and the poor condition of their troops, of the Major taken prisoner and of William gone up to fight (though unaware as Thomas' substitute), and that the large cotton shipment whose proceeds were to redeem the Northern held shares in Quantness has been impounded by the French against payment for a ram being built there to break the Union blockade. As the Union army announces conscription, Thomas is confronted with the arrest of the young man who had mugged him, a casualty of the mines, and amidst lofty declarations of refusal to surrender his destiny to chance, and a further dose of Plato on justice versus the appearance of justice (Republic, Book II at 359) this time delivered in Mr Bagby's disreputable brogue espousing the latter position, Thomas sends the young man up in his place and departs for France once more in pursuit of justice. The act concludes with a highly theatric interlude featuring Mr Bagby musing over the dead on the edge of the Antietam battlefield as night falls.

The rest of the play is of less consequence in the matter at bar. The war ended, Mr Bagby has acquired the controlling shares in Quantness and is now an official in Washington where Thomas, having been interned on the ram Sphynx at sea all this time, returns seeking damages from the government. Bagby's price is his signing papers incriminating Mr Kane who is nearby awaiting execution as a spy; and the prison scene that follows not merely mirrors the last days of Socrates, but lifts the Crito almost bodily intact. Refusing Bagby's condition, Thomas ventures back to Quantness where having learned of the death of his two substitutes, one of them William, in the bloodiest single day of the war, he realizes he has been used by those around him in their efforts to fulfill their own destinies, thereby robbing him of his own, and the play's final scene claws for the heights of Greek tragedy as envisaged in the words of C M Bowra (Attic Tragedy at 101) 'because in his fight against insuperable odds he shows all his nobility of character and is nonetheless defeated.'

The picture opens with a decrepit horse and buggy carrying two silent passengers, an aging woman and a handsome, intense young man, through a variety of bad weather and unpromising vistas to pause and then enter at a gate labeled Cross Creek. As he stands and snaps the whip imperiously they proceed up the moss-hung drive to an elaborate antebellum mansion where a black house slave disdainfully points them on their way, and for a moment we glimpse a ravishingly beautiful young woman in negligee watching from behind a curtain as the buggy retreats back down the drive and is next seen pulling up before a small farm house in bad need of repair. A long montage sequence follows in which the young man is seen hammering, splitting, driving posts, planting tobacco, assisted by a young black evidently a slave who is also shown by lamplight at the woman's knee learning with the Bible's help to read and write. Thus far the entire story is told in dumb show, heightened by musical effects, until the day of his dramatic sexually charged encounter with the ravishing young woman glimpsed in the opening scene and even more so now, on horseback, where he is out hunting; their acquaintance rapidly ripens into love and marriage, and he moves into Cross Creek with her jealous, vindictive brother Jake and her vain, drunken father, who assumes the rank of major with the dawn of the Civil War where they go up, leaving the sniveling brother behind. The battle at Ball's Bluff is next portrayed with all the ferocity that modern motion picture techniques and special effects are capable of producing and which need not be detailed here, except to observe that the Major appears to stay well out of the action into which his son in law, whose name we have since learned is Randal, plunges with admirable not to say bloodthirsty zeal. Returning home, Randal learns from his mother of the death in the North of a wealthy coal baron uncle whom she has taught him to despise for having cheated his father of the legacy to which he now, as the only surviving relative, may lay claim as she urges him to do. Similarly, he is urged on by the Major who, we learn in a fiery scene between father and daughter, has accumulated heavy gambling debts and sees his son in law's good fortune as a way out, conniving meanwhile to satisfy the new Confederate draft by sending his own son Jake up in Randal's place. Leaving his wife behind at her own wish, Randal proceeds north to take over the coal empire where, with the collusion of the mines' wily manager Carlucci, he brutally suppresses a strike by the miners against their unhuman working conditions, contemptuously sending one of them up as his substitute when he is threatened by a draft by the Union army. Unwilling to risk his new empire by returning to Cross Creek as the war draws closer threatening both his wife and mother, only the Major is there recuperating from a minor wound with an abundance of drink when a marauding band abruptly materializes to shoot him dead after degrading him mercilessly, tormenting the older woman beyond endurance and then in a prolonged scene reveling in its own depiction of cruelty raping the younger one in almost clinical detail. All this however has been in mere preparation for the scenes which follow depicting the war's bloodiest confrontation in the Battle of the Antietam, which exhausts every conceivable cinematic possibility for the exploitation of blood and gore concluding, amidst the moans of the dying at nightfall, with Randal's spectral appearance on the battlefield where among the day's twenty odd thousand casualties he stumbles upon the corpses of his two substitutes locked in mortal combat. The rest of the picture seeks simply to lend dramatic credibility to Randal's eventual self destruction with his discovery of certain letters drawn by defendants from the public domain but which, finding no parallel in plaintiff's play, is of no consequence here.

The defendants are in the business of providing motion picture entertainment in Hollywood, California. Erebus, headed by studio chief B F Leva for almost two decades, a rare event in that mercurial milieu, is well known for its lavishly budgeted 'blockbuster' offerings. Kiester is an independent producer and director whose recent Africa extravaganza Uruburu, containing scenes aptly tagged 'Not for the squeamish,' made over $300 million and his top professional reputation. While denying allegations of fraud as set forth in plaintiff's Third Cause of Action, Kiester concedes that he began his career as a television producer in New York under his given name Jonathan Livingston, later to be known as Jonathan L Siegal, and upon arriving in Hollywood taking the name Constantine Kiester. It was to the defendant under the first of these names plaintiff contends that he originally submitted his playscript, receiving it back with a curt note of rejection, an occurrence of which defendant denies any recollection and in any event did not solicit. Defendants contend that having determined that the motion picture market was ready for a spectacular treatment of the Civil War, given the historic success of Gone With the Wind and its projected sequel by a rival studio, they cast about for a story that would provide a suitable vehicle for an actor named Bredford, just then not employed. To this end Kiester contacted a former schoolmate named John Knize whom he remembered as a Civil War 'buff' who provided the story idea and at Kiester's request expanded it into a treatment. On the strength of this treatment Kiester contracted with Erebus to produce and direct the picture, assigning preparation of the screenplay to Knize and, between them, choosing Afhadi, Railswort, Schultz and Probidetz to help him, the first three with the scenario, the fourth with the dramatic production. All these five were examined by deposition; all denied that they had ever encountered, known of, read or used the play in any way whatever; all agreed that they had based the picture on material in the public domain provided by Knize. To meet these denials, the plaintiff appeals to the substantial similarity between passages in the picture and those parts of the play which are original with them.

In granting summary judgment to defendant, the district judge felt that story idea central to the play was not sufficiently novel to create 'property interest' entitled to protection under New York law in action against the motion picture makers for unfair competition and unlawful use, misappropriation and conversion; that notwithstanding the author's alleged submission of his play to defendant there was no evidence of any intent to contract with regard to the said play by defendant and thus its alleged unlawful use could form neither any basis for action for breach of implied contract, nor any basis for plaintiff's unjust enrichment action, nor for fraud action in that the defendants could not have enriched themselves at the author's expense on the ground that 'plaintiff's alleged submissions lack the requisite novelty under applicable law' and so falling into the public domain where he could not be defrauded of property he did not own.

Plaintiff argues that in granting defendant's motion for summary judgment the court below erred in misunderstanding the applicable law and in deciding this case should have applied a different body of doctrine. The courts have frequently debated whether laws of unfair competition are similar enough to copyright jurisdiction in its aims to be preempted by Federal copyright law, to which defendant argues that preemption is not absolute in the area of intellectual property. However under the doctrine of pendent jurisdiction a Federal court may take jurisdiction over a State law if, as established by the Supreme Court in United Mine Workers v. Gibbs, that State law claim rises out of a 'common nucleus of operative fact' with the Federal claim, and here plaintiff argues for such a common nucleus residing in all his claims rising from defendant's use of his playscript. His entitlement to copyright thereof is undisputed under 17 U.S.C. 303 dealing with the transition between the Copyright Acts of 1909 and 1976, the play having been written before the 1976 Act became effective but never published thus furnishing him this protection.

Both the issues of originality and novelty were raised before the district court by defendant asserting lack of novelty as a defense to all of plaintiff's claims, the judge holding that the latter applied whereas the former did not and that even if the issue of originality did apply plaintiff would lose since though defendants might have used the play they had taken only what the law allowed, that is, those general themes, motives or ideas where there could be no copyright and that in any case if they did copy this constituted fair use, embracing the famous dictum that even if a law does not apply, if it did the result would be thus. Should it emerge that the judge below focused on superficial differences or mere disguise ignoring identities of locale, motivation and similar persuasive factors the matter would be remanded to the district court for review; or further, if the judge assumed copying and failed to pursue the question whether similarities between the works were substantial enough to raise triable issues of fact concerning infringement thereby depriving plaintiff of trial, this would constitute an abuse of discretion.

Whereas the low threshold of originality as opposed to novelty had already been clearly established by this court (See Alfred Bell & Co. v. Catalda Fine Arts, Inc. 191 F.2d 99, 2d Circ. 1951), under the 1976 Copyright Act it is now explicit in the statute that copyright subsists in 'original works of authorship,' and it is the task of this court to determine whether the issue of novelty or originality applies in the case before us.

In an appeal bearing certain striking resemblances to the case at bar, Judge Learned Hand disputed the issue of novelty more than a generation ago in observing at the outset that '[w]e are to remember that it makes no difference how far the play was anticipated by works in the public demesne which the plaintiffs did not use. The defendants appear not to recognize this, for they have filled the record with earlier instances of the same dramatic instances and devices, as though, like a patent, a copyrighted work must be not only original, but new. That is not however the law as is obvious in the case of maps or compendia, where later works will necessarily be anticipated. At times, in discussing how much of the substance of a play the copyright protects, courts have indeed used language which seems to give countenance to the notion that, if a plot were old, it could not be copyrighted.' Sheldon et al. v. Metro-Goldwyn Pictures Corp. et al., 81 F.2d 49, quoting London v. Biograph Co. (C.C.A.) 231 F. 696. Defendant-appellees in the instant case have pursued a similar course, and the district court has joined with their pursuit, conjuring up once more this spectre of novelty in arguments relying heavily on citations from a more recent case in which the judge determined this to be the 'sole issue' before the court in granting defendants' motion for summary judgment, and affirmed in the review by the appeals court limiting its decision to whether there was 'no genuine issue as to any material fact' entitling defendants to 'judgment as a matter of law.' Fed. R. Civ. P.56(c). Murray v. National Broadcasting Co. Inc., 671 F. Supp. 236 (S.D. N.Y. 1987), quoting Anderson v. Liberty Lobby, Inc., 477 U.S. 242, 248-49 (1986). In so arguing, defendants in the case before us have sought and found refuge in a decision embracing property rights in an idea, thus narrowing the issue to those mean constraints which the district court had then proceeded to analyze in light of the New York Court of Appeals decision in Downey v. General Foods Corp., 31 N.Y.2d 56, 334 N.Y.S.2d 874, 286 N.E.2d 257 (1972) Affirmed (1988) establishing the general proposition that '[l]ack of novelty in an idea is fatal to any cause of action for its unlawful use' therewith granting defendants' motion for summary judgment. In tying the case at bar to the Procrustean bed of *Murray* as refined by further pruning at the hands of this court, plaintiff is disabled from pursuing the triable issue of infringement of a copyrighted work wherein novelty rightly construed is a contributing but not the controlling factor and where, for that matter, we may take notice of Pratt, C.J. dissenting in *Murray* 'convinced that the novelty issue in this case presents a factual question subject to further discovery and ultimate scrutiny by a trier of fact.'

In deciding Nichols v. Universal Pictures Corporation (45 F.2d at 121) Judge Hand stated '[i]t is of course essential to any protection of literary property, whether at common law or under the statute, that the right cannot be limited literally to the text, else a plagiarist would escape by immaterial variations... When plays are concerned, the plagiarist may excise a separate scene (citations omitted); or he may appropriate part of the dialogue (citation omitted). Then the question is whether the part so taken is "substantial," and therefore not a "fair use" of the copyrighted work; it is the same question as arises in the case of any other copyrighted work. (Citations omitted.) But when the plagiarist does not take out a block in situ, but an abstract of the whole, decision is more troublesome.' Further, in *Murray*, this court has conceded 'that even novel and original ideas to a greater or lesser extent combine elements that are themselves not novel. Originality does not exist in a vacuum.' And as stated in Edwards & Deutsch Lithographing Co. v. Boorman, 7th Circ., 15 F.2d 35, 36, 'The materials used are all old and in the public domain, but the selection, the ordering and arrangement, are new and useful, and copyrightable. In deciding the question of infringements, the first and most obvious thing to do is to compare the productions themselves. The copyrightable feature of appellant's production being a particular plan, arrangement and combination of materials, the identity of such plan, arrangement and combination of similar materials, found in appellee's production, not only suggests, but establishes, the claim of copying.' See Universal Pictures Co. v. Harold Lloyd Corporation 162 F.2d 354.

The defendants took for their mise en scène the same locale, the same two fragmented families contrasting privilege and penury, the same leading roles and the same protagonist's relationships with them. Both Thomas and Randal are fueled by indignation; both escape their humiliating circumstances through marriage to the plantation heiress next door, whose father is a Confederate major and whose brother takes their place at the battlefront unbeknownst to them; both travel north on the same mission and send substitutes from the mines up in their place, to the same fate and in the same battle; finally, both are saddled by a bleak embittered mother who holds the key to their family injustice in the form of the intestate uncle. The differences are not of character but of dimensions, convenience or mere disguise; thus Thomas is an ambitious young man of intellectual leanings caught at cross purposes and fully aware of the ethical fine points at stake in his demand for justice, whereas Randal is cast in a simpler mould, reflecting the vacant stare of the motion picture audience in its warm acquaintance with greed undiluted by any exercise of the intellect let alone the bewildering thicket of Socratic dialogue. Where the play has in mind to edify, the picture sets out to entertain; thus Giulielma, Thomas' touching and desolate bride, finds her tempestuous full bosomed counterpart on the screen composed to arouse those appetites that will find their vicarious reward in the rape scene. Similarly, the sympathetic stage portrait of the Major as a genteel if self serving Southern aristocrat not unfamiliar in the literature, becomes that of a scheming rural drunk familiar from the small screen of television, and his son a mean figure of weakness and spite who is portrayed on the stage as a complex mixture of thwarted and divided love and loyalties. Even the part of Mr Bagby, a study in the business as usual corruption that ushered in Reconstruction and flourishes among us today as the beau ideal, is taken by a comic Italian stereotype reflecting, perhaps, no more than the mirth provoking possibilities provided by each successive wave of immigration, where were the story set in our own time his name would be Jimenez. Only the mother remains the same consistently unpleasant presence from one incarnation to the next, though her message delivered at the opening of the play does not come until later in the picture with its full impact when the two have parted company altogether. The Negro boy at her knee in the play has all but disappeared in the picture, there being no need to explore Rousseau's views on freedom; and Mr Kane of the play is entirely absent from the picture where Crito would be as unhappy a stranger as King Tut.

The main action of the play commences well after that of the picture, with the hero's return from battle to the news of his inheritance. Rather than marking a difference however, this draws them the closer, since the play's opening dialogue summing up all that has gone before now reads like the scenario written for and played out in the picture. From the mother's bleak recounting of the event, we behold on the screen the hero driving their shabby equipage up the plantation drive 'as if he owned the place' only to be sent on his way by a disdainful black to the dilapidated farm, where their struggle against adversity is depicted in the ensuing montage as a long pantomime of privation with musical flourishes unaided by the spoken word. The first voice we hear is that of the ravishing heiress next door, taking him by surprise while out hunting though from her demeanor and subsequent actions we gather that she is not. In calculated contrast to Thomas' poetic recounting of this scene in the play, where his humiliation out hunting food for the table confronted the girl's wayward loneliness, the man on the screen turns the tanned and perspiring badges of his low estate to advantage bringing her down from her arrogant seat on a pawing stallion to be found in short order undoing his overalls and, in the phrase that has caught currency from its high Joycean literary pedigree, 'making a man of him.' Following a lavish wedding and his installation at Cross Creek with his bride's unsavoury relations, the clouds of war loom over the happy couple, preparing us for the full scale screen spectacle of battle at Ball's Bluff.

We may note that at this point in the picture the main action of the play has not even begun, and nothing has been offered by defendants as evidence taken from the public domain, yet we need only come this far in tracking the picture to the play to arouse our doubts regarding 'the particular plan, arrangement and combination of materials' in defendants' product in the light of Nutt v. National Institute Incorporated for the Improvement of Memory, 2d Circ., 31 F.2d 236, 238 where the court observed, '[c]opying is not confined to a literal representation but includes various modes in which the matter of any publication may be adopted, imitated or transferred with more or less colourable alteration.' The matter of dialogue versus action portrayed, or as alleged in the instant case employed as a blueprint for such portrayal, has enjoyed many variations in infringement actions, quoting the author's description of the infringing scene in Chappell & Co. v. Fields, 2d Circ., 210 F. 864 where '[i]n the plaintiff's play the idea that B was deliberately bound to the track with the intention of having him killed by the train was conveyed by the joint effect of the language spoken and movements performed in accordance with the written directions; while in the defendant's play the same idea was conveyed solely by the language uttered. The action, the narrative, the dramatic effect, the impression created and the series of events in the two scenes were identical.' Thus '[w]e have often decided that a play may be pirated without using the dialogue. (Sheldon v. Metro-Goldwyn Pictures, supra, citations omitted.) Were it not so, there could be no piracy of a pantomime, where there cannot be any dialogue; yet nobody would deny to pantomime the name of drama. Speech is only a small part of a dramatists' means of expression; he draws on all the arts and compounds his play from words and gestures and scenery and costume and from the very locks of the actors themselves.' Yet even as here quoting Judge Hand in their defense, appellees rather strengthen the case for the plaintiff as they have done elsewhere 'by setting out dissimilarities, changes, omissions, additions, and variations... different characters, different dialogues, and different costumes which were used to effect a different purpose. Evidence of these differences is relevant upon the question of infringement, but if such differences are shown to exist, the question remains for the trier of fact to decide the issue.' Pellegrini v. Allegrini, D.C., 2 F.2d 610. Where a grant of summary judgment may be precluded by evidence of substantial differences between two works because such evidence would demand a trial on the issue of substantial similarity, should we follow the procedure of the court below assuming copying we must determine whether there are differences which are not extensive enough to show that there is no substantial similarity between the play and the picture as a matter of law. Thus in Fleischer Studios, Inc. v. Ralph A. Freundlich, Inc., 2d Circ., 73 F.2d 276, 278, cert. denied 294 U.S. 717, 55 S.Ct. 516, 79 L.Ed. 1250, the court found the test of infringement to be whether the work is 'recognizable by an ordinary observer as having been taken from the copyrighted source. Such is an infringement... Slight difference and variations will not serve as a defense.' As in the case at bar, '[s]urely the sequence of these details is pro tanto the very web of the author's dramatic expression; and copying them is not "fair use..." Again these details in the same sequence embody more than the "ideas" of the play; they are its very raiment.' And see Chicago Record-Herald C. v. Tribune Association, 7th Circ., 275 F. 797, 799, in which it is said that the unauthorized use, copy or appropriation is not to be neutralized on the plea that 'it is such a little one.'

If this de minimis defense cannot prevail, then neither can defendants' copious recital of omissions, variations and incidents foreign to both the play and the public domain. The simple handshake transformed on the screen to a heaving ejaculatory introduction between the leading couple is after all classic, in the vulgar sense, 'Hollywood' usage of a property assuming of course that the rights to the context of the handshake have first been secured, just as the picture's entirely gratuitous rape scene is an excusatory contrivance for the obligatory nudity presumably contemplated in the female star's seven figure contract. 'Incident springs out of character, and having occurred it alters that character,' writes the English novelist E M Forster, and 'characters, to be real, ought to run smoothly, but a plot ought to cause surprise.' Thus in the play we see plot emerging from character, whereas in the picture the characters are mere puppets of the plot, and defendants will prosper no better with reciting prolonged instances of the play's dialogue which do not occur in the picture, than in pointing the accusing finger at plaintiff for his cavalier lifting of dialogue and even whole scenes from the works of Plato, for as elucidated by Judge Hand in Sheldon v. Metro-Goldwyn Pictures, supra: 'Borrowed the work must indeed not be, for a plagiarist is not himself pro tanto an "author"; but if by some magic a man who had never known it were to compose anew Keats's Ode on a Grecian Urn, he would be an "author," and, if he copyrighted it, others might not copy that poem, though they might of course copy Keats's. (Citations omitted.) True, much of the picture owes nothing to the play... but that is entirely immaterial; it is enough that substantial parts were lifted; no plagiarist can excuse the wrong by showing how much of his work he did not pirate. We cannot avoid the conviction that, if the picture was not an infringement of the play, there can be none short of taking the dialogue.'

It becomes clear beyond peradventure that the district court abused its discretion in granting defendants' motion for summary judgment dismissing a complaint containing triable issues of fact including that of novelty, to which the issue was largely reduced, relying heavily on Murray v. National Broadcasting Company, supra, as argued in defendants' representations of 'fair use' making no finding in the instant case on whether they actually used the play or not. In this connection we again find Pratt C.J., dissenting in *Murray*, persuasive in his observation that 'there is no evidence indicating NBC knew anything of the program idea until Murray submitted it' and '(even though plaintiff's idea was in public domain, no evidence that defendant knew about or would have discovered the idea except through plaintiff's proposal; hence the "idea was novel" as far as defendant was concerned.'

Plaintiff's Fourth, Fifth, Sixth and Seventh Causes of Action relate to defendants' alleged infringement of plaintiff's copyrighted property. Plaintiff's Fourth Cause of Action is for unjust enrichment. In his Fifth Cause of Action plaintiff claims fraud and conspiracy between defendants Erebus and Kiester in the non-performance clause of their contract. Plaintiff's Sixth Cause of Action charges naked theft of characters and sequences to be found nowhere in material presented in discovery as from the public domain. In his Seventh Cause of Action which is against Kiester and his head writer Knize only, plaintiff claims misrepresentation, deceit and fraudulent conduct in the misappropriation and conversion of copyrighted material on deposit at certain public institutions, and of material obtained under false pretenses from plaintiff some years earlier. Plaintiff's Eighth Cause of Action is directed against the writing team assembled by the producer holding them liable as joint tort feasors in this action.

Plaintiff's First Cause of Action claiming his original and prevailing proprietary interest in the main character of the story by virtue of its depiction of his own grandfather, whom he had indeed known as a small child and some of whose papers and effects remain in his possession, was dismissed by the trial judge holding that such grounds even if justiciable could not survive the entry of the story itself into the public domain through turn of the century press clippings, subsequent publication in Western North Carolina Sketches and elsewhere. We concur. In dismissing plaintiff's Second Cause of Action for breach of an implied contract, the judge cites Murray v. National Broadcasting Co., supra, quoting Miller v. Schloss, 218 N.Y. 400, 406, 407, 113 N.E. 337 (1916) stating that '[a] contract cannot be implied *in fact* where the facts are inconsistent with its existence; or against the declaration of the party to be charged... The assent of the person to be charged is necessary and unless he has conducted himself in such a manner that his assent may fairly be inferred he has not contracted,' and, as in *Murray*, '[t]he facts in this case do not support a finding of an intent to contract. On the contrary, the complaint alleges NBC's express rejection of plaintiff's proposal,' in this case the infringed work. Again we concur, as we do also with the dismissal of plaintiff's Third Cause of Action alleging fraud on the part of Kiester in his repeated changes of name to conceal his original access to the play under his original identity, since we find in defendant's Third Affirmative Defense of these name changes 'for professional reasons' expressed in his own indelicate choice of words 'I'm a Jew the minute I step off the plane in L.A.' to carry with them the vulgar ring of truth.

The Ninth Cause of Action contains the charges 'that the fraudulent conduct on the part of the defendants as herein alleged was willful, wanton, malicious and in utter disregard of the rights of the plaintiff causing him mental and professional distress and that as a result he is entitled to compensatory and treble or punitive damages, an accounting, a constructive trust for plaintiff's benefit on all profits and gross revenues from The Blood in the Red White and Blue, an injunction stopping its showing unless and until he is credited with his originative role in its creation, interest, costs and reasonable attorney's fees.' Responding to plaintiff's charge of unjust enrichment at the expense of the possibility of the sale or production of his play elsewhere, defendant has claimed in oral argument that plaintiff has received such an offer since filing his complaint, but absent clear evidence to this effect we must dismiss defendant's claim as hearsay. That it is a 'unique, artistic property' there can be no doubt, since notwithstanding and despite the district court's dismissal rejecting plaintiff's claims on these grounds, it is so described in the remedies section of the development agreement drawn between Erebus Entertainment Inc. and producer director Constantine Kiester, defendants, giving Kiester the right to prevent the loss of this 'unique, artistic property' making certain that if his relationship with Erebus faltered this novel idea and property would be protected from disclosure. That its bare skeleton exists in the public domain may be granted, but only in the face of the persuasive argument that but for plaintiff's submission it is hugely unlikely that defendants would have come upon it there in the form of newspaper accounts appearing in the Gastonia Tribune, Gastonia, North Carolina, on June 4 and July 2, 1903, and January 14, 1904, and the Rutherfordton Sun for June 4, 1903, or the gist of these accounts gathered in the slim locally published Western North Carolina Sketches a half century ago. Yet even assuming this vast unlikelihood to have taken place, and whatever defendants may have applied to their purpose from the various papers and letters on file at a university library, where again plaintiff established his copyright, no evidence has been presented of the bleak mother figure common to both the play and the picture appearing in these confines of the public domain; nor of an intestate uncle (the original of the protagonist inherited from his wealthy grandfather); nor of the cheek by jowl wretched farmhouse with the extravagant plantation; nor of its proprietary major; nor its heiress wife bawdy or otherwise; nor a conniving brother in law; nor even a runaway slave; nor finally a scheming Irish figure of fun or his Italian counterpart; stereotypical as these roles may be, to find their corresponding parts in 'such plan, arrangement and combination of similar materials' coincidental taxes credulity beyond any imaginable bounds. Thus where defendant-appellees urge the defense of 'public domain' claiming that all material in that category may be used repeatedly without charge of infringement, that claim is limited by the court in Fred Fisher, Inc. v. Dillingham, D.C., 298 F. 145, 146, 150 as follows: 'Any subsequent person is, of course, free to use all works in the public domain as sources for his compositions. No later work though original, can take that from him. But there is no reason in justice or law why he should not be compelled to resort to the earlier works themselves, or why he should be free to use the composition of another, who himself has not borrowed. If he claims the rights of the public, let him use them; he picks the brains of the copyright owner as much whether his original composition be old or new. The defendant's concern lest the public should be shut off from the use of works in the public domain is therefore, illusory; no one suggests it. That domain is open to all who tread it; not to those who invade the closes of others.'

Defendant-appellee Knize, and by turn writers Afhadi, Railswort, Schultz and Probidetz, in seeking to escape liability, urge that they are not liable as infringers in that they 'had nothing to do with the production, release, or exhibition of the alleged infringing screenplay,' and that they received no profits therefrom, relying on Washingtonian Publishing Co. v. Pearson, 78 U.S. App. D.C. 287, 140 F.2d 465 to the effect that authors are not liable for profits which other infringers derive from the infringement, discussing *profits* only. There is no merit in the contention that Knize is in no way connected or responsible for the infringements in the public showing of the alleged infringing film and is not liable for *damages* sustained by plaintiff for his deliberate misappropriation of plaintiff's property, or in his claim that a mere employee or workman or servant is not liable for damages for the infringement of his employer, or in the convenient lapses of memory as to who contributed what at the story conferences where the screenplay was concocted and developed. Quoting Sheldon v. Metro-Goldwyn Pictures, supra, 'in concluding as we do that the defendants used the play pro tanto, we need not charge their witnesses with perjury. With so many sources before them they might quite honestly forget what they took; nobody knows the origin of his inventions; memory and fancy merge even in adults. Yet unconscious plagiarism is actionable quite as much as deliberate.'

In allowing the issue of novelty as necessary to create a property right in an idea in accordance with New York State's unfair competition law to prevail in this case, defendant's heavy reliance on *Murray* appears to have been swallowed whole in the court below where both judge and counsel for plaintiff appear to have overlooked its irrelevance, leading us to the inescapable conclusion that in failing to recognize this defense as entirely without merit the district judge has misunderstood, misinterpreted and misapplied the law in obligating this court to review this frivolous defense on appeal.

The decree will be reversed and an injunction will go against the picture together with a decree for damages and an accounting. The plaintiff will be awarded an attorney's fee in this court and in the court below, both to be fixed by the district court upon the final decree.

Decree reversed.

—I simply can't describe it Harry, can you hear me? holding the phone closer, —I mean I drove in here with these immense suits of women's underwear billowing on clotheslines strung up out on the veranda Ilse's brought her sister out here with her, she has to be led around to find a good strong chair she's already smashed one sitting down in the kitchen to peel potatoes while Oscar marches around stroking his new beard and waving a cigar giving orders, poor Lily's a perfect wreck, he's out there on the lawn right now playing with that horrid dog and there are travel brochures all over the place, he thinks we should all take a trip up the Nile and visit Luxor, the whole house smells like cabbage and... Well my God of course he's read it, he's reread it a thousand times since I brought it out here he must know it by heart, gestures and all you'd think it was Hamlet, licking his lips over every phrase and he'll stop to mutter the play's the thing to catch the conscience of the king of course he means Father, I showed him! as though he'd done it all himself and then this box of trout shows up with a... Of trout, a box of frozen Norwegian trout and a fatuous note dripping with congratulations, so pleased we could see this landmark case to a successful conclusion it's all perfectly revolting but of course money's the one thing on his mind now, how many million he's going to collect when they... oh. Oh, well I'll tell him that, God knows whether he can contain himself he wanted to go out and buy a new car just like ours this morning until I wait, wait there's somebody at the door, Lily? Will you see who that, what? About what billings Harry, you just said... well what in God's name has Trish got to do with it, Bill Peyton can't blame you if she hasn't even come up with her retainer yet can he? Tell him to talk to his brilliant Mister Mudpye he's the one who's been herding her through every courtroom from here to... well of course losing this appeal has cast a cloud over his brilliant career there, it should have brought down a thunderstorm, you're the one who said he was too quick aren't you? that he takes shortcuts? sets up the game as if he's the only player? did you ever tell Bill Peyton that? I mean my God Harry I don't care one damn about Mister Mudpye's brilliant career, after the ride he's given poor Oscar? I care about yours, I mean I'm your wife aren't I Harry? When will you be... what kind of a conference, you mean things can come to a screeching halt at the very last minute because somebody suddenly gets the bright idea for a settlement they could have come up with five years ago and the taxpayers pay for the whole idiotic perfor... No now listen Harry I mean I'm not entirely stupid. One of your socalled parties deducts millions in legal costs every year as a business expense and the other one has never paid taxes in its entire parasitic life then who makes up the difference? Who pays for these bombs and battleships and these fools with nothing better to do than play golf on the moon eating ham sandwiches while people are sleeping in the streets and, what is it Lily.

—They're delivering this big fish tank Oscar sent for and they want to know where to...

—Well for God's sake don't let them bring it in here, tell them to, Harry? I've got to go, they're delivering a... no, not more fish no a fish tank, an aquarium Oscar can't live without Harry take care of yourself please, please because the rest of it doesn't matter it's nonsense, millions of dollars of nonsense because I, because you matter Harry you matter to me and, and that's, yes I'm coming!

—I think Oscar wants it over by those windows where the...

—It is not going over by those windows! They can, tell them to put it down in the laundry where the, Oscar? as the doors clattered down the hall —and for God's sake leave the dog outside, they are not bringing your fish farm in here, it can go down...

—No but wait Christina, the fish like light and...

—Well put it in the sunroom! And close the door to the kitchen, the whole place smells like a tenement in Minsk it's like a scene out of, marching around in your father's old suit crowing over putting one over on him because you think he turned his back on you like one of those dreadful Karamazovs and tell Ilse to sew up the hem there, it's hanging loose in the back or just find a safety pin to go with that scraggly beard hiding the battle scar you were so proud of where nothing's left to hide. I mean maybe now you can shave and bathe and get a fresh start, I don't think you've slept since I got here.

—How could I! with this? he came brandishing the dogeared pages —God, how long I've waited. People spend their lives like that waiting for something to happen and change things, and they die like that, waiting.

—You'd better wait yourself before you take off for Luxor, that was Harry on the phone. He said they'll appoint a master to execute that decree you're waving around and compute your damages so don't start buying new cars, you don't know what you'll end up with. You've got a stack of bills over there to choke a horse while we sit here eating corned beef and cabbage as though we were living on that grand teaching salary of yours and now you haven't even got that.

—That salary! that miserable salary month after month just to remind me what injustice really was, this is worth all the salaries they ever paid Christina! I've earned it haven't I? slapping the pages against his opened hand, —living out here like beggars in this broken down old house with the wind coming in through the cracks in the wainscotting, feel it, right here you can feel it, the veranda caving in and the driveway out there like an obstacle course and those bills, yes, to get out of debt and to stay out! to make choices instead of being forced to them, will the car last as long as a new set of tires no, a new car new tires all of it new! his hands trembling, twisting up the pages —all of it...

—If you last as long as a new set of teeth with anything left after those bills you're so eager to pay, that crate of fish your friend Sam probably expects a check in the next mail.

—Fine. Let him have it, it's not my...

—My God Oscar, somebody you were ready to sue for malpractice ten minutes ago now you're ready to pay him God knows how much because he sends you a crate of dead fish? You've forgotten that battle royal right where you're standing? Harry trying to get him off the hook ends up in a car accident and the whole thing almost cost me my marriage, it was either fraud or negligence wasn't it? if it was true then it's just as true now isn't it? and you don't remember a word of it?

—I remember Harry said if I'd won it wouldn't have made any difference, now I've won haven't I? Besides, I don't...

—Care no, you don't care, pay him whatever he...

—I don't have to! That's what I'm trying to tell you Christina, they have to, it's out of my hands. Kiester and Erebus and the rest of them, they have to pay him it's right here in the decision, didn't you see it? riffling over coffee stains, tea streaks, wine washed declensions —right here at the end. The plaintiff will be awarded an attorney's fee in this court and in the court below both to be fixed by the district court upon there, billings disbursements depositions prepositions all of it, the more the better, limousines, airplanes, Mister Basie flying around the country buying drinks for the house in the Beverly Wilshire all of it, give them a nice tax writeoff isn't that what you said?

—It's revolting. It's all perfectly revolting.

—Well what's, why is it revolting what's...

—While he sits in prison somewhere making brooms for a dollar a day and you think that's all right?

—I didn't say it was right. It's the chance he took isn't it? Lying for his bar exam he knew he might get caught sooner or later didn't he? It's not my...

—He chanced it for you! He could have told you to take their settlement couldn't he? like I wanted you to, so did Harry and you would have too but he had more guts than any of us, sitting right there while we acted like mice, you mean you plan to lose I asked him? Win or lose, and that sweet smile of his, win or lose we'll take them on the appeal.

—And we did, it's only just isn't it? Where it says right here in the decree the district judge and counsel for plaintiff both overlooked the irrelevance of their defense? Sitting right there with the clock running every minute running up his billings and...

—And you think he ever saw one penny of it? Off God only knows where while Sam spends it salmon fishing in Norway I mean who ran up his billings, sitting here hour after hour reading your play to him and getting that gang from your classroom in to mumble the parts? My God what he put up with, because he cared about it Oscar, listening to you, reasoning with you he had more faith in it than all the rest of...

—No listen Christina, turning the whole thing upside down you...

—Like your new pal Jerry? Turning the whole thing upside down explaining to you what your own play is really all about? Blacks and Jews and God knows what else, breaking your bones while the man who really fought for you is...

—Well I can't help it! It's just the way the whole system works, there's nothing I can do about it is there? Besides we don't know he's in prison making brooms that's just something Harry said, he takes off right in the middle of things and you act like his keeper, off on the run he could be anywhere. He could be anywhere.

—On the run hunted down while Sam goes fishing and you sail up the Nile after all he did for you, think about it.

—Why! Nothing I can do, why should I think about it.

—Because he was your friend!

—But, no listen Christina don't get so upset, I...

—He was your friend Oscar! She'd found a wad of tissue somewhere, clearing her throat —I mean my God, how many have you got.

—Well I, I can't help what people will do, I...

—People will do anything. She blew her nose sharply, turned away gazing out over the pond, caught herself with a sniff —people will string up long underwear and smell up your house with oh, Lily. Will you tell me whose inspiration this corned beef and cabbage was?

—It was, it's something her sister, Ilse's sister it's something she likes to cook and she wanted to feel useful so...

—If you want to feel useful yourself I think I'd like a drink.

—There's those cases of wine Oscar ordered, do you...

—I said a drink Lily, there's some scotch isn't there? And pour one for yourself, if you still think you're seeing mice in the kitchen you probably need it.

And there was, as she said later, —enough to feed an army, or at least get that crew through the night, I mean of course they'll eat in the kitchen and if you brought her out here to peel potatoes and help with the laundry she's simply got to learn to use the dryer, the place looked like a Bedouin encampment drying their tents out there blown on the rising winds flinging gulls willy nilly against a grey sky heavy with the threat of snow where a ragged skein of wild ducks unraveled high above the blunt bursts of a shotgun somewhere down the pond all of it giving way to dark, and the stillness that finally shrouded the house itself till the day woke flaming the east like a cauldron, woke the thud and clamber of footsteps on bare floors and the stairs, his own muted in slippers pacing the room end to end with those stained pages clutched rolled like a stave freighted with anticipation simmering in his wake liable to any intrusion of triumph or calamity or sheer inconsequence, intimate or abruptly outlandish as the sparkling apparition of a police car standing there in the drive before his eyes.

—Oscar? came her voice from somewhere, near to following him up the hall when she came in but she stopped looking out up the angle of the veranda arrested there by the sight of the uniform, voices borne in on a draft from the doors till they clattered closed, —well? What was that all about.

—A policeman.

—Well obviously. Selling tickets to the policemen's ball?

—No, no they found the car, they found my car Christina. It's been impounded by the insurance company that's who took it away.

—Thank God, I hope we never have to...

—No but that's not the point, the police have a report that it was in an accident where the victim was seriously injured and they're after me because I'm the owner and didn't report it so...

—Well if nobody reported it then who reported it?

—I did, I reported the stolen car but the accident wasn't...

—Oh Lily, thank God bring a pot of tea will you? I don't know how much more of this I can go back to the beginning Oscar. When you were in the hospital raving about your little man in the black suit taking messages for the other side and...

—Don't talk about it no, I might have died I don't want to think about it, what if I'd died before all this happened! brandishing the tattered stave at her —and I'd never have...

—Well obviously if you'd died it wouldn't have happened.

—That's what I mean! My work, it would never be heard of, it would just disappear as though it had never existed, as though I'd never lived.

—Would it matter? I mean you'd be sitting over there on the other side happy as a clam wouldn't you? all this earthly nonsense of cars and lawsuits and the stupidity you despise so much...

—That's not it he said, pacing away and then more slowly, back to her —but it is, isn't it. Because my work, it would exist wouldn't it, its only claim to existence would be in this fraudulent counterfeit this, this vulgar distorted forgery and the thing itself, the original immortal thing itself would never be...

—Would it matter? She was off pounding sofa pillows into shape, setting them right, —meanwhile what do you plan to do about your stolen car and the...

—Christina I'm talking to you! I'm trying to talk about something that, can't you listen? for a minute?

—Well my God Oscar, that's what this world is isn't it? I mean you're not on the other side yet are you? Talking about immortality I've thought you always treated it as a monstrous joke, listening to that harangue with your new friend Jerry over which came first, madness or religion and this frenzy over God and the afterlife that's what they're all about isn't it? these hordes of people going to church on Sunday and your revolting movie travesty during the week? Is that what you...

—That's it yes! Sunday mass nailing down their immortality one day a week so they can waste the rest of it on trash, or the ones who squander it piling up money like a barrier against death while the artist is working on his immortality every minute, everything he creates, that's what his work is, his immortality and that's why having it stolen and corrupted and turned into some profane worthless counterfeit is the most, why it's sacrilege, that's what sacrilege really is isn't it? Isn't that really why I got into all this?

—Frankly Oscar, the way you've been waving that court decree around waiting to hear about your damages I thought it might have something to do with money.

—Well of course it does! Because that's the only language they understand, I've said that a thousand times haven't I? that that's the only way I can be vindicated?

—Meanwhile maybe you can help her with that tray, just put it down over there Lily. I heard the phone earlier, it wasn't Harry was it?

—I would have called you no, it was Daddy. He said there's something very important he has to talk to me about after all this trouble and everything since tragedy struck so it must be finally about we're going to get reconciled like I've been praying for.

—You? praying?

—No I just meant really hoping, you know.

—I'm afraid I do, you and Oscar here both being vindicated with a good price tag on it because that's what we're really talking about isn't it.

—Well that's, he just said they're coming up here him and Mama with something very important to talk about and...

—No no I agree, I mean my God there's nothing more important than a dollar in the bank to make people take you seriously is there Oscar, it's a language we all speak isn't it but they certainly can't stay here, the place is turning into a menagerie and that ghastly little dog, where is it.

—I think it's under that couch in the sunroom where I'm sleeping, it likes to get under things. I think it's scared of getting stepped on.

—I don't blame it with those two, what in God's name are they doing out there now.

—I think there's still all that corned beef and...

—No! the first thing in the morning, we've got to have a civilized meal in this house, we've got to go shopping the first thing in the morning.

It was Harry. On the phone? yes, first thing in the morning, seasoned from her end by little more than —my God, all of it? and —I shudder to think of it, you were right Harry yes, the person he thinks he is it's almost frightening but... Yes I'll tell him that... I'll tell him that yes, if I can just make it penetrate God knows what he'll... yes, it's frightening... and she hung up the phone both hands holding it down as though it might erupt again before she could temper her voice with the calm that filled her gaze out there over the pond where a serenity of swans skirted the skin of ice left by the night, clearing her throat to call —Oscar? waiting, and again, back on the sofa —Oscar?

—Yes he's coming, came from far down the hall, from the sunroom —wait a second, let me button this back up, and fix your pants.

—Where were you? when he appeared, straightening his collar.

—Just, in the library looking for, you remember this letter? had it in his hand in fact, —from this lawyer named Preswig? That's why they took the car, the insurance company, because we're suing them as the accident victim so I'd better call him so he can call the police before they arrest me.

—Please, sit down for a minute. No one's going to arrest you.

—A hit and run accident, that's what the police...

—Will you please sit down? But he was already at the phone, gasping, muttering, finally banging it down. —Well?

—Mister Preswig is no longer with us they said, of all the, and that summons I got where's that summons, because if the insurance company is suing the...

—Oscar listen to me! They've settled your damages.

—But the hospital bills and what about the car, they...

—I'm not talking about your car. I'm talking about your immortal soul, now sit down. Harry called. You've been awarded all the profits on the motion picture The Blood in the Red White and Blue.

—But that's, Christina that's millions.

—Now listen, sit down. Harry said that of course they'll...

—But that's millions! I can't sit down no, Lily? That's millions Christina, those newspaper clippings when it opened where are they, you remember it gave all those box office figures the first week it, where is she. Lily!

—For God's sake stop shouting. It's not over with, can you just sit down for a minute and let that penetrate? Harry said of course they'll appeal the master's decision to try to get the award reduced and...

—Yes call Harry, why didn't you call me? Let me call Harry and...

—He's not there Oscar, he was in a hurry. He had to get this company helicopter up to Westchester for one of these endless conferences, now...

—Oscar? are you okay?

—He's not okay Lily, he's about to go through the ceiling, now...

—But it's millions! All the profits, the court's awarded me all the profits suppose they do reduce it a little it's millions, it's still millions isn't it? isn't that what I said? that that's the only language they understand? Now where's the, where's my, what was I looking for.

—God only knows, that summons? Have you looked in this mess on the sideboard? Bills, statements, travel folders, glossy new car brochures and—what's this.

—Oh that's this little package that came for Oscar yesterday, I just put it there and forgot to...

—Well give it to me! but she'd already torn it open. —It's mine Christina give it to me!

—I don't believe it.

—No listen, I just sent away for them to see what they...

—I don't believe it. Hiawatha's Magic Mittens, made from genuine simulated my God Oscar. Wear 'em with the furside there isn't any furside, they're plastic. Your own personalized pair of look at them, they're for a six year old and look. A little song book. Your own book of brand new songs to sing when you put on Minjekahwun and set forth to do battle with the West Wind, with the mighty Mudjekeewis, when you rend the jutting crag of the fatal black rock Wawbeek I mean my God, you're not six years old any more are you?

—I said they're mine! Give them to me, now I can, listen. I can settle things once for all now can't I? so I won't owe Father a thing? I can buy this place myself so he can't sell it right out from under us, it was never really his anyway was it? so we won't have the bank and the mortgage and repair the veranda, put in a new driveway and that real estate woman peeking in the windows whenever we, listen. Listen, call her, tell her I'm prepared to make an offer who is she, I'll call her myself.

—Oscar sit down! You're not calling anyone, you're not prepared to make an offer on an old shoe, I told you Harry said it's not over with didn't I? that they're figuring out ways right now to get your award reduced? I mean Father's got enough on his plate with this Senate committee and the mess in his courtroom over this wrongful death case, apparently that insane law clerk is sending you a copy of his instructions to the jury just to make things more difficult for everyone since that seems to be his main purpose in life and, what is it now Lily.

—That's where Reverend Bobby Joe is at that trial because that's why Daddy's coming up here so we can get reconciled without him making restitution to the Lord with his hand on my...

—For God's sake be still, go and see if the mail's come yet will you? And here, hand him these damn mittens and his little book, if he's going to sing a dirge for the mighty Mudjekeewis he'll need them.

INSTRUCTIONS TO THE JURY

In the case of Fickert v. Ude, U.S. District Court, S.D. Va. Misc. 88687

CREASE, DISTRICT JUDGE

You have heard a suit for damages in a case alleging wrongful death brought by the plaintiff Earl Fickert, of Hog Corners, Mississippi, against the defendant Rev. Elton Ude, residing in this federal jurisdiction, for the loss of plaintiff's minor child Wayne Fickert, on October 25, 1985.

As members of the jury and thus of this court, you have been offered evidence by both parties which it will be your duty to sift through for the facts. During these deliberations, you will also consider the sometimes conflicting testimony of the many witnesses which will be yours to evaluate according to your best judgment, unclouded by either prejudice or sentiment.

You understand that this is a civil and not a criminal case. In other words, it is a suit brought by one private citizen against another, and the fact that a death is involved does not mean that the defendant, if found guilty, would be subject to criminal penalties leading to his imprisonment or worse, but limited to the payment of money damages to the plaintiff. Before you retire, it is my duty to assist your deliberations by providing you with the controlling points of law which must guide you in reaching your verdict, to the exclusion of all other considerations.

On the unchallenged evidence there is no doubt that the decedent suffered death by drowning, having delivered himself into the hands of the defendant for immersion in the flowing waters of the Pee Dee River for the purpose of baptism in the Christian faith according to usage and custom, and that he was abruptly borne away by the river's current in the course of this ordeal which he did not survive.

You have heard the tragic event recounted in some detail by the defendant, and you may review his testimony in the light of that of other witnesses and of the evidence. On no account, however, are you to allow either the emotional outbursts from the spectators attending this trial, notably that provoked by defendant's son resulting in the courtroom being cleared, or any stories, gossip or other innuendo you may have encountered in the past regarding defendant's earlier alleged adventures with the law, to influence your deliberations.

We repeat, this is not a trial for murder or even manslaughter. There has been no evidence or even a suggestion of deliberate intent on defendant's part to harm the victim of this unfortunate episode. Thus, you are asked first to determine the actual cause of death and its relation to the possibility of negligence on defendant's part in the event. Clearly the testimony of one witness, for example, in an effort to simplify matters with the words "he just got drownded" will not suffice. The medical reports do indeed verify drowning as the proximate cause of death, but was there an intervening cause beyond the control of the defendant which might have brought this about?

Let us suppose your near neighbor lights a bonfire during a strong wind which blows sparks onto your property, setting fire to your house. You would certainly find him negligent, not to say stupid, in that he should have known better. But suppose the day he lights his fire is still and calm, and only later a high wind suddenly rises carrying the fire's embers to your house and property with the same result. This is known as an intervening cause, since it acts upon a situation orginating with your neighbor but, as he would certainly argue, with a result he had not anticipated. How long had he lived there, and how familiar was he with the vicissitudes of the weather you inevitably shared, where a high wind might suddenly come up from nowhere on the finest of days? In other words, the standard of law regarding negligence embraces the idea of a risk to others which can be foreseen by a reasonable man, since if he cannot anticipate any harm coming from his actions, he can't be held liable for injuries that may result. Is the Pee Dee River known for sudden surges of its current at this particular site, in certain seasons, or at certain times of day, sufficient to sweep away the thrashing figure of an eighty pound boy? Or was this an abrupt departure from the river's habits brought on by flooding in the waters above, or by some other mighty force?

These factors are part of the evidence before you together with the defendant's testimony, supported by a veritable horde of witnesses, that innumerable such baptisms have been conducted at this site without dire consequences, and you are instructed to disregard as irrelevant that testimony citing the death of an unattended cow, two dogs, and the handful of pigs rumoured to have accommodated Jesus in Matthew 8:32 as latter day hosts to devils rushed to their destruction in these waters.

While under the law a suit for negligence places the burden of the standard of care on the defendant, it may also rest on another foot, however small, in this case that of the decedent Little Wayne as he was known to the community. How aware was he of the risk to himself posed by this ceremony, and whatever the degree or lack of his awareness did he consent to his part in it freely and voluntarily? There is a basic principle of the common law expressed in the Latin tongue as volenti non fit injuria. That means no wrong is done to someone who is willing, and if you know there are risks the law can't protect you from your own foolishness if you go ahead with it. From the evidence and testimony of witnesses, the decedent readily consented to undertake his part in this fatal ordeal, that he enthusiastically and even joyously embraced the prospect of baptism in the Lord's service and had, in fact, looked forward to that transforming moment from the tender age of four. Under the circumstances we cannot, of course, hear his own testimony as to his awareness, or the lack of it, of any risk he might face, and here the law is our guide.

Under the laudable doctrine of this venerable Christian sect from which it takes its name, baptism is deferred until an age when the candidate is believed able to understand the depths of this commitment, unlike those widespread cults of mainly foreign origin wherein infants are handed over to the designs of the Almighty well before they are weaned. Under the law, the age at which an individual is considered capable of the assumption of risk has varied from one court to another and is often set at fourteen, but it is usually a question for the jury to decide. In doing so however, the jury must realize that if he is capable of understanding the risk involved and goes ahead with it anyhow, he will share in the responsibility for its consequences, in this case his own destruction. This is called contributory negligence, and will largely relieve the defendant of his own. On the other hand, given the facts of a situation containing elements of duress, in other words of various pressures from family, friends and the community which a minor finds himself unable to resist, he has in effect been given a choice of evils by the defendant, and while his conduct may indicate his consent, the facts in the situation may persuade us otherwise. Consequently, the court here instructs the jury to find that the decedent will be found not to have assumed the risk, or to have relieved the defendant of the duty to protect him.

In discharging this duty of care placed on him by the law, we have no evidence that the defendant knowingly misrepresented any aspect of the situation to the decedent. Due to the swift current and the suddenness of its action we see no indication of a last clear chance when the decedent might have been saved or have saved himself. We have only conflicting testimony as to whether the defendant knew the boy could not swim, and the suggestion that alcohol may have played a part in the defendant's conduct has been stricken from the record. There are certain things we can never know, and during your deliberations you are urged to bear in mind the words of an eminent jurist of a bygone era. 'The law,' wrote Justice Holmes, 'takes no account of the infinite varieties of temperament, intellect, and education which make the internal character of a given act so different in different men. It does not attempt to see men as God sees them, for more than one sufficient reason.'

Thus far we have gone on the premise that the defendant acted entirely on his own. At the same time however, we are all aware that he has never presented himself to this court, to the decedent or to the world at large as other than a willing and devoted servant of a most demanding master, to whom his life and works are dedicated. He is widely held as a servant in the Lord's employ, and a diligent member of his working staff.

We reach far back in the history of English law, from which we draw our own, for the doctrine linking the master to damage and injury caused by his servant, and holding the master liable even when done intentionally, so long as it was carried out within the scope of the servant's employment. While we have before us neither direct testimony from the defendant's employer, nor any means of obtaining it, regarding the terms or even the fact of this employment, the defendant's own sworn statement to having been 'called' into the Lord's service is uncontested. He has elsewhere been reported to have spoken directly with his employer, and referred to in contemporary accounts of the event before us as 'the dynamic leader of Christian Recovery for America's People' in his call for 'the opening salvo in God's eternal war against the forces of superstition and ignorance throughout the world and elsewhere.' There can be no question that, in bringing a new soul into the fold through the baptismal ceremony, he was engaged on his master's business much as, we may recall in Luke 2:49, this selfsame master at age twelve found lagging behind at the temple in Jerusalem by his anxious parents, rebuked them saying 'Wist ye not that I must be about my Father's business?' and not, in the words of a later English jurist, 'going on a frolic of his own.' In carrying out this solemn assignment, even were there reliable testimony that this omniscient master must have been aware of the risk and told his servant to act carefully, the law still holds him liable for a prevailing share in the consequences. In other words, the master may not delegate responsibility for the servant's acts to him, since under the terms of their relationship he remains ultimately responsible for protecting his servant. This must hold the more true where the instrument of imminent catastrophe is the master's to control, as must the crest and current of the Pee Dee River have been for one who had shown himself capable of stilling a great tempest to save a ship from foundering by merely rebuking the winds and the sea in Matthew 8:26, with which I am sure you are all familiar.

In pursuing your deliberations, I must pause to recall your attention to one more item of testimony which you are instructed to disregard. That is the heated attempt by one witness to indict Satan for meddling in this situation, drawn from the evidence of contemporary records quoting defendant's mention of 'the great deceiver Satan' causing him to doubt the Lord's purpose. As was held in an earlier case before a district court in Pennsylvania, in which the plaintiff accused Satan of ruining his prospects by placing obstacles in his path, thereby depriving him of his constitutional rights, the complaint was dismissed for its failure to discover Satan's residence within the judicial district, or instructions for the U.S. Marshal needed to serve the summons, and the failure to meet legal requirements necessary to maintain a probable class action, since the class would be so numerous that getting them all together for this purpose would be impractical. I may add that this information could be useful to any of you contemplating a similar recourse in your own difficulties, as the commotion which greeted this testimony in the courtroom provoked by defendant's son indicated to be a serious possibility.

While the allocation of damages should not be allowed to direct your verdict, you must be clear on the law as it views these matters. In general, the damages awarded to the legal beneficiaries in the death of a child are based on his earnings, services and contributions at the time, and more problematically on the loss of whatever prospective economic benefits he might have been expected to provide had his life not been cut short. This is governed by such elements as life expectancy, health, habits, character, and perhaps particular talents in profitable fields of enterprise. It is quite possible for the cost of rearing, maintaining and educating a child to outweigh the expected benefits, leaving him for all practical purposes worthless. Furthermore, since awards for sentimental family relationships are generally forbidden, and survivors may not seek damages for mental suffering or grief, he may even end with a negative value, going so far as to tempt the defendant, where contributory negligence is involved, to turn the tables and sue for recovery himself.

The future of each mortal being is wrapped in an impenetrable mist, most especially that of a boy who has scarcely embarked upon life's journey. In the annals of law we find, here a substantial award made for a boy of seven who showed promise as a cartoonist, there for another the near certainty of an impressive income in his consuming ambition to become a dentist. Still, in a country where a chief executive is paid a million dollars' salary for managing an automobile company that loses a billion that same year, the odds are hard to call. The decedent might one day have abandoned his calling and, like Babbitt, found it elsewhere in the malodorous realm of real estate development, might have become a writer at the mercy of publishers and starved in a garret or ended it on the spot, might have been lost at sea or gone up as a soldier, become a drunkard and a public charge. We can only speculate with the evidence before us.

The decedent's earnings at the time of death had been gained mainly by picking berries, and his carefully husbanded estate amounted to $4.36, having bought new clothing especially for the baptismal ceremony from his own savings. This earthly estate would appear to corroborate the testimony we have heard quoting Matthew 6:19–21, that he was unconcerned with laying up treasures on earth but rather 'in heaven, where neither moth nor rust doth corrupt, and where thieves do not break through nor steal: for where your treasure is, there will your heart be also.' In the defendant's testimony from the record at the time of the event, 'recalling the day Wayne Fickert made his decision for Christ,' he saw him 'going forth one day from the Christian Recovery Bible Mission School to take the Lord's word to the very farthest reaches of the world.' There, high in the Himalayas, he might have been a priest aspiring to no more than a begging bowl; elsewhere, in the urban din below, he might have pursued the course of rabbi looking forward to a hundred thousand a year; but the humble faith of his fathers, who appear to have been numerous, promised no such economic benefits in computing an award for damages to the survivors since you must exclude from your deliberations any speculation involving the vast sums accumulated by those in the Lord's service who are currently in jail for confusing his assets with their own, or even those still at large living on the scale of the automobile executive who, like the elder John D Rockefeller teaching his Sunday school classes, regard themselves simply as the Lord's stewards.

Under the State of South Carolina statutes authorizing civil actions for wrongful acts causing death, such actions shall be for the benefit, among other relatives not here represented, 'of the parent or parents, and if there be none such' for the heirs at law and so forth. Both parents are parties to this action, the father Earl Fickert as plaintiff, and by joinder the boy's mother Billye. You are here instructed to dismiss the latter's claim on the grounds of contributory negligence on her part, in the assumption of risk in providing her consent as evidenced at the time by 'her tearful gratitude that her son had been baptized and entered the waiting arms of the Lord in a state of grace,' and on the further grounds of her remarriages since the event, reclaiming her name as the boy's mother for the sole purpose of participating in this action.

Damages will go to the original plaintiff, whose scurrilous testimony and profane demeanor throughout the trial leave no doubt that consent to his son's baptism, had he known of it, must have been the last thing in what we may arguably call his mind. The amount of the award will not be diminished by the usual claims for medical and funeral expenses, there having been none for the former and the latter, including the fried chicken and refreshments served for the occasion, were assumed by the defendant's assembled congregation. This leaves only the loss of the boy's clothing, a blue suit, shirt and tie bought at a cost of $18.76 at JC Penney which he insisted upon wearing under his baptismal smock, and the award will be made in that amount plus one dollar for punitive damages.

—Laying up treasures in heaven! did you see that Christina? He wouldn't read my play, no, but that's where he got it, he took it right out of my prologue.

—It's faintly possible he's read the Bible himself Oscar. I mean he's had ninety five years to get through it hasn't he?

—Well he, all right then maybe the Old Testament, the last thing he did was throw God out of his courtroom and you saw what happened, now he's bringing Jesus in at the back door. He doesn't even get through the third book of the New Testament does he? leading this jury by the hand like kindergartners on a field trip so he can point the finger right at him? Master and servant, master and man, he's just trying to stir them up.

—But he already did Oscar, came from the sofa in the flickering light of the silenced screen where a leggy blonde who had found relief from hemorrhoids cycled down a country lane and passed them beaming —when Daddy called last night? and he said they're coming up here without Reverend Bobby Joe because your daddy put him in jail for thirty days for contempt of court for getting up and shouting for the Lord Jesus to come and...

—Well my God Lily Father would give Jesus thirty days if he could, are you watching that thing? If you're not turn it off, now what is this mess.

—No wait, those are plants for my fish tank.

—Then take them in and plant them, now what about this heap...

—First I have to fix the light in it and the aerator and...

—I said what are you going to do with this heap of mail, look at it. Everybody on earth must have read about your great award.

—I've looked at it Christina. That's why I'm getting a secretary.

—That's ridiculous, Lily can read can't she? You can open an envelope can't you Lily? doing so herself, —the National Speakers Association invites you to join our panel of distinguished Americans who are in constant demand for speaking engagements and God help us, I hope you've learned that lesson, what you need is a wastebasket. As a high achiever who appreciates the finer things in life, you are invited to join a select circle of...

—Will you just stop standing there and tearing things up? There might be something important.

—A pre-approved credit line with a string of Handichecks for your immediate convenience, do you need a secretary simply to throw things away? What we need is a housekeeper, loading those two on that bus for the Bronx was the happiest day of my life. You can boil a lobster can't you Lily, after that revolting trout we deserve something civilized, I mean what we need is a cook. Now, with a sweep of her emptied hand —will you clean up all that before I lose my mind? All that, before a bottle of Chablis smoothed their way for the lobster, butter running down his thumb onto the white tablecloth, before the light and the aerator were installed and the plants submerged in the tank, before another delivery brought more bills and anonymous personalized invitations and a script indecently titled from a playwriting hopeful thirsting for production and before another rushed a lone angelfish in a plasticized transparency to take up residence among the water sprite and Ludwigia and wavering fronds of Spatterdock enveloped in silence and the eerie illumination neither day nor night, spooky was the word for it as his hand glided over her breasts, now could he feel it? in a whisper, the lump there? because it seemed to have moved, as his hand did preoccupied elsewhere, as hers did now filling with promise abruptly kept with a gasp and a shudder echoed in a moan before he rose from her unsteadily to find the stairs in the dark with the stealth of a schoolboy, all that before the night winds rose with a moaning echo down the chimney blowing in a new day.

Tea, and toast, —and this, she said, holding out the shred of something, —it was on the floor in there.

—Well what is it.

—Those mittens, he chewed up those dumb magic mittens.

—Well my God don't tell Oscar, I'd forgot all about him. Where is he, have you looked for him?

—He's usually under something. Pookie? trailing her voice down the hall, peering under things, and on into the kitchen where —it must have choked, discovered rigid behind the kitchen stove —right where I keep seeing this mouse. She's never even called.

—She will Lily. She will.

And when, eventually, she did, —Who? No this is Lily... Oh hi, sure I remember, that day you came out here with that big picnic and that man with the... with a little white dog? No, I... Oh. Oh, well maybe if you advertise in the paper, they... No I just thought if he was worth a lot maybe somebody kidnaped him and...

—Here, give me that. Trish? what... oh. Oh what a shame... No I, but he, I mean he must be around somewhere, he... and you're sure you didn't take him to Aspen? Maybe he's right there at Bunker's, I mean you ought to have another look before you call in private detectives he, he might be under something, maybe Jerry... Oh. Oh my God... about losing his job yes but why in God's name is he angry at Oscar, I mean... No that's the most ridiculous thing I ever heard, he hasn't spoken to his father in ages and... but... No, but... Trish it's the most ridiculous thing I've ever heard it's absolutely paranoid, he's... I said he's more than just a little bit crazy, that show he put on out here breaking Oscar's bones you were here Trish, you were right here and... Who, Oscar? now wait a... Wait just a minute Trish! Of course Oscar's a bit eccentric but for you to use a word like... Certainly not! and I don't want to hear another... Well I'm sure you'll find it, just keep looking under things! and their eyes met the moment she hung up, holding each other's steadily until she said —what did you do with it.

—I threw it in the pond.

And she sat there simply tapping her foot until the tight line of her lips broke with —Well. Here's the mad poet himself.

—Was that call for me?

—It was not.

—No but listen, I'm expecting a call from...

—I just said it was not didn't I! My God, putting up with this nonsense day after day, your friend Jerry thinks there's a conspiracy. He thinks Father wrote the brief for your appeal, it was much too clever and thorough for the young country lawyer who showed up there in the appeals court so he checked and found he was from Father's jurisdiction and the whole thing turns into a conspiracy, I mean isn't that what paranoia is simply all about?

—But what do you mean, it turns into a conspiracy. That day he came out here and we talked about my play and the...

—Between you and Father! He thinks you think the way he would, he's giving you credit for being much more cunning than you really are that's why he's outraged, because you took him in, because you put one over on him pretending you didn't know anything about it when you'd already gone to Father for help and you and Father set up the whole thing.

—But I, it never occurred to me, I...

—And why didn't it! Marching around here with your magic mittens and the whole, I told you to call him didn't I?

—But I still don't see what the, why did he call you, why would Mudpye call you and make up something like...

—Did I say that? You don't listen, did I say he'd called me? Trish called, it was Trish more muddled than ever babbling away with a drink or two because dear Jerry lost the appeal and is losing his bonus and may lose his job till I had to hang up, babbling on about appeals and briefs she doesn't know a brief from a, from a banana it's all nonsense. It's all perfect nonsense.

—But maybe, listen Christina maybe Harry can find out what it's all about couldn't he? Can you call him and...

—My God if he was in town do you think I'd be sitting here with you two? He's in a motel up in Westchester standing by at these idiotic conferences doing exactly nothing but running up the client's billings and...

—Listen...

—propping up Bill Peyton in the cocktail lounge with some topless...

—I said listen! Will you listen to me? can't you see what happened? that he did it himself, can't you see? That Father exploded when he got hold of that lower court decision and tore their case to pieces in a brief he sent some local lawyer up here to the appeals court with? He didn't even, there didn't have to be any conspiracy he just did it! God that's what he's like isn't it? He doesn't conspire he doesn't have to conspire with anybody even with me, I told you he'd read it didn't I? my play, I always knew he'd really read it but never told me, he never really told me anything even when I, when he knew I was digging in the chair cushions for change that fell out of his pockets, I know he knew but he never said anything and that made it worse, I'd just see him looking at me sometimes like he did that terrible day with the birch tree and that made it worse listen, listen I've got to call him. I've got to call him I, how badly I...

—Oscar wait, will you just sit down and try to think it through before you do anything? But he was already up punching numbers, spilling the phone, muttering broken syllables into it and finally standing there intent, his shoulders fallen hanging it up. —Why don't you sit down and make sure of the number while you...

—Of course it was the right number, after all these years? It was just some, his law clerk's out sick and that was some bailiff or something, he's in court, he's on the bench says this loafer and just hangs up before I can leave a message, it was always like that. Even when I'd leave a message I never knew if Father got it, even back then when I'd call and call I never knew if he heard me and now, and now...

—And now will you please just sit still and try to collect yourself? I mean after all you're just guessing aren't you? Will you wait till you can find out what really happened? wait till Harry's turned loose and can take time to get it all straight before you...

—But I've waited! Waiting on Harry waiting on Sam I thought it was some lawyer of Sam's but then Harry said no, no that's what's so terrible I've waited! Mudpye and Harry and Sam and, yes and Basie all of them with some patched up ideas while Father's been there standing by me all the time! He's kept his faith in me when I'd lost mine in him and, and the things I've said, a lot on his plate of course he's got a lot on his plate when I thought he'd turned his back on me because I wasn't worth his, because I wasn't, I wasn't was I! his face gone suddenly buried in his hands —God I, I'm just so ashamed.

—Oscar... both of them at once, but he broke away from their hands on him, one on a wrist, one seized on a quivering shoulder,

—Listen! We'll get it produced. Did I tell you? I didn't tell you did I, in yesterday's paper this project of his has fallen through, the School for Scandal because Nipples wanted to use the English actor from the London production they'd called splendid and unforgettable over there but American Actors' Equity said he was too obscure to merit a work permit for Broadway and he'd have to use an American actor so he quit, he just canceled the whole thing that means he's free! That means the biggest director in the whole English speaking theatre and with his name we won't have any trouble renting a theatre and getting it produced, that's a nice irony isn't it? Mudpye himself out here telling me it should be up there on the stage just the way I wrote it before they turned it into that cheap parody on the screen?

—Cheap? And what makes you think the backers for this classic English revival will put their money into some Civil War hodgepodge by somebody they've never...

—We don't need them! We don't need their money Christina and don't call it a hodgepodge! I can put up the backing myself can't I? All those dreams I had of taking Father to opening night, we talked about it once remember? when I told you why I wrote it in the first place? why I wanted to do something that would please him, that would make him proud of me sitting there together on opening night the way I wrote it celebrating our history and Grandfather getting to the heart of everything we, of everything and all this time, all this time he's had more faith than I have and now I can make it up, all my miserable doubts in him I can atone for all of it, this whole glorious production up there on the stage with Quantness and the stars glittering over the battlefield for Bagby's soliloquy at the second act curtain, with a Giulielma who's not some slut but the desolate girl the way I wrote her all of it, all of it the way I wrote it and the prison scene in the last act, Kane in prison in the last act not some Jewish peddler but man's whole shattered conscience, the moral imperative the way I wrote him before they stole it, all the profits! That's the irony, that's the delicious irony, the profits from this revolting travesty backing this whole real spectacle of justice and war and destiny and human passion, not the passion of a gang rape or...

—Speaking of delicious irony, what are we doing about dinner.

—What do you, Christina I'm talking about something!

—So am I Oscar. I mean my God it's turning into a lecture, it's a shame you can't see the movie yourself and join that panel of distinguished Americans in constant demand for speaking engagements to ladies' clubs in Des Moines on the corruption of lust and language and true human passion in a movie you haven't even seen?

—I don't have to see it! I'm talking about the passion of ideas not her hands down there unbuttoning his trousers making a man of him, the passion of the whole riddle of human existence and...

—So are they Oscar.

—And why can't I see it, I told you I'm getting a car didn't I? a new car? If it's not showing out here we can drive into town and see it, Harry's not there we can all stay at your place while I look up John Nipples and...

—You can't stay there Oscar, Harry may be through any day and you can't see the movie, neither can your ladies in Des Moines, nobody can.

—What do you mean, it's the biggest box office success in...

—The injunction against exhibitors distributors Kiester and all of them from showing it till this mess is...

—What injunction, what...

—Your injunction Oscar. You got all the profits you also got an injunction against showing it till this whole mess is cleaned up.

—But the, wait what about my, if it's not showing anywhere what about my profits!

—Exactly. Now why don't you sit down and collect yourself before you ride off in all directions renting theatres and buying new cars till you know what you're doing, get things straightened out with Father. That's what you've been carrying on about isn't it?

—Yes and Oscar it's not the money anyway is it, it's like Daddy coming up here for us to get reconciled after everything got all screwed up with these misunderstandings where everything just kept getting worse like you and your daddy and maybe even he and Daddy could get together and we could all have this wonderful recon...

—Lily will you be still! Not about money my God, I mean you're as bad as he is, all this handwringing and tears and carrying on about atonement and getting reconciled while he's standing here trying to reconcile all the profits and you're whining about that insurance on the death instrument the day tragedy struck of course it's about money! That's all it's about, that's all anything's about, now we've got that small roasting chicken haven't we? It ought to go in the oven unless we all plan to starve to death here nibbling the crumbs of Oscar's delicious immortality, destiny and passion and the riddle of human existence what we need is a cook.

—Oh look, look!

—My God Lily what is it now.

—No out there Christina, look. Look, it's snowing.

And where they looked next morning the frozen pond was gone in an unblemished expanse of white under a leaden sky undisturbed by the flight of a single bird in the gelid stillness that had descended to seize every detail of reed and branch as though time itself were frozen out there threatening the clatter of teacups and silver and the siege of telephoning that had already begun with —well when, just tell me when I can talk to him, will you tell him I called? as he slammed it down. —His law clerk, I think he'd been drinking.

—At this hour?

—At any hour, working for Father for forty years you could get in the habit. I ask him about my appeal and sending that lawyer up here with the brief and he just chuckles and tells me Father's ripping his knickers on this idiotic Cyclone Seven case and asks if I got those jury instructions in the case of the boy that got drownded and whether I've seen any good movies lately, I couldn't even...

—What was the name of that lawyer in your accident case, this last letter you got? she broke through a rustle of newspaper without listening, —did you see this?

—What. It was Jack, Jack something...

—Preswig? thrusting the pages at him, —This may interest you.

—Wait, I need my glasses.

—You need a handkerchief, I think you're getting a cold. Your friend Mister Preswig was arrested for digging a three foot pothole in the middle of the night up on Third Avenue where a client had had a serious accident, maybe that's why the girl told you he's no longer with us.

—But he, they sent me a bill yesterday for sixteen hun...

—What did you expect, you're suing the hit and run driver who ran over you aren't you?

—No I'm suing his, I mean my, I'm suing the insurance company for the owner of the car who are suing the, I think they're suing the dealer, the original dealer who's suing the car's maker it's all in the letter I got with this bill about a postponement for that summons to appear as a witness against the, I'd better call them... and the siege went on, from —Mister Mohlenhoff? This is... well can you tell me when he'll be in? to —Nipples yes, I'm trying to reach Sir John Nip... well can you tell me when he'll be in? his voice growing hoarse as the day wore on, —then can you simply tell them I called! till the one time it rang back just at suppertime, —It's always at suppertime, hello? And when he joined them at the table a minute later, —some idiot doing a survey in our area who understands I am the owner of a house with a septic tank.

—The veal's a little dry Lily, do you think we could have some more wine?

—Oh. It's right here, it gets dark so early it's like eating in the middle of the night, seizing his wrist bolt upright there in the eerie light of the fish tank with —What's that! It was nothing he told her, a woodpecker out on the shingles. —Well it scared me. Why do you always have to go upstairs after, that dumb fish staring at us and this spooky tap tap tap out there like the police in the movie just before they broke the door down all of it scares me, it might be Al out there why can't you go to sleep right here, I mean by now she knows what we do in here doesn't she? Can't you, no here, give me your hand. There. Feel it?

—Well for God's sake Lily see a doctor, came at her next morning over burnt crusts of the last of the bread and the scrapings of ginger preserve, —you've heard of a mammogram haven't you? Is Oscar down yet? as though that might have made any difference, day fading into day like the snow receding, porous and pocked by the passage of rabbits, gone altogether with a night of rain leaving the yellowed grass of the lawn where a squirrel came scratching haphazard, cocked upright its tail atremor with indecision and off again on some frantic search of its own, leaving her gazing out over the still pond where two, three white tail deer broke cover on the opposite shore and were gone, her hands twisting one in the other behind her, —it's the waiting, the waiting, vulnerable to any such intrusion of sheer inconsequence, of triumph or calamity as abruptly outlandish by the time the day's light had begun to fade as the still apparition of a car standing there deep green in the drive square before her eyes —my God! Harry? Where are you.

—He called while you were up taking a...

—He's here Lily, where is he.

—He can't be, he called while you were up taking a bath and said he'd be out day after...

—He's here, our car standing out there can't you see it? God I hope nothing's wrong, he...

—But it's not. It's Oscar's.

—What's Oscar's.

—That new car out there, they delivered it while you were up taking a...

—It can't be! catching her balance on the arm of the sofa where she came down heavily, —that's the most ridiculous, where is he.

—He's in there laying down with his cold, it's practically laryngitis he can hardly...

—Will you simply tell me what's going on here! He can't buy a car, he hasn't got the money to buy a car like that what do you mean Harry called, why didn't you call me.

—Because he was in this real hurry, all he wanted to say was to tell you he'd be...

—He said he's coming out here?

—That's what I'm telling you, can't you just listen! He's coming out tomorrow with something about Oscar's appeal he said may not please him so not to get into it with Oscar before he talks to him so he doesn't get the wrong idea with them showing the movie on television and all that.

—And all what! on television my God how did, when.

—I don't know, he didn't...

—Well can't you look in the paper? Where's the paper.

—I don't know, he just said Oscar ought to be restrained till...

—From what, out buying new cars without even, that car out there how can he pay for it, he can't even...

—All he said was they just needed the down payment and he was in there looking in the trash for those Handichecks you threw out.

—Where's the paper. It's not on tonight is it? Ought to be restrained my God, he doesn't know about it yet does he? I mean don't mention it to him till we have to or he won't be fit to live with.

—You know what I bet you a dollar? with an abrupt clatter of heels toward the hall leaving open the odds and the hazard itself so certain of returning a minute later with the winning hand holding —the paper, see? blazoning it forth paged open to Gala Television Premiere, the magnificent soul searing Civil War epic starring Robert Bredford and —see? He's already seen it.

—What did he say, when is it.

—He's asleep. It's not till tomorrow.

—Thank God. And I mean don't wake him up she said, her voice drowning with exhaustion like the day out there draining away over the pond, the same words lain in wait through the night to charge daybreak with a burst of panic —for God's sake don't wake him up! where she stood holding the phone, —Harry? I don't know what we'll tell him just hurry, as soon as you can yes just hurry! hanging it up —now, the paper, where is it.

—Right there where we were looking at it yester...

—Today's! Today's paper has it come yet? My God Lily don't stand there, get a coat and go out for it! Quickly! doing up the dishabille of the gown she'd slept in with the same distracted intensity she'd turn to the pages of the paper now she had her hands on it, —the obituary page, you've got the business section there, look in the index.

—Is this it?

—Yes, give it to me yes she said almost a whisper, sinking back on the sofa —this is it, staring as fixed as the black words staring back at her there, THOMAS L. CREASE, 97, VETERAN JURIST, the unsparing finality of the bold letters belying the hesitating retinue of finer shades in the halftone likeness peering over her shoulder at —Lily? will you, just make some tea will you?

—I put the water on. He looks real young doesn't he.

—Well my God it's an old picture, I mean it was probably taken before you were born. Judge Thomas L. Crease, a veteran of almost a half century on the Federal bench and the son of a legendary Supreme Court justice for whom he clerked as a youth, died yesterday in his chambers at the district court here. He was ninety seven years old and succumbed to a massive heart attack, according to his law clerk who was with him at the time. As highly regarded by his colleagues for his wide grasp and strict interpretation of constitutional law as for the fastidious language with which he framed that idiot, why didn't he call us! With him at the time, he could have picked up the phone right there in the Judge's chambers and called us couldn't he? What time is it now, I'll try to call him before we have Oscar on our hands here, I don't think we need to tell him just yet Lily. For his own sake, God knows what state he's in and Harry's coming out, I think we can wait till then when I've talked to this law clerk, he probably sat right down and poured a stiff drink when it happened thank God he didn't call, he would have got Oscar and we would have been up all night weeping and wailing, I mean it had to happen sooner or later there's nothing to go to pieces about, he was almost a hundred years old wasn't he? Where are you going, you're not going to wake him up are you?

—No, I think the water's boiling for the...

—Well just try to be as quiet as you can, I want to make this call and find out what arrangements he's making down there before the juices start flowing and he sets up a state funeral, and some toast if there's any bread? And by the time the tray came rattling uneasily up the hall she'd hung up the phone and was back with the paper, —of course he doesn't answer but it's all right here at the end anyhow thank God. His appointment to the U.S. Court of Appeals which, where is it. Regarded by his colleagues as intransigent and even somewhat eccentric, his fierce judicial commitment to First Amendment rights occasionally collided with an equally strong sense of privacy in such intemperate outbursts off the bench as 'Damn the public's right to know!' This disposition found similar expression elsewhere in his habit of destroying early drafts of his judicial opinions threatening to place him at the mercy of collectors and biographers, echoing Justice Holmes in his wish to be known only by the final product with the observation that how he got there was his own affair, an approach carried through to the last in his stipulation, according to his law clerk, for immediate cremation with no funeral services of any sort and the forbidding of a grave marked by a cross or any other such barbaric instrument of human torture well thank God, I mean that takes care of that. There's no toast?

—There's no bread.

—Hand me my cup, I'm going up and get dressed, you'd better get something on before the oh, get the phone, if it's Harry again...

—Hello? who... Oh. It's him.

—Harry?

—It's this law clerk, he...

—Here give it to me. Hello? He's not up yet, this is... yes, Christina. I just saw it in the paper, I mean why didn't you call us yesterday when it happened, we... Well I know there's nothing we could have done but my God! Letting us just happen to stumble on it in the paper like every Tom Dick and... Harry? my husband Harry you called him? When was... well when did he call you!

—I just heard Oscar coughing in there, I think he's awake.

—Just a minute. Take him something Lily here, take him this cup of tea and make him stay in bed until we, hello? Well I know that yes, I know that it's right here in the paper isn't it? I have to learn there's no funeral by reading it in the paper like a million other... Well I'm sure you've been catching them faster than you can string them down there but my God after all we, what? up here? Why are you coming up here, we... You? you mean he made you his executor? but, but... Well my God I know we're the next of kin! I mean why in God's name did he make you his... Well if it's that simple an estate and you've already filed his will for probate what do we... what papers to sign, we... I said I know we're the survivors! My God, do we need you to tell us we're the beneficiaries of course we're the beneficiaries! Now... well when, when are you coming, we can... No now don't be ridiculous you can't come on the bus, you can fly up here and... on a plane, you can fly up here on a plane can't you? and we'll send a car to the... Well a lot of people have never flown before I mean my God the woods down there must be full of them, you... I know the bus is cheaper! We'll pay your air fare we're not penniless are we? I mean you can charge it to the estate you're the executor aren't you? We'll send a car to the airport to meet you and... no I appreciate it thank you, I appreciate your trying to save the estate's money but that's hardly the... Well I'm sure whatever these personal effects are you can get them on the plane, if you can't you can ship them up later but I mean don't bring up things like all his old clothes, if there's one thing we don't need here it's a closetful of... Well fine. If there are a lot of needy folks there fine, give them whatever you... and his books yes, you can simply ship those later can't you? I mean I'm sure they're no earthly use to people who probably never reached third grade or can even... No I have to go, will you call? when you've made your travel arrangements and we'll see that someone meets you? Now, Lily? Lily!

—He's getting up anyway, I couldn't...

—I'm sure all this will keep until Harry gets out here with some bad news of his own, isn't that what he told you yesterday when he called?

—Only something about Oscar's appeal that he said may not please him before he sees the...

—Well of course that's a lawyer's delicate way of putting things, I mean he could say it may not please you to learn that we think you have cancer thank God he's coming out here, imagine Father making that law clerk his executor? Taking the bus, I mean he'd certainly been drinking or he's particularly dense, telling me that we're the survivors the whole world knows it, it's right here at the tail end isn't it? with a flourish of the paper, —Judge Crease was married to the daughter of a wealthy Long Island architect and landowner, the former Winifred Riding, and following her early death for a second time to a Mrs Mabel, a Mrs? that's my mother, what do they mean a Mrs! Surviving are his son, Oscar L thank God they didn't say Oswald, Oscar L Crease, a historian and playwright well that should please him, who resides on Long Island, and a stepdaughter, Christina Lutz, of Manhattan and Lily, get the phone if it rings before he does, it might be the newspapers or God knows who and put this out of sight somewhere will you? I mean speaking of survivors there'll be plenty of time for it if we're all still in one piece after his gala television premiere tonight, now what time is it. I had some tea didn't I? Where did you, oh. Oscar, here, sit down here, here's a pillow. You look perfectly awful.

—Well I am! Wouldn't you be? breaking off in a torrent of coughing, seizing the arm of the sofa where he came down unsteadily. —Where's my paper.

—The paper's right here, just relax. Some hot tea Lily, I'm sure this is cold by now anyway, and...

—Not today's paper, yesterday's! I had it in there, that ad for the movie who took it.

—Without milk Lily, and put a little whisky in it, it's right here somewhere Oscar I'm sure you've read it a thousand times and Lily? put a little in mine too will you?

—A magnificent soul searing epic here it is, they all ought to be shot. Did you see this? gasping, a hand pressed at his heaving chest —this whole revolting...

—Just try to be patient till this evening, I'm sure it will be far worse than you imagine. Harry's coming out later to cheer you up.

—The war torn saga of a man fleeing destiny for a woman's love, introducing the magnificent Nordic-Eurasian discovery Anga Frika in her first starring look at her! The war torn, why is he coming out here, has something happened?

—I'm sure he'll tell you when he gets here, now for the love of God stop torturing yourself and here, here's this morning's paper you can read about three teenagers slain in drug shootout while we, no I'll get it sit still! and she was up holding the phone as grudgingly impatient as her tone, turn left, go straight, turn right through the gate, fourth drive on the left —some woman for your job as a secretary, you put an ad in the local paper?

—I told you didn't I? all this correspondence and bills and the phone...

—And you plan for her to pay your bills, how do you plan to pay her, you can talk on the phone yourself can't you?

—I need a secretary to talk to other people's secretaries! Right now I have to try to reach...

—With a voice like that you shouldn't try to reach anyone, you sound like a...

—Well there, you see? isn't that what I just said? the renewed splurge of coughing giving way to a wheeze that settled him back against the cushions glaring at the three teenagers slain in drug shootout until a steaming cup rattling its saucer came down beside him and where were his glasses? rustling the pages past global strife from Londonderry to Chandigarh, raising his emptied cup with the mute appeal of the toothless Tibetan hoisting a begging bowl at him on page sixteen and on through the smug scoldings of the editorial redoubt to a hissing demand from the flurry of paper for —the business section? Christina?

—I heard you, what on earth do you want with the business section.

—Something here on tearing down a Broadway theatre to build a pizza palace, it says continued on page D sixteen that's the business section where is it.

—God only knows, they forgot to put it in. Do you want an omelette for lunch?

—I want the business section!

—Well I don't have it! Here, you can read your mail while I finish dressing, a brand new law firm entering your life. Will you ask Lily to fix you something when you're ready? and she fled for the stairs before he could tear the envelope open beyond reach of the howl of her name and a gagging sound almost like laughter still echoing when she came down.

—It's, look, look you won't believe it.

—I'm sure I will. Who are you suing now.

—No they're suing me! The O'Neill estate Christina, the estate of Eugene O'Neill they're suing me for infringing that old chestnut Mourning Becomes Electra, of all the...

—All the profits yes, I really don't want to hear about it. I'm sure they'll love the movie.

—No they're suing them too, they're suing all of us, they're...

—I said I don't want to hear about it! When Harry gets here you can share it with him, now where's Lily, we'll need to do some shopping. Have you had anything to eat? We need bread and, yes and whisky, we'll certainly need more scotch before all this is over, Lily? Will you bring in a blanket or something to put over him while we're out? do you hear me? And popcorn for this evening, it sounds like the kind of a movie you watch eating popcorn.

—Wait, Christina? he gasped out minutes later, pulling the quilt up under his chin —will you get me some ice cream? did you hear me? But whether she had or not, all he heard was that door up the hall clattering closed, fumbling among the cushions to snap the screen to life with Indians, cavalry, the sound of gunfire; white faces, dreadlocks, the sound of gunfire; bank guards, men in hats, the sound of gunfire; choppers, flaming hooches, snapping off the crash of gunfire as his eyes flickered closed and his mouth fell open hungering for breath which gradually subsided as his hand twitched and fell still as the shadows cast over him by the sun streaming in from a sudden break in the clouds out there, sudden as a shadow the shape of a man standing over him —No who are you!

—I'm fine Oscar. Wake you up?

—I, I, oh. Oh, Harry.

—Sound like you picked up a little cold someplace. Where is everybody.

—Who. Oh. They went out didn't they. Can you hand me those, that box of tissues there? and a cough brought him struggling upright, —an awful way to start the day.

—Well, can't be too surprised though can you? He'd put his case down by a chair and stood there peeling off his coat, —comes along sooner or later as it must to all men as they say, taking it pretty well though aren't you.

—A little hard to breathe yes, but it's mainly the cough, my throat feels like sandpaper.

—I meant your, you've talked to Christina?

—She's not much help. I asked her to get me some ice cream but I don't think she heard me.

—But she, oh, yes I see, yes you, you haven't seen the paper?

—This morning's? It's right there somewhere, tearing down the old Century theatre to build a pizza palace for the barbarians waiting at the gate listen Harry, I've got to talk to you before they get back and it all turns into a circus listen, this movie? you've seen that ad haven't you? this soul searing Civil War epic and their great Nordic-Eurasian discovery with her shirt open? Tonight, the gala television premiere they're showing it tonight how can they, you'll still be here?

—What I came out here to talk to you about Oscar, they...

—But how can they show it on television, the movie theatres can't show it with that injunction can they?

—That's what I came out to talk to you about, they...

—And this letter where is it, the Eugene O'Neill estate wants to sue me they're suing the studio Kiester all of us what did they do, wait for my profits to start rolling in and then show up with a lawsuit? that's laches isn't it? didn't you tell me about laches?

—Look Oscar, part of what I came out here to talk to you about, just let me get my coat off? and he sank down slowly in the chair, —now...

—But this injunction, they can't...

—Got it lifted once the appeals court ruled on your master's decree on the profits and the accounting, show it anywhere they want to. This one time television exposure they're probably trying to bring the exhibitors back to life, afraid of breach of contract suits from these tie-ins, merchandising rights, T shirts, games, spinoffs, comic strips like your dog Spot and Cyclone Seven, novelization with Anga Frika's tits on the cover probably already on the racks at the airports, You've seen the movie now read the book and if there's no movie they're up the...

—No but what, wait, what book there wasn't any book.

—What's called novelization Oscar, look. Somebody writes a novel and the studio buys the rights, runs it through a dozen script writers before they get their final shooting script they pay some hack seven or eight hundred dollars to turn into a novel in time to get it on the racks when the movie's released, works both ways. Read the book now see the movie.

—But there already is a novel, you said they buy the rights to a novel and...

—Not what's up there on the screen is it? Get through the squabbles between the writers the director the stars and what you end up with's probably miles away from where it started, just confuse the man at the airport who's looking for Anga Frika's tits and...

—But the book they, what happens to the novel they bought in the first place to...

—Dead in the water. You think any studio's going to sign a contract with a droit morale clause in it? Point here is they're trying to cut their losses, get back on track with their tie-ins and spinoffs start their cash flow moving again that's what I've come out here to talk to you about, now...

—Yes, yes good I'm glad to hear it I was getting worried I even, that new car out there you saw it, I just made the first payment and...

—No new car out there Oscar, all I saw when I drove in was an old brown...

—No it's out there, it's just like yours it's a new, wait, they took it. They took it! They took it shopping they didn't even ask me, I haven't even driven it myself yet and she took it without even asking.

—A little reckless Oscar, a car in that price range you...

—No she'll drive carefully but, but she could have asked me couldn't she?

—I mean getting it in the first place, talked to your friend Lily there when I called and told her you'd better show a little restraint until the...

—Yes! Yes that's why I'm relieved but the main thing, listen. My play, I'll be able to produce it myself now, isn't that the marvelous irony in the whole thing? This piece of, sitting here tonight eating popcorn watching this piece of trash on television paying to put my play up there on the stage where it should have been in the first place yes the worse the movie is the better, the more tawdry, vulgar, bloody it is the better, that's justice isn't it? if you want poetic justice?

—Oscar look, that's what I came out to...

—No but the point of it, the whole point of it Harry listen. All this trouble and pain and years of misunderstanding with Father it's been mainly my fault, it's all been my fault for having no faith in him because I thought he didn't have any in me and this play and all of it when he was standing behind me all the time because that's true isn't it? that he wrote the appeal?

—Had to be, it had his handprints all over it that's what had Mudpye climbing the walls, little bastard expected to get up there with his long fancy oral argument and give those shrewd old hands on the bench a lesson in State law preempting the Federal statutes I don't think they gave him three minutes. One look at that appeal brief they didn't doubt for a second it had come from a colleague, never prove it of course but I think they knew where it came from, turned Mudpye's performance upside down on its face and left him out in the cold that's why he's out for blood in the second round here. I could have called you but I thought I'd better wait till I could come out and run through it with you in case you've got any questions, afraid you won't be too pleased with what they've come up with here reviewing the master's decree on your damages.

—Who. All the profits yes, they who.

—The appeals court Oscar, look. You understand how this whole legal proceeding works don't you? He had out a folder, snapping the case closed on his lap —what you've got here, this is your final decree from the Second Circuit entered on the accounting they directed when they reversed the district court and it went to the master to determine your award, mind if I turn this thing off? and he was up again in the flickering light of the silent screen where a lively fellow fled the torments of diarrhea in what appeared to be an international airport, —told you they'd come back trying to get your award reduced didn't I? and he sat down again, now at the foot of the sofa opening the folder —now, you see here. You were awarded all the profits they made from exhibiting the picture The Blood in the Red White and Blue and the question is whether that was correct.

—Well of course it was, they stole my work and have to give me all their profits in damages it's that simple, isn't it?

—No. They insist that the profits should have been apportioned. Here, that the recovery of the author of a copyrighted work ought to be limited to those profits which result from its exploitation; and that since the value of the picture here depended only in very small measure upon those parts which the defendants have been found to have lifted, they should be accountable for only a correspondingly small part of the...

—Well that's, they can't do that no that's ridiculous, they stole it didn't they?

—Point is Oscar, all right look. Write a poem, somebody lifts it, publishes it elsewhere with his name on it simple case of plagiary, same words printed on a piece of paper, a movie's something else, the profits come from the people who pay to see it with the hope of enjoyment don't they? He thrust the stapled pages at the quavering hand on the quilt, —here, look. That enjoyment, which is one source of its further popularity, is made up of many factors: the actors, the work of the producer and director, the story, the scenery and costumes. The attraction and the hope which first draws them are principally aroused by advertisements, and the reputation of the stars and the producing company. These factors have no unit common to all, and are therefore incommensurable; in that, the situation is not different from the usual case of copyright infringement where the pirated material has been mixed with matter in the public domain. They've usually just tried to get the net profits down as low as possible, what the court's saying this time is that no matter how little the defendants say the value of the picture depends on what they stole, it's right here, the infringer carries the burden of disentangling the contributions of the several factors which he has confused. Your appeal didn't bring up that point and here, the court undertook sua sponte to declare that the plaintiff should recover all the profits and they moved to modify that so they could prove the value of their own contribution, move over a little so I can get my jacket off will you?

—Their own contribution! gone in a spasm of coughing, —nothing but a lot of, of...

—Gets into patent accountings here where the infringer has to separate the profits from his own contribution where it's just as unfair here to cast the infringer for all the profits as it would be to deny the patentee or the author any recovery because he can't separate his own contribution so the court puts the burden on them, you see? riffling through the pages, —what this whole thing is all about?

—No.

—All right, look. They claim everything they can and throw in the kitchen sink, some of it's allowed some of it isn't. Down here for instance, whether the profits from showing it outside the United States should be included, the court holds that the plaintiff, you the plaintiff, had an equitable interest in the negatives the minute they were made in this country where it was a tort so the law impresses them with a constructive trust. Here the master has used the cost of production as the basis for figuring the distribution cost the defendants have put in under overhead expenses they've tried to spread over their other pictures and the court holds for the master, same thing here where they've disallowed a five million dollar studio overhead item for stories or screenplays they bought that were failures or weren't made at all I, just let me get up for a minute? drawing away from the seething breath mingling with his own, —little early for a drink but that's a long drive out here, just give me a minute while you run through the rest of this?

—Harry? when he came back swirling ice in a glass, standing there loosening his tie —listen, I can't read all this, interest disallowed on a loan made to Erebus from one of their subsidiaries where the master has included in the overhead only the interest on the plant investment used in making the picture? that overhead that doesn't assist in the production of the infringement shouldn't be credited to the infringer and this allowance for continuities that were scrapped and pictures that were made but never shown and all the rest of, and this. And this Harry? legal costs? where the master allows only those legal expenses directly incurred by the, but that's me! I mean that's you, that's your law firm defending them against me for stealing my...

—No look Oscar, a lot of legal expenses go into a...

—No listen Harry that's Mudpye getting paid to sit right here for that deposition twisting around everything I said so I'm supposed to be paying him hundreds of thousands of dollars for cutting my own throat while the...

—Not the way it works Oscar, he was probably priced out at around one eighty an hour but they'd be billed by the firm for...

—Yes for destroying everything I, for destroying me!

—No look Oscar, look, all kinds of legal expenses connected with a venture like this one, contracts, leases, insurance all just the nuts and bolts of the industry, not an art form it's an industry you see that by now don't you? and he sat back in the chair at a safe distance —you can see it right there. They can only charge back what they bought and paid for making the picture, but they can't charge for their work exploiting what they stole and that's where the court is protecting you but they didn't steal the battle at Antietam did they? Cast of thousands all those special effects how many millions do you think they...

—But they stole it from me! And Ball's Bluff, they were both in my play and they...

—Went over this back at the start didn't we? that you can't copyright the Civil War? You don't show the battle at Ball's Bluff in your play do you? They just talk about it, you don't show Antietam it happens offstage, you see what I mean? The basic plot, the general skeleton it was already in the public domain wasn't it? A man hires substitutes on both sides in the Civil War, they're both killed in the same battle and he goes off the deep end as some sort of moral suicide who...

—Well he, no, no he doesn't really go off the deep end but...

—But what was the proportion of the gross receipts of the movie that could be credited to your play, that's what the court is trying to untangle here. Expert testimony from producers and exhibitors ran from five to twelve percent, one of them said nothing at all. A hit play, a best seller that would have been different but your play Oscar, your play just wasn't in that class was it.

—Class! How can you, listen. Where do I come out that's all. Just tell me where I come out.

—Right there somewhere, look at the last paragraph before the...

—Just tell me!

—Twenty percent, Oscar. One fifth of the net profits.

—Twen, twenty percent of...

—Of the net.

—Of the net.

—A fifth of the net profits on the picture look, they probably keep two sets of books anyway, one for the SEC and the IRS and the stockholders and the other to suit the fifty page net profit definition in their standard contract so you won't be taking home millions but the real damn point is, whole God damn point is where we live now, all been trying to tell you that from the start haven't we? Don't have to tell you you know it, you know it better than the rest of us, why you've fought it so hard while the rest of us just swallow hard and look for another dollar so we can be entertained and take our minds off it, why people go to the movies isn't it? to see Anga Frika show us her Nordic-Eurasian tits not some moral agonizing over questions that don't have answers? That's what this proceeding's about, what the whole of the law's all about, questions that do have answers, sift through all the evidence till you come up with the right ones.

—The right ones! One fifth of the, how can you say the right ones! We won didn't we? we won the appeal?

—The right ones within the framework of the law, Oscar. Won the appeal yes, they stole from your work. Question now is how much they stole, and how much they did steal contributed to the picture in relation to their own contribution, just went over that didn't we? Look. The Blood in the Red White and Blue is a spectacular, a ninety million dollar spectacular, blockbuster whatever you want to call it, the more tawdry vulgar and bloody the better, you just said that yourself didn't you? why these mobs of people have poured in to see it? what that ad you just showed me, what forty million dollars in advertising promises them? The stars, the track record of the studio, the producer, director who gave them Uruburu with the man's face smashed with a sledgehammer? the top box office draw of an actor like Bredford and their sensational Anga Frika with tits nobody's seen before? That's why she gets a straight contract three million dollar deal while Bredford takes twenty four million off the top and Kiester around six, any movie, could be a movie about the Borgias with her as Lucrezia and Bredford playing Michelangelo, Solomon and the Queen of Sheba, the French revolution and a tale of two titties that's why the expert witnesses they brought in call them the controlling factors in the movie's success.

—No but the, what expert witnesses, where did they...

—Just told you, producers and exhibitors here, here's the citation Section 70, Title 35, U.S. Code, 35 U.S.C.A. that opinion or expert testimony should be competent upon the issue, apparently without regard to where the burden of proof might for the moment lie, goes on to say the court is justified in basing its decrees on...

—But they're the ones who said my play contributed only five or ten percent and one of them said nothing at all because it wasn't a Broadway hit? Producers and exhibitors what do you expect them to say they're part of the, they're already on the other side they're part of the snake pit with the studio and Kiester and...

—That's why they're experts Oscar look, problem's spelled out right here. The plaintiffs, that's you, plaintiffs called no witnesses to rebut this testimony, and if their failure to do so was because of the commanding position of the defendants in the industry, they did not prove it. We must therefore assume that the testimony represents the best opinion of the calling but look, you've still got an advantage under the Copyright Act, gives the court the power to award you damages in lieu of actual damages and profits as they put it. Give you the job of showing actual money damages would be hopeless, ask you to sort out who contributed what you'd be completely at sea and never recover a dime that's why the burden falls on the infringer and that's what this is all about, expert witnesses and all the rest of it. Stars, producers, director, supporting players, extras, scenery and locations, set designers, cinematographers, special effects, composer, costumers, it's a costume drama isn't it? makeup, hairdressers, point is there's a pretty fair market value established for all these services and the story is just one more element where development may run through ten writers and twenty versions of the script and the original concept, the story idea is left in the dust. One of their experts here calls it mundane, another one says it's frail so they try to put a price on it, on your contribution, fair market value for the...

—Like the hairdresser.

—Like the hairdresser, look. They see a thousand ideas a day, even good ideas don't always make good movies, they buy one and stake millions on it hoping for some big success and that's up to the development and execution of the final product, the rest is goods and services.

—Like the hairdresser.

—All right look, the...

—Like the no, no it's outrageous. It's an outrage Harry, goods and services like your hairdresser when a theatrical, when one of the biggest theatre directors around is interested in it as a play? Sir John Nipples, that puts real value on it doesn't it? Even Mudpye said that, what a great success it can be on the stage directed by Sir John Nip...

—You told Mudpye that? that he was interested?

—Well I, more or less yes, just that he wanted to read it and...

—And there goes your claim for damages destroying its other commercial possibilities good God Oscar, you told Mudpye that? Told you he was out for blood didn't I? and you handed him that on a platter? What else did you tell him, never did file that assault and battery case against him did you?

—Not yet no, not yet but now I'm...

—Look, not giving you legal advice here just a friendly tip, forget it. Talk about your expert witnesses he'd have the whole AMA in there wearing your guts for garters, all he's assaulting here's your pocketbook. They offered you a two hundred thousand dollar settlement didn't they? and you turned it down? That's the figure they're using now to base their estimated purchase price on.

—But it's not a, there never was a purchase price they stole it, they didn't even try to purchase it they...

—I know that! and he was on his feet again, rattling the naked ice cubes in his glass —look. I just told you that's where your advantage under the Copyright Act comes in didn't I? gives the court power to award you damages in lieu of actual damages and profits? That's what this one fifth of the net is all about, the court passing up their fair market value claim for services like the hairdresser and trying to give you some room to move in with a percentage of their net profits.

—When Bredford gets what did you say? twenty five million? and Kiester another six?

—Off the top Oscar, I said off the top, they have gross participation deals, percentage of the gross cash receipts that come in from the movie theatres, networks, cable, home video, foreign exhibitors, net they figure on an accrual basis after their negative costs and distribution, advertising the rest of...

—Harry?

—where a little of their creative accounting comes in like their twenty percent royalty to the distributor who's already their subsidiary and the interest on...

—Harry listen!

—Fine but, running dry here just give me a minute? and he was gone rattling the ice cubes, safely afloat again when he came back to stand over the gasping figure on the sofa with almost a sigh, —now what.

—On this decree, right here on the decree it says Bone, Judge Bone he's the one who granted my appeal isn't he? giving me all the profits and now he's turned it upside down with this one fifth of the...

—Put it in the hands of the master to come up with the accounting Oscar, what we've just been talking about here, they moved to reduce your award with all these exhibits separating their contribution from yours and Bone's court reversed the decree that was based on the assumption that, look. You sued for infringement because they stole your play for their movie, that your entire play was your contribution to their gross receipts, but they...

—But they did! It's right there in that original opinion isn't it? tracking the play and the movie scene for scene and the...

—They stole your play but they didn't use all of it, that's what this business of apportioning these contributions is all about can't you understand! He drank off half the glass with one hand, waving the other —have to go through it all again? separating the material they pirated from what they mixed with it from the public domain in the whole development process, ten or twenty script rewrites and your last act, they claim they didn't use anything from your last act at all and there's a third of your contribution gone right there.

—Well at least, Father's seen it and at least he'll have the chance to finally see the real thing if I can manage it, even if it takes all of this fifth of what's left of their plunder because that's the thing, that's really the important thing.

—Maybe he will, Oscar... and his hand came down gently on the shoulder sagging before him there on the sofa, resting there and suddenly squeezing it tightly before he stood away and finished his drink as the doors clattered open up the hall, —maybe he will.

—Harry you're here! Will you come and help Lily with these bundles? and as he came near, prolonging their close embrace —have you talked to him?

—Just this decision in his lawsuit, I...

—Oh. I thought maybe you'd get it over with while we were gone. Oscar? she broke away, —how do you feel.

—Didn't think it was my place to dive right into it without...

—I feel fine Christina. You took my car. Why did you take my car without telling me, without even asking me.

—My God Oscar, there are worse things believe me. Get him some more tissues will you Lily? and do something about that quilt? He looks like one of those homeless out sleeping on the grates, maybe you can finally shave off that ghastly excuse for a beard now and make a fresh start. Harry hasn't done much to cheer you up has he, you look like the wrath of God. I got you some ice cream.

—Harry has not cheered me up Christina. Do you want to hear what he's told me?

—No. I mean look at him, he hasn't got much to cheer about

himself, you look exhausted Harry, have Bill Peyton and his gang finally turned loose what's left of you to live like a human being?

—Whole case is pretty well cleaned up yes, still some dickering going on between the accountants but my end of it's finished until the...

—Well thank God, have you had anything to eat? She was half out of her coat and suddenly pulled it on as though a chill had come over her, —Oscar? looking down on him there, —you haven't eaten have you? pulling her coat off again slowly —I thought, before we talk I thought you might, I thought we all might want something to eat I mean I'm famished, I haven't had a thing since that tea this morning do you, can I fix you an omelette or, or a...

—Ice cream.

—But just ice cream? Don't you want, where are you going? as he stood up unsteadily, dragging the quilt toward the hall, —don't you want some...

—Ice cream! I'm going to the bathroom and then I'm going in there and lie down.

—Yes well, Lily can bring it in to you yes, Lily? watching him out of sight —my God, I don't know how to, it's going to be so difficult Harry I don't...

—And you, and you Christina! his arm suddenly round her holding her close —God, it's not easy for you here, here let me get a tissue just, you're marvelous it's just as bad for you.

—Oh, I'm sorry I didn't mean to...

—No come in Lily, come in, take him some ice cream in there will you? wiping her eyes, stepping free to blow her nose hard —and then we, and then you can help me fix something to, in the kitchen you can help me in the kitchen and, what time is it. I think I'll have a drink.

At the time of his death, Judge Crease had only the night before handed down his last decision in a First Amendment case dealing with the notorious outdoor steel sculpture known as —you've read all this, Christina? he said when she reappeared and sat down beside him, her face fallen over the glass she held in both her hands.

—I don't know, I read part of it I don't know what I read.

—First chance I've had to read through it myself, didn't think I should dive right into it with Oscar before we had a chance to sit down and...

—Well we're sitting down Harry, I mean he'll have to hear about it sooner or later won't he? I wish you'd eat something, and she was as abruptly back up on her feet, —I'm going upstairs and lie down, leaving him sitting there staring at the drink she'd left behind untouched, eat something? but what, struggling to restore a day that was completely losing its shape and even the sun itself, already dislocated by the season, coming and going in the clouds out there losing track of it as he reached for the glass and settled back in the cushions, broke his neck getting out here and everybody simply disappears as he tipped the glass up to his lips simply because it was here in his hand, trapped by the words in the obituary column demanding to be read simply because here they were propped up before him, according to his law clerk who was with him at the time. As highly regarded by his colleagues for his wide grasp and strict application of constitutional law as for the elaborate language with which he framed his judicial decrees, Judge Crease was a jurist in the tradition of Justice Oliver Wendell Holmes Jr, whom he frequently quoted in his legal opinions, and with whom his father had served on the Supreme Court where the two were often in conflict over demands for justice by the elder Crease confronted by Holmes' dedication to the reason and practicality of the common law in its lack of sentimentality in applying rules of conduct regardless of hardship. Their differences, however, took second place to the bond forged between them by their service in the Civil War, which has recently formed the backdrop for a popular motion picture said to be drawn on the youthful adventures of Justice Crease in that historic conflict. At the time of his death, raising the glass for another deep swallow, silence infringing the shadows around him like the burden placed on the infringer to separate his contribution from the public domain in this enfeebled effort to disentangle the words floating before his eyes from the sensuous warmth lapping at his dwindling concentration At the time of his death...

—He looks real young doesn't he.

—What! he started almost upright, splashing the drink on his hand, on the crease in his trousers.

—Oh I'm sorry! I didn't know you were sleeping I'm sorry, wait a second, and before he could finish off the drink if simply to get rid of it she was down beside him with a tissue dabbing at the back of his hand. —I know it's this old picture of him, they probably took it before I was even born, she came on, setting the emptied glass aside to dab at his wrist, the warmth of her knee pressing carelessly against his —I'm always amazed when somebody dies like that how the newspaper can sit down and write this long story with everything about him practically overnight, it would take me a month.

—Not quite the way it works, he told her, letting the knee he'd sharply withdrawn come back to rest against hers, against the soft length of her thigh against his as he sank back in the cushions clearing his throat, breathing deeply the cool scent of soap mingling with perspiration from the careless buttoning of her blouse, probably wrote this obituary itself before she was born, anyone of any promise or prominence they're prepared well ahead and kept updated in the morgue he went on, short of breath, that's what they call it, the morgue where these files are kept for the day death comes along and they can simply write in the lead, after a long illness, in a plane crash, in the warm glow of low lights and lowered voices in the funeral home exchanging condolences and appointments for lunch, for drinks, for some affirmation to deny and obliterate the reality that had brought them together with another at distinct and ultimate odds on a couch somewhere, in a bed, no mystical conjunction of death and eros here as she bent closer over him to go at the spot on his trousers with the damp tissue, his hand brushing her shoulder as though for it to slip lower dislodging a button would be the most natural thing in the world reeling round him baring her breast to his lips in the act of restoring nature's equation with a new life, simply part of the natural order of things for her hand diligently rubbing away the wet crease there to stray scarcely its own breadth to undo his trousers discovering the pulsing source of her deliverance already obediently evident in its lair to redress the balance of natural law in all its practicality and lack of sentimentality, regardless of hardship.

He woke with a start to a voice saying —Don't wake him, poor thing he's exhausted, has he had anything to eat? the lights snapping on like some whirling galaxy infringing upon the darkness that had settled round him there struggling under the burden of disentangling the contributions of the pirated warmth of her thigh and the lingering soap scent drenched with perspiration from his own, gone to unrequited rest now where he straightened his trousers sitting up.

—Harry?

—Oh, Oscar yes, what...

—I've been thinking about what you said earlier, about the court leaving it up to them to disentangle their contribution from mine? from my play? He came shuffling by dragging the quilt to pull it over him coming down in a heap in a chair —the last act? that they hadn't even used it? You said a third, there goes a third of my contribution but it's not a third, it's a very short act, just the dénouement it's just three scenes, three very short scenes and if they didn't use it, Mudpye said he hadn't even read it did you know that? did I tell you that?

—Probably Basie didn't hand it over, surrender as little as possible and if they didn't ask for it he's under no duty to hand it over, must have known they were on safe ground with whatever their writers dreamed up for an ending.

—Dreamed up! What could they, they took whatever they wanted from what they claimed was the public domain but where else would they look, the letters and papers in that decrepit historical society down there that's trying to sue me that's not the public domain is it? Basie said he'd tried to register them for copyright but Father had already done it, Father had got in there before him and done it.

—Then they're yours Oscar, copyright passed right to you per stirpes like anything else he...

—Yes but meanwhile Father...

—Meant to say I, meant to say will pass to you, the title will pass to you when he, probably to you and Christina if you're both his legal benefic...

—Because if they didn't use that or any of my last act how could they make any sense of it, the whole thing builds toward the last act that's what any play is about isn't it?

—Can't help you there Oscar, haven't seen their exhibits just what's here in the decree. All these special effects, they may end it snatching everybody up to meet the Lord in the clouds when the trumpet sounds for the second coming while we sit here tonight eating popcorn in a rain of fire and brimstone, about time for the news isn't it? Mind if I turn this on? He was up and already halfway across the room, —have you seen Christina?

—They're doing something in the kitchen Harry listen, they've claimed they never read the last act but if we see things in the movie tonight that...

—No sit still, just going to see what they're up to out there I'm suddenly really hungry, bring you anything? safely beyond reach now of the fit of coughing he left behind where the screen burst into life with Yummy! a waffle crowned with peanut butter being drenched in maple syrup and a blare of music that pursued him all the way to the kitchen table ravages of crusts and torn muffins, heels of cheese, wilted butter, jam, soggy remnants of an omelette and a sprinkling of spilled sugar or it might have been salt, empty cups, glasses, juice cartons, an oily sardine tin and sodden tea bags, olive pits, crumpled napkins, spoons and a butter smeared carving knife where the two of them sat, greeting his gratuitous inquiry, —Are you eating? with an equally senseless response.

—Oh Harry, are you up? He may want a bite of something Lily.

—Does he want that omelette or should I make a new one.

—Some hot tea, he looks like he needs it.

—Or maybe he wants some soup, there's this can of tomato soup? both their vacant gazes fixed on him where he'd sat down between them chewing on a bite of something.

—I can't even think about supper, I don't think anyone will care about it at this point anyhow. Is Oscar up, Harry?

—In there watching the news, can't you hear it? he muttered to the distant echo of gunfire, reaching for another crust.

—Have you said anything to him yet? I mean it had to happen sooner or later, he was almost a hundred years old and the smoking and drinking on top of it, I do wish you'd take better care of yourself Harry you've lost weight. I mean you should really make a point of eating three full meals a day, are you still taking those pills? are you? He nodded, spooning up the last cold shred of omelette —because God knows what tonight will, oh Lily! We forgot the popcorn.

—I better clean up here anyway before we, what was that.

—What was that!

—Christina Harry Christina quickly! Come here quickly!

—My God I knew it! chairs scraping, crusts cup and the carving knife gone to the floor —I knew it!

—Look! The flaming effigy swung closer in a floodlit melee of flying rocks and beer cans, Stars, Bars and Stripes asunder, signs and placards brandished and trampled, GOD IS JUDGE aloft and IMPEACH smouldering on the judicial robes —what do they, look!

—It had to happen sooner or later Oscar, I mean he was almost...

—What did! What are they doing all this again for! they...

—What the media's all about Oscar, pictures make the news, no fun showing an old judge writing a landmark legal opinion but they get an excuse to show their old file tape full of rum and riot, burning crosses, burning flags stir the pot and they've got a feature story, any excuse to stir up the flames of hatred and...

—But what excuse, I didn't hear the...

—He died, Oscar.

—But we, I mean my God we thought you knew.

—Father? died? The screen had simmered down to display a new denture cleaner and brightener —Lily? you said he, he died?

—Thought they'd, thought you'd just heard it on the news in there Oscar, we...

—But he, how do you know? his voice sunk near a whisper, staring fixedly now at a new itch fighting shampoo —how do you know!

—It was in the paper Oscar, we just didn't quite, Lily will you get him something? a drink or, I mean it had to happen sooner or later didn't it he was almost a hundred and, or just some wine Lily?

—It was not in the paper! I read the paper and it was not in the paper!

—In the one I brought out with me Oscar might have been a, probably a later edition, thought you'd probably want to get this business of your appeal out of the way before you...

—Well where is it? The paper, where is it!

—I'll get it Oscar here, this whole long story look. He looks real young here doesn't he.

—Lily for God's sake will you, just do as I asked you and some glasses, bring some more glasses will you? and flinging a hand at the bloody aftermath and weeping mothers of three teenagers slain in drug shootout —and will you turn that thing off!

—Gave him a nice long obit there though didn't they, never knew he'd clerked for your grandfather on the High Court Oscar, probably where he got all his...

—Where they got all their nonsense about madness and, did you read it all? just like what we just saw, long distinguished career but instead they rattle on about that ridiculous mob scene down there, at the time of his death. Judge Crease had only the night before handed down his last decision in a First Amendment case dealing with the notorious outdoor steel sculpture known as Cyclone Seven, overshadowing his long and distinguished career on the Federal bench in clouds of public controversy reaching his court in various guises, most recently the highly publicized 'Spot decision' and another just adjudicated in a related matter involving trademark infringement by a manufacturer of novelty mittens, repeatedly subjecting him to a campaign of vilification as a cold-blooded unAmerican atheist in a tumult culminating in his being burned in effigy. These events had obstructed his appointment to the U.S. Court of Appeals, widely viewed in light of his advanced age as an interim political appointment, which was cleared yesterday morning by the Senate Judiciary Committee following the abrupt collapse of the virulent opposition led by Senator Orney Bilk who had gone so far as to call for his impeachment. Reached for comment today, Senator Bilk said no, listen to this! Did you read it?

—Good obit isn't it, didn't quite finish it but...

—Listen! Spurred by his constituents' expressions of respectful affection for Judge Crease in the handling of a recent case of wrongful death, Senator Bilk stated that 'In exemplifying the highest ideals of our great American judicial system without fear of favor, Judge Thomas Crease leaves us all in his eternal debt, and like his illustrious father before him, now he belongs to the ages' did you, God! did you read that Harry? Did you see that?

—Just give him the glass Lily and, wait you'd better just bring in another bottle.

—Christina did you hear that! Now he belongs to the, it's revolting.

—Well my God it's true isn't it? I mean he was really a great...

—But from a mouth like that, those glorious words in a dirty mouth like Bilk's he's never said a decent, never told the truth in his life every low rotten thing he's ever said about Father about Grandfather all of us now he's got the, the brazen insolence a moment like this to dare to try to, it's revolting he ought to be shot.

—Politics Oscar, just politics, sees where the parade is heading and jumps in front to lead it, pretty startling turnaround but people have short memories first thing a politician learns, jump right in and give them new ones, got an election coming up remember that, that's all he...

—Remember it! That's what I, listen. Listen, you know what he'll do if we don't stop him? The funeral Harry, Father's funeral he'll come to the funeral and take it over for himself, come to bury Caesar that, that bastard will get up there with the American flag and the Stars and Bars and launch into a harangue about the sacred rights of this mob of honest citizens black folk and white alike under the glorious canopy of the US Constitution that he...

—Oscar?

—Don't interrupt me Christina listen! Thank God I thought of it, Christian values of our great republic that Father defended with his life to the very last breath God gave him and now he belongs to the ages if we don't stop him, we've got to do something before it's too late call them, call the...

—Oscar! Now listen to me, there's not going to be one, sit still and try to relax there's not going to be a funeral and that takes care of that, now...

—What do you, who said there's not! He was an important man Christina a great man of course he'll have a, he ought to have a state funeral after a career like that he's part of history, you think there aren't important people in the bar who'll want to get up and pay a few words of tribute like I will? I owe him at least that don't I? Don't I? And you want to sit there and decide he won't have a funeral just because you...

—What! because what! Because he wasn't my own father? Be, because I came in here like a, dragged in here by my mother like an orphan who never...

—Oscar quit it! She's already real upset can't you see that? She didn't decide it anyway he did, your daddy did it's right there in that thing you're reading if you'd just read it before you start yelling and blaming everybody read it, read it! but she snatched it away —right here, it's right here someplace where it says here, in his stipu, his stipulation according to his law clerk for immediate cremation with no funeral services of any sort and forbidding a grave marked by a cross or, hand her some of those tissues while you're standing there will you?

—I, I'm sorry Christina I didn't mean, if you'd told me I...

—You ought to be Oscar, you ought to be sorry she...

—No it's, I'm all right Lily it's all right I, thanks, I mean I should have explained Oscar, he's Father's executor this law clerk is, Father named him his executor in his will so he's just carrying out Father's wishes and...

—But no funeral that's not, is that right Harry? Harry?

—What? Oh, the funeral yes matter of fact, I don't think it's binding, put it in a will it just expresses the wishes of the decedent he'd like a Viking funeral, put to sea in a flaming ship or sent up in a rocket or nothing at all but his wishes end with him, not like bequeathing a house or a diamond bracelet doesn't bind the survivors to anything but their own sentimental whatever they decide, no funeral but they can send the remains up in a rocket whatever they...

—Yes well there! There Christina, we can do whatever we, Christina? We can still, if it's not too late we can still do it I'll call him, we can still...

—Oscar please, will you simply, simply sit down and try to relax? clearing her throat, blowing her nose in the handful of tissue —I'm sure it's too late. I'm sure he went right ahead and followed Father's instructions like he's followed them down there for thirty years.

—Yes but Harry just said, he should have asked us shouldn't he? He's a law clerk he should know that, he must know these wishes aren't binding on the survivors he's not even, he's just a clerk a law clerk he had no right doing that without asking us, we could, he's a law clerk he should know we could probably sue him if we...

—Oscar for the love of God! Will you stop talking about suing people? can't you see where it's already got you? Where's, Lily where are you going.

—I'm making you some tea.

—I think I want a drink, I...

—I said I'm making you some hot tea didn't I? and she was gone.

—Look at it this way Oscar. Talk about your Senator Bilk turning things into a tent show the old Judge was way ahead of you, exactly what he knew could happen that's probably why he put in that stipulation, have to give him credit don't you? Big state funeral you talked about you might even get a Justice from the High Court but you'd get Bilk and the rest of the political trash with the media in there exercising their First Amendment rights to turn it into a public spectacle with a few rocks and beer cans from their file tapes thrown in for entertainment value because that's what their business is, it's not news it's entertainment. That's just what we were talking about earlier isn't it? what your movie lawsuit's all about? what this whole country's really all about? tens of millions out there with their candy and beer cans and this inexhaustible appetite for being entertained? Anything they can get their hands on, talk about bread and circuses that's...

—All right Harry please, that's enough now please. That's enough.

—All right Christina but, Harry listen, naming this law clerk his executor he's not even part of the family, he drinks and...

—Name anybody he wanted to Oscar, anybody he'd trust to carry out the provisions of his will exactly as he wrote it, take it through probate and...

—He trusted him all right, Father trusted him but what about us, we don't even know him he drinks and...

—One place the law's absolutely clear, catch an executor pulling any fast ones he's in a hell of a lot of trouble and if anybody knows that your law clerk does.

—Well but, and do we have to pay him?

—Estate pays him, don't know the laws down there could be up to three percent unless he elects to waive it or...

—Oh Lily thank God here, just put the cup here, Oscar? will you just let all this rest for a while? It's a simple estate it's a perfectly simple will, we're the joint beneficiaries we always took that for granted didn't we? And I mean you of all people, the way you've felt about Father talking about him standing by you and all the rest of it shouldn't you be the very first one to respect his wishes? let him go like he wanted to instead of some Viking funeral and God knows what else?

—I didn't mean that Christina, a Viking funeral I just thought, he could have made me his executor couldn't he? if he trusted this law clerk down there with a drink in his hand more than he...

—Well my God you drink don't you? will you look at that bottle beside you that was full a few minutes ago?

—Yes all right but, but he could have named Harry couldn't he? Harry's a lawyer, that three percent to keep that three percent in the family couldn't he?

—No wait Christinia, look Oscar. You've got somebody down there who knows the courts, knows the State laws can get the will through probate with drinks in both hands, an estate as simple as this one a few legal papers he can clean the whole thing up without a lot of...

—Yes but how do you know, you both keep saying it's a simple estate how do you know it is, maybe there are things we don't even...

—Don't worry about it, I asked him to send up a copy of the will and...

—You mean you've talked to him?

—We've both talked to him Oscar. Harry called him first thing and I talked to him later, he's bringing some papers up here and Father's personal effects that's about all there is, now...

—But why didn't you tell me!

—They just told you didn't they? I mean honest you're going to drive everybody crazy like this Oscar, how she's been tiptoeing around all day trying not to upset you, you okay Christina? You want to go in and lay down before the movie?

—Oh my God, that!

—No wait it's almost time! Turn it on it's right after the news, I have to go to the bathroom turn it on! as he heaved up and away, leaving them to the vision of a lady in impeccable lingerie stirred by a gentle breeze over phantom breasts smiling serenely on an unruffled landscape of a country morning after a satisfactory bout with an overnight laxative, all of them ensconced in varied degrees of discomfort by the time he reappeared to recover the sanctuary of the sofa where he came down unsteadily aping the writhings of the middleaging arthritic on the screen enduring languorous massage with a heat penetrating unguent and a Florida backdrop Kissing Pain Goodbye when suddenly the room shook with the sound of cannon fire, the screen with a tumult of plunging horses, flaring rockets and the Stars and Bars and men, men —look! as

The Blood in the Red White and Blue

unfurled before them, going up in flames for the stark parade of names sprung from briefs, dockets, decrees, each more hateful than the last till finally the smoke cleared, the music died and now the room echoed with the clop clop of a horse and carriage seen approaching up a drive adroop with Spanish moss from the pillared veranda of an antebellum mansion by an imposing liveried black —there he is! that's that, that Button that friend of Basie's, his brow arching disdainfully as a decrepit horse and buggy bearing an aging woman and a handsome intense young man standing to snap his whip imperiously came close for an exchange of unheard words to be pointed scornfully on their way, glimpsed from behind a curtain by a ravishingly beautiful young woman in negligee —there she is! he hissed after their retreat back down the drive, pulling up before a small farm house badly in need of repair as a musical mélange of sombre chords appropriated from the alcoholic ramblings of Stephen Foster seeped in to set the tone for a long montage of hammering, wood splitting and split rail fencing, the decrepit horse yielding the buggy's traces for the plough under a blistering sun rows of tobacco leaves, stands of corn, rivulets of sweat connoting manlydom on white skin and servitude on the black knelt by lamplight at the old woman's knee tracing the Beatitudes of Matthew 5 with a black finger on the white page escorted by the pirated strains of a gospel hymn yet to be written and, nearer to hand from the sofa gasps of recognition and wheezes of impatience rising on the wings of the gamebird smashed by the burst of a shotgun to scurry frantically through the brown grasses fleeing for the crevice of a stone wall from what was happening, the clatter of hooves, the crash of underbrush, Hunting Musique! With Horns and with Hounds I waken the Day And hye to my Woodland walks away, tempestuously bosomed, flaming hair'd, where Mars destroys and I repair, Take me, take me, while you may, Venus comes not ev'ry Day, three million dollars worth of stardom buskin'd in finest calf, twilled thighs spread wide astride the pawing stallion looming over him he rais'd a mortal to the skies; She drew an angel down undoing the front of his overalls, Flush'd with a purple grace he shows his honest face mingling the sweating badges of his low estate with perspiration born of highborn sport beading her open breasts. Now gives the hautboys breath; he comes, he comes provoking here a giggle, there a gasp of outrage at —this clumsy, vulgar, did you see it! That scene I wrote in all its classic simplicity turned into trash dragged through the mud in the most vulgar clumsy, the whole thing right from the start, my whole prologue they used the dialogue for their scenario right from the start, did you see it Harry?

—What? clearing his throat, recovering his gaze from the salt swells of the carelessly buttoned feast nearby no more attainable than those his eyes had strayed from on the screen at the sound of that giggle, —oh. Satire Oscar, they're just satirizing the whole genre don't you think? the plaintive tones of the oboe given way to a vocal frenzy heralding a long forgotten movie star gnashing gleaming dentures at her small audience confiding how she kept them in place.

—We forgot the popcorn.

—Is there any more ice cream?

—That's always their escape Harry, make a real mess they pretend they did it on purpose and call it satire.

—More wine? A very Merry, Dancing, Drinking, Laughing, Quaffing, and unthinking Time not long in coming with the wedding at Cross Creek where soon enough The Sprightly Green In Woodland Walks, no more is seen; Arms and Honour Set the Martial Mind on Fire, And kindle Manly Rage. Plenty, Peace, and Pleasure fly; Sound the Trumpet, Beat the Drum, Sound a Reveille, Sound, Sound, —too loud, will you turn it down a little? as the secular masque of the old order took its farewell in the orotund tones of a Union commander and Lover of Poetry high on a bluff above the Potomac shaking an officer's hand with 'I congratulate you, sir, on the prospect of a battle,' uncostumed artifice of breast and sinew given place to brawn and those sweet beads of perspiration to rank sweat, the curried stallion in the Woodland Walks to a drayhorse mired on the bank below and that lone shotgun's burst to the crash of small arms fire from the higher ground in the woods beyond through gunsmoke lain like a pall over his green regiments, and echoing Sir Walter Scott with a bugle blast worth a thousand men the Lover of Poetry went down with a Rebel bullet through his heart, his prospect of a battle gone withershins in a tumultuous rout down the steep bluff for four small boats to carry them back across the wide river white as a hailstorm with bullets fired from the abandoned heights and of those thousand men nine hundred lost, shot, drowned, or left for prisoners on the dark Virginia shore.

—God!

—Oscar? you okay?

—That was stunning! he gasped, lurching upright to fill his emptied glass —exactly yes, exactly what it was like! as though he'd been there himself that late October day in eighteen sixty one, a boy cheering when the Lover of Poetry turned on the Twentieth Massachusetts with 'Boys, you want to fight, don't you?' —as though they really were there, they must have been they must have filmed it right there at the real Ball's Bluff that was clever, telling it from the Union side that was clever, that great flatboat turning over and the drowning soldiers being shot to pieces right at the end, did you see that right at the end? that wounded man left behind on the beach? filling his glass again, —that was Holmes, that could have been the young Oliver Wendell Holmes wasn't it, he was a lieutenant in the Twentieth Massachusetts wounded at Ball's Bluff just like that wasn't he? gasping, pausing for breath, —left behind on the beach just like that wasn't he? raising his glass to the screen where just then a car came careening round a bend with the reckless abandon of a drunk at the wheel and an exhortation to buy one.

—You got quite carried away Oscar didn't you, I thought you...

—Well the battle, the battle they, that was clever, the Confederates you hardly ever got a look at them, just a flag or two and their shapes through the trees and the smoke except for this, this ridiculous Major on horseback with a swill from his flask and the, and our hero the one playing my character Thomas when he gets hit, this ridiculous actor playing Grandfather he's twice the...

—Well my God Oscar he's not playing your character Thomas, he's never heard of your grandfather he's...

—Well he's twice too old! And he can't act he's as wooden as a, he can't even act he's a stick, stands there reading his lines there's nothing in his face at all it's just a face and he, now! Look, look at him with his scar this is where it's supposed to begin, this is where my play opens coming home with his battle scar it's the first line in the prologue isn't it? his own hand rising to brush at his stubbled cheek —where a cab driver bit him? and that voice, it's as lifeless as he is just listen to it.

—If you keep talking this way how can we listen to the...

—You don't have to! he seized up the bottle, —will you look at him? pouring the last of it —he's supposed to be seething with excitement and indignation, this letter his mother just gave him he's supposed to be exulting over the death of this uncle who'd humiliated him and cheated his father and now it's all his, it's revenge for the humiliation heaped on him since the day he was born and he's acting the part like a, like Father used to say? And he stabbed him in the back with a wet sock! No wonder Father hated it, seeing Grandfather played by this sullen morose, God, if Father could have seen it. If he could have seen what I saw there.

—Well it's not going to get any better is it, I mean you've read those reviews, do we have to suffer through it? We can just turn it off, there's no reason to get in a state over...

—I am not in a state! and he sank back muttering imprecations, finishing his glass and gasping with the effort of fighting off the creatures of his own invention travestied before his eyes narrowing at the unctuous duplicity in the Major's embrace of his hero's scarred wooden counterpart urging him north to claim what was now rightfully his and rescue the decaying plantation from the burden of gambling debts revealed in a vicious encounter belowstairs with his own lamed and sniveling son about to be shipped off as a substitute for the transgressor to unnamed battlefields beyond this one above where even now in canopied splendour none but the brave deserved the fair tempestuously breasted, flaming haired, her glistening thighs spread wide astride what now, flushed with a purple grace, was rightfully hers.

—Oscar where are you going? In answer he brandished the emptied wine bottle at a woman on the screen astride a mechanical marvel who had lost 118 pounds in just three weeks, —Lily? He'll never make it, will you bring in another? and to the startled look she drew —just go ahead, I mean my God at this point he probably deserves it.

A light glissando greeted her return with the threat of comic relief set up against the bleak prospect of a Northern mining shaft as she perched on the sofa's arm inexpertly manipulating the corkscrew. —Here, give it to me! his impatience less with her and the bottle which he had by the neck without a glance than for the figure now filling the screen in cunning parody of the manager of the mines, Bagby's obsequious brogue gone for the flagrant guile of old Calabria wheedling, remonstrating, cajoling and patronizing the new master by turns, now for his misguided notions of fairness in dealing with the striking miners, now for the uses of influence in getting ahead, breaking off for a highly theatrical interlude of mugging and arson and here came the playful glissando again as new comic possibilities emerged in the parade of petty thieves, rumpots, fugitives from wives and creditors and a brace of Chippewa Indians being cursorily questioned, pummeled, browbeaten, paid and fleeced as recruits for the Union army by the mine manager in his time away from raising stores of vermifuges, decorative sabres, trusses and mule feed cut with sand in the patriotic cause.

—Oscar be careful, that's going to spill.

—What? he looked up startled, righted the bottle against a cushion beside him and sank back muttering —listen! his impatience burst at her abrupt intrusion on the unwilling suspension of disbelief that seemed gradually to have come over him, the polished scorn of his defenses eroded by the desecration prospering before his eyes, enveloping his senses pillaged into submission to this version of his own creations, until at last the plot's device calling for the draft notice for the Union forces enmeshed his reluctant hero's ignoble counterpart in the fatal decision to send up a hapless boy from the mines as a substitute provoked no more than what might have been a wheeze of acquiescence or even in fact, one of satisfaction with this glancing shot at his own dwindling contribution even now, with another pull at his glass, dissolving altogether before his eyes in the mists of a country morning where a curtain stirred by a gentle breeze over a bared shoulder might have signaled the return of testimonial relief after a satisfactory bout with an overnight laxative but for the ominous rise of a cello and the burst of gossamered breasts suddenly and splendidly real as she flung a cape round her shoulders and cried out.

—Harry? are you awake?

—Here it comes Oscar, what you've been waiting for a tale of two...

—Lily where are you going.

—I already saw this part.

—See if there's any more juice while you're up, will you? And in a tumult of broken crockery and unsheathed blades, shouts of laughter and screams of despair, trampled gossamer, torn clothing high and low, plunging buttocks and tangles of limbs, howls of torment and triumph and a single gunshot, it all came true. —My God! she whispered, as the still life of wizened hands clutching a Bible, a bloodsoaked major's cockade crowning a sightless eyeball and the faintly heaving breasts of despoiled nudity faded away before the sparkling overtures of a sometime movie star pursuing the active life with a tennis racket no longer hampered by incontinence, and they woke to the clatter of glassware on a kitchen tray.

—Oscar? you want some of this juice? He sat licking his lips, stirred to filling his wineglass from the bottle tucked beside him.

—I really think we've had enough, don't you?

—No! he gasped getting breath, raising his glass unsteadily —there's still Antietam, the battle at Antietam.

—I think I'm going up, I'm exhausted. Harry?

—Really earned her three million there didn't she.

A recreation vehicle careening through mud, a man with lower back pain, that decrepit couple on a bed warping and heaving at the touch of a button, and the sharp notes of a bugle cutting through the suddenly surging rumble of cannon fire in the half dark brought him bolt upright like a trooper, —now! splashing the drink on his knee —look! That's Hooker, on horseback that's Joe Hooker on the ridge up here with his I Corps looking south toward the, can you see it? that little white spot, the Dunker church you can't really see it yet it's only five thirty in the morning almost a mile away where those flashes of fire from Jackson's artillery are coming from now Stuart's joining in, Jeb Stuart's horse artillery on a hill down by the Hagerstown road shelling us up here on the ridge and down there, that big farmhouse right here that's Miller's farmhouse where the what are you doing!

—Turning it down Oscar, it's getting louder and...

—Of course it's getting louder! The Union artillery's opening up for Hooker's attack, he's sending Rickett's division on his left through the East Woods and Doubleday's down the Hagerstown road with Meade in between now you can see them, his skirmish lines coming down the slope toward the cornfield and Miller's farm it's light enough now to look! in the cornfield look! Bayonets glittering through the leaves where the Rebels are waiting to, it's starting! It's starting! Torn to pieces look at them, the skirmish lines blown to pieces from the cornfield and Miller's farm so much smoke you can hardly see where the, where's the, here they are yes here they are! Six gun batteries look at the horses, six horse teams pulling them in at a gallop and the bugle calls they know what they mean, these old war horses they know what they mean look at that, thirty six guns lined up blasting the cornfield with canister now that boom! boom! in the distance, McClellan's long range guns up back of the Antietam oh it's glorious, crossfire tearing the cornfield to pieces Rebels going down whole ranks of them blown to bits now we're coming in, Meade's down the center of the line and Rickett's infantry from the East Wood smoke so thick you can hardly look! Did you see him? didn't you see him? the substitute from the mines there just for a second? he'd be in one of Meade's Pennsylvania regiments wouldn't he? God, it's glorious! he gasped, coming forward breathing heavily, gripping the edge of the sofa as the carnage grew even louder —what? I can't hear you!

—Because you're tipping over the, be careful! she came down beside him catching the falling bottle, —if you'd just stop bouncing up and down you'd...

—Give it to me give it to me! He filled his glass, drank it off and filled it again to the shouts and fire from the cornfield —there! a man's shoulder blown off —look out! too late, the boy in butternut hit full in the open mouth, mere boys, mere boys in homespun and blue in a screaming frenzy of bayonets and shellfire —unbelievable, it's unbelievable look at that! Half the regiment wiped out at thirty feet we're taking the cornfield there's Meade, there's Meade in the midst of it there's Meade look at the flags, battle flags the Sixth Wisconsin, Pennsylvania regiments and three hundred of the Twelfth Massachusetts with two hundred casualties now! We're almost there, the Dunker church Georgia boys trying to get over the fence pffft! shot like laundry hung on a line listen! The Rebel yell listen to it, Hood's division counterattack makes your blood run cold they're coming through! Driving us back they're driving us back, A P Hill coming in from the East Wood I mean D H, D H Hill's division right into the, ooph! Battery B, six old brass cannon it's Battery B charging straight into it look at that! Double rounds of canister hitting them at fifty feet the whole Rebel column's blown to pieces blood everyplace, blood everyplace that's Mansfield, wild white beard's got to be General Mansfield Hooker sending him in with his XII Corps riding down the line waving his hat hear them cheering he's, yes he's hit, horse is down and Mansfield's hit in the stomach God, get him off the field!

—Ouch!

—What's the...

—You hit me Oscar, can't you sit...

—Didn't mean to look out! Hooker, his foot smashed he's riding to the rear, brought in nine thousand men he's lost twenty five hundred killed and wounded and half Lee's forces are casualties where's the, where are we where's my glass.

—It's empty, why don't you just try to...

—Fill it up then! Signal flags wagging where are we, the creek down there's the Antietam down below yes we're up here with McClellan running the whole show there he is, with the telescope there he is, Hooker's I Corps shattered his whole right wing's collapsed where's Sumner, sending in Sumner's II Corps to turn Lee's flank watch the mess he makes of it, eighteen thousand men he's got three divisions, one can't get started one gets lost and Sedgwick's division's hit on three sides, Rebel brigades out of nowhere cutting down half the Thirty Fourth New York, two thirds of the Fifty Ninth wiped out could have ended right there if he'd broken Lee's flank but only a third of his forces get in there and leave two thousand dead and wounded in the West Wood while the Twentieth Massachusetts marches out with the look, look that's Holmes! wounded again yes the same man isn't it? the one they left on the beach at Ball's Bluff? You can hardly see the, it's terrible, watching it all on this tiny screen we should have one as big as this room seeing it in a theatre look at it, we're supposed to be looking out over forty acres, twelve thousand dead and wounded in barely four hours it's not even ten o'clock in the morning.

—Anyway I'm just real glad it's over Oscar, you're getting all sweaty and...

—But it's not! It should be but it's not, if they'd broken Lee's flank there the whole war would be over but the worst is now, right now you've seen it look at them! Parading down the slope bayonets flashing in the sun straight for D H Hill's regiments hidden in the sunken road I thought you'd seen it, the Bloody Lane you said you'd seen it!

—That's where I closed my eyes.

—All right go ahead, go ahead I'll tell you what's happening any minute, any minute there! a crash of fire filled the sunken road end to end —the whole Union first rank blown to pieces God, look at them! He had hold of a cushion pounding it, pounding it —McClellan's long range guns smashing the Rebel artillery look, the gunner's legs blown to aphh! the horses, shells tearing the artillery horses to pieces God it's awful, smoke down here in the sunken road you can't even see what they, they've stopped them! We've stopped their advance, the whole no, don't look, don't look piles of arms and legs men laid out on the straw they've made this barn a hospital surgeons covered with blood and arms and legs stacked up like my glass, where's my glass! gurgling, coughing, he filled it again crushing the cushion in his lap —finally! Sumner's Third Division finally getting here to relieve French God it goes on, it goes on, D H Hill breaking through the gap there it goes, there it goes the whole Confederate line collapsing why can't he send in his reserves and end the whole thing! McClellan's got ten thousand men up there send them in! send them in! he pounded the cushion —he won't, Lee's lines completely shredded McClellan could break right through but he still thinks he's outnumbered, seventy thousand men to Lee's forty thousand it's hardly noon he could end the war right here, Porter's whole V Corps sitting up on a hill playing cards all day and they won't send them in! he sank back getting breath, wiping a hand across his brow —all down hill from now on, all down hill, here comes Burnside two or three places he could ford the creek but he wants that little bridge the idiot. You idiot! he cried out suddenly and sank back again muttering imprecations as two regiments rushed the bridge under heavy fire, eyes glazing over as the bridge was engulfed in a tumult of men and horses, carts and wagons trying to cross it at once, heavy firing on the road toward Sharpsburg —he could still do it, twelve thousand men what's the matter with him! one unsteady hand holding the empty glass, the other searching the cushions as his breathing subsided, shoulders fallen in defeat.

—It's empty Oscar, don't...

—Well get, get another then! he gasped, —never fired a shot, a third of his army never fired a shot all gone to pieces, Lee withdrawing could have cut him off at the Potomac never fired a shot. Harry? his eyes dimming, —where's Harry.

—He's right there Oscar, I think he went to sleep, are you okay?

—Never fired a shot he mumbled, as the blood splashed leaves of corn and corpses, mouths open in full cry and shattered limbs and guns catching the last sunlight passed before them and twilight sparkled in pools of blood in the sunken road, caught the last glimmer of frenzy in the eyes of the horses turned toward the dying heavens in the stillness enveloping the dark as the descending darkness enshrouded the stillness vouched in a low sound of moaning, pierced by a scream as a fire, now another, and another, pierced the dark bursting the bloated bellies of the horses and the moaning rose with the careful tread of burial details in the cornfield, the East Wood, West Wood, Miller's farm and Roulette's and Piper's and the Dunker church and, slow and cautious as their tread, these impassable last fierce embraces in the sunken road —Harry? you okay? in a kind of panic—what's this? What's this! as a figure materialized with a terrible slowness, the pale scar livid on the pale cheek brooding down upon two bloodied faces twinned in this final agony more real than they'd been in life whining, whimpering, limping to this, eyes rolling from the mineshafts now wide and emptied —look! as the spectre faded, —look...

—It's spooky.

—Lily?

—Oh! You scared me, I thought you're upstairs asleep.

—Asleep? with this racket? and she snapped off the sound silencing a languorous blonde caressing the length of a shiny car fender as though it were a stalwart thigh. —Oscar? What's he mumbling about.

—He just fought the whole war.

—And are these the dead soldiers? she came picking up the empty bottles, —Harry? coming down on the arm of his chair, stroking his forehead —do you want to come up now? But still none of them moved as the sun rose silently flooding the pitted columns where a curtain stirred by a gentle breeze through a broken pane for a glimpse of bare tables, empty chairs as shadows moved among them, a spiffy four-in-hand coming up the overgrown drive beneath the weeping mosses and a lone figure carrying a carpetbag mounting the steps to pound on the door under their vacant stares through the broken pane flashes of red hair disheveled over features frozen in translucent beauty and an open bodice sheltered behind the scarred chalkwhite countenance confronting the florid entrance of the visitor finally rousing her to —what on earth is going on! with the hazy approach of a black figure up the wide lawn gradually becoming distinct as she restored the sound at the instant of a gunshot from somewhere and from nowhere the gentle swells of a symphonic mutilation of what might have been Swing Low, Sweet Chariot, as the end credits crept their way onto the emptied screen. —Oscar?

—What happened! He lurched upright gaping at the credit crawl, special effects, technical advisors, costumes, makeup, wranglers...

—God only knows, will you help me with him Lily?

—Harry look! There she is, the hairdresser there she is!

—What? what?

—No grab his arm, just help me get him down the hall.

—Never fired a shot.

—His shirt's really soaking, we can cover him up in the library okay?

—Stabbed him in the back with a wet sock.

—And get a wet cloth to wipe his face, I mean my God he's really had a very long day.

Far out across the silence of the pond some number, five or six, of swans composed a copse of white so still they might be frozen in the ice there in a morning sun so pale it seemed the cold's mere manifest serving to make it visible when here, along the nearer shore, came a string of wild duck their brilliant green of head and neck a luminescence, given the stingy sun, that must be all their own in orangelegged parade order past dowdy mates blown like withered clumps of vegetation marching puffed up against the cold in muted dignity abruptly desecrated, as she turned from the window, shorn and profaned on the silent screen where a black and tattered cartoon duck hurled a stick marked dynamite into the cartoon hunter's blind. —Lily? didn't I turn this off before I went up last night? and she did so, —oh good, you've made tea. I thought Harry was down here.

—He's in the kitchen making coffee.

—Well I've got to thank you for cleaning up in there, I dreaded facing it. And for straightening up in here, my God what a night.

—I thought you did.

—But I've just come down. You haven't waked Oscar have you?

—He's not in there.

—In the library? and he's not in your, well where in God's name is he, no just put the tray there by the window. He certainly can't have gone for a walk he'd catch pneumonia, I mean after last night he must feel like the wrath of God you don't think he, oh Harry. Have you seen him?

—Who.

—Who! Who do you think, the man in the moon?

—You mean Oscar? He sat down carefully balancing his cup, —haven't seen him, haven't seen a soul.

—You've been up for simply hours haven't you? It's almost noon, sitting here watching the Saturday morning cartoon shows?

—Matter of fact I...

—But you cleaned up the mess in the kitchen, that was sweet.

—Haven't touched a thing Christina, matter of fact I...

—My God! tea splashing all over the tray —it's gone! Look, his car is gone, look! as though at something to see rather than not to see.

—Maybe he went to, just went out to get the paper or something?

—Paper's right here I just finished it, he must have brought it in.

—Well of course he didn't go out to get the paper or something! He's not even, didn't you hear anything? didn't you hear him?

—I keep the pillow over my head when that crazy woodpecker starts and then that spooky fish gets...

—Stop it both of you, I mean my God he could have gone anywhere, the shape he was in last night he was ready to, he could be a hundred miles away he could be anywhere.

—Just that battle scene got him going Christina, bottle or two of wine I wouldn't worry about his...

—The way he was hitting everything I even have this bruise on my knee, waving his arms around it was like Al watching the Redskins with his sixpack yelling send him in! send him in! waving his arms and...

—Lily for God's sake can you be still! Wouldn't worry about him it's freezing out there, I mean he could be in jail somewhere he could be in the hospital with an accident couldn't he? You know all about that don't you Harry? Does he know how to drive that thing? has he ever driven ours?

—Look Christina, call the police you'll have to sign a complaint and if they pick him up they'll arrest him, start calling hospitals all you'll get will be the usual tanked up...

—Well what are we supposed to do, sit here? just sit here till some hospital in Georgia calls us?

—Or the police in Hoboken or he walks in the door, sit here and have some more coffee look, it was still warm when I came down he can't be far, don't hear anything before I have to leave we can worry about it then.

—Where are you going.

—Get some more coffee.

—I mean when you have to leave! Why do you have to leave?

—Just going to tell you. I talked to Bill Peyton earlier he wants to sit down and go over a few things before he...

—Bill Peyton Bill Peyton! It's Saturday Harry it's Saturday, why do you have to see Bill Peyton on Saturday!

—Leaving town tomorrow, something's come up in Aspen he's got to straighten out and I think he wants to talk about this senior partnership before he goes.

—Going to Aspen when Oscar may be in a ditch somewhere bleeding to death? If they want to make you a senior partner he can send you your diploma and then go skiing in Aspen and straighten out a few topless waitresses all he wants to can't he?

—Not that simple Christina look, sit down try to be patient, anybody bleeding to death I can cancel in an instant. Here's the problem, whole scene right now's like sailing through the strait of Messina between Scylla and Charybdis. You make partner, make senior partner with a fine old reputable white shoe firm used to mean you were set for life, now you've got the sea monster's cave on one side and a whirlpool on the other, liability as a partner you're on board risking being devoured by these monstrous suits and government regulators or sucked under and drowned in the unemployment pool.

—Well my God Harry, I mean they can't fire you, you said once...

—Talking about being sucked under when the whole ship goes down Christina, last few years eight or ten top firms have gone down and a dozen more ready to go right now, small firms wiped out all over the place, expartners out on the street who shed their blood for the firm in worries and legal battles brought on by some venerable old senior partner billing four hundred fifty an hour for making bad decisions they had nothing to do with while he puts in for twenty five hundred hours over the year, takes home about a third of the million that he brings in to the firm to pay out overhead and bonuses on the rest of the three hundred million pouring in from all their other accounts and then the senior partners sit down under the Christmas tree and share the profits.

—Well what makes you think Swyne and, where are you going.

—Told you, make some more coffee.

—Lily can make some more coffee and Lily? some more tea, and if you'll clean up that tray? I mean what makes you think they can blame you if the old tub sinks, you're not running General Motors are you?

—Don't understand Christina look, that's the point. You're not protected by limited liability like you are with a corporation, state regulations on these partnership forms you're wide open, the firm's liable means you're liable, insurance protection's like throwing your drowning sailor a lifesaver, a firm with two hundred lawyers at five or six thousand a head there's over a million in premiums right there. All those massive firings a while ago firms like mine were hiring right out of law school fattening up on those billion dollar mergers and takeovers, wild real estate deals, fancy office space and computer networks for these multinational accounts whole thing dries up overnight and the government regulators step in catch some monstrous financial institution cooking their books and we're part of the act because we'd advised them so down go earnings and blue ribbon reputations paying out fines and settlements on these suits by the Justice Department and a few thousand bitter investors first thing you know you're...

—Harry?

—You're paying these million, five million dollar claims from your own pocket, tens of millions in coverage but you've kept raising your deductibles to meet your premiums up twenty percent last year probably another twenty or thirty this one and zero for your legal costs fighting these malpractice suits growing like weeds wherever you...

—Harry! I mean why are you telling me all this about millions in deductibles and God knows else I can't even...

—Just told you Christina! Firm's liable means the partners are liable, big firm gets sued means you're not just accountable for your own work you're stuck for the work of other partners you've probably never even met.

—Well that's the most ridic, I mean you never told me all this I don't even...

—Didn't want to drag you through it, you don't even want to hear it all now do you? What I'm trying to tell you, risking everything you've got, home, pension rights, bonus profit shares everything you own, why our friend Sam there owns nothing but the clothes on his back, town house, cars, sailboat, summer place they're building right over here in Southampton put it all in his wife's name.

—Charming Harry, perfectly charming.

—What do you mean charming, what else could he...

—I mean our friend Sam Harry! I mean these malpractice suits springing up like weeds I mean you standing right there talking Oscar out of bringing a malpractice suit worried about Sam, about our friend Sam and this whole revolting self regulating conspiracy is that when he did it?

—Did what, I don't...

—Put everything in his wife's name so he wouldn't have to give Oscar anything but the shirt off his back and a box of dead fish how can you tell me this!

—Not talking about Sam I'm talking about us, things go sour we could be in the same...

—We? you're putting everything in my name is that how all this started?

—Started with me sitting down with Bill Peyton didn't it? Started with, tell you what it started with it started when I heard Mudpye had turned down partner, broke his neck to make partner they just handed it to him and he turned it down, had second thoughts and he turned it down. Breaking mine for senior partner I'm having a few second thoughts too, tell Bill Peyton I want to see the firm's balance sheets, bank borrowings, pension liabilities, insurance, problem clients, just take your friend Trish probably in for a few hundred thousand by now hasn't put up a dime what's she going to do, wait till they sue her?

—They may just wait until she sues them.

—Not funny Christina now look, I brought her in there and...

—My God I know it's not funny! I mean you look Harry, you brought her in there and all your fine venerable old senior partners could see was dollar signs, they knew she's a problem client Bill Peyton knew it everybody knows it, she'd sue the Queen of England if it occurred to her and you're going to talk to Bill Peyton about bank loans and balance sheets and these millions in deductibles on this insurance they've got on you? and you think you can trust...

—Not on me Christina no, on the firm, I've got half a million with them but that's just life insurance, these tens of millions I'm talking about are the firm, liability for the...

—For the firm while the firm takes your last drop of blood chewing pills, pouring drinks, car accidents my God do we have to go over all this again? Risking everything you own when Bill Peyton pulls a fast one and you think you can trust him talking about bank loans and balance sheets and God knows what you think you can trust any of them? All of it, the whole thing the whole atmosphere's mistrust, every breath you take no put it down here Lily, give him his coffee he needs it, nothing but mistrust, mistrust, mistrust, did you bring sugar?

—What it's all about Christina, if everyplace you looked here wasn't ridden with mistrust you wouldn't have one lawyer for every five hundred people mostly can't afford one anyway, whole country conceived in competition rivalry bugger thy neighbor, the whole society's based on an adversary culture what America's all about, you want to get into dialectical materialism supposed to be Marxist theory but we're the...

—I don't want to get into dialectical anything Harry, I mean my God we know that people will do anything and, listen. Listen! as those glass doors clattered closed —well thank God, Lily help him will you, give him your chair Harry give him your coffee he's pale as a sheet, my God without a coat look at him I mean he's probably caught pneumonia, can you tell me? what would drive any sane person out of the house at dawn in this weather, can you tell me?

—I went for a ride Christina. I wanted to go for a ride. Do you know what those men are doing in the trees out at the end of our drive?

—Men in the trees, will you pull that quilt up over his knees Lily? He's shivering, of course he feels perfectly ghastly, he probably doesn't remember a thing.

—Oh yes, yes, every second of it it was glorious! He came forward splashing coffee on the quilt —when Hooker brought up those six batteries of cannon? His officers riding out front with their sabres flashing setting up the firing line it was stunning, all the guns opening up at once raking the cornfield, those bayonets gleaming in the smoke and blood spattered all over the green corn they lost half their force, the Confederates lost half their force, it was glorious.

—While we're losing our minds here worrying about you in jail or a ditch somewhere catching pneumonia, for God's sake will you sit still and drink your coffee? Where are you going! Lily can get it for you.

—Going where Lily can't go for me. Hooker took over two thousand casualties Harry, two hours they never stopped for a second, twenty five hundred casualties in that bloody cornfield they never stopped for a second.

—My God look at him, a gallon of wine it still hasn't worn off if he drove like he's walking we're lucky he's alive, why he got up and put on that blue suit and a necktie to go for a ride he looks like he lost ten pounds overnight, he's white as a sheet.

—Because he's shaved, Christina. It's because he's shaved.

—Well no wonder he looks odd, I mean thank God he got rid of that asinine excuse for a beard, he looks like a schoolboy on his way to a funeral, that's what they're for aren't they? isn't that what funerals are for? her voice fallen abruptly to a tone as vague as the steps taking her aimlessly toward the windows, —all the hurt and anger and making up for these miserable notions of guilt, isn't that what funerals are for? to simply roll up all these confused feelings in a ball and, and simply fill the gaping hole that Father's left in our lives? I mean no wonder he looks numb babbling about blood on the corn and men in the trees, depriving him of that, it's like a last parting slap in the face from Father denying him that.

—Going too far Christina, probably never occurred to the old man the way he felt about these sentimental tributes and all your mealymouthed claptrap about the resurrection and the life just trying to spare everybody the embarrass...

—Harry he never spared anyone a thing in his life! He was the most, one of the most selfish men who ever lived, the law was the only thing that was alive for him people were just its pawns look at us! Look at poor Oscar and his whole, going back to that whole sad business about his mother it was simply coldblooded, Father was always coldblooded right to the end ordering up this cremation without even a fare-thee-well? a shiver shawling her own shoulders there gazing out over the frozen silence of the pond that would suffice, if he had had to perish twice, that poem about fire and ice whose was it, Yeats? that for destruction ice was great? but he had chosen for the fire, and then some line about desire? or hate?

—What? what did you say?

—No nothing, nothing I was, nothing.

—Clean getaway Christina, nothing that strange about it is there? Strip away the poetry and off to the crematory, time comes I hope you'll do as much for me.

—Don't joke about it! His whole world caving in around him and, Oscar? are you all right?

—Joke was on him, wasn't it? He'd paused there in the doorway doing up the front of his trousers, —the last laugh?

—What are you talking about.

—Bilk, that Neanderthal Senator Bilk, Father beat him to the wire on that impeachment didn't he? Stabbed him in the back with a cat's shinbone, you remember that Harry?

—Oscar just sit down, have you eaten anything?

—Have your choice of fathers, we just saw Holmes shot through the neck when the Twentieth Massachusetts was hit on three sides didn't we? so that smug autocrat could preen himself at the breakfast table at his son's expense, you've read that haven't you Harry? My Hunt after 'The Captain'? Self serving piece of sentimental humanism at his son's expense published in the Atlantic before the blood was dry on those piles of amputated limbs he loved it, Doctor Oliver Wendell Holmes he loved every minute of it.

—Well we've simply got to eat something, where's Lily.

—Got to get started Christina, I'll eat something later when I, I thought you'd come in with me.

—Obviously I can't can I? I mean this law clerk coming up here with God knows what for us to sign I hardly know what I'm doing.

—Don't have to rush it do you? Get Bill Peyton out of the way we can clear up any questions but it all looks simple enough, death and taxes, same old things people spend their lifetimes trying to outsmart, this place goes to you and Oscar with whatever's in the estate unless he's made some eccentric bequests somewhere, client we had left everything to fight against circumcision but...

—Harry? do you know how it ended?

—Probably a good bank balance somewhere Oscar, Federal judge's salary over a hundred thousand a year and expenses nothing but whisky and cigarettes? He was up pulling on his jacket, —hell of an irony isn't it? Federal judge at a hundred thousand with this stream of hotshot lawyers pulling down half a million, a million shouting at him showing off to the client sitting there guilty as hell he collects win or lose?

—No, no I couldn't figure that out. All the crying and moaning and those bodies piled up in the Bloody Lane with that sort of spectre standing there ankle deep in pools of blood looking down on the two dead substitutes? Because that was the whole point wasn't it, because Grandfather never appeared on the battlefield that was the point, it was Bagby who stumbled on their corpses at the end of act two but then what happened. I got confused, how did they end it? Did John Israel show up at Quantness right at the end? because I got confused and...

—Oh, got to confess Oscar I dozed off, pretty strenuous day for all of us and I...

—The whole scene with Kane in prison that's right out of the Crito in my last act I'll get it, you can read it I'll get it.

—Can't right now, I've got to get started. Where's Christina.

—But, all right, you don't have to. That's all right Harry you don't have to, it doesn't really matter does it? He came down unsteadily on the sofa —I just thought, you're not really missing anything but, no that's all right.

—Not what I meant Oscar, look.

—No no it's all right, it doesn't really matter does it, just a lot of, it's all those ideas I had that got in the way it's all sort of stiff and old fashioned, characters making speeches and, those ideas that just got in the way that's what happened, it doesn't matter.

—Look, I don't want to read it till I can give it my full attention that's what I mean, few things I've got to clear up so we can take time to sit down and do it right, you follow me?

—Because I just thought maybe I, I thought with no funeral service or stone or anything maybe I could still try to...

—Far as that goes nothing to prevent you from putting up a stone or a monument for him is there? Put it right out here on your grounds overlooking the pond if you want to? Make a lot more sense than lined up with a lot of crosses and stone angels, far as that goes you can always arrange a memorial service any kind you want to, these secular times that's what most civilized people do anyhow isn't it?

—But a fifth of the net, you probably couldn't mount much of a production on a fifth of the net could you, when you don't even know how much it will amount to?

—Tried to explain that to you Oscar, what that in lieu of phrase is in there for, keeps things halfway fair so the judge has the discretion to make an award in lieu of damages when their creative accounting comes up with a fifth of nothing but I don't get the connection between the...

—It's all right Harry no, it's all right I just thought maybe, kind of a memorial service because he wouldn't see it, he wouldn't be there to see it done the way I always hoped he would but I thought maybe it could be kind of a way to make things up to him for...

—Oscar can't you see! coming down suddenly almost a blow on the shoulder hunched there before him —you've done it? He'd read it hadn't he? stood by you didn't he? He came through for you with that brief he came up with for your appeal? did what he had to do and you've done what you had to do, you plan to carry around this load of guilt on your head for the rest of your life? what he tried to free you from while he was alive and now his death has finally done it, you're liberated! That's what this is all about, what a father's death is all about, any father, mine was a, when I was in law school he died when I was in law school yes he, he had a small business making mattresses always in the red, debt and bankruptcy broke his neck putting me through college and law school where people fail and drop out like flies afraid I'd think he'd failed, afraid he'd disappoint me if he couldn't back me up that was the worst of it because my real fear was disappointing him if I did fail, killing ourselves because we were afraid of disappointing each other, can't you see?

—Yes but, but my father was...

—They're all fathers! Never got to see me graduate even then I felt like somehow I'd let him down, never saw me make partner and I felt like I could never make it up to him till I finally realized I could never be afraid of disappointing him again, only of disappointing myself I'd been freed! Free to win or lose, drop out and fail throw the whole thing over if I think it's what I should do right now, run for president or hang for murder you've been liberated! hands on both shoulders bent over him now almost shaking him —you're free! All those years of being on trial, of fear of disappointment and betrayal and being judged he's dead Oscar! The Judge is dead!

—Harry what, is everything all right?

—What? He straightened up sharply —oh, fine Christina yes, everything just fine.

—Well he hardly looks...

—No no, just fine aren't you Oscar? standing over him there rubbing his hands like some fighter's trainer scanning the battered hulk after the final round, —he'll be fine.

—Well I've made you sort of a sandwich for the drive in and Harry, will you do something for me? Will you get to the dentist and do something about this tooth? You were up and down half the night it's driven me crazy, I mean if you won't do it for yourself will you do it for me?

—Try to squeeze it in Christina, first chance I get, say goodbye to Lily where is she, in the kitchen? and he was off down the hall, a look back over his shoulder coming in straight for the cupboard, —a little toothache medicine, don't mind do you Lily?

—Sure. You okay? She watched him tip the bottle up a moment longer, that close to him backed up against the sink there, watched him drink it down, clear his throat, looking at her.

—Got to thank you for everything Lily, you've been terrific putting up with all this and, and take care of him, of both of them will you? his arm suddenly around her pressed hard against him, a hand out as though to steady himself reeling with that scent of soap and perspiration beading her forehead where he kissed her, and her upper lip kissing her there, recovering his hand lingering at her breast as though to save its memory as he backed off getting breath —and, and yourself, take care of yourself will you? leaving her flushed, getting her own breath, off up the hall scarcely pausing to embrace those shoulders slumped on the sofa seizing his case and his coat and his wife by a wrist out through the doors clattering behind them for another sharp embrace out there on the steps as though fleeing something too close for comfort without a look back to the bleak wave of a hand in the window, still there when she came back in.

—My God it's cold! She stood grinding one hand in the other, sniffing as after some fugitive scent gone before she could grasp it, looking about. —Well. You straightened up in here this morning didn't you. That was thoughtful.

—What?

—And the kitchen. I simply couldn't have faced it.

—But, but Christina? he turned looking anxiously past her. —Where's the dog!

—Well it's, I mean my God Oscar it's been gone for ages.

—But, where is it.

—Oh, Lily? Oscar's asking about the dog, have you seen it?

—Maybe somebody stole it or, no maybe they just came and...

—Well I think we can all breathe a sigh of relief, I'd better shop for supper before it gets dark, Oscar? do you want to drive? But he'd turned back to the window where a shudder seemed to run through him, framed there against the fading light. —Never mind, Lily? maybe you can turn on his nature program for him and just, and keep him company?

—It's Saturday.

—Well, you can just, she can just fix you some soup while I'm out Oscar try to relax, there's nothing we can do.

—All of a sudden, it's just strange all of a sudden having him gone.

—Of course it is, it's strange and difficult for all of us but we've simply got to get used to it don't we? People do after all, I mean it happens to everyone doesn't it? Sooner or later, I mean it had to happen sooner or later didn't it? And almost a hundred years after all, I mean...

—I meant Harry. I meant, I just meant having someone to talk to. Wait! Don't move!

—My God what is it now.

—Look! no be quiet, look! down there at the pond's frozen edge where three deer appeared casually chewing at growth in the dead grasses, their white tails blurting as a fourth emerged behind them all the larger for lofting his antlers alert to movement anywhere, to threat anywhere beyond them in a halt bringing up a foreleg poised disdainfully staring directly at him —look! he gasped again —how, how elegant!

—Where's my, Lily? have you seen my beige coat? her heels sharp crossing the room, —I'll look for some sole if they're still open, or flounder? and will you put on some potatoes to boil? heels clattering up the hall —I mean I'm quite ready just to go for a drive myself.

And here behind him, —Oscar? a hesitant hand on his sleeve as that clatter of heels closed on the clatter of those doors up the hall, —you want to come in and lay down? But he stood frozen there as the emptied waste he looked out on, left alone with the remains of the day until it was gone with the burst of lights at the stairs, in the halls, in the kitchen, white wine and white flounder and boiled potatoes on the clatter of white china plates at the kitchen table given over to the clatter of dishes at the sink and to stillness at last spreading the darkness in another dimension, greying with the seepage of dawn, shattered by the ring of the phone.

—It's him.

—God it's Harry, I knew it!

—At that telephone out on the highway, no. It's this law clerk.

—I don't believe it! in a flurry of coats nonetheless —no I'll go, wake Oscar will you? No don't, don't it's not even daylight but some tea when I'm back and turn up the heat, he'll be frozen. I don't believe it! but a minute later the roar of the car out there nonetheless, and she was gone.

—What happened?

—It's this law clerk Oscar, she went to get him. You okay? He sat down heavily, pulling the quilt over his knees, sipping tea when she brought it, gaining his feet when she blurted —here they are.

—Lily? can you help us here? and get him some hot tea he's frozen, he got a ride in a truck from the airport God knows how he found us, can you help us Oscar? Give him your quilt and wait, drag this big one inside, be careful the string's breaking. I think he wants to go to the bathroom, will you show him? skewing an old Gladstone bag ahead of her with one foot —and take this, and will someone turn up the heat? when he'd returned buttoning up the gap of his trousers to settle in an armchair here they were in their various stages of hasty undress like some depraved version of Christmas morning, dawn breaking through the frosted panes and the creak of the heat coming up arrayed round this frayed apparition of Christmas past or, worse, one yet to come, grounded in a beaver collared overcoat from ranging across the starry heavens where he'd got himself locked in the airborne toilet missing the complimentary victualing being supplanted now in a rash of tea and crusts where he bent forward to open the yellowed pebblegrained old Gladstone, their faces those of aging children in that instant where vestiges of eager anticipation disappeared as he pulled out a bottle sheathed in a much darned green sock to meliorate the cup that cheers but not inebriates, spilling a carpet slipper and sending a coffee can rolling across the floor toward the unadorned fireplace. He needn't have brought it, —I mean we've plenty of coffee, would you rather have coffee? Coffee? no, this was the ashes he told her, they'd tried to palm off a hundred dollar urn on him that would have made the Judge mad as hell, the whole cremation arranged and paid in full twenty years ago signed sealed and delivered —but my God! she thrust it at arm's length —I mean what shall we do with it? laying the can up on the mantle. Well, you couldn't do better than human ash for making fine dishware, that fancy English bone china they fire and powder up animal bones but he knew a man that had them to make a chop plate with his wife's ashes and every time he sat down and said grace before dinner he'd —Oscar, can't you do something? I mean, I mean we can put him in the library, will you take his things? and gesturing at the mantle —and that, for God's sake will you take that in there too? waking the mists of memory to reveal that somewhere, China or someplace like that, it was said when a great man dies it was like a whole library burning down, he'd burned all the Judge's papers first thing like he'd been instructed to do but just to think of all kinds of things heaped up there for almost a century that never even got put down on paper lost and gone forever right up there in that coffee can, now wouldn't a nice fire in the fireplace cheer things up? —Please! Can't we stop talking about fire before he burns down the whole, Lily when you've dressed will you help me in the kitchen while I go up and get something on? And there some minutes later over a glutinous mass churning on the stove —what in God's name is that.

—It's that old vanilla pudding we got when your friend came out here with the...

—Anything hot yes, I mean a few more pulls at the bottle he's got wrapped in that old sock we can put ham gravy on it and he won't know the difference, of course I suppose that means getting a ham.

—But how long will he be here?

—Well we've got to put him up overnight don't we? I mean after a trip like that I'm sure he expects, oh Oscar. What's going on in there.

—He's watching cartoons on television Christina, listen. You're aware that's Father's coat he's got on aren't you?

—Why, do you want it? And that battered old Gladstone bag that was Father's too wasn't it? God knows what else he's got in it, I think I smell something burning. I mean bringing a can of human ashes as a house present he may plan to spend Christmas with a roaring fire in the fireplace it's all he can talk about now, don't you smell something? Burning bones and papers and libraries he's, no! No he's smoking in there Oscar go in and stop him! he's a pyromaniac go in there and stop him before he burns the place to the ground will you? Lily I'm going up the back way and lie down until we can go shopping, if he gets hungry you can give him some of your pudding and start a list will you? Ham, put down ham and, and grits, don't they eat grits?

—What are those.

—God only knows, just write it down will you? slipping off her shoes to find her way up the dark stairs as stealthily as she came down them when the empty kitchen had waked to the full light of day, through the hall to tap at the sunroom and lead out through the butler's pantry and the tradesman's entrance round to start the car with a bare murmur leaving the house and barren hearth behind.

—Where have you been!

—Well Oscar where does it look like we've been, let him take that one Lily it's heavy, it's got the ham in it. Will you help her?

—You've been gone since, slipping out without even telling me it doesn't take three hours to buy a ham. Why did you buy a ham. I don't like ham, I never liked ham and I don't like...

—Will you simply take it in? or do you want to stand out here in the cold reciting poetry, it's Sunday Oscar. We had to drive sixteen miles down the highway to find a place open in that revolting shopping mall with every bloated obese local specimen pushing mountains of inedible junk food wherever you wait, hold the door will you Lily? That bag's splitting, will you see what he dropped? as they reached the kitchen, —just put it all down there.

—But what are these?

—Can't you read the label? It says Tater Skins doesn't it?

—And Black Bean Nacho Chips, Fried Hog Rinds why did you, Cream of Wheat? Does anyone here eat Cream of Wheat?

—For grits Oscar, they didn't have grits so...

—But grits are corn, hominy grits are made from ground corn.

—Fine! Put ham gravy on it and he'll be fine, I mean my God Oscar we can do something to make him feel at home short of burning the house down can't we? He's not smoking in there is he?

—No, he just brought those packages of Picayunes that Father left because he thought I might like them. He wants to know what we do for fun around here. He thinks the place is gloomy. He says if we'll put a pool table in there he'll show me a few tricks.

—Put in a, I mean my God how long does he expect to stay! He was just bringing up some papers and things for us to sign wasn't he? about the will? I mean Father left more than a few packages of Picayunes didn't he?

—He brought Father's decision in that case about Spotskin and

Hiawatha's Magic Mittens, do you want to hear about little James B suing his father as guardian over the royalties and a local court appointing his lawyer J Harret Ruth as his conservator? about the thrilling success of his father's junkyard theme park The American Way as a tourist attraction till a three year old got locked in an old fashioned icebox? about little James B himself hailed before Wink County Court over his mastiff and salukis fighting making the night hideous with their howls? He brought this latest Cyclone Seven First Amendment decision where Szyrk and the Village reversed their positions before two little kids drove a pickup truck into it just before he came up here and...

—Please! I don't want to hear about it, I mean you're the one who was longing for someone to talk to weren't you?

—I didn't say somebody to listen to did I? I tried to talk to him about the movie, about how the whole thing ended and he said at Appomattox he thought I meant the war so when I told him the war could have ended right there at Antietam if McClellan had sent in his reserves or if Burnside hadn't made such a mess of that bridge crossing and pulled up short of Sharpsburg when Lee's lines were destroyed or if they'd cut off Lee's retreat that night across the Potomac at Boetler's Ford we would have...

—Lily turn on the oven will you? I suppose we have to bake this thing I've never fixed one, it probably tells you on the wrapper God knows how long it will take.

—He usually has dinner around four thirty Christina, he said...

—At four thirty! We're not running a nursing home here, you can fix him a nice plate of Tater Skins and try to straighten out all this business about Father, that's why he came up here isn't it?

—No but that's what I'm trying to tell you, he finally admitted he didn't know how it ended, he said Father got up and walked out after that great battle scene when that ghostly spectre appeared standing there brooding over those two corpses in the Bloody Lane that was supposed to be Grandfather and when I said maybe that was why Father was upset with me for exploiting the family and Grandfather if he thought I wrote the script like it said in the newspaper and I asked him to read my last act he said he...

—My God, just hand me that bag of Tater Skins and a napkin, do I have to do it myself like everything else around here? and over a shoulder as she reached the hall —Lily, we'll eat when we usually do if he can make it to the table, put the ham in when the oven gets hot and then read the directions and some yams in with it, they're in that bag on the floor.

Bake uncovered on a rack in preheated 325° oven ½ hour to the pound, remove 1 hour before it is done and cut away rind, score with diagonal gashes, dot with cloves and glaze with 1¼ cups brown sugar, 1 tsp dry mustard, 2 tblsp vinegar, garnish with pineapple slices.

—But what about the gravy?

—There wasn't any, there was just this what looked like this little piece of tar in the bottom of the pan so I threw it out.

—Well we've got to eat, get him in to the table will you Lily? And you can start carving this thing Oscar, I mean there's no sense hauling it in there it's enough for an army, hand me a glass will you? And where's the scotch, I mean I don't dare take it in to the table for obvious reasons God, I wish Harry were here, don't cut yourself. Has she put out the silver? And for God's sake keep the wine at your end of the table, we'd better put it in a carafe just the sight of a bottle could, oh Lily. Are we ready?

—He's asleep.

—Well wake him up!

—I can't. I poked him a little and he just sort of moaned with that empty bag of Tater Skins in his hand, he looks sort of yellow.

—I mean you don't think he's had a seizure or something do you? did you feel his pulse? Oscar go and see.

—No I just, I didn't want to touch him it's sort of spooky, he...

—Don't be ridiculous, Oscar put that knife down and do something.

—I am not going in there and feel his pulse Christina. Why did you give him that whole bag of Tater Skins, no wonder he's turned yellow, you can take these plates in Lily I'll bring the...

—Why on earth should she take the plates in, I mean we can sit down and eat right here in peace and quiet now can't we? Whatever made me think I could sit down with him in there to straighten out these papers we have to sign for Father's estate, every time he dug for them in that awful Gladstone bag he came up with something else, didn't we fix a vegetable? I thought we had some peas, those instructions he gave the jury over that wretched child that drowned letting Jesus in at the back door when he'd just finished throwing God out of the courtroom when that odious dog was killed? I mean Harry thought they'd be livid when he practically indicted Jesus for manslaughter but they came out singing his praises for respecting their intelligence of course they hardly understood a word he said, throwing in a Latin phrase or two they thought he was speaking in tongues, Jesus he talked English didn't he? her voice rising to the nasal cadences of far off Stinking Creek —right there in the Bible where he cast those devils into a herd of swine that ran into the sea and drowned just like the time those pigs old Jim Harps had to run and get drowned right there in the Pee Dee where the county agent said it was probably swine fever got to them, did you take those yams out? They're probably burnt to a crisp, not that it matters at this point pour some wine will you, Lily? Talking to them in their own language with that story about the bonfire sparks blowing over and setting the neighbor's house afire same thing with old Frank somebody, set a trash fire blew right over and burned Goody's corncrib down to the ground wouldn't pay him a red cent, I can't possibly eat all this Oscar here, take it back. They liked how he got at them Catholics too, baptising their young before they're hardly off the tit I mean my God, respecting their intelligence? Just a good thing they had a fine man like the Judge to hold this trial, had it down there at Wink County Court with some jury from Tatamount and Stinking Creek where everybody knowed how Billye Fickert shacked up with that fertilizer salesman before she married Hoddy Coops after Earl took off for Mississippi when they run him out for throwing lye down Hoddy's well a jury like that would have give the whole store away, can you tell me how Father could have put up with that for thirty years? can you?

—No wait Christina, that doesn't make sense giving the whole store away to somebody who...

—That's what I'm telling you! None of it makes sense, naming this, this babbling lunatic his executor? I mean you think there may not be something to it? that talk about madness running in the family when that loathsome Senator Bilk was ready to impeach him? burning his effigy down there one day and what a great man he was the next when Bilk feels the wind change blowing his trash fire over to burn down Goody's corncrib so he grabs Father's ghost for his reelection campaign while his law clerk sits in there eating

Tater Skins with a spicy story about Old Lardass he wanted to tell me when I finally gave up, you can try again in the morning I simply haven't the strength.

—No but wait, don't you want...

—I'm exhausted Lily, I can't eat another bite just hand me my glass, I'm going up the back way and if Harry calls? already slipping off her shoes —will somebody wake me?

—I never even knew those stairs were back there.

—But then you never had servants either did you, oh and Oscar? pausing there in the shadows —for the love of God, make sure he's got no cigarettes when you put him in the library for the night, I mean he'll burn it down and then tell us it's just like a great man dying.

—It's spooky she whispered, to the fading creak of treads and risers gone so long untrodden up the dark stairs, taken up when darkness had stilled through the kitchen itself and the bare floorboards of the halls, the hesitant opening of a bathroom door and the wavering trickle that followed, the shuffle of carpet slippers and the distant clatter of a fallen spoon pulling the pillow over her head till at last the eery light of the fishtank yielded to the sunroom reclaiming its name with a day soft as spring and the echo of raucous laughter down the hall.

—What in God's name is that.

—He's in there watching a game show.

—At this hour? Oscar take him some coffee and get him started digging out those papers we're to sign before he gets his hands on that vile green sock again, Lily? What's this mess on the stove.

—He must have made Cream of Wheat when he was up in the night.

—And the ham, did we leave the ham out? It looks like somebody'd gone at it with an axe.

—Maybe it was these mice that I...

—Lily there are no damn mice you're just seeing shadows, I mean did you hear him out there?

—Maybe he didn't turn the light on, I heard these noises and this shuffling in the hall when the bathroom door squeaked and this trickle trickle trickle every time he went in there because he left the door open, it was spooky.

—Well it's more than spooky, as soon as Oscar digs out these papers to sign we can drive him to the airport, I mean we can't live huddled here in the kitchen like hostages while he sits in there looking like death warmed over cradling that sock in his lap watching game shows and, Harry hasn't called has he?

—That was Reverend Bobby Joe about Daddy, where he just got out of jail down there? banging the saucepan in the sink, scraping the dregs, muttering —they ought to of kept him there.

—Your daddy's full of surprises isn't he, you can throw out those yams too they're burnt to a crisp.

—It's not him no, it's Reverend Bobby Joe that was in jail for yelling at that trial of that boy that got drowned when Daddy was coming up here to get reconciled? So now he can't come because he's going in the hospital for this big operation where Reverend Bobby Joe's down there giving him all this spiritual comfort getting him right with the Lord in case the Lord calls him and if I should go down there and...

—Yes, well meanwhile you can go in and see if Oscar's getting anywhere before the Lord calls all of us, I mean you'd think he could simply pick up the phone and tell me what's going on, I am his wife aren't I? Driving out of here like a madman for some kind of showdown with Bill Peyton you can never have a showdown with Bill Peyton, are we out of milk again? I mean that's why he's their managing partner, pats you on the back, tells you a joke, you're off for a chat with the firm's psychiatrist and suddenly you realize he's thrown you both ends of the rope up there on the bridge waving goodbye while you're not waving you're drowning, now where are you going.

—In to see whether Oscar...

—Never mind, I'll do it myself like everything else here, and those crumbs and God knows what under the table when you sweep up? already through the door with —Oscar? and up the hall —where are you! but here before her loomed only the solitary figure seated in the halo of the screen busied just then with a woman gnashing gleaming dentures with her secret for keeping them in place taken up, as though on cue, in a grimace of clamping in the real thing that stopped her dead. —But, but where's Oscar? At this a hand came up to flutter fingers stained with a generation of Picayunes off in the direction of the pond, the sea, the tired waves vainly breaking, where hopes were dupes fears might be liars, could they turn this thing off so they could get down to business? breaking through the mists of God only knew what lost soliloquy still trembling on his lips to bring him forward gasping over the gaping Gladstone and hand over a clutch of letters in a faded hand bound up with twine which she thrust aside with the emptied Black Bean Nacho Chips bag from the floor, he'd brought some papers up here for them to sign hadn't he? her free hand scribbling a lavish signature on the air but wait, those letters? The Judge had wrenched them away from those old biddies at the historical society, threatened them with perdition if they didn't hand them over when some black showed up down there trying to register them for copyright, maybe should have burned them like the rest of the Judge's papers but once they'd burned the Judge himself they weren't rightly his anymore but the survivors', looked up the law on it right there in 17 U.S. Code 201(d)(1) where copyright ownership may be bequeathed by will or pass as personal property, couldn't copyright them once he'd burned them up could they? right there in Section 203(a)(2)(c) where the rights of the author's children and grandchildren are in all cases divided among them and exercised on a per stirpes basis just thought he ought to explain it doing his duty as executor right to the letter, those old biddies had already let some outsider in to read them where they had no business to was when the Judge read them the riot act and —Please! she beseeched him, half across the room now to toss the packet on the heap of bills and brochures, threats and glossy invitations to prospects of still further threats crowding the sideboard —you, thank you you, thank you for taking such care but, yes but now what you want us to sign and get it over with so you can get back to your, to get home we can take you to the airport or whatever you, or the bus if you...

—Christina?

—Well my God Oscar where have you been! I thought you, who's that.

—Yes it's Mrs, it's that real estate woman Christina, she's got a prospect waiting out in her car and I've tried to tell her there's some misunderstanding because when I called her we...

—This is ridiculous, I mean why on earth did you let her in.

—I thought it was somebody answering my ad for a secretary and...

—I just said ridiculous didn't I? and she turned on the woman with —what made you think the place was for sale?

—Why, I've been here before you know, and when your husband called I thought the first thing I could do was to...

—He is not my husband! and the second thing you can do is to be on your way.

—No that's quite all right, I've plenty of time and it's such a beautiful day. You don't mind if I look around a little do you? smiling the lipstick on her teeth —such a charming site, and just look at the view! flinging a handful of red nails at the pond out there as though already embarked on a sale —or if you're only thinking of renting? Because you'd need a good deal of work done wouldn't you, that front porch to start with it's positively dangerous and old Mister Paintbrush to brighten things up, it's a little gloomy in here isn't it but...

—It is not for rent! now...

—Oh I understand perfectly, and for a sale of course you wouldn't need to bother, buyers always have their own ideas it would just be throwing your money away and I wouldn't let that happen to you would I.

—God knows what you'd let happen to us, Oscar you started all this now do something!

—Yes I tried to explain, when I called we just wanted some sort of appraisal because the property belonged to my father and...

—And this is Dad? she swooped at him red in tooth and claw cowering there in the armchair, life preserver muffled in a much darned brown sock in his lap at the ready —I, I should have known yes it's, the nose? she backed off warily —I'd say, I'd say a whisker over three million? out of harm's way now, —yes, say three million two with this sweeping view over the pond and the swans, look at them! You can't find this anymore with these wetland setbacks, this four acre piece right up here across your driveway that just went for two million six with no view at all, did you know the people?

—We did not, why in God's name would anyone pay two and a half million the house is a perfect rats' nest.

—Oh it's not for the house they'll tear that down in a wink, it's for the site, it's quite an exclusive area here and right on the pond even if it's only a cove there where they can't take the trees down for the hundred and fifty foot setback and all they'd see is a mudflat even if they could but they'll cut down everything else, they'll have to for the house they've planned by this famous post modern architect, a regular showplace, they're very wealthy needless to say I think they made it in parking garages and...

—But those were probably the men I saw in the trees there Christina, they must have been surveyors and...

—It all sounds perfectly revolting, I mean you don't become wealthy building parking garages you simply get rich there's quite a difference, chopping down everything in sight to build a showplace out here it sounds quite sickening, you can find your way out can't you?

—Oh they're going to landscape, I've heard they've put aside a million just for landscaping it should give real estate values here a real boost and, oh! It's been such a pleasure talking to you I almost forgot my poor client sitting out there in the car, you don't mind if I bring him in just for a moment to see your lovely view? It's such a beautiful day and...

—I do mind! Oscar for God's sake will you see her to the door?

—Oh no, no, I can find my way, another time then? Such a pleasure meeting you, you have my number yes and while I think of it you'll want to do something about your driveway out there won't you, I almost hit a deer coming in they are such pests, they'll chew up everything in sight till not a tree's left standing.

—Now where was I! She stood with her fingertips pressed to her temples until the doors up the hall clattered closed —my God, such a beautiful day! Just to get that odious woman's voice out of my head, now where was I.

—I thought you were finding these papers for us to sign and...

—I thought that's why I sent you in here an hour ago, now will you sit right down there with him and get it over with before I come back? I'm going out for a walk.

Such a beautiful day! or what had been till that odious woman's voice reduced it to an epithet, and she shook her head as though to empty it of that jangling echo of words cluttering all that lay about her coming down the lawn toward the pond, toward the swans look at them! but they were already a distant trail of white across the water fled, like her, to rescue their serenity from a raucous visitation as she descended to the narrow strand, picking her way more slowly now the sandy edge gave way to reeds, to shoals of mud, to stagnant pools where suddenly the crows burst in a rage of cries that drowned her own, where a step further would have trampled what had been a sort of face snaggle toothed and staring up from eye sockets plucked clean, staggering back to recover her foot from the paw gently stirred there on the still backwater her balance almost lost again blinded by the flats of her hands, deprived like the breath she gasped for retreating to the hard crest of the road leading her away past those silent hulks shuttered for winter and on to the dunes looking far down the beach to the cut where turning the pond brackish came silent, flooding in, the main, a stiff breeze harassing her every retraced step and garbled metaphor the long way back under those mangled pines strewn with the jangling echoes of a million just for landscaping to clatter up the steps of that perilous veranda and the doors closing behind her, and her name reaching her the length of the hall, —Is that you Christina? You had a phone call, it was...

—Harry? When is he coming out.

—No, no Lily said it was somebody from his office, they said it was urgent and...

—Well if it's so urgent couldn't he have simply picked up the phone and called me himself? No I've told you what's urgent haven't I? signing these things and getting this memento mori with his green sock out of here, have you done anything about it?

—Yes I, it's a brown sock now he said something about a hair of the dog and...

—I, don't tell me about a hair of the dog! just, some tea, some hot tea.

—She'll get it but listen, there's only one thing for us to sign Christina that's all, it's a waiver and consent saying we won't contest the will so it can be probated that's all he brought.

—Well it can't be! Coming all the way up here just for, couldn't he have mailed it? both of them closing in —I mean, simply have mailed it? coming down on the sofa, the strength gone out of her —oh Lily, thank God bring me some tea will you?

—You okay? You look real pale.

—I'm, please just, just bring me a drink.

—There was this call for you, they said can you come right in there they sounded real serious, they...

—All right I'll call them! Now will you do as I ask? and she was back up for the phone, Mister Lutz? All right, Mister Peyton then? out of town? both of them? but who was the, —what? I said I'm his wife aren't I? This is ridiculous, why don't you know how to reach them! finally banging it down —my God, you never heard such confusion, they all sound scared out of their wits I mean no wonder Harry thinks the whole ship may go down. Sailing in there to confront Bill Peyton over pensions and balance sheets, if they're forcing him out can't he simply call me? already assailing the phone again —you see? He's not answering, I suppose I've got to simply go in, driving all of us out of our minds he'll be standing there in a towel naked with a drink in one hand like the last time just didn't want to upset me, stupid predicament he got himself in no reason he should bother me with it, nothing I could have done with my hands full out here running this madhouse find my sweater will you, Lily? I thought you were making tea, the beige one, Oscar stop standing there, he found this idiotic paper to be signed didn't he? Well where is it.

—With the will, here, he wants us to read the will before we sign to make sure we under...

—But I thought it was already probated, I mean why in God's name would we contest it if we're the sole beneficiaries, equal shares and per stirpes and the rest of that nonsense?

—There's a bequest in there for him Christina, a bequest for five hundred dollars and he must be afraid that we'd...

—And that's why he came all the way up here? My God I've never heard such a miserable, where's a pen, can we get this ridiculous business over with?

—When it's signed by a witness and...

—Well Lily can write her name can't she? Has he got a pen? and she stood over him searching deep among worn folds of worsted, reminded of a case down there where they had an old night watchman who couldn't write signed his pension checks with his thumbprint till somebody noticed he must be over a hundred and ten years old with the checks still coming through and when they investigated they found his thumb in a bottle of formaldehyde up on a kitchen shelf with the green tomato preserves and —just give me the pen!

—But Christina wait, you're not taking my car are you? one step behind her up the hall —you can't just leave us here you can wait for him to call, can't you? and at the door —you're just using this! You're just using it as an excuse to get away and leave us with...

—Exactly.

Name three African countries beginning with C.

—You ought to get on one of those Oscar.

—One of what! he snapped over the clamour of the studio audience greeting Cameroon.

—He's already up to almost four thousand dollars, they let you choose your own category and you could...

—Listen, we've got a game show going right here, she just drove out with my car how are we going to get him out of here, I don't know when she'll be back we've got to shop for food and...

—You want a ham sandwich?

What breed of African antelope is named after an American car? And the din went on interspersed with graphic portrayals of lower back pain and laxatives, arthritic fingers and acid stomach, incontinence and hemorrhoids each summoning a moan of satisfaction embracing fellowship with this geriatric fraternity in armchairs, loungers and contorting mattresses throughout the land gnashing dentures over Black Bean Nacho Chips and Tater Skins with another pull at the brown sock as afternoon displaced the morning and the conquest of Africa eighteen thousand dollars the richer had long since given way to the interminable war between the animal and vegetable kingdoms on the nature program where a potato leaf under attack by a caterpillar provoked a lethal case of indigestion in its assailant and a belch from the solitary audience intruded upon with suggestions for his departure by bus? by plane? He must have got a round trip ticket hadn't he? as mountain pine beetles busy boring out lodgings to lay eggs for a new generation in the mighty ponderosa pine were assailed by a noxious flow of resin engulfing the tiny nursery, they could even call a cab to get him to the airport while the weather was still fine, it could change overnight with a storm, a blizzard, marooned here with the ham whose aroma even now crept near lending its pungent emphasis to a coyote tobacco plant rewarding a jack rabbit's ravin with a severe attack of diarrhea, she'd found this can of creamed corn in the recipe book where it told you how to make these ham croquettes for supper when darkness had set in and the flowering clusters of wild parsnip flooding their grazing predators with poison had been displaced by Serbs slaughtering Croats on the evening news.

—Well he's dead isn't he? she said as he gasped scraping the last of his croquette into the trash. —He was floating around on top of the fishtank so I threw him away. You think I should go down there Oscar? I tried to call Mama before they do this operation on him only they were busy getting all this spiritual counseling in case the Lord calls him so I hardly know what I'm doing. You think you should go in there and feel his pulse? With those ashes he's got in that can up there on the shelf by your grandfather's picture in that black smock thing we can just leave this croquette and everything out here on the table for when he gets up in the night, you want to finish this wine? He gets up about five times and you hear this trickle trickle trickle in there, couldn't he close the bathroom door and just get it all done at once like everybody else? Old men, he muttered something about old men pouring off the last of the wine, a gland called the prostate that can swell up when men get old and cut off the flow from the bladder so —that's what Daddy has! she'd got her breath again, —this operation where they're going inside him and cut if off that's why I'm scared, you think I should go down there? A fairly common operation from all he'd heard, the real danger was cancer, if they got in there and found —cancer? What about me! she took up later pressing his hand to her breast there in the half dark —feel it? did it get any bigger? Well? she'd been told to have an x-ray hadn't she? a mammogram? —I'll go tomorrow, I'll go when she brings the car back out tomorrow.

—She hasn't even called has she? His hand warmed to its task, to the neighboring breast —I don't know when she'll come back, she just used that call for an excuse to get out of here, out of this madhouse she called it it was just an excuse, Harry will be there with a towel around him and a drink in his hand they're probably having a great time right now at some fancy...

—Listen! She stalled his hand rounding her thigh till the shuffle of carpet slippers had passed in the hall —no, there's something wrong Oscar, the way they sounded when they called, will you turn off that light in the fishtank? as the faint sound of a trickle reached them, —it's spooky.

A heavy mist pierced by sporadic gunfire waking the day, waking the sleeper to a confusion of realms with a fleeting white disc up there that might have been the sun or the moon confounding the day shapelessly enveloped out over the pond obscuring the opposite shore colliding with history as spectacle, the shotgun blasts with Hooker's opening volleys through the morning mists down on Jackson's two divisions bestriding the Hagerstown pike where by midmorning the slaughter was done, the attack repulsed and the mist burned away by the sun as it proved to be now over heels of toast and more tea meliorated by today's hair of the dog muffled in a much darned black sock all hopelessly aswirl for lack of a recipe to bring the ingredients together in some grand design illuminating the whole in this battle all tactics and no strategy, leaving no course open but getting to choose your own category in history as a game show.

What famous Civil War general was shot down and killed by his own men? abruptly conjuring history costumed as theatre: We are speaking of General Jackson, sir! clamouring through the clutter of blasted hopes and grand intentions, history as madness, the God-driven man who knows without question and acts, but admire him? riding forth in the dusk hand pointed heavenward to organize the pursuit rolling up the Union flank at Chancellorsville in one of the most brilliant manoeuvres in history as war, seizing death in victory and his commander left crippled without his right arm's divinely sanctioned audacity to prolong the slaughter for two more years staring its futility square in the face embracing war as madness with his General Ewell was it? who thought he was a bird? did bird songs and ate birdseed?

What three famous men living or dead have had the first name Rudolph.

Hitler? —Good God! he muttered, backing off furtively from the solitary audience propped up before the screen there in a litter of crusts and glossy wrappings —Good God! again, bursting into the kitchen, —can such stupidity really exist?

—You said you wanted somebody to talk to didn't you?

—I didn't mean him I meant, I mean him yes, plain as the nose on his face when Lee lost Jackson the whole cause was lost but he wouldn't face it, he kept the slaughter going for two more whole years, half starved boys without shoes in their first long pants blown to bits at Vicksburg, Chattanooga, the Wilderness, that old fool in there with his fried hog rinds talking about the noble cause it was vanity, vanity that's all it was, look at Gettysburg. Lee might have taken Meade at Gettysburg but he couldn't get his act together, do you think Pickett would have led that insane charge if Jackson had been around taking his orders direct from the Almighty?

—I don't know Oscar, but we're out of bread.

—Have you looked? We can't be out of everything.

—There's this jar of olives.

—We'll starve him out, he muttered, coming down heavily on a wooden chair to seize the wine bottle there on the bare kitchen table and cling to it like a stanchion, —he wants some more Tater Skins when we go shopping how does he think we, will you hand me a glass? I never knew anyone could be so selfish even Christina, I can't even reach her. When I called there I got some awful woman who said she was Harry's sister I didn't know he had one, when I said where's Christina she said she didn't know or give a damn and hung up, what about your friend's car the one with red hair?

—He dumped her so she needed it back, all he wanted off her was what he got off of me but just wait! You can hire a cab can't you?

—To go shopping for Tater Skins? splashing wine on her hand where she set down the glass, —we can't even...

—We can starve him out Oscar but what about us, am I supposed to just sit here eating Cream of Wheat while you get the DT's drinking all this wine?

Bent unsteadily over the basin for a late afternoon shave the ultimate confusion of realms collided upstairs and down, reaching for a towel all unawares as he'd been of that excursion laid out erect beside her on a bed littered with cans of shoe polish that he was, as real as anything, this very instant walking naked into the junkyard of the mind here in the sunroom where sleep tempered the soft rise and fall of her belly and the descent of an intinerant hand idly scratching the warm crest mounting the vulvate den massed thick with hairs like some mortal Gorgon spread for the thrust of an impudent tongue in the shaving mirror turning to search a drawer for a clean shirt from the sticky doings in that marshy venereal bog where Dionaea muscipula closed the spined hinges of pudendal lips summoning up the legendary vagina dentata as he zipped up his trousers on their oblivious tenant, a faint whimper and flick of her tongue the only avowal of his visit, licking her lips and her hand rising gently kneading her breast coming over on her side where time passed over her unbroken and unheard as his footsteps down the stairs, her face still buried in the pillow when his howl burst down the hall full upon her starting her up crying out —I'm coming! where he stood as though turned to stone staring wide with horror at the screen, fifty, a hundred of them writhing in a ball round eyes mirroring nothing in this mating frenzy of darting tongues' search for the scented female among them seizing him by a rigid arm stumbling down the hall beside her to the kitchen drawn up panting, both of them, recrimination prompting her abrupt recovery with —so there! didn't I tell you? That's what it will be like!

—But what, what are you talking about!

—On your nature program in there, only the next time you'll really be seeing them! as she thrust the wine bottle from reach, —and Oscar? now fully recovered, —I need some money.

—But, good God so do...

—I have to go down there Oscar. Because I've been thinking about poor Daddy all alone down there with only Mama and this big operation where you don't know what can happen if tragedy strikes and we'd never had this chance to get reconciled like you and your daddy I'd never forgive myself. You want some coffee?

—No. Yes! Of all the, if tragedy strikes it's a common operation happens all the time there's no reason you no, no the only reason you want to go it's just an excuse, it's just like Christina it's just an excuse to get out of here and leave me with this this, with him in there and...

—Well what am I doing here anyway? What am I even doing here! It's spooky. If I came to help you out back when you were alone and get away from Al I can get away from him down there can't I? Because what am I supposed to do, you have to go in there and talk to him and pack him up to go home if you want to wait till she gets back because you already got done what he came up here for about your daddy's will and everything didn't you? and there's my poor daddy down there I don't even know if he's got one, where it was always Bobbie everything was for Bobbie and all this insurance mess on that Porsche he bought him now he hasn't got

Bobbie anymore with this big operation where the Lord might call him I have to be by his side don't I? I'm his daughter aren't I?

—You've waited this long, you can wait till she gets back can't you? and we get things straightened out here?

—I just told you Oscar, you can go in there and straighten him out right now. You said you think she's out having a good time with Harry someplace why should she hurry back out to this madhouse she called it and I'll need some money, I'm going in and pack.

—No wait, wait! but she was gone, and he sat muttering over his coffee finally digging in pockets to rescue a Picayune from a crumpled packet up lighting it at the stove to puff at it without apparent pleasure till a distant fanfare invited him up the hall into a brand new confusion of realms superseding the revelations of the nature program where that mass of male red-sided garter snakes, writhing in a lusty tempest of confusion brought on by one witty fellow among them oozing a female scent to entice their frantic courtship enlivened its own chances to line itself up along the back of the real thing when she raised her tail and the curtain on the spicy story going the rounds down there putting Old Lardass out of the race, seemed some homo's showed up claiming they'd had sex together at five dollars a throw five or six times in the back seat of a green Chevy back when the Senator was soldiering over at Fort Bragg and there's Bilk all fussed up denying it but this homo has it all down chapter and verse, time place license number and all, called himself Daisy back then got up as a girl all perfumed up with a blonde wig and left lipstick all over Orney's drawers smelling like a rose, had to confess he recollected Daisy all right he'd bragged about her to his buddies never knew the difference till this homo's arrested dressed in those black skirts like a priest for those altar boys and shows up asking Old Lardass to get him off for old times' sake or he'll —Listen! I don't want to hear about it now, I have to talk to you! or he'll tell the whole world about —listen! What was that! and he was back down the hall where she stood in the kitchen trembling over the puddled breakage of the teapot smashed on the floor. —No it's all right, turn on some lights before you step on the, what are you doing!

—That! and a dinner plate smashed at his feet, —and that! but he'd caught her hand and the teacup with it —oh I told you, didn't I tell you?

—But who? and he got her to a chair, an arm round her quivering shoulders, elbows plunged on the table and a dishcloth stifling her sobs —what happened?

—It's Daddy!

—But, but wait, wait just try to, there's nothing you could have done just try to let yourself...

—I called Mama to say I was coming down there and and, and...

—No just try to, try to relax there's nothing you could have done is there? his hand tightening on her shoulder standing over her there, pressing her close —you knew it was going to be a serious operation and...

—I should have gone down there! I should have gone while there was still time I told you didn't I? where I still could have talked them out of it and got reconciliated before it was too late?

—Well you couldn't have, listen. When the doctors say an operation's necessary you can't talk them out of it and, and you shouldn't because, you can't blame yourself you shouldn't even try because they, because that's what it was for, to save his life that's what the operation was for and if he died while they...

—If who died.

—But, your father, you...

—I just talked to him.

—Yes I, I know, I know and, and I'm sure he heard you aren't you? a hand dubiously stroking her temple, —I'm sure he...

—Jesus Christ Oscar what are you talking about! She wrenched away from him, wiping her tears and staring at him —who said he was dead! I said I just talked to him didn't I?

—But, but I thought...

—And he God damn well heard me too so did she, so did Mama! I told her I'm calling to tell her how worried I am about Daddy and I'm coming right down there so she puts Daddy on the phone too and I'm telling them both how I miss them and how I finally realize how selfish I've been and I'm coming down there so we can be together and reconcile everything like we used to be because I'm their only daughter without Bobbie there with them in their hour of need so they get all weepy about how happy they are the Lord has let me see the light about being selfish and ungrateful after all they've done for me and, and up in the cupboard there get me some whisky, it's up there in the cupboard will you?

—Yes just, yes but...

—Just get it! So how happy they are for me that I've seen the light and don't have to come down there and shouldn't worry because Bobbie's there with them in spirit on the right hand of the Lord where he's waiting for them to join him and how happy it will make me to know they just wrote this new will giving everything to Reverend Bobby Joe's church so they know they'll be with Bobbie on the other side and no, don't put water in it! Just give it to me, and would I please talk to Reverend Bobby Joe who's right there all the while giving them this spiritual comfort from the Lord's merciful bounty and the sneaky slimeball wants to give me some too, I could kill him! She drank it off and banged the glass down on the table. —I could kill him.

—No but listen, your daddy's not, he's still alive isn't he? back to smoothing her hair with his hand —once he's had this operation, it's a pretty routine procedure they can still change their minds when he gets over the...

—Leave me alone! she caught his wrist with a strength that almost brought him down —change their minds they haven't got any minds left, do you think they'd be buying tickets to join Bobbie on the other side if they did? I'd like to just tell Bobbie what I, where is he. Where is he Oscar, your little man in the black suit you can go back to that hospital and give him a message to take over there and tell Bobbie what I think of this whole mess!

—No relax, try to relax, he didn't take the messages anyhow he was just looking for terminal cases who'd take them for you, do you want some coffee? I just saw some spaghetti in the cupboard, I'd better go in there and see whether the old...

—Let him take it then! Let him take the message he's on his way over anyway isn't he? He can take one for Mama and Daddy too when they show up telling me they won't need money over there when I need it right here on this side unless he's already there, you better feel his pulse first with that black sock in his lap in there watching snakes on the television and bringing us those ashes he's the messenger, isn't he? I'm going in and lay down.

He sat there staring at the bottle his gaze as empty as the glass she'd left behind with her fevered phantasmagoria he suddenly struck through reaching for it to pour a drink swallowed at a gulp and another, rising more hazily on the smoke of a Picayune stealthily up the hall past the dark cavity of the library into the chill beyond where nothing moved but the durable fugitive from halitosis still harvesting dead leaves with a bamboo rake made in a Chinese prison giving way, by the time he'd grasped the vacancy of the armchair there and filled it, to the refreshing carnage of the evening news, each respite for relief from acid stomach, aching back, bad breath and bleeding gums prompting another foray to the kitchen, another car chase, another siege of gunfire as fact blurred into fiction until at last he roused himself and lumbered unsteadily down the hall to where she lay lips parted as though ravished, an arm flung out and her still breasts undefended coming down to pull off his shoes and his trousers and sprawl beside her, his heavy breathing broken by a cough and hers an answering moan subsiding to a silence as unbroken as the long slow pace of night wrapping the house so that, when it came, the streak of light out there seemed rather to confirm than breach the darkness as the dull throb of the car's engine closing in left a stillness the more intense when it abruptly stopped. —What's that! he came up on an elbow, —listen! he caught her shoulder, sinking back, until the clatter of a door brought him full upright —someone's out there!

One after another the lights were coming on up the hall, and from the cavernous dark behind him —Oscar? Who is it.

—It's just Christina he called back, watching her sit down loosening her coat, simply looking at him across the room as over a great distance, clutching a worn book in her hands, all she'd brought.

—It's chilly in here, she said finally.

—Well of course it's chilly Christina it's the middle of the night, what did you ex...

—You'd better get some trousers on before you catch another cold and, oh Lily. I'm sorry, I woke you didn't I.

—Of course you woke her you woke both of us, it's the middle of the...

—You don't look well, Lily. Are you all right?

—She's had some bad news Christina, she's had a bad disappointment, you can see she's been crying can't you?

—No I'm okay I'm just, do you want some tea or something? You look cold.

—I'm a little bit hungry.

—Well we're all hungry Christina, we couldn't go shopping without a car could we? The way you drove my car out of here without even, without even calling we didn't know when you'd be back, there's nothing here but a box of spaghetti we can't go shopping in the middle of the night can we? I've been trying to call you and you wouldn't even answer that message I left on your machine, all I got was some woman who said she was Harry's sister what was she doing there, she hung up in my face I didn't even know he had one.

—Her name is Masha. He had two.

—Did she tell you I called? You knew what things were like out here, you could have called couldn't you? just to tell us when you'd be back so we wouldn't, so we'd know what was going on? or at least had him call? just had Harry call couldn't you?

—Harry's dead, Oscar.

—Well if he, if that's all he, what? No, what did you say?

—I'd rather not say it twice.

—But, no. No that's, no but wait Christina that's not what I, no! broken off by a rush and a cry of such anguish behind him that he was left standing there as though his blood had frozen.

—Oh God. Go and see to her, will you?

—But...

—Go and help her! her own hands coming up to bury her face —and for God's sake Oscar put on some trousers!

When he came back in fumbling with his clothes she was standing at the window gazing out at the dull glow in the sky far over the pond and he hesitated, and sat down on the sofa. —What happened? and after a moment she turned, sniffing into a tissue.

—Have you been smoking in here?

—Good God Christina I asked you what happened!

—And I just told you I'd rather not repeat it didn't I? She blew her nose sharply, —will you turn up the heat in here? It's cold as a tomb.

—I mean how did he, you know what I mean! We've been worried about you I've called and I just get this sister, this Masha hanging up in my face what's it all about, will you tell me?

—She's loathsome, they both are, the other one's a simpering little thing called Norrie poking around the apartment behind doors and plants I finally asked her what she was looking for, just that painting I gave you Christina, I thought you might have it hanging somewhere? A perfectly hideous thing of a sunset she'd painted herself for a wedding present that made it mean more than just spending a lot of money on some old Rembrandt and she wanted it back, can you imagine? We always wanted warm friendly relations with you when you joined the family but you always seemed so distant because we never had them in to dinner my God, joined the family! while both of them are looking at me as though I'd poisoned him Harry couldn't stand them either, Masha's husband Leo trying to pull him in on some sleazy real estate deal the one time they met he's a slumlord in Cleveland, shows her off in so much jewelry on her it looks fake painted up like a two dollar whore in there right now going through my cosmetics, she's...

—But why are they, what are they doing there! You mean you just walked out and left them in your...

—I told you didn't I! I couldn't stand the sight of them the, these dirty little looks between them, you and Harry weren't having any problems were you Christina? She's mean as a snake, Masha, both of them blaming me like ten of them trying to corner me that place all glass and mirrors and chrome that had been so, been so glorious when Harry and I, when I came in and he was standing there in a towel and the light and, and I had to get out I just had to get out!

—But they, is that all you brought with you? that book? Why did you...

—I don't know why I brought it! I just saw it there and, and...

—Oscar leave her alone!

—But all I wanted to know was...

—Just quit it! tea splashing from the cup in her haste across the room where their hands clasped one in the other, and the battered copy of Hard Times went to the floor.

—God Lily thank you I, I'm just exhausted, I...

—Listen! catching their breath for the shuffle of carpet slippers far down the hall and, as they sank down slowly, a distant trickle, trickle.

—My God is that, is he still here?

—He's still here! I told you Oscar, didn't I tell you? she hissed —he's the one! He's the one that brought it into this house with those ashes and his black sock and the snakes he's the one, she whispered.

—Lily listen you're just upset, we've got the car back now, when the time comes we can work things out but it's still the middle of the...

—Oscar look out the window it's not the middle of the night! Get him out of here! he's, I told you he's the messenger he can take it someplace else before he takes us all to the other side with him, get his clothes and get him in the car and get him out of here, he's done enough hasn't he? Look at her, look at Christina she's coming to pieces right in front of your eyes while you sit there asking these dumb questions, will you go put some clothes on and get him dressed while he's still up on his feet? Drink that while it's hot Christina and then go up and lay down, I'm going in and wash my face.

Now with dawn breaking through the frosted panes and the creak of the heat rising he came forth buttoning the gap in his trousers like some frayed apparition of old Saint Nick caught out, the last of the Magi surrounded by childhood betrayed in faces drained of all illusion as she skewed the plundered Gladstone toward the hall —and get him that coat Oscar with the fur collar on it.

—But that coat was...

—Just get it! herding him ahead of her now, —Christina? are the keys in the car?

—Yes but let Oscar do it, he can take the...

—He can stay here you might need him, can I take your coat?

—Yes here but, no I just need to sleep for God's sake take him with you and, Lily? will you pick up some food?

And as the doors clattered behind them —Get his arm, put him in the back he can sleep back there, can't he? and watching the fumbling at the brake, the ignition —my God here, let me drive or we'll never get there.

—But where, where are we going? he asked gripping the dashboard as they careened up the pitted drive.

—To the airport where do you think, you said he has his round trip ticket didn't you? as they swerved out into the road —and turn on some music will you? in case he should start to talk? and so they roared out onto the empty highway to the lowering strains of the Verklärte Nacht until she stabbed at the switch and engulfed them in noise more attuned to the speed of the car.

—What was wrong with that.

—It was spooky! she snapped back, her teeth clenched tight as her hands on the wheel headlong as though fleeing the sun rising behind them to the blare of brass and pounding bass and even voices raised in screams sounding almost human carrying them, relieved along the way by the usual complement of shopping suggestions, storm window and used car sales, television repair and septic tank rejuvenation, to the posted exit westward where —look, she muttered to him, the land was bright with the lights of —the main terminal, stay here with him while I go in and check it out will you? and she blazed into the curb cutting off a stretch limousine with this dark green status symbol of conspicuous consumption emerging from it with a disdainful toss of the blonde haired leisure class only to be reclaimed by her own once inside among the milling suppliants for Coach Class dodging from one line to another, trying Information and finally surrendering to Snack Bar where her approach was threatened by the friendly advances of a large ungainly dog.

—Pookie stop it! in a flurry of mink —get down now don't, my God it's you! That glorious day we had in the country, it's Lily isn't it? Pookie stop it, you see he remembers you doesn't he, I mean it's rather sweet because he doesn't seem to remember me he can't even remember his own name now get down! with a futile tug at the braided leash —he's just trying to thank you isn't he!

—Me? gathering back her skirt from the dripping muzzle, —but...

—I mean you must think me simply gauche never to have called to thank you myself for your marvelous inspiration, I put ads in the papers the way you suggested offering a reward really more of a ransom and a most unsavoury young man appeared at my door quite unshaven in clothing that looked like he slept on the grates of course it may be the latest fashion I scarcely know anymore and I hardly recognized him, Pookie I mean he had him on a rope and my mind wasn't quite clear I'd been at a party with some Tibetans drinking yak milk the night before and he seemed rather larger than I'd remembered him God knows what they'd been feeding him I mean he's really quite enormous isn't he but thank God he doesn't bark and yap like he used to and the young man seemed quite content with my five hundred dollars, I mean there wasn't a peep out of him when we were robbed two nights later but tell me, how are you all how is Oscar.

—He's okay, he's right out in the...

—Out in the country oh I know, it restores your faith in human nature not having to see anyone, I've been helping Bunker do over his country place and I can't tell you how the creative spirit takes wings simply choosing new slipcovers, of course the place is bedlam because they've torn up the floor to put in the new bar with the space behind it for his barman a good foot lower since Bunker can't bear to look up at him and he's putting in an entire carpentry shop where his handyman can repair the furniture that gets broken at his parties without the outrageous prices and haggling these antique restorers put you through Pookie! get down! Will you tell dear Teen that's why I haven't called her? I've simply been up to my eyes with these decorators and upholsterers and God knows what since the day we were married and I hope she wasn't annoyed at not being invited, I mean you only get married for the fourth time once but Bunker's lawyers wanted to get it out of the way this year on account of his taxes since I've had these marvelous losses wherever you look, will you just hold him for a moment? and she thrust out the leash, digging in her purse.

—But I have to go, I...

—Oh I know, it's down there on the left isn't it awful, I mean it always comes on you in public places like this God knows what you can catch.

—Get down quit it! Quit it!

—Pookie stop it! I just have to find my ticket to see where I'm going, there simply hasn't been a moment to get him spayed will you tell Teen that's why I haven't called? I mean I'd just seen her father's picture in the paper the old Judge, I don't remember what it was all about I think he'd done something terribly important and of course I haven't dared call dear Larry when I'm right in the midst of suing his ridiculous law firm behaving simply abominably over these bills and I really can't help blaming it is Larry, isn't it? because he got me mixed up with them in the first place but I haven't said a word because it might upset Teen whenever I've tried to call him they say he's out or in court of course I know he's simply trying to avoid facing me when they tell me he's away they can hardly expect me to believe them can they?

—Ouch! no, I think you can believe them this time...

—Pookie stop it! a ribbon of tickets fluttering in one hand as she yanked back the leash with the other —I mean after all self preservation's nine tenths of the law really, isn't it? and she was left clutching the ticket with —my God, Rio?

Outside at the curb, the policeman looming over the baleful figure huddled alone in the car's front seat looked up sharply from his summons pad to the disheveled onslaught of blonde hair, coat flying loose as she pulled up short for the moment it took her to seize the situation and rush at him with —Officer! pointing haphazard down the platform at a man who might have been fleeing for a tiled refuge from the throes of diarrhea —he stole my purse! and, the pursuit so joined, turned back to the car. —Where is he?

—Gone. I told him we'd wait for his... but she was already round the other side of the car.

—We're waiting for nothing! to the squeal of a cab's brakes behind them as she swept into the stream of traffic leading out to the highway full into the rising sun.

—You're driving too fast. What took you so long in there.

—A woman with a dog.

—But why did...

—I told you! Their course veered to the blare of horns as she reached up for the sunshade —a crazy woman with a dog!

—I thought you were finding out about his flight, I had to sit out there with him while he...

—What's that? where her eye caught the glitter of gold snapping open and closed in his hand.

—This? It's my grandfather's watch, it was in his pocket he almost forgot to give it to me. I had to sit out there with him while he dragged me through the whole thing again, Father getting furious when he saw that lower court decision where Mudpye put one over on that stupid woman judge and what fools we were not to spot the trap they laid for us letting us sue in district court here instead of California preempting the Federal statutes and getting it in under New York law and not even following through with an appeal, what kind of nitwits were my lawyers anyhow? This old bugger tried to run them down but they told him my lawyer had gone fishing and they didn't know anything about that black who showed up down there trying to register those family letters for copyright so Father sat down and did it himself. He knew Judge Bone, knew he'd see right through it but he sat down and wrote out the appeals brief himself and sent that local kid lawyer up here with it, that was Father. You want something done right you do it yourself, he could have called me couldn't he? what I was going through? May have thought I was a, that I was a damn fool that's what he said, that I was just a damn fool but I wasn't venal, that I'd sold out the family and Grandfather writing that movie he knew they were just using it to block his seat on the circuit court with the madness and all the rest of it but, and then he told me, when I said maybe Father thought I was a damn fool but, but he came through for me didn't he? snapping the watch case open, snapping it closed hard and clutching it there —that he cared about me, that he did it because he cared enough about me to...

—Is it gold?

—Is, it what. Is what gold.

The car veered again as she glanced down, her hands tight on the wheel and the sun catching the perspiration beading her lip. —You could sell it, she said. —You could sell it and buy something.

—Sell it! His hand closed tighter as though it were being wrenched from him —it was my, I told you, it was my grandfather's I used to, when he put on his evening clothes he used to let me change it from his suit to that black waistcoat with the quilted buttons and and, and sell it? What could I ever buy to replace that! the only thing I've got left in this whole terrible, this whole sad story, the only one who ever really cared for me and...

—You could buy me a nice watch, she said in a voice as hard and level as the road ahead.

—You? he gasped, —buy you?

—With a gold band.

—But how can you say, but I never heard anything so, so cold blooded and sel...

—And selfish! You want to hear somebody cold blooded and selfish Oscar you better just listen to yourself. That's all you can talk about is yourself, Jesus Christ! I mean yourself and your father he's dead and your grandfather he's dead and this raw deal you got on this play you wrote about this war that happened a thousand years ago that's like some sickness where everybody's been nursing you through it till we all catch it and the whole house is like living in this hospital out of the past, it's the past all of it's the past! All of it's...

—God listen, slow down, you're driving too fast we'll be...

—All of it! with an extra burst of speed bearing down on the white station wagon carrying four nuns and the license **HAIL MARY** a mile a minute before them —while you sit there like you're ready to cry clinging onto this old watch like it's some magic charm and these ashes you're saving up there in that coffee can? All of it, all of it should have gone right in the grave where it belongs with that messenger we should have put on the plane for the other side before it was too late.

—Who do you, what do you mean too late we're rid of him aren't we?

—I mean Jesus Christ Oscar who do you think I mean! the sun glistening on her trembling lip, on her open throat looking up to the rearview mirror, surging ahead, —who the hell do you think!

—No but, yes but listen, we don't even know what happened, she didn't tell us did she? Maybe she, maybe there's some misunderstanding, all she talked about was his sisters how awful Harry's sisters are when I asked her, she wouldn't just leave them alone in their apartment like that if he, if something like that happened would she? when all she could talk about was this Masha using her cosmetics and look out! both his hands seizing the dashboard —you're too close! you're, listen do you want me to drive? you're...

—Did you see her Oscar? did you look at her? I mean did you really look at her? walking in there like some zombie sitting there staring at us don't you know what somebody looks like in a state of shock? don't you ever go to the movies? I mean look at me, do you ever look at me? her own eyes flashing back to the rearview mirror as the traffic grew heavier with the end of the divider streaming before them, behind them, toward them and past in a blur of speed —do you! With Daddy going in for this big cancer operation with this sleazeball Reverend Bobby Joe fucking me out of every cent with this cancer I've got right here in my breast you think is just some plaything how am I supposed to pay for that if I've got it! her eyes fixed on the mirror now —oh this bastard, this bastard.

—God Lily listen slow down, you're...

—With Al out there in the woods trying to shoot down that shit Kevin screwing my girlfriend from long lines look at him! this bastard behind me he keeps trying to pass me look at him! her hands on the wheel white across the knuckles —bastard look at him. Snap your seatbelt.

—Well good God let him pass! his own hand gripping the dash as he looked back at the glare of sunlight on the windshield and the flared nostril snout of the BMW almost within reach —let him! as with no more torque at the wheel than she might have used straightening a picture, righting a teacup, the image coming up behind them veered from sight and was gone in a shearing crash as she swerved for the exit.

—Just don't say it! her voice hoarse with calm before words could shape the sound clogging his throat, sweat glistening on her forehead and her lips clenched tight as her hands on the wheel guiding them now at the pace of a Sunday afternoon drive past brown aprons of lawn and Chic's Auto Body, chain link and post and rail, Dunkin' Donuts, Fred's Foto and used car pennants to draw up unobtrusively among the shopping carts littering the R Dan Snively Memorial Parking Lot.

—What are we doing here?

—She said to pick up some food didn't she? Give me some money.

—But we can wait till we're...

—Just give me some money! and he watched her brisk walk toward the sliding doors slumped there in the silence, the watch moist in the grip of his hand, until it was broken by the distant whine of police sirens coming nearer, coming from all directions, closing his eyes to the screech of an ambulance, opening them wide with confusion at the bustle of grocery bags and the slam of the car's door as she came in beside him and threaded the way back out to the street past Jim's Place, Clips 'n Grooms, Laundr-o-Mat, Biggie's Hideaway, pink flamingos and a plastic madonna in the hideaway blue of an upended bathtub on brown aprons of lawn till he could safely ask —Don't you want me to drive? confident of her scornful silence gliding boldly into the traffic stream on the highway pursued like a distant echo by the howl of an ambulance rapidly overflowing in a burst of flashing lights as it took shape bearing down like the Furies to scream past in a tumult of light and noise —God! do you think anybody...

—I said don't say it, Oscar. Reach in the top of that bag back there will you? reaching her own unseeing hand to bring the radio to life with an opening chord of Bruckner, to take what he handed her and tear open the cellophane wrap with her teeth, —the sun got in my eyes, okay? she said biting into the Hostess Twinkie, her eyes dead ahead, chewing slowly to the soaring cadences of his ninth symphony which, even in its unfinished state, carried them all the way to the road off the highway, to the byroad, to the gate past **STRANGERS ARE REQUESTED NOT TO ENTER** without another word between them until she turned, climbing the veranda steps emptyhanded to say —and bring in the newspaper will you? pointing a foot at it there and leaving the doors open for him struggling with the groceries behind her.

—What do you mean happened to notice them!

—Oh! I thought you're upstairs sleeping.

—I'm on the phone with these, these vultures, make some tea will you Lily? Norrie? I said what do you mean she happened to notice them, she wouldn't happen to notice them unless she'd been digging through his shirt drawer would she? What does she... well my God if she thinks they'd suit Leo she can go out and buy him some can't she? and tell her I know every single one of Harry's neckties and I don't... No! I mean my God they're cashmere, how do you know they wouldn't fit Oscar you've never even met him! meant to ask me what? Of course I left suddenly I thought you were both right behind me, what does she... Well my God I certainly do mind Norrie! I mean there are hotels all over town aren't there? What does she... I don't know! I don't know whether I'm going to keep it or not I mean it's not really your business is it? Who? who did, what... well she has no business talking to him about all that, put her on the phone where is she, she... then call her out of the bathroom! what in God's name makes her think I won't need my cosmetics I'm still alive aren't I? Put her on the, Masha? what did... No, she just told me Bill Peyton called what did he... Well God damn it Masha he has no business discussing that with you! You don't know a damn thing about Harry's health or his... because I made the decision! It's what he wanted and I made the decision my God I'm his wife aren't I? It was his... no I have not seen the paper and I don't like the implication that I... of course he had one, of course I've seen it we drew it up together and... why! What do they think is in it! Tell Leo and your father they can read it when it's probated and it becomes a public document everybody can read it, now I'd... No. No I'd just like you both to leave right now and make sure the door locks behind you, and don't... what? Hello? oh that bitch! she slammed it down and sat staring at him. —What's all that.

—It's just groceries, we stopped and...

—Well you're not going to leave them in the middle of the living room floor are you?

—No, no I just put them down to...

—You look like hell, Oscar. Have you been drinking?

—Have I, now? but it's still...

—Where in God's name have you been.

—Well we, you know, we just took him to the airport and...

—That bitch! She just happened to notice those Turnbull and Asser shirts going through every drawer in the place, she can go out and buy some for Leo herself can't she? What in God's name I thought I was doing walking out and leaving them there I thought they were right behind me, would I mind if Masha stays there tonight she doesn't get to New York often and wants to get in some shopping, my God don't they have stores in Cleveland?

—It's awfully hot in here Christina, you don't mind if I turn down the...

—Thank God Lily here, put it down here will you? and as the cup came down trembling —you look pale, are you all right?

—I'm just, I'm okay.

—It tastes a little, did you put something in it?

—I put some whisky in it.

—I think it's just relief Christina, finally having him out of here it's been quite a, quite a relief not starting the day with a game show we've been...

—What in God's name are you talking about, is that the paper? today's paper?

—I just brought it in yes, it's...

—Well give it to me! and will you get those damn groceries out of here as I asked you? tearing through the pages —in the entertainment section where is it, that sweet tone of hers as though he'd just won a medal, have you seen this morning's paper? with that edge to it sounding like we both really knew I'd poisoned him for the insurance money and had him cremated to hide the, no. My, my God no! the paper gone down in a heap and the teacup smashed to the floor before they could reach her.

—Christina here, let me...

—I'm all right! she broke free straightening up, straightening the page —it's the, it's just the picture I've never seen it he looks, he almost looks like somebody I never, who I never... she cleared her throat sharply —well there, you see? It's Bachrach, it's back when he first made partner they send them to Bachrach for the, to impress their clients I'm sorry Lily, have you seen my bag? There are some tissues in it.

—No but listen Christina you don't have to read it now, you...

—Why can't I read it now! I mean I, those vultures have read it haven't they? everybody else has read it? A prominent member of the New York bar and a senior partner in the prestigious law firm Swyne and they got right in there didn't they, that's Bill Peyton getting the firm right in the first line, the cause of death was not disclosed though he had reportedly been in ill health recently where did they get that. Where in God's name did they get that.

—No listen Christina, try to...

—Did they call here? did they call me? I'm his wife aren't I? They got his age right at least, Mister Lutz was born in Chicago where his father, an early innovator in the textile industry cut-throat operator would be more like it, went on to make a fortune in the home furnishing business where he expected his son to follow and where did they dig this up, conduct resulting in his dismissal from a series of Ivy League colleges and a brush with divinity school combined with his consuming interest in poetry, which his father condemned as an unprofitable vocation for 'sissies,' led to an irreparable breach between them which never my God, I mean he never told me that's what they fought over you can leave that Lily, I'll clean it up later.

—Sit still. Just move your foot.

—his interest in the law inspired by a growing sense of injustice which he later ascribed to his reading of Dickens, whom he had taken up with a view to becoming a novelist if you can imagine that, Harry a novelist?

—There's nothing strange about that Christina, every young...

—Move your foot, Oscar.

—after working his way through law school and serving with a number of small public interest law firms became increasingly disillusioned with the law as an instrument of justice and this is more like him, yes, to regard it as a vehicle for imposing order on the unruly universe depicted by Dickens that's more like Harry isn't it, what he saw all around him, initiating his rapid climb in the complex field of corporate law where his talent for...

—No but wait Christina, all this part about working his way through law school and his father's...

—And while you're out there Lily would you mind bringing me another cup I'll try to be more careful, to his recent appointment as the youngest senior partner in the century old history of the blue ribbon firm Swyne and here comes Bill Peyton of course, a little commercial for the firm like that carnival barker breaking in with his cure for acid stomach, where managing partner William T B Peyton labeled his recent successful efforts in resolving the legal battles between the Pepsi-Cola interests and the Episcopal Church of America, which have run into the tens of millions of dollars over a decade, as the most brilliant bringing to bear of fundamental constitutional issues in the age old conflict between free enterprise America and the pills, the whisky, runins with the firm's psychiatrist and a car accident thrown in he doesn't mention all that does he? just what they got off his resume and a nice sales pitch for that blue ribbon conspiracy of thieves?

—No but they got everything else wrong didn't they, about that irreparable breach with his father and working his way through...

—Divinity school no, no he actually told me once he'd gone through a phase looking for easy answers survived by his wife, Christina; two vultures, Eleanor Lutz of New Rochelle and Marian...

—Christina listen, it's not...

—All right, sisters! Eleanor Lutz of New Rochelle and Marian Ragow of Cleveland, Ohio; and his father, Stanley Lutz of Lake Forest, Illinois asking me to see Harry's will as though he'd left them a dime with that simpering Norrie asking if I planned to keep the penthouse while Masha sniffs around hinting my taste for luxury drove him to...

—Christina listen! Survived by his father they've got it all wrong, his father's been dead for years he died when Harry was still in law school, he...

—That's ridiculous, what in God's name makes you think that.

—He told me, Harry told me the last time we talked, we were talking about fathers and sons disappointing each other and he told me about his father's debt and bankruptcies breaking his neck to put him through law school afraid of disappointing him if he failed and he didn't live to see him graduate, his father never saw him make partner and he still felt like he'd let him down, he...

—You must have misunderstood him Oscar, I mean my God they've been estranged for years, his father lives like a king out there he's never made less than a million a year and when we got married those two vultures moved right in like a, talk about Regan and Goneril poisoning the old man so they'd split the inheritance two ways instead of three sucking up to him with me as the snake in the garden I told you didn't I? that she's mean as a snake, Masha? talk about a forked tongue asking me if Harry and I were having problems and talking to Bill Peyton as though we were on our way to the divorce court I know she did, trying to turn this whole business of his cremation into a cheap murder mystery simply because she wasn't told? because I went ahead with it without consulting them I'm the next of kin aren't I? what, what God damn business was it of theirs!

—But why didn't you...

—Because it's what he wanted! because there was some mixup everything was jumbled and confused and they called me about the, his wife as next of kin about the disposal of, about what to do with the remains I didn't know they'd be so quick about it was what he wanted you heard him, didn't you? A clean getaway right here talking about Father? standing right here strip away the poetry and off to the crematory when the time comes I hope you'll do the same for me when the, the time came! No, no the thought of him being drained and laid out dressed up like some kind of a, lying there alone with his eyes closed and those two vultures hovering over him a week later, a month later the skin falling away from his...

—Christina please, you're only making it...

—that, that marvelous face and the, the empty eye sockets staring out at, my God I'm his, I was his wife wasn't I?

—Christina don't, sit down what are you doing! but she was already up with the phone, blowing her nose hard.

—If they think they're going to bring some kind of lawsuit over it because that's what they talked about, that snake Masha I know that's what she talked to him about and, hello? clearing her throat again sharply —Mister Peyton please, this is... hello? away from his desk well where is he? This is Christina Lutz, I... leave my number he's got my number, tell him to... He knows damn well what it's in reference to! Tell him to call me! and she stood there holding the phone tipped like an emptied cup, staring out over the pond.

—But he, why would he have told me all that Christina why did he, why would he have lied to me?

She stood staring out over the pond for moments longer before she turned to him sitting there, his shoulders fallen, the watch closed tight in his hands. —I think, I think he was just trying to help, Oscar. He was, Harry was awfully fond of you, you knew that didn't you? she said coming over to him, resting a hand on his fallen shoulder —trying to help you through a bad time that was all, he meant it for your own good he knew what you were going through, I think he admired you, that he really admired what you'd tried to do because he'd tried it himself that's what he used to say, about failing at something worth doing because there was nothing worse for a man than failing at something that wasn't worth doing in the first place simply because that's where the money was, it was always the money...

—Christina? You ought to drink that and go up and get some sleep, and Oscar? looking at them both the way she'd looked at those cars on the highway, in the rearview mirror, listening the way she'd listened to those siren howls without blinking an eye —why don't you go in and lay down while I air out the bathroom and the library I'll be back later, I'm going down and get this x-ray over with, all right? the same detached calm hardening her voice later over the flaming pyre of vehicles on the evening news, over the blazing picture in the next morning's paper before he could shape the catch in his throat into words —just don't say it, Oscar.

—No, I was only going to...

—Well my God Lily, look at who's out there tearing down the highways at seventy miles an hour, what's appalling's not this mass incineration but that there's not one every five minutes, I mean half of them are functional illiterates the other half are geriatric, arthritic, insomniac, drugged and sedated with crippling headaches, cramps, diarrhea frustration and just plain rage trying to prove something it's just amazing anybody's left alive, Oscar you look like the last roe of shad what are you trying to say.

—Only that he called this morning, that Bill Peyton called before you were up to tell you these insurance company investigators will probably want to talk to you, that they've asked for Harry's medical records and his psychiatric evaluation and the whole...

—And what does he want me to do! her empty cup coming down hard on the saucer, —tell them Harry was relaxed? carefree? happily married? no money worries, just an occasional beer never forgot his own address or left his keys in the door, loved his job and his fellow workers, loyal and true to the firm and ready to go down with the ship?

—It wasn't like that no, no he sounded really concerned like they're doing everything possible to force this claim through, the insurance company's one of their clients they've even got a partner on the board but he said it's a highly regulated industry where there are all these legal constraints so there can't be any grounds for doubt about an improper payment if they think, if anybody thought it was a, that he did it on purpose if some stockholder tried to sue them for...

—Well that's the most, it's ridiculous it's simply ridiculous, I'm the one they're afraid will bring a lawsuit for the stress they put him under driving him round the bend with his caseload and these threats making him liable for their own idiotic mistakes and all the rest of it that would reflect badly on the firm's image and their whole miserable self regulating conspiracy, no. No, they'll put their paid psychiatrist up there swearing that he was unstable and bring in that car accident running that dizzy tramp into a storm drain to show he was a selfdestructive personality with a yen for car crashes and I ordered the cremation to destroy the evidence I told you didn't I? that Bill Peyton and Masha were pulling something? you heard me right here on the phone with her what was she doing digging in his shirt drawer where he kept his cash, in the bathroom going through my cosmetics no, she was probably going through the medicine cabinet looking for Harry's pills, I mean she'd do anything to see me done out of this half million life insurance that's about all he left me with, I told you she was mean as a snake didn't I? Didn't I?

—I just wish you'd stop talking about snakes.

—And I mean it's not even really the money, it's what's right. It's simply what's right that's what Harry always, that's what killed him.

—Christina? his bewildered voice echoing his irresolute struggle half to his feet as though he might have, as though he should have sprung to her rescue with some sort of dubious embrace from the desolation that had come down like a pall with her silence, so alone there hands covering her eyes until she brought them down abruptly exposing him to a stare so vacant he sank back reprieved by the vacancy taken up in the hollow of her voice.

—Where did she go?

—Lily? rescued himself now —to the kitchen? sparked by this diversion —I think she went to the kitchen yes, she...

—I'd never have pictured her taking it this hard would you? She looks like she'd been hit by a train.

—What the, oh. She's upset yes she's been quite upset since we, since she had some bad news, all her hopes about reconciliation with this fool of a father of hers he's just told her he's leaving all his money to this ridiculous church to be reunited with Bobbie on the other side, he's going in for a serious operation and if the Lord calls him to the other side in the midst of it he...

—Oscar! the clatter of a tray breaking in on him with —you want to quit talking about the other side? Here. I made some eggs.

—That was sweet Lily, where are yours.

—I ate already. Oscar I need thirty dollars.

—You, what for, what...

—My God Oscar just give it to her! What business is it of yours, hand me my purse Lily it's right there on the sideboard.

—I have to pay them for this x-ray before they'll tell me what they found there.

—God knows what they'll find for thirty dollars, where on earth did you find them.

—It's this place I just saw up on the highway next to that Chinese restaurant? There's this new sign in this empty storefront that says Urgent Medical Care so I just went in. They do passport photos and chiropractors there too.

—It sounds like a dime store raffle, I mean if you'd waited we could have gone to a proper hospital and here, you'd better take fifty just in case.

—That's the trouble I've waited, they said maybe I've waited too long where they'll have to do this biopsy. They do them there too, you need anything? gone up the hall without waiting for an answer, but here she was again. —Oscar? You better come out here.

Lights flashing red, yellow, red were emerging from the bare trees skirting the driveway like the blind end of some alien juggernaut lumbering inexorably into the open, some vast image out of Spiritus Mundi moving its slow thighs, its bones of iron shuddering convulsively with a grinding of gears as a flatbed truck took shape bearing a naked tenant merrily riding its back like some wounded avatar of the automotive deity celebrating a convalescent visit.

—Wait! he came down waving his arms —what are you doing! where two men were already dismounted unfastening the chains —not there no, you can't leave it there put it, just put it, put it someplace...

—They can put it over in those trees Oscar, so I can get out.

—Over there! Put it over under those trees so we can get out! and the thing heaved into motion again rattling its chains, dropping its tracks, winching the red Sosumi down into a clump of serviceberry bush.

—Christina! he came pounding down the hall —did you see that? and on to the kitchen —where are you! with a passing glimpse into the disheveled sunroom —Christina? back now staring at the silent phone, he picked it up and put it down again muttering —Mohlenhoff, Schriek Mohlenhoff and, no, Prestig? over digging in the litter on the sideboard, envelopes, bills, brochures, folders spilling under his hands still muttering —wig yes, Preswig? but the one that stopped him, lips silently shaping its return Lepidus, Shea & —it's not even opened! he whispered, patting pockets for his glasses till he found them coming down slowly on the sofa and tearing it open like a man with an appetite, turning each page more quickly as though to wipe away the taste of the one before it, moistening his lips against the searing bite of each paragraph until the last leaving him sitting there with his burning mouth agape, only to suck in his breath like some cooling draft and start again with the first pungent savoury, rehearsing each course more slowly as those spiced with figures caught him gasping for breath finally getting to his feet as empty as he'd sat down and beginning to pace the room, tapping the scrolled pages against his thigh like the menu of some Barmecidal feast standing there at the window staring vacantly out over the pond.

—Well? What are you going to do about it.

—What? he turned as though seized from behind —about what! I've been calling you where have you been.

—You needn't be upset, I went out for a little fresh air and I don't want that old car on this property, things look shabby enough around here. What are you going to do about it.

—You shouldn't go out like that, you've got nothing on but a sweater you'll catch pneumonia Christina that's not why I'm upset, look at this! brandishing the pages, the torn envelope —when did it come, I just happened to find it on that pile over there couldn't somebody have told me?

—I'm not your secretary Oscar neither is Lily, I mean might it occur to you we could have other things on our minds? and she sat down with the weariness draining her voice, the dulled look of her eyes on him —if it's something so important that...

—Well it is! It's my, it's the final award in my lawsuit look at it!

—I saw it Oscar, I just told you I don't want it on the property.

—What do you, not that one Christina my play! My big lawsuit against Kiester and The Blood in the no, no you're just being smart aren't you you know what I'm talking about, you're just trying to, to belittle it aren't you.

—Don't be silly no, I'd forgotten all about it.

—Forgot! how could, there. There, you're just ridiculing it like some stupid case of No Fault case of, forgot all about it! brandishing the pages at her —look at it it's a travesty, they make a movie that's a vulgar travesty and now they make a travesty of the whole judicial process, read it!

—I don't want to read it Oscar.

—Well then don't! They took in three hundred and seventy million dollars it says it right here in the socalled master's accounting and they're claiming the movie lost eighteen million how could it! Three hundred seventy million dollars in gross receipts and I was supposed to get all the profits till they got away with apportioning my share only to what they stole from me when we didn't show up to contest it because Sam had gone fishing and Basie was busy somewhere making brooms? What Harry called their creative accounting, all the profits and suddenly they're figuring the fair market value of what they stole calling it goods and services down there with the hairdresser and they decide to give me a fifth of the market value because the rest of it's in the public domain and the success of the movie was due to everybody but the creator of the idea that was frail to begin with and my claim to it is tainted anyway because they didn't steal my last act, the scenarist made up the whole resolution of the story from historical sources he says he dug up somewhere? So the master's accounting here says they're using the ratio of two point five of the gross receipts to costs whatever that means, seven million for Kiester and how many million for that stick of an actor Bredford with another three million for Anga Frika's tits and forty million more for advertising them? No wonder they lost eighteen million.

—I mean you scarcely need me to make a mockery of it then do you, I thought you'd got some kind of an award.

—I did! I end up getting look at it, it's not even two hundred thous it's not even enough for these legal bills it's just Harry trying to cheer me up with all his talk about the court's discretion making me an award in lieu of actual damages and profits what can I do about it, I can't ask Harry can I?

—No you can't, Oscar.

—But, no I didn't mean...

—You didn't mean what! Blaming him as though he'd, as though he's gone to Bermuda on a vacation? blaming Sam who went fishing and Basie for sitting in prison somewhere making brooms? My God think about it! You said they grossed three hundred and seventy million dollars? you said you thought you were going to get all the profits? you said they cut that down to one fifth and their creative accounting shows they lost eighteen million? If they'd based your award on actual damages and profits you'd have twenty percent of nothing wouldn't you? You'd have a fifth of minus eighteen million is that what you want? you'd owe them three and a half million dollars is that what you want?

—Well that's, no that's absurd Christina that's insane, it's...

—Think about it! I mean my God you can be glad you may come out with enough to buy yourself one last bottle of your Pinot Grigio, will you stop waving those papers around and weeping over money is that all you can think about? when we, when there are real things to weep over?

—No, Christina? and this time he was up, his arms wide in embrace but so was she, turning her back on him in her hard stride toward the windows —I'm sorry, I didn't mean...

—I mean we're not going hungry, are we? she said from there, gazing out over the still pond —we're hardly destitute after all.

—Well you're not. With whatever Harry left and this life insurance, I don't think it even gets taxed and it's more than twice this miserable award of mine with these legal bills and all those medical expenses that...

—I'll believe that when I see it, expect a free lunch from Bill Peyton with Masha out there spitting in the soup I'll believe it when I can taste it.

—Well I told you what he said on the phone didn't I? He really sounded upset about it Christina. They're using all the pressure they can to get this settlement and they have the leverage, an old line firm like that with all their prestige they really have the leverage and it's not even costing them anything out of their own pocket is it? You just said they're afraid of anything that would reflect badly on the firm's image they're protecting that too aren't they? the way Harry always talked about protecting the firm? That's what it was all about even if he'd died with just the change in his pocket and you've got the penthouse, you've still got the penthouse in there too haven't you?

—I don't know what I've got Oscar! she finally turned on him —my God, you sound like that idiot Norrie will I keep the penthouse. Harry handled all of it, the mortgage, financing all I know is we bought it at the top of the market and he certainly didn't die with just the change in his pocket! And I mean my God if he'd been a senior partner, if they'd made him one a year or two ago like they should have he'd be billing four or five hundred dollars an hour and sitting under the Christmas tree with the other senior partners sharing the profits on the millions pouring in from every case the firm handles he had nothing to do with, we'd be...

—Like mine.

—What do you mean like mine, he'd be...

—I said like mine Christina! I said he'd be sharing the blood money that movie paid them for stealing my work and running up my legal bills and destroying everything I...

—Oscar that's ridiculous, I mean Harry didn't know they were hiring his firm to defend their...

—That's what you just said! that he'd be sharing the profits from leaving me with twenty percent of nothing to buy one last bottle of Pinot Grigio while you're sitting up there in a penthouse with...

—Oscar that's enough! I mean my God that's just the way that whole marvelous self regulating conspiracy works, there's nothing he could do about it and nobody's sitting in a penthouse, we're sitting right here and I mean we're certainly not destitute are we? Here's Father's estate if that clown can stay sober long enough to get it together, he told Harry it should come to over five million, five and a half I mean we're not going to go hungry are we?

—Yes but it's, that includes this house, most of his estate is in this property Christina. All I have of whatever's left in that Maryland trust now without Father there doling it out will go to upkeep and paying the taxes here like my mother meant it for so I'd always be sure to have the...

—Have what Oscar! her arms suddenly flung out embracing beam and scantling, hearth and newel, casement lights and dark wainscot —are you starting all this again?

He'd sunk down there on the sofa staring at her like a child, —but what...

—All of it! This property and this old house where my mother dragged me in like an orphan, sorting out what's yours and what's mine? My insurance claim and your ridiculous award, my bank and your mother's trust, my penthouse and this place that's yours because it was hers, Winifred Riding daughter of a wealthy Long Island architect and landowner when she married your father my God Oscar it's a hundred years ago! Your sainted mother it's history, it's all just history! and she turned back to the window, looking out over the pond —playing like we did as children by the shores of Gitche Gumee? stilled by that unheard of coldness, that intolerable winter on the shining Big-Sea-Water passed the swan, the Mahnahbezee, Mahng the loon with clangorous pinions, the blue heron, the Shuh-shuh-gah, —all your outrage over Father, how you've fought since we were children? bringing back his youth of passion and the beautiful Wenonah stooping down among the lilies as a car door slammed outside, up the hall the glass doors clattered followed by the snap of footsteps wayward as the Minnehaha with her moods of shade and sunshine, eyes that smiled and frowned alternate, all he'd told to old Nokomis was his fight with Mudjekeewis, not a word of Laughing Water.

—I swear, I'll kill him! she burst in at them tearing off her coat, —Oscar? I'm going to need to have seven hundred dollars.

—Well but wait, I...

—What in God's name for, Lily. I mean they didn't find...

—I'll kill him, I swear it! These implants he put in they said one of them ruptured, that's what this lump was they said if I don't take it out I'll have all this silicone jelly running all through my body you know what it cost me? I mean it was Al, he wanted me to have big ones it was Al all the time he said once so he could play telephone with them he didn't care what it cost so that's where he got me this fancy Doctor Kissinger, the same one you were talking about that time? with that friend that brought that Mister Mudpye out here looking down my front I just saw her at the airport, she said to tell you she got married.

—Well I'm hardly surprised, I mean people will do anything but...

—I mean I just need you to loan it to me Oscar because I'll be able to pay you back because I'm going to sue him, I can still feel his squishy hands on them I'll sue him for everything he's got so I don't even need to care about Daddy's money anymore if the Lord calls him and this Reverend Bobby Joe gets his slimy hands on it because I'm going to sue him too.

—Yes but I mean my God Lily, at least you can be happy it didn't turn out to be cancer after all, you...

—Why should I be happy, I mean if it was who am I supposed to sue? Oscar? turning on him arms akimbo, her small fists jammed against her hips —what's the matter, you mad at me or something? and I mean look, you didn't even eat my eggs.

—He's upset about something else Lily, he found a letter in that mess over on the sideboard that nobody bothered to give him and...

—Who's supposed to hand it to him, some secretary? and she was already over there sweeping the heap together —you want to help me clean it up?

—Later yes, it's high time isn't it. I think I feel a draft, is something open?

—Now. I mean now. I told you I'm airing out that smelly bathroom and the library didn't I? and those sheets that have to go in the wash, you want to keep this Oscar? where you're invited to join this panel of distinguished Americans discussing vital issues of the day at the National Speakers Association?

—No, but...

—Or this camping equipment and patio furniture? Here's your hearing date in a product liability action by Ace Fidelity Worldwide against Sosumi Motors regarding injuries...

—They postponed that no, put it, put it somewhere...

—It's already somewhere that's the trouble.

—There's a blue folder someplace, put it...

—This? Overdue. Overdue. Overdue?

—Those are, yes, those are just bills put it...

—The Bursar's Office informs you that a lien has been placed against your salary as of...

—Well what are you going to do about that Oscar, have you called them?

—No, it's that ambulance chaser who...

—And that sleazeball, I'm going to sue him too unless Al gets him first, tulip bulbs? boating equipment? Luxor, you going to Luxor?

—My God Lily just throw it all out, it's...

—Wait what's that.

—Hobbytime?

—Yes no keep it, it's my fishtank keep it, give it to me.

—Over whose dead body, here's your father's obituary you want to keep that?

—Well good God of course, it's...

—You can put it with those ashes in there, you keeping them too?

—Well good God yes!

—From Schriek Mohlenhoff & Shransky, it says statement.

—It's a bill just put it with the, but there's another one I'm looking for from them somebody named Preswig I have to call him, he...

—Then why don't they just call it a bill, you want to keep this thing? Opinion of the Court, James B, minor, v. Spotskin?

—Yes keep it, yes, it's Father's decision in the...

—Ladies Historic Preservation Society that can go, Dear Doctor Crease that can go, Here's Gunnin' for You that slimeball Mickey Mouse was I ever dumb. You have been selected by the board of directors for your biographical entry in the exclusive new volume Five Thousand Important American Men?

—No stop it, throw it out it's...

—Here's a bunch of these real old letters tied up with this dirty string, throw it...

—No wait Lily, I forgot all about it Oscar it's those old letters Father pried out of that bogus historical society, our charming visitor dug them out of that old Gladstone with his assorted bottles and gamy socks in one of his half sober moments hellbent on reading me the letter of the law, U.S. Code this and per stirpes that rescuing them from the furnace with the rest of Father's papers while he sat here ready to burn down the house with those vile Picayunes.

—Oscar? the packet came sailing through the air —you can put them with your ashes in there and here, Hiawatha's Magic Songbook? and some old letter from your Ace insurance company, you want it? Oscar?

—My God give it to him, Oscar call them and find out who dumped that car out there, I told you I want it off the property didn't I? will you call them? right now? And Lily that's really enough for now, just throw the rest of it out and let us get our breath.

—I'm going down and do the laundry, you want to bring down your sheets from upstairs?

—I said isn't this enough! I mean my God we're all exhausted, I'm still spinning with those awful voices of Harry's sisters and his whole, and, and his obituary in the paper like something you just happen to read in the paper and tomorrow there's another paper and nobody, and Oscar look at him sitting there with his lapful of trash all his wildest hopes for his award from the appeals court gone up in smoke, gone up in some bookkeeper's creative accounting my God can't we just, can't we do the laundry tomorrow and just stop and, and have a cup of tea and get our breath?

—That's all we do around here Christina! We sit around and have a cup of tea and catch our breath, there's nothing you can do about Harry anymore is there? there's nothing Oscar can do about this lousy reward he got for this play is there? there's nothing I can do about Daddy cutting me off like some orphan till he gets to the other side is there? or get my breasts fixed up till I get some money to pay for it is there? I mean it's like some crazy Halloween where we sit around here waiting for dark surrounded by these ghosts waiting for supper turning into this bunch of mummies waiting for the evening news with all these things we can't do anything about so that's why you have to do something about something you can do something about like the laundry, Oscar? You want to get a wastebasket for all that crap over there you're throwing away and bring in a broom to sweep up around here?

—Yes but wait Lily, I mean there's something you certainly can do something about immediately and get yourself into a proper hospital for this business about your implants, I mean my God to let a thing like money stop you? I can write a check right now can't I?

—That's not what I meant Christina. I mean I never meant for you to offer to pay for it, it was my own dumb fault wasn't it? letting them do that to me? just so Al could have a good time with...

—Don't be ridiculous. I mean you can't wait to sue Doctor Kissinger while this gel's running around plugging up every crack and cranny in your body God knows what would happen.

—They said this one lady lost her hair and her memory and she's so worn out she can hardly do anything.

—Well my God we can't have you going around the house like that can we, now let's have some tea while Oscar makes his call before it gets dark and we can think about supper.

Frozen fishcakes? and freeze dried, what were they, **just add contents of package to 1 cup of cold water bringing to a full boil while stirring gently, turn heat down and simmer for 2 minutes. For a thicker sauce add less water, for a thinner sauce add more water, serve piping hot with your favorite fish, meat or other choice. For a delicious variation sprinkle with grated Parmesan cheese and season to taste following** hard upon the visual banquet of Sikhs killing Hindus, Hindus killing Muslims, Druses killing Maronites, Jews killing Arabs, Arabs killing Christians and for a delicious variation Christians killing each other seasoned to taste and served piping hot by the snappy dresser on the evening news but, frozen fishcakes? —Because they were cheap, she said up scraping plates, and later, in the pall fallen over the room, the dark casements and the cold hearth, the only movement a fugitive couple kissing on the silent screen and the unascribed bleat of digestive juices —you know what I never understand here? where all this time we're stuck together in this house, that I don't ever see you read? I mean with all those books in there in the library and these ideas and people from books you're always talking about where all anybody reads around here is the paper and bills and the crosswords and this junk mail and the dumb television but I mean books? reading a book?

—Yes we, we used to, Lily we used to, we used to do a lot of things. We used to play the piano up there, four hand pieces for the piano, that little Mozart sonata, the sonata in D? her voice taking up with an almost desperate eagerness —within three bars he'd flatted the G, Oscar? It was so long ago.

—No, no every time we did it you failed to play the A on time Christina, that's what I remember. We'd have to start again because you'd fail to play the A on time.

—Well my God it happened when we changed places too didn't it? because you couldn't turn the page fast enough to give us the next phrase?

—Because you always wanted to play the upper part, because you were supposed to be the stronger pianist so you'd always take the upper part because you said it was harder, it's just more strident that's all Christina. You took it because it dominates, the upper part always dominates that's why you took it.

—It was the pedals Oscar, because the lower part takes the foot pedals and back when we were first learning you always wanted...

—It wasn't like that, Christina. That wasn't it at all.

—I've never seen that, I wish I could see you playing it.

—Hear us Lily, hear us but with the music room locked off like all the rest of them to save heat and God only knows when it was tuned last, the sounding board's probably warped with all the dampness out here and, and it was all so long ago. When we read everything then didn't we, we even read Shakespeare aloud sometimes but Oscar would never go to a performance would you Oscar, he'd only read it. They showed Henry the Fifth on television not long ago and he turned it off sputtering after five minutes.

—Because it's on the page! he suddenly erupted, —it's always been that way, the silent beautiful words coming off the page together to stop and listen to them to, to savour them without some vain fool in a costume prancing around up there just getting in their way, any of them! Once more unto the breach, dear friends, once more God it sends a chill down your spine doesn't it? Christina? but she'd gone silent, her still hands arched up to her face leaving only her cold eyes staring somewhere back, staring within, and she shivered.

A little touch of Harry in the night.

When they came out next morning she was gone: the morning's paper, tea cold in a cup and even some mail there on the kitchen table, a pale sun well up in the sky and now up the hall the clatter of doors.

—Oscar? There's this little man in a black suit out here to see you.

—No wait! don't...

—Frank Gribble, Ace Worldwide Fidelity, may I come in? You remember me Mister Crease? We got your message yes, thank you for calling. How are we feeling. May I sit down? and he'd done so, flattening a plastic portfolio on his lap, —I hope your pain is all a thing of the past? and he had out a yellow pad, —now. Let's not take too much of your valuable time Mister Crease. Just a paper or two here for you to sign and we can put this whole episode behind us, a lot of water has gone under the bridge but the mills of the gods, as they say? Now. Will you bring me up to date?

—I think the last thing I, I've got a letter here somewhere from my lawyer who...

—A Mister Preswig yes, I have a communication from him here but I believe he's no longer in the picture? digging into the portfolio and bringing forth papers —we understand that he has found employment elsewhere and in the interests of expediency I thought if I simply dropped in on you we could work things out together without all the bother and expense of further legal proceedings which seem calculated to merely muddy the waters as they say and to save you the costly annoyance of going to trial?

—Well yes by all means, I...

—By all means yes, yes we are in agreement then aren't we, after all our friendship goes all the way back to my hospital visit before these lawyers came between us simply to line their own pockets as they say? or as we say I should say, which is to say you could hardly be blamed for disclaiming the generous No Fault provision of your coverage which had come into being for the protection of persons like yourself over the vigorous opposition of the powerful lobby of trial lawyers like the one who took your case originally.

—Well he ought to be shot yes, he...

—I'm afraid that would only introduce new complications not included under your coverage, now to return to the matter at hand. When he filed to have you disclaim your No Fault coverage we had no recourse but to claim immunity as insurers of the car's owner and you are now seeking to recover under your coverage as the accident victim?

—More or less, yes.

—Yes. This motion filed on your behalf seeks to ensure that the controversy will take place in an adversary context since the court would lack jurisdiction to render judgment without adversary parties appearing before it whether, I have a few notes here from our legal department may I refer to them? bringing forth a sheaf of papers, licking a thumb —whether natural or artificial persons yes, you as plaintiff claiming bodily injuries being recognized as a natural person.

—Well what else would...

—Of course yes, as a party named in the record they've apparently listed them here under several categories, necessary parties, formal parties, indispensable parties, proper parties, indispensable parties being of course necessary parties who must take part in an action either as defendants or plaintiffs and indispensable parties those who must be included in an action in order for it to proceed, both of them signifying parties who should be joined in a proceeding though there has been some disagreement over the degree of such obligation expressed by the word should.

—Mister Gribble, I think...

—I agree yes, words always cause such problems don't they when it becomes less a matter of their actual meaning than their interpretation, take the word should here, I use it quite frequently myself without thinking twice about the...

—Mister Gribble listen! I'm quite busy, can't we cut through all this talk about parties and come to the point?

—But that's why I've come all the way out here to see you Mister Crease, I had a terrible time finding the place but we want to be certain of protecting your legal rights before you sign anything in your pursuit of justice, I believe you used that phrase yourself the last time we...

—Before signing what.

—Yes we'll come to that, but first may we clear up this matter of one person as both plaintiff and defendant in the same action? licking his thumb again, flurrying pages —suing in one capacity and defending in the other which creates certain problems, if you follow me.

—But I'm the victim, you just said that yourself didn't you? that I'm suing as the victim?

—Of course, yes, which means you need to find the defendant guilty of negligence as the proximate cause of your injuries, but that is to say even once negligence is established, since the scope of the defendant's liability can be no greater than the duty of care he owes to the plaintiff, he has not breached his duty if he has no duty and therefore he has no liability, and so in this case I suppose you would take the position that you owe a duty of care to yourself?

—Well obviously, that's what the whole...

—Do you happen to serve in the capacity of a public officer anywhere Mister Crease? licking his thumb again, turning pages.

—As what? Good God no, why.

—Because apparently the rule is confined to natural persons and as an individual you could join in a suit against yourself as a public officer, because this is where things get somewhat complicated. As they say here, whether an action is in contract or in tort, you see what I mean, the rule that one person cannot take the position of both plaintiff and defendant will not apply so long as the case does not add up to one party against himself. To put it in plain language you might almost say that this is a suit between who you are and who you think you are, the question being which one is the plaintiff and which one is the defen...

—Well I, here where are my glasses, give me that! and he seized the fluttering pages. —Do you know Montaigne?

—I'm afraid not no, is he someone you...

—Where he says it's a hard task to be always the same man? flipping a page over —there is as much difference between us and ourselves as there is between us and other people, they're practically quoting Montaigne right here aren't they? Since the presumption is in favour of the judgment, even though the plaintiff and defendant bear the same name it is presumed they are different persons?

—I see your point Mister Crease, but bringing in your friend as a third party can only complicate things further unless, of course, he might join the suit as a formal party in establishing negligence as the proximate cause of your...

—Of whose negligence, that's what this is all about isn't it? I'm the victim aren't I?

—Yes yes of course, but I think you'll see something in there about contributory negligence that needs clearing up? When the plaintiff's injuries are equally likely to have been caused by his own improper conduct and standing in front of the vehicle Mister Crease, by standing directly in front of the vehicle with the hood raised restricting your vision when you tampered with the wiring in order to start it might be considered improp...

—No wait, wait a minute, I don't like the word tampered there Mister Gribble. I was simply wait, here it is, contributory negligence is never a defense to strict liability but often the opposite is held? They'll have it both ways won't they, if it can be shown that the user was proceeding against a known unreasonable danger I was simply trying to start the damn car wasn't I? or this? in making no use of the product except to be injured by it do you think I'm mad?

—I think no, no I don't think we should take that course Mister Crease I don't think it's included in your coverage and...

—All right listen, here it is listen, that a damage-feasant motor vehicle may be joined as a party in an action against the driver of the vehicle.

—But I understand there was no driver?

—I was the driver I simply wasn't driving, how could I drive it without starting it.

—I see your point yes but, yes we probably should have a lawyer here to help us with these finer distinct...

—We don't need one, you just said that yourself didn't you? It's all here look, even the citation Brown v. Quinn 220 S.C. 426, 68 SE.2d 326 and the damage-feasant motor vehicle, it's standing right outside there didn't you see it?

—I did yes, yes but suing the car would not be exactly the...

—We're not suing the car! We're joining the damn thing as a party in the action a necessary indispensable formal proper artificial person do you want some coffee or something? tea? Lily, are you out there?

—No, no thank you I know how busy you are, I haven't wanted to take so much of your valuable time Mister Crease but it seemed only fair to you to review the range of legal complications you might confront in a long drawn out expensive lawsuit which we wish to help you avoid, and of course under the circumstances the possibility cannot be ruled out that your suit as the victim might not prevail as a party who should be joined in a, there's that word should again, would you mind giving me back those papers?

—And would you mind, Mister Gribble, first would you mind simply telling me what it is you want me to sign?

—Why I, yes of course I have it right here somewhere it's just a release that will save us all a good deal of...

—Is that all?

—The release yes, yes and then there's an affidavit in connection with your...

—And listen, what about that summons I got as a witness with companies all over the globe and some kind of postponement that...

—That's exactly what I was coming to yes, yes rather than put you through the grueling cross examinations such a trial would subject you to this simple affidavit will relieve you of any further obligations and we can put the whole matter behind us, here we are. It simply states that you were injured by the product, which is to say the damage-feasant motor vehicle in this case, that your injury came about because the product was defective and that its defects existed when it left the hands of the defendant.

—What defendant. Oh Lily, will you bring me something? just a glass of wine or something?

—I hadn't wanted to take more of your valuable time getting into all these details Mister Crease but you see you are only a part of the bigger picture which threatens to get out of control and may go on for years involving a whole series of defendants. When your second attorney Mister Preswig filed your motion as the victim against the car's owner this in turn brought Ace Worldwide Fidelity in as his or your insurer where it might possibly have ended.

—Well why didn't it!

—Because liability attaches to anyone who sells the product going back to its manufacturer including the makers of parts supplied by others since it is marketed under the manufacturer's name, if you follow me? Our legal department sought out the person you bought it from who had joined the Navy and so proceeded against the dealer from whom he'd purchased it new and the dealer then sued the wholesaler who has brought suit against the manufacturer who in turn is suing the assembler of the defective component parts whose makers are as you observed in your summons as a witness in the suit being brought against them by the assembler all over the globe as you put it, however. As you were notified that trial has been postponed since these component parts makers abroad turn out to be largely subsidiaries or joint ventures with American companies which must all be sorted out before matters can proceed to the Supreme Court where it all appears to be headed.

—Good God! he sank back with the glass in his free hand, —did you hear all that Lily?

—I heard enough.

—Wait sit down, listen. The whole thing sounds like a, it sounds like the house that Jack built. Will you tell me why you've dragged me through this whole insane rigmarole of indispensable parties and artificial persons and now this global car chase you refer to as the big picture?

—Yes yes of course Mister Crease. I thought it would be useful to review the wide range of complex issues and prolonged expensive procedures which would no doubt prove exhausting in your weakened condition resulting from your little adventure which will be lifted from your shoulders when you sign these papers and can go on to your important work with this entire matter behind you, going to sleep at night with the added satisfaction you might say of putting bread on many tables for years to come, I have a pen right here and...

—Wait what in the hell are you talking about, putting bread on many tables.

—Just joking yes, yes a figure of speech as they say, I meant the legal profession of course, lawyers all over the land and abroad, pita bread, bagels, baguettes you may even see some children put through college if the...

—No wait a second Oscar, I mean what about our table Mister Dribble.

—Please.

—What about all these doctor bills and the hospital and even just that chair over there he had to ride around in.

—Yes, yes but I believe you both understand that Ace Worldwide has already gone to considerable expense and faces still further financial sacrifice in our efforts to relieve Mister Crease of the intolerable burdens I have just gone to all this trouble to outline for you which can all be dismissed with a stroke of the pen yes, yes I have one right here, sign there at the bottom and your daughter as witness under the...

—She is not my daughter! and will you stop this yes yes every time you speak?

—Yes oh, I'm sorry yes it's just habit, when I joined Worldwide we were given this fine Dale Carnegie course free, I'm sure being a scholar that you're familiar with his work? when he speaks of using the approach perfected by the ancient Greek philosopher Socarides in getting the yes yes response from his...

—God. Listen, why me Mister Gribble, will you tell me?

—But you started the whole thing after all Mister Crease, the rest of us are just out here picking up the...

—What if he doesn't sign this stuff.

—Yes as I say, we would just have to let things make their difficult way through the courts and I must caution you the other parties, especially the manufacturer have very deep pockets.

—So do you Mister Dribble, so what about these doctor bills and all.

—I'll be glad to discuss it with my office when I take the signed release and affidavit back in yes, yes I think it quite likely they'll be willing to make some sort of voluntary contribution toward...

—You can discuss it right here. I mean I'm not talking about some voluntary contribution I'm talking about the doctor bills and the hospital and the therapist and his lost income, what about his lost income, I'm talking about the whole thing and that chair over there too or all you'll take back to your office is your hat and your ass.

—I ah, yes I don't think I had a hat did I? bent over the plastic portfolio on his lap —now that you speak of it yes, yes in fact I may happen to have brought along something that, what we call a letter of agreement you might say deals with these contingencies if you insist on having it all down in black and...

—That's what I'm doing aren't I? Here Oscar, read it.

—Though in the atmosphere of trust we generally enjoy with our clients it hardly seems necessar...

—You reading it Oscar?

—Yes but, wait where it says here agree to satisfy obligations for fully verified medical and custodial care of a general nature directly resulting from...

—No wait a second, put in all. Put in all obligations, take out that crap about of a general nature and put in all medical care and wait a second, put in dental, put in...

—Well I hardly think...

—You think you're going to get run over like that without practically getting your teeth knocked out? I mean you hear the way he's talking?

—Yes I, yes but I thought it might be the wine, he...

—You want him to sign this stuff or not. And wait a second, what about his loss of earnings in there.

—I believe the ah, I believe the formula is eighty percent up to one thousand dollars monthly but oh, just a moment I brought along a camera somewhere to record the, to satisfy our examiners with evidence of what was described in the claim as permanent significant disfigurement marring the natural expression so as to attract attention referring as I recall to a facial scar which, would you mind turning your face this way Mister Crease? I'm afraid I don't detect any trace of...

—How do you know what his natural expression looks like, you want us to sign this stuff? Just put in there a thousand dollars monthly, go ahead and sign it Oscar.

—It seems somewhat irregular but...

—And you too, you sign it we all sign it what about copies.

—Copies?

—I said copies didn't I? so everybody gets a copy? in a flurry of pen and papers until they sank back for a moment leveling their stares, hers at the collapse on the sofa, his at the floor and the third of them down her blouse until she stood pulling it close.

—Yes I should, I mean I'd better be off yes, it's been a pleasure meeting you both with the opportunity to serve you in the best traditions of Ace Worldwide where our clients always, I didn't bring a hat did I?

—Wait a second.

—But, no but please I think we've cleared everything up haven't we? jamming the papers he'd retrieved back where they'd come from, —the claims are pouring in from that holocaust on the highway near the airport and I'm far behind schedule, you have my phone num...

—It's just this one question, where my brother got killed in this car crash?

—Oh I, I see and, and he was a client of ours too?

—No it's just this question, he got killed in this car my daddy gave him the money to buy it with so then when tragedy strikes there's this religious reverend that steps right in there calling it the death instrument and he talks Daddy into giving all this insurance money from Bobbie to the Lord to cleanse it to make sure him and Mama will get to join Bobbie on the other side when they get there too where it should be mine right here on this side where I need it, I mean I'm his daughter aren't I?

—I see yes, but of course it's your daddy's prerogative to leave his money as he sees fit, that is to say if you were his wife you would be entitled to one third, in some states even half but...

—How could I be his wife, he's already got Mama doesn't he? So I want to sue him.

—But I don't think that would succeed is what I meant to say, unless you could have him declared incompetent, it's not at all uncommon for children to be cut out of their parents' wills and of course his will wouldn't even take effect until he'd passed on because he...

—I don't mean sue Daddy I mean suing this reverend! Daddy's going in for this big operation and if the Lord calls him right in the middle of it then what. If he shows up over there and can't join Bobbie or maybe can't even find him in the crowd then what.

—I think what she's talking about is something in the line of a malpractice suit Mister Gribble.

—But, I see. Might I suggest another approach? his voice abruptly taking a softer, almost intimate tone —if I may take a few more moments of your valuable time? as he sat down again peeling open a separate pocket of the portfolio on his lap. —Of course your feelings are quite understandable, but have you considered weighing them against the spiritual comfort you might enjoy by yielding these funds to the Lord's service in an unselfish gesture of love for your departed brother?

—Are you kidding? and I mean look, suppose Daddy is incontinent but he never gets there anyway because when he gets there he finds out there is no other side then what, where he already paid off this reverend didn't he? and you don't call that malpractice?

—But in such a suit there might be a, as I say I'm not an expert in the law but I think as the plaintiff your daddy's suit from the other side against the reverend would face the problem of jurisdiction, and...

—I'm talking about me suing him right here on this side where he's taking this money that ought to be mine for something he doesn't come through with.

—But you couldn't really prove that he doesn't come through.

—Could he prove that he did?

—Sounds more like breach of contract now, doesn't it Gribble? and the glass came down emptied. —Is this all the wine?

—It's right there by your foot Oscar. Could he?

—Well but first Miss ah, Lily if I may? He was pulling forth booklets and pamphlets ablaze with flaming colour, radiant with cerulean blues —at least from my long experience with automobile liability policy, the credibility of the parties to the contract in such an action is of primary importance. Of course we have God's own unimpeachable word for the existence of the heavenly realm you refer to as the other side, and in the words of third John sixteen which I'm sure you have known by heart since childhood, where is it now, yes here. For God so loved the world, that he gave his only begotten Son, that whosoever believeth in him should not perish, but have everlasting life. In other words assuming that your daddy...

—You're not a Mormon there are you Gribble? They stack them up like cordwood there on the other side, talk about finding a face in the crowd they've hollowed out a mountain out west somewhere full of genealogies that go right back to Methus...

—I'm not no, I'm not a Mormon Mister Crease but I do belong to a serious Pentecostal Bible study group in fact I was about to ask you both to join us some evening, I think your contributions to the discussion would be greatly...

—Having our discussion right here, find another glass for Mister Gribble will you Lily? Preaching the inerrancy of scripture I think he'll take a little wine for his stomach's sake?

—No thank you no, no we never preach I'm only suggesting that if her daddy has stood up before witnesses to the truth and declared his faith in the belief so beautifully expressed in the simple words of this gospel and he should, in the course of events he does arrive on the other side unable to find her brother there? he came on turning to her with growing appetite licking his lips as his eyes dropped slightly from hers —isn't it very possible that not having made a similar avowal of faith Bobbie may have gone elsewhere?

—Very good Mister Gribble, even though of course we're both aware that John is generally regarded as the least reliable of the gospels?

—Perhaps in certain minor historical details, but...

—But here he is with his contract for everlasting life, we'd call him an interested party? promising in the Lord's name this immunity from death unless Bobbie here has failed to live up to this provision of belief and his immune system breaks down, he's nonsuited I think it's called and he's tossed out of court.

—Put in these terms I think he's made my point nicely, don't you? looking back at her eyes glittering with satisfaction, even cunning, taken up in a tone almost patronizing in its strained levity with —after all you could hardly bring your breach of contract suit against God naming him as an artificial person with his only begotten son as a necessary party now, could you? and he was suddenly busied unfurling a folder overflowing with stick figures tumbling into a blazing abyss —let me show you an artist's rendering of...

—Right here on earth Mister Gribble, she's talking about suing this slippery reverend in Federal court under diversity of citizenship right there in a neighboring jurisdiction and it's just a damned shame my father's not still on the bench, sue him as a public official and his church would be held liable wouldn't it? filling his glass again, —if you want a nice parallel to your scripture there right here on earth just take AIDS.

—But that's not, I think you're straying a little far afield, people dying of AIDS aren't...

—That's what it's all about Gribble they don't die of AIDS, they die from some regular old fashioned germ like pneumonia or tuberculosis because their immune system's broken down like this lack of belief or the loss of it, same thing isn't it? Acquired immune deficiency syndrome and they both end in death, your immune system collapses and some germ like this reverend steps in and finishes the job.

—I really think your ah, your parallel is quite far fetched, people dying of terrible diseases like cancer and...

—It's all metaphor Gribble, it's all metaphor! There's no cancer germ is there? No, no cancer's it's an expression of life gone wild, these exuberant living cells suddenly cutting loose, multiplying all over the place having a grand time they're all metaphors for reality right here on earth, people who've outlived it roaming around with what we used to call old timers' disease and...

—My God, what's going on.

—Christina! I didn't hear you come in where have you been, sit down and join us we're talking about whether Lily's daddy will bump into Bobbie when he gets to the other side and...

—If he bumps into Harry that will straighten him out, Lily will you take this package? Be careful, it can spill.

—Or Father! if he bumps into Father he'll be...

—I think I'd better be going now is that my coat? He was up jamming papers, folders, pamphlets together —and let me thank you for...

—Lily walk the poor man out will you whoever he is, and Oscar for God's sake settle down.

—But where have you been. The last time you took my car like that you didn't even...

—It's my car Oscar, I left yours in, hello? She was already at the phone —yes, give me Mister Peyton please, God what a day look at it out there, an hour ago the sun was, hello? All right then listen, give him a message when he... This is Christina Lutz now listen to me. I've just sent him something very important please see that he gets it, it's got urgent and personal written all over it the minute he shows up, do you under... He'll know what it's in reference to! Tell him to call me in the country the minute he, what? What do you mean what country this country! He's got the number and... it's Lutz! Christina Lutz l u t z Lutz! Mrs Harry Lut... exactly. I'm glad you read the papers, my God! she slammed it down —of all the, she saw that nice picture of him in the paper, isn't that what I told you? Yesterday's news you wrap the fish in where's Lily, I got some lovely halibut after those ghastly fishcakes, you don't think it will snow do you? will you look at those clouds? The wind almost blew me off the road when I, oh Lily? Who in God's name was that.

—Him! He asked me can I slip off to some prayer breakfast with him to tell you to update your homeowner policy for the porch out there while he's getting around where he can look right down my front and...

—I'll take you right after lunch it's all arranged, I got some lovely chowder did I give it to you when I came in? I don't think you should eat a lot before they put you under, I used Bunker's name that old pickled friend of Trish's and they're squeezing you in they'd just had a cancellation, you can take that plaid robe of mine and a nightgown I mean I assume you don't own one I've never seen you in anything but your, what's that bottle doing there. Oscar? by your feet?

—No now listen Christina, before you start...

—Just get me a glass will you? What time is it. I'd love to see them try to squirm out of this one, I'll put Doctor Chichester right up there on the stand and send their precious white shoe image straight to the bottom.

—No but listen Christina, we don't even know who...

—Of course you don't, neither did I nobody did till his bill came this morning, Harry always said when you went to him his bill would be waiting in your mailbox before you got home thank God he sent a copy out here this time, he's a dentist Oscar he's been Harry's dentist for years thank you Lily, just fill it up will you? The day it happened, that tooth that had been driving us both crazy keeping us up at night you remember when he drove out of here? and I told him for God's sake to get it tended to and he said he'd try to squeeze it in? Would you go in and have a tooth scraped out and a temporary cap put on it if you knew you wouldn't be around tomorrow? Would you? She stood there drawn up against the windows her coat flung wide as though braving the winds shaking the pine boughs beyond her, sweeping two black crows across a grey sky sullen with the threat of snow that came on in a flurry and was gone by the time their lunch was and the car had retreated up the driveway leaving him standing there staring after it as though they might never return —but I could hardly just drop her on the doorstep like some sort of foundling, could I? she said when she did, —I mean you could have put a light on out there for me couldn't you? Have there been any calls? None, no. And what had he been doing? Nothing really, just, nothing. The sparkling surf broke down a dazzling beach where a cruise ship lay in the azure waters offshore and immaculate liveried blacks served exotic drinks to tawny blondes dancing the night away on the silent screen —I mean you can't spend day after day pacing up and down here muttering about that ridiculous award of yours, it's all over with isn't it? you came out with something didn't you? You can tell your friend Sam there you'll pay their disbursements they're all listed separately on that idiotic bill of his aren't they? Basie buying drinks for the house and a fortune in postage stamps and he can whistle for the rest, she told me you'd cleared up your medical bills with that idiot from the insurance company and even some new teeth I mean my God, I can't wait to see whether Bill Peyton will jam Harry's dentist's bill down their big time insurance company's throat and make them cough up the poor thing was so upset when the hospital demanded payment in advance, all fifteen hundred she thought it would be seven nobody'd mentioned the operating room and the anesthesiologist and the rest of those vultures with their free toothbrush and printed menu I wasn't even thinking when I picked up that lovely halibut, that she wouldn't be here to help with supper God knows what we'll have with it, I think there are some capers,

I'll simply do it in butter, and a white sauce? and some of your white wine here, and boiled potatoes served up, after the last shot was heard round the world on the evening news, on white china plates in the sepulchral silence of the kitchen left there in the sink when she switched off the lights behind them leading back up the hall to interrupt a famous actress done up as a nun in the midst of her orisons with —you're not going to watch this thing are you? snapping it off as she passed for the stairs —because I'm simply exhausted, I'm going up and read something and Oscar? that heap of papers and those letters you wanted to keep when she tried to clean up in here you put them right back on the sideboard, will you do something with them? throw them out or put them back with that mess in the library where they belong? and where a reading lamp would stay lighted far into the night.

Toast, but no butter, tea but no milk in it both gone for the white sauce the night before, Oscar? but no response in her rush for the phone, for the hospital later than she'd thought when she came down only to be left stranded in a white corridor's passing parade of motley looking no worse off than what you'd dodge in the street till a familiar beige coat hurried toward her —just to get my ass out of here before they charge us for another day, they wake me up at five o'clock this morning I still didn't eat anything but some ow! as they swerved for a corner and again finally pitching up the cratered driveway —no I'm okay, they're just a little sore that's all, their heels clattering up the steps, down the bare hall echoing the emptiness pervading the house like a sudden chill, —Oscar? Where are you.

—Oscar? God only knows, there's some canned soup I brought in yesterday just sit down. Oscar? I mean he can't have gone out he's probably in the kitchen, French onion or tomato. Lily?

—He's in there, Christina.

—He's in where, ask him if he wants...

—In the library. He's just sitting in there. He looked right straight at me like he never saw me before he didn't even move, it's spooky.

—Don't be ridiculous, I mean he can't have been drinking this early can he? Oscar? as they reached the doorway together, —what is it. You look like you've been sitting there like that all night, what's the matter. Will you answer me? beside him now shaking his shoulder, reaching down to catch the papers spilling from his lap when her wrist was seized so hard she almost came down on him —my God! breaking away as he leaned down slowly to pick them up letter by letter —what is going on! He was standing up heavily now, the papers crushed up in one hand reaching the other to turn off the reading lamp.

—It's a farce, Christina. It's just a farce.

—Well of course it is! What is! following him out —what is a farce.

He'd got all the way up the hall and as far as the windows, standing there looking out over the pond before he said quietly —I've been lied to all my life.

—But what... she broke off, sitting down slowly, both of them sitting down silently watching him framed there against the sky shattered with an exaggerated gesture turning upon them as though the footlights had just come up.

—When we came back from France like beggars looking for a new exile and you sent me up there to see him? his voice quavering with indignation —coming in here in your fine French clothes demanding your rights he said to me when I asked him for the money he owed my father when I'd spent the morning trimming frayed cuffs pinning up the hem on my father's threadbare coat to look fit to call, five hundred dollars! in a gasp of outrage subsiding to a murmur muttering —to lay up treasures in heaven Thomas while you seek here below, on a sharp intake of breath —Only justice! As a farce yes, play it as farce because that's what it is isn't it!

—Oscar what's happened, I don't under...

—I just told you didn't I? that I've been lied to all my life? No, no I cast myself a hundred years too early didn't I, with those tragic heroics of John Dryden's, sound the trumpet! beat the drum! when it was farce all the time, Sir John would have grasped that if only he'd read it, if only I'd got it to Sir John Nipples he would have played it as farce when his School for Scandal fell through, with Sir Lucius O'Trigger, yes. Sir Lucius O'Trigger playing Thomas based on a true story no, here's the true story! thrusting the letters at them crushed in his hand where one of them fell as it trembled there, and another —these letters, these damned letters those old ladies were sitting on in that historical society down there till Father got hold of them here's the true story, the whole sad, miserable pitiful true story. Laying up treasures in heaven where moth and rust corrupt and thieves break through and steal she was lying all the time! It's all here in these letters whining, begging, broken promises and more promises no wonder they hid them away because she'd married the wrong brother, she'd married the drunk. Grandfather's father the charming, weak, careless dandy it calls him in one of them, one of the letters here gambling away everything and dying of drink as a diplomatic flunkey in the embassy job his brother'd got for him as a last resort God, the words I put in their mouths! When my father died in an embassy post where they gave him nothing, no promotions and let him rot there till it was over and we came back to beg from his brother what was really ours? How's that for farce! That loathsome hypocritical old woman lying through her teeth, poisoning Grandfather against his uncle who'd worked and fought his way up as a mine owner your uncle never gave things away she says, not a smile not a penny and his own brother lying dead and buried in a foreign land? The one line I got right there, where Thomas says to her it's as though you cherish injustice, the one line I got right for all the wrong reasons because it's all here in one of these letters, Grandfather storming in demanding his rights from an uncle who didn't owe him a thing but maybe he admired his brashness, maybe he saw his own driving obstinate will in this angry young man and decided to give him a chance, that broken down farm and three hundred dollars just barely a chance to see what he could make of it knowing he'd been lied to by that loathsome old woman protecting her useless husband and herself for ever marrying him that's the true story! And Father knew it. Father knew it all the time didn't he, that his father'd been lied to and that's where it all came from, the battlefield hero and the distinguished career on the High Court bench up there beside Justice Holmes because he'd been lied to like I have, like I have.

—Oscar...

—Like I've been lied to all my life.

—Oscar can't you see? can't you see that Father was only protecting his own father? because he knew how you idolized your grandfather and how much your grandfather loved you that's what he tried to protect isn't it? for your own good my God, I mean the way Father came through for you didn't he? with that appeal writing the whole thing up and sending somebody up here to win your appeal for you, coming through for you standing behind you having faith in you like you realized that day saying you'd lost yours in him? Can't you see all that?

—No, he whispered, and he leaned down to pick up the letters that had fallen abruptly wrenching them all between his hands straightening up to cross the room slowly and throw them all together into the empty hearth. —No I never told you, that day we took him to the airport, when we took the law clerk to the airport sitting in the car and he found Grandfather's watch in a pocket he'd forgotten to give me and I said something like that to him, that Father's coming through with his love for me showing it that way without asking anything in return and he chuckled. He just chuckled as though it was all, as though it was all just a farce no, no he said, the Judge never gave a damn for things like that, all that sentimentality or the movie you wrote he knew they were just using it to keep him off the circuit court he never blamed you, he may have thought you were a fool but he never thought you were venal and he didn't draw up that appeal for love of anybody, not you or anybody no. It was love of the law. When he got his hands on that decision he was mad as hell. He acted like the closest person in his life had been raped, like he'd come on the body of the law lying there torn up and violated by a crowd of barbarians, what was the matter with you? What in hell was wrong with your lawyers not following it up, letting a wide open trap that was laid for you slip by them for this new judge to fall into, he had me on the phone and then he grabbed it himself trying to run down this lawyer that handled your case there, he's no longer with the firm they told him same thing they told me, we have no record of his whereabouts and hung up. Want it done right you do it yourself that was him all right, your father, had me up for two nights digging out every citation that applied and a hundred more to be sure patching up that appeals brief with them like bandages wherever there was a scratch on this body he held dearer than his own life or yours or anyone else's, this love he had for the law and the language however he'd diddle them both sometimes because when you come down to it the law's only the language after all and, and

I can still smell the whisky on him and the smoke and hear his rasping voice shut up in the car there together, and what better loves could a man have than those to get him through the night.

She cleared her throat at last, squaring her shoulders back straightening up and clearing her throat sharply as though the deep breath she took were his by some sort of contagion to straighten him up clearing his throat for the words to free them from a spell driven, finally, to break it weakly with her own, to say —Oscar, it's all history now. It's all just, history.

—I've been lied to all my life.

—Oscar? You know that place I went to first up on the highway where they have this urgent medical care in these empty storefronts? and that brought his eyes up warily —you know what I just thought of?

—I don't need urgent med...

—No I don't mean that, there's this new place right next to it like a pet store where they have birds and canaries and these different kind of fish for the home aquarium the sign says, you want to go up there and see?

He stared at her there for a moment, and then —I'm going to have a nap. I'm going into the library and have a nap.

—Have you eaten anything Oscar? or some soup? but he was past them, —Lily where are you going.

—I'm going up there anyway.

—Well get some milk and some butter while you're out will you? Lily? are you all right? Don't you want me to...

—No I'm okay. I just thought maybe this will get his mind off things, you know? and she caught up the coat plunging up the hall, out into the winds wild with rapine from a look at her out there blonde hair flying, skirts branches boughs flung high and wide with no more malice than purpose till they seemed to discover the house itself and join forces to summon sheets of rain descending with a vengeance blowing the pathetic fallacy to shreds for anyone cowered inside fighting to be delivered from things nothing could be done about in sleep or in doing something that something could be done about like the dishes in the kitchen sink and opening a can of soup over the moaning hinges of a loosened shutter and the clatter of a door banging somewhere, of heels down the bare hall and —It's me.

—My God. You're soaked.

—What do you expect? She held up a glassine envelope, —look.

—What is it, I don't see anything.

—It's these guppies, they're real tiny so that's why they're only fifteen cents apiece so I got ten of them.

—My God.

—Well I mean anyway it's a start, isn't it? and minutes later she was back dripping fistfuls of yellowed water sprite, sodden Ludwigia and despondent fronds of Spatterdock across the kitchen floor, couldn't she do all this somewhere else? get rid of it in the bathroom? as a bucket of algae tinted water came by, just flush it down the toilet? rerouting those that followed past the door of the library where he finally appeared standing there watching them pass as a diverting eye witness episode of flood relief wedged between those of a more intimate nature on the evening news until she set one down at his feet with —you want to help me, Oscar?

—And Lily? from the kitchen, —the milk? and the butter? But she'd forgot them on this consuming mission to get his mind off things and was there another pail someplace? as the bucket brigade came about with each fresh gallon bearing a new lease of life for the goggling eyed tenants where their gigantic new landlord grudgingly restored the basic services of light and aeration, pH balance, filtration and an agreeable temperature sprinkled with krill and daphnia floating down upon them like the manna in the wilderness till another trip up the highway brought in a cohort of discus gleaming turquoise and red and cobalt blue bearing down like the Egyptians before green seafans, shaving brush and a fresh canopy of water sprite beckoned the promised land right down ten centuries to a Crusaders' castle lofting its plastic battlements among the brown flecked young leaves of the Amazon swordplant —so they can hide in there if they want, isn't it cute?

Cute or not, —God knows whether it's getting his mind off things I mean he wanders around the house as though he hasn't got one left, ask him a question and he simply mumbles. Something in the paper this morning I thought would amuse him about that revolting Senator Bilk's campaign seeking the support of the Gay Alliance when that story of his adventure with the transvestite came out? and that Iowa congressman who joined him trying to impeach Father resigning from the House over charges that he's actually illiterate, can't write anything but his name and reads at the second grade level while his loyal staff have carried him through seven straight terms before anyone noticed so he's setting himself up as a political consultant my God how Harry would have loved it, I mean it's almost Dickensian but Oscar simply muttered and asked if the mail had come yet, has it? All I've seen is a letter saying they're going to repossess his new car because he hasn't made the payments and I mean my God we don't need two exactly alike do we? I'd told him I left his in town when I drove Harry's out here and remind me to call the garage and tell them to send someone out with it, they can repossess it and drag that red eyesore that started the whole thing away while they're at it, things look shabby enough around here don't they?

—I think somebody's out there knocking at the door.

—Well let Oscar get it, where is he.

—I think he was in there watching a game show.

—If it's another COD air express delivery of live barracuda will you go and get rid of them? Instead she was back a minute later juggling the tall bulbous pink of a potted amaryllis —for us? Who in God's name would, give me the note on it will you? tearing it open —my God. I mean Bill Peyton? Talked to Harry's dentist and his bill clinches it, insurance people are paying up and I'll keep you informed, thanks a million Bill. Well thank God. I mean it's really quite hideous isn't it? snipping the thick leaves free —but they're quite expensive and of course that's Bill Peyton, send you the most barbarous looking plant in Christendom and it's not even that, I mean I think they're from Africa and that's hardly Christendom but it was probably that dense secretary of his who sends them out to their blue ribbon clients every day and of course, if you stop for a minute and think about it? as another snap of the scissors gave her the chance to do —it's the first civilized gesture I've ever had from him but he's really just putting a pretty face on it for fear of my lawsuit isn't he. I mean that dentist appointment of Harry's has them dead to rights and he couldn't do a damn thing about it even if he wanted to, now what was I talking about. I've had something on my mind since I woke up that's been driving me crazy all day because I can't remember what it is.

—We need to shop for supper.

—Well that's certainly not what woke me up, you haven't run through that cash I put in the towel drawer have you?

—How could I? It's this bunch of hundred dollar bills and all I've used it for was some groceries and his fishes.

—I mean thank God I had my wits about me when those two vultures were going through every drawer in the place, that Masha picking through Harry's Turnbull and Asser shirts where he kept enough cash not to have to bother cashing checks every ten minutes if she got there before I did I'd simply have died. What do you think he wants for supper.

—Oscar? He doesn't care, I already asked him and he just says whatever you're having.

—Well he hardly eats at all so it doesn't really matter does it. Do you think he'd like fish?

—You ask him that and he'll just say he wants big ones.

—Like Al.

—Like, what?

—No I'm sorry Lily that was crude, I thought I was making a joke but...

—No I meant for his tank in there but I didn't tell you, when I just called up my girlfriend from long lines? and she told me Al found out that they caught this woman that stole my purse down at Palm Beach with all my cards and ID and everything so they're holding her for this adultery case he's's got against that shit Kevin. I hope she's black.

—What in God's name makes you say a thing like that!

—I shouldn't of said it, I was just thinking that would fix that shit Kevin because he doesn't like them. He's prejudiced.

—Well that's hardly a reason to, my God wait a minute. That was it, that was the dream that woke me up and I started to put together the whole wait, wait for me I've got to talk to Oscar before we go out.

—I'll put this stuff in the dryer while you're...

—Oscar? she burst up the hall —Oscar listen to me! breaking in on him sunk deep in the sofa there chewing on something —will you turn that thing off? I want to talk to you.

—I'm watching it he said, without raising his eyes from a tiger salamander making a meal of another tiger salamander it had just killed.

—I woke up this morning from a dream about Mister Basie, I can't even remember what it was but I woke up thinking about that law clerk telling you how angry Father got over the trap Mudpye laid for that judge and what fools your lawyers were not to catch it or even follow it up, you remember? she came on over the proposal that members of one's own species might make the most nutritious meals, —how they were told your lawyer had disappeared and, are you listening? When the food supply runs out and the only ones around are your own species, why go hungry? —I mean can't you see what happened, Oscar? that it was really Basie who laid the trap? Sitting here with the clock running and he kept saying we'll take them on the appeal, that the Second Circuit likes reversing district judges to keep them on their toes didn't he say that? and that Harry said Judge Bone on the appeals court was a crusty old misogynist he'd seen him take a smart young woman lawyer right off at the knees once like this new woman judge just to teach her a lesson, don't you think Basie knew it too? Now a three-spine stickleback lurked guarding fertilized eggs while his mate cruised around the screen destroying nests and eating eggs lining up new opportunities to mate, —won't go into the legal niceties Basie said, we'll take them on the appeal don't you remember? He knew Mudpye was a quick study, Harry said he was too quick he'd have the answer before he got the question and Basie knew it. He knew Mudpye had done his homework and was vain and full of himself I mean by going and marrying Trish? and with that kind of money behind them he knew he could lose your case if he played it their way, can you see what I'm saying? What he saw just then were two acorn woodpeckers sharing a nest where one laid an egg and the other one ate it —so instead of taking a chance on losing the case even if he brought out the error, that would have been the end of it, you can always lose a law case remember? So he let it pass, he let their error pass on purpose so he could base the appeal on it that was the real trap! That was the trap he laid for all of them and they jumped right into it, now don't you see? But what he saw now was the Australian red-back spider jumping into the female's jaws in the midst of mating which he continued undismayed as she chewed at his abdomen, munching the last of the Twinkie —there! Based on a true story Oscar that's the true story, I know it is! He held back for the appeal because he knew he could win it and it all fell to pieces when he couldn't show up to handle it himself off making your brooms or on the run God only knows where have you heard what I've said Oscar? that he wasn't just smart and a lawyer and a really decent man have you heard what I've told you?

—You ready to go Christina?

—What? Oh. What's the use yes, I mean my God Oscar think about it will you? He wasn't just a smart lawyer and a sweet natured man a real man, he was our friend! seizing up her coat for the door, —think about it! and leaving him there in the throes of battle among the notorious burying beetles over the corpse of a mouse nicely scraped and embalmed by the victorious couple for their young to eat and then eating the young when they hatched to ensure the survivors of enough food for a stalwart new generation to start the whole thing all over again, inducing a stupor that lasted till he heard his name in full cry with a bang at the doors.

—Mister Crease? when he finally got them opened to the glad hand of —your friend Jack Preswig, a foot in the doors shuddering closed against him —no wait, hold on! May I come in? wedging his foot more firmly —all right then but let me explain, I'm in a new line of work Mister Crease and I think you can use me, won't cost you a dime just let me explain. I got out of the law, just to set your mind at rest, nothing but dog eat dog thought I'd better quit while I still had a spark of decency left in me. It's the biggest swindle ever invented, a regular cesspool of human greed, the side you see of people makes you ashamed of the human race I'll tell you, your best friends will eat you alive and I finally just couldn't face that man in the mirror so I got out, kept a few contacts because without them you're dead and that's where I heard about this problem you're having. I see the old red baron parked in the weeds out there but I hear this new car you leased is up for repossession because you can't make the payments and I think I can save you a lot of headaches, let me explain Mister Crease won't cost you a nickel. You get the bank and the loan people and the insurers after you they'll have you for lunch, destroy your credit rating job prospects liens foreclosure everything near and dear they're cannibals Mister Crease, they're all cannibals now here's how we work. It's a dark green Jag XJ6, five forty nine a month on a thirty six month lease, right? got all the particulars right here, you just leave it standing right here in the driveway with the keys handy, wake up some morning and it's gone, call the police report a stolen vehicle and you're home free. What? didn't hear you, what?

—Go away.

—You don't pay a thing no, must have misunderstood me I just said it won't cost you a penny that's the beauty of it. They're the ones who pay, I just said they're all cannibals aren't they? All the same breed let them chew each other's bellies out, you just blow the whistle on your stolen vehicle I'll take care of the paper work and you don't ever have to give it another, who's this? not yours too is it? as a small black car pulled up, —not the lady of the house is it? for the bulk already clambering up the steps red, with what forty years before might have been a cheerleader's smile and wave of the hand, in tooth and claw.

—I hope you're not showing this person the property, Mister Crease? We wouldn't want to see you make a hasty decision you could regret later, would we. I have a gentleman waiting in my car who is prepared to make a very attractive offer. He's a friend of the lovely little family who are going to be your new neighbors right up the driveway, I think they plan to start clearing the site this week and he'd like to get himself located here as soon as possible, he's flying out to the coast tonight and...

—What's he offering.

—He is thinking in the neighborhood of, who are you? Who is this person, Mister Crease?

—My name is Preswig, Madame. Jack Preswig, I'm an attorney, I've represented Mister Crease in other legal matters and we've just finished discussing a transaction where he stands to benefit substantially, now what is your client's offer.

—He's a very busy man and doesn't like to waste time haggling with third parties Mister Prestig, and so I'll be brief, he has to fly out to the coast tonight for a very important meeting and he...

—What's his offer.

—I know it's slightly below the sum we discussed on my last visit Mister Crease, when I met your charming wife and that dear old man, your father wasn't it? But my client is a very busy man, he makes deals in the millions every day I'm sure you'll recognize his name when you see it and he's offering two million seven on the spot.

—You can't be serious Madame, or possibly I misunderstand? You must be referring to another of Mister Crease's holdings and not this magnificent property before our eyes? I have a client in my practice, three of them in fact, who are looking around the area and wouldn't blink at five million, a high prestige neighborhood like this there's another million right there. You saw the sign at the gate out there strangers requested not to enter? All these exclusive old enclaves are gone, this is not the kind of subdivision you're used to dealing with Madame, the place has been in the Crease family for generations and it's plainly not a distress sale, Mister Crease obviously doesn't need the money but I don't think he can consider any...

—Mister Crease excuse me, let me say that my...

—He really can't consider anything less than five mil...

—My client, Mister Crease, is prep...

—Five million six.

—Mister Crease, my client is prepared to write a check on the spot. There won't be a day wasted on banks, mortgages and all those silly time consuming details, his attorneys will take care of the title insurance and the usual formalities and I think we can have a closing almost overnight, I think I mentioned that he's a very busy man he has a dinner meeting with some top industry executives out on the coast tonight and...

—Let's not waste any more of Mister Crease's valuable time standing out here in the cold, Madame. He won't consider a laughable sum like your two million seven for a minute. You couldn't build a place like this today for less than ten, just look at the gentle curve of these slate roofs it's all handwork, every single slate, you don't find workmanship like that anymore it's practically a landmark, two million seven? It's worse than laughable Madame, it's an insult, go down and tell your client Mister Crease takes it as a gross insult. If he wants to make a serious offer we can give you another minute to get his best price, I'm a busy man myself so will you please hurry? and he drew closer watching her unwieldy efforts to do just that down the cascading steps, his foot wedged more firmly in the door with —I'll tell you Mister Crease, a real stroke of luck I was here for this, these real estate people almost make you ashamed of the human race, a regular cesspool of human greed it's all the biggest swindle ever invented right down there with your insurance racket nothing but dog eat dog, I've got to leave any minute now a big commission right down the line but don't listen to anything less than five million firm, if he wants it he'll take it, just get a look at her she's just told him she thinks she can talk you down to four million a real steal at the price they're cannibals all of them, don't see how she can face herself in the mirror, what do you say.

—Please go away.

—Oh Mister Crease, Mister Crease? she renewed her assault up the steps without pausing for breath —I have wonderful news for you. I've been able to talk him up to your original asking price of three million two, half right now on the spot and the rest at closing he's waiting right there with his checkbook in his hand and...

—Where'd you get this three million two asking price.

—We discussed it on an earlier occasion as the fair market value Mister Prestig, I'm afraid you're not very well acquainted with the real estate market in this area and the slump we've been in is...

—You're talking about condos and housing developments Madame, there's no slump in properties like this one look at the view, you won't get that anymore with these wetland setbacks, the privacy alone is worth a couple of million because money can't buy it, I'm a busy man I've got to get going but I'll be glad to handle your closing if they come up with a reasonable figure Mister Crease here, take my card, you'll see I've got a new number? sidling round to recover his foot and slip a hundred dollar bill into the breast pocket folds —glad we worked out this other arrangement just leave the rest of it to me, keep in touch.

—Well! Now we can talk, if you allow me to say so Mister Crease I hate to see a gentleman like yourself bullied that way. Lawyers just seem to try to complicate things and some of them can really scrape the bottom of the barrel when they...

—Will you go away?

—Yes it won't take us a minute without him interfering now will it. I wouldn't argue for a moment about the value of the site and the location in this prestige area since that's really all my client is interested in, with all your Mister Prestig's talk about slate roofs and landmarks but the place is old and in bad repair isn't it, this very porch where we're standing is ready to fall on our heads but that's unimportant because he plans to tear the whole thing down anyway and start fresh with this famous postmodern architect who's doing the place on the corner right down to the carpets and picture frames it will be quite a showplace, he has his checkbook in his hand Mister Crease and offers like this may never come again, certainly not from these imaginary clients who won't blink at five million but will try to jew you down the minute you...

—Get out of here.

—But, what? She stepped aside as he strode past her for the edge of the veranda where he stood undoing his trousers —I don't...

—Didn't you hear me? He paused there with his hand digging deep in his underclothes. —If you don't get out of here right now I'll throw you down these steps do you hear me? and if I see your painted pig face on this property again I'll, I'll have you for lunch.

—I, my God! she got hold of the railing as he turned away without a glance after her headlong clamber down the steps and the roar of her car swerving aside for one bearing down on the driveway ahead.

—Who in God's name was that.

—Some crazy woman. Did we forget milk? as they came to a halt and silenced, staring at him standing at the end of the veranda directing a steaming arc down on the withered grass below.

—Oscar! not even raising his eyes to them with the slamming doors of the car —stop it! My God he hasn't done this since he was eight years old, Oscar? as they reached the steps together —I said stop it! He used to try to write his name on the snow that way, come inside right now it's cold out here! Will you tell me what in God's name's going on? she came up after him, —who was that woman! but he ambled on back through the doors doing up his trousers to leave her standing there in the grip of the cold for the grocery bags handed to her up the steps, down the hall and through to the silent kitchen: butter, oyster mushrooms, broccoli, feta cheese, pesto, elbows braced on the table there and her face sunk in her hands, pickled ginger? Ponentine olive spread?

—What's all this stuff, sun dried tomatoes? unsalted pignolias?

—God only knows Lily, I mean I just took whatever I saw, I thought we could get him interested in meals again I must have been thinking of that day Mister Basie came out here with those carrots in the Spanish style, I hardly know what I'm doing. That performance just now out there on the veranda he must be into the wine again, where is he now.

—He's in there with his fishes.

—Well God help us. I mean at least they don't make any noise.

Neither the red scream of sunset blazing on the icebound pond nor the thunderous purple of its risings on a landscape blown immense through leafless trees off toward the ocean where in flocks the wild goose Wawa, where Kahgahgee king of ravens with his band of black marauders, or where the Kayoshk, the seagulls, rose with clamour from their nests among the marshes and the Mama, the woodpecker seated high among the branches of the melancholy pine tree past the margins of the pond neither rose Ugudwash, the sunfish, nor the yellow perch the Sahwa like a sunbeam in the water banished here, with wind and wave, day and night and time itself from the domain of the discus by the daylight halide lamp, silent pump and power filter, temperature and pH balance and the system of aeration, fed on silverside and flake food, vitamins and krill and beef heart in a patent spinach mixture to restore their pep and lustre spitting black worms from the feeder when a crew of new arrivals (live delivery guaranteed, air freight collect at thirty dollars) brought a Chinese algae eater, khuli loach and male beta, two black mollies and four neons and a pair of black skirt tetra cruising through the new laid fronds of the Madagascar lace plant.

And now where was he? He must have gone someplace because the car wasn't out there in the driveway, setting off a new round of muttering about the last time this happened, calling the hospitals, calling the police in Hoboken was it? lying in a ditch somewhere and in he walked frozen to the gills it was probably these damn fish again, he'd probably gone up to that place on the highway to get them something for lunch —I mean my God they're eating us out of house and home, can't we do something about this mess in the refrigerator? Ground beef heart and baby brine shrimp mixed up in here with the pickled ginger and sun dried tomatoes, he's got bloodworms and crabmeat and medicines for their parasite bacteria and fungus problems right in with the feta cheese and that Ponentine olive spread that cost God knows how much and what's that on the shelf over the sink, that plastic cup that says cole slaw there's something floating in it, will you throw it out? I've been looking at it for a week.

—No don't! That's mine Christina, that's my jelly implants.

—Well what in God's name are they doing here, are you keeping them for souvenirs?

—They told me to keep them for evidence when I went up there to get my stitches out, I told you I'm going to sue that slimeball didn't I? And they told me they're putting together this big class action lawsuit against him and this whole bunch of doctors and this company that made the jelly if I start to lose my hair and my memory like this other lady I was scared to tell you, there's something else I was scared to tell you Christina. See I thought when you paid them that fifteen hundred dollars up at the hospital that that was for everything but they said that was just the room and the operating room and the anasthesist and the television rental and the free toothbrush but the doctor's separate. This doctor which took them out is separate.

—What do you mean he's separate.

—Fifteen hundred dollars but...

—Fine. When you win your big lawsuit against the doctor who put them in you can pay the doctor who took them out now let's not talk anymore about it, I want to get, listen. Did you hear that?

—It's these big trucks way out at the end of the driveway, you know that little house that was back there in the trees? It's gone. Right overnight the whole house, it's...

—Not the trucks no it's, listen. It's Oscar! He's, my hands are wet go in there and see what in God's name's going on will you? and Lily? ask him if he's eaten? but she was gone, leaving nothing but the distant rumble of the trucks until her heels came clattering down the hall again.

—He's calling the police, Christina. He's calling to report a stolen car.

—I'll kill him! she whispered, twisting the dishtowel in her hands like a throat —he's, no be still! I told you to remind me to call the garage in town to bring his car out here didn't I? flinging it down —where is he. Oscar? and through the door —where is he! the phone trembling in her own hands now stabbing out a number, her voice sunk to a deadly calm as she got on with —Carlos or

José, one of them can drive it out here can't he? today? or tonight then? My God I mean, all right here are the directions, will you write them down?

—I'm making some tea when you're done, all right? and when she brought it in, —what are you so mad at Oscar for.

—Because he, just because I am! Where is he!

—How come you're blaming him then! He's just trying to help out isn't he? I mean we always leave the keys in the car here don't we? Is it his fault if somebody steals it?

—Because I, because he's driving me crazy Lily, everything is, those trucks out there now before it's even light when I come down and he's already in there with his bowl of cereal he hardly eats anything else, all he asked for last time I went shopping was peanut butter and another box of it, I try to talk to him I ask him if he wants tea or some toast and he just goes on shoveling it down and puts on his glasses reading the back of the cereal box till he finally asks me if there's any mail, I mean it's practically dawn and is there any mail! and back in the kitchen —have you seen his latest?

—No but wait a second, I forgot to...

—These tiny sea horses he sent away for roaming in and out of the windows of that idiotic castle in there the way he roams around the house here himself like some lost soul, I mean God only knows what he expects after this thing that came for him yesterday, did you see it? reaching behind the cereal box —from Saint Pancras School, Dear Professor Crease I thought they were inviting him to lecture on the...

—No but wait a second, there's a...

—I mean can you imagine? Your colleague, Doctor J Madhar Pai, has given your name as a reference on his application to join our faculty as Psychological Counselor and Senior Proctor for the Sixth Form. He would also supervise the School's athletic program, chapel attendance and any disciplinary...

—No but wait a second Christina there's a...

—qualities of moral fibre and leadership embracing traditional values, best embodied on the playing fields of Saint Pancras where emphasis is placed not on winning but rather on how you play the game, and we will appreciate your candid appraisal of his suitability in these capacities and for taking an active role in our lively academic community. Your comments will be held in the strictest

I mean my God people will do anything, the very thought of Trish ending up on the lively playing fields of...

—No but listen Christina something came yesterday certified I put up here over the sink and forgot to...

—Well thank God. I mean I'd begun to think Bill Peyton expected me to sit here staring at that rotting amaryllis till the end of, throw it out will you? tearing open the envelope barely in her hands —it looks like the bowels of a, oh my God.

—But what...

—Just be still! She folded back a page, folded back another, —where is he.

—Oscar? He probably went back up to his old room on the top floor with his rock collection, he even slept up there last night did you know that? He was...

—Well call him! folding back each page more slowly than the last until she suddenly got up herself storming back up the hall to the foot of the stairs —Oscar! in a near collision there —sit down. Just be quiet and listen to this, will you sit down? doing so herself, getting her breath —that, that insufferable law clerk my God, a simple estate! He's whipped together the final accounting on Father's estate, I'll say he's whipped it together right across our naked backs, will you look at it? But she made no sign of giving it up, pausing again for breath which dwindled with the balance of the principal (assets listed on page 3 here below) totaling $5,649,500, less the following, in Federal tax, $2,065,000; in New York State tax (location of house only, less mortgage), $284,500; executor's fee, court costs, filing and attorneys' fees, $100,000; personal bequest, $500; leaving to the residual legatees in equal shares the amount of $3,199,500 —well my God Oscar why are you staring at me like a, can't you see what this means? It means the house. It means these treasury notes and deposit certificates and the cash and everything else all go for taxes and that drunken fool's executor's fee passing along what's left to his courthouse cronies because this house is the bulk of the estate, three point two million! This property assessed at three point two million and he's probably already drunk up every cent of the five hundred dollars he took out of it sitting down there on a hundred thousand as his executor's fee my God, a hundred thousand dollars for this? suddenly on her feet brandishing the papers —and what he's scribbled at the foot here just to be cute? over seizing the phone now, —puts him in mind of old Justice Holmes he says, left most of his estate to the U.S. Treasury I mean aren't we doing practically the same damn thing? punching out numbers —handing the IRS two million dollars with the veranda caving in and not a penny for paint or even fixing our driveway, hello? Yes, Bill Peyton please, if they expect us to keep a roof over our heads while they, who? Well who are you I, what? sputtering her own name —and who are you! Lenny what? Yes, yes tell him I got his lovely plant but when does he expect to send me the... I said when! and she stood tapping her foot till she hung it up with a choked out —thank you. Some flunky named Lenny telling me it's at the top of Bill Peyton's agenda coming out here in a day or two with some of Harry's papers he thinks we'd like to keep, I mean if he dares show his face without that insurance check in his hand I'll, I'm going to have a drink.

—What shall I...

—Don't ask me Lily do what you want to! There's that flounder for supper I'm going in to get a drink, now where did he go? but she raged past the dim room festooned with blankets without a glance in at the figure looming in the cadaverous pallor of the halide lamp tapping a teaspoon of God only knew what over the blades of the Amazon sword plant, settling on the Madagascar lace where the recent wave of immigrants seemed to have thinned considerably since their arrival as a glittering turquoise discus passed trailing a shred of black skirt from its jaws and the sea horses, gliding past the walls of the castle with all the diminutive rectitude of the knights of King Richard the Lionhearted raising the siege at Acre, only for it to fall once again to the gleaming ranks of the Saracens a century later ending the last Crusade and, with it, the kingdom of Jerusalem, were now nowhere to be seen.

—He said he's not hungry for us to go ahead and eat. He's in there now watching some mystery with a peanut butter sandwich.

—Well I'm simply exhausted, it's been dark for hours I'm going up as soon as we're done. Will you tell me what those blankets are doing strung up in the sunroom?

—Because I can't sleep with that spooky light in there, like it's always daytime in the middle of the night.

Day for night, good cop bad cop, undercover sleuth tracks serial killer, incest victim seeks revenge, heavy metal star on killing spree and the screen ablaze with an overturned patrol car, flashing lights merging with the late night news, spy in mafia drug orbit and the door battered in: police! freeze!

—Well my God where is he, I thought he was down here.

—No it's real Christina, there's somebody out there! as the red and blue lights flashed across the walls and the pounding on the door continued.

—Well open it!

—Mrs Crease? We picked up your car, you want to come out and identify it?

—But who, what time is it? She stared at the policeman half her age weighted down with the hardware strung at his waist —I mean I'm not even awake, I can't go out there now I'm not even dressed.

—We picked up Pedro there riding around the neighborhood, he says he was lost but he doesn't speak much English, probably just took it out to do a little partying. You leave the keys in it?

—I don't, Pedro who, I mean yes it's our car I can see it from here but who's Pedro.

—Just meant one of your Hispanics, probably one of them working on that site out at the corner of the driveway and he happened to spot it, they're checking him out now for drugs and alcohol. You can come down in the morning and sign a complaint.

—Yes all right I, what time is it I'm still half asleep.

—It's one twenty Mrs Crease, just take your time. He's not going anywhere.

—Yes I, good night and thank you.

She was down the next morning with the first rumble of trucks out there on that site at the corner of the driveway raised to a dull roar with the arrival of backhoes and bulldozers suddenly pierced by the scream of a chainsaw, —well can't you hear it Oscar? It's enough to wake the dead! I mean do you hear anything in that little room on the top floor? God knows why you want to sleep up there you'll freeze to death, did you hear that racket last night when the police brought the car back? I was barely awake I didn't know what was happening, the whole thing is like some wild dream now where are you going. Do you think you could clean up after yourself when you're done in here? If you won't sit down at the table with us like the last civilized man couldn't you at least put your dishes in the sink and throw out these crusts and empty milk cartons?

doing so herself as her voice followed him through the door before she wiped up the spilt milk, swept the floor and made tea, sitting there staring at the back of the cereal box.

—Are you okay?

—I'm not okay Lily nothing is okay, will you listen to this? You talk about nobody in the house reading, do you want to hear what he's been reading? Win big prizes. Official entry form. If you're the grand prize winner you'll take your whole family on a fun filled vacation to Disney World. Second prize winners take home a family bicycle set. The more times you enter the more chances you, what are you looking for.

—I just need some money for this delivery out there? she said digging in the towel drawer. —He just got some more fishes.

—Well can't he pay for them himself?

—I don't know, he said he found a quarter and a penny in the cushion of that big chair from when Harry was out here but...

—That's ridiculous, I mean you've seen that hundred dollar bill sticking out of the breast pocket of that old jacket he wears haven't you? God knows where he got it, when I asked him he said he had some riddles too, what gets harder to catch the harder you run? What can run but can't walk, where in God's name is he now.

—He's out there watching this man that's looking at the car, maybe you better go out and...

—Oh my God I forgot all about it, is it the police? and by the time she got out there the engine was already running, coming down waving her arms —wait a minute! Who are you, what are you doing! Mrs Crease was it? He'd come to repossess the car, they'd been duly notified —but you can't no it's my, Oscar come down here! Make, model, license, registration inspection stickers it all checked, sorry to inconvenience her, rolling up the window as it moved away, just doing his job —oh my God, oh my God.

—Christina what happened! Who was it!

—Oh my God! she whispered, coming slowly back up the steps —what I've done, what I've done, I didn't know what I was doing! suddenly moving quickly down the hall —Quickly! with the phone in her hand turning it up for the number pasted there —hello, yes hello, hello. Last night, you brought a car out here last night a stolen car, I thought it was my car that had been stolen but the man who was driving it, the man you arrested, he's... Crease yes that's right but the man you... he what? No but where, where did they take him, he's... oh my God. But what will happen to him! oh my God she whispered, finally hanging it up. —No. No no no. Pedro, just one of your Hispanics I wasn't thinking, I wasn't even thinking! It was one of the boys from the garage, it was Oscar's car it was José or Carlos driving it out here and I didn't even...

—But why didn't you just tell them that, why did...

—Because he's gone! Because his papers weren't right so they called the Immigration Service who came and took him away, just doing their job, all of them just doing their job and they'll probably deport him for, for just doing his job?

—But wait a second Christina, maybe you can...

—I can't do a damn thing! When I could just pick up the phone and call Harry? He'd know what to do, he'd know exactly what to do and where is he! and she got unsteadily to her feet echoing —where is he, reaching up to open the cabinet.

—I don't think you should have a drink Christina, it's still early and...

—I don't care what you think Lily. I don't care if it's still early. I don't care if it's the day or the night I don't, God will it stop! at the scream of a chainsaw —just doing their jobs like those maniacs out there tearing out the bowels of the earth cutting down every living thing and where is he! with her glass up the hall as the trucks continued to rumble out there through the trees still standing in their path, out over the pond where she stared for a full minute stirred by a west wind blowing toward the ocean before she swallowed her drink and —no, listen...

—Just those trucks and...

—No listen! Don't you hear it? broken notes of a piano far away flatting the G within three bars, holding her breath till the A came in, late, starting again —he's up there Lily! He's up in the music room get him my God, he'll freeze to death go and get him! putting down her emptied glass to go for the door.

—Mrs Lutz? Hi. I'm Lenny.

—You're what?

—Lenny Wu? I'm a new associate at Swyne & Dour Mrs Lutz. Mister Peyton had to go out of town and he entrusted me to bring this out to you because it was the top of his agenda when I called you, remember? Can I come in?

—Well, come in yes, come in I didn't, yes come in please! leading him through to take off his coat and sit down snapping open the brass mounts of a briskly new monogramed attaché case in calf. —Can I get you something? some tea or...

—No. No thank you Mrs Lutz I trust I'm not disturbing you, I had a little difficulty finding the place but...

—No that's all right please! I appreciate your coming all the way out here to bring the...

—It's my privilege I assure you Mrs Lutz. Mister Peyton asked me to convey his deepest apologies for not coming himself. He was deeply attached to your husband both as a colleague and friend as I'm sure you know, and the loss is a terrible blow to the entire firm, both that of a brilliant legal mind and to its enduring reputation for probity and adhering to the highest standards of...

—I'm quite aware of the firm's image thank you, now...

—I'm sure you are Mrs Lutz! In the light of that, it occurred to Mister Peyton on the occasion of cleaning out your husband's desk that you might like to keep his papers which comprise a sort of memorial to his service and to his prominent place in the profession. I'm sure you have your own wonderful memories of your marriage to such a brilliant legal mind but we thought...

—Please. I was not married to a legal mind though I must say it often seemed like it, I was married to a man. Now if you don't terribly mind I'd like to get down to...

—I'm sorry Mrs Lutz! I didn't mean to, to intrude I was only expressing my admiration for his, for your husband's brilliant handling of some of the firm's leading courtroom victories, this one in particular that I, I do hope you understand? as he seemed to seek refuge from her dulled gaze burrowing in the sheaf of papers —that I'm sure you'll want to keep, this one in particular it's really enough in itself to immortalize him in the annals of First Amendment law for the life of the, the case he'd just brought to its triumphant conclusion when he, at his demise I'm sure you're familiar with it, what the press has labeled the Pop and Glow case?

—My God yes, but please don't...

—No I'm sure I have it here, just their vulgar shorthand for bringing a landmark case in the hundreds of millions down to the harried level of the general public who delight in trivializing anything they cannot understand, treating another landmark case striking at the heart of our constitutional rights cited here in his brief somewhere I'm sure I, when his citation of Carson v. Here's Johnny Portable Toilets is treated as a comical diversion like they've attached this Pop and Glow label to Episcopal Church of America v. Pepsico confronting the exclusionary clause in the First Amendment breaching the wall between church and, I know you'll want to read it Mrs Lutz it's brilliant unless of course, unless perhaps you've read it already?

—My God no, but...

—Yes I'll find it here, just give me a moment? as he riffled through the sheafs of paper and began to pile them on the floor at his feet —alleging that in devising the trade name Pepsi-Cola the defendants had deliberately contrived an obvious and infringing anagram of Episcopal hoping to profit from some subliminal confusion in the minds of the consumer public, thus enhancing the value of their worldwide bottling franchises and their marketing skills by exploiting the plaintiff's historical success in proselytizing its spiritual wares honed down through the centuries thereby defaming the venerable image of the church in attributing to it mercenary motives indistinguishable from the promotional campaigns for a soft drink which, you see I know his brief practically by heart it's the most skillfully...

—I see yes, but really...

—Oh just a moment, here's something I was told to call your special attention to? waving a fresh handful of papers at her, —the complaint by this woman and her insurance company's attorneys against your husband's estate regarding an automobile accident in which he allegedly left the scene after causing...

—Please just, just put it down somewhere and...

—I know you're familiar with it Mrs Lutz, I only meant to say that the services of the firm are of course at your dispos...

—Please! Will you get on with the...

—Of course yes I'm sorry, as I say I'll find it in a moment, it's the most skillfully argued brief I've encountered since we read Cardozo's opinion in Palsgraf v. Long Island Railroad last year in law school there where your husband summarizes the defendant's allegation portraying the suit by the church as a gesture born of desperation to keep its head above water with its dwindling coffers and membership welcoming homosexual priests and ordaining women to attract the same worldwide constituency of brand name loyalists who, which clearly lay the groundwork for the final resolution of the case, there's hardly an argument he failed to, I can't have left it behind I was reading it again just before I left the office but if, I can send it to you can't I? as the pile at his feet mounted. —The striking parallel he draws with the fierce marketing innovation for the New Coke forced to go back to Classic Coke, even to citing regional thorns like R C Cola with the Roman Catholic campaign to recover its faithful from the alienation brought on by the desperate effort of the Second Vatican Council lowering its standards to reach out to the multitude by doing the mass in local jargon like allowing the orthodox to make a meal kosher by holding a telephone over it with a rabbi's voice at the other end, you see I was brought up Catholic Mrs Lutz and this touches a special chord in my oh, just a moment yes, quite off the subject but this is important, I think you may have heard mention of it? bringing him to his feet flourishing the intimidating document —regarding the infringement suit against your husb, your brother I mean being brought by the Eugene O'Neill estate for alleged...

—I have heard mention of it yes and I don't want to again! Will you please simply...

—I didn't mean to distract you Mrs Lutz I'm sorry, I was told to bring it out here for his immediate attention if you could be so good as to place it in his hands? commencing to pace the room as though loath to chance placing it in hers, —since he is named as codefendant in this suit being brought by the same estate against our client springing from the original case our client successfully defended against him notwithstanding, our firm wishes to offer its services as a courtesy in what promises to be a rather prolonged course of litigation of sufficient importance to all concerned for it to be handled by one of our senior partners should he, unless that is to say he has already retained counsel elsewhere? his rapid pacing before her now verging on prancing as he stopped abruptly with —I, excuse me Mrs Lutz I, is there a bathroom I might use? bringing her to her feet as abruptly to hurry him down the hall and make her own way hastily on to the kitchen where she clung to the edge of the sink for a moment before she reached up for the bottle and a glass to drink it straight down, getting her breath with a long swallow of water before she returned her unsteady composure to confront his full recovery seated back in the chair gesturing an empty hand, —I put it there on the sideboard Mrs Lutz. I only wished to add the note of deep regret felt throughout the firm that your husband could not be with us to see the fortunate outcome of his major role in breaking the deadlock leading to an amicable settlement between the parties. Everyone from the senior partners down agrees that his unsparing efforts laid the groundwork for the firm to proceed with the complex terms of the merger being negotiated between their marketing and evangelical arms but as I said earlier, this inclination of the press to turn momentous events into comical diversions pandering to the jaded tastes of their readers, anything you may read about a plan to use the soft drink in the communion service is purely a...

—Oh Lily come in yes, thank God. Just sit down we're, this child has come out from Harry's office to bring us his...

—Please excuse me yes how do you do, I'd just finished telling Mrs Lutz about my admiration for her husband's handling of his last important case, I believe the only aspect that remains to be unraveled is the effect the merger may have in the Middle East markets and on cola enthusiasts of the Jewish faith but it's hoped they'll let bygones be bygones and feelers have already gone out to the Jews for Jesus who, but I'm afraid I could go on and on and...

—I'm afraid you could too, but you're not going to. I want to know about Harry's life insurance.

—Oh yes, yes I'm afraid I don't know all the details but I heard Mister Peyton speaking about it, he was especially appreciative of your coming up with your husband's dental bill which solved the situation immediately and the entire matter's been settled.

—Well where's the check.

—The check?

—The check for a half million dollars for Harry's life insurance!

—But, but I assume it's been absorbed by the firm, our bookkeepers are sometimes a little slow with...

—What do you mean absorbed by the firm! I'm his wife his, I'm his widow aren't I? He told me he had a half million dollar life insurance policy and I'm...

—But you, I'm afraid you don't understand Mrs Lutz. It was paid to the firm as beneficiary since the firm held the policy and had paid all the premiums in light of his, of how valuable he was to the firm's standing in the profession as a partner and, yes and the tragedy of his loss on the very eve of his...

—Where is the check!

—I think maybe you better just leave, Mister...

—But I, I didn't realize there was any misunderstanding over the, I can't tell you how badly I feel I'd so looked forward to meeting you Mrs Lutz and we wanted to assure you again that the firm will be glad to be of service in these pending matters I spoke of regarding...

—Is this your coat?

—Thank you yes but, but in spite of this little disappointment I wanted to thank Mrs Lutz for her, for my great admiration for her hus, for Harry I should say Harry everyone called him Harry even the secretaries and the, being new there I can't say I knew him well but whenever I saw his tall patrician figure coming down the hall he'd always give me a smile of encourage...

—Harry?

—Yes everyone called him Har...

—My God, Harry? She was looking at him hard —tall, patrician he was stocky with black hair he was no taller than you are!

—He oh, oh I'm sorry again Mrs Lutz he, no. No that's not the Harry I knew.

—The, what did you say?

—He, that he, I said I'm sorry Mrs Lutz. That's not the Harry I knew.

—Lily do something!

—I said you better go didn't I? I said go! slamming the open case at him —now go! Get out of here! Christina? you okay? You want me to get you a drink?

She choked out a whisper over the clatter of the doors echoing down the hall, motionless but for the quiver of a hand caught abruptly in the other and held tight there till she reached it up to seize the glass hovering before her. —He knew it all the time didn't he! she broke out suddenly clearing her throat with the drink, —a pill and a scotch and a pill destroying himself right before my eyes he knew exactly what he was doing. Married to such a brilliant legal mind yes and where is he now! staring fixed at the sheafs of paper tumbled in a heap on the floor there beside the empty chair. —Now what are you doing.

—All these papers, you want me to put them in the library with the...

—Burn them.

—But I thought maybe you wanted to keep them in there with the...

—I said burn them! in a burst that brought her to her feet, turning her back to stand staring out over the pond where the west wind tore its surface in waves toward the ocean, laying the brown grasses flat along its icebound edge as she put her emptied glass on the sill. —What's that on the floor over there under the sideboard, that manila folder it's been there for days.

—That's his last act, he was reading it before and...

—Before what! Just do something with it will you? Laying up his treasure in heaven where moths break through and steal I mean my God, talk about a following shade of care I just got the bill for that cremation they didn't waste any time, twelve hundred seventy one dollars and fifty cents with another hundred fifty nine for the crematory charge and where would I like the remains sent my God, that bookshelf up there with Father and the ashes of this lasting memorial to his prominent place in the legal profession I said burn them didn't I? I thought you were getting me a drink.

—But Christina you just...

—Did you hear me! And some matches? But when the pale drink appeared she was standing at the hearth staring at the papers already ablaze round the edges —who favour fire? But if he had to perish twice that ice was, strip away the poetry and off to the crematory and then some line about desire? or hate?

—It's Frost, Christina.

—What? bringing her round sharply —my God Oscar where have you been!

—You thought it was Yeats Christina. It's Robert Frost. Some say the world will end in fire, Some say in ice. From what I've...

—I don't give one damn who it is, how long have you been standing there! catching her balance against the chair —and what's that thing.

—Remember it? this canoe I made from that birch tree down by the pond? I just found it up with my...

—Give it to me! Here, get rid of it will you? flinging an arm toward the fire as he held it closer sitting down slowly, staring at her bent down shaking the smouldering pages aflame —with this mess of the past where it belongs? Immortalizing him in the annals of First Amendment law he knew what he was doing all the time, drawing up our will leaving everything to the survivor, a mortgage on a penthouse that has to be sold to pay it and a half dozen eggs in the...

—Christina?

—A pill and a drink and a pill destroying himself in front of my eyes he knew what he was doing, half a million dollars to prop up the firm's image while I survive on a half dozen...

—But Christina? if you'd died, Christina? his voice abruptly plodding as his logic —and your will left everything to each other, if you'd died first? Then half this house would be Harry's now, it would be half mine and...

—Oscar my God don't be morbid! I didn't die he did and stop looking at me like that, Lily get that napkin and wipe his chin he looks half witted, Harry died and I'm standing right here in front of you with my, where's that drink never mind, I'll get it myself!

—But if you had Christina! echoed after her heels down the hall, —he'd be standing right here in front of me with, he'd be buying my half from me with my own blood money from his senior partner share because I can't buy his half can I? so he can sell it to some west coast millionaire who'll tear it down to build a showplace like that nightmare on the corner where the screaming of the chainsaws suddenly brought him to his feet, to the window where he stood cradling the wrecked canoe, wiping his face with the dry napkins where she stood up close beside him with her shock of loose blonde hair fallen on her beaded forehead and the beading on her lips bare of any trace of lipstick and her fragrance from her blouse loosely buttoned pressed against him, he'd been lied to all his life, just as he'd appeared to triumph with a farce sprung from a lie in a fight to prove his courage by the old man driven back to the earth's remotest border, from his refuge as an immortal offering to share his kingdom, ruler of the North-West wind, the homewind, the Keewaydin shifting now on the surface of the pond laying low the yellowed grasses where so long ago the birch tree rustling in the breeze of morning laid aside its white skin wrapper as she pressed herself against him in the shadow of the pine trees, made a bed with boughs of hemlock where the squirrel, Adjidaumo, from his ambush in the oak trees watched with eager eyes the lovers, watched him fucking Laughing Water and the rabbit, the Wabasso sat erect upon his haunches, watched him fucking Minnehaha as the birds sang loud and sweetly where the rumble of the trucks drowned the drumming of the pheasant and the heron, the Shuh-shuh-gah gave a cry of lamentation from her haunts among the fenlands at the howling of the chainsaws and the screams of the wood chipper for that showplace on the corner promising a whole new order of woodland friends for the treeless landscape, where Thumper the Rabbit and Flower the Skunk would introduce the simpering Bambi to his plundered environment and instruct him in matters of safety and convenience by the shining Big-Sea-Water, by the shores of Gitche Gumee where the desolate Nokomis drank her whisky at the fireside, not a word from Laughing Water left abandoned by the windows, from the wide eyed Ella Cinders with the mice her only playmates as he turned his back upon them with his birch canoe exulting, all alone went Hiawatha.

Out over the pond a strange gloom had descended and the wide lawn slipped into the water as though it were flooding, not a cloud in the sky to fault for the sudden change in the light where the far bank was gone abruptly in a dull strip of grey and the middle distance seemed to advance and recede, the whole pond to heave as it ebbed from the foot of the lawn in a rising swell toward the other side like some grand seiche coming over it rocked by a catastrophe in the underworld, wavering as the swell returned, retreating in a massive unbroken rhythm like the tipping from side to side of a giant bowl as she clung with a hand to the sill swept by a wave of vertigo suddenly gathering her blouse to her throat to turn away gasping for breath in the cloud of smoke curling toward her from the fireplace. —Christina? She stood there for a moment still till shaken by a cough, eyes watering from the smoke looking for something, anything to prod the smouldering heap into flames, seizing the manila folder rolled like a stave bent down to thrust it at the embers raising a blue flame that crept along the margin and leaped to yellow life as she stood away from the blaze empty-handed in the smoke and the stillness broken only by the sound of footsteps somewhere, suddenly calling out —Christina? as the silence broke all about her with the crash of a door.

—Oscar stop! where he'd burst out from behind it —stop it! Stop I can't, no stop tickling me I can't breathe! I can't, Lily! Lily come here quickly I can't, Lily help me!